The Correspondence of Henry David Thoreau

The preparation of this volume was in part made possible by grants from the American Council of Learned
Societies and the Rutgers University Research Council.

To Marjorie Harding *and* Margaret Bode

Acknowledgments

We are indebted to many persons for aid in the compilation and annotation of this edition. Mr. Harding is particularly grateful to the members of his graduate committee and of the faculty at Rutgers University: Professors Richard Amacher, L. Ethan Ellis, Robert Falk, J. Milton French, Alfred Kellogg, and Rudolf Kirk, for their patience and advice in the editorial work. Mr. Bode wishes to acknowledge the assistance of Professor Leon Howard of the University of California at Los Angeles, the encouragement of Professor Charles Murphy and Dean Leon P. Smith of the University of Maryland, and the secretarial help of Miss Marie Harris, Mr. Harry Kroitor, and Mrs. George Leith. For giving us access to the manuscripts in their collections and providing photostats, microfilms, and typescripts of them, we are indebted to the librarians of Abernethy Library at Middlebury College; the Berg Collection of the New York Public Library; the Boston Public Library; the Boston Society of Natural History; the Bruce Museum of Greenwich, Connecticut; the Buffalo and Erie County Public Library; the Chapin Library of Williams College; the Columbia University Library; the Concord Antiquarian Society; the Concord Free Public Library; the Edward L. Doheny Memorial Library at St. John's Seminary, Camarillo, California; the Essex Institute of Salem, Massachusetts; the Folger Shakespeare Library; the Fruitlands Museum; the Gunn Memorial Library of Washington, Connecticut; the Harvard College Library; the Harvard University Archives; the Historical Society of Pennsylvania; the Henry E. Huntington Library and Art Gallery of San Marino, California; the Iowa State Department of History and Archives; the Massachusetts Historical Society; the Middlesex School of Concord, Massachusetts; the Morgan Library; the New York Historical Society; the New York Public Library; the University of Notre Dame Library; the Princeton University Library; the University of Rochester Library; the Scripps College Library; the University of Texas Library; and the Yale University Library. For permitting us to print manuscripts in their private collections, we wish to express our appreciation to Professor Lawrence Averill of Wiscasset, Maine;

Mr. C. Waller Barrett of New York City; Mr. Daniel Bernstein of New York City; Mrs. Robert Bowler of Plymouth, Massachusetts; Mr. Percy Brown of Cleveland, Ohio; Mr. Richard Cholmondeley, Baschurch, Shropshire, England; Mr. John L. Cooley of Pleasantville, New York; Mr. William Cummings of St. Paul, Minnesota; Mr. Raymond Emerson of Concord, Massachusetts; Goodspeed's Book Shop Inc., of Boston, Massachusetts; Mr. and Mrs. Herbert Hosmer of Concord, Massachusetts; Mr. Leonard Kleinfeld of Forest Hills, Long Island; Mr. Albert E. Lownes of Providence, Rhode Island; the late Mr. Daniel Gregory Mason of New Canaan, Connecticut; Mrs. Frank L. Mather, Jr. of Princeton, New Jersey; Mr. Robert Miller of Bristol, Rhode Island; the Scribner Book Store of New York City; Mr. Frank Walters of Hollis, New Hampshire; the late Mr. Edward H. Wannemacher of Philadelphia, Pennsylvania; and Mrs. Hilda Wheelwright of Bangor, Maine. For permitting us to reprint letters for which they hold the copyright, we are indebted to the *Atlantic Monthly;* the Attic Press of Richmond, Virginia; the Bibliographical Society of America; Mr. Henry Seidel Canby of Deep River, Connecticut; the Ralph Waldo Emerson Memorial Association; the Emerson Society; Miss Edith Guerier of Brighton, Massachusetts; the Houghton Mifflin Company; the *New England Quarterly;* G. P. Putnam's Sons of New York City; the *Saturday Review;* and the Vermont Botanical Club. For permission to publish the letters of Theo Brown, we are indebted to the present Mr. Theo Brown of Moline, Illinois; for the letters of Ellery Channing, to Mr. Henry Channing of Boston, Massachusetts; of Thomas Cholmondeley, to Mr. Richard Cholmondeley of Baschurch, Shropshire, England; of Mr. and Mrs. Ralph Waldo Emerson, to the Ralph Waldo Emerson Memorial Association; of Daniel Ricketson, to Miss Edith Guerier of Brighton, Massachusetts; of Mr. and Mrs. Nathaniel Hawthorne, to Mr. Manning Hawthorne; of Henry James, Sr., to Mr. William James of New York City; of Mrs. Horace Mann, to the present Mr. Horace Mann; of Mr. and Mrs. Bronson Alcott, to Mr. Frederic Wolsey Pratt of Concord, Massachusetts; of Sarah Alden Ripley, to Mr. John W. Ames, Jr.; of Franklin Sanborn, to the late Mr. F. B. Sanborn of Westfield, New Jersey; of Charles Scribner, to Mr. Charles Scribner, Jr. of New York City; and of the unpublished letters of Moncure Conway, to Miss Eleanor Conway Sawyer. We are also indebted to Mr. Henry Seidel Canby for information and good counsel; to Professor William Charvat of Ohio State University for access to correspondence in the Ticknor & Fields letter books; to Professor James R. Naiden of the University of Washington for checking Sanborn's translation of Thoreau's one letter in Latin; to Professor Ralph L. Rusk of Columbia University for permitting examination of the photostats he collected for his edition of the Emerson letters; and for aid in locating and annotating various letters, to Professor James Beard, Miss Eva Brook, Mr. Van Wyck Brooks, Professor Kenneth Cameron, Mr. Benton Hatch, Professor

ACKNOWLEDGMENTS

George Hendrick, Mrs. Herbert Hosmer, Professor Albert Kerr, Professor Joseph Jones, Professor Jay Leyda, Professor Joseph Slater, and Mrs. Caleb Wheeler. We are also grateful to the librarians of the Concord Free Public Library, the State University Teachers College at Geneseo, New York, the Huntington Library, the Library of Congress, the New York Public Library, the University of North Carolina Library, the Princeton University Library, and the Rutgers University Library for their continued and willing assistance. Then too, we wish to express our gratitude to the many members of the Thoreau Society who helped to locate manuscript letters.

The research necessary to produce our edition was furthered by grants-in-aid from Rutgers University to Mr. Harding and from the American Council of Learned Societies to Mr. Bode.

Walter Harding
State University Teachers College
at Geneseo, New York

Carl Bode
University of Maryland

April 1958

Contents

Illustrations

The History of Thoreau's Published Correspondence

Although scattered letters by Thoreau have been published in numerous books and articles, only two major editions of his letters have appeared. Neither of these is inclusive; neither attempts to add the letters written to Thoreau. Ralph Waldo Emerson edited the first compilation, *Letters to Various Persons*, in 1865, only three years after Thoreau's death. His purpose, as he told Thoreau's sister Sophia, was to exhibit "a most perfect piece of stoicism." To that end he omitted from some of the letters "private or personal references." Many letters he simply omitted entirely. Sophia Thoreau protested and insisted on inserting letters that would show "some tokens of natural affection." She said that "it did not seem quite honest to Henry" to omit such passages. Emerson said, though, that she had "marred his classic statue"; and the matter was referred to James T. Fields for settlement. He proposed a compromise that retained a few of the letters she had inserted. So says Sanborn in his *Henry D. Thoreau* (pp. 305–6).

Emerson's edition was, then, highly selective. He included only sixty-five letters. "Verbal corrections" were made. The recipients were frequently identified only by initials, and there were no indications of excisions. No doubt Emerson's intentions were of the best, since he was doing what he thought most likely to insure Thoreau's fame and emphasizing what he thought to be Thoreau's strongest point. But he succeeded only in producing a distorted picture, forgetting all the warmer qualities "needed to balance the fundamental stoicism which Emerson perceived in his friend." It was this edition that gave James Russell Lowell the opportunity to denounce Thoreau as cold and humorless. In the *Atlantic* for October 1865 Thomas Wentworth Higginson similarly

xiii

complained of these letters: "There is almost no private history in them; and even of Thoreau's beloved science of Natural History, very little." Apparently only Bronson Alcott was satisfied with the edition. He commented in his *Journals* (p. 374): "The most remarkable addition to epistolary literature that we have had; a book likely to be read and prized as are Marcus Antoninus, Pliny, Plutarch, and the delightful works of that class, for years to come. Indeed, I may say, the book is unique for the weight of wit, the high moral tone, the surpassing insights, and the fast hold it shows alike on thoughts and persons. The style, too, is as remarkable as the rest, and altogether proves the remarkable gifts of the man and the author. Thoreau is sure of living while New England survives and Nature continues to interest mankind." Perhaps because Alcott knew Thoreau so well as a person, he was able to see the humanity in the letters. Today's reader is apt to find Emerson's edition of the letters unsatisfactory.

In 1894 Franklin Benjamin Sanborn, another friend and neighbor of Thoreau, edited a more comprehensive volume under the title *Familiar Letters of Henry David Thoreau*. It contains 130 letters—more or less, for Sanborn's kind of editing makes it hard to tell—by Thoreau (increased to about 140 in the 1906 edition, entitled simply *Familiar Letters*, Volume VI of *The Writings of Henry David Thoreau*) and fragments from a few letters to him. All the letters in Emerson's edition are included, many in more detailed form. It was Sanborn's announced intention "to give the world . . . a fuller and more familiar view of our friend" than that afforded by the Emerson edition. For this purpose he chose "many letters and mere notes, illustrating his domestic and gossipy moods . . . and even the colloquial vulgarity . . . that he sometimes allowed himself."

Although Sanborn's edition was twice the size of Emerson's, it likewise aimed at neither completeness nor accuracy. It omitted many letters published elsewhere, even some published by Sanborn himself. He was guided in his editing by the practice, then common, of revising and polishing the originals to suit the style of the day. Hardly a letter was left untouched. In one letter, chosen at random, there are over 100 changes in punctuation, grammar, spelling, and wording. Although these changes do not as a rule alter the meaning, they do give us a false idea of Thoreau's style. Moreover, in a few of the letters the changes are so drastic that the original can scarcely be recognized at first glance. An excellent example is the letter to Horace Greeley of May 19, 1848,

as a comparison of the manuscript in the Boston Public Library with Sanborn's transcription will show. Furthermore Sanborn sometimes gave two different versions of the same letter. For example, he printed one version of the letter written to Thoreau by James Elliot Cabot on May 27, 1847, in his *Henry D. Thoreau* and a second in *Familiar Letters of Thoreau*. The two versions overlap in parts, but each contains material not in the other. Because the original manuscript has disappeared, we have to be satisfied with a mosaic of the two and wonder about the original letter. Sanborn was also careless about dates. He occasionally dated the same letter differently in different printings, as for example the letter of February 12, 1843 from Emerson, which he dated correctly in the *Atlantic*, but February 10, 1843 in *Bronson Alcott at Alcott House*. In *Familiar Letters of Thoreau* he quoted a portion of a letter of December 2, 1847 from Emerson and a part of another letter of March 25, 1848, entering them together as one letter dated February 1848, halfway between the two. Sanborn forces the student to question the dating of many of the letters he handled.

Sanborn published elsewhere, as we have seen, a number of letters from Thoreau's correspondence. He printed a large portion of the Thoreau-Greeley correspondence in his 1882 biography of Thoreau, including twenty-three letters from Greeley and one from Thoreau. In 1892 he printed thirty-one letters (as he counted them) from the Emerson-Thoreau correspondence in two installments in the *Atlantic Monthly*. He also scattered other letters to and from Thoreau throughout his various books and articles, too often with little regard to appropriateness. Unfortunately all these printings display the same faults that mar his editions of the letters. Exactly how many letters Sanborn changed drastically we shall never know, for many of the manuscripts have disappeared. Yet with all his faults as an editor—faults more the product of the time than of the man—he compels our gratitude for a great many letters from Thoreau's correspondence that we might otherwise never have known.

Although the Emerson and the Sanborn volumes have been the only major editions of Thoreau's correspondence, over the years several small groups of his letters have appeared in print and remain as important source material. One of these is *Some Unpublished Letters of Henry D. and Sophia E. Thoreau*, edited by Dr. Samuel Arthur Jones in 1899. It contains the brief correspondence with Calvin Greene, Thoreau's Michigan disciple, later reprinted in Sanborn's edition of 1906. Dr. Jones

Explanatory Note

Any editor of manuscript materials is immediately faced with the problem whether he is to aim his text at the general reader or the scholar. In this edition we have attempted to satisfy both without compromising the purposes of either. We have tried to make the texts of the letters as readable as possible for the layman and as accurate as possible for the scholar. For clarity therefore we have occasionally had to insert identifications of individuals, places, and other matters mentioned. But every such addition has been set off in brackets. In the rare instances where reproduction of an oddity in the original irresistibly suggests an overlooked printer's error we have permitted ourselves a cautionary "[*sic*]." The only silent change we have made in the text is the omission of a few obviously inadvertently repeated words. Our treatment, we hope, will enable the layman to find a readable text and the scholar to construct an accurate reproduction.

Wherever possible we have based our texts on the original manuscripts. Occasionally we have been forced to resort to microfilms or photostats, and still more rarely to transcripts made by individuals on whom we could depend. (Every such transcript is indicated by the insertion of the word "typescript" immediately after the identification of the manuscript source.) Only as a last resort, when unable to trace a manuscript, have we depended on a printed source, and in that event we have tried to determine the most accurate printed version available.

The letters have been placed in chronological order according to the date of writing. Where there are two or more letters for a single day they have been arranged alphabetically by author or recipient. The letters not exactly dated have been entered as close as possible to the probable date of composition. A letter dated only by month appears at the end of that month; one dated only by year at the end of that year. If

a letter can be dated only before or after a certain date, it will be found immediately before or after that date. If a letter has no date at all and we have not found any clue to its date, it will be found at the end of the book.

We have tried to include in this edition every letter written by or to Thoreau for which any of the text still exists. (In our "Henry David Thoreau: A Check List of His Correspondence," *Bulletin of the New York Public Library*, LIX, May 1955, 227–52, we have also listed many letters that once existed but have since disappeared; also the letters misdated by other editors.) The only exceptions that we know of—we should be sanguine indeed if we were to assert that no other letters may at some later date come to light—are some letters in the possession of Professor Raymond Adams of Chapel Hill, North Carolina, who has not seen fit to release them for our use.

We have given each letter a heading that indicates, if the letter were written by Thoreau, to whom it was written, or, if it were written to Thoreau, by whom it was written. Any of this information about which there is doubt we have followed with a question mark.

Although we have been careful to follow the paragraphing indentions of the original letters, we have not attempted to indicate the *exact* spacing of the heading, close, and paragraph indention; these have been blocked and formalized.

Many of the letters we have followed with brief annotations. In these we have tried to make a compromise between the kind of information the general reader wants and the kind the specialist asks. What one reader will need, another will not; there is no perfect answer to the problem of annotation. For the reader's convenience we have repeated some of the information from letter to letter.

At the end of each letter (or of the notes on it) we have indicated the source of our text. For some of the more frequent sources we have used abbreviations, a chart of which follows this explanatory note. If the text of a letter is first printed here, the source is followed by the words "previously unpublished." It should also be noted that many letters not so marked contain new material, for earlier editors have often printed cut versions of them.

At the beginning of each year we have inserted, to help place the letters in their proper context, a brief note indicating some of Thoreau's activities for the year and some of the events in the world around him.

Abbreviations and Major Sources

Abernethy	The Abernethy Library of American Literature, Middlebury College; Manuscript
Atlantic	*The Atlantic Monthly*
Berg	The Henry W. and Albert A. Berg Collection, New York Public Library; Manuscript
Cholmondeley	"Thoreau and His Friend Thomas Cholmondeley," edited by F. B. Sanborn, *The Atlantic Monthly*, LXXII (December 1893), 741–56
Emerson Letters	*The Letters of Ralph Waldo Emerson*, edited by Ralph L. Rusk, six volumes (1939)
Emerson-Thoreau	"The Emerson-Thoreau Correspondence," edited by F. B. Sanborn, *The Atlantic Monthly*, LXIX (May–June 1892), 577–96 and 736–53
Familiar Letters	*Familiar Letters*, enlarged edition, edited by F. B. Sanborn; Volume VI in The Manuscript Edition of *The Writings of Henry David Thoreau* (1906)
Familiar Letters of Thoreau	*Familiar Letters of Henry David Thoreau*, edited by F. B. Sanborn (1894)
Harvard	The Harvard University Library; Manuscript
Hosmer	The Alfred Hosmer Collection, Concord Free Public Library; Manuscript
Huntington	The Henry E. Huntington Library; Manuscript
Lownes	The Albert E. Lownes Collection; Manuscript
Morgan	The Pierpont Morgan Library; Manuscript
New York	The New York Public Library; Manuscript not in the Berg Collection
Ricketson	*Daniel Ricketson and His Friends*, edited by Anna and Walton Ricketson (1902)

The Correspondence of Henry David Thoreau

A Word to the Reader of These Letters

There is relatively little in Henry David Thoreau's life that is not reflected in the correspondence gathered here. You can understand him better after looking at the letters he wrote and the letters he received. Thoreau in college, Thoreau at Walden, Thoreau in love, struggling to break into the periodicals, lecturing, surveying, moralizing, asserting his independence, are all to be seen in this correspondence. Many of a person's letters are answers to those received; few are best understood purely by themselves. Almost equally important is the fact that the letters someone receives help to make clear the kind of world he is involved in. Consequently we have inserted all available letters addressed to Thoreau; and when we include both sides of a correspondence, the result is a kind of biography. It is a life in letters, not in any unlimited sense, but a life in letters nevertheless.

The Thoreau Correspondence

1836

The population of the United States was 15,423,108, and the watchword was "Progress." Texas won its independence. President Andrew Jackson looked about him fiercely while the conservatives purpled in spite of the fact that this was his last year in office. Daniel Webster was already the leading statesman, or politician, of New England. Massachusetts kept a wary eye on Jackson although it did not completely surrender to Webster's Olympian look. The food the people ate was more abundant than it was to be the next year; but it swam in grease, as a good many travelers from abroad sadly observed, and it was bolted with vigor. At Harvard College the fare was reputed to be a little worse than elsewhere. That may have been merely student libel, however. Out of Concord came Emerson's provocative little book *Nature*.

Henry Thoreau had things to complain about at Harvard in this, his junior year, besides the food. As a member of the unusually unruly class of 1837, he found several matters, academic and other, not to his taste. Nevertheless he did well in languages (Harvard had some broad offerings here, including even Portuguese), literature (he was to become one of the best-read men of his time), and mathematics. He was sick during a good deal of the year; he dropped out May 28 and did not return until fall. Yet he found some friends and was less of a solitary, as the lively tone of his college correspondence shows, than tradition has made him out to be.

Cambridge May 30, 1836

Dear Thoreau,

After nine days of constant rain, we have some prospect of pleasant weather. I cannot describe my feelings of joy, rapture, and astonishment, but you may have some idea of the effect produced on me, from the fact that to this circumstance alone, you owe the present letter.

I have somewhere seen an essay, to prove that a man's temper depends greatly on the weather; I will not however give the arguments brought forward to prove this important fact for two reasons.

Firstly because it appears to me self evident; and secondly because I don't intend to write a theme, but a letter.

Strange that any person in his sober senses, should put two such sentences as the above in a letter, but howsomedever, "what's done cant be helped."

Everything goes on here as regular as clock work, and it is as dull as one of Dr Ware's sermons. (A very forcible comparison that, you must allow).

The Davy Club got into a little trouble the week before last, from the following momentous circumstance.

Hen. Williams gave a lecture on Pyrotechny, and illustrated it with a parcel of fire works he had prepared in the vacation. The report spread through college, that there was to be a "display of fire works," and on the night of their meeting the Davy room was crowded, and those unfortunate youths who could not get in, stood in the yard round the windows. As you may imagine, there was some slight noise on the occasion. In fact the noise was so slight, that Bowen heard it at his room in Holworthy.

This worthy, boldly determined to march forth and disperse the "rioters." Accordingly in the midst of a grand display of rockets, et cetera, he stept into the room, and having gazed round him in silent

4

astonishment for the space of two minutes, and hearing various cries of, —Intrusion—Throw him over—Saw his leg off—Pull his wool &c &c he made two or three dignified motions with his hand to gain attention, and then kindly advised us to "retire to our respective rooms." Strange to say he found no one inclined to follow this good advice, and he accordingly thought fit to withdraw.

There is (as perhaps you know) a law against keeping powder in the college buildings.

The effect of "Tutor Bowens" intrusion was evident on the next Monday night, when Williams and Bigelow were invited to call and see President Quincy, and owing to the tough reasoning of Bowen, who boldly asserted that "powder was powder," they were each presented with public admonition.

We had a miniature volcanoe at Websters lecture the other morning, and the odours therefrom, surpassed all ever produced by Araby the blest.

Imagine to yourself all the windows and shutters of the above named lecture room closed, and then if possible stretch your fancy a little farther and conceive the delightful scent produced by the burning of nearly a bushel of Sulphur, Phospuretted Hydrogen, and other still more pleasant ingredients.

As soon as the burning commenced there was a general rush to the door, and a crowd collected there, running out every half minute to get a breath of fresh air, and then coming in to see the volcanoe.

"No noise nor nothing."

Bigelow and Dr Bacon manufactured some "laughing gas," and administered it on the Delta. It was much better than that made by Webster.

Jack Weiss took some as usual. King, Freshman, took a bag, and produced surprising effects, merely by running into all the unhappy individuals he met, who seemed by no means desirous of his company. Wheeler, Joe Allen, and Hildreth, each received a dose. Wheeler proceeded to dance for the amusement of the company, Joe signalized himself by jumping over the Delta fence, and Sam raved about Milton Shakespeare Byron &c. Sam took two doses. It produced great effect on him. He seemed to be as happy as a mortal could desire, talked with Shakespeare, Milton &c, and seemed to be quite at home with them. It was amusing to trace the connexion of his ideas, and on the whole he afforded greater entertainment than any other person there, it affected

him however very strongly, and he did not get over it till he was led off the Delta and carried into Wheelers room; he was well enough however next day.

This letter containeth a strange mixture.

All possible allowance must be made for want of time, not being accustomed to letter writing &c &c.

Hope you are all well, at home.

Yours truly
A. G. Peabody.

This earliest extant letter to Thoreau was written by one of his class-mates. Thoreau was now probably in Concord on an enforced vacation because of ill health, possibly an early attack of tuberculosis. Henry Williams, Henry Jacob Bigelow, John Bacon, John Weiss, Charles Stearns Wheeler, William Allen, and Samuel Tenney Hildreth were also members of Thoreau's class, and John King was of the class of 1839. Dr. Henry Ware was Professor of Pulpit Eloquence and the Pastoral Care; John White Webster, then Erving Professor of Chemistry and Miner-alogy, later achieved great notoriety by murdering a Dr. Parkman. Francis Bowen was a Harvard tutor. According to Sanborn, The Life of Henry David Thoreau *(p. 57), the Davy Club was a "chemical so-ciety." MS., Morgan.*

To HENRY VOSE

Concord, July 5, 1836.

Dear Vose,

You will probably recognize in the following dialogue a part which you yourself acted.

Act 1st

Scene 1st.

T. Come, Vose, let's hear from a fellow now and then.

V. We—ll, I certainly will, but you must write first.

6

T. No, confound you, I shall have my hands full, and moreover shall have nothing to say, while you will h[av]e bon-fires, gunpowder plots, and deviltry enough to back you.

V. Well, I'll write first, and in the course of our correspondence we can settle a certain other matter.

Now 'tis to this "certain other matter" alone that you are indebted for this epistle. The length and breadth, the height and depth, the sum & substance of what I have to say, is this. Your humble servant will endeavor to enter the Senior Class of Harvard University next term, and if you intend taking a room in College, and it should be consistent with your pleasure, will joyfully sign himself your lawful and proper "Chum."

Should the case be otherwise, you will oblige him much if you will request that sage doughface of a Wheeler to secure me one of the following rooms. Agreeably to his polite offer.

H. 23
St. do
H. 27
St. do
St. 28
H. do

Look well to the order.

I shall expect to hear from you forthwith. I leave it to you to obtain a room, should it be necessary.

Yrs Matter-of-factly
D H Thoreau

This earliest extant letter by Thoreau was written to a Harvard classmate and fellow Concordian who later became a justice of the Superior Court of Massachusetts. A "doughface," which is what Thoreau calls Charles Stearns Wheeler in this letter, was a Northerner who supported the South. "H" was Holworthy and "St" Stoughton, both Harvard dormitories. MS., Huntington.

To CHARLES WYATT RICE

Concord, August 5, 1836

Friend Rice,

You say you are in the hay field: how I envy you! Methinks I see thee stretched at thy ease by the side of a fragrant rick with a mighty flagon in one hand, a cold slice in the other, and a most ravenous appetite to boot. So much for haying. Now I cannot hay nor scratch dirt, I manage to keep soul and body together another way. I have been manufacturing a sort of vessel in miniature, not a *eusselmon nea* [well-benched ship] as Homer has it, but a kind of oblong bread-trough.

In days of yore, 'tis said, the swimming alder Fashioned rude, with branches lopped and stript of its smooth coat, Where fallen tree was not and rippling stream's vast breadth Forbade adventurous leap, the brawny swain did bear secure to farthest shore.

The book has passed away, and with the book the lay, which in my youthful days I loved to ponder. Of curious things it told, how wise men three of Gotham In bowl did venture out to sea, And darkly hints their awful fate.

If men have dared the main to tempt in such frail barks, why may not wash-tub round or bread-trough square oblong Suffice to cross the purling wave and gain the destin'd port?

What do you think these capitals mean? When I begin to feel bluey, I just step into my hog-trough, leave care behind, and drift along our sluggish stream at the mercy of the winds and waves.

The following is an extract from the log-book of the *Red Jacket*, Captain Thoreau:

Set sail from the island—the island! how expressive!—reached Thayer's after a tedious voyage, having encountered a head wind during the whole passage—waves running mountain high, with breakers to leeward—however, arrived safe, and after a thorough outfit, being provided with extra cables, and a first-rate birch mainmast, weighed anchor at 3 p.m., August 1, 1836, N.S., wind blowing N.N.E.

The breeze having increased to a gale, tack'd ship and prepared for emergencies. Just as the ship was rounding point Dennis a squall stuck [*sic*] her, under a cloud of canvas, which swept the deck. The aforesaid mast went by the board, carrying with it the only mainsail. The vessel

8

being left at the mercy of the waves was cast ashore on Nashawtuck beach. Natives—a harmless, unoffensive race, principally devoted to agricultural pursuits—appeared somewhat astonished that a stranger should land so unceremoniously on their coast.

Got her off at twenty minutes of four, and after a short and pleasant passage of ten minutes arrived safely in port with a valuable cargo.

"Epistolary matter," says Lamb, "usually comprises three topics, news, sentiment and puns." Now as to news I don't know the coin—the newspapers take care of that. Puns I abhor and more especially deliberate ones. Sentiment alone is immortal, the rest are short-lived—evanescent.

Now this is neither matter-of-fact, nor *pungent*, nor yet sentimental—it is neither one thing nor the other, but a kind of hodge-podge, put together in much the same style that mince pies are fabled to have been made, i.e. by opening the oven door, and from the further end of the room, casting in the various ingredients—a little lard here, a little flour there—now a round of beef, and then a cargo of spices—helter skelter.

I should like to crawl into those holes you describe—what a crowd of associations 'twould give rise to! "One to once, gentlemen."

As to Indian remains, the season is past with me, the Doctor having expressly forbidden both digging and chopping.

My health is so much improved that I shall return to C. next term if they will receive me. French I have certainly neglected, Dan Homer is all the rage at present.

This from your friend and classmate,
D. H. Thoreau.

P.S. It would afford me much pleasure if you would visit our good old town this vacation; *in other words, myself.*

Don't fail to answer this forthwith; 'tis a good thing to persevere in well doing.

How true it is that the postscript contains the most important matter, invariably.

Text, Two Thoreau Letters, *printed by E. B. Hill (Mesa, Arizona, 1916).*

9

her Library, has constrained me. I have had the offer and opportunity of several places, but the distance or smallness of salary were objections. I should like to hear about Concord Academy from you, if it is not engaged. Hoping that your situation affords you every advantage for continuing your mental education and development I am

with esteem & respect
Yr classmate & friend
James Richardson Jr

P.S. I hope you will tell me something about your situation, state of mind, course of reading, &c; and any advice you have to offer will be gratefully accepted. Should the place, alluded to above, be filled, any place, that you may hear spoken of, with a reasonable salary, would perhaps answer for your humble serv't

—R—

James Richardson, another of Thoreau's Harvard classmates, turned to the ministry after doing some teaching and attended Harvard Divinity School. Thoreau had graduated August 16, 1837. Reverend Barzillai Frost was pastor of the Unitarian Church, Concord. Samuel Hoar was chairman of the Concord school committee. Charles Beck was a professor of Latin at Harvard. Reverend Daniel Kimball kept a boarding school in Needham. Although some have questioned the story of Thoreau's teaching in the Concord public schools, this letter authenticates it. MS., Berg.

To HENRY VOSE
Concord Oct 13th 37

Friend Vose
You don't know how much I envy you your comfortable settlement—almost sine-cure—in the region of Butternuts. How art thou pleased with the lay of the land and the look of the people? Do the rills tinkle and fume, and bubble and purl, and trickle and meander as thou

12

expectedest, or are the natives less absorbed in the pursuit of gain than the good clever homespun and respectable people of New England?

I presume that by this time you have commenced pedagoguersing in good earnest. Methinks I see thee, perched on learning's little stool, thy jet black boots luxuriating upon a well-polished fender, while round thee are ranged some half dozen small specimens of humanity, thirsting for an idea:

> Pens to mend, and hands to guide.
> Oh who would a schoolmaster be?

Why I to be sure. The fact is, here I have been vegetating for the last three months. "The clock sends to bed at ten, and calls me again at eight." Indeed I deem "conformity one of the best arts of life." Now should you hear of any situation in your neighborhood, or indeed any other, which you think would suit me, such as your own, for instance, you will much oblige me by dropping a line on the subject, or, I should rather say, by making mention of it in your answer to this.

I received a catalogue from Harvard, the other day, and therein found Classmate Hildreth set down as assistant instructor in Elocution, Chas Dall divinity student—Clarke and Dana law do, and C. S. W[heeler] resident graduate. How we apples Swim! Can you realize that we too can now moralize about College pranks, and reflect upon the pleasures of a college life, as among the things that are past? Mays't thou ever remember as a fellow soldier [in] the campaign of 37

Yr friend and classmate

Thoreau

PS   I have no time for apologies.

Thoreau's former Harvard classmate Vose was now teaching school in upstate New York in the little village of Butternuts. Hildreth, Dall, Clarke, Dana, and Wheeler were other members of that same class of 1837. In the last line of this letter the bracketed word is torn out of the manuscript. MS., Berg.

From HENRY VOSE

Butternuts Oct. 22nd, 1837.

Friend Thoreau

I received by yesterday's mail your favor of the 13th. with great pleasure, and proceed at once to indite you a line of condolence on your having nothing to do. I suspect you wrote that letter during a fit of ennui or the blues. You begin at once by expressing your envy of my happy situation, and mourn over your fate, which condemns you to loiter about Concord, and grub among clamshells. If this were your only source of enjoyment while in C. you would truly be a pitiable object. But I know that it is not. I well remember that "antique and fish-like" office of *Major* Nelson, [to whom and Mr Dennis and Bemis, and J Thoreau I wish to be remembered]; and still more vividly do I remember the fairer portion of the community in C. If from these two grand fountainheads of amusement in that ancient town, united with its delightful walks and your internal resources, you cannot find an ample fund of enjoyment, while waiting for a situation, you deserve to be haunted by blue devils for the rest of your days.

I am surprised that, in writing a letter of two pages and a half to a friend and "fellow soldier of the —37th" at a distance of 300 miles, you should have forgotten to say a single word of the news of C. In lamenting your own fate you have omitted to even hint at any of the events that have occurred since I left. However this must be fully rectified in your next. Say something of the *Yeoman's Gazette* and of the politics of the town and county, of the events, that are daily transpiring there, &c.

I am sorry I know of no situation whatever at present for you. I, in this little, secluded town of B. am the last person in the world to hear of one. But If I do, you may be assured that I will inform you of it at once, and do all in my power to obtain it for you.

With my own situation I am highly pleased. My duties afford me quite as much labor as I wish for, and are interesting and useful to me. Out of school hours I find a great plenty to do, and time passes rapidly and pleasantly.

Please request friend W. Allen to drop me a line and to inform of his success with his school. You will please excuse the brevity of this:

14

but as it is getting late, and everybody has been long in bed but myself, and I am deuced sleepy I must close. Write soon and long, and I shall try to do better in my next.

Yours truly,
Henry Vose.

It is difficult to identify the various persons mentioned by Vose in this letter. They probably include Albert H. Nelson and Bowman W. Dennis, two Concord youths of Thoreau's age, and William Allen of Thoreau's Harvard class. "Grub among clamshells" may refer to Thoreau's favorite pastime of searching for Indian arrowheads. MS., Morgan.

To HELEN THOREAU

Concord Oct 27 1837

Dear H.

Please you, let the defendant say a few words in defense of his long silence. You know we have hardly done our own deeds, thought our own thoughts, or lived our own lives, hitherto. For a man to act himself, he must be perfectly free; otherwise, he is in danger of losing all sense of responsibility or of self-respect. Now when such a state of things exists, that the sacred opinions one advances in argument are apologized for by his friends, before his face, lest his hearers receive a wrong impression of the man,—when such gross injustice is of frequent occurrence, where shall we look, & not look in vain, for men, deeds, thoughts? As well apologize for the grape that it is sour,—or the thunder that it is noisy, or the lightning that it tarries not. Farther, letterwriting too often degenerates into a communing of facts, & not of truths; of other men's deeds, & not our thoughts. What are the convulsions of a planet compared with the emotions of the soul? or the rising of a thousand suns, if that is not enlightened by a ray?

Your affectionate brother,
Henry

15

Helen, the eldest of the Thoreau children, is the least known member of the family. Born October 22, 1812, she died June 14, 1849. For a few years she taught in various schools, but most of her life was spent in the family home. This earliest extant letter to a member of the Thoreau family was written while Helen was in Taunton, where her maternal relatives the Dunbars lived. Sanborn identifies the recipient (Familiar Letters of Thoreau, p. 12). Emerson first intended to include the letter in his collection, but at the last minute dropped it out. MS., Berg, copy in Emerson's hand.

To JOHN THOREAU

Musketaquid two hundred and two summers—two moons—eleven suns since the coming of the Pale Faces. Tahatawan—Sachimausan—to his brother sachem—Hopeful—of Hopewell—hoping that he is well.

Brother, it is many suns that I have not seen the print of thy moccasins by our council fire, the Great Spirit has blown more leaves from the trees and many clouds from the land of snows have visited our lodge—the earth has become hard like a frozen buffalo skin, so that the trampling of many herds is like the Great Spirit's thunder—the grass on the great fields is like the old man of eight winters—and the small song-sparrow prepares for his flight to the land whence the summer comes.

Brother—I write thee these things because I know that thou lovest the Great Spirit's creatures, and wast wont to sit at thy lodge door—when the maize was green—to hear the bluebird's song. So shalt thou in the land of spirits, not only find good hunting grounds and sharp arrowheads—but much music of birds.

Brother. I have been thinking how the Pale Faces have taken away our lands—and was a woman. You are fortunate to have pitched your wigwam nearer to the great salt lake, where the pale-Face can never plant corn.

Brother—I need not tell thee how we hunted on the lands of the Dundees—a great war-chief never forgets the bitter taunts of his ene-

mies. Our young men called for strong water—they painted their faces and dug up the hatchet. But their enemies the Dundees were women —they hastened to cover their hatchets with wampum. Our braves are not many—our enemies took a few strings from the heap their fathers left them, and our hatchets were buried.—But not Tahatawan's—his heart is of rock when the Dundees sing—his hatchet cuts deep into the Dundee braves.

Brother—there is dust on my moccasins—I have journeyed to the White lake in the country of the Ninares. The Long-knife has been there—like a woman I paddled his war-canoe. But the spirits of my fathers were angered.—the waters were ruffled and the Bad Spirit troubled the air.

The hearts of the *Lee*-vites are gladdened—the young Peacock has returned to his lodge by Nawshawtuck. He is the medicine of his tribe, but his heart is like the dry leaves when the whirlwind breathes. He has come to help choose new chiefs for the tribe in the great council house when two suns are past.—There is no seat for Tahatawan in the council-house. He lets the squaws talk—his voice is heard above the warwhoop of his tribe, piercing the hearts of his foes—his legs are stiff, he cannot sit.

Brother, art thou waiting for spring that the *geese* may fly low over thy wigwam? Thy arrows are sharp, thy bow is strong. Has Anawan killed all the eagles? The crows fear not the winter. Tahatawans eyes are sharp—he can track a snake in the grass, he knows a friend from a foe—he welcomes a friend to his lodge though the ravens croak.

Brother hast thou studied much in the medicine books of the Pale-Faces? Dost thou understand the long talk of the great medicine whose words are like the music of the mocking bird? But our chiefs have not ears to hear him—they listen like squaws to council of old men—they understand not his words. But Brother, he never danced the war-dance, nor heard the warwhoop of his enemies. He was a squaw—he staid by the wigwam when the braves were out, and tended the tame buffaloes.

Fear not, the Dundees have faint hearts, and much wampum. When the grass is green on the great fields, and the small titmouse returns again we will hunt the buffaloe to gether.

Our old men say they will send the young chief of the Karlisles who lives in the green wigwam and is a great medicine, that his words may

17

be heard in the long talk which the wise men are going to hold at Shawmut by the salt-lake. He is a great talk—and will not forget the enemies of his tribe.

14th sun.

The fire has gone out in the council house. The words of our old men have been like the vaunts of the Dundees. The Eaglebeak was moved to talk like a silly Pale-Face, and not as becomes a great war-chief in a council of braves. The young Peacock is a woman among braves—he heard not the words of the old men—like a squaw, he looked at his medicine paper. The young chief of the green wigwam has hung up his moccasins, he will not leave his tribe till after the buffaloe have come down on to the plains.

Brother this is a long talk—but there is much meaning to my words. they are not like the thunder of canes when the lightening smites them.

Brother I have just heard *thy talk* and am well pleased thou are getting to be a great medicine.

The Great Spirit confound the enemies of thy tribe.

Tahatawan
his mark

It is clear that Thoreau always admired and loved his elder brother John, whose tragic death from lockjaw in 1842 left a deep impression on him. This letter, written in what is supposedly conventionalized Indian dialect, gives a sidelight on the brothers' interest in Indian lore. Thoreau writes as Tahatawan, the mythical(?) sachen (according to Sanborn, Familiar Letters of Thoreau, p. 19) of the Musketaquid or Concord River.

Sanborn has furnished the following annotations: "The White lake in the country of the Ninares" is White Pond in the district called Nine-Acre Corner; the "Lee-vites" were a family living on Lee's Hill or Nashawtuck, where the old Tahatawan lived at times before the English settled in Concord in September 1635; the "real date" of this letter is November 11–14, 1837, and between those two days the Massa-

18

chusetts state election was held; the council house was the Boston State House, to which the Concord voters were electing deputies; "Eagle-Beak" was doubtless Samuel Hoar, Concord's leading citizen; the "great medicine whose words are like the music of the mocking bird" may have been the mellifluous but rather shallow orator Edward Everett; and the "young chief of the Karlisles" was Albert Nelson, son of a Carlisle physician, who began to practice law in Concord in 1836. MS., Berg.

To ORESTES BROWNSON

Concord Dec 30th 1837.

Dear Sir—

I have never ceased to look back with interest, not to say satisfaction, upon the short six weeks which I passed with you. They were an era in my life—the morning of a new *Lebenstag*. They are to me as a dream that is dreamt, but which returns from time to time in all its original freshness. Such a one as I would dream a second and a third time, and then tell before breakfast.

I passed a few hours in the city, about a month ago, with the intention of calling on you, but not being able to ascertain, from the directory or other sources, where you had settled, was fain to give up the search and return home.

My apology for this letter is to ask your assistance in obtaining employment. For, say what you will, this frostbitten 'forked carrot' of a body must be fed and clothed after all. It is ungrateful, to say the least, to suffer this much abused case to fall into so dilapidated a condition that every northwester may luxuriate through its chinks and crevices, blasting the kindly affections it should shelter, when a few clouts would save it. Thank heaven, the toothache occurs often enough to remind me that I must be out patching the roof occasionally, and not be always keeping up a blaze upon the hearth within, with my German and metaphysical cat-sticks.

But my subject is not postponed *sine die.* I seek a situation as

teacher of a small school, or assistant in a large one, or, what is more desirable, as private tutor in a gentleman's family.

Perhaps I should give some account of myself. I would make education a pleasant thing both to the teacher and the scholar. This discipline, which we allow to be the end of life, should not be one thing in the schoolroom, and another in the street. We should seek to be fellow students with the pupil, and we should learn of, as well as with him, if we would be most helpful to him. But I am not blind to the difficulties of the case; it supposes a degree of freedom which rarely exists. It hath not entered into the heart of man to conceive the full import of that word—Freedom—not a paltry Republican freedom, with a *posse comitatus* at his heels to administer it in doses as to a sick child—but a freedom proportionate to the dignity of his nature—a freedom that shall make him feel that he is a man among men, and responsible only to that Reason of which he is a particle, for his thoughts and his actions.

I have even been disposed to regard the cowhide as a nonconductor. Methinks that, unlike the electric wire, not a single spark of truth is ever transmitted through its agency to the slumbering intellect it would address. I mistake, it may teach a truth in physics, but never a truth in morals.

I shall be exceedingly grateful if you will take the trouble to inform me of any situation of the kind described that you may hear of. As referees I could mention Mr Emerson—Mr [Samuel] Hoar—and Dr [Ezra] Ripley.

I have perused with pleasure the first number of the 'Boston Review.' I like the spirit of independence which distinguishes it. It is high time that we knew where to look for the expression of *American* thought. It is vexatious not to know beforehand whether we shall find our account in the perusal of an article. But the doubt speedily vanishes, when we can depend upon having the genuine conclusions of a single reflecting man.

Excuse this cold business letter. Please remember me to Mrs Brownson, and dont forget to make mention to the children of the stern pedagogue that was—

> [Sincerely and truly yours,
> Henry D. Thoreau.]

P. S.   I add this postscript merely to ask if I wrote this formal epistle. It absolutely freezes my fingers.

*Brownson was a vigorous and aggressive minister who believed that
moral reform should be accompanied by political reform. Without,
he affirmed, changing his basic position, he went through several religious conversions before ending as a Roman Catholic. He was a social
radical in his early thirties when Thoreau came to stay at his house late
in 1835. Thoreau had been allowed a brief leave of absence from his
studies at Harvard that he might teach school for a term and make a
little money. Brownson was living in Canton, Massachusetts, and
Thoreau was sent there to see about an opening. He was interviewed
and recommended by Brownson, whose children were attending the
Canton school, and Brownson liked him so well that he took him into
his home. Brownson edited the* Boston Quarterly Review. MS., University of Notre Dame Library; *closing salutation missing from manuscript
and copied from printed text in Henry F. Brownson's* Orestes A. Brownson's Early Life, *pp. 204–6.*

1838

The House of Representatives, resolutely closing its eyes to the future, resolved to receive no more antislavery petitions. The *Great Western,* first steamship built for transatlantic service, left Bristol on its maiden voyage April 8 and docked at New York April 23. Under the will of John Smithson half a million dollars was paid into the United States Treasury for the founding of the Smithsonian Institution. (Congress was to be surprisingly tardy in using the money.) Chief Black Hawk died in Iowa. A treaty of commerce and navigation was signed with Sardinia. Every railroad in our country was constituted a post route. The banks, after some bitter disagreements, decided to resume specie payments. Lieutenant Charles Wilkes, of the Navy, in command of a fleet of six vessels, was commissioned to explore the Pacific Ocean and the southern seas.

In need of work and looking for it, Thoreau joined with his brother John to open a private school for small boys. It was housed for a short time on the site of the present Concord Public Library. Henry taught the children classics, mathematics, and nature study. He made his first trip to Maine. He found time to lecture before the Concord Lyceum; his first lecture was called "Society." To judge by the scraps preserved, it was characteristically critical. In his *Journal* he wrote some original verse, quoted from the classics, reflected on life, and mourned the loss of a tooth.

To JOHN THOREAU

Concord, February 10, 1838.

Dear John,—

Dost expect to elicit a spark from so dull a steel as myself, by that flinty subject of thine? Truly, one of your copper percussion caps would have fitted this nail-head better.

Unfortunately, the "Americana" has hardly two words on the subject. The process is very simple. The stone is struck with a mallet so as to produce pieces sharp at one end, and blunt at the other. These are laid upon a steel line (probably a chisel's edge), and again struck with the mallet, and flints of the required size are broken off. A skillful workman may make a thousand in a day.

So much for the "Americana." Dr. Jacob Bigelow in his "Technology" says, "Gunflints are formed by a skillful workman, who breaks them out with a hammer, a roller, and steel chisel, with small, repeated strokes."

Your ornithological commission shall be executed. When are you coming home?

Your affectionate brother,
Henry D. Thoreau.

Text, Familiar Letters of Thoreau, *pp. 20–21.*

To JOHN THOREAU

Concord, March 17th 1838

Dear John,

Your box of relics came safe to hand, but was speedily deposited on the carpet I assure you. What could it be? Some declared it must be Taunton herrings Just nose it sir. So down we went onto our knees and commenced smelling in good earnest, now horizontally from this corner to that, now perpendicularly from the carpet up, now diagonally, and finally with a sweeping movement describing the entire circumference. But it availed not. Taunton herring would not be smelled. So we e'en proce[e]ded to open it *vi et chisel*. What an array of nails! Four nails make a quarter four quarters a yard,—i faith this isn't cloth measure. Blaze away old boy, clap in another wedge, then!—There! softly she begins to gape—Just give that old stickler with a black hat on a hoist. Aye! W'ell [*sic*] pare his nails for him. Well done old fellow there's a breathing hole for you. "Drive it in," cries one, "rip it off," cries another. Be easy I say. What's done, may be undone Your richest veins don't lie nearest the surface. Suppose we sit down and enjoy the prospect, for who knows but we may be disappointed? When they opened Pandora's box, all the contents escaped except hope, but in this case hope is uppermost and will be the first to escape when the box is opened. However the general voice was for kicking the coverlid off.

The relics have been arranged numerically on a table. When shall we set up housekeeping? Miss Ward thanks you for her share of the spoils, also accept many thanks from your humble servant *"for yourself."*

I have a proposal to make. Suppose by the time you are released, we should start in company for the West and there either establish a school jointly, or procure ourselves separate situations. Suppose moreover you should get ready to start previous to leaving Taunton, to save time. Go *I* must at all events. Dr Jarvis enumerated nearly a dozen schools which I could have—all such as would suit you equally well. I wish you would write soon about this. It is high season to start. The canals are now open, and travelling comparatively cheap. I think I can borrow the cash in this town. There's nothing like trying

Brigham wrote you a few words on the eig[h]th which father took the liberty to read, with the advice and consent of the family. He wishes you

24

to send him those [numbers] of the library of health received since— 38, if you are in Concord, othe[rw]ise, he says, you need not trouble you[rse]lf about it at present. [H]e is in C and enjoying better health than usual. But one number, and that you have, has been received.

The bluebirds made their appearance the 14th day of March—robins and pigeons have also been seen. Mr. E[merson] has put up the bluebird box in due form.

All send their love.   From

Y'r aff. brother
H. D. Thoreau

John, still in Taunton, had shipped to Concord a box of Indian relics (*Thoreau's* Journal, I, 454). *Miss Prudence Ward was a boarder in the Thoreau household. Dr. Edward Jarvis, according to Sanborn* (Familiar Letters of Thoreau, *p. 23*), *was born in Concord in 1803 and went to Louisville in April 1837. He knew the Thoreau boys well and gave them good hopes of success in Ohio or Kentucky as teachers. But their plan was never carried through. Since Brigham was a common name in Concord, no specific identification can well be made. The* Library of Health *was probably the Boston periodical published from 1837 to 1843. Emerson in his* Journals (*IX, 360*) *says of the bluebird house: "John Thoreau, Jr., one day put up a bluebird box on my barn,—fifteen years ago, it must be,—and there it is still with every summer a melodious family in it, adorning the place and singing his praises." MS., Huntington. Words and letters torn from the manuscript in the third from the last paragraph have been replaced within brackets.*

From JOSIAH QUINCY

Sir,—

The school is at Alexandria; the students are said to be young men well advanced in ye knowledge of ye Latin and Greek classics; the requisitions are, qualification and *a person who has had experience in*

school keeping. Salary $600 a year, besides washing and Board; duties to be entered on ye 5th or 6th of May. If you choose to apply, I will write as soon as I am informed of it. State to me your experience in school keeping.

Yours,
Josiah Quincy.

Josiah Quincy, the president of Harvard, came to Thoreau's aid in his quest for a school. He first wrote a letter of recommendation (San-born's Henry D. Thoreau, *p. 61):*

Harvard University, Cambridge, March 26, 1838.

To Whom It May Concern,—
I certify that Henry D. Thoreau, of Concord, in this State of Massachusetts, graduated at this seminary in August, 1837; that his rank was high as a scholar in all the branches, and his morals and general conduct unexceptionable and exemplary. He is recommended as well qualified as an instructor, for employment in any public or private school or private family.

Josiah Quincy, President of Harvard University.

A few weeks later he followed it with the letter to Thoreau recommending a school in Alexandria, Virginia, which, Sanborn suggests, might have been the Episcopal Theological Seminary there. Miss Prudence Ward, in a letter to her sister on April 13, 1838, comments on the offer: "He is willing to take it . . . if accepted" (Sanborn, The Life of Henry David Thoreau, *p. 201); Sanborn dates the letter April 12, 1838. Quite evidently Thoreau's offer was not accepted. Text, Sanborn's* Henry D. Thoreau, *pp. 61–62.*

To JOHN THOREAU

Concord July 8th 38—

Dear John,

We heard from Helen today and she informs us that you are coming home by the first of August, now I wish you to write, and let me know exactly when your vacation takes place, that I may take one at the same time. I am in school from 8 to 12 in the morning, and from 2 to 4 in the afternoon; after that I read a little Greek or English, or for variety, take a stroll in the fields. We have not had such a year for berries this long time—the earth is actually blue with them. High blu[e]berries, three kinds of low—thimble and rasp-berries, constitute my diet at present. (Take notice—I only diet between meals.) Among my deeds of charity I may reckon the picking of a cherry tree for two helpless single ladies who live under the hill—but i' faith it was robbing Peter to pay Paul—for while I was *exalted* in charity towards them, I had no mercy on my own stomach. Be advised, my love for currants continues .The only addition that I have made of late to my stock of ornithological information—is in the shape, not of a Fring. Melod. but surely a melodious Fringilla—the F. Iuncorum, or rush sparrow. I had long known him by his note but never by name. Report says that Elijah Stearns is going to take the town school.

I have four scholars, and one more engaged. Mr. Fenner left town yesterday. Among occurrences of ill omen, may be mentioned the falling out and cracking of the inscription stone of Concord monument. Mrs. Lowell and children are at Aunt's. Peabody walked up last Wednesday—spent the night, and took a stroll in the woods. Sophia says I mu[st] leave off and pen a few lines for her to Helen. S[o] Good bye. Love from all and among them yr

aff' brother
H D T

Here Thoreau is writing about the private school he opened in Concord the month before. His brother John soon joined him in the enterprise. The Sophia referred to is Henry's younger sister; Helen is the older

*one. Augustus Goddard Peabody was the former Harvard classmate
who wrote the earliest letter to Thoreau that we have. MS., Lownes.
Words mutilated in the last paragraph of the manuscript have been
replaced within brackets.*

To HELEN THOREAU

Concord Oct. 6th—38.

Dear Helen,

I dropped Sophia's letter into the box immediately on taking
yours out, else the tone of the former had been changed.

I have no acquaintance with "Cleavelands First Lessons," though I
have peeped into his abridged grammar, which I should think very
well calculated for beginners, at least, for such as would be likely to
wear out one book, before they would be prepared for the abstruser
parts of Grammar. Ahem! As no one can tell what was the Roman pro-
nunciation, each nation makes the Latin conform, for the most part,
to the rules of its own language; so that with us, of the vowels, only a
has a peculiar sound.

In the end of a word of more than one syllable, it is sounded like ah—
as pennah, Lydiah Hannah, &c. without regard to case.—but da is never
sounded dah because it is a monosyllable.

All terminations in es and plural cases in os, as you know, are pronounced long—as homines (hominēse) dominos (dominōse) or in
English Johnny Vose. For information see Adam's Latin Grammar—before the Rudiments This is all law and gospel in the eyes of the world
—but remember I am speaking as it were, in the third person, and
should sing quite a different tune, if it were I that made the quire. However one must occasionally hang his harp on the willows, and play on
the Jew's harp, in such a strange country as this.

One of your young ladies wishes to study Mental Philosophy—hey?
well tell her that she has the very best text book that I know of already
in her possession. If she do not believe it, then she should have bespoken
a better in another world, and not have expected to find one at "Little

28

and Wilkins'." But if she wishes to know how poor an apology for a Mental Philosophy men have tacked together, synthetically or analytically, in these latter days—how they have squeezed the infinite mind into a compass that would not nonpluss a surveyor of Eastern Lands—making Imagination and Memory to lie still in their respective apartments, like ink stand and wafers in a la[dy's] escritoire—why let her read Locke or Stewart, or Brown. The fact is, Mental Philosophy is very like poverty—which, you know, begins at home; and, indeed, when it goes abroad, it is poverty itself.

Chorus. I should think an abridgment of one of the above authors, or of Abercrombie, would answer her purpose. It may set her a-thinking.

Probably there are many systems in the market of which I am ignorant.

As for themes—say first "Miscellaneous Thoughts"—set one up to a window to note what passes in the street, and make her comments thereon; or let her gaze in the fire, or into a corner where there is a spider's web, and philosophize—moralize—theorize, or what not.

What their hands find to putter about, or their minds to think about, —that let them write about. To say nothing of Advantages or disadvantages—of this, that, or the other. Let them set down their ideas at any given Season—preserving the chain of thought as complete as may be.

This is the style pedagogical.

I am much obliged to you for your piece of information. Knowing your dislike to a sentimental letter I remain

Yr affectionate brother,
H D T

A sidelight on Thoreau's Transcendental—or pre-Transcendental—ideas is cast by the slighting reference to John Locke, Dugald Stewart, and Thomas Brown in this pedagogical letter. Locke became an object of scorn for the Transcendentalists because he stressed the superiority of knowledge acquired through the senses over knowledge acquired from within. The Scottish philosophers Stewart and Brown, however, taught that all of us have a "common sense" that lets us know the truth of some things our five regular senses could never tell us. The Transcendentalists were well agreed that the knowledge from within was superior to, and

transcended, any knowledge gained from without. MS., Berg. Part of a word torn from the fifth paragraph of the manuscript has been replaced within brackets.

Note. A belatedly discovered letter of 1838 is printed on page 656.

From EMERSON

My dear Sir,

    Will you not come up to the Cliff this P.M. at any hour convenient to you where our ladies will be greatly gratified to see you & the more they say if you will bring your flute for the echo's sake; though now the wind blows.

                                    R. W. E.

Monday 1 o'clock P.M.

By February of 1838 Emerson and Thoreau had become friendly; by April they were walking together to the Cliff, that is to say the southern side of Concord's Fair Haven Hill. Their friendship, however, was probably still maturing, as Emerson's formal salutation shows. Indeed, in February of 1839 Emerson will still head a letter to Thoreau "My dear Sir"; and it will take Thoreau almost ten years before he can bring himself to start a letter with Emerson's given name. On February 23, 1848 he will finally write: "Dear Waldo,—For I think I have heard that that is your name." This note of Emerson's was probably written on Monday, November 12, 1838, when H. G. O. Blake, who was to become one of Thoreau's most devoted correspondents, came to visit Emerson. A walk to the Cliff and "social music" were among their activities. Another possible but less likely date, also advanced by Rusk (Emerson Letters, II, 174), is June 29, 1840. MS., Berg.

30

1839

The Whigs nominated William Henry Harrison. The Mormons, forced out of Missouri, sent their agents to buy land on the Illinois side of the Mississippi for the new city of Nauvoo. W. F. Harnden started the first express between Boston and New York. A treaty of navigation and commerce was signed between Texas and France. Men's trousers, after having been almost skintight and somber in the earlier years of the decade, were now being cut with luxurious fullness out of plaids. The bloodless Aroostook War between Maine frontiersmen and Canadian trespassers took place, the president having even been given authority to send troops to Maine to protect the sanctity of the frontier. A petition from settlers on the Willamette River asking the United States to take formal possession of Oregon was laid before the Senate. Congress passed a law prohibiting dueling and one abolishing imprisonment for debt in certain circumstances.

Thoreau, in his *Journal* for this year, set down more verses, as well as several pages on bravery and a few paragraphs about love and friendship. A page and a half contains a brief itinerary, with such comments as "Camped in Merrimack, on the west bank, by a deep ravine" and "Ascended the mountain and rode to Conway." These scraps of sentences are all we have at this point about what later became one of the most famous of American journeys, the one transcendentalized in *A Week on the Concord and Merrimack Rivers*. The other major event of the year was Thoreau's falling in love. Ellen Sewall, a pretty girl from a nearby town, came to visit the Thoreau household. Thoreau's brother John, Henry's companion on the excursion up the rivers, fell in love with her too. The triangle was not resolved until the next year.

Friday, 15 Feb.

My dear **Sir**

The dull weather and some inflammation still hold me in the house, and so may cost you some trouble. I wrote to Miss Fuller at Groton a week ago that as soon as Saturday (tomorrow) I would endeavor to send her more accurate answers to her request for information in respect to houses likely to be let in Concord. As I know that she & her family must be anxious to learn the facts, as soon as may be, I beg you to help me in procuring the information today, if your engagements will leave you space for this charity.

My questions are

1. Is Dr. Gallup's house to be vacant shortly, &, if so, what is the rent?
   It belongs, I believe, to Col. Shattuck.
2. What does Mrs Goodwin determine in regard to the house now occupied by Mr. Gourgas? Since, if she do not wish to apply for that house, I think that will suit Mrs. F. If it is to be had, what is the rent?
   Col. Shattuck is also the owner of this house.
3. What is the rent of your Aunts' house, & when will it be rentable?
4. Pray ask your father if he knows of any other houses in the village that may want tenants in the Spring.

If sometime this evening you can without much inconvenience give me an answer to these queries, you will greatly oblige your imprisoned friend

R. W. Emerson

In the spring of 1839 Margaret Fuller was house-hunting in Concord, and Emerson called on Thoreau to assist in the search. Sanborn tenta-

tively misdated the letter 1840. Rusk (Emerson Letters, II, 182), however, points out that this letter was clearly written on the same day, February 15, 1839, as one from Emerson to Margaret Fuller. Concordians mentioned are Dr. William Gallup, Colonel Daniel Shattuck, Mrs. Amelia Goodwin, and Francis R. Gourgas. Thoreau's aunts were the Misses Jane and Maria Thoreau, who lived in what is now part of the Colonial Inn. MS., Hosmer.

From EMERSON

Dear Sir,

    Mrs Brown wishes very much to see you at her house tomorrow (Saturday) Evening to meet Mr Alcott. If you have any leisure for the Useful Arts, L. E. is very desirous of your aid. Do not come at any risk of the Fine.

R. W. E.

The Mrs. Brown mentioned here is undoubtedly Emerson's sister-in-law, Lucy Jackson Brown. A quiet and sensitive woman, older than Thoreau, she made for him a good friend and listener. His poem "Sic Vita" was for her, and he later sent her some idealistic letters. Rusk suggests that since Alcott was not yet a resident of Concord, Thoreau may have met him for the first time as a result of Mrs. Brown's invitation. L. E. is undoubtedly Lidian Emerson. This note was apparently an afterthought to be sent with the letter given just above. Rusk notes (Emerson Letters, II, 183) that he has seen a copy of the letter accompanied by a copy of the note, and the note is preceded by this introduction "[inclosed a scrap of paper on wh. is written]." MS., Berg, copy in J. E. Cabot's hand.

1840

President Van Buren ordered a ten-hour day for government workers, to the announced regret of a number of prominent politicians. We fought the Seminole Indians in Florida. Harrison and John Tyler conducted a remarkably successful log-cabin-and-hard-cider political campaign and defeated Van Buren. S. F. B. Morse introduced photography into America. The population of the United States exceeded 17,000,000 —including 14,189,705 whites, 2,487,355 slaves, and 386,293 free Negroes. The craze for phrenology continued. Women's bonnets underwent a decided change; the large flaring brims popular during the past decade were cut back and the bonnets came down rather far over the ears. In our architecture "American Gothic," inspired by Sir Walter Scott's novels, was the fashion. Bronson Alcott moved to Concord.

Thoreau broke into print with a poem about Ellen Sewall's brother, which the Transcendentalist magazine, the *Dial*, published in its July number. Ellen's and Henry's love affair ripened, but early in November —under orders from her father—Ellen wrote to Henry rejecting him. (This letter has unfortunately disappeared.) "I never felt so badly at sending a letter in my life," she maintained. In his *Journal* Thoreau philosophized and wrote about nature, adding some obscure personal allusions every now and then. Margaret Fuller, who was editing the *Dial*, rejected Thoreau's essay "The Service" in December. "Yet I hope you will give it me again," was the suggestion she added.

Concordiae, Dec. Kal. Feb. AD. MDCCCXL.

Care Soror,

Est magnus acervus nivis ad limina, et frigus intolerabile intus. Coelum ipsum ruit, credo, et terram operit. Sero stratum linquo et maturè repeto; in fenestris multa pruina prospectum absumit, et hîc miser scribo, non currente calamo, nam digiti mentesque torpescunt. Canerem cum Horatio, si vox non faucibus haeserit—

"Vides, ut altâ stet nive candidum
   Nawshawtuct, nec jam sustineant onus
      Silvae laborantes, geluque
      Flumina constiterint acuto
   Dissolve frigus, ligna super foco
   Large reponens; etc."

Sed olim, Musâ mutatâ, et laetiore plectro,

—"neque jam stabulis gaudet pecus, aut arator igni,
      Nec prata canis albicant pruinis,
   Jam Cytherea choros ducit Venus, imminente lunâ;"

Quum turdus ferrugineus ver reduxerit, tu, spero, linques curas scholasticas, et negotio religato, desipere in loco audebis, aut mecum inter inter sylvas, aut super scopulos Pulchri-Portus, aut in cymba super lacum Waldensem, mulcens fluctus manu, aut speciem miratus sub undas.

Bulwerius est mihi nomen incognitum, unus ex ignobile vulgo, nec refutandus nec laudandus. Certe alicui nonnullam honorem habeo qui insanabili Cacoëthe scribendi teneatur.

Species flagrantis Lexingtonis non somnia deturbat? At non Vulcanum Neptunumque culpemus cum superstitioso grege. Natura curat animalculis aequê ac hominibus; cum serena, tum procellosa amica est.

Si amas historiam et fortia facta heroûm non depone Rollin, precor, ne Clio offendas nunc, nec illa det veniam olim.

Quos libros Latinos legis? legis, inquam, non studes. Beatus qui potest suos libellos tractare et saepe perlegere sine metu domini urgentis! ab otio injurioso procul est; suos amicos et vocare et dimittere quandocunque velit potest. Bonus liber opus est nobilissimum hominis! Hinc ratio non modo cur legeres sed cur tu quoque scriberes. Nec lectores carent; ego sum. Si non librum meditaris, libellum certê. Nihil posteris proderit te spirâsse et vitam nunc lenîter nunc asperê egisse, sed cogitâsse praecipue et scripsisse.

Vereor ne tibi pertaesum hujus epistolae sit; Necnon alma lux caret,

"Majoresque cadunt altis de montibus umbrae."

Quamobrem vale, imô valete, et requiescatis placidê Sorores. [M]emento scribere.

H. D. Thoreaus.

Care Sophia,

Samuel Niger crebris aegrotationibus, quae agilitatem et aequum animum abstulêre, obnoxius est; iis temporibus ad cellam descendit et [multas horas (ibi) manet.

Flores, ah crudelis pruina! parvo leti discrimine sunt. Cactus frigore ustus est, gerania vero adhuc vigent.

Conventus sociabiles hac hieme reinstituti fuere. Conveniunt ad meum domum mense quarto vel quinto, ut tu hic esse possis. Matertera Sophia cum nobis remanet; quando urbem revertet non scio. Gravedine etiamnum, sed non tam aegre, laboramus.]

Adolescentula E. White apud pagum paulisper moratur. Memento scribere intra duas hebdomedas.

Te valere desiderium est
Tui Matris C. Thoreaus.

Amanuense, H. D. T.
[P. S. Epistolam die solus proxima expectamus.]

MS., Morgan; *bracketed portions are from* Familiar Letters of Thoreau, *pp. 32–33. The manuscript is torn and a portion of the original letter missing. The postscript should appear on the manuscript, but does not:*

whether Sanborn found an extra scrap of paper originally appended to the manuscript is not known. Sanborn translated this letter in his edition of Familiar Letters of Thoreau. *His translation, with a few corrections, follows:*

Concord, January 21, 1840.

Dear Sister,

There is a huge snowdrift at the door, and the cold inside is intolerable. The very sky is coming down, I guess, and covering up the ground. I turn out late in the morning, and go to bed early; there is thick frost on the windows, shutting out the view; and here I write in pain, for fingers and brains are numb. I would chant with Horace, if my voice did not stick in my throat,—

> See how Nashawtuck, deep in snow,
> Stands glittering, while the bending woods
> Scarce bear their burden, and the floods
> Feel arctic winter stay their flow
>
> Pile on the firewood, melt the cold,
> Spare nothing, etc.

But soon, changing my tune, and with a cheerfuller note, I'll say,—

> No longer the flock huddles up in the stall, the plowman
> bends over the fire,
> No longer frost whitens the meadow;
> But the goddess of love, while the moon shines above,
> Sets us dancing in light and in shadow.

When Robin Redbreast brings back the springtime, I trust that you will lay your school-duties aside, cast off care, and venture to be gay now and then, roaming with me in the woods, or climbing the Fairhaven cliffs,—or else, in my boat on Walden, let the water kiss your hand, or gaze at your image in the wave.

Bulwer is to me a name unknown,—one of the unnoticed crowd, attracting neither blame nor praise. To be sure, I hold any one in some esteem who is helpless in the grasp of the writing demon.

Does not the image of the Lexington afire trouble your dreams? But

37

we may not, like the superstitious mob, blame Vulcan or Neptune. Nature takes as much care for little animals as for mankind; first she is a serene friend, then a stormy friend.

If you like history, and the exploits of the brave, don't give up Rollin, I beg; thus would you displease Clio, who might not forgive you hereafter. What Latin are you reading? I mean *reading*, not studying. Blessed is the man who can have his library at hand, and oft peruse the books, without the fear of a taskmaster! he is far enough from harmful idleness, who can call in and dismiss these friends when he pleases. An honest book's the noblest work of Man. There's a reason, now, not only for your reading, but for writing something, too. You will not lack readers,—here am I, for one. If you cannot compose a volume, then try a tract. It will do the world no good, hereafter, if you merely exist, and pass life smoothly or roughly; but to have thoughts, and write them down, that helps greatly.

I fear you will tire of this epistle; the light of day is dwindling, too,—

"And longer fall the shadows of the hills."

Therefore, good-by; fare ye well, and sleep in quiet, both my sisters! Don't forget to write.

H. D. Thoreau.

Dear Sophia,

Sam Black (the cat) is liable to frequent attacks that impair his agility and good-nature; at such times he goes down cellar, and stays many hours. Your flowers—O, the cruel frost! are all but dead; the cactus is withered by cold, but the geraniums yet flourish. The Sewing Circles have been revived this winter; they meet at our house in April or May, so that you may then be here. Your Aunt Sophia remains with us,—when she will return to the city I don't know. We still suffer from heavy colds, but not so much. Young Miss E. White is staying in the village a little while. Don't forget to write within two weeks.

That you may enjoy good health is the prayer of

Your mother,
C. Thoreau.

H.D.T. was the scribe.
P.S. We expect a letter next Sunday.

Helen was teaching in Roxbury. Nashawtuck is the largest hill near the center of Concord. The steamer Lexington *was destroyed by fire in Long Island Sound January 13, 1840, with a loss of many lives. Aunt Sophia Dunbar was Thoreau's mother's sister and a resident of Boston. The book referred to is* Ancient History *by Charles Rollin.*

To HELEN THOREAU

Concord, June 13, 1840.

Dear Helen,—

That letter to John, for which you had an opportunity doubtless to substitute a more perfect communication, fell, as was natural, into the hands of his "transcendental brother," who is his proxy in such cases, having been commissioned to acknowledge and receipt all bills that may be presented. But what's in a name? Perhaps it does not matter whether it be John or Henry. Nor will those same six months have to be altered, I fear, to suit his case as well. But methinks they have not passed entirely without intercourse, provided we have been sincere though humble worshipers of the same virtue in the mean time. Certainly it is better that we should make ourselves quite sure of such a communion as this by the only course which is completely free from suspicion,—the coincidence of two earnest and aspiring lives,—than run the risk of a disappointment by relying wholly or chiefly on so meagre and uncertain a means as speech, whether written or spoken, affords. How often, when we have been nearest each other bodily, have we really been farthest off! Our tongues were the witty foils with which we fenced each other off. Not that we have not met heartily and with profit as members of one family, but it was a small one surely, and not that other human family. We have met frankly and without concealment ever, as befits those who have an instinctive trust in one another, and the scenery of whose outward lives has been the same, but never as prompted by an earnest and affectionate desire to probe deeper our mutual natures. Such intercourse, at least, if it has ever been, has not condescended to the vulgarities of oral communication, for the ears are

39

provided with no lid as the eye is, and would not have been deaf to it in sleep. And now glad am I, if I am not mistaken in imagining that some such transcendental inquisitiveness has traveled post *thither*,—for, as I observed before, where the bolt hits, thither was it aimed,—any arbitrary direction notwithstanding.

Thus much, at least, our *kindred* temperament of mind and body—and long *family*-arity—have done for us, that we already find ourselves standing on a solid and natural footing with respect to one another, and shall not have to waste time in the so often unavailing endeavor to arrive fairly at this simple ground.

Let us leave trifles, then, to accident; and politics, and finance, and such gossip, to the moments when diet and exercise are cared for, and speak to each other deliberately as out of one infinity into another,—you there in time and space, and I here. For beside this relation, all books and doctrines are no better than gossip or the turning of a spit.

Equally to you and Sophia, from

> Your affectionate brother,
> H. D. Thoreau.

Helen was still teaching school in nearby Roxbury and, according to Sanborn, was apparently being assisted by Sophia Thoreau. Text, Familiar Letters of Thoreau, *pp. 37–39.*

To?

Concord June 20th 1840.

Dear Sir,

I have made inquiry of sundry songlovers and songwrights in the neighborhood, with a view to your proposals, with what result, favorable or unfavorable, will appear. Mr. Wood pronounces in his cool experienced way that the scholars will not be forthcoming—for why? The town or parish contemplate a school the next winter which should be public, and open equally to old and young—learned and unlearned. The people, he says, have been accustomed to look to the parish for

these things, and to them a dollar even has lost some of its weight when it has passed once through the assessors' hands.

Mr Whiting, the Superintendent of the Sabbath School, affirms that there are whole platoons of children, whom the parish would be glad to have in a condition to do singing, but have never yet accomplished the thing by voting it, or once correctly pitching the tune. So he stands ready to render smooth official assistance by public notice to the school—and the like.

But of what avail all this ballancing of reasons—depend upon it nothing good was ever done in accordance with, but rather in direct opposition to—advice. Have you not the sympathy of parish votes— that it will have singing? Or rather have you not the assurance of your own resolution that you will give it them at any rate?

Mr. Wood then, who more than any man has gaged all throats— Juvenile and senile—in the vicinity—raises the cold water bucket.

Mr. Whiting—and Nelson and others rely mainly on the incalculable force there is in a man—who has sternly resolved to do what is in him to do,—the phial of laudanum—and nodding poppy—and Concord river running nine times round—to the contrary notwithstanding.

At present I read in the faces of the children neither encouragement nor discouragement they having had no hint of the future.

Yrs to command
Henry D. Thoreau.

MS., Massachusetts Historical Society; *previously unpublished.*

From MARGARET FULLER

1st Dec.

I am to blame for so long detaining your manuscript. But my thoughts have been so engaged that I have not found a suitable hour to reread it as I wished till last night. This second reading only confirms my impression from the first. The essay is rich in thoughts, and I should

be *pained* not to meet it again. But then the thoughts seem to me so out of their natural order, that I cannot read it through without *pain.* I never once feel myself in a stream of thought, but seem to hear the grating of tools on the mosaic. It is true, as Mr. E[merson] says, that essays not to be compared with this have found their way into the Dial. But then these are more unassuming in their tone, and have an air of quiet good-breeding which induces us to permit their presence. Yours is so rugged that it ought to be commanding. Yet I hope you will give it me again, and if you see no force in my objections disregard them.

S. M. Fuller

Direct and to the point, this letter from Margaret Fuller, probably from Jamaica Plain, accompanied the returned manuscript of Thoreau's essay on "The Service," which he had submitted for publication in the Dial. The essay was finally published in 1902 by Charles E. Goodspeed of Boston. Sanborn's Life of Henry David Thoreau *dates the letter 1840. Since the manuscript of "The Service" is itself dated July 1840, Sanborn is probably correct. MS., Morgan.*

1841

Henry Clay fought in the Senate to establish the Whig program, which he had shrewdly termed the "American System," only to see an important part of it vetoed by Tyler, who had just succeeded to the presidency on Harrison's death and was proving that you cannot always count on what a vice-president will do after he becomes president. Horace Greeley began to publish the *New-York Tribune*. The first passenger train was run on the Erie Railroad. John C. Fremont reached Sutter's Fort in California. Calomel was still one of the doctors' favorite remedies; patent medicines, making enormous claims almost without exception, probably killed a good many more persons than they cured. Among the typical nostrums were Dr. Leidy's Vegetable Febrile Elixir and Goelicke's Matchless Sanative, whose effectiveness produced "Trembling among American Physicians." Brook Farm, one of the most famous American communistic experiments, was founded by the Transcendentalists.

Starting at the end of April Thoreau solved his problem of making a living by going to work at R. W. Emerson's house. His job was to be a caretaker, a friend, and a handyman. It is a tribute to Emerson's unassuming greatness that Thoreau accepted the job and continued in it for two years. He also lectured on the lyceum platform, though he found, he confesses for the *Journal*, that in "a public performer, the simplest actions, which at other times are left to unconscious nature, as the ascending a few steps in front of an audience, acquire a fatal importance and become arduous deeds." He wrote a good deal in the *Journal* and published three interesting poems in the *Dial*. He acquired a disciple in a Buffalo law student, Isaiah Williams. His esteem grew, it appears, for both Mrs. Emerson and her sister Mrs. Lucy Brown.

From EMERSON

My dear Henry

We have here G. P. Bradford, R. Bartlett, Lippitt C S Wheeler & Mr Alcott. Will you not come down & spend an hour?

Yours,

R W E

Thursday P. M.

Emerson's guests are identified by Rusk (Emerson Letters, II, 409–12) *as George Partridge Bradford, one of Emerson's best friends; Robert Bartlett, then a tutor at Harvard; George Warren Lippitt, a member of the senior class at the Harvard Divinity School; Charles Stearns Wheeler, Thoreau's Harvard classmate; and Bronson Alcott. Though Emerson's note is undated, the general course of his biography and correspondence makes June of 1841 the most probable date. The circumstances—especially the gathering of these particular guests in Emerson's household at this particular time—support this date. MS., Berg.*

To MRS. LUCY BROWN

Concord, July 21, 1841.

Dear Friend,—

Don't think I need any prompting to write to you; but what tough earthenware shall I put into my packet to travel over so many hills, and thrid so many woods, as lie between Concord and Plymouth? Thank fortune it is all the way down hill, so they will get safely carried; and yet it seems as if it were writing against time and the sun to send

44

a letter east, for no natural force forwards it. You should go dwell in the West, and then I would deluge you with letters, as boys throw feathers into the air to see the wind take them. I should rather fancy you at evening dwelling far away behind the serene curtain of the West,—the home of fair weather,—than over by the chilly sources of the east wind.

What quiet thoughts have you nowadays which will float on that east wind to west, for so we may make our worst servants our carriers, —what progress made from *can't* to *can*, in practice and theory? Under this category, you remember, we used to place all our philosophy. Do you have any still, startling, well moments, in which you think grandly, and speak with emphasis? Don't take this for sarcasm, for not in a year of the gods, I fear, will such a golden approach to plain speaking revolve again. But away with such fears; by a few miles of travel we have not distanced each other's sincerity.

I grow savager and savager every day, as if fed on raw meat, and my tameness is only the repose of untamableness. I dream of looking abroad summer and winter, with free gaze, from some mountain-side, while my eyes revolve in an Egyptian slime of health,—I to be nature looking into nature with such easy sympathy as the blue-eyed grass in the meadow looks in the face of the sky. From some such recess I would put forth sublime thoughts daily, as the plant puts forth leaves. Now-a-nights I go on to the hill to see the sun set, as one would go home at evening; the bustle of the village has run on all day, and left me quite in the rear; but I see the sunset, and find that it can wait for my slow virtue.

But I forget that you think more of this human nature than of this nature I praise. Why won't you believe that mine is more human than any single man or woman can be? that in it, in the sunset there, are all the qualities that can adorn a household, and that sometimes, in a fluttering leaf, one may hear all your Christianity preached.

You see how unskillful a letter-writer I am, thus to have come to the end of my sheet when hardly arrived at the beginning of my story. I was going to be soberer, I assure you, but now have only room to add, that if the fates allot you a serene hour, don't fail to communicate some of its serenity to your friend,

Henry D. Thoreau.

No, no. Improve so rare a gift for yourself, and send me of your leisure.

45

Mrs. Brown, a sister of Emerson's second wife, was boarding with the Thoreau family as early as 1837, when Thoreau composed his first love poem, "Sic Vita," for her. Text, Familiar Letters of Thoreau, *pp. 40–43.*

To MRS. LUCY BROWN

Concord, Wednesday evening, September 8, [1841.]

Dear Friend,—

Your note came wafted to my hand like the first leaf of the Fall on the September wind, and I put only another interpretation upon its lines than upon the veins of those which are soon to be strewed around me. It is nothing but Indian Summer here at present. I mean that any weather seems reserved expressly for our late purposes whenever we happen to be fulfilling them. I do not know what right I have to so much happiness, but rather hold it in reserve till the time of my desert.

What with the crickets and the crowing of cocks, and the lowing of kine, our Concord life is sonorous enough. Sometimes I hear the cock bestir himself on his perch under my feet, and crow shrilly before dawn; and I think I might have been born any year for all the phenomena I know. We count sixteen eggs daily now, when arithmetic will only fetch the hens up to thirteen; but the world is young, and we wait to see this eccentricity complete its period.

My verses on Friendship are already printed in the "Dial"; not expanded but reduced to completeness by leaving out the long lines, which always have, or should have, a longer or at least another sense than short ones.

Just now I am in the mid-sea of verses, and they actually rustle around me as the leaves would round the head of Autumnus himself should he thrust it up through some vales which I know; but, alas! many of them are but crisped and yellow leaves like his, I fear, and will deserve no better fate than to make mould for new harvests. I see the stanzas rise around me, verse upon verse, far and near, like the mountains from Agiocochook, not all having a terrestrial existence as yet, even as some of them may be clouds; but I fancy I see the gleam of

46

some Sebago Lake and Silver Cascade, at whose well I may drink one day. I am as unfit for any practical purpose—I mean for the further-ance of the world's ends—as gossamer for ship-timber; and I, who am going to be a pencil-maker to-morrow, can sympathize with God Apollo, who served King Admetus for a while on earth. But I believe he found it for his advantage at last,—as I am sure I shall, though I shall hold the nobler part at least out of the service.

Don't attach any undue seriousness to this threnody, for I love my fate to the very core and rind, and could swallow it without paring it, I think. You ask if I have written any more poems? Excepting those which Vulcan is now forging, I have only discharged a few more bolts into the horizon,—in all, three hundred verses,—and sent them, as I may say, over the mountains to Miss Fuller, who may have occasion to remember the old rhyme:—

> "Three scipen gode
> Comen mid than flode
> Three hundred cnihten."

But these are far more Vandalic than they. In this narrow sheet there is not room even for one thought to root itself. But you must consider this an odd leaf of a volume, and that volume

> Your friend
> Henry D. Thoreau.

Text, Familiar Letters of Thoreau, *pp. 43–45; the date 1841 is supplied by Sanborn.*

From ISAIAH T. WILLIAMS

Buffalo N.Y. Sept. 24, 1841—

Mr. D. H. Thoreau
My dear Sir,

Your kind offer to receive and answer any communications from me, is not forgotten. I owe myself an apology for so long neglecting to

avail myself of so generous an offer. Since I left Concord I have hardly found rest for the sole of my foot. I have followed the star of my destiny till it has, at length, come and stood over this place. Here I remain engaged in the study of Law— Part of the time I have spent in New Hampshire part in Ohio & part in New York and so precarious was my residence in either place that I have rarely known whither you might direct a letter with any certainty of its reaching me.

When I left Concord I felt a strong desire to continue the conversation I had so fortunately commenced with some of those whom the Public call Transcendentalists. Their sentiments seemed to me to possess a peculiar fitness. Though full of doubt I felt I was fed & refreshed by those interviews. The doctrines I there heard have ever since, been uppermost in my mind—and like balmy sleep over the weary limbs, have they stolen over me quite unawares. I have not embraced them but they have embraced me—I am led, their willing captive. Yet I feel I have but yet taken the first step. I would know more of this matter. I would be taken by the hand and led up from this darkness and torpidity where I have so long groveled like an earthworm. I know what it is to be a slave to what I thought a Christian faith—and with what rapture do grasp the hand that breaks my chains—& the voice that bids me—live.

Most of the books you recommended to me I was not able to obtain— "Nature" I found—and language can not express my admiration of it. When gloom like a thick cloud comes over me in that I find an amulet that dissipates the darkness and kindles anew my highest hopes. Few copies of Mr Emerson's Essays have found their way to this place. I have read part of them and am very much delighted with them. Mr. Park's German I have also found and as much as I should have shrunk from such sentiments a year ago—half, so I already receive them. I have also obtained "Hero Worship"—which of course I read with great interest and as I read I blush for my former bigotry and wonder that I have not known it all before wonder what there is in chains that I should have loved them so much— Mr. E's oration before the Theological Class at Cambridge I very much want. If you have it in your possession, allow me to beg you to forward it to me & I will return it by mail after perusing it. Also Mr. Alcott's "Human Culture." I will offer no apology for asking this favor—for I know you will not require it.

I find I am not alone here, your principals are working their way even in Buffalo—this emporium of wickedness and sensuality. We look to

the east for our guiding star for there our sun did rise. Our motto is that of the Grecian Hero—"Give but to see—and Ajax asks no more."

For myself my attention is much engrossed in my studies—entering upon them as I do without a Public Education—I feel that nothing but the most undivided attention and entire devotion to them will ensure me even an ordinary standing in the profession. There is something false in such devotion. I already feel its chilling effects I fear I shall fall into the wake of the profession which is in this section proverbially bestial. Law is a noble profession it calls loudly for men of genius and integrity to fill its ranks. I donot aspire to be a great lawyer. I know I cannot be, but it is the sincere desire of my heart that I may be a true one.

You are ready to ask—how I like the West. I must answer—not very well—I love New England so much that the West is comparatively odious to me. The part of Ohio that I visited was one dead level—often did I strain my eyes to catch a glimpse of some distant mountain—that should transport me in imagination to the wild country of my birth, but the eternal level spread itself on & on & I almost felt myself launched forever. Aloud did I exclaim—"My own blue hills—O, where are they!" —I did not know how much I was indebted to them for the happy hours I'd passed at home. I knew I loved them—and my noble river too— along whose banks I'd roamed half uncertain if in earth or heaven—I never shall—I never can forget them all—though I drive away the re- membrances of them which ever in the unguarded moments throngs me laden with ten thousands incidents before forgotten & so talismanic its power—that I wake from the enchantment as from a dream. If I were in New England again I would never leave her but now I am away—I feel forever—I must eat of the Lotus—and forget her. Tis true we have a noble Lake—whose pure waters kiss the foot of our city— and whose bosom bears the burdens of our commerce—her beacon light now looks in upon me through my window as if to watch, lest I should say untruth of that which is her nightly charge. But hills or mountains we have none.

My sheet is nearly full & I must draw to a close—I fear I have already wearied your patience. Please remember me to those of your friends whose acquaintance I had pleasure to form while in Concord—I en- gaged to write your brother—Mr Alcott also gave me then the same privilege—which I hope soon to avail myself of. I hope sometime to visit your town again which I remember with so much satisfaction—yet with so much regret—regret that I did not earlier avail myself of the

49

acquaintances, it was my high privilege to make while there and that the lucubrations of earlier years did not better fit me to appreciate & enjoy. I cheer myself with fanning the fading embers of a hope that I shall yet retrieve my fault that such an opportunity will again be extended to me and that I may once more look upon that man whose name I never speak without reverence—whom of all I most admire —almost adore—Mr Emerson—I shall wait with impatience to hear from you.

Believe me

ever yours—
Isaiah T. Williams.

Isaiah Williams, now a young law student in Buffalo, had resided for a while in Concord, teaching school, and had formed a friendship with Thoreau. Emerson, in his letter to Margaret Fuller of June 7, 1843, calls him "very handsome very intelligent" and adds "whom I wish you could see." Among books to which Williams refers are Emerson's famous little volume, the 1836 Nature, *Edwards Amasa Park's* Selections from German Literature *(1839), and Bronson Alcott's* Doctrine and Discipline of Human Culture *(1836).* Rusk *(Emerson Letters III, 180 n.) confuses Isaiah Williams with a Charles H. S. William. MS., Berg, copy made by Thoreau's disciple H. G. O. Blake; previously unpublished.*

To MRS. LUCY BROWN

Concord, October 5, 1841.

Dear Friend,—

I send you Williams's letter as the last remembrancer to one of those "whose acquaintance he had the pleasure to form while in Concord." It came quite unexpectedly to me, but I was very glad to receive it, though I hardly know whether my utmost sincerity and interest can

50

inspire a sufficient answer to it. I should like to have you send it back by some convenient opportunity.

Pray let me know what you are thinking about any day,—what most nearly concerns you. Last winter, you know, you did more than your share of the talking, and I did not complain for want of an opportunity. Imagine your stove-door out of order, at least, and then while I am fixing it you will think of enough things to say.

What makes the value of your life at present? what dreams have you, and what realizations? You know there is a high table-land which not even the east wind reaches. Now can't we walk and chat upon its plane still, as if there were no lower latitudes? Surely our two destinies are topics interesting and grand enough for any occasion.

I hope you have many gleams of serenity and health, or, if your body will grant you no positive respite, that you may, at any rate, enjoy your sickness occasionally, as much as I used to tell of. But here is the bundle going to be done up, so accept a "good-night" from

Henry D. Thoreau.

Text, Familiar Letters of Thoreau, *pp. 45–46.*

To ISAIAH T. WILLIAMS

Concord Sept. 8th 1841

Dear Friend

I am pleased to hear from you out of the west, as if I heard the note of some singing bird from the midst of its forests, which travellers report so grim and solitary— It is like the breaking up of Winter and the coming in of Spring, when the twigs glitter and tinkle, and the first sparrow twitters in the horizon. I doubt if I can make a good echo— Yet it seems that if a man ever had the satisfaction to say once entirely and irrevocably what he believed to be true he would never leave off to cultivate that skill.

I suppose if you see any light in the east it must be in the eastern

state of your own soul, and not by any means in these New England States. Our eyes perhaps do not rest so long on any as on the few who especially love their own lives—who dwell apart at more generous intervals, and cherish a single purpose behind the formalities of society with such steadiness that of all men only their two eyes seem to meet in one focus. They can be eloquent when they speak—they can be graceful and noble when they act. For my part if I have any creed it is so to live as to preserve and increase the susceptibleness of my nature to noble impulses—first to observe if any light shine on me, and then faithfully to follow it. The Hindoo Scripture says, "Single is each man born; single he dies; single he receives the reward of his good, and single the punishment of his evil deeds."

Let us trust that we have a good conscience The steady light whose ray every man knows will be enough for all weathers. If any soul look abroad even today it will not find any word which does it more justice than the New Testament,—yet if it be faithful enough it will have experience of a revelation fresher and directer than that, which will make that to be only the best tradition. The strains of a more heroic faith vibrate through the week days and the fields than through the Sabbath and the Church. To shut the ears to the immediate voice of God, and prefer to know him by report will be the only sin. Any respect we may yield to the paltry expedients of other men like ourselves—to the Church—the State—or the School—seems purely gratuitous, for in our most private experience we are never driven to expediency. Our religion is where our love is. How vain for men to go musing one way, and worshipping another. Let us not fear to worship the muse. Those stern old worthies—Job and David and the rest, had no Sabbath-day worship but sung and revelled in their faith, and I have no doubt that what true faith and love of God there is in this age will appear to posterity in the happy system of some creedless poet.

I think I can sympathize with your sense of greater freedom.— The return to truth is so simple that not even the nurses can tell when we began to breathe healthily, but recovery took place long before the machinery of life began to play freely again when on our pillow at midnoon or midnight some natural sound fell naturally on the ear. As for creeds and doctrines we are suddenly grown rustic—and from walking in streets and squares—walk broadly in the fields—as if a man were wise enough not to sit in a draft, and get an ague, but moved buoyantly in the breeze.

It is curious that while you are sighing for New England the scene of our fairest dreams should lie in the west—it confirms me in the opinion that places are well nigh indifferent. Perhaps you have experienced that in proportion as our love of nature is deep and pure we are independent upon her. I suspect that ere long when some hours of faithful and earnest life have imparted serenity into your Buffalo day, the sunset on lake Erie will make you forget New England. It was the Greeks made the Greek isle and sky, and men are beginning to find Archipelagos elsewhere as good. But let us not cease to regret the fair and good, for perhaps it is fairer and better to   them.

I am living with Mr. Emerson in very dangerous prosperity. He gave me three pamphlets for you to keep, which I sent last Saturday. The "Explanatory Preface" is by Elizabeth Peabody who was Mr. Alcott's assistant, and now keeps a bookstore and library in Boston. Pray let me know with what hopes and resolutions you enter upon the study of law—how you are to make it a solid part of your life. After a few words interchanged we shall learn to speak pertinently and not to the air. My brother and Mr Alcott express pleasure in the anticipation of hearing from you and I am sure that the communication of what most nearly concerns you will always be welcome to Yours Sincerely

H. D. Thoreau

Isaiah T. Williams Buffalo, N.Y.

Although Thoreau had moved to the Emerson house the preceding April, we find here the first reference to the fact in his letters. Method of Spiritual Culture: Being an Explanatory Preface to the Second Edition of Record of a School *(1836) is the booklet referred to. The letter, clearly in answer to Williams's of September 24, should have been dated October. MS., Berg, copy in H. G. O. Blake's hand; the blank space at the end of the next to the last paragraph comes from his copy; previously unpublished.*

To RUFUS W. GRISWOLD

Concord Oct. 9th 1841.

Dear Sir,

     I am sorry that I can only place at your disposal three small poems printed in the "Dial"—that called "Sympathy" in no. 1.—"Sic Vita" in no. 5—and "Friendship" in no. 6. If you see fit to reprint these will you please to correct the following errors?
In the second stanza of "Sympathy"
                   for posts read ports.
" "   5th   "   " breeze " haze.
"   "   "   the eyes " *our* eyes
"   "   "   " worked " works.
"   13th   "   " dearest " truest.
"   4th   "   " "Friendship"
                   for our read one.
"   10th   "   " warden " warder.
I was born in Concord, Massachusetts, in 1817, and was graduated at Harvard University, in 1837.

                                Yrs respectfully
                                Henry D. Thoreau.

A note clipped to the manuscript identifies it as corrections for an edition (probably the first) of The Poets and Poetry of America, *but none of Thoreau's poems appeared in that or any other of Griswold's anthologies.* MS., Berg.

Concord Oct. 9th 1841.

Dear Sir,
              I am sorry that I can only
place at your disposal three small
poems printed in the "Dial"— that called
"Sympathy" in No. 1.— "Sic Vita" in No. 5.
and "Friendship" in No. 6. If you
see fit to reprint these will you please to
correct the following errors?
In the second stanza of the "Sympathy"
                              for posts read ports.
    "   "   5th.   "   "   " breeze " bare
              "   "   the eyes " our eyes
    "   "   "   worked " works.
    "   13"   "   "   " dearest " truest.
    "   4"   "   "   "Friendship"
                              for own read one.
    "   10th.   "   "   warden " warder.

I was born in Concord, Massachusetts,
in 1817, and was graduated at Harvard
University, in 1837.
                    Yrs respectfully
                    Henry D. Thoreau.

55

From MARGARET FULLER

18 Oct 1841,

I do not find the poem on the mountains improved by mere compression, though it might be by fusion and glow.

Its merits to me are a noble recognition of nature, two or three manly thoughts, and, in one place, a plaintive music. The image of the ships does not please me originally. It illustrates the greater by the less and affects me as when Byron compares the light on Jura to that of the dark eye of woman. I cannot define my position here, and a large class of readers would differ from me. As the poet goes on to

> Unhewn, primeval timber
> For knees so stiff, for masts so limber"

he seems to chase an image, already rather forced, into conceits.

Yet now that I have some knowledge of the man, it seems there is no objection I could make to his lines, (with the exception of such offenses against taste as the lines about the humors of the eye &c as to which we are already agreed) which I would not make to himself. He is healthful, sure, of open eye, ready hand, and noble scope. He sets no limits to his life, nor to the invasions of nature; he is not wilfully pragmatical, cautious, ascetic or fantastical. But he is as yet a somewhat bare hill which the warm gales of spring have not visited. Thought lies too detached, truth is seen too much in detail, we can number and rank the substances embedded in the rock. Thus his verses are startling, as much as stern; the thought does not excuse its conscious existance by letting us see its relation with life; there is a want of fluent music. Yet what could a companion do at present unless to tame the guardian of the Alps too early. Leave him at peace amid his native snows. He is friendly; he will find the generous office that shall educate him. It is not a soil for the citron and the rose, but for the whortleberry, the pine or the heather. The unfolding of affections, a wider and deeper human experience, the harmonizing influences of other natures will mould the man, and melt his verse. He will seek thought less and find knowledge the more. I can have no advice or criticism for a person so sincere, but if I give my impression of him I will say He says too constantly of nature She is mine; She is not yours till you have been more hers. Seek the lotus, and take a draught of rapture. Say not so confidently All places,

56

all occasions are alike. This will never come true till you have found it false.

I do not know that I have more to say now, Perhaps these words will say nothing to you. If intercourse should continue, perhaps a bridge may be made between two minds so widely apart, for I apprehended you in spirit, and you did not seem to mistake me as widely as most of your kind do. If you should find yourself inclined to write to me, as you thought you might, I dare say many thoughts would be suggested to me; many have already by seeing you day by day. Will you finish the poem in your own way and send it for the Dial. Leave out 'And seems to *milk* the sky"

The image is too low. Mr Emerson thought so too. Farewell. May Truth be irradiated by Beauty! — Let me know whether you go to the lonely hut, and write me about Shakspeare, if you read him there. I have many thoughts about him which I have never yet been led to express.

Margaret F.

The pencilled paper Mr E. put into my hands. I have taken the liberty to copy it You expressed one day my own opinion that the moment such a crisis is passed we may speak of it. There is no need of artificial delicacy, of secrecy, it keeps its own secret; it cannot be made false. Thus you will not be sorry that I have seen the paper. Will you not send me some other records of the good week.

Once again Margaret Fuller rejected a manuscript that Thoreau had submitted for publication in the Dial. *The poem was "With frontier strength ye stand your ground," eventually included in his essay "A Walk to Wachusett" and published in the* Boston Miscellany *for January 1843. Thoreau accepted some of Miss Fuller's suggestions in his final version, but ignored others. The "lonely hut" is probably a reference to the Hollowell Farm, which Thoreau was talking of purchasing, rather than to any intent thus early to go to Walden. The "good week" indicates that he was already working on his first book. The reference to Byron is to* Childe Harold's Pilgrimage, *Canto III, Stanza XCII. MS., University of Texas Library.*

From ISAIAH T. WILLIAMS

Buffalo N. Y. Nov 27 1841—

My dear Friend

I feel rebuked as I draw your most interesting letter from my file and sit down to answer it—that I have so long delayed so grateful a task—For though I surely get away from the world & Law long enough to enter within myself and inquire how I am—how I feel and what sentiments and what response my heart gives out in answer to your voice whose notes of sweetest music comes from that "Land of every land the pride Beloved of Heaven o'er all the World beside" "That spot of earth divinely blest—That dearer sweeter spot than all the rest" Yet—when weary and heart sick—when disgusted with the present—and memory, as if to give relief, retires to wander in the 'Graveyard of the past'—she passes not unmindful nor lingers briefly around that spot where more than in any other I feel I first tasted of that bread I hope will yet nourish my youth strengthen my manhood—cheer and solace "whe[n] the daughters of music are brought low."

Time's devastating hand is beginning already to obliterate the traces of my youthful feelings—and I am becoming more & more contented with my present situation and feel less and less a desire inexorable to return and be a child once more.

This I suppose to be the natural tendency of the circumstances in which I *am* placed. Man's ends are shaped for him and he must abide his destiny. This seems a little like futility—yet, how can we avoid the conclusion that the soul is shaped by circumstances and many of those circumstances beyond man's control? I think that could I always be "true to the dream of Childhood" I should always be happy—I can imagine circumstances in which I think I might be so—but they are not my present circumstances—these are my fate—I would not complain of them did they not war against what I feel to be my highest interest and indeed I will not as it is, for I know not what is my highest good—I know not the goal whither I am bound, and as I donot know but all is well as far as the external is concerned I will trust to the author of my being— the author and creator of those beautiful fields and woods I so much enjoy in my morning and evening walks—the author of the glorious lake sunsets—that all is well. I have already half answered your interrogat-

ing in relation to my hopes and feelings as I enter upon the study of Law—With so little knowledge—so a—stranger in its walks—with my face only set toward the temple just spying its tapering finger pointing to the heavens as the throne of its justice—its golden dome glittering as though it were the light of that city which "has no need of a candle neither the light of the Sun" —not yet passed under its gateway—or wandered among the trees and flowers of its paradisean garden—viewed the stones of its foundation or laid hold of its massy pillars. I hardly know what to hope or how to feel at all—I must say, if I would speak truly, that I do not "burn with high hopes" Tis not that "the way seems steep and difficult" but that "the event is feared"; tis the prospect of a life in "daily contact with the things I loath" I love the profession It presents a boundless field—a shoreless ocean where my bark may drift —and bound & leap from wave to wave in wild but splendid rays— without the fear of rock or strand. Yet I chose it not so much for the love I bore it for I knew that in it my intercourse must be with the worst specimens of humanity—as knowing that by it I might get more knowl- edge, dis[c]ipline and intellectual culture than in any other which I could choose simply as a means of livelihood—have more time to devote to literature and philosophy—and, as I have said, be better prepared in- tellectually for progress in these pursuits than in any other branch of business followed simply to provide for the bodily wants— So—you see— this profession I chose simply as a means to enable me to pursue what I most delight in—and for that end I think it the wisest selection I could make I know this motive will not lead me to any eminence in the profes- sion—yet I donot know as I wish to be great in that respect even if I could— My books tell me that on entering the profession I must bid adieu to literature—everything and give up myself wholy to Law— I thought I would do so for a time—and I sat down to Blackstone with a heavy heart. Adieu ye Classic halls. My Muse adieu! I wept—as I took perhaps my last look of her—her *form* lessening in the distance—she cast her eye over her shoulder to rest once more on me. O, it was all pity, love and tenderness—I called aloud for her—but she hastened on— grieved, she heeded not my call— It was too much— What ever might by standing as a Lawyer—I would not turn my back to literature— philosophy theology or poetry—Would give them their place & Law its place—A thousand thanks for the pamphlets you forwarded me. I have read them with great pleasure—and shall read them many times more. The Oration at Waterville I very much admire—it is circulating among

Mr. E's admirers in this place who all express great admiration of it—Human Culture I admire more and more as I read it over. I loaned it to a young man who told me on returning it that he had almost committed it to memory—and wished the loan of it again as soon as the other friends had read it.

I have read some of your poetry in the Dial—I want to see more of it—it transports me to my childhood and makes everything look as playful as when first I looked upon them in my earliest morning. I only wish it were more liquid—smooth I should admire Pope's Homer if it were for nothing but that it flows so smoothly.

Remember me affectionately to the friends in Concord and believe me

ever yours
I. T. Williams

The works referred to are Emerson's Method of Nature *(1841), a lecture before the Society of Adelphi at Waterville College in Maine, and Bronson Alcott's* Doctrine and Discipline of Human Culture *(1836). Thoreau's poems "Sic Vita" and "Friendship" had appeared in the* Dial *of July and October. MS., Berg, copy in H.G.O. Blake's hand; previously unpublished.*

1842

Charles Dickens arrived in Boston on a visit to America. The patent for a sewing machine was granted to one John Greenough. Massachusetts passed a law reducing the number of hours children under twelve might work in factories to ten a day. The Florida legislature instructed its delegate in Congress to press for a law that would authorize rewards for Indian scalps and for every Indian taken alive. With the signing of the Webster-Ashburton treaty the United States and Great Britain settled the boundaries between Maine and the Canadian provinces. President Tyler continued to veto bills. Through Congressman John Quincy Adams the intransigent citizens of Haverhill petitioned for a peaceful dissolution of the Union. The New York Philharmonic Orchestra gave its first concert. Nathaniel Hawthorne moved to Concord with his bride, his "dove."

The death of John Thoreau in January was a blow that it took Henry years to overcome. It brought him into a community of sorrow with the Emersons, for their little son Waldo died during the same month. Thoreau went on working around the Emerson household, but found plenty of time to write and live his own life too. He had not yet abandoned the writing of verse—a few of his best poems were still to be finished—but he was already concentrating on his prose. There he found ampler scope for his ideas. His prose rhythms and his images became more disciplined and more artful. The *Dial* found space for his first real essay, "Natural History of Massachusetts," as well as for a backlog of his poems. His *Journal* for the year as now in print begins with some thoughts on the bravery of virtue, runs to references to Sir Walter Raleigh and Chaucer, continues principally with a variety of reflections about nature, and ends on Sunday, April 3, with more praise for virtue. The rest of the *Journal* for 1842 has not been published. Thoreau's letters for the year are few, but several are unusually moving.

To MRS. LUCY BROWN

Concord March 2nd 1842.

Dear Friend,
I believe I have nothing new to tell you, for what was news you have learned from other sources. I am much the same person that I was, who should be so much better; yet when I realize what has transpired, and the greatness of the part I am unconsciously acting, I am thrilled, and it seems as if there were now a history to match it.

Soon after John's death I listened to a music-box, and if, at any time, that even had seemed inconsistent with the beauty and harmony of the universe, it was then gently constrained into the placid course of nature by those steady notes, in mild and unoffended tone echoing far and wide under the heavens. But I find these things more strange than sad to me. What right have I to grieve, who have not ceased to wonder?

We feel at first as if some opportunities of kindness and sympathy were lost, but learn afterward that any *pure grief* is ample recompense for all. That is, if we are faithful;—for a spent grief is but sympathy with the soul that disposes events, and is as natural as the resin of Arabian trees. — Only nature has a right to grieve perpetually, for she only is innocent. Soon the ice will melt, and the blackbirds sing along the river which he frequented, as pleasantly as ever. The same everlasting serenity will appear in this face of God, and we will not be sorrowful, if he is not.

We are made happy when reason can discover no occasion for it. The memory of some past moments is more persuasive than the experience of present ones. There have been visions of such breadth and brightness that these motes were invisible in their light.

I do not wish to see John ever again — I mean him who is dead — but that other whom only he would have wished to see, or to be, of whom he was the imperfect representative. For we are not what we are, nor do we treat or esteem each other for such, but for what we are capable of being.

62

As for Waldo, he died as the mist rises from the brook, which the sun will soon dart his rays through. Do not the flowers die every autumn? He had not even taken root here. I was not startled to hear that he was dead;—it seemed the most natural event that could happen. His fine organization demanded it, and nature gently yielded its request. It would have been strange if he had lived. Neither will nature manifest any sorrow at his death, but soon the note of the lark will be heard down in the meadow, and fresh dandelions will spring from the old stocks where he plucked them last summer. I have been living ill of late, but am now doing better. How do you live in that Plymouth world, now-a-days?—Please remember me to Mary Russell.—You must not blame me if I do *talk to the clouds*, for I remain

Your Friend,
Henry D. Thoreau.

Thoreau's beloved brother John died suddenly of lockjaw on January 11. The death of little Waldo Emerson, Thoreau's favorite, occurred two weeks later on January 27. The shock to Thoreau was profound, and for more than a month he wrote neither letters nor Journal. *Mary Russell of Plymouth later became the wife of Thoreau's friend and fellow student at Harvard, Marston Watson. MS., Harvard; a note in longhand across the top of the letter reads "To Mrs. L. C. Brown an invalid, Mrs Emerson's sister."*

To EMERSON

Concord March 11th 1842

Dear Friend,

I see so many "carvels licht, fast tending throw the sea" to your El Dorado, that I am in haste to plant my flag in season on that distant beach, in the name of God and King Henry. There seems to be no oc-

casion why I who have so little to say to you here at home should take pains to send you any of my silence in a letter—Yet since no correspondence can hope to rise above the level of those homely speechless hours, as no spring ever bursts above the level of the still mountain tarn whence it issued—I will not delay to send a venture. As if I were to send you a piece of the house-sill—or a loose casement rather. Do not neighbors sometimes halloo with good will across a field, who yet never chat over a fence?

The sun has just burst through the fog, and I hear blue-birds, song-sparrows, larks, and robins down in the meadow. The other day I walked in the woods, but found myself rather denaturalized by late habits. Yet it is the same nature that Burns and Wordsworth loved the same life that Shakspeare and Milton lived. The wind still roars in the wood, as if nothing had happened out of the course of nature. The sound of the waterfall is not interrupted more than if a feather had fallen.

Nature is not ruffled by the rudest blast—The hurricane only snaps a few twigs in some nook of the forest. The snow attains its average depth each winter, and the chic-adee lisps the same notes. The old laws prevail in spite of pestilence and famine. No genius or virtue so rare & revolutionary appears in town or village, that the pine ceases to exude resin in the wood, or beast or bird lays aside its habits.

How plain that death is only the phenomenon of the individual or class. Nature does not recognize it, she finds her own again under new forms without loss. Yet death is beautiful when seen to be a law, and not an accident—It is as common as life. Men die in Tartary, in Ethiopia —in England—in Wisconsin. And after all what portion of this so serene and living nature can be said to be alive? Do this year's grasses and foliage outnumber all the past.

Every blade in the field—every leaf in the forest—lays down its life in its season as beautifully as it was taken up. It is the pastime of a full quarter of the year. Dead trees—sere leaves—dried grass and herbs— are not these a good part of our life? And what is that pride of our autumnal scenery but the hectic flush—the sallow and cadaverous countenance of vegetation—its painted throes—with the November air for canvas—

When we look over the fields are we not saddened because the particular flowers or grasses will wither—for the law of their death is the law of new life Will not the land be in good heart *because* the crops die

down from year to year? The herbage cheerfully consents to bloom, and wither, and give place to a new.

So it is with the human plant. We are partial and selfish when we lament the death of the individual, unless our plaint be a paean to the departed soul, and a sigh as the wind sighs over the fields, which no shrub interprets into its private grief.

One might as well go into mourning for every sere leaf—but the more innocent and wiser soul will snuff a fragrance in the gales of autumn, and congratulate Nature upon her health.

After I have imagined thus much will not the Gods feel under obligation to make me realize something as good

I have just read some good verse by the old Scotch poet John Bellenden—

> "The fynest gold or silver that we se,
>   May nocht be wrocht to our utilitie,
>   Bot flammis keen & bitter violence;
>   The more distress, the more intelligence.
>   Quhay sailis lang in hie prosperitie,
>   Ar sone oureset be stormis without defence."

From your friend
Henry D. Thoreau

Emerson had gone to New York—not Philadelphia, as Sanborn states in his Scribner's Magazine *version of the letter (XVII, March 1895, 352–53)—to deliver a series of lectures when Thoreau wrote this first extant letter to him. MS., Berg.*

To ISAIAH T. WILLIAMS

Concord March 14th 1842

Dear Williams,

I meant to write to you before but John's death and my own sickness, with other circumstances, prevented. John died of the lock-jaw, as you know, Jan. 11th I have been confined to my chamber for a month with a prolonged shock of the same disorder—from close attention to, and sympathy with him, which I learn is not without precedent. Mr. Emerson too has lost his oldest child, Waldo, by scarlet fever, a boy of rare promise, who in the expectation of many was to be one of the lights of his generation.

John was sick but three days from the slightest apparent cause—an insignificant cut on his finger, which gave him no pain, and was more than a week old—but nature does not ask for such causes as man expects—when she is ready there will be cause enough. I mean simply that perhaps we never assign the sufficient cause for anything—though it undoubtedly exists. He was perfectly calm, ever pleasant while reason lasted, and gleams of the same serenity and playfulness shone through his delirium to the last. But I will not disturb his memory. If you knew him, I could not add to your knowledge, and if you did not know him, as I think you could not, it is now too late, and no eulogy of mine would suffice—For my own part I feel that I could not have done without this experience.

What you express with regard to the effect of time on our youthful feelings—which indeed is the theme of universal elegy—reminds me of some verses of Byron—quite rare to find in him, and of his best I think. Probably you remember them.

"   "No more, no more! Oh never more on me
"   The freshness of the heart can fall like
     dew
"   Which out of all the lovely things we see,
"   Extracts emotions beautiful and new,
"   Hived in our bosoms like the bag o' the bee,
"   Think'st thou the honey with these objects
     grew

> "   Alas! 'Twas not in them, but in thy power,
> "   To double even the sweetness of a flower.
>
> "   No more, no more! Oh! never more, my heart!
> "   Cans't thou be my sole world, my universe
> "   Once all in all, but now a thing apart,
> "   Thou canst not be my blessing, or my curse;
> "   The illusion's gone forever—"

It would be well if we could add new years to our lives as innocently as the fish adds new layers to its shell—no less beautiful than the old. And I believe we may if we will replace the vigor and elasticity of youth with faithfulness in later years.

When I consider the universe I am still the youngest born. We do not *grow* old we *rust* old. Let us not consent to be old, but to die (live?) rather. Is Truth old? or Virtue—or Faith? If we possess them they will be our *elixir vitæ* and fount of Youth. It is at least good to remember our innocence; what we regret is not quite lost— Earth sends no sweeter strain to Heaven than this plaint. Could we not grieve perpetually, and by our grief discourage time's encroachments? All our sin too shall be welcome for such is the material of Wisdom, and through her is our redemption to come.

'Tis true, as you say, "Man's ends are shaped for him," but who ever dared confess the extent of his free agency? Though I am weak, I am strong too. If God shapes my ends—he shapes me also—and his means are always equal to his ends. His work does not lack this completeness, that the creature consents. *I* am my destiny. Was I ever in that straight that it was not sweet to do right? And then for this free agency I would not be free of God certainly—I would only have freedom to defer to him He has not made us solitary agents. He has not made us to do without him Though we must "abide our destiny," will not he abide it with us? So do the stars and the flowers. My destiny is now arrived—is now arriving. I believe that what I call my circumstances will be a very true history of myself—for God's works are complete both within and without—and shall I not be content with his success? I welcome my fate for it is not trivial nor whimsical. Is there not a soul in circumstances?—and the disposition of the soul to circumstances—is not that the crowning

circumstance of all? But after all it is *intra*-stances, or how it stands within me that I am concerned about. Moreover circumstances are past, but I am to come, that is to say, they are results of me—but I have not yet arrived at my result.

All impulse, too, is primarily from within The soul which does shape the world is within and central.

I must confess I am apt to consider the trades and professions so many traps which the Devil sets to catch men in—and good luck he has too, if one may judge. But did it ever occur that a man came to want, or the almshouse from consulting his higher instincts? All great good is very present and urgent, and need not be postponed. What did Homer—and Socrates—and Christ and Shakspeare & Fox? Did they have to compound for their leisure, or steal their hours? What a curse would civilization be if it thus ate into the substance of the soul— Who would choose rather the simple grandeur of savage life for the solid leisure it affords? But need we sell our birthright for a mess of pottage? Let us trust that we shall be fed as the sparrows are.

"Grass and earth to sit on, water to wash the feet, and fourthly, affectionate speech are at no time deficient in the mansions of the good"

You may be interested to learn that Mr. Alcott is going to England in April.

That you may find in Law the profession you love, and the means of spiritual culture, is the wish of your friend

Henry D. Thoreau.

The impact of John's death upon Thoreau is well indicated by the account of his "sympathetic lockjaw" in this letter. The quotation from Byron is from Don Juan, Canto the First, *CCXIV, CCXV. MS., Berg, copy in H. G. O. Blake's hand; previously unpublished.*

THE CORRESPONDENCE OF THOREAU

From ISAIAH T. WILLIAMS

Buffalo June. 23, 1842—

Dear Thoreau
    I have not written you for a long time—but I am not going to
apologize for of course you only wish to hear when & what I wish to
write The poor thoughts that have occupied my busy little mind since
I last wrote you have been many & often had I seen you should I have
inflicted upon your ear the sad narration of them, or at least some of
them—& I donot know why I should withhold any of them they were sent
by a power above me, at the beck & bidding of another did they come &
go— I know that men have but little to do with the affairs of this world—
still I feel a responsibility to myself for all things that befall me in life
—though to no other. To live this life well I feel a strong desire. I also
feel a presentiment that I shall fail in part—if not totally fail to do so.
I donot know what it is to live well—or how to do it if I did—between
idid and idea I swing like a pendulum—I know 'tis weakness, yet such
I am—But I must not disgust you by talking too much of myself. & I
know it is not well to afflict myself with my own image. Still it is prety
much all I know— the source of most I have ever learned. Perhaps this
has been my fault— I have often repented & as often sinned again—
What a succession of falls is life! I wonder if that is the object of it—&
this that we may know how to stand when it is past—I donot suppose
it is of any use to speculate about life—we know but little of it & if it
were well for us to know it would be taught us. & I am coming more &
more every day to the settled practicable belief that the true mode of
life is to live & do from moment to moment the duty or labor before us
with no questions about its fitness or end and no thought for the morrow. I sometimes think further—that it is also best to be of men & like
them while with them—to love what they love be interested in what
they are interested—share their hopes & joys their dejection & sorrows
—seek the ends & have the objects of pursuit that they have take their
fortunes in life as I must in death & when the curtain shall have fallen—
have to think my fortune & fate is & has ever been that of my race—I
fear it will be a hard one if it is, but "such is the sovereign doom & such
the will of Jove" Of one thing I am certain—My race have an indisputa-
ble claim upon my best— all the services I am able to render while I live

69

—I will not withhold from them the pittance due from me— With this thought before me I have endeavoured to join in the reforms of the day—I make Temperance speeches, such as they are—at any rate the best I can—I go to Sabbath School & talk to & endeavour to instruct the children what I can— & where-ever I see an opportunity to do any thing for others I have a kind of general design to lend my aid—though not to interfere with my duties to myself. Whether I am taking the best course to benefit myself & others— that is the question— Yet if I do as well I know— & know as well as I can I shall never accuse myself. After all I am not wholly satisfied with myself or with this view of things I fear there is something beyond & higher I ought to know & seek— Is it given to man in this state of existence to be satisfied? Is not this very dissatisfaction but the breathing of an immortal nature that whispers of eternal progress? Shall not hope change this very dissatisfaction into the highest fruition? Say to me in reply what these desultory thoughts suggest to your mind— & as my sheet is nearly full I will say a few words more & fold & forward it for your perusal.

Your letter of March 14 gave me much pleasure though I need not say that I sympathize with you most deeply in the loss you sustain by the death of your brother— I knew him but little—yet I thought I had never met with a more flowing generous spirit— It was not fitted for a cold & hard hearted world like this— in such a nature do I see a strong assurance of a better existence when this is over. Ever will his name float down my memory untainted by those folies & crimes. I am forced to associate with those of so many of my race. And Mr Emerson—how did he endure the loss of his child? It was a cruel stroke—did his philosophy come to his aid as does the Christian Faith to administer consolation to the bereaved? I wish to know what were his feelings. for the consolations that a christian faith offers the bereaved & afflicted is one of its strongest holds upon my credulity. If there is consolation from his philosophy in trials like those—it will do much toward settling my belief—I wish to know minutely on this point. I think much on Death & sometimes doubt if my early impressions upon that subject are ever effaced—The fear of it occasions a thousand folies—I feel it is unmanly— but yet "that undiscovered country" Who shall tell us whether to fear —or desire it?

As to myself—I am less homesick than at first though I am not satisfied with the west. nor quite with my profession. Perhaps I ought to be

I often think my feelings foolish. Do you think engaged in the practice of law the best way of spending ones life? Let me hear from you soon. I will not be so remiss in my future correspondence—

Yours
I. T. Williams

MS., Berg; *copy in H. G. O. Blake's hand; previously unpublished.*

From JAMES RICHARDSON, JR.

Friend Thoreau

I have been desirous of sending to some of my mystic brethren— some selections from certain writings of mine, that wrote themselves, when "I was in the spirit on the Lord's Day." Some of these are so utterly and entirely out of all my rational faculties, that I can't put *any* meaning in them; others I read over, and learn a great deal from. This, I send you, seems to be a sort of Allegory—When you return it, will you be so kind as to tell me all that it means, as there are some parts of it I do not fully understand myself—I have a grateful remembrance of the moments I saw you in. Mr Emerson too I have less awe of, and more love for, than formerly His presence has always to me something infinite as well as divine about it. Mrs Emerson I am very desirous of knowing. Your family give my love to—

James Richardson jr

December 9 Dy College Cam.

Richardson, a classmate of Thoreau, after trying his hand at school teaching returned to Cambridge to attend the Divinity School, from which he graduated in 1845. His selections that accompanied the letter have disappeared; they were probably returned to him by Thoreau. There is no clue to their specific contents. Richardson attended the

71

Divinity School for three years: he might have written this letter during any one of them, but his addressing it in care of Emerson suggests that he wrote it while Thoreau was in the Emerson household. Thoreau started working for Emerson in April 1841 and continued for the greater part of the next two years. In May 1843 he left Concord for Staten Island to tutor William Emerson's boy. This letter probably belongs, then, to 1842, the only year that in its final month saw both Richardson at Harvard and Thoreau at Emerson's. MS., Morgan; previously unpublished.

1843

In January Francis Scott Key died. The House of Representatives rejected the resolution offered by J. M. Botts to impeach President Tyler. In the spring Daniel Webster, Secretary of State, retired majestically from the Cabinet. The Bunker Hill Monument was dedicated. The John Fremont expedition sighted Pike's Peak. A Mormon revelation of July 12 sanctioned plural marriage. The National Liberty Party of abolitionists, assembled in convention at Buffalo, nominated James G. Birney for president of the United States and Thomas Morris for vice-president. Congress voted $30,000 to help Morse establish the first telegraph line between Washington and Baltimore.

The beginning of this year found Thoreau at a low point. He had exhausted his possibilities in the Emerson household, he believed that his poetry was drying up, and he recognized that he needed to earn a living—preferably with his pen. Since mid-nineteenth-century America allowed no really good writer to do that, the best that could be arranged was a compromise. Emerson got Thoreau a job as tutor in William Emerson's family on Staten Island. This was not to be hard work, and it was to give Thoreau a chance to test the New York literary market. The test did not turn out too well. It was not that he had no success at all—actually he managed to publish three pieces, two in the *Democratic Review* and one in the *Boston Miscellany*—but he was not nearly successful enough. The *Journal* for 1843 is not in print, but we can get a good notion of Thoreau's aims and attitudes from the many letters that survive. The typical letter of this year shows both Thoreau's liveliness and his frustration.

Concord Jan 16 1843

Dear Richard

I need not thank you for your present for I hear its music, which seems to be playing just for us two pilgrims marching over hill and dale of a summer afternoon—up those long Bolton hills and by those bright Harvard lakes, such as I see in the placid Lucerne on the lid—and whenever I hear it, it will recall happy hours passed with its donor.

When did mankind make that foray into nature and bring off this booty—? For certainly it is but history that some rare virtue in remote times plundered these strains from above, and communicated them to men. Whatever we may think of it, it is a part of the harmony of the spheres you have sent me, which has condescended to serve us Admetuses—and I hope I may so behave that this may always be the tenor of your thought for me.

If you have any strains, the conquest of your own spear or quill to accompany these, let the winds waft them also to me.

I write this with one of the "primaries" of my osprey's wings, which I have preserved over my glass for some state occasion—and now it affords.

Mrs. Emerson sends her love—

Yr friend,
Henry D. Thoreau

Richard Fuller was a younger brother of Margaret Fuller and of Ellen, the wife of Thoreau's friend Ellery Channing. It seems probable that the gift of the music box was made in return for Thoreau's tutoring to help young Fuller enter Harvard, where he was now a junior sophister.

Apollo forced to serve King Admetus was one of Thoreau's favorite symbols; here he gives it an unusual turn. MS., John Cooley (typescript).

———————

To MRS. LUCY BROWN

Concord Jan 24th 1843

Dear Friend,

The other day I wrote you a letter to go in Mrs Emerson's bundle but as it seemed unworthy I did not send it, and now to atone for that I am agoing to send this whether it be worthy or not—I will not venture upon news for as all the household are gone to bed—I cannot learn what has been told you. Do you read any noble verses now a days—or do not verses still seem noble? —For my own part they have been the only things I remembered—or that which occasioned them—when all things else were blurred and defaced. All things have put on mourning but they—for the elegy itself is some victorious melody and joy escaping from the wreck.

It is a relief to read some true book wherein all are equally dead—equally alive. I think the best parts of Shakspeare would only be enhanced by the most thrilling and affecting events. I have found it so. And so much the more as they are not intended for consolation.

Do you think of coming to Concord again?—I shall be glad to see you—I should be glad to know that I could see you when I would.

We always seem to be living just on the brink of a pure and lofty intercourse which would make the ills and trivialness of life ridiculous. After each little interval, though it be but for the night, we are prepared to meet each other as gods and goddesses.—I seem to have lodged all my days with one or two persons, and lived upon expectation—as if the bud would surely blossom—and so I am content to live.

What means the fact—which is so common—so universal—that some soul that has lost all hope for itself can inspire in another listening soul an infinite confidence in it, even while it is expressing its despair—?

I am very happy in my present environment—though actually mean

enough myself and so of course all around me—Yet I am sure we for the most part are transfigured to one another and are that to the other which we aspire to be ourselves. The longest course of mean and trivial intercourse may not prevent my practising this divine courtesy to my companion. Notwithstanding all I hear about brooms and scouring and taxes and house keeping—I am constrained to live a strangely mixed life —As if even Valhalla might have its kitchen. We are all of us Apollo's serving some Admetus.

I think I must have some muses in my pay that I know not of—for certain musical wishes of mine are answered as soon as entertained— Last summer I went to Hawthorne's suddenly for the express purpose of borrowing his music box, and almost immediately Mrs. H proposed to lend it to me. The other day I said I must go to Mrs. Barrett's to hear hers—and lo straightway Richard Fuller sent me one for a present from Cambridge. It is a very good one. I should like to have you hear it. I shall not have to employ you to borrow for me now. Good night.

from your affectionate friend
H. D. T.

MS., Folger Shakespeare Library.

To EMERSON

Concord, January 24, 1843.

Dear Friend, —

The best way to correct a mistake is to make it right. I had not spoken of writing to you, but as you say you are about to write to me when you get my letter, I make haste on my part in order to get yours the sooner. I don't well know what to say to earn the forthcoming epistle, unless that Edith takes rapid strides in the arts and sciences—or music and natural history—as well as over the carpet; that she says "papa" less and less abstractedly every day, looking in *my* face,—which

may sound like a *Ranz des Vaches* to yourself. And Ellen declares every morning that "papa *may* come home to-night"; and by and by it will have changed to such positive statement as that "papa came home *larks* night."

Elizabeth Hoar still flits about these clearings, and I meet her here and there, and in all houses but her own, but as if I were not the less of her family for all that. I have made slight acquaintance also with one Mrs. Lidian Emerson, who almost persuades me to be a Christian, but I fear I as often lapse into heathenism. Mr. O'Sullivan was here three days. I met him at the Atheneum [Concord], and went to Hawthorne's [at the Old Manse] to tea with him. He expressed a great deal of interest in your poems, and wished me to give him a list of them, which I did; he saying he did not know but he should notice them. He is a rather puny-looking man, and did not strike me. We had nothing to say to one another, and therefore we said a great deal! He, however, made a point of asking me to write for his Review, which I shall be glad to do. He is, at any rate, one of the not-bad, but does not by any means take you by storm,—no, nor by calm, which is the best way. He expects to see you in New York. After tea I carried him and Hawthorne to the Lyceum.

Mr. Alcott has not altered much since you left. I think you will find him much the same sort of person. With Mr. Lane I have had one regular chat *à la* George Minott, which of course was greatly to our mutual grati- and edification; and, as two or three as regular conversations have taken place since, I fear there may have been a precession of the equinoxes. Mr. Wright, according to the last accounts, is in Lynn, with uncertain aims and prospects,—maturing slowly, perhaps, as indeed are all of us. I suppose they have told you how near Mr. Alcott went to the jail, but I can add a good anecdote to the rest. When Staples came to collect Mrs. Ward's taxes, my sister Helen asked him what he thought Mr. Alcott meant,—what his idea was,—and he answered, "I vum, I believe it was nothing but principle, for I never heard a man talk honester."

There was a lecture on Peace by a Mr. Spear (ought he not to be beaten into a ploughshare?), the same evening, and, as the gentlemen, Lane and Alcott, dined at our house while the matter was in suspense,— that is, while the constable was waiting for his receipt from the jailer, —we there settled it that we, that is, Lane and myself, perhaps, should agitate the State while Winkelried lay in durance. But when, over the

audience, I saw our hero's head moving in the free air of the Universalist church, my fire all went out, and the State was safe as far as I was concerned. But Lane, it seems, had cogitated and even written on the matter, in the afternoon, and so, out of courtesy, taking his point of departure from the Spear-man's lecture, he drove gracefully *in medias res,* and gave the affair a very good setting out; but, to spoil all, our martyr very characteristically, but, as artists would say, in bad taste, brought up the rear with a "My Prisons," which made us forget Silvio Pellico himself.

Mr. Lane wishes me to ask you to see if there is anything for him in the New York office, and pay the charges. Will you tell me what to do with Mr. [Theodore] Parker, who was to lecture February 15th? Mrs. Emerson says my letter is written instead of one from her.

At the end of this strange letter I will not write—what alone I had to say—to thank you and Mrs. Emerson for your long kindness to me. It would be more ungrateful than my constant thought. I have been your pensioner for nearly two years, and still left free as under the sky. It has been as free a gift as the sun or the summer, though I have sometimes molested you with my mean acceptance of it,—I who have failed to render even those slight services of the *hand* which would have been for a sign, at least; and, by the fault of my nature, have failed of many better and higher services. But I will not trouble you with this, but for once thank you as well as Heaven.

Your friend,
H. D. T.

Emerson was in Philadelphia delivering lectures and visiting his friend W. H. Furness. Incidentally, he had Furness try to find a publisher for the Week. *Edith was Emerson's daughter; O'Sullivan was editor of the* Democratic Review *(see letter from O'Sullivan of July 28, 1843); and Charles Lane and Henry G. Wright were English friends of Alcott who later joined in his experiment at Fruitlands. (It is possible, however, that Thoreau is referring to Henry C. Wright, the American reformer.) Alcott's refusal to pay taxes was similar in purpose to Thoreau's refusal during the war with Mexico. Thoreau refers to* My Prisons *in his essay* "Civil Disobedience," *too. Pellico was a noted Italian dramatist jailed*

*for revolutionary activities in his homeland; one of the American trans-
lations of* My Prisons *was printed in Cambridge in 1836.* Text, Emerson-
Thoreau, *pp. 578–79; the bracketed additions are Sanborn's.*

To MRS. LUCY BROWN

Concord, Friday evening, January 25, 1843.

Dear Friend,—

Mrs. Emerson asks me to write you a letter, which she will put
into her bundle to-morrow along with the "Tribunes" and "Standards,"
and miscellanies, and what not, to make an assortment. But what shall
I write? You live a good way off, and I don't know that I have anything
which will bear sending so far. But I am mistaken, or rather impatient
when I say this,—for we all have a gift to send, not only when the year
begins, but as long as interest and memory last. I don't know whether
you have got the many I have sent you, or rather whether you were
quite sure where they came from. I mean the letters I have sometimes
launched off eastward in my thought; but if you have been happier at
one time than another, think that then you received them. But this that
I now send you is of another sort. It will go slowly, drawn by horses over
muddy roads, and lose much of its little value by the way. You may have
to pay for it, and it may not make you happy after all. But what shall be
my new-year's gift, then? Why, I will send you my still fresh remembrance of the hours I have passed with you here, for I find in the remembrance of them the best gift you have left to me. We are poor and
sick creatures at best; but we can have well memories, and sound and
healthy thoughts of one another still, and an intercourse may be remembered which was without blur, and above us both.

Perhaps you may like to know of my estate nowadays. As usual, I find
it harder to account for the happiness I enjoy, than for the sadness
which instructs me occasionally. If the little of this last which visits me
would only be sadder, it would be happier. One while I am vexed by
a sense of meanness; one while I simply wonder at the mystery of life;
and at another, and at another, seem to rest on my oars, as if propelled

by propitious breezes from I know not what quarter. But for the most part I am an idle, inefficient, lingering (one term will do as well as another, where all are true and none true enough) member of the great commonwealth, who have most need of my own charity,—if I could not be charitable and indulgent to myself, perhaps as good a subject for my own satire as any. You see how when I come to talk of myself, I soon run dry, for I would fain make that a subject which can be no subject for me, at least not till I have the grace to rule myself.

I do not venture to say anything about your griefs, for it would be unnatural for me to speak as if I grieved with you, when I think I do not. If I were to see you, it might be otherwise. But I know you will pardon the trivialness of this letter; and I only hope—as I know that you have reason to be so—that you are still happier than you are sad, and that you remember that the smallest seed of faith is of more worth than the largest fruit of happiness. I have no doubt that out of S——'s death you sometimes draw sweet consolation, not only for that, but for long-standing griefs, and may find some things made smooth by it, which before were rough.

I wish you would communicate with me, and not think me unworthy to know any of your thoughts. Don't think me unkind because I have not written to you. I confess it was for so poor a reason as that you almost made a principle of not answering. I could not speak truly with this ugly fact in the way; and perhaps I wished to be assured, by such evidence as you could not voluntarily give, that it was a kindness. For every glance at the moon, does she not send me an answering ray? Noah would hardly have done himself the pleasure to release his dove, if she had not been about to come back to him with tidings of green islands amid the waste.

But these are far-fetched reasons. I am not speaking directly enough to yourself now; so let me say *directly*

From your friend,
Henry D. Thoreau.

Lacking the manuscripts, we cannot check Sanborn's dating of this letter to Mrs. Brown or of the one dated January 24; however, the two letters largely parallel each other in contents and give a reader the feeling that they are almost two drafts of the same letter. Or it may be,

if we judge from the opening sentence, that the letter Sanborn dated the 25th was actually the one that Thoreau wrote first and then said he did not mail. The 25th was not a Friday, but a Wednesday; Friday the 20th and Friday the 27th are two possibilities. Text, Familiar Letters of Thoreau, *pp. 53–56.*

From EMERSON

Carlton House: New York Feb 1843

My dear Henry,

I have yet seen no new men in N. Y. (excepting young Tappan) but only seen again some of my old friends of last year. Mr. Brisbane has just given me a faithful hour & a half of what he calls his principles, and he shames truer men by his fidelity & zeal, and already begins to hear the reverberations of his single voice from most of the States of the Union. He thinks himself five of W. H. Channing here, as a good Fourierist. I laugh incredulous whilst he recites (for it seems always as if he was repeating paragraphs out of his master's book) descriptions of the self-augmenting potency of the Solar System which is destined to contain 132 bodies, I believe and his urgent inculcation of our Stellar *duties.* But it has its kernal of sound truth and its insanity is so wide of New York insanities that it is virtue and honor.

I beg you my dear friend to say to those faithful lovers of me who have just sent me letters which any man should be happy & proud to receive—I mean my mother & my wife that I am grieved that they should have found my silence so vexatious, I think that some letter must have failed for I cannot have let ten days go by without writing home I have kept no account but am confident that that cannot be. Mr. Mackay has just brought me his good package & I will not at this hour commence a new letter but you shall tell Mrs. E. that my first steps in N. Y. in this visit seem not to have been prudent & so I lose several precious days. 11 Feb. A Society invited me to read my Course before them in the Bowery on certain terms one of which was that they guaranteed me a thousand auditors. I referred them to my brother William

81

who convenanted with them. It turned out that their Church was a dark inaccessible place a terror to the honest & fair citizens of N. Y. & our first lecture had a handful of persons & they all personal friends of mine from a different part of the city.

But the Bereans felt so sadly about the disappointment that it seemed at last on much colloquy not quite good-natured & affectionate to abandon them at once but to read also a second lecture & then part. The second was read with faint success & then we parted. I begin this evening anew in the Society Library where I was last year. This takes more time than I could wish, a great deal—I grieve that I cannot come home. I see W. H. Channing & Mr James at leisure & have had what the Quakers call "a solid season," once or twice. With Tappan a very happy pair of hours & him I must see again. I am enriched greatly by your letter & now by the dear letters which Mr Mackay had bro't me from Lidian Emerson & Elizabeth Hoar and for speed in part & partly because I like to write so I make you the organ of communication to the whole household & must still owe you a special letter. I dare not say when I will come home as the time so fast approaches when I should speak to the Mercantile Library. Yesterday eve, I was at Staten Island where William had promised me as a lecturer & made a speech at Tompkinsville. Dear love to My Mother I shall try within 24 hours to write to my wife.

Thanks thanks for your love to Edie. Farewell!

R Waldo E

From Philadelphia Emerson had traveled as far back as New York on has way to Concord. Among the persons he reports seeing are William Tappan, a youthful admirer; Albert Brisbane, father of the Hearst columnist and the leading American exponent of a kind of streamlined Fourierist communism; W. H. Channing, a Christian Socialist, minister, and the nephew of the great Unitarian William Ellery Channing; and Henry James, the father of the novelist and the psychologist. The Mr. Mackay that Emerson mentions is identified by Rusk (Emerson Letters, III, 24 n.) as Tristram Barnard Mackay. There are reports on the Berean course of lectures in the New-York Daily Tribune *of February 7–10, 1843 and on the New York Society Library course in the issues of February 11–22. Emerson started his brief Mercantile Library course Febru-*

ary 28. Photostat of MS., Columbia University Library. Sanborn says (Familiar Letters of Thoreau, *p. 67*) *that the beginning date for this letter is February 4 and that this and one other have the terminal date February 12. Since we have the letter for the 12th and our text agrees with Sanborn's description, we conjecture that the terminal date for the letter begun on the 4th is February 11. Lest we rely too heavily on Sanborn, however, we should note that he inserts "February 10" between the first and second paragraphs of the present letter, though it is lacking in the manuscript.*

To EMERSON

Concord, February 10, 1843.

Dear Friend,—

    I have stolen one of your own sheets to write you a letter upon, and I hope, with two layers of ink, to turn it into a comforter. If you like to receive a letter from me, too, I am glad, for it gives me pleasure to write. But don't let it come amiss; it must fall as harmlessly as leaves settle on the landscape. I will tell you what we are doing this now. Supper is done, and Edith—the dessert, perhaps, more than the desert—is brought in, or even comes in *per se;* and round she goes, now to this altar, and then to that, with her monosyllabic invocation of "oc," "oc." It makes me think of "Langue d'oc." She must belong to that province. And like the gipsies she talks a language of her own while she understands ours. While she jabbers Sanscrit, Parsee, Pehlvi, say "Edith go bah!" and "bah" it is. No intelligence passes between us. She knows. It is a capital joke,—that is the reason she smiles so. How well the secret is kept! she never descends to explanation. It is not buried like a common secret, bolstered up on two sides, but by an eternal silence on the one side, at least. It has been long kept, and comes in from the unexplored horizon, like a blue mountain range, to end abruptly at our door one day. (Don't stumble at this steep simile.) And now she studies the heights and depths of nature

On shoulders whirled in some eccentric orbit
Just by old Pestum's temples and the perch
Where Time doth plume his wings.

And how she runs the race over the carpet, while all Olympia applauds, —mamma, grandma, and uncle, good Grecians all,—and that dark-hued barbarian, Partheanna Parker, whose shafts go through and through, not backward! Grandmamma smiles over all, and mamma is wondering what papa would say, should she descend on Carlton House some day. "Larks night" 's abed, dreaming of "pleased faces" far away. But now the trumpet sounds, the games are over; some Hebe comes, and Edith is translated. I don't know where; it must be to some cloud, for I never was there.

Query: what becomes of the answers Edith thinks, but cannot express? She really gives you glances which are before this world was. You can't feel any difference of age, except that you have longer legs and arms.

Mrs. Emerson said I must tell you about domestic affairs, when I mentioned that I was going to write. Perhaps it will inform you of the state of all if I only say that I am well and happy in your house here in Concord.

Your friend,
Henry.

Don't forget to tell us what to do with Mr. [Theodore] Parker, when you write next. I lectured this week. It was as bright a night as you could wish. I hope there were no stars thrown away on the occasion.

Thoreau's lecture dealt with Sir Walter Raleigh; it was delivered to the Concord Lyceum on February 8. This letter, not mailed for a few days, was finally enclosed with that of February 12. Text, Emerson-Thoreau, pp. 579–80.

84

From EMERSON

New York 12 Feby

My dear Henry,

I am sorry I have no paper but this unsightly sheet this Sunday eve. to write you a message which I see must not wait—The Dial for April.—What elements shall compose it? What have you for me? What has Mr. Lane? Have you any Greek translations in your mind? Have you given any shape to the comment on Etzler? (It was about some sentences on this matter that I made someday a most rude & snappish speech, I remember, but you will not, & must give the sentences as you first wrote them.) You must go to Mr Lane with my affectionate respects & tell him that I depend on his most important aid for the new number, and wish him to give us the most recent & stirring matter he has. If (as he is a ready man) he offers us anything at once, I beg you to read it, & if you see & say decidedly that it is good for us you need not send it to me: but if it is of such quality that you can less surely pronounce, you must send it to me by Harnden. Have we no more news from Wheeler? Has Bartlett none?

I find Edw. Palmer here studying medicine & attending medical lectures. He is acquainted with Mr. Porter whom Lane & Wright know & values him highly. I am to see Porter. Perhaps I shall have no more time to fill this sheet, if so, farewell

Yours,
R. Waldo E.

It was the April 1843 number of the Dial *that Thoreau edited for Emerson. The leading article was one on Bronson Alcott's works by Charles Lane. None of Thoreau's translations from the Greek was included, and his review of Etzler was submitted instead to the* Democratic Review. *Charles Stearns Wheeler was a classmate of Thoreau at Harvard, Robert Bartlett one of Wheeler's close friends. Edward Palmer was a one-time Boston clergyman; Sanborn evidently confuses him with the Joseph Palmer of Fruitlands. Harnden & Co. ran an express service between Boston and New York and also connected with the Concord stage at the Earl Tavern in Boston. MS., Hosmer.*

To EMERSON

February 12, 1843.

Dear Friend, —

As the packet still tarries, I will send you some thoughts, which I have lately relearned, as the latest public and private news.

How mean are our relations to one another! Let us pause till they are nobler. A little silence, a little rest, is good. It would be sufficient employment only to cultivate true ones.

The richest gifts we can bestow are the least marketable. We hate the kindness which we understand. A noble person confers no such gift as his whole confidence: none so exalts the giver and the receiver; it produces the truest gratitude. Perhaps it is only essential to friendship that some vital trust should have been reposed by the one in the other. I feel addressed and probed even to the remote parts of my being when one nobly shows, even in trivial things, an implicit faith in me. When such divine commodities are so near and cheap, how strange that it should have to be each day's discovery! A threat or a curse may be forgotten, but this mild trust translates me. I am no more of this earth; it acts dynamically; it changes my very substance. I cannot do what before I did. I cannot be what before I was. Other chains may be broken, but in the darkest night, in the remotest place, I trail this thread. Then things cannot *happen*. What if God were to confide in us for a moment! Should we not then be gods?

How subtle a thing is this confidence! Nothing sensible passes between; never any consequences are to be apprehended should it be misplaced. Yet something has transpired. A new behavior springs; the ship carries new ballast in her hold. A sufficiently great and generous trust could never be abused. It should be cause to lay down one's life,—which would not be to lose it. Can there be any mistake up there? Don't the gods know where to invest their wealth? Such confidence, too, would be reciprocal. When one confides greatly in you, he will feel the roots of an equal trust fastening themselves in him. When such trust has been received or reposed, we dare not speak, hardly to see each other; our voices sound harsh and untrustworthy. We are as instruments which the Powers have dealt with. Through what straits would we not carry this little burden of a magnanimous trust! Yet no harm could possibly

come, but simply faithlessness. Not a feather, not a straw, is entrusted; that packet is empty. It is only *committed* to us, and, as it were, all things are committed to us.

The kindness I have longest remembered has been of this sort,—the sort unsaid; so far behind the speaker's lips that almost it already lay in my heart. It did not have far to go to be communicated. The gods cannot misunderstand, man cannot explain. We communicate like the burrows of foxes, in silence and darkness, under ground. We are undermined by faith and love. How much more full is Nature where we think the empty space is than where we place the solids!—full of fluid influences. Should we ever communicate but by these? The spirit abhors a vacuum more than Nature. There is a tide which pierces the pores of the air. These aerial rivers, let us not pollute their currents. What meadows do they course through? How many fine mails there are which traverse their routes! He is privileged who gets his letter franked by them.

I believe these things.

Henry D. Thoreau.

Text, Emerson-Thoreau, *pp. 580–81.*

To EMERSON

Concord, February 15, 1843.

My dear Friend,—

I got your letters, one yesterday and the other to-day, and they have made me quite happy. As a packet is to go in the morning, I will give you a hasty account of the Dial. I called on Mr. [Charles] Lane this afternoon, and brought away, together with an abundance of good will, first, a bulky catalogue of books without commentary,—some eight hundred, I think he told me, with an introduction filling one sheet,—ten or a dozen pages, say, though I have only glanced at them; second, a review—twenty-five or thirty printed pages—of Conversations on the

Gospels, Record of a School, and Spiritual Culture, with rather copious extracts. However, it is a good subject, and Lane says it gives him satisfaction. I will give it a faithful reading directly. And now I come to the little end of the horn; for myself, I have brought along the Minor Greek Poets, and will mine there for a scrap or two, at least. As for Etzler, I don't remember any "rude and snappish speech" that you made, and if you did it must have been longer than anything I had written; however, here is the book still, and I will try. Perhaps I have some few scraps in my Journal which you may choose to print. The translation of the Æschylus I should like very well to continue anon, if it should be worth the while. As for poetry, I have not remembered to write any for some time; it has quite slipped my mind; but sometimes I think I hear the mutterings of the thunder. Don't you remember that last summer we heard a low, tremulous sound in the woods and over the hills, and thought it was partridges or rocks, and it proved to be thunder gone down the river? But sometimes it was over Wayland way, and at last burst over our heads. So we'll not despair by reason of the drought. You see, it takes a good many words to supply the place of one deed; a hundred lines to a cobweb, and but one cable to a man-of-war. The Dial case needs to be reformed in many particulars. There is no news from [Charles Stearns] Wheeler, none from [Robert] Bartlett.

They all look well and happy in this house, where it gives me much pleasure to dwell.

Yours in haste,
Henry

Text, Emerson-Thoreau, *pp. 581–84* (*where Sanborn adds the letter of February 16 as a postscript*).

To EMERSON

Wednesday Evening

Dear Friend

I have time to write a few words about the Dial. I have just received the first 3 signatures—which do not yet complete Lane's piece. He will place five hundred copies for sale at Munroe's bookstore—Wheeler has sent you two full sheets—more about the German universities—and proper names which will have to be printed in alphabetical order for convenience.—what this one has done that one is doing—and the other intends to do—Hammer Purgstall (von Hammer) may be one for aught I know. However there are two or three things in it as well as names—One of the works of Herodotus is discovered to be out of place. He says something about having sent to [James Russell?] Lowell by the last steamer a budget of Literary news which he will have communicated to you ere this.

Mr Alcott has a letter from [John] Heraud and a book written by him—The Life of Savonarola—which he wishes to have republished here —Mr Lane will write a notice of it. The latter says that what is in the N. Y. post office *may* be directed to Mr. Alcott.

Miss [Elizabeth] Peabody has sent a "Notice to the readers of the Dial"—which is not good.

Mr [E. H.] Chapin lectured this evening—but so rhetorically—that I forgot my duty, and heard very little.

I find myself better than I have been—and am meditating some other method of paying debts than by lectures and writing which will only do to talk about—If anything of that "other" sort should come to your ears in N. Y. will you remember it for me?

Excuse this scrawl which I am writing over the embers in the dining room. I hope that you live on good terms with yourself and the gods—

Yrs in haste

Henry.

MS., Berg. *Although no date other than "Wednesday Evening" appears on the manuscript, Sanborn has assigned the letter to February 16, 1843.*

To EMERSON

Concord, February 20, 1843.

My dear Friend,—

I have read Mr. Lane's review, and *can* say, speaking for this world and for fallen man, that "it is good for us." As they say in geology, time never fails, there is always enough of it, so I may say, criticism never fails; but if I go and read elsewhere, I say it is good,—far better than any notice Mr. Alcott has received, or is likely to receive from another quarter. It is at any rate "the other side," which Boston needs to hear. I do not send it to you, because time is precious, and because I think you would accept it, after all. After speaking briefly of the fate of Goethe and Carlyle in their own countries, he says, "To Emerson in his own circle is but slowly accorded a worthy response; and Alcott, almost utterly neglected," etc. I will strike out what relates to yourself, and, correcting some verbal faults, send the rest to the printer with Lane's initials.

The catalogue needs amendment, I think. It wants completeness now. It should consist of such books only as they would tell Mr. [F. H.] Hedge and [Theodore] Parker they had got; omitting the Bible, the classics, and much besides,—for there the incompleteness begins. But you will be here in season for this.

It is frequently easy to make Mr. Lane more universal and attractive; to write for instance, "universal ends" instead of "the universal end," just as we pull open the petals of a flower with our fingers where they are confined by its own sweets. Also he had better not say "books designed for the nucleus of a *Home* University," until he makes that word "home" ring solid and universal too. This is that abominable dialect. He has just given me a notice of George Bradford's Fénelon for the Record of the Months, and speaks of extras of the Review and Catalogue, if they are printed,—even a hundred, or thereabouts. How shall this be arranged? Also he wishes to use some manuscripts of his which are in your possession, if you do not. Can I get them?

I think of no news to tell you. It is a serene summer day here, all above the snow. The hens steal their nests, and I steal their eggs still, as formerly. This is what I do with the hands. Ah, labor,—it is a divine institution, and conversation with many men and hens.

Do not think that my letters require as many special answers. I get one as often as you write to Concord. Concord inquires for you daily, as do all the members of this house. You must make haste home before we have settled all the great questions, for they are fast being disposed of. But I must leave room for Mrs. Emerson.

Yours,
Henry.

A new name in this correspondence is Hedge's. He was a Unitarian minister and one-time Harvard professor who became a leader in the movement to spread German culture and idealistic philosophy throughout New England. Although never really a Transcendentalist himself, he remained a close friend of the most notable Transcendentalists and met with them whenever he could; indeed, they called their first Transcendental group Hedge's Club because it gathered when he came to town from Maine. Text, Emerson-Thoreau, pp. 584–85. Mrs. Emerson added a lively postscript, worth reprinting for its story about Thoreau:

My dear Husband,—

Thinking that Henry had decided to send Mr. Lane's manuscript to you by Harnden to-morrow, I wrote you a sheet of gossip which you will not ultimately escape. Now I will use up Henry's vacant spaces with a story or two. G. P. Bradford has sent you a copy of his Fénelon, with a freezing note to me, which made me declare I would never speak to him again; but Mother says, "Never till next time!" William B. Greene has sent me a volume of tales translated by his father. Ought there to be any note of acknowledgment? I wish you may find time to fill all your paper when you write; you must have millions of things to say that we would all be glad to read.

Last evening we had the "Conversation," though, owing to the bad weather, but few attended. The subjects were: What is Prophecy? Who is a Prophet? and The Love of Nature. Mr. Lane decided, as for all time and the race, that this same love of nature—of which Henry was the champion, and Elizabeth Hoar and Lidian (though L. disclaimed possessing it herself) his faithful squiresses—that this love was the most subtle and dangerous of sins; a refined idolatry, much more to be dreaded than gross wickednesses, because the gross

sinner would be alarmed by the depth of his degradation, and come up from it in terror, but the unhappy idolaters of Nature were deceived by the refined quality of their sin, and would be the last to enter the kingdom. Henry frankly affirmed to both the wise men that they were wholly deficient in the faculty in question, and therefore could not judge of it. And Mr. Alcott as frankly answered that it was because they went beyond the mere material objects, and were filled with spiritual love and perception (as Mr. T. was not), that they seemed to Mr. Thoreau not to appreciate outward nature. I am very heavy, and have spoiled a most excellent story. I have given you no idea of the scene, which was ineffably comic, though it made no laugh at the time; I scarcely laughed at it myself,—too deeply amused to give the usual sign. Henry was brave and noble; well as I have always liked him, he still grows upon me. Elizabeth sends her love, and says she shall not go to Boston till your return, and you must make the 8th of March come quickly.

From ELIZABETH PEABODY

Boston, Feb. 26, 1843.

My Dear Sir:

I understand you have begun to print the *Dial,* and I am very glad of it on one account, viz., that if it gets out early enough to go to England by the steamer of the first of the month (April) it does not have to wait another month, as was the case with the last number. But I meant to have had as a first article a letter to the "Friends of the *Dial,*" somewhat like the rough draft I enclose, and was waiting Mr. Emerson's arrival to consult him about the name of it. I have now written to him at New York on the subject and told him my whys and wherefores. The regular income of the *Dial* does not pay the cost of its printing and paper; there are readers enough to support it if they would only subscribe; and they will subscribe if they are convinced that only by doing so can they secure its continuance. He will probably write you on the subject.

I want to ask a favor of you. It is to forward me a small phial of that black-lead dust which is to be found, as Dr. C. T. Jackson tells me, at a

certain lead-pencil manufactory in Concord; and to send it to me by the first opportunity. I want lead in this fine dust to use in a chemical experiment.

Respectfully yours,
E. P. Peabody.

P. S. I hope you have got your money from Bradbury & Soden. I have done all I could about it. Will you drop the enclosed letter for Mrs. Hawthorne into the post-office?

Mr. Henry D. Thoreau, Concord.

Since Thoreau speaks of Miss Peabody's letter to the "Friends of the Dial" in his letter to Emerson of February 16, 1843, it is quite possible that Sanborn has misdated this letter to Thoreau by several weeks. Thoreau did not include her paper in the April issue. The lead pencil manufactory was certainly that of Thoreau's father. Text, Sanborn, "A Concord Note-Book," The Critic, XLVIII (April 1906), 346.

To RICHARD FULLER

Concord, April 2, 1843.

Dear Richard,—

I was glad to receive a letter from you so bright and cheery. You speak of not having made any conquests with your own spear or quill as yet; but if you are tempering your spear-head during these days, and fitting a straight and tough shaft thereto, will not that suffice? We are more pleased to consider the hero in the forest cutting cornel or ash for his spear, than marching in triumph with his trophies. The present hour is always wealthiest when it is poorer than the future ones, as that is the pleasantest site which affords the pleasantest prospects.

What you say about your studies furnishing you with a "mimic

idiom" only, reminds me that we shall all do well if we learn so much as to talk,—to speak truth. The only fruit which even much living yields seems to be often only some trivial success,—the ability to do some slight thing better. We make conquest only of husks and shells for the most part,—at least apparently,—but sometimes these are cinnamon and spices, you know. Even the grown hunter you speak of slays a thousand buffaloes, and brings off only their hides and tongues. What immense sacrifices, what hecatombs and holocausts, the gods exact for very slight favors! How much sincere life before we can even utter one sincere word.

What I was learning in college was chiefly, I think, to express myself, and I see now, that as the old orator prescribed, 1st, action; 2d, action; 3d, action; my teachers should have prescribed to me, 1st, sincerity; 2d, sincerity; 3d, sincerity. The old mythology is incomplete without a god or goddess of sincerity, on whose altars we might offer up all the products of our farms, our workshops, and our studies. It should be our Lar when we sit on the hearth, and our Tutelar Genius when we walk abroad. This is the only panacea. I mean sincerity in our dealings with ourselves mainly; any other is comparatively easy. But I must stop before I get to 17thly. I believe I have but one text and one sermon.

Your rural adventures beyond the West Cambridge hills have probably lost nothing by distance of time or space. I used to hear only the sough of the wind in the woods of Concord, when I was striving to give my attention to a page of Calculus. But, depend upon it, you will love your native hills the better for being separated from them.

I expect to leave Concord, which is my Rome, and its people, who are my Romans, in May, and go to New York, to be a tutor in Mr. William Emerson's family. So I will bid you good by till I see you or hear from you again.

Margaret Fuller's brother, attending Harvard, according to Sanborn "desired to know something of Thoreau's pursuits there." Text, Familiar Letters of Thoreau, *pp. 77–79.*

Concord April 11th 1843

Friend Vose,

Vague rumors of your success as a lawyer in Springfield have reached our ears in Concord from time to time, and lately I have heard other news of interest regarding you from our mutual acquaintance Mrs. Jackson of Boston—All which concerns an old school—and class-mate. [William?] Davis too is with you seeking his fortune also—please give my respects to him.

The last time you wrote to me in days gone by, I think you asked me to write you some political news, to enliven your residence in that drear Chenango country—but alas I could hardly be sure who was President already—still less who was about to be— And now I have to trouble you with matters of far different tenor.—To be short—my sisters—whom per-haps you remember—who for the last three or four years have been teaching a young-ladies school in Roxbury—with some *eclat* and satis-faction, and latterly have passed a long vacation here, are desirous to establish themselves in one of those pleasant Connecticut river towns —if possible, in Springfield. They would like, either to take charge of some young-ladies school already established, or else, commencing with the few scholars that might be secured, to build up such an insti-tution by their own efforts—Teaching, besides the common English branches, French, Music, Drawing, and Painting.

And now I wish to ask if you will take the trouble to ascertain if there is any opening of the kind in your town, or if a few scholars can be had which will warrant making a beginning.

Perhaps Davis' profession acquaints him with this portion of the statistics of Springfield—and he will assist us with his advice.

Mr [Samuel] Hoar, Mr Emerson and other good men will stand as referees.

I hear of no news of importance to write you—unless it may be news to you that the Boston and Fitchburg railroad passing through this town, is to be contracted for directly—I am going to reside in Staten-Island this summer. If you will answer this as soon as convenient you will oblige

Your Classmate and well-wisher

Henry D. Thoreau.

Thoreau's Harvard classmate was now beginning his profitable legal career. MS., Lownes; previously unpublished.

From ELLERY CHANNING

My Dear Thoreau

     I leave with you a schedule of repairs & improvements, to be made on the Red Lodge before I move into it, & upon the place generally.

Cellar, sand put in enough to make it dry—under-pinned with stone, pointed inside & out. New cellar stairs to be put.

Bank to be made round the house, round well, & in woodshed. (This is to [be] sodded after planting.)

House interior. Kitchen-floor painted, & the woodwork of the kitchen. All the plastering white-washed. Lock to be put on front-door. Glass reset where broken. New sill put to front-door & back-door, & steps if necessary. Leaky place about chimney, caused by pinning up the house, to be made tight.—A new entry laid at front door.

Washroom—to be white-washed—& a spout made from sink long enough to carry off dirty water, so as to keep it from running into well.

Well. To be cleaned out, inner stones reset (as I understand the Captain told you originally)—an outside wall to be built up, high enough to keep out all wash; this outside wall to be filled round. A new pump to be put in & to pump up good, clean, fresh water.

The Acre to be measured, & fenced around with a *new* four rail fence. The acre to be less wide than long.

Privy.—To be moved from where it is now, behind the end of the barn, the filth carried off, & hole filled in. The privy to be whitewashed & have a new door, & the floor either renewed or cleaned up.—

Barn. (not done at once as I understood) New sill, & pinned up, so as to make it dry.

In May 1843 Ellery Channing, nephew of the great Unitarian divine and later to become Thoreau's most intimate friend, moved with his

family to the little Red Lodge on the Cambridge Turnpike beyond Emerson's house. While the lodge was being repaired Channing wanted to stay with his family in Cambridge; and he already felt close enough to Thoreau to ask him to supervise the repair work. This letter contains the general list of repairs. The one from Channing to Thoreau of May 1, 1843 seems to be something of a supplement, including much additional personal material and (at least in the partial text we have) only a reminder that the banks around the lodge should be sodded. Of the two letters, the present one is probably the earlier. MS., Abernethy (typescript); previously unpublished.

From ELLERY CHANNING

An autograph letter from Channing to Thoreau dated from Cambridge May 1, 1843 is described in the *Stephen H. Wakeman Collection* sale catalogue under Item 997 as being "3 pp. 4to" and addressed to Thoreau in care of Emerson. The catalogue notes that "he addresses Thoreau in one of the sentences as 'O my beloved Thoreau.'" Channing is said in this letter to have asked Thoreau to have the banks around the house Channing had just bought (in Concord) sodded to keep the sand from blowing into the rooms. He adds: "See them [then?], O beloved Thoreau, how greatly convenient a house of one's own will be!" He also writes to Thoreau that he is sending him what the catalogue calls a "Greek book," which will keep him reading Greek half a year. In his last sentence Channing writes: "So many have been your benevolences that my wish is too shallow to know how to bring you into my debt. Only so much, as offering you a shelter under my roof, when I may have one, can show effect." The letter is described as accompanying a copy of the *Week* that Thoreau presented to Channing.

From ELIZABETH HOAR

Boston, May 2, 1843

Dear Henry,—

The rain prevented me from seeing you the night before I came away, to leave with you a parting assurance of good will and good hope. We have become better acquainted within the two past years than in our whole life as schoolmates and neighbors before; and I am unwilling to let you go away without telling you that I, among your other friends, shall miss you much, and follow you with remembrance and all best wishes and confidence. Will you take this little inkstand and try if it will carry ink safely from Concord to Staten Island? and the pen, which, if you can write with steel, may be made sometimes the interpreter of friendly thoughts to those whom you leave beyond the reach of your voice,—or record the inspirations of Nature, who, I doubt not, will be as faithful to you who trust her in the sea-girt Staten Island as in Concord woods and meadows. Good-bye, and εὖ πράττειν [fare well], which, a wise man says, is the only salutation fit for the wise.

Truly your friend,
E. Hoar.

Elizabeth Hoar, daughter of Concord's most prominent family, had long been an intimate friend of the Emersons, through whom she became more familiar with her old schoolmate Thoreau. Text, Familiar Letters of Thoreau, *pp. 138–39n.*

To MRS. JOHN THOREAU

Castleton, Staten Island, May 11, 1843.

Dear Mother and Friends at Home,—

We arrived here safely at ten o'clock on Sunday morning, having had as good a passage as usual, though we ran aground and were de-

tained a couple of hours in the Thames River, till the tide came to our relief. At length we curtseyed up to a wharf just the other side of their Castle Garden,—very incurious about them and their city. I believe my vacant looks, absolutely inaccessible to questions, did at length satisfy an army of starving cabmen that I did not want a hack, cab, or anything of that sort as yet. It was the only demand the city made on us; as if a wheeled vehicle of some sort were the sum and summit of a reasonable man's wants. "Having tried the water," they seemed to say, "will you not return to the pleasant securities of land carriage? Else why your boat's prow turned toward the shore at last?" They are a sad-looking set of fellows, not permitted to come on board, and I pitied them. They had been expecting me, it would seem, and did really wish that I should take a cab; though they did not seem rich enough to supply me with one.

It was a confused jumble of heads and soiled coats, dangling from flesh-colored faces,—all swaying to and fro, as by a sort of undertow, while each whipstick, true as the needle to the pole, still preserved that level and direction in which its proprietor had dismissed his forlorn interrogatory. They took sight from them,—the lash being wound up thereon, to prevent your attention from wandering, or to make it concentre upon its object by the spiral line. They began at first, perhaps, with the modest, but rather confident inquiry, "Want a cab, sir?" but as their despair increased, it took the affirmative tone, as the disheartened and irresolute are apt to do: "You want a cab , sir," or even, "You want a nice cab, sir, to take you to Fourth Street." The question which one had bravely and hopefully begun to put, another had the tact to take up and conclude with fresh emphasis,—twirling it from his particular whipstick as if it had emanated from his lips—as the sentiment did from his heart. Each one could truly say, "Them's my sentiments." But it was a sad sight.

I am seven and a half miles from New York, and, as it would take half a day at least, have not been there yet. I have already run over no small part of the island, to the highest hill, and some way along the shore. From the hill directly behind the house I can see New York, Brooklyn, Long Island, the Narrows, through which vessels bound to and from all parts of the world chiefly pass,—Sandy Hook and the Highlands of Neversink (part of the coast of New Jersey)—and, by going still farther up the hill, the Kill van Kull, and Newark Bay. From the pinnacle of one Madame Grimes' house the other night at sunset, I could see almost round the island. Far in the horizon there was a fleet of sloops bound up the Hudson, which seemed to be going over the

edge of the earth; and in view of these trading ships, commerce seems quite imposing.

But it is rather derogatory that your dwelling-place should be only a neighborhood to a great city,—to live on an inclined plane. I do not like their cities and forts, with their morning and evening guns, and sails flapping in one's eye. I want a whole continent to breathe in, and a good deal of solitude and silence, such as all Wall Street cannot buy,— nor Broadway with its wooden pavement. I must live along the beach, on the southern shore, which looks directly out to sea,—and see what that great parade of water means, that dashes and roars, and has not yet wet me, as long as I have lived.

I must not know anything about my condition and relations here till what is not permanent is worn off. I have not yet subsided. Give me time enough, and I may like it. All my inner man heretofore has been a Concord impression; and here come these Sandy Hook and Coney Island breakers to meet and modify the former; but it will be long before I can make nature look as innocently grand and inspiring as in Concord.

Your affectionate son,
Henry D. Thoreau.

On May 6, 1843 Thoreau left his family and departed for Staten Island to become the tutor of William Emerson's son Haven. A complete account of the Staten Island stay is given in an article by Max Cosman, "Thoreau and Staten Island" in The Staten Island Historian, VI *(January–March, 1943), 1 ff.* Text, Familiar Letters of Thoreau, *pp. 80–83. Sanborn notes the letter as being addressed to both Thoreau's mother and his father, but gives no authority.*

From HENRY JAMES

New York   May 12 1843   21 Washington Place

My dear Sir—

I feel indebted to Mr Emerson for the introduction he has given me to you. I hope you will call at my house when you next come to the city and give me some of the good tidings wherewith you are fraught from Concord. I am in at all hours & shall be glad to see you at any. I am liable I believe to be called to Albany any day between now and next Thursday—though when I do go I shall stay but a day. Remember when you come over I am at 21 Wash. *Place,* a little street running from the Washington Square to Broadway, flanked on one corner by the University, and on the opposite by a church. You will easily find it. Meanwhile I remain

Yours truly
H. James

Mr H D Thoreau

On May 6, 1843 Emerson had written to Henry James, Sr.: "A friend of mine who has been an inmate of my house for the last two years, Henry D. Thoreau, is now going (tomorrow) to New York to live with my brother William at Staten Island, to take charge of the education of his son. I should like both for Mr. Thoreau's and for your own sake that you would meet and see what you have for each other. . . . If you remain in the city this summer, which seemed uncertain, I wish you would send your card to him through my brother at 64 Wall Street." On May 11 James had replied: "I shall right gladly welcome Mr. Thoreau for all our sakes to my fireside, or any preferable summer seat the house affords—and will so advise him at once." (See Ralph Barton Perry, The Thought and Character of William James, *I, 44–46.) Thoreau accepted the invitation before many weeks and reported on the meeting in his letter to Emerson of June 8, 1843. MS., Morgan; previously unpublished.*

From EMERSON

Concord Sunday Eve. 21 May, 1843

My dear Friend,

Our Dial is already printing & you must, if you can, send me something good by the 10th of June certainly, if not before. If William E can send by a private opportunity, you shall address it to Care of Miss Peabody 13 West Street, or, to be left at Concord Stage office. Otherwise send by Harnden, W. E. paying to Boston & charging to me. Let the pacquet bring letters also from you & from Waldo & Tappan, I entreat. You will not doubt that you are well remembered here, by young, older, & old people and your letter to your mother was borrowed & read with great interest, pending the arrival of direct accounts & of later experiences especially in the city. I am sure that you are under sacred protection, if I should not hear from you for years. Yet I shall wish to know what befals you on your way.

Ellery Channing is well settled in his house & works very steadily thus far & our intercourse is very agreeable to me. Young Ball has been to see me & is a prodigious reader & a youth of great promise,— born too in the good town. Mr Hawthorne is well; and Mr Alcott & Mr. L. are resolving a purchase in Harvard of 90 acres. Yours affectionately,

R. W. Emerson

My wife will reopen my sealed letter, but a remembrance from her shall be inserted.

Thoreau had a variety of items in the belated April 1843 Dial. *Giles Waldo, like William Tappan, was—as Thoreau explained in a letter of May 22 to his sister Sophia—a young friend of Emerson. For Emerson's further account of the visit of Benjamin Ball see his* Journals, VI, 396–99. *Alcott and Lane established their Fruitlands community soon after this letter was written. MS., Morgan.*

To MRS. R. W. EMERSON

Castleton, Staten Island, May 22, 1843.

My dear Friend,—

I believe a good many conversations with you were left in an unfinished state, and now indeed I don't know where to take them up. But I will resume some of the unfinished silence. I shall not hesitate to know you. I think of you as some elder sister of mine, whom I could not have avoided,—a sort of lunar influence,—only of such age as the moon, whose time is measured by her light. You must know that you represent to me woman, for I have not traveled very far or wide,—and what if I had? I like to deal with you, for I believe you do not lie or steal, and these are very rare virtues. I thank you for your influence for two years. I was fortunate to be subjected to it, and am now to remember it. It is the noblest gift we can make; what signify all others that can be bestowed? You have helped to keep my life "on loft," as Chaucer says of Griselda, and in a better sense. You always seemed to look down at me as from some elevation—some of your high humilities—and I was better for having to look up. I felt taxed not to disappoint your expectation; for could there be any accident so sad as to be respected for something better than we are? It was a pleasure even to go away from you, as it is not to meet some, as it apprised me of my high relations; and such a departure is a sort of further introduction and meeting. Nothing makes the earth seem so spacious as to have friends at a distance; they make the latitudes and longitudes.

You must not think that fate is so dark there, for even here I can see a faint reflected light over Concord, and I think that at this distance I can better weigh the value of a doubt there. Your moonlight, as I have told you, though it is a reflection of the sun, allows of bats and owls and other twilight birds to flit therein. But I am very glad that you can elevate your life with a doubt, for I am sure that it is nothing but an insatiable faith after all that deepens and darkens its current. And your doubt and my confidence are only a difference of expression.

I have hardly begun to live on Staten Island yet; but, like the man who, when forbidden to tread on English ground, carried Scottish ground in his boots, I carry Concord ground in my boots and in my hat,—and am I not made of Concord dust? I cannot realize that it is the

103

roar of the sea I hear now, and not the wind in Walden woods. I find more of Concord, after all, in the prospect of the sea, beyond Sandy Hook, than in the fields and woods.

If you were to have this Hugh the gardener for your man, you would think a new dispensation had commenced. He might put a fairer aspect on the natural world for you, or at any rate a screen between you and the almshouse. There is a beautiful red honeysuckle now in blossom in the woods here, which should be transplanted to Concord; and if what they tell me about the tulip-tree be true, you should have that also. I have not seen Mrs. Black yet, but I intend to call on her soon. Have you established those simpler modes of living yet?—"In the full tide of successful operation?"

Tell Mrs. Brown that I hope she is anchored in a secure haven and derives much pleasure still from reading the poets, and that her constellation is not quite set from my sight, though it is sunk so low in that northern horizon. Tell Elizabeth Hoar that her bright present did "carry ink safely to Staten Island," and was a conspicuous object in Master Haven's inventory of my effects. Give my respects to Madam Emerson, whose Concord face I should be glad to see here this summer; and remember me to the rest of the household who have had vision of me. Shake a day-day to Edith, and say good night to Ellen for me. Farewell.

For a note on the relationship of Thoreau and Lidian Emerson see his letter of June 20, 1843. For Elizabeth Hoar's "bright present" see her letter of May 2, 1843. "Hugh the gardener" was Hugh Whelan, who later purchased and attempted to rebuild Thoreau's Walden hut. The Concord almshouse was just across the meadow in back of the Emerson house. Mrs. Rebecca Black was a New York friend of Emerson frequently mentioned in his letters and journals as a "spiritual woman" (for example, Emerson Letters, III, 23). Madam Emerson was Emerson's mother, who lived with him in Concord. Text, Familiar Letters of Thoreau, pp. 89–92.

To SOPHIA THOREAU

Castleton, Staten Island, May 22nd -43

Dear Sophia,

I have had a severe cold ever since I came here, and have been confined to the house for the last week with bronchitis, though I am now getting out, so I have not seen much in the botanical way. The cedar seems to be one of the most common trees here, and the fields are very fragrant with it. There are also the gum and tulip trees. The latter is not very common, but is very large and beautiful, having flowers as large as tulips and as handsome. It is not time for it yet. The woods are now full of a large honeysuckle in full bloom, which differs from ours in being red instead of white, so that at first I did not know its genus. The painted cup is very common in the meadows here. Peaches, and especially cherries, seem to grow by all the fences.

Things are very forward here compared with Concord. The apricots growing out of doors are already as large as plums. The apple, pear, peach, cherry and plum trees, have shed their blossoms. The whole Island is like a garden, and affords very fine scenery. In front of the house is a very extensive wood, beyond which is the sea, whose roar I can hear all night long, when there is no wind, if easterly winds have prevailed on the Atlantic. There are always some vessels in sight—ten, twenty, or thirty miles off and Sunday before last there were hundreds in long procession, stretching from New York to Sanday [sic] Hook, and far beyond, for Sunday is a lucky day.

I went to New York Saturday before last. A walk of half an hour, by half a dozen houses along the Richmond road, ie. the road that leads to R—— on which we live—brings me to the village of Stapleton, in South- field, where is the lower dock; but if I prefer I can walk along the shore three quarters of a mile further toward New York, to Quarantine, village of Castleton, to the upper dock, which the boat leaves five or six times every day, a quarter of an hour later than the former place. Further on is the village of New Brighton and further still Port Richmond, which villages another steamboat visits.

In New York I saw Geo. Ward, and also Giles Waldo and William Tappan, whom I can describe better when I have seen them more—They are young friends of Mr Emerson. Waldo came down to the Island to

see me the next day. I also saw the Great Western, the Croton Water-
works, and the picture gallery of the National Academy of Design. But
I have not had time to see or do much in N. Y. yet.

Tell Miss [Prudence] Ward I shall try to put my microscope to a good
use, and if I find any new and pressible flower, will throw it into my
common place book. Garlic, the original of the common onion, grows
like grass here all over the fields, and during its season spoils the cream
and butter for the market, as the cows like it very much. Tell Helen
there are two schools just established in this neighborhood, with large
prospects, or rather designs, one for boys, and another for girls. The
latter by a Miss Errington—and though it is very small as yet—will keep
my ears open for her in such directions—The encouragement is very
slight.

I hope you will not be washed away by the Irish sea. Tell mother I
think my cold was not wholly owing to imprudence. Perhaps I was
being acclimated.

Tell father that Mr Tappan whose son I know—and whose clerks
young Tappan and Waldo are—has invented and established a new
and very important business—which Waldo thinks could allow them to
burn 99 out of 100 of the stores in N. Y. which now only offset and cancel
one another. It is a kind of intelligence office for the whole country—with
branches in the principal cities, giving information with regard to the
credit and affairs of every man of business in the country. Of course it is
not popular at the South and West. It is an extensive business, and will
employ a great many clerks.

Love to all—not forgetting Aunt and Aunts—and Miss and Mrs. Ward.

Yr Affectionate Brother

Henry D. Thoreau.

*Thoreau had been ill in February, and perhaps the trip to Staten Island
brought on an attack of bronchitis, an early indication of his chronic
tendency to consumption. Possibly he felt that the sea air at Staten
Island would help his condition; anyway, he soon recovered from his
cold. The "Irish sea" is the influx of laborers to help build the railroad
from Boston to Fitchburg. MS., Berg.*

Castleton, Staten Island, May 23d.

My Dear Friend,

I was just going to write to you when I received your letter. I was waiting till I had got away from Concord. I should have sent you something for the Dial before, but I have been sick ever since I came here—rather unaccountably, what with a cold, bronchitis, acclimation &c—still unaccountably. I send you some verses from my journal which will help make a packet. I have not time to correct them—if this goes by Rockwood Hoar. If I can finish an account of a winter's walk in Concord in the midst of a Staten Island summer—not so wise or true I trust —I will send it to you soon.

I have had no "later experiences" yet. You must not count much upon what I can do or learn in New York. I feel a good way off here—and it is not to be visited, but seen and dwelt in. I have been there but once, and have been confined to the house since. Every thing there disappoints me but the crowd—rather I was disappointed with the rest before I came. I have no eyes for their churches and what else they find to brag of. Though I know but little about Boston, yet what attracts me in a quiet way seems much meaner and more pretending than these—Libraries—Pictures—and faces in the street—You don't know where any respectability inhabits.—It is in the crowd in Chatham street. The crowd is something new and to be attended to. It is worth a thousand Trinity Churches and Exchanges while it is looking at them—and will run over them and trample them under foot one day. There are two things I hear, and am aware that I live in the neighborhood of—The roar of the sea— and the hum of the city. I have just come from the beach (to find your letter) and I like it much. Every thing there is on a grand and generous scale—sea-weed, water, and sand; and even the dead fishes, horses and hogs have a rank luxuriant odor. Great shad nets spread to dry, crabs and horse-shoes crawling over the sand—Clumsy boats, only for service, dancing like sea-fowl on the surf, and ships afar off going about their business.

Waldo and Tappan carried me to their English alehouse the first Saturday, and Waldo spent two hours here the next day. But Tappan I have only seen I like his looks and the sound of his silence. They are

confined every day but Sunday, and then Tappan is obliged to observe the demeanor of a church goer to prevent open war with his father.

I am glad that Channing has got settled, and that too before the inroad of the Irish. I have read his poems two or three times over, and partially through and under, with new and increased interest and appreciation. Tell him I saw a man buy a copy at Little and Brown's. He may have been a virtuoso—but we will give him the credit.

What with Alcott & Lane & Hawthorne too you look strong enough to take New York by storm. Will you tell L. if he asks, that I have been able to do nothing about the books yet.

Believe that I have something better to write you than this. It would be unkind to thank you for particular deeds

Yr friend
Henry D Thoreau

Rockwood Hoar, later a distinguished judge, was the brother of Eliza-beth Hoar. None of Thoreau's poems was included in the July issue of the Dial: *there is no indication of what ones he sent to Emerson at this time. He was evidently too late in completing "A Winter Walk," since it was not published till the October issue. Ellery Channing's first volume,* Poems, *had just been published. Thoreau attempted to help Lane sell his library to raise money for Fruitlands. The final disposition of the books is accounted for in the Lane letter of February 17, 1846. MS., Huntington.*

To HELEN THOREAU

Castleton Staten Island May 23d 43

Dear Helen,

In place of something fresher I send you the following verses from my journal, written some time ago.

Brother where dost thou dwell?
What sun shines for thee now?

[1843]

Dost thou indeed farewell?
    As we wished here below.

What season didst thou find?
    Twas winter here.
Are not the fates more kind
    Than they appear?

Is thy brow clear again
    As in thy youthful years?
And was that ugly pain
    The summit of thy fears?

Yet thou wast cheery still,
    They could not quench thy fire,
Thou didst abide their will,
    And then retire.

Where chiefly shall I look
    To feel thy presence near?
Along the neighboring brook
    May I thy voice still hear?

Dost thou still haunt the brink
    Of yonder river's tide?
And may I ever think
    That thou art at my side?

What bird wilt thou employ
    To bring me word of thee?
For it would give them joy,
    'Twould give them liberty,
To serve their former lord
    With wing and minstrelsy.

A sadder strain has mixed with their song,
    They've slowlier built their nests,
Since thou art gone
    Their lively labor rests.

Where is the finch—the thrush,
    I used to hear?

109

Ah! they could well abide
The dying year.

Now they no more return,
I hear them not;
They have remained to mourn,
Or else forgot.

"Brother where dost thou dwell?" is the tribute to John Thoreau, who died in January 1842. The seventh stanza probably refers to the interest in ornithology shared by the brothers. MS., Abernethy (typescript).

To EMERSON

Staten Island, June 8, 1843.

Dear Friend,—

I have been to see Henry James, and like him very much. It was a great pleasure to meet him. It makes humanity seem more erect and respectable. I never was more kindly and faithfully catechised. It made me respect myself more to be thought worthy of such wise questions. He is a man, and takes his own way, or stands still in his own place. I know of no one so patient and determined to have the good of you. It is almost friendship, such plain and human dealing. I think that he will not write or speak inspiringly; but he is a refreshing forward-looking and forward-moving man, and he has naturalized and humanized New York for me. He actually reproaches you by his respect for your poor words. I had three hours' solid talk with him, and he asks me to make free use of his house. He wants an expression of your faith, or to be sure that it is faith, and confesses that his own treads fast upon the neck of his understanding. He exclaimed, at some careless answer of mine, "Well, you Transcendentalists are wonderfully consistent. I must get hold of this somehow!" He likes Carlyle's book, but says that it leaves him in an excited and unprofitable state, and that Carlyle is so

110

ready to obey his humor that he makes the least vestige of truth the foundation of any superstructure, not keeping faith with his better genius nor truest readers.

I met Wright on the stairs of the Society Library, and W. H. Channing and Brisbane on the steps. The former (Channing) is a concave man, and you see by his attitude and the lines of his face that he is retreating from himself and from yourself, with sad doubts. It is like a fair mask swaying from the drooping boughs of some tree whose stem is not seen. He would break with a conchoidal fracture. You feel as if you would like to see him when he has made up his mind to run all the risks. To be sure, he doubts because he has a great hope to be disappointed, but he makes the possible disappointment of too much consequence. Brisbane, with whom I did not converse, did not impress me favorably. He looks like a man who has lived in a cellar, far gone in consumption. I barely saw him, but he did not look as if he could let Fourier go, in any case, and throw up his hat. But I need not have come to New York to write this.

I have seen Tappan for two or three hours, and like both him and Waldo; but I always see those of whom I have heard well with a slight disappointment. They are so much better than the great herd, and yet the heavens are not shivered into diamonds over their heads. Persons and things flit so rapidly through my brain, nowadays, that I can hardly remember them. They seem to be lying in the stream, stemming the tide, ready to go to sea, as steamboats when they leave the dock go off in the opposite direction first, until they are headed right, and then begins the steady revolution of the paddle-wheels; and *they* are not quite cheerily headed anywhither yet, nor singing amid the shrouds as they bound over the billows. There is a certain youthfulness and generosity about them, very attractive; and Tappan's more reserved and solitary thought commands respect.

After some ado, I discovered the residence of Mrs. Black, but there was palmed off on me, in her stead, a Mrs. Grey (quite an inferior color), who told me at last that she was not Mrs. Black, but her mother, and was just as glad to see me as Mrs. Black would have been, and so, forsooth, would answer just as well. Mrs. Black had gone with Edward Palmer to New Jersey, and would return on the morrow.

I don't like the city better, the more I see it, but worse. I am ashamed of my eyes that behold it. It is a thousand times meaner than I could have imagined. It will be something to hate,—that's the advantage it

will be to me; and even the best people in it are a part of it and talk coolly about it. The pigs in the street are the most respectable part of the population. When will the world learn that a million men are of no importance compared with *one* man? But I must wait for a shower of shillings, or at least a slight dew or mizzling of sixpences, before I explore New York very far.

The sea-beach is the best thing I have seen. It is very solitary and remote, and you only remember New York occasionally. The distances, too, along the shore, and inland in sight of it, are unaccountably great and startling. The sea seems very near from the hills but it proves a long way over the plain, and yet you may be wet with the spray before you can believe that you are there. The far seems near, and the near far. Many rods from the beach, I step aside for the Atlantic, and I see men drag up their boats on to the sand, with oxen, stepping about amid the surf, as if it were possible they might draw up Sandy Hook.

I do not feel myself especially serviceable to the good people with whom I live, except as inflictions are sanctified to the righteous. And so, too, must I serve the boy. I can look to the Latin and mathematics sharply, and for the rest behave myself. But I cannot be in his neighborhood hereafter as his Educator, of course, but as the hawks fly over my own head. I am not attracted toward him but as to youth generally. He shall frequent me, however, as much as he can, and I'll be I.

Bradbury told me, when I passed through Boston, that he was coming to New York the following Saturday, and would then settle with me, but he has not made his appearance yet. Will you, the next time you go to Boston, present that order for me which I left with you?

If I say less about Waldo and Tappan now, it is, perhaps, because I may have more to say by and by. Remember me to your mother and Mrs. Emerson, who, I hope, is quite well. I shall be very glad to hear from her, as well as from you. I have very hastily written out something for the Dial, and send it only because you are expecting something,— though something better. It seems idle and Howittish, but it may be of more worth in Concord, where it belongs. In great haste. Farewell.

Henry D. Thoreau.

The forthright father of William and Henry James, who interested Thoreau very much, met him with a directness that almost equaled

Thoreau's own. The book by Carlyle was apparently Past and Present, *just published in its first American edition in Boston at Emerson's behest. Wright may have been either Alcott's English friend Henry G. Wright or Henry C. Wright, the American reformer. Wymond Bradbury was a member of the Boston publishing house of Bradbury, Soden, & Co., which published Thoreau's essay* "A Walk to Wachusett" *in the* Boston Miscellany *and then ignored his requests for payment.* Text, Emerson-Thoreau, *pp. 587–88.*

To MR. AND MRS. JOHN THOREAU

Castleton, Staten Island, June 8th 1843

Dear Parents,

I have got quite well now, and like the lay of the land and the look of the sea very much—only the country is so fair that it seems rather too much as if it were made to be looked at. I have been to N.Y. four or five times, and have run about the island a good deal. Geo. Ward when I last saw him, which was at his house in Brooklyn, was studying the daguerreotype process, preparing to set up in that line. The boats run now almost every hour, from 8 A.M. to 7 P.M. back and forth, so that I can get to the city much more easily than before. I have seen there one Henry James, a lame man, of whom I had heard before, whom I like very much, and he asks me to make free use of his house, which is situated in a pleasant part of the city, adjoining the University. I have met several people whom I knew before, and among the rest Mr Wright, who was on his way to Niagara.

I feel already about as well acquainted with New York as with Boston, that is about as little, perhaps. It is large enough now and they intend it shall be larger still. 15th Street, where some of my new acquaintances live, is two or three miles from the battery where the boat touches, clear brick and stone and no give to the foot; and they have layed out though not built, up to the 149th Street above. I had rather see a brick for a specimen for my part such as they exhibited in old times. You see it is quite a day's training to make a few calls in different parts of the city. (to say nothing of 12 miles by water and three by land,

113

ie. not brick and stone) especially if it does not rain shillings which might interest omnibuses in your behalf. Some Omnibuses are marked "Broadway—Fourth Street"—and they go no further—others "8th Street" and so on, and so of the other principal streets. This letter will be circumstantial enough for Helen.

This is in all respects a very pleasant residence—much more rural than you would expect of the vicinity of New York. There are woods all around.

We breakfast at half past six—lunch if we will at twelve—and dine or sup at five. Thus is the day partitioned off. From 9 to 2 or thereabouts I am the schoolmaster—and at other times as much the pupil as I can be. Mr and Mrs Emerson & family are not indeed of my kith or kin in any sense—but they are irreproachable and kind.

I have met no one yet *on the Island* whose acquaintance I shall actually cultivate—or hoe around—unless it be our neighbor Capt. Smith —an old fisherman who catches the fish called moss-bonkers—(so it sounds) and invites me to come to the beach where he spends the week and see him and his fish.

Farms are for sale all around here—and so I suppose men are for purchase.

North of us live Peter Wandell—Mr Mell—and Mr. Disusway (dont mind the spelling) as far as the Clove road; and south John Britton— Van Pelt and Capt Smith as far as the Fingerboard road. Behind is the hill, some 250 feet high—on the side of which we live, and in front the forest and the sea—the latter at the distance of a mile and a half.

Tell Helen that Miss Errington is provided with assistance. This were as good a place as any to establish a school if one could wait a little. Families come down here to board in the summer—and three or four have been already established this season.

As for money matters I have not set my traps yet, but I am getting the bait ready. Pray how does the garden thrive and what improvements in the pencil line? I miss you all very much. Write soon and send a Concord paper to

Yr affectionate son
Henry D. Thoreau

MS., New-York Historical Society.

From CHARLES LANE

Dear Friend,—

    The receipt of two acceptable numbers of the "Pathfinder" reminds me that I am not altogether forgotten by one who, if not in the busy world, is at least much nearer to it externally than I am. Busy indeed we all are, since our removal here; but so recluse is our position, that with the world at large we have scarcely any connection. You may possibly have heard that, after all our efforts during the spring had failed to place us in connection with the earth, and Mr. Alcott's journey to Oriskany and Vermont had turned out a blank,—one afternoon in the latter part of May, Providence sent to us the legal owner of a slice of the planet in this township (Harvard), with whom we have been enabled to conclude for the concession of his rights. It is very remotely placed, nearly three miles beyond the village, without a road, surrounded by a beautiful green landscape of fields and woods, with the distance filled up by some of the loftiest mountains in the State. The views are, indeed, most poetic and inspiring. You have no doubt seen the neighborhood; but from these very fields, where you may at once be at home and out, there is enough to love and revel in for sympathetic souls like yours. On the estate are about fourteen acres of wood, part of it extremely pleasant as a retreat, a very sylvan realization, which only wants a Thoreau's mind to elevate it to classic beauty.

    I have some imagination that you are not so happy and so well housed in your present position as you would be here amongst us; although at present there is much hard manual labor,—so much that, as you perceive, my usual handwriting is very greatly suspended. We have only two associates in addition to our own families; our house accommodations are poor and scanty; but the greatest want is of good female aid. Far too much labor devolves on Mrs. Alcott. If you should light on any such assistance, it would be charitable to give it a direction this way. We may, perhaps, be rather particular about the quality; but the conditions will pretty well determine the acceptability of the parties without a direct adjudication on our part. For though to me our mode of life is luxurious in the highest degree, yet generally it seems to be thought that the setting aside of all impure diet, dirty habits, idle thoughts, and selfish feelings, is a course of self-denial, scarcely to be encountered or even thought of in such an alluring world as this in which we dwell.

Besides the busy occupations of each succeeding day, we form, in this ample theatre of hope, many forthcoming scenes. The nearer little copse is designed as the site of the cottages. Fountains can be made to descend from their granite sources on the hill-slope to every apartment if required. Gardens are to displace the warm grazing glades on the south, and numerous human beings, instead of cattle, shall here enjoy existence. The farther wood offers to the naturalist and the poet an exhaustless haunt; and a short cleaning of the brook would connect our boat with the Nashua. Such are the designs which Mr. Alcott and I have just sketched, as, resting from planting, we walked around this reserve.

In your intercourse with the dwellers in the great city, have you alighted on Mr. Edward Palmer, who studies with Dr. Beach, the Herbalist? He will, I think, from his previous nature-love, and his affirmations to Mr. Alcott, be animated on learning of this actual wooing and winning of Nature's regards. We should be most happy to see him with us. Having become so far actual, from the real, we might fairly enter into the typical, if he could help us in any way to types of the true metal. We have not passed away from home, to see or hear of the world's doings, but the report has reached us of Mr. W. H. Channing's fellowship with the Phalansterians, and of his eloquent speeches in their behalf. Their progress will be much aided by his accession. To both these worthy men be pleased to suggest our humanest sentiments. While they stand amongst men, it is well to find them acting out the truest possible at the moment.

Just before we heard of this place, Mr. Alcott had projected a settlement at the Cliffs on the Concord River, cutting down wood and building a cottage; but so many more facilities were presented here that we quitted the old classic town for one which is to be not less renowned. As far as I could judge, our absence promised little pleasure to our old Concord friends; but at signs of progress I presume they rejoiced with, dear friend,

Yours faithfully,
Charles Lane.

The Pathfinder *mentioned in this pastoral letter from Harvard, Massachusetts, was a weekly journal of politics, literature, drama, and music.*

It first appeared on February 25, 1843 in New York. Text, Sanborn's Henry Thoreau, pp. 137–40. Sanborn, for one, dates the letter June 9 there and June 7 in his memoir of Alcott published eleven years later in A. Bronson Alcott: His Life and Philosophy, II, 377. Lacking the manuscript and satisfactory internal evidence, we know nothing against the date Sanborn gave first.

From EMERSON

Concord, 10 June 1843

Dear Henry,

It is high time that you had some token from us in acknowledgment of the parcel of kind & tuneful things you sent us, as well as your permanent right in us all. The cold weather saddened our gardens & our landscape here almost until now but todays sunshine is obliterating the memory of such things. I have just been visiting my petty plantation and find that all your grafts live excepting a single scion and all my new trees, including twenty pines to fill up interstices in my "Curtain," are well alive. The town is full of Irish & the woods of engineers with theodolite & red flag singing out their feet & inches to each other from station to station. Near Mr Alcott's the road [Fitchburg R. R.] is already begun.—From Mr. A. & Mr Lane at Harvard we have yet heard nothing. They went away in good spirits having sent "Wood Abram" & Larned & Wm Lane before them with horse & plough a few days in advance of them to begin the Spring work. Mr. Lane paid me a long visit in which he was more than I had ever known him gentle & open, and it was impossible not to sympathize with & honor projects that so often seem without feet or hands. They have near a hundred acres of land which they do not want, & no house, which they want first of all. But they account this an advantage, as it gives them the occasion they so much desire of building after their own idea. In the event of their attracting to their company a carpenter or two, which is not im-

117

possible, it would be a great pleasure to see their building which could hardly fail to be new & beautiful. They have 15 acres of woodland with good timber. Ellery Channing is excellent company and we walk in all directions He remembers you with great faith & hope thinks you ought not to see Concord again these ten years, that you ought to grind up fifty Concords in your mill & much other opinion & counsel he holds in store on this topic. Hawthorne walked with me yesterday p.m. and not until after our return did I read his "Celestial Railroad" which has a serene strength which one cannot afford not to praise,—in this low life.

Our Dial thrives well enough in these weeks. I print W. E. C[han-ning]'s "Letters" or the first ones, but he does not care to have them named as his for a while. They are very agreeable reading, their wisdom lightened by a vivacity very rare in the D.—[Samuel G.] Ward too has sent me some sheets on architecture, whose good sense is eminent. I have a valuable manuscript—a sea voyage from a new hand, which is all clear good sense, and I may make some of Mr Lane's graver sheets give way for this honest story. otherwise I shall print it in October. I have transferred the publishing of the Dial to Jas. Munroe & Co. Do not, I entreat you, let me be in ignorance of anything good which you know of my fine friends Waldo & Tappan. Tappan writes me never a word. I had a letter from H. James, promising to see you, & you must not fail to visit him. I must soon write to him, though my debts of this nature are perhaps too many. To him I much prefer to talk than to write. Let me know well how you prosper & what you meditate. And all good abide with you!

R. W. E.

15 June

Whilst my letter has lain on the table waiting for a traveler, your letter & parcel has safely arrived. I may not have place now for the Winter's Walk in the July Dial which is just making up its last sheets & somehow I must end it to-morrow—when I go to Boston. I shall then keep it for October, subject however to your order if you find a better disposition for it. I will carry the order to the faithless booksellers. Thanks for all these tidings of my friends at N. Y. & at the Island & love to the last. I have letters from Lane at "Fruitlands" & from Miss Fuller at Niagara. Miss F. found it sadly cold & wet rainy at the Falls.

The curtain, according to Sanborn, was a group of pine trees set out east of Emerson's house to break the wind. Channing's "Letters" is "The Youth of the Poet and the Painter"; Ward's paper is "Notes on Art and Architecture," both in the July Dial. *"A Winter Walk" was postponed to the October number. The advance party at Fruitlands consisted of Samuel Larned, Abraham Everett, and Charles Lane's son.* MS., Berg.

To MRS. EMERSON

Staten Island June 20th 1843

My very dear Friend,

I have only read a page of your letter and have come out to the top of the hill at sunset where I can see the ocean to prepare to read the rest. It is fitter that it should hear it than the walls of my chamber. The very crickets here seem to chirp around me as they did not before. I feel as if it were a great daring to go on and read the rest, and then to live accordingly. There are more than thirty vessels in sight going to sea. I am almost afraid to look at your letter. I see that it will make my life very steep, but it may lead to fairer prospects than this.

You seem to me to speak out of a very clear and high heaven, where any one may be who stands so high. Your voice seems not a voice, but comes as much from the blue heavens, as from the paper.

My dear friend it was very noble in you to write me so trustful an answer. It will do as well for another world as for this. Such a voice is for no particular time nor person, and it makes him who may hear it stand for all that is lofty and true in humanity. The thought of you will constantly elevate my life; it will be something always above the horizon to behold, as when I look up at the evening star. I think I know your thoughts without seeing you, and as well here as in Concord. You are not at all strange to me.

I could hardly believe after the lapse of one night that I had such a noble letter still at hand to read—that it was not some fine dream. I

looked at midnight to be sure that it was real. I feel that I am unworthy to know you, and yet they will not permit it wrongfully.

I, perhaps, am more willing to deceive by appearances than you say you are; it would not be worth the while to tell how willing—but I have the power perhaps too much to forget my meanness as soon as seen, and not be incited by permanent sorrow. My actual life is unspeakably mean, compared with what I know and see that it might be —Yet the ground from which I see and say this is some part of it. It ranges from heaven to earth and is all things in an hour. The experience of every past moment but belies the faith of each present. We never conceive the greatness of our fates. Are not these faint flashes of light, which sometimes obscure the sun, their certain dawn?

My friend, I have read your letter as if I was not reading it. After each pause I could defer the rest forever. The thought of you will be a new motive for every right action. You are another human being whom I know, and might not our topic be as broad as the universe. What have we to do with petty rumbling news? We have our own great affairs. Sometimes in Concord I found my actions dictated, as it were, by your influence, and though it lead almost to trivial Hindoo observances, yet it was good and elevating.

To hear that you have sad hours is not sad to me. I rather rejoice at the richness of your experience. Only think of some sadness away in Pekin—unseen and unknown there. What a mine it is. Would it not weigh down the Celestial empire, with all its gay Chinese? Our sadness is not sad, but our cheap joys. Let us be sad about all we see and are, for so we demand and pray for better. It is the constant prayer and whole Christian religion. I could hope that you would get well soon, and have a healthy body for this world, but I know this cannot be—and the Fates after all, are the accomplishers of our hopes. Yet I do hope that you may find it a worthy struggle, and life seems grand still through the clouds.

What wealth is it to have such friends that we cannot think of them without elevation. And we can think of them any time, and any where, and it costs nothing but the lofty disposition. I cannot tell you the joy your letter gives me—which will not quite cease till the latest time. Let me accompany your finest thought.

I send my love to my other friend and brother, whose nobleness I slowly recognize.

Henry

*This beautifully affectionate letter is one of the most controversial
Thoreau ever wrote. Was he in love with Lidian Emerson when he
wrote it? Canby (Thoreau, p. 160) feels that in it Thoreau "was peril-
ously close to love, by any definition" and uses it as the keystone of his
theory that "Thoreau was what the common man would call in love
with Emerson's wife" (p. 163). Dr. Raymond Adams in reviewing Canby's Thoreau (American Literature, XII [March, 1940], 114) says on
the other hand: "I think Mr. Canby shows that there was a slight
mother-fixation about the Thoreau-Lidian Emerson relationship, but
nothing more." Unfortunately neither of the letters that Mrs. Emerson
wrote before and after receiving this letter has survived. They might
have helped to answer the question. To almost anyone who will read
the text with an open mind, this is a love letter. MS., Bruce Museum,
reproduced through the courtesy of Miss Nellie P. Bigelow.*

To MRS. JOHN THOREAU

Staten Island July 7th

Dear Mother,

    I was very glad to get your letter and papers. Tell Father that
circumstantial letters make very substantial reading, at any rate. I like
to know even how the sun shines and garden grows with you.

    I did not get my money in Boston and probably shall not at all. Tell
Sophia that I have pressed some blossoms of the tulip tree for her. They
look somewhat like white lilies. The magnolia too is in blossom here.
Pray have you the Seventeen year locust in Concord? The air here is
filled with their din. They come out of the ground at first in an imperfect state, and crawling up the shrubs and plants, the perfect insect
burst[s] out through the bark. They are doing great damage to the fruit
and forest trees. The latter are covered with dead twigs, which in the distance looks like the blossoms of the chestnut. They bore every twig of
last year's growth in order to deposit their eggs in it. In a few weeks the

eggs will be hatched, and the worms fall to the ground and enter it—and in 1860 make their appearance again. I conversed about their coming this season before they arrived. They do no injury to the leaves, but beside boring the twigs—suck their sap for sustenance. Their din is heard by those who sail along the shore—from the distant woods. Phar-r-r-a oh —Pha-r-r-aoh. They are departing now. Dogs, cats and chickens subsist mainly upon them in some places.

I have not been to N.Y. for more than three weeks.—I have had an interesting letter from Mr Lane, describing their new prospects.—My pupil and I are getting on apace. He is remarkably well advanced in Latin and is well advancing.

Your letter has just arrived. I was not aware that it was so long since I wrote home; I only knew that I had sent five or six letters to the town. It is very refreshing to hear from you—though it is not all good news— But I trust that Stearns Wheeler is not dead. I should be slow to believe it. He was made to work very well in this world. There need be no tragedy in his death.

The demon which is said to haunt the Jones family—hovering over their eyelids with wings steeped in juice of poppies—has commenced another campaign against me. I am "clear Jones" in this respect at least. But he finds little encouragement in my atmosphere I assure you—for I do not once fairly lose myself—except in those hours of truce allotted to rest by immemorial custom. However, this skirmishing interferes sadly with my literary projects—and I am apt to think it a good day's work if I maintain a soldier's eye till nightfall. Very well it does not matter much in what wars we serve—whether in the Highlands or the Lowlands—Everywhere we get soldiers' pay still.

Give my love to Aunt Louisa—whose benignant face I sometimes see right in the wall—as naturally and necessarily shining on my path as some star—of unaccountably greater age and higher orbit than myself. Let it be inquired by her of George Minott—as from me—for she sees him—If he has seen any pigeons yet—and tell him there are plenty of Jacksnipes here.—As for William P. the "worthy young man"—as I live, my eyes have not fallen on him yet. I have not had the influenza— though here are its head-quarters—unless my first week's cold was it. Tell Helen I shall write to her soon. I have heard Lucretia Mott—This is badly written—but the worse the writing the sooner you get it this time—from yr affectionate son H. D. T.

The "interesting letter from Mr Lane" is probably that of June 9[?], 1843. Stearns Wheeler, Thoreau's Harvard classmate and friend, died in Leipzig on June 13, 1843. He had gone abroad to study in the German universities. Mrs. Thoreau's maternal grandparents were the Joneses. Thoreau's Uncle Charlie Dunbar inherited the sleepiness of the Jones family; as Thoreau once reported, he was known to have fallen asleep while shaving. A full account of Thoreau's seeing Lucretia Mott will be found in his letter to Helen Thoreau of July 21, 1843. The "money in Boston" was the Boston Miscellany *debt (see Elizabeth Peabody's letter of February 26, 1843). Aunt Louisa Dunbar lived with the Thoreaus from 1830 on. George Minott was Thoreau's Concord farmer friend. The unnamed year is plainly 1843. MS., Huntington.*

To MR. AND MRS. R. W. EMERSON

Staten Island July 8th —43

Dear Friends,

I was very glad to hear your voices from so far. I do not believe there are eight hundred human beings on the globe—It is all a fable; And I cannot but think that you speak with a slight outrage and disrespect of Concord, when you talk of fifty of them. There are not so many. Yet think not that I have left all behind—for already I begin to track my way over the earth, and find the cope of heaven extending beyond its horizon—forsooth, like the roofs of these Dutch houses. Yet will my thoughts revert to those dear hills and that *river* which so fills up the world to its brim, worthy to be named with Mincius and Alpheus still drinking its meadows while I am far away. How can it run heedless to the sea, as if I were there to countenance it—George Minott too looms up considerably—and many another old familiar face—These things all look sober and respectable. They are better than the environs of New York, I assure you.

I am pleased to think of Channing as an inhabitant of the grey town. Seven cities contended for Homer dead. Tell him to remain at least long enough to establish Concord's right and interest in him. I was be-

123

ginning to know the man. In imagination I see you pilgrims taking your way by the red lodge and the cabin of the brave farmer man, so youthful and hale, to the still cheerful woods—

And Hawthorne too I remember as one with whom I sauntered in old heroic times along the banks of the Scamander, amid the ruins of chariots and heroes. Tell him not to desert even after the tenth year. Others may say "Are there not the cities of Asia?"—but what are they? Staying at home is the heavenly way.

And Elizabeth Hoar—my brave townswoman to be sung of poets— if I may speak of her whom I do not know.

Tell Mrs Brown that I do not forget her going her way under the stars through this chilly world—I did *not* think of the wind—and that I went a little way with her. Tell her not to despair—Concord's little arch does not span all our fate—nor is what transpires under it law for the universe.—

And least of all are forgotten those walks in the woods in ancient days—too sacred to be idly remembered—when their aisles were pervaded as by a fragrant atmosphere—They still seem youthful and cheery to my imagination as Sherwood and Barnsdale—and of far purer fame.—Those afternoons when we wandered o'er Olympus—and those hills, from which the sun was seen to set while still our day held on its way.

> "At last he rose and twitched his mantle blue;
> To-morrow to fresh woods and pastures new"

I remember these things at midnight at rare intervals—

But know, my friends, that I a good deal hate you all in my most private thoughts—as the substratum of the little love I bear you. Though you are a rare band and do not make half use enough of one another.

I think this is a noble number of the Dial. It perspires thought and feeling. I can speak of it now a little like a foreigner. Be assured that it is not written in vain—it is not for me. I hear its prose and its verse— They provoke and inspire me, and they have my sympathy. I hear the sober and earnest, the sad and cheery voices of my friends and to me it is like a long letter of encouragement and reproof—and no doubt so it is to many another in the land. So don't give up the ship—Methinks the verse is hardly enough better than the prose—I give my vote for the Notes from the Journal of a Scholar—and wonder you dont print them faster. I want too to read the rest of the Poet and the Painter. Miss

124

Fuller's is a noble piece, rich extempore writing—talking with pen in hand—It is too good not to be better even. In writing conversation should be folded many times thick. It is the height of art that on the first perusal plain common sense should appear—on the second severe truth—and on a third beauty—and having these warrants for its depth and reality, we may then enjoy the beauty forever more.—The sea piece is of the best that is going—if not of the best that is staying—You have spoken a good word for Carlyle.—As for the "Winter's Walk" I should be glad to have it printed in the D. if you think it good enough, and will criticise it—otherwise send it to me and I will dispose of it. I have not been to N. Y. for a month and so have not seen W[aldo] and T[appan]. James has been at Albany meanwhile. You will know that I only describe my personal adventures with people—but I hope to see more of them and *judge* them too. I am sorry to learn that Mrs. E. is no better. But let her know that the Fates pay a compliment to those whom they make sick—and they have not to ask what have I done

Remember me to your mother, and remember me yourself as you are remembered by

H. D. T.

I had a friendly and cheery letter from Lane a month ago.

Hate as a basis for love plus some shrewd comments on the Dial *are two of the noteworthy things about this letter. Nor should the fact that Lidian Emerson is now merely included with her husband under the heading of "Dear Friends" be overlooked. It may be surmised, as it is by Canby, that Lidian had just given Thoreau's emotional letter of June 20 a cold reply and that the present letter represents a corresponding return to moderation by Thoreau himself.*

Sanborn (Hawthorne and His Friends, p. 37) *identifies "the cabin of the brave farmer man" as that of Edmund Hosmer. "The Notes from the Journal of a Scholar" was by C. C. Emerson. Margaret Fuller's piece was "The Great Lawsuit." The "sea piece" was probably B. P. Hunt's "Voyage to Jamaica." Emerson's "good word for Carlyle" was a review of* Past and Present. MS., Berg.

From EMERSON

Concord 20 July 1843

Dear Henry,

Giles Waldo shall not go back without a line to you if only to pay part of my debt in that kind long due. I am sorry to say that when I called on Bradbury & Soden nearly a month ago, their partner in their absence informed me that they could not pay you at present any part of their debt on account of the B. Miscellany. After much talking, all the promise he could offer, was, "that within a year it would probably be paid," a probability which certainly looks very slender. The very worst thing he said was the proposition that you should take your payment in the form of B. Miscellanies! I shall not fail to refresh their memory at intervals. We were all very glad to have such cordial greetings from you as in your last letter on the Dial's & on all personal accounts. Hawthorn & Channing are both in good health & spirits & the last always a good companion for me, who am hard to suit, I suppose. Giles Waldo has established himself with me by his good sense. I fancy from your notices that he is more than you have seen. I think that neither he nor W. A. T[appan] will be exhausted in one interview. My wife is at Plymouth to recruit her wasted strength but left word with me to acknowledge & heartily thank you for your last letter to her. Edith & Ellen are in high health, and as pussy has this afternoon nearly killed a young oriole, Edie tells all comers with great energy her one story, "Birdy—sick." Mrs. Brown who just left the house desires kindest remembrances to you whom "she misses," & whom "she thinks of." In this fine weather we look very bright & green in yard & garden though this sun without showers will perchance spoil our potatoes. Our clover grew well on your patch between the dikes & Reuben Brown adjudged that Cyrus Warren should pay 14.00 this year for my grass. Last year he paid 0. All your grafts of this year have lived & done well. The apple trees & plums speak of you in every wind. You will have read & heard the sad news to the little village of Lincoln of Stearns Wheeler's death. Such an overthrow to the hopes of his parents made me think more of them than of the loss the community will suffer in his kindness diligence & ingenuous mind. The papers have contained ample notices of his life & death.—I saw Charles Newcomb the other day at Brook Farm, & he expressed his great grati-

fication in your translations & said that he had been minded to write you & ask of you to translate in like manner—Pindar. I advised him by all means to do so. But he seemed to think he had discharged his conscience. But it was a very good request. It would be a fine thing to be done since Pindar has no adequate translation in English equal to his fame. Do look at the book with that in your mind, while Charles is mending his pen. I will soon send you word respecting The Winter Walk. Farewell.

R. W. Emerson.

Charles Newcomb, one of the minor Transcendentalists, was a member of Brook Farm. Reuben Brown and Cyrus Warren were Concord residents. Thoreau eventually translated some fragments from Pindar and published them in the January 1844 Dial. MS., *photostat in the possession of the Columbia University Library.*

To HELEN THOREAU

Staten Island July 21st 43

Dear Helen,

I am not in such haste to write home when I remember that I make my readers pay the postage—But I believe I have not taxed you before—I have pretty much explored this island—inland and along the shore—finding my health inclined me to the peripatetic philosophy— I have visited Telegraph Stations—Sailor's Snug Harbors—Seaman's Retreats—Old Elm Trees, where the Hugonots landed—Brittons Mills —and all the villages on the island. Last Sunday I walked over to Lake Island Farm—8 or 9 miles from here—where Moses Prichard lived, and found the present occupant, one Mr Davenport formerly from Mass.— with 3 or four men to help him—raising sweet potatoes and tomatoes by the acre. It seemed a cool and pleasant retreat, but a hungry soil. As I was coming away I took my toll out of the soil in the shape of arrowheads—which may after all be the surest crop—certainly not affected by drought.

I am well enough situated here to observe one aspect of the modern world at least—I mean the migratory—the western movement. Sixteen hundred imigrants arrived at quarantine ground on the fourth of July, and more or less every day since I have been here. I see them occasionally washing their persons and clothes, or men women and children gathered on an isolated quay near the shore, stretching their limbs and taking the air, the children running races and swinging—on their artificial piece of the land of liberty—while the vessels are undergoing purification. They are detained but a day or two, and then go up to the city, for the most part without having *landed* here.

In the city I have seen since I wrote last—W. H. Channing—at whose house in 15th St. I spent a few pleasant hours, discussing the all absorbing question—What to do for the race. (He is sadly in earnest—about going up the river to rusticate for six weeks—and issues a new periodical called The Present in September.)—Also Horace Greeley Editor of the Tribune—who is cheerfully in earnest.—at his office of all work—a hearty New Hampshire boy as one would wish to meet. And says "now be neighborly"—and believes only or mainly, first, in the Sylvania Association somewhere in Pennsylvania—and secondly and most of all, in a new association to go into operation soon in New Jersey, with which he is connected.—Edward Palmer came down to see me Sunday before last. As for Waldo and Tappan we have strangely dodged one another and have not met for some weeks.

I believe I have not told you anything about Lucretia Mott. It was a good while ago that I heard her at the Quaker Church in Hester St. She is a preacher, and it was advertised that she would be present on that day. I liked all the proceedings very well—their plainly greater harmony and sincerity than elsewhere. They do nothing in a hurry. Every one that walks up the aisle in his square coat and expansive hat—has a history, and comes from a house to a house. The women come in one after another in their Quaker bonnets and handkerchiefs, looking all like sisters and so many chic-a-dees—At length, after a long silence, waiting for the spirit, Mrs Mott rose, took off her bonnet, and began to utter very deliberately what the spirit suggested. Her self-possession was something to say, if all else failed—but it did not. Her subject was the abuse of the Bible—and thence she straightway digressed to slavery and the degradation of woman. It was a good speech—transcendentalism in its mildest form. She sat down at length and after a long and decorous silence in which some seemed to be really digesting her words, the elders

shook hands and the meeting dispersed. On the whole I liked their ways, and the plainness of their meeting house. It looked as if it was indeed made for service. I think that Stearns Wheeler has left a gap in the community not easy to be filled. Though he did not exhibit the highest qualities of the scholar, he possessed in a remarkable degree many of the essential and rarer ones—and his patient industry and energy—his reverent love of letters—and his proverbial accuracy—will cause him to be associated in my memory even with many venerable names of former days. It was not wholly unfit that so pure a lover of books should have ended his pilgrimage at the great book-mart of the world. I think of him as healthy and brave, and am confident that if he had lived he would have proved useful in more ways than I can describe—He would have been authority on all matters of fact—and a sort of connecting link between men and scholars of different walks and tastes. The literary enterprises he was planning for himself and friends remind one of an older and more studious time—so much then remains for us to do who survive.

Tell mother that there is no Ann Jones in the directory. Love to all— Tell all my friends in Concord that I do not send m[y lov]e to them but retain it still.

Your affectionate brother
H. D. T.

Moses Prichard was a former Concord resident. This may have been Thoreau's first meeting with Greeley, who was later to become so help- ful in selling Thoreau's essays to the various magazines. Greeley was, as always, interested in all community experiments from Brook Farm to the phalanxes. Ann Jones was probably a cousin of Mrs. Thoreau. MS., Huntington. The bracketed matter replaces portions torn from the manuscript.

From J. L. O'SULLIVAN

New York, July 28, 1843.

My dear Sir,

I am very sorry that with so much in it that I like very much there are others in the paper you have favored me with which have decided me against its insertion. I trust, however, soon to hear from you again,—especially should I like some of those extracts from your Journal, reporting some of your private interviews with nature, with which I have before been so much pleased. That book of Etzler's I had for some time had my mind upon to review. If you have got it, I should be very much obliged to you for a sight of it, and if you would not object I think it very likely that some addition & modification made with your concurrence would put your review of it into the shape to suit my peculiar notion on the subject. Articles of this nature are not in general published in the D[emocratic] R[eview] on the responsibility of the individual name of the author, but under the general impersonality of the collective "we"—(the name of the author being usually indicated in pencil on the Index in the copies sent to the editors of newspapers). This system renders a certain pervading homogeneity necessary, inviting often the necessity of this process of editorial revision, or rather communication.

Very Respectfully Yours,

J. L. O'Sullivan

I am at present staying out of town. When I return to the city, if you are still in these latitudes, I shall hope to be afforded the pleasure of renewing the acquaintance begun under the auspices of our common friend Hawthorne.

While Thoreau was living on Staten Island he made a constant round of the periodical publishers in an attempt to place his work. In general he was not successful. O'Sullivan, however, printed a little sketch of Thoreau's called "The Landlord" in the October 1843 number of the

Democratic Review *and the review of* The Paradise within the Reach of All Men, *by J. A. Etzler, under Thoreau's title of "Paradise (to be) Regained" in the November number.* MS., Berg; *previously unpublished.*

To MRS. JOHN THOREAU

Staten Island, August 6, 1843.

Dear Mother,—

As Mr. William Emerson is going to Concord on Tuesday, I must not omit sending a line by him,—though I wish I had something more weighty for so direct a post. I believe I directed my last letter to you by mistake; but it must have appeared that it was addressed to Helen. At any rate, this is to you without mistake.

I am chiefly indebted to your letters for what I have learned of Concord and family news, and am very glad when I get one. I should have liked to be in Walden woods with you, but not with the railroad. I think of you all very often, and wonder if you are still separated from me only by so many miles of earth, or so many miles of memory. This life we live is a strange dream, and I don't believe at all any account men give of it. Methinks I should be content to sit at the back-door in Concord, under the poplar-tree, henceforth forever. Not that I am homesick at all,—for places are strangely indifferent to me,—but Concord is still a cynosure to my eyes, and I find it hard to attach it, even in imagination, to the rest of the globe, and tell where the seam is.

I fancy that this Sunday evening you are poring over some select book almost transcendental perchance, or else "Burgh's Dignity," or Massillon, or the "Christian Examiner." Father has just taken one more look at the garden, and is now absorbed in Chaptelle, or reading the newspaper quite abstractedly, only looking up occasionally over his spectacles to see how the rest are engaged, and not to miss any newer news that may not be in the paper. Helen has slipped in for the fourth time to learn the very latest item. Sophia, I suppose, is at Bangor; but Aunt Louisa, without doubt, is just flitting away to some good meeting, to save the credit of you all.

It is still a cardinal virtue with me to keep awake. I find it impossible to write or read except at rare intervals, but am, generally speaking, tougher than formerly. I could make a pedestrian tour round the world, and sometimes think it would perhaps be better to do at once the things I *can*, rather than be trying to do what at present I cannot do well. However, I shall awake sooner or later.

I have been translating some Greek, and reading English poetry, and a month ago sent a paper to the "Democratic Review," which, at length, they were sorry they could not accept; but they could not adopt the sentiments. However, they were very polite, and earnest that I should send them something else, or reform that.

I go moping about the fields and woods here as I did in Concord, and, it seems, am thought to be a surveyor,—an Eastern man inquiring narrowly into the condition and value of land, etc., here, preparatory to an extensive speculation. One neighbor observed to me, in a mysterious and half inquisitive way, that he supposed I must be pretty well acquainted with the state of things; that I kept pretty close; he did n't see any surveying instruments, but perhaps I had them in my pocket.

I have received Helen's note, but have not heard of Frisbie Hoar yet. She is a faint-hearted writer, who could not take the responsibility of blotting one sheet alone. However, I like very well the blottings I get. Tell her I have not seen Mrs. Child nor Mrs. Sedgwick.

Love to all from your affectionate son.

Mrs. Thoreau's reading was James Burgh's Dignity of Human Nature *and Massillon's* Sermons. *The latter, translated from the French by Dickson, is listed in Thoreau's 1840 catalogue of his own books (San-born's* Life of Henry David Thoreau, *p. 510). J. A. C. Chaptal was the author of a much-translated book on the technical applications of chemistry. Thoreau's father was probably studying some aspects of the graphite processes for his pencil manufactory. Sophia was visiting her cousins the Thatchers in Bangor. Frisbie Hoar, then a student at Harvard, was later a United States senator. Lydia Maria Child and Catherine M. Sedgwick were popular writers of the day.* Text, Familiar Letters of Thoreau, *pp. 117–20.*

To EMERSON

Staten Island Aug 7th 1843

My Dear Friend,

I fear I have nothing to send you worthy of so good an opportunity. Of New-York I still know but little, though out of so many thousands there are no doubt many units whom it would be worth my while to know. Mr James talks of going to Germany soon with his wife—to learn the language. He says he must know it—can never learn it here—there he may absorb it and is very anxious to learn beforehand where he had best locate himself, to enjoy the advantage of the highest culture, learn the language in its purity, and not exceed his limited means. I referred him to Longfellow—Perhaps you can help him.

I have had a pleasant talk with [W. H.] Channing—and Greeley too it was refreshing to meet. They were both much pleased with your criticism on Carlyle, but thought that you had overlooked what chiefly concerned them in the book—its practical aim and merits.

I have also spent some pleasant hours with W[aldo] & T[appan] at their counting room, or rather intelligence office.

I must still reckon myself with the innumerable army of invalids—undoubtedly in a fair field they would rout the well—though I am tougher than formerly. Methinks I could paint the sleepy God more truly than the poets have done, from more intimate experience. Indeed I have not kept my eyes very steadily open to the things of this world of late, and hence have little to report concerning them. However I trust the awakening will come before the last trump—and then perhaps I may remember some of my dreams.

I study the aspects of commerce at the Narrows here, where it passes in review before me, and this seems to be beginning at the right end to understand this Babylon.—I have made a very rude translation of the Seven Against Thebes and Pindar too I have looked at, and wish he was better worth translating. I believe even the best things are not equal to their fame. Perhaps it would be better to translate fame itself—or is not that what the poets themselves do? However I have not done with Pindar yet. I sent a long article on Etzler's book to the Dem Rev six weeks ago, which at length they have determined not to accept as they could not subscribe to all the opinions, but asked for other matter—

purely literary I suppose. O'Sullivan wrote me that articles of this kind
have to be referred to the circle, who, it seems are represented by this
journal, and said something about "collective we," and "homogeneity"—
Pray dont think of Bradbury and Soden any more

> "For good deed done through praiere
> Is sold and bought too dear I wis
> To herte that of great valor is."

I see that they have given up their shop here.

Say to Mrs. Emerson that I am glad to remember how she too dwells
there in Concord, and shall send her anon some of the thoughts that
belong to her. As for Edith—I seem to see a star in the east over where
the young child is.—Remember me to Mrs. Brown.

Yr friend
Henry D. Thoreau.

*Thoreau's translations from Pindar went into the January 1844 Dial.
Furthermore, as we know, O'Sullivan accepted the review of Etzler's
book after all as well as a "purely literary" piece, "The Landlord," and
both were in print before winter. MS., Berg.*

———————

To MRS. JOHN THOREAU

Tuesday Aug 29th-43

Dear Mother,

Mr Emerson has just given me a short warning that he is about
to send to Concord, which I will endeavor to improve—I am a good
deal more wakeful than I was, and growing stout in other respects—so
that I may yet accomplish something in the literary way—indeed I
should have done so before now but for the slowness and poverty of the
Reviews themselves. I have tried sundry methods of earning money in
the city of late but without success. have rambled into every book-

sellers or publisher's house and discussed their affairs with them. Some propose to me to do what an honest man cannot—Among others I conversed with the Harpers—to see if they might not find me useful to them—but they say that they are making fifty thousand dollars annually, and their motto is to let well alone. I find that I talk with these poor men as if I were over head and ears in business and a few thousands were no consideration with me—I almost reproach myself for bothering them thus to no purpose—but it is very valuable experience—and the best introduction I could have.

We have had a tremendous rain here—last Monday night and Tuesday morning—I was in the city at Giles Waldo's—and the streets at daybreak were absolutely impassable for the water. Yet the accounts of the storm which you may have seen are exaggerated, as indeed are all such things to my imagination.

On sunday I heard Mr [Henry Whitney] Bellows preach on the island—but the fine prospect over the bay and narrows from where I sat preached louder than he—though he did far better than the average, if I remember aright.

I should have liked to see Dan. Webster walking about Concord, I suppose the town shook every step he took—But I trust there were some sturdy Concordians who were not tumbled down by the jar, but represented still the upright town. Where was Geo. Minott? he would not have gone far to see him. Uncle Charles should have been there—he might as well have been catching cat naps in Concord as anywhere. And then what a whetter up of his memory this event would have been! You'd have had all the classmates again in alphabetical order reversed—and Seth Hunt & Bob Smith—and he was a student of my fathers—and where's Put now? and I wonder, you, if Henry's been to see Geo. Jones yet— A little account with Stow—Balcolm—Bigelow—poor miserable to-a-d (sound asleep) I vow you—what noise was that?—saving grace—and few there be—That's clear as preaching—Easter Brooks—mora[lly] depraved—How charming is divine p[hi]losophy—Some wise and some otherwise—Heighho! (Sound asleep again)

Webster's a smart fellow—bears his age well—how old should you think he was—you does he look as if he were ten years younger than I?

I met, or rather was overtaken by Fuller, who tended for Mr [Phineas] How, the other day in Broadway— He dislikes New York very much.— The Mercantile Library—ie its librarian—presented me with a stran-

ger's ticket for a month—and I was glad to read the reviews there—and Carlyle's late article.—In haste

from yr affectionate son
Henry D. Thoreau

I have bought some pantaloons—and stockings show no holes yet Thin pantaloons cost $2.25 ready made.

According to Sanborn (Familiar Letters of Thoreau, p. 104), Daniel Webster had been retained in the once well-known Wyman case of a bank officer charged with fraud and spent several days in the Concord courthouse. Uncle Charles Dunbar, a great admirer of Webster, was notorious for his sleepiness. MS., Morgan. Bracketed portions replace material torn from the manuscript.

From EMERSON

Concord, September 8, 1843.

Dear Henry,—

We were all surprised to hear, one day lately, from G. Waldo, that you were forsaking the deep quiet of the Clove for the limbo of the false booksellers, and were soon relieved by hearing that you were safe again in the cottage at Staten Island. I could heartily wish that this country, which seems all opportunity, did actually offer more distinct and just rewards of labor to that unhappy class of men who have more reason and conscience than strength of back and of arm; but the experience of a few cases that I have lately seen looks, I confess, more like crowded England and indigent Germany than like rich and roomy Nature. But the few cases are deceptive; and though Homer should starve in the highway, Homer will know and proclaim that bounteous Nature has bread for all her boys. To-morrow our arms will be stronger; to-

136

morrow the wall before which we sat will open of itself and show the new way.

Ellery Channing works and writes as usual at his cottage, to which Captain Moore has added a neat slat fence and gate. His wife as yet has no more than five scholars, but will have more presently. Hawthorne has returned from a visit to the seashore in good spirits. Elizabeth Hoar is still absent since Evarts's marriage. You will have heard of our Wyman Trial and the stir it made in the village. But the Cliff and Walden, which know something of the railroad, knew nothing of that; not a leaf nodded; not a pebble fell. Why should I speak of it to you? Now the humanity of the town suffers with the poor Irish, who receives but sixty, or even fifty cents, for working from dark till dark, with a strain and a following up that reminds one of negro-driving. Peter Hutchinson told me he had never seen men perform so much; he should never think it hard again if an employer should keep him at work till after sundown. But what can be done for their relief as long as new applicants for the same labor are coming in every day? These of course reduce the wages to the sum that will suffice a bachelor to live, and must drive out the men with families. The work goes on very fast. The mole which crosses the land of Jonas Potter and Mr. Stow, from Ephraim Wheeler's high land to the depot, is eighteen feet high, and goes on two rods every day. A few days ago a new contract was completed,—from the terminus of the old contract to Fitchburg,—the whole to be built before October, 1844; so that you see our fate is sealed. I have not yet advertised my house for sale, nor engaged my passage to Berkshire; have even suffered George Bradford to plan a residence with me next spring, and at this very day am talking with Mr. Britton of building a cottage in my triangle for Mrs. Brown; but I can easily foresee that some inconveniences may arise from the road, when open, that shall drive me from my rest.

I mean to send the Winter's Walk to the printer to-morrow for the Dial. I had some hesitation about it, notwithstanding its faithful observation and its fine sketches of the pickerel-fisher and of the woodchopper, on account of *mannerism,* an old charge of mine,—as if, by attention, one could get the trick of the rhetoric; for example, to call a cold place sultry, a solitude public, a wilderness *domestic* (a favorite word), and in the woods to insult over cities, whilst the woods, again, are dignified by comparing them to cities, armies, etc. By pretty free omissions, however, I have removed my principal objections. I ought to

say that Ellery Channing admired the piece loudly and long, and only stipulated for the omission of Douglas and one copy of verses on the Smoke. For the rest, we go on with the Youth of the Poet and Painter and with extracts from the Jamaica Voyage, and Lane has sent me A Day with the Shakers. Poetry have I very little. Have you no Greek translations ready for me?

I beg you to tell my brother William that the review of Channing's poems, in the Democratic Review, has been interpolated with sentences and extracts, to make it long, by the editor, and I acknowledge, as far as I remember, little beyond the first page. And now that I have departed so far from my indolence as to write this letter, I have yet to add to mine the affectionate greetings of my wife and my mother.

Yours,
R. W. Emerson.

Miss Hoar, according to Sanborn, had attended the marriage of her cousin, W. M. Evarts, later a senator from New York. Peter Hutchinson was a Concord resident. According to Sanborn again, Emerson removed "two pages or so" from "A Winter Walk" before printing it in the Dial. *Captain Abel Moore owned the Red Lodge in which Ellery Channing now lived. George Bradford, one of the minor Transcendentalists, had been a resident at Brook Farm. Further details of the house for Mrs. Brown may be found in Emerson's letter to brother William of this same date (Emerson Letters, III, 205–6). The triangle is the present site of the Concord Antiquarian Society. The house for Mrs. Lucy Brown was never built. Text, Emerson-Thoreau, pp. 592–93.*

To EMERSON

Staten Island, September 14, 1843.

Dear Friend,—

Miss Fuller will tell you the news from these parts, so I will only devote these few moments to what she does not know as well. I was ab-

sent only one day and night from the Island, the family expecting me back immediately. I was to earn a certain sum before winter, and thought it worth the while to try various experiments. I carried the Agriculturist about the city, and up as far as Manhattanville, and called at the Croton Reservoir, where indeed they did not want any Agriculturist, but paid well enough in their way. Literature comes to a poor market here, and even the little that I write is more than will sell. I have tried the Democratic Review, the New Mirror, and Brother Jonathan. The last two, as well as the New World, are overwhelmed with contributions which cost nothing, and are worth no more. The Knickerbocker is too poor, and only the Ladies' Companion pays. O'Sullivan is printing the manuscript I sent him some time ago, having objected only to my want of sympathy with the Communities.

I doubt if you have made more corrections in my manuscript than I should have done ere this, though they may be better; but I am glad you have taken any pains with it. I have not prepared any translations for the Dial, supposing there would be no room, though it is the only place for them.

I have been seeing men during these days, and trying experiments upon trees; have inserted three or four hundred buds (quite a Buddhist, one might say). Books I have access to through your brother and Mr. Mackean, and have read a good deal. Quarles's Divine Poems as well as Emblems are quite a discovery.

I am very sorry Mrs. Emerson is so sick. Remember me to her and to your mother. I like to think of your living on the banks of the Millbrook, in the midst of the garden with all its weeds; for what are botanical distinctions at this distance?

Your friend,
Henry D. Thoreau.

In an attempt to earn more money Thoreau tried, completely unsuccessfully, to sell subscriptions to the American Agriculturist, *founded the year before and published in New York City. The other publications mentioned were more urbane New York periodicals. H. S. McKean was librarian of the Mercantile Library Association, from which Thoreau was being allowed to borrow books. Thoreau's interest in Quarles is*

shown particularly by quotations throughout his works. Shortly after writing this letter Thoreau characterized Quarles in his note of October 16 to Lidian Emerson. Text, Emerson-Thoreau, *pp. 593–94.*

From MARGARET FULLER

Mr. Emerson has written a very fine poem, you will see it in the Dial. Ellery [Channing] will not go to the West. He regrets your absence, you, he says, are the man to be with in the woods.

This quotation from a two-page folio letter appears in the catalogue of the Willard sale (Charles F. Libbie & Co.; February 15–16, 1910), where it is dated only 1843 and described as a "fine intimate letter." We believe, however, that the manuscript is the same one that came up for sale at least once more.

The Stephen H. Wakeman Collection *sale catalogue, under Item 984, lists "an autograph letter signed, 2pp. folio, September 25, 1873 [1843], from Margaret Fuller to Henry Thoreau, relating to the poem 'Ode of Beauty.' " Emerson's poem "Ode to Beauty," which Thoreau criticized for him in a letter dated October 17, 1843, was printed in the* Dial *of October 1843. Margaret Fuller had returned from her tour of the West on September 19 and then "visited around." She went on to Brook Farm, and a letter from Emerson to her is postmarked Concord, October 10 and superscribed to her in care of George Ripley at Brook Farm (Emerson Letters, III, 211). Consequently we feel that the month and day are correctly given in the Wakeman catalogue, except that the "4" in the year was mistaken for a "7."*

Certainly the two references in the sales catalogues do not conflict; we suggest that both describe the same letter.

To MRS. JOHN THOREAU

Staten Island Oct 1*st* 43

Dear Mother,
    I hold together remarkably well as yet, speaking of my outward
linen and woolen man, no holes more than I brought away, and no
stitches needed yet. It is marvellous. I think the Fates must be on my
side, for there is less than a plank between me and—Time, to say the
least. As for Eldorado that is far off yet. My bait will not tempt the rats;
they are too well fed. The Democratic Review is poor, and can only
afford half or quarter pay—which it *will* do—and they say there is a Ldy's
Companion that pays—but I could not write anything companionable.
However, speculate as we will, it is quite gratuitous, for life never the
less, and never the more, goes steadily on, well or ill fed and clothed,
somehow, and "honor bright" withal. It is very gratifying to live in the
prospect of great successes always, and for that purpose, we must leave
a sufficient foreground to see them through. All the painters prefer distant prospects for the greater breadth of view, and delicacy of tint.—But
this is no news, and describes no new conditions. Meanwhile I am som-
nambulic at least—stirring in my sleep—indeed, quite awake. I read a
good deal and am pretty well known in the libraries of New York. Am
in with the Librarian, one Dr [Philip J.] Forbes, of the [New York]
Society Library—who has lately been to Cambridge to learn liberality,
and has come back to let me take out some untake-out-able-books,
which I was threatening to read on the spot. And Mr [H. S.] Mackean,
of the Mercantile Library, is a true gentleman—a former tutor of mine—
and offers me every privilege there. I have from him a perpetual stranger's ticket, and a citizen's rights besides—all which privileges I pay
handsomely for by improving.
    A canoe-race "came off" on the Hudson the other day, between Chip-
peways and New Yorkers, which must have been as moving a sight as
the buffalo hunt which I witnessed. But canoes and buffaloes are all
lost, as is everything here, in the mob. It is only the people have come to
see one another. Let them advertise that there will be a gathering at
Hoboken—having bargained with the ferry boats, and there will be,
and they need not throw in the buffaloes.
    I have crossed the bay 20 or 30 times and have seen a great many

141

immigrants going up to the city for the first time—Norwegians who carry their old fashioned farming tools to the west with them, and will buy nothing here for fear of being cheated.—English operatives, known by their pale faces and stained hands, who will recover their birth-rights in a little cheap sun and wind,—English travellers on their way to the Astor House, to whom I have done the honors of the city.—Whole families of imigrants cooking their dinner upon the pavements, all sunburnt—so that you are in doubt where the foreigner's face of flesh begins—their tidy clothes laid on, and then tied to their swathed bodies which move about like a bandaged finger—caps set on the head, as if woven of the hair, which is still growing at the roots—each and all busily cooking, stooping from time to time over the pot, and having something to drop into it, that so they may be entitled to take something out, forsooth. They look like respectable but straightened [sic] people, who may turn out to be counts when they get to Wisconsin—and will have their experience to relate to their children.

Seeing so many people from day to day one comes to have less respect for flesh and bones, and thinks they must be more loosely [word torn out] of less firm fibre, than the few he had known. It must have a very bad influence on children to see so many human beings at once—mere herds of men.

I came across Henry Bigelow a week ago, sitting in front of a Hotel in Broadway, very much is [sic] if he were under his father's own stoop. He is seeking to be admitted into the bar in New York, but as yet, had not succeeded. I directed him to Fuller's store, which he had not found, and invited him to come and see me, if he came to the island. Tell Mrs & Miss [Prudence] Ward that I have not forgotten them, and was glad to hear from George [Ward] with whom I spent last night, that they had returned to C.—Tell Mrs Brown that it gives me as much pleasure to know that she thinks of me and my writing as if I had been the author of the piece in question; but I did not even read the papers I sent. The Mirror is really the most readable journal here. I see that they have printed a short piece which I wrote to sell in the Dem Review, and still keep the review of Paradise that I may include in it a notice of another book by the same author, which they have found, and are going to send me.—I dont know when I shall come home—I like to keep that feast in store—Tell Helen that I do not see any advertisement for her—and I am looking for myself—If I could find a rare opening, I might be tempted to try with her for a year till I had payed my debts; but for such I am

sure it is not well to go out of N. Eng. Teachers are but poorly recompensed even here.—Tell her and Sophia (if she is not gone) to write to me—Father will know that this letter is to him as well as to you—I send him a paper which usually contains the news—if not all that is stirring—all that has stirred—and even draws a little on the future. I wish he would send me by and by the paper which contains the results of the Cattleshow. You must get Helen's eyes to read this—though she is a scoffer at honest penmanship yr affectionate son

Henry D. Thoreau

The Henry Bigelow mentioned was a young Concordian five years Thoreau's junior. The short piece was "The Landlord," in the Democratic Review *for this month. The "Paradise" review was in the November issue. The buffalo hunt was a Barnum publicity stunt. Barnum made a fortune by chartering all the ferries to Hoboken.* MS., Huntington.

To MRS. EMERSON

Staten Island Oct 16th 1843

My Dear Friend,

I promised you some thoughts long ago, but it would be hard to tell whether these are the ones. I suppose that the great questions of Fate, Freewill, Foreknowledge absolute, which used to be discussed in Concord are still unsettled. And here comes Channing with his "Present," to vex the world again—a rather galvanic movement, I think. However, I like the man all the better, though his schemes the less. I am sorry for his confessions. Faith never makes a confession.

Have you had the annual berrying party, or sat on the Cliffs a whole day this summer? I suppose the flowers have fared quite as well since I was not there to scoff at them, and the hens without doubt keep up their reputation.

I have been reading lately what of Quarles's poetry I could get. He

was a contemporary of Herbert, and a kindred spirit. I think you would like him. It is rare to find one who was so much of a poet and so little of an artist. He wrote long poems, almost epics for length, about Jonah, Esther, Job, Samson & Solomon, interspersed with meditations after a quite original plan. Shepherd's Oracles, Comedies, Romances, Fancies and Meditations—the Quintessence of Meditation, and Enchiridions of Meditations all divine,—and what he calls his Morning Muse, besides prose works as curious as the rest. He was an unwearied Christian and a reformer of some old school withal. Hopelessly quaint, as if he lived all alone and knew nobody but his wife, who appears to have reverenced him. He never doubts his genius;—it is only he and his God in all the world. He uses language sometimes as greatly as Shakspeare, and though there is not much straight grain in him, there is plenty of tough crooked timber. In an age when Herbert is revived, Quarles surely ought not to be forgotten.

I will copy a few such sentences as I should read to you if there. Mrs Brown too may find some nutriment in them!

Mrs Emerson must have been sicker than I was aware of, to be confined so long, though they will not say that she is convalescent yet though the Dr pronounces her lungs unaffected.

How does the Saxon Edith do? Can you tell yet to which school of philosophy she belongs—whether she will be a fair saint of some Christian order, or a follower of Plato and the heathen? Bid Ellen a good night or a good morning from me, and see if she will remember where it comes from. And remember me to Mrs Brown and your mother and Elizabeth Hoar.

Yr friend
Henry.

Canby notes in his Thoreau (p. 160) *the complete change in temper in this letter from that of June 20, 1843, and asserts: "She must have written him a cooling epistle," since he now deals with the very "petty rumbling news" that he earlier felt no need to write down. The Present was W. H. Channing's new and enthusiastic magazine. MS., Berg.*

To EMERSON

Staten Island Oct 17th

My Dear Friend,

I went with my pupil to the Fair of the American Institute, and so lost a visit from Tappan whom I met returning from the Island. I would have liked to hear more news from his lips, though he had left me a letter, and the Dial which is a sort of circular letter itself. I find [Ellery] Channing's letters full of life and enjoy their wit highly. Lane writes straight and solid like a guide-board, but I find that I put off the Social Tendencies to a future day—which may never come. He is always Shaker fare, quite as luxurious as his principle will allow. I feel as if I were ready to be appointed a committee on poetry, I have got my eyes so whetted and proved of late, like the knife-sharpener I saw at the Fair certified to have been in constant use in a gentleman's family for more than two years. Yes, I ride along the ranks of the English poets casting terrible glances, and some I blot out, and some I spare.

Mackean has imported within the year several new editions and collections of old poetry, which I have the reading of but there is a good deal of chaff to a little meal, hardly worth bolting. I have just opened Bacon's Advancement of Learning for the first time, which I read with great delight. It is more like what Scott's novels were than anything.

I see that I was very blind to send you my manuscript in such a state, but I have a good second sight (?) at least. I could still shake it in the wind to some advantage, if it would hold together. There are some sad mistakes in the printing.—It is a little unfortunate that the Ethnical scripture should hold out so well, though it does really hold out. The Bible ought not to be very large. Is it not singular that while the religious world is gradually picking to pieces its old testaments, here are some coming slowly after on the sea-shore picking up the durable relics of perhaps older books, and putting them together again?

Your letter to contributors is excellent and hits the nail on the head. It will taste sour to their palates at first no doubt, but it will bear sweet fruit at last.

I like the poetry, especially the Autumn verses. They ring true. Though I am quite weather beaten with poetry having weathered so many epics of late. The Sweep Ho sounds well this way. But I have a

good deal of fault to find with your ode to Beauty. The tune is altogether unworthy of the thoughts. You slope too quickly to the rhyme, as if that trick had better be performed as soon as possible or as if you stood over the line with a hatchet and chopped off the verses as they came out—some short and some long. But give us a long reel and we'll cut it up to suit ourselves. It sounds like a parody. "Thee knew I of old" "Remediless thirst" are some of those stereotyped lines. I am frequently reminded, I believe of Jane Taylors Philosopher's Scales and how the world

"Flew out with a bounce"

which—"yerked the philosopher out of his cell." or else of "From the climes of the sun all war-worn and weary." I had rather have the thoughts come ushered with a flourish of oaths and curses. Yet I love your poetry as I do little else that is near and recent—especially when you get fairly around the end of the line, and are not thrown back upon the rocks.—To read the lecture on the Comic, is as good as to be in our town meeting or Lyceum once more.

I am glad that the Concord farmers have plowed well this year, it promises that something will be done these summers. But I am suspicious of that Brittonner who advertises so many cords of *good* oak, chestnut and maple wood for sale—*Good!* aye, good for what? And there shall not be left a stone upon a stone. But no matter let them hack away—The sturdy Irish arms that do the work are of more worth than oak or maple. Methinks I could look with equanimity upon a long street of Irish cabins and pigs and children revelling in the genial Concord dirt, and I should still find my Walden wood and Fair Haven in their tanned and happy faces.—I write this in the corn field—it being washing day—with the inkstand Elizabeth Hoar gave me—though it is not redolent of corn-stalks, I fear.

Let me not be forgotten by Channing & Hawthorne nor our graysuited neighbor under the hill.

Yr friend
H. D. Thoreau

Charles Lane wrote both the "A Day with the Shakers" and "Social Tendencies" for the October Dial. *Thoreau's manuscript was "A Winter Walk," which Emerson edited for that* Dial. *The "Ethnical Scriptures"*

were selections from the Chinese by Thoreau, a part of his long-dreamed-of anthology of the world's scriptures. The "Autumn verses" were by Ellery Channing; the "Sweep Ho" by Ellen Hooper; the "lecture on the Comic" by Emerson. For Elizabeth Hoar's inkstand see her letter of May 2, 1843. "The gray-suited neighbor under the hill" was Edmund Hosmer. MS., Berg.

To HELEN THOREAU

Staten Island Oct 18*th* 43

Dear Helen,

What do you mean by saying that "we have written eight times by private opportunity"? Is'nt it the more the better? and am I not glad of it? But people have a habit of not letting me know it when they go to Concord from New York. I endeavored to get you The Present, when I was last in the city, but they were all sold—and now another is out, which I will send if I get it. I did not send the Dem Rev because I had no copy, and my piece was not worth fifty cents.—You think that [W. H.] Channing words would apply to me too, as living more in the natural than the moral world, but I think that you mean the world of men and women rather and reformers generally. My objection to Channing and all that fraternity is that they need and deserve sympathy themselves rather than are able to render it to others. They want faith and mistake their private ail for an infected atmosphere, but let any one of them recover hope for a moment, and right his *particular* grievance, and he will no longer train in that company. To speak or do any thing that shall concern mankind, one must speak and act as if well, or from that grain of health which he has left.—This Present book indeed is blue, but the hue of its thoughts is yellow.—I say these things with the less hesitation because I have the jaundice myself, but I also know what it is to be well. But do not think that one can escape from mankind, who is one of them, and is so constantly dealing with them.

I could not undertake to form a nucleus of an institution for the development of infant minds, where none already existed—It would be

147

too cruel, and then as if looking all this while one way with benevolence, to walk off another about ones own affairs suddenly!—Something of this kind is an unavoidable objection to that.

I am very sorry to hear such bad news about Aunt Maria, but I think that the worst is always the least to be apprehended—for nature is averse to it as well as we. I trust to hear that she is quite well soon   I send love to her and to Aunt Jane.

Mrs Emerson is not decidedly better yet, though she is not extremely sick. For three months I have not known whether to think of Sophia as in Bangor or Concord, and now you say that she is going directly. Tell her to write to me, and establish her whereabouts, and also to get well directly—And see that she has something worthy to do when she gets down there, for that's the best remedy for disease. [Four fifths of pp. 3–4 are cut away; at the top of p. 4 these lines follow:] judge that the prospect was as good as anywhere in the west—and yet I think it very uncertain, though perhaps not for anything that I know [page cut] unless that she got [page cut; and the conclusion of the letter follows in the margin of p. 1:] Tell Father and mother I hope to see them before long—

yr affectionate brother
H. D. Thoreau.

MS., Huntington.

From EMERSON

Concord, Oct 25, 1843—

Dear Henry,—

I have your letter this evening by the advent of Mrs [Timothy] Fuller to Ellery C and am heartily glad of the robust greeting. Ellery brought it to me & as it was opened wondered whether he had not some right to expect a letter. So I read him what belonged to him. He is usually in good spirits & always in good wit, forms stricter ties with George

Minott, and is always merry with the dulness of a world which will not support him. I am sorry you will dodge my hunters, T[appan] & W[aldo]. T. is a very satisfactory person only I could be very willing he should read a little more. he speaks seldom but easily & strongly, & moves like a deer. H James too has gone to England—I am the more sorry because you liked him so well. In Concord no events. We have had the new Hazlitt's Montaigne which contained the "Journey into Italy"—new to me, & the narrative of the death of the renowned friend Etienne de la Boétie. Then I have had Saadis' *Gulistan* Ross's translation; and Marot; & Roman de la Rose; and Robert of Gloucester's rhymed chronicle. Where are my translations of Pindar for the Dial? Fail not to send me something good & strong. They send us the "Revista Ligure," a respectable magazine from Genoa; "la Democratie Pacifique," a bright daily paper from Paris; the Deutsche Schnellpost,—German New York paper; and Phalanx from London; the New Englander from New Haven, which angrily affirms that the Dial is not as good as the Bible. By all these signs we infer that we make some figure in the literary world though we are not yet encouraged by a swollen publication list. Lidian says she will write you a note herself. If as we have heard, you will come home to Thanksgiving, you must bring something that will serve for Lyceum lecture—the craving thankless town!

Yours affectionately,
Waldo Emerson—

Thoreau's translations from Pindar were printed in the January 1844 Dial and more in the April number. The magazines mentioned were received in exchange for the Dial. *In response to Emerson's request Thoreau delivered a lecture on "The Ancient Poets" before the Concord Lyceum November 29, 1843. MS., Berg.*

To HENRY SWASEY MCKEAN

Mr McKean
    [Would you] be kind [and let] me take [your "C]hapman's Trans[lation] of the Greek Pastoral [Poe]ts" & "Ossian's Genuine Remains"?

Yrs resply
Henry D. Thoreau.

MS., Abernethy. *The bracketed portions are torn from the manuscript and we have followed the reading assumed by Kenneth Walter Cameron,* The Transcendentalists and Minerva, *II, 371–72. Mr. Cameron assumes, quite rightfully, we believe, that this letter was written about November 1, 1843, to Henry Swasey McKean, librarian of the Mercantile Library of New York City.*

From EMERSON

Thursday P. m.

Dear Henry,
    I am not today quite so robust as I expected to be & so have to beg that you will come down & drink tea with Mr Brownson & charge yourself with carrying him to the Lyceum & introducing him to the Curators. I hope you can oblige thus far.

Yours,
R. W. E.

Though the note is dated only "Thursday," November 23, 1843 was, as Rusk points out (Emerson Letters, III, 225), *the only time that Orestes Brownson delivered a lecture before the Concord Lyceum on a*

Thursday. Thoreau probably returned from Staten Island in the middle of November; the date is not known. MS., Huntington.

From MRS. NATHANIEL HAWTHORNE

Mr Thoreau,

Will you be kind enough to take to New York the letter to Mr O'Sullivan, & if it be convenient for you, to carry my letter to Boston? If you cannot call at West St, it is just as well to put it into the Boston Post Office.

S A. Hawthorne.

Dec. 3, 1843

Thoreau returned to Staten Island after the Thanksgiving period in Concord, but his stay was not long. Emerson wrote his brother on December 17, 1843 (Rusk, Emerson Letters, III, 228–29) indicating that Thoreau had once more returned to Concord. Probably this brief trip was to wind up his business affairs in New York.

This note from Hawthorne's wife contained a letter for the editor of the Democratic Review, *who had published both Hawthorne and Thoreau, and one probably for Mrs. Hawthorne's sister Elizabeth Peabody, who ran a little bookstore at 13 West Street in Boston. The Hawthornes, in the Old Manse in Concord, were fairly well acquainted with Thoreau. MS., Morgan; previously unpublished.*

From CHARLES LANE

Boston Decr 3/43

Dear friend

As well as my wounded hands permit I have scribbled something for friend Hecker which if agreeable may be the opportunity for entering into closer relations with him; a course I think likely to be mutually encouraging, as well as beneficial to all men. But let it reach him in the manner most conformable to your own feelings.

That from all perils of a false position you may shortly be relieved and landed in the position where you feel "at home" is the sincere wish of yours most friendly

Charles Lane

Henry Thoreau

Isaac Hecker, idealistic, enthusiastic, but troubled, had been a baker in New York and after that a seeker of truth in various places. From January 1843 he lived at Brook Farm off and on for several months; then he went to Fruitlands, Alcott's and Lane's vegetarian utopia, where he became friendly with Lane. Now he was back in New York working at the family bakery, thinking about religion and corresponding with the utopians he had met. Lane's final sentence probably signifies his hope that Thoreau would shortly leave his mundane tutoring at William Emerson's (as he had done) and return to Transcendental Concord. The Earl House, to which Lane directed his note, was the Boston tavern where mail and packages to or from Concord were transferred; Harnden's Express, in particular, which ran over the Boston-New York route, made its Concord connections here. MS., Fruitlands *Museum, Harvard, Massachusetts.*

1844

The Whigs nominated Henry Clay. The Democrats nominated James Polk, and the news was carried to Washington by Morse's telegraph. The chief issue was the annexation of Texas. Polk favored it and won. William Miller, founder of the Millerite sect, set October 23 as the day the world would end; the Millerites crowded the hilltops in their white robes and waited. Succeeding Joseph Smith, who had been murdered in the jail in Carthage, Illinois, Brigham Young was elected president of the Mormon Church. In the House of Representatives old John Quincy Adams carried the repeal of the gag rule against discussions of slavery. A hairdresser's fashion note during the year stated: "A most irresistible coiffure is a wreath of periwinkles with pendant sprigs of flowers mingled with the curls at each side of the face or if the hair is worn in bands the wreath may be most becoming, arranged around the head with small bunches of flowers and leaves hanging from the coil at the back."

Thoreau, now back from New York, made pencils. Thereby he gained a living, but the trouble was—as he told Emerson in March—that he could do only one thing at a time. If he made pencils during the day, he could not help making them at night when he was supposed to be studying and writing. He lent his father a hand in the construction of the "Texas House." He accidentally helped to set a fire that burned off a hundred acres or more of Concord woodlots and got him cursed for it, on and off, for many years. In summer he went on a walking trip through the Hoosacs and Catskills with his good if highly eccentric friend Ellery Channing. The *Journal* for '44, like the one for '43, is missing; Thoreau's letters for this period are few. Not one is extant for the first six months. The main correspondence is with the young Transcendentalist Isaac Hecker. All in all, Thoreau left little in the way of written record for the year. It was a year of preparation that looked forward to the classic sojourn at Walden Pond.

Henry Thoreau

It was not altogether the circumstance of our immediate physical nearness, tho this may [have] been the consequence of a higher affinity, that inspired us to commune with each other. This I am fully sensible since our seperation [*sic*]. Oftentimes we observe ourselves to be passive or cooperative agents of profounder principles than we at the time ever dream of.

I have been stimulated to write to you at this present moment on account of a certain project which I have formed in which your influence has no slight share I imagine in forming. It is to work our passage to Europe, and to walk, work, and beg, if needs be, as far when there as we are inclined to do. We wish to see how it looks. And to court difficulties, for we feel an unknown depth of untried virgin strength which we know of no better way at the present time to call into activity and so dispose of. We desire to go without purse or staff, depending upon the all embracing love of God, Humanity, and the spark of courage imprisoned in us. Have we the will we have the strong arms, and hands, to work with, and sound feet to stand upon, and walk with. The heavens shall be our vaulted roof, and the green Earth beneath our bed, and for all other furniture purposes. These are free and may be so used. What can hinder us from going but our bodies, and shall they do it. We can as well deposit them there as here. Let us take a walk over the fairest portions of the planet Earth and make it ours by seeing them. Let us see what the genius and stupidity of our honored fore fathers have heaped up. We wish to kneel at their shrines and embrace their spirits and kiss the ground which they have hallowed with their presence. We shall prove the dollar is not almighty and the impossible moonshine. The wide world is before us beckoning us to come let us accept and embrace it. Reality shall be our antagonist and our lives if sold not at a good bargain for a certainty.

How does the idea strike you? I prefer at least to go this way before going farther in the woods. The past let us take with us. We reverence,

we love it, but forget not that our eyes are in our face set to the beautiful unimagined future. Let us be Janus faced with a beard and beardless face. Will you accept this invitation? Let me know what your impressions are. As soon as it is your pleasure.

Remember me to your kind family. Tomorrow I take the first step towards becoming a *visible* member of the Roman Catholic Church.

If you and your good family do not become greater sinners I shall claim you all as good catholics, for she claims all baptized infants; all innocent children of every religious denomination; and all grown up Christians who have preserved their baptismal innocence, though they make no outward profession of the Catholic faith; are yet claimed as her children by the Roman Catholic Church.

Yours Very Truly
Isaac Hecker

N. Y. Thursday July 31. /44

A good deal had happened to Hecker since the previous December when Charles Lane mentioned him in a note to Thoreau. Hecker had come to Concord in April in order to study Latin and Greek under a schoolmaster friend of his and Emerson's, George Partridge Bradford. He had roomed at the Thoreau house at a cost of seventy-five cents a week. There he had found Mrs. Thoreau motherly and Henry learned and stimulating. Hecker had gone back to New York in June, his religious problem settled in his mind, to join the Catholic Church. MS., Huntington.

To ISAAC HECKER

Concord Aug. 14th 44

Friend Hecker,

I am glad to hear your voice from that populous city and the more so for the tenor of its discourse. I have but just returned from a pedestrian excursion, some what similar to that you propose, *parvis componere magna*, to the Catskill mountains, over the principal moun-

tains of this state, subsisting mainly on bread and berries, and slumbering on the mountain tops. As usually happens, I now feel a slight sense of dissipation. Still I am strongly tempted by your proposal and experience a decided schism between my outward and inward tendencies. Your method of travelling especially—to *live* along the road—citizens of the world, without haste or petty plans—I have often proposed this to my dreams, and still do— But the fact is, I cannot so decidedly postpone exploring the *Farther Indies,* which are to be reached you know by other routs and other methods of travel. I mean that I constantly return from every external enterprise with disgust to fresh faith in a kind of Brahminical Artesian, Inner Temple, life. All my experience, as yours probably, proves only this reality.

Channing wonders how I can resist your invitation, I, a single man —unfettered—and so do I. Why—there are Roncesvalles, the cape de Finisterre, and the three kings of Cologne; Rome, Athens, & the rest— to be visited in serene untemporal hours—and all history to revive in one's memory as he went by the way with splendors too bright for this world— I know how it is. But is not here too Roncesvalles with greater lustre? Unfortunately it may prove dull and desultory weather enough here, but better trivial days with faith than the fairest ones lighted by sunshine alone. Perchance my wanderjahre has not arrived. But you cannot wait for that. I hope you will find a companion who will enter as heartily into your schemes as I should have done.

I remember you, as it were, with the whole Catholic church at your skirts— And the other day for a moment I think I understood your relation to that body, but the thought was gone again in a twinkling, as when a dry leaf falls from its stem over our heads, but instantly lost in the rustling mass at our feet.

I am really sorry that the Genius will not let me go with you, but I trust that it will conduct to other adventures, and so if nothing prevents we will compare notes at last.

Yrs &c

Henry D. Thoreau.

Thoreau's walking tour of the Berkshires and the Catskills with Ellery Channing is recounted in the chapter called "Tuesday" in A Week on the Concord and Merrimack Rivers. *MS., Huntington.*

From ISAAC HECKER

I know not but that I shall receive an answer to the letter I sent you a fortnight ago before you will receive this one, however as the idea of making an indefinite pedestrian tour on the other side of the Atlantic has in all possible ways increased in my imagination and given me a desire to add a few more words on the project I will do it in the hope of stimulating you to a decision. How the thought has struck you I know not, its impractibility or impossibility in the judgment of others would not I feel assured deter you in any way from the undertaking, it would rather be a stimulus to the purpose I think in you as it is in me. Tis impossible; Sir, therefore we do it. The conceivable is possible, it is in harmony with the inconceivable. we should act. Our true life is in the can-not, to do what we can do is to do nothing, is death. Silence is much more respectable than repetition. The idea of making such a tour I have opened to one or two who I thought might throw some light on the subject. I asked the opinion of the Catholic Bishop [John Mc-Closkey] who has travelled considerable in Europe but I find that in every man there are certain things within him which are beyond the ken & counsel of others. The age is so effeminate that it is too timid to give heroic counsel. It neither will enter the kingdom of heaven or have others to do so. I feel, and believe you feel so too, that to doubt the ability to realize such a thought is only worthy of a smile & pity. We feel ourself mean in conceiving such a feasable [*sic*] thing and would keep it silent. This is not sufficient self abandonment for our being, scarce enough to affect it. To die is easy, scarce worth a thought, but to be and live is an inconceivable greatness. It would be folly to sit still and starve from mere emptiness, but to leave behind the casement in battling for some hidden idea is an attitude beyond conception a monument more durable than the chisel can sculptor. I imagine us walking among the past and present greatness of our ancestors (for the present in fact the present of the old world to us is ancient) doing reverence to their remaining glory. If tho I am inclined to bow more lowly to the spiritual hero than the exhibition of great physical strength still not all of that primitive heroic blood of our forefathers has been lost before it reached our veins. We feel it exult some times as tho it were cased in steel and the huge broad axe of Co[e]ur de Lion seems glitter[i]ng before us and we awake in another world as in a dream. I know of no

other person but you that would be induced to go on such an excursion. The idea and yourself were almost instantaneous. If needs be for a few dollars we can get across the ocean. The ocean, if but to cross this being like being it were not unprofitable. The Bishop thought it might be done with a certain amount of funds to depend on. If this makes it practible for others to us it will be but sport. It is useless for me to speak thus to you for if there are reasons for your not going they are others than these.

You will inform me how you are inclined as soon as practible. Half inclined I sometimes feel to go alone if I cannot get your company. I do not know now what could have directed my steps to Concord other than this. May it prove so. It is only the fear of death makes us reason of impossibilities. We shall possess all if we but abandon ourselves.

Yours sincerely
Isaac—

NY. Aug 15– |44
To Henry Thoreau.

On Friday, August 2, 1844, Hecker was baptized into the Roman Catholic Church. Anxious to be on his way and not aware that Thoreau was vacationing, Hecker repeats his invitation. MS., Huntington.

To ISAAC HECKER

I improve the occasion of my mothers sending to acknowledge the receipt of your stirring letter. You have probably received mine by this time. I thank you for not anticipating any vulgar objections on my part— *Far* travel, very *far* travel, or travail, comes near to the worth of staying at home— Who knows whence his education is to come! Perhaps I my drag my anchor at length, or rather, when the *winds* which blow *over* the deep fill my sails, may stand away for distant ports—for now I seem to have a firm *ground* anchorage, though the harbor is low-shored enough, and the traffic with the natives inconsiderable—I may be away to Singapoor by the next tide.

I like well the ring of your last maxim—"It is only the fear of death makes us reason of impossibilities"—and but for fear death itself is an impossibility.

Believe me I can hardly let it end so. If you do not go soon let me hear from you again.

Yrs in great haste

Henry D. Thoreau

It is clear that this letter was written not long after August 15. Hecker added to the manuscript: "The proposition made to Thoreau was to take nothing with us, work our passage acrost the Atlantic, and so through England France, Germany and Italy. I. T. H." Within a year Hecker had gone abroad and joined the order of the Redemptorist Fathers at St. Trond in Belgium. Thus the brief acquaintance came to an end. MS., Huntington.

To JAMES MUNROE & CO.

Concord Oct 14th

James Munroe & Co,

Please to send me a dozen copies of Mr. Emerson's Address by the bearer—

Yrs respectfully
Henry D. Thoreau.

This note is probably a request for copies of Emerson's Address . . . *on the Anniversary of the Emancipation of the Negroes in the British West Indies (Boston: James Munroe, 1844). When Emerson delivered the address in Concord August 1, the local church authorities refused him the use of their buildings. Thoreau secured the old Concord courthouse for him and rang the bell to gather a crowd. MS., Boston Public Library, previously unpublished. The date supplied by the Boston Public Library, 1844, is confirmed by the reference to Emerson's Address.*

1845

Postage on letters was reduced to five cents for 300 miles and ten cents for greater distances. The recipient still paid the postage. Texas was annexed by a joint resolution of the houses of Congress. Our dispute with Britain over the Oregon boundary began to warm up; President Polk devoted to it a fifth of his message to Congress. Pittsburgh and New York City were devastated by fires. Capital stock in the famous Lowell knitting mills was valued at $10,850,000. The average wage of women workers there, in addition to board, was $1.75 a week, and there were 6,320 women working in the mills. The Infidel Convention assembled at the New York Coliseum in May, with about 500 persons attending. The socialist Robert Owen, in addressing them, mentioned that he disliked the appellation of "Infidel" and recommended instead "Friends of Universal Mental Freedom and Unlimited Charity."

And Thoreau, on July 4, went to live beside Walden Pond.

New York March 5, 45

My dear Thoreau

The hand-writing of your letter is so miserable, that I am not sure I have made it out. If I have it seems to me you are the same old sixpence you used to be, rather rusty, but a genuine piece.

I see nothing for you in this earth but that field which I once christened "Briars"; go out upon that, build yourself a hut, & there begin the grand process of devouring yourself alive. I see no alternative, no other hope for you. Eat yourself up; you will eat nobody else, nor anything else.

Concord is just as good a place as any other; there are indeed, more people in the streets of that village, than in the streets of this. This is a singularly muddy town; muddy, solitary, & silent.

They tell us, it is March; it has been all March in this place, since I came. It is much warmer now, than it was last November, foggy, rainy, stupefactive weather indeed.

In your line, I have not done a great deal since I arrived here; I do not mean the Pencil line, but the Staten Island line, having been there once, to walk on a beach by the Telegraph, but did not visit the scene of your dominical duties, Staten Island is very distant from No. 30 Ann St.

I saw polite William Emerson in November last, but have not caught any glimpse of him since then. I am as usual offering the various alternations from agony to despair, from hope to fear, from pain to pleasure. Such wretched one-sided productions as you, know nothing of the universal man; you may think yourself well off.

That baker,—Hecker, who used to live on two crackers a day I have not seen, nor Black, nor Vathek [Vethake?], nor Danedaz nor [Isaiah] Rynders, or any of Emerson's old cronies, excepting Henry James, a little fat, rosy Swedenborgian amateur, with the look of a broker, & the brains & heart of a Pascal.—Wm Channing I see nothing of him; he is the dupe of good feelings, & I have all-too-many of these now.

161

I have seen something of your friends, Waldo, and Tappan, I have also seen our goodman "McKean," the keeper of that stupid place of the "Mercantile Library." I have been able to find there no book which I should like to read.

Respecting the country about this city, there is a walk at Brooklyn rather pleasing, to ascend upon the high ground & look at the distant ocean. This is a very agreeable sight. I have been four miles up the island in addition, where I saw, the bay; it looked very well, and appeared to be in good spirits.

I should be pleased to hear from Kamkatscha occasionally; my last advices from the Polar Bear are getting stale. In addition to this, I find that my corresponding members at Van Dieman's land, have wandered into limbo. I acknowledge that I have not lately corresponded very much with that section.

I hear occasionally from the World; everything seems to be promising in that quarter, business is flourishing, & the people are in good spirits. I feel convinced that the Earth has less claims to our regard, then formerly, these mild winters deserve a severe censure. But I am well aware that the Earth will talk about the necessity of routine, taxes, &c. On the whole, it is best not to complain without necessity.

Mumbo Jumbo is recovering from his attack of sore eyes, & will soon be out, in a pair of canvas trousers, scarlet jacket, & cocked hat. I understand he intends to demolish all the remaining species of Fetishism at a meal; I think it's probable it will vomit him. I am sorry to say, that Roly-Poly has received intelligence of the death of his only daughter, Maria; this will be a terrible wound to his paternal heart.

I saw Teufelsdrock a few days since; he is wretchedly poor, has an attack of the colic, & expects to get better immediately. He said a few words to me, about you. Says he, that fellow Thoreau might be something, if he would only take a journey through the "Everlasting No," thence for the North Pole. By God," said the old clothes-bag "warming up," I should like to take that fellow out into the Everlasting No, & explode him like a bomb-shell; he would make a loud report. He needs the Blumine flower business; that would be his salvation. He is too dry, too confused, too chalky, too concrete. I want to get him into my fingers. It would be fun to see him pick himself up." I "camped" the old fellow in a majestic style.

Does that execrable compound of sawdust & stagnation, Alcott still prose about nothing, & that nutmeg-grater of a Hosmer yet shriek about

nothing,—does anybody still think of coming to Concord to live, I mean new people? If they do, let them beware of you philosophers.

Ever yrs my dear Thoreau

W E C

This Carlyleish letter from Ellery Channing gives the first direct reference to Thoreau's Walden experiment. "Briars" was the Emerson woodlot on Walden Pond where Thoreau before the month was over started to erect his cabin. Mumbo Jumbo, according to Canby (Thoreau, p. 252), was Horace Greeley, the editor of the New-York Tribune and at the moment Channing's employer. Sanborn (Henry D. Thoreau, p. 210) suggests that Teufelsdröckh was "the satirical man in the writer himself." (Sartor Resartus, thanks to Emerson, had recently been published in America.) Holbrook Jackson (Dreamers of Dreams, p. 248 n.) suggests: "Blumine represents the love motive in Carlyle's Sartor Resartus which brought colour and music into the heart of Teufelsdröckh: 'Thus did soft melodies flow through his heart; tones of an infinite gratitude; sweetest intimations that he also was a man, that for him also unutterable joys had been provided.' Sartor Resartus, chap. v, 'Romance.'" Canby (p. 214), basing his judgment on Sanborn's incomplete version of the letter, mistakenly substitutes Alcott for Charles Lane and Hosmer for Alcott. MS., Abernethy (typescript).

To THE EDITOR OF *The Liberator*

Concord, Mass. March 12th, 1845.

Mr. Editor:

We have now, for the third winter, had our spirits refreshed, and our faith in the destiny of the Commonwealth strengthened, by the presence and the eloquence of Wendell Phillips; and we wish to tender to him our thanks and our sympathy. The admission of this gentleman into the Lyceum has been strenuously opposed by a respectable portion

of our fellow-citizens, who themselves, we trust, whose descendants, at least, we know, will be as faithful conserver of the true order, whenever that shall be the order of the day,—and in each instance, the people have voted that they *would hear him,* by coming themselves and bringing their friends to the lecture room, and being very silent that they *might* hear. We saw some men and women, who had long ago *come out, going in* once more through the free and hospitable portals of the Lyceum; and many of our neighbors confessed, that they had had a 'sound season' this once.

It was the speaker's aim to show what the State and above all the Church, had to do, and now, alas! have done, with Texas and Slavery, and how much, on the other hand, the individual should have to do with Church and State. These were fair themes, and not mistimed; and his words were addressed to 'fit audience, *and not* few.'

We must give Mr. Phillips the credit of being a clean, erect, and what was once called a consistent man. He at least is not responsible for slavery, nor for American Independence; for the hypocrisy and superstition of the Church, nor the timidity and selfishness of the State; nor for the indifference and willing ignorance of any. He stands so distinctly, so firmly, and so effectively, alone, and one honest man is so much more than a host, that we cannot but feel that he does himself injustice when he reminds us of 'the American Society, which he represents.' It is rare that we have the pleasure of listening to so clear and orthodox a speaker, who obviously has so few cracks or flaws in his moral nature—who, having words at his command in a remarkable degree, has much more than words, if these should fail, in his unquestionable earnestness and integrity—and, aside from their admiration at his rhetoric, secures the genuine respect of his audience. He unconsciously tells his biography as he proceeds, and we see him early and earnestly deliberating on these subjects, and wisely and bravely, without counsel or consent of any, occupying a ground at first, from which the varying tides of public opinion cannot drive him.

No one could mistake the genuine modesty and truth with which he affirmed, when speaking of the framers of the Constitution,—'I am wiser than they,' who with him has improved these sixty years' experience of its working; or the uncompromising consistency and frankness of the prayer which concluded, not like the Thanksgiving proclamations, with —'God save the Commonwealth of Massachusetts,' but God dash it into a thousand pieces, till there shall not remain a fragment on which a man

can stand, and dare not tell his name—referring to the case of Frederick —————; to our disgrace we know not what to call him, unless Scotland will lend us the spoils of one of her Douglasses, out of history or fiction, for a season, till we be hospitable and brave enough to hear his proper name,—a fugitive slave in one more sense than we; who has proved himself the possessor of a *fair* intellect, and has won a colorless reputation in these parts; and who, we trust, will be as superior to degradation from the sympathies of Freedom, as from the antipathies of Slavery. When, said Mr. Phillips, he communicated to a New-Bedford audience, the other day, his purpose of writing his life, and telling his name, and the name of his master, and the place he ran from, the murmur ran around the room, and was anxiously whispered by the sons of the Pilgrims, 'He had better not!' and it was echoed under the shadow of Concord monument, 'He had better not!'

We would fain express our appreciation of the freedom and steady wisdom, so rare in the reformer, with which he declared that he was not born to abolish slavery, but to do right. We have heard a few, a very few, good political speakers, who afforded us the pleasure of great intellectual power and acuteness, of soldier-like steadiness, and of a graceful and natural oratory; but in this man the audience might detect a sort of moral principle and integrity, which was more stable than their firmness, more discriminating than his own intellect, and more graceful than his rhetoric, which was not working for temporary or trivial ends. It is so rare and encouraging to listen to an orator, who is content with another alliance than with the popular party, or even with the sympathising school of the martyrs, who can afford sometimes to be his own auditor if the mob stay away, and hears himself without reproof, that we feel ourselves in danger of slandering all mankind by affirming, that here is one, who is at the same time an eloquent speaker and a righteous man.

Perhaps, on the whole, the most interesting fact elicited by these addresses, is the readiness of the people at large, of whatever sect or party, to entertain, with good will and hospitality, the most revolutionary and heretical opinions, when frankly and adequately, and in some sort cheerfully, expressed. Such clear and candid declaration of opinion served like an electuary to whet and clarify the intellect of all parties, and furnished each one with an additional argument for that right he asserted.

We consider Mr. Phillips one of the most conspicuous and efficient

champions of a true Church and State now in the field, and would say to him, and such as are like him—'God speed you.' If you know of any champion in the ranks of his opponents, who has the valor and courtesy even of Paynim chivalry, if not the Christian graces and refinement of this knight, you will do us a service by directing him to these fields forthwith, where the lists are now open, and he shall be hospitably entertained. For as yet the Red-cross knight has shown us only the gallant device upon his shield, and his admirable command of his steed, prancing and curvetting in the empty lists; but we wait to see who, in the actual breaking of lances, will come tumbling upon the plain.

The Concord Lyceum invited Wendell Phillips to speak on slavery. He was known to hold radical views, and two of the curators resigned in protest. Thoreau was chosen to fill one of the vacancies. Phillips delivered his lecture March 11. Thoreau immediately wrote a report in the form of a letter to William Lloyd Garrison, editor of the Liberator, *who printed it.* Text, The Liberator, March 28, 1845.

1846

Captain S. B. Thornton and sixty dragoons, riding out from General Zachary Taylor's encampment on the Rio Grande, were attacked by Mexican soldiers—the formal opening of the Mexican War that Polk had been waiting for. Commodore J. D. Sloat raised the American flag at Monterey and proclaimed the annexation of California. The Pennsylvania Railroad was incorporated. The last of the Mormons left Illinois on the great western trek. The phalanstery at Brook Farm, the community's largest building, burned down and brought to earth with it the whole utopian experiment. Dr. William Morton was the first successful user of ether as an anesthetic. The Jacob Donner party left Springfield, Illinois, for California.

Although Thoreau continued to make Walden his residence, it actually became during this year less of a home and more of a headquarters. He spent more time back in Concord than he had spent the season before; he wandered through the countryside a good deal; and he traveled up into the Maine woods in late summer. But he seems to have kept on writing as richly as when he lived beside the Pond. The composition of the *Week* went ahead solidly; so did the early work on *Walden*. Moreover, the night Thoreau stayed in jail because he refused as a matter of principle to pay the poll tax gave him the fuel for the later lecture and essay "Civil Disobedience." This was a year rich in both action and its results in writing. There are few letters and only scraps of the *Journal*, but there is little need for more.

From CHARLES LANE

New York February 17 / 46

Dear Friend

The books you were so kind as to deposit about two years and a half ago with Messers Wiley and Putnam have all been sold, but as they were left in your name it is needful in strict business that you should send an order to them to pay to me the amount due. I will therefore thank you to enclose me such an order at your earliest convenience in a letter addressed to your admiring friend,

Charles Lane
Post Office New York City.

In 1843 Thoreau had been commissioned to take Lane's books to New York and sell them, that Lane might pay the debts incurred in the Fruitlands experiment conducted with Bronson Alcott. (See also letter of May 23, 1843, to Emerson.) MS., Leonard Kleinfeld; the manuscript is addressed, incidentally, to "Henry D. Thoreau, Sylvan, favored by A. B[ronson] A[lcott]."

From CHARLES LANE

Boonton, N. J., March 30, 1846.

Dear Friend,—

If the human nature participates of the elemental I am no longer in danger of becoming suburban, or super-urban, that is to say, too

urbane. I am now more likely to be converted into a petrifaction, for slabs of rock and foaming waters never so abounded in my neighborhood. A very Peter I shall become: on this rock *He* has built *his church*. You would find much joy in these eminences and in the views therefrom.

My pen has been necessarily unproductive in the continued motion of the sphere in which I have lately been moved. You, I suppose, have not passed the winter to the world's unprofit.

You never have seen, as I have, the book with a preface of 450 pages and a text of 60. My letter is like unto it.

I have only to add that your letter of the 26th February did its work, and that I submit to you cordial thanks for the same.

Yours truly,
Chas. Lane.

I hope to hear occasionally of your doings and those of your compeers in your classic ploughings and diggings.

To Henry D. Thoreau,
Concord Woods.

Text, Familiar Letters of Thoreau, *pp. 147–48.*

From HORACE GREELEY

New York, Aug. 16, 1846.

My dear Thoreau,

Believe me when I say that I *mean* to do the errand you have asked of me, and that soon. But I am not sanguine of success, and have hardly a hope that it will be immediate if ever. I hardly know a soul that could publish your article all at once, and "To be continued" are words shunned like a pestilence. But I know you have written a good thing about Carlyle—too solidly good, I fear, to be profitable to yourself or attractive to publishers. Didst thou ever, O my friend! ponder on the

significance and cogency of the assurance, "Ye cannot serve God and Mammon," as applicable to Literature—applicable, indeed, to all things whatsoever. God grant us grace to endeavor to serve Him rather than Mammon—that ought to suffice us. In my poor judgment, if any thing is calculated to make a scoundrel of an honest man, writing to sell is that very particular thing.

Yours, hastily,
Horace Greeley.

Remind Ralph Waldo Emerson and wife of my existence and grateful remembrance.

Thoreau met Horace Greeley sometime during his sojourn on Staten Island in 1843. Greeley was interested in all the activities of the Transcendentalists, and the two became friends. Eventually Greeley became an unofficial literary agent for Thoreau and helped him to place many of his articles in magazines. This, the earliest extant letter between the two, concerns Thoreau's essay "Thomas Carlyle and His Works," which eventually found publication in Graham's Magazine *for March and April 1847. MS., Lownes.*

From HORACE GREELEY

I learned to-day, through Mr. [Rufus] Griswold, former editor of "Graham's Magazine," that your lecture is accepted, to appear in that magazine. Of course it is to be paid for at the usual rate, as I expressly so stated when I inclosed it to [George R.] Graham. He has not written me a word on the subject, which induces me to think he may have written you. Please write me if you would have me speak further on the subject. The pay, however, is sure, though the amount may not be large, and I think you may wait until the article appears, before making further stipulations on the subject.

170

Text, Sanborn's Henry D. Thoreau, pp. 219–20. Sanborn dates the letter September 30, 1846.

From HORACE GREELEY

My Friend Thoreau,—

I know you think it odd that you have not heard further, and, perhaps blame my negligence or engrossing cares, but, if so, without good reason. I have to-day received a letter from Griswold, in Philadelphia, who says: "The article by Thoreau on Carlyle is in type, and will be paid for liberally." "Liberally" is quoted as an expression of Graham's. I know well the difference between a publisher's and an author's idea of what *is* "liberally"; but I give you the best I can get as the result of three letters to Philadelphia on this subject.

Success to you, my friend! Remind Mr. and Mrs. Emerson of my existence, and my lively remembrance of their various kindnesses.

Yours, very busy in our political contest,

Horace Greeley.

Text, Sanborn's Henry D. Thoreau, pp. 221–22. The letter is dated October 26, 1846 by Sanborn.

1847

It was resolved to light the nation's Capitol and its grounds with gas. The use of postage stamps was inaugurated. The Massachusetts legislature resolved that "the present war with Mexico has . . . the triple object of extending slavery, of strengthening the 'slave power,' and of obtaining the control of the free states." Thoreau did not dissent. The Mexican War ended triumphantly for our country, with an almost unbroken string of victories. At the Battle of El Molino del Rey Ulysses S. Grant was made a brevet first lieutenant for gallant conduct. In the Senate John Calhoun moved that Congress had no right to prohibit slavery under the Constitution. The Mormons founded the City of the Great Salt Lake. The wheat crop was average in quantity but, at least in the eyes of some patriots, unsurpassed in quality. Black claw-hammer coats with capacious pockets in the tails were popular; the young men about town added bright plaid waistcoats.

Except for some minor revisions and additions, the *Week* was now finished; by the end of the year at least four publishers had turned it down. In September Thoreau left Walden Pond, having still several more lives to live, and was again invited to stay at Emerson's. Emerson himself started for Europe, and Henry remained behind as handyman to the household, but now on a firmer and easier basis than before. Lidian Emerson valued his presence; so did the children. He published another magazine article, but still found the progress slow in spite of Horace Greeley's help. The writing of *Walden* continued. Stimulated by his communication with the great Swiss scientist Louis Agassiz, who was teaching at Harvard, Thoreau's interest in nature study grew. The Transcendentalist was developing into the naturalist.

172

To EVERT A. DUYCKINCK

Concord, Jan 14, 1847.

Dear Sir—
    Will you please inform Mr. [John] Wiley that I have concluded to wait a fortnight for his answer. As I should like to make some corrections in the Mss. in the meanwhile, I will thank you if you will send it to me by Harnden's express to Boston and by Adams' to Concord and I will return it in ten days.

Yrs &c.,
Henry D. Thoreau

This letter, written for the information of the head of Wiley & Putnam, the New York publishers and booksellers, was probably addressed to Duyckinck: Thoreau's later correspondence with the firm was through Duyckinck. Thoreau had apparently submitted an early draft of the Week *and now wished it returned for revision. For further details of this correspondence see the letter to Duyckinck of May 28, 1847. Augustus Adams ran a local express from Concord to the City Tavern in Boston.* Text, *Adrian Joline,* Rambles in Autograph Land, *p. 293.*

From HORACE GREELEY

New York Feb. 5th, 1847.

My dear Thoreau:
    Although your letter only came to hand to-day, I attended to its subject yesterday, when I was in Philadelphia on my way home from

Washington. Your article is this moment in type, and will appear about the 20th inst. as *the leading article* in Graham's Mag. for next month. Now don't object to this, nor be unreasonably sensitive at the delay. It is immensely more important to you that the article should appear thus (that is, if you have any literary aspirations,) than it is that you should make a few dollars by issuing it in some other way. As to lecturing, you have been at perfect liberty to deliver it as a lecture a hundred times if you had chosen—the more the better. It is really a good thing, and I will see that Graham pays you fairly for it. But its appearance there is worth far more to you than money.

I know there has been too much delay, and have done my best to obviate it. But I could not. A Magazine that pays, and which it is desirable to be known as a contributor to, is always crowded with articles, and has to postpone some for others of even less merit. I do this myself with good things that I am not required to pay for.

Thoreau, do not think hard of Graham. Do not try to stop the publication of your article. It is best as it is. But just set down and write a like article about Emerson, which I will give you $25 for if you cannot do better with it; then one about Hawthorne at your leisure, &c. &c. I will pay you the money for each of these articles on delivery, publish them when and how I please, leaving to you the copyright expressly. In a year or two, if you take care not to write faster than you think, you will have the material of a volume worth publishing, and then we will see what can be done.

There is a text somewhere in St. Paul—my scriptural reading is getting rusty—which says 'Look not back to the things which are behind, but rather to these which are before,' &c. Commending this to your thoughtful appreciation, I am,

Yours, &c.
Horace Greeley

Regards to Mr. and Mrs. Emerson.

Thoreau's difficulties with the Carlyle article were not at an end even with the receipt of this letter. More than a year later Graham's Magazine had still not paid for it. (See Greeley's letter of April 3, 1848.) Despite Greeley's comment about lecturing, Thoreau apparently used the article for a lecture only once, on February 4, 1846, before the Concord

Lyceum. He never wrote about Hawthorne and Emerson for publication, as Greeley suggested, probably because he did not wish to profit by his friendship for them. This letter marks the first of several attempts by Greeley to help Thoreau get a book published. MS., Abernethy (typescript).

To HORATIO R. STORER

Concord Feb. 15th 1847

Dear Sir,

I have not forgotten your note which I received sometime since. Though I live in the woods I am not so attentive an observer of birds as I was once, but am satisfied if I get an occasional night of sound from them. My pursuits at present are such that I am not very likely to meet with any specimens which you will not have obtained. Moreover, I confess to a little squeamishness on the score of robbing their nests, though I could easily go to the length of abstracting an egg or two gently, now and then, and if the advancement of science obviously demanded it might be carried even to the extreme of deliberate murder.

I have no doubt that you will observe a greater number of species in or near the College yard than I can here. I have noticed that in an open country where there are but few trees, there are more attractions for many species of birds than in a wooded one. They not only find food there in greater abundance, but protection against birds of prey; and even if they are no more numerous than elsewhere, the few trees are necessarily more crowded with nests. Many of my classmates were quite successful in collecting birds nests and eggs and they did not have to go far from the college-yard to find them— I remember a pigeon-woodpecker's nest in the grove on the east side of the yard, which annually yielded a number of eggs to collectors, while the bird steadily supplied the loss like a hen, until my chum demolished the whole with a hatchet. I found another in the next field chipped nearly two feet into a solid stump. And in one of the fields near the yard I used to visit daily in the winter the dwelling of an ermine-weasel in a hollow apple tree. But of

course one must be a greater traveller than this if he would make anything like a complete collection.

There are many whipporwills & owls about my house, and perhaps
with a little pains one might find their nests. I hope you have more
nimble and inquisitive eyes to serve you than mine now are— However,
if I should chance to stumble on any rarer nest I will not forget your
request. If you come to Concord again, as I understand you sometimes
do, I shall be glad to see you at my hut—. Trusting that you will feather
your own nest comfortably without stripping those of the birds quite
bare—I am

Yrs

Henry D. Thoreau

*Storer, a member of the Harvard class of 1850, studied under Agassiz
and Asa Gray and was a promising naturalist. His report on the fishes
of Nova Scotia and Labrador was published the year he graduated.
However, in 1853 he took an M.D. at the Harvard Medical School and
for the rest of his professional life was a practicing gynecologist.
Thoreau, in addressing his letter, either misread or forgot Storer's correct middle initial and recorded it as B. MS., Abernethy (typescript).*

From HENRY WILLIAMS

Boston, March 1, 1847.

Dear Sir,

The following inquiries are made agreeably to a vote passed at
the Last Annual Meeting of the Class, with a view to obtain authentic
information concerning each one of its members, and to enable the
Secretary to record facts now easily obtainable, but which, from year
to year, it will be more and more difficult to collect.

You are respectfully requested to answer the questions proposed, as
fully as may be convenient and agreeable to you, and to add such other

176

facts concerning your life, before or after entering College, as you are willing to communicate. The answers are to be recorded in the Class Book for future reference.

Please to address Henry Williams, Jr., Boston; *post paid.*

Very Respectfully and Truly Yours,

Henry Williams, Jr., Class Secretary.

1. When and where were you born?
2. Where were you fitted for College, and by whom?
3. If married, when, where, and to whom?
4. What is your profession? If learned, with whom studied? If mercantile, where and with whom begun?
5. What are your present employment, and residence?
6. Mention any general facts of importance before or since graduating.

A form letter sent out by the secretary of Thoreau's Harvard Class of 1837. Thoreau did not reply until September 30, 1847. MS., Harvard.

From JAMES ELLIOT CABOT

I carried them immediately to Mr. Agassiz, who was highly delighted with them [, and began immediately to spread them out and arrange them for his draughtsman. Some of the species he had seen before, but never in so fresh condition; others, as the breams and the pout, he had seen only in spirits, and the little tortoise he knew only from the books. I am sure you would have felt fully repaid for your trouble, if you could have seen the eager satisfaction with which he surveyed each fin and scale.] He said the small mud-turtle was really a very rare species, quite distinct from the snapping-turtle. The breams and pout seemed to please the Professor very much. [Of the perch Agassiz remarked that it was almost identical with that of Europe, but distinguishable, on close examination, by the tubercles on the sub-

177

operculum. . . . More of the painted tortoises would be acceptable. The snapping turtles are very interesting to him as forming a transition from the turtles proper to the alligator and crocodile. . . . We have received three boxes from you since the first.] He would gladly come up to Concord to make a spearing excursion, as you suggested, but is drawn off by numerous and pressing engagements.

Few newcomers to America were able to establish themselves here more swiftly and brilliantly than Agassiz. He arrived in Boston from Europe at the beginning of October 1846. Thanks to his excellent reputation, he was engaged by the Lowell Institute of Boston to give one of its series of lectures. His first course, "Lectures on the Plan of the Creation, Especially in the Animal Kingdom," was highly successful. He was very well paid for it, and he followed it with another, by private subscription, on glaciers, which gave him more money and more renown. More important to him, America offered him a virgin field for scientific discoveries, and he was happy to stay once he realized that he could support himself. He settled in Boston and soon filled his house with scientific specimens and interested researchers. Then early in 1848 he lost his professorship in Switzerland because of a change of government and was offered the chair of Natural History at Harvard's Lawrence Scientific School.

Young Cabot acted as Agassiz's conscientious assistant and secretary. His "Life and Writings of Agassiz" appeared in the Massachusetts Quarterly Review *for December 1847.*

In the spring of 1847 Thoreau collected many specimens of fish and reptiles for Agassiz and shipped them to Cabot. This letter was written shortly after the receipt of the first shipment. Two different extant versions of it are here pieced together. Text, Sanborn's Henry D. Thoreau, *pp. 243–44, for the unbracketed portions;* Familiar Letters of Thoreau, *p. 156, for the bracketed. They are dated May 3, 1847. The following note by Agassiz to Cabot is added in* Familiar Letters of Thoreau.

"I have been highly pleased to find that the small mud turtle was really the Sternothaerus odoratus, *as I suspected,—a very rare species, quite distinct from the snapping turtle. The suckers were all of one and*

178

the same species (Catastomus tuberculatus); *the female has the tubercles. As I am very anxious to send some snapping turtles home with my first boxes, I would thank Mr. T. very much if he could have some taken for me."*

To JAMES ELLIOT CABOT

Concord, May 8, 1847.

Dear Sir,—

I believe that I have not yet acknowledged the receipt of your notes, and a five dollar bill. I am very glad that the fishes afforded Mr. Agassiz so much pleasure. I could easily have obtained more specimens of the *Sternothaerus odoratus;* they are quite numerous here. I will send more of them erelong. Snapping turtles are perhaps as frequently met with in our muddy river as anything, but they are not always to be had when wanted. It is now rather late in the season for them. As no one makes a business of seeking them, and they are valued for soups, science may be forestalled by appetite in this market, and it will be necessary to bid pretty high to induce persons to obtain or preserve them. I think that from seventy-five cents to a dollar apiece would secure all that are in any case to be had, and will set this price upon their heads, if the treasury of science is full enough to warrant it.

You will excuse me for taking toll in the shape of some, it may be, impertinent and unscientific inquiries. There are found in the waters of the Concord, so far as I know, the following kinds of fishes:—

Pickerel. Besides the common, fishermen distinguish the Brook, or Grass Pickerel, which bites differently, and has a shorter snout. Those caught in Walden, hard by my house, are easily distinguished from those caught in the river, being much heavier in proportion to their size, stouter, firmer fleshed, and lighter colored. The little pickerel which I sent last, jumped into the boat in its fright.

Pouts. Those in the pond are of different appearance from those that I have sent.

Breams. Some more green, others more brown.

179

Suckers. The horned, which I sent first, and the black. I am not sure whether the *Common* or *Boston sucker* is found here. Are the three which I sent last, which were speared in the river, identical with the three *black suckers,* taken by hand in the brook, which I sent before? I have never examined them minutely.

Perch. The river perch, of which I sent five specimens in the box, are darker colored than those found in the pond. There are myriads of small ones in the latter place, and but few large ones. I have counted ten transverse bands on some of the smaller.

Lampreys. Very scarce since the dams at Lowell and Billerica were built.

Shiners. Leuciscus chrysoleucas, silver and golden. What is the difference?

Roach or *Chiverin, Leuciscus pulchellus, argenteus,* or what not. The *white* and the *red.* The former described by Storer, but the latter, which deserves distinct notice, not described, to my knowledge. Are the minnows (called here *dace*), of which I sent three live specimens, I believe, one larger and two smaller, the young of this species?

Trout. Of different appearance in different brooks in this neighborhood.

Eels.

Red-finned Minnows, of which I sent you a dozen alive. I have never recognized them in any books. Have they any scientific name?

If convenient, will you let Dr. Storer see these brook minnows? There is also a kind of dace or fresh-water smelt in the pond, which is, perhaps, distinct from any of the above. What of the above does M. Agassiz particularly wish to see? Does he want more specimens of kinds which I have already sent? There are also minks, muskrats, frogs, lizards, tortoise, snakes, caddice-worms, leeches, muscles, etc., or rather, *here they are.* The funds which you sent me are nearly exhausted. Most fishes can now be taken with the hook, and it will cost but little trouble or money to obtain them. The snapping turtles will be the main expense. I should think that five dollars more, at least, might be profitably expended.

The authority Thoreau cites is David H. Storer, A Synopsis of the Fishes of North America (*1846*). Text, Familiar Letters of Thoreau, *pp. 150–53.*

[1847]

From JAMES ELLIOT CABOT

[Mr.] Agassiz was [very] much surprised and pleased at the extent of the collections you sent during his absence in New York; [the little fox he has established in comfortable quarters in his backyard where he is doing well.] Among the fishes there is one, and probably two, new species. The fresh-water smelt he does not know. He is very anxious to see the pickerel with the long snout, which he suspects may be the *Esox estor,* or Maskalongé; he has seen this at Albany. . . . As to the minks, etc., I know they would all be very acceptable to him. When I asked him about these, and more specimens of what you have sent, he said, "I dare not make any request, for I do not know how much trouble I may be giving to Mr. Thoreau; but my method of examination requires many more specimens than most naturalists would care for."

The letter is dated May 27, 1847 by Sanborn. Text, Familiar Letters of Thoreau, *pp. 156–57; bracketed portions are from another version of the letter given in Sanborn's* Henry D. Thoreau, *p. 244.*

———

To EVERT A. DUYCKINCK

Concord May 28 -47

Dear Sir,

    I should not have delayed sending you my manuscript so long, if I had not known that delay would be no inconvenience to you, and advantage to the sender. I will remind you, to save time, that I wish to be informed for what term the book is to be the property of the publishers, and on what terms I can have 30 copies cheaply bound in boards without immediate expense.—If you take it—It will be a great convenience to me to get through with the printing as soon as possible, as I wish to take a journey of considerable length and should not be willing that any other than myself should correct the proofs.

181

If you will inform me as soon as may be, whether you want the manuscript, and what are the most favorable terms on which you will print & publish it, you will greatly oblige

Y'rs &c
Henry D. Thoreau.

Thoreau, having completed his first book, the Week, *while at Walden Pond, had now started it on an unsuccessful round of the publishers. (Duyckinck was with Wiley & Putnam, 161 Broadway.) After continued rejection Thoreau thoroughly revised the book. He did not get it published until 1849. The "journey of considerable length" was apparently never taken, for Thoreau left Walden in early September and settled down to live with the Emersons again. MS., New York; previously unpublished.*

To JAMES ELLIOT CABOT

Concord, June 1, 1847.

Dear Sir,—

I send you 15 pouts, 17 perch, 13 shiners, 1 larger land tortoise, and 5 muddy tortoises, all from the pond by my house. Also 7 perch, 5 shiners, 8 breams, 4 dace? 2 muddy tortoises, 5 painted do., and 3 land do., all from the river. One black snake, alive, and one dormouse? caught last night in my cellar. The tortoises were all put in alive; the fishes were alive yesterday, *i. e.,* Monday, and some this morning. Observe the difference between those from the pond, which is pure water, and those from the river.

I will send the light-colored trout and the pickerel with the longer snout, which is our large one, when I meet with them. I have set a price upon the heads of snapping turtles, though it is late in the season to get them.

If I wrote red-finned eel, it was a slip of the pen; I meant red-finned

minnow. This is their name here; though smaller specimens have but a slight reddish tinge at the base of the pectorals.

Will you, at your leisure, answer these queries?

Do you mean to say that the twelve banded minnows which I sent are undescribed, or only one? What are the scientific names of those minnows which have any? Are the four dace I send to-day identical with one of the former, and what are they called? Is there such a fish as the black sucker described,—distinct from the common?

Text, Familiar Letters of Thoreau, *pp. 153–54.*

From JAMES ELLIOT CABOT

(June 1.)

Agassiz is delighted to find one, and he thinks two, more new species; one is a Pomotis,—the bream without the red spot in the operculum, and with a red belly and fins. The other is the shallower and lighter colored shiner. The four dace you sent last are *Leuciscus argenteus.* They are different from that you sent before under this name, but which was a new species. Of the four kinds of minnow, two are new. There is a black sucker (*Catastomus nigricans*), but there has been no specimen among those you have sent, and A. has never seen a specimen. He seemed to know your mouse, and called it the white-bellied mouse. It was the first specimen he had seen. I am in hopes to bring or send him to Concord, to look after new *Leucisci,* etc.

Text, Familiar Letters of Thoreau, *p. 157; Sanborn prints only this fragment.*

To EVERT A. DUYCKINCK

Concord July 3d 1847.

Dear Sir,
    I sent you my Mss. this (Saturday) morning by Augustus Adams' and Harnden's expresses, and now write this for greater security, that you may inform me if it does not arrive duly. If Mr. [George P.] Putnam is not likely to return for a considerable time yet, will you please inform

Yrs &c
Henry D. Thoreau.

MS. New York; *previously unpublished.*

To EVERT A. DUYCKINCK

Concord, July 27th, 1847.

Dear Sir
    It is a little more than three weeks since I returned my mss. sending a letter by mail at the same time for security, so I suppose that you have received it. If Messrs Wiley & Putnam are not prepared to give their answer now, will you please inform me what further delay if any, is unavoidable, that I may determine whether I had not better carry it elsewhere—for time is of great consequence to me.

Yours respectfully
Henry D. Thoreau

MS., Fruitlands Museum, Harvard, Massachusetts; *previously unpublished.*

To JAMES MUNROE & CO.

Concord Aug 28th 1847

Dear Sir,

Mr Emerson has showed me your note to him and says that he thinks you must have misunderstood him. If you will inform me how large an edition you contemplated, and what will be the whole or out-side of the expense—(The book is about the size of one vol of Emerson's essays)—I will consider whether I will pay one half the same (or what-ever of my part one half the profits has failed to pay)—*at the end of six months after the day of publication,* if that is agreeable to you. This arrangement to affect only one edition. The MSS is quite ready and is now in New York.

Please answer this as soon as convenient.

Yours &c.
Henry D. Thoreau

P S. I should have said above that I decline your proposition as it now stands.

MS., Historical Society of Pennsylvania.

To HENRY WILLIAMS, JR.

Concord Sept 30th 1847

Dear Sir,

I confess that I have very little class spirit, and have almost forgotten that I ever spent four years at Cambridge. That must have been in a former state of existence. It is difficult to realize that the old routine is still kept up. However, I will undertake at last to answer your questions as well as I can in spite of a poor memory and a defect of in-formation.

1st then, I was born, they say, on the 12th of July 1817, on what is called the Virginia Road, in the east part of Concord.

2nd I was fitted, or rather made unfit, for College, at Concord Academy & elsewhere, mainly by myself, with the countenance of Phineas Allen, Preceptor.

3d I am not married.

4th I dont know whether mine is a profession, or a trade, or what not. It is not yet learned, and in every instance has been practised before being studied. The mercantile part of it was begun *here* by myself alone.

—It is not one but legion. I will give you some of the monster's heads. I am a Schoolmaster—a Private Tutor, a Surveyor—a Gardener, a Farmer—a Painter, I mean a House Painter, a Carpenter, a Mason, a Day-Laborer, a Pencil-Maker, a Glass-paper Maker, a Writer, and sometimes a Poetaster. If you will act the part of Iolas, and apply a hot iron to any of these heads, I shall be greatly obliged to you.

5th My present employment is to answer such orders as may be expected from so general an advertisement as the above—that is, if I see fit, which is not always the case, for I have found out a way to live without what is commonly called employment or industry attractive or otherwise. Indeed my steadiest employment, if such it can be called, is to keep myself at the top of my condition, and ready for whatever may turn up in heaven or on earth. For the last two or three years I have lived in Concord woods alone, something more than a mile from any neighbor, in a house built entirely by myself.

6th I cannot think of a single general fact of any importance before or since graduating

Yrs &c

Henry D Thoreau

P S. I beg that the Class will not consider me an object of charity, and if any of them are in want of pecuniary assistance, and will make known their case to me, I will engage to give them some advice of more worth than money.

MS., Harvard.

186

To SOPHIA THOREAU

Concord, October 24, 1847.

Dear Sophia,—

I thank you for those letters about Ktaadn, and hope you will
save and send me the rest, and anything else you may meet with relating to the Maine woods. That Dr. Young is both young and green too
at traveling in the woods. However, I hope he got "yarbs" enough to
satisfy him. I went to Boston the 5th of this month to see Mr. Emerson
off to Europe. He sailed in the Washington Irving packet ship; the same
in which Mr. [F. H.] Hedge went before him. Up to this trip the first
mate aboard this ship was, as I hear, one Stephens, a Concord boy, son
of Stephens the carpenter, who used to live above Mr. Dennis's. Mr.
Emerson's stateroom was like a carpeted dark closet, about six feet
square, with a large keyhole for a window. The window was about as
big as a saucer, and the glass two inches thick, not to mention another
skylight overhead in the deck, the size of an oblong doughnut, and
about as opaque. Of course it would be in vain to look up, if any con-
templative promenader put his foot upon it. Such will be his lodgings
for two or three weeks; and instead of a walk in Walden woods he will
take a promenade on deck, where the few trees, you know, are stripped
of their bark. The steam-tug carried the ship to sea against a head wind
without a rag of sail being raised.

I don't remember whether you have heard of the new telescope at
Cambridge or not. They think it is the best one in the world, and have
already seen more than Lord Rosse or Herschel. I went to see Perez
Blood's, some time ago, with Mr. Emerson. He had not gone to bed,
but was sitting in the woodshed, in the dark, alone, in his astronomical
chair, which is all legs and rounds, with a seat which can be inserted
at any height. We saw Saturn's rings, and the mountains in the moon,
and the shadows in their craters, and the sunlight on the spurs of the
mountains in the dark portion, etc., etc. When I asked him the power
of his glass, he said it was 85. But what is the power of the Cambridge
glass? 2000!!! The last is about twenty-three feet long.

I think you may have a grand time this winter pursuing some study,—
keeping a journal, or the like,—while the snow lies deep without. Winter
is the time for study, you know, and the colder it is the more studious

187

we are. Give my respects to the whole Penobscot tribe, and tell them that I trust we are good brothers still, and endeavor to keep the chain of friendship bright, though I do dig up a hatchet now and then. I trust you will not stir from your comfortable winter quarters, Miss Bruin, or even put your head out of your hollow tree, till the sun has melted the snow in the spring, and "the green buds, they are a-swellin'."

From your
Brother Henry.

Thoreau's sister was visiting her Bangor cousins again. Perez Blood was an amateur Concord astronomer, according to Sanborn. Thoreau had befriended the Penobscot Indians when he made his first journey to the Maine woods in the summer of 1846. Text, Familiar Letters of Thoreau, *pp. 158–60.*

To EMERSON

Concord, November 14, 1847.

Dear Friend,—

I am but a poor neighbor to you here,—a very poor companion am I. I understand that very well, but that need not prevent my *writing* to you now. I have almost never written letters in my life, yet I think I can write as good ones as I frequently see, so I shall not hesitate to write this, such as it may be, knowing that you will welcome anything that reminds you of Concord.

I have banked up the young trees against the winter and the mice, and I will look out, in my careless way, to see when a pale is loose or a nail drops out of its place. The broad gaps, at least, I will occupy. I heartily wish I could be of good service to this household. But I, who have only used these ten digits so long to solve the problem of a living, how can I? The world is a cow that is hard to milk,—life does not come so easy,—and oh, how thinly it is watered ere we get it! But the young

bunting calf, he will get at it. There is no way so direct. This is to earn one's living by the sweat of his brow. It is a little like joining a community, this life, to such a hermit as I am; and as I don't keep the accounts, I don't know whether the experiment will succeed or fail finally. At any rate, it is good for society, so I do not regret my transient nor my permanent share in it.

Lidian and I make very good housekeepers. She is a very dear sister to me. Ellen and Edith and Eddy and Aunty Brown keep up the tragedy and comedy and tragic-comedy of life as usual. The two former have not forgotten their old acquaintance; even Edith carries a young memory in her head, I find. Eddy can teach us all how to pronounce. If you should discover any rare hoard of wooden or pewter horses, I have no doubt he will know how to appreciate it. He occasionally surveys mankind from my shoulders as wisely as ever Johnson did. I respect him not a little, though it is I that lift him up so unceremoniously. And sometimes I have to set him down again in a hurry, according to his "mere will and good pleasure." He very seriously asked me, the other day, "Mr. Thoreau, will you be my father?" I am occasionally Mr. Rough-and-tumble with him that I may not miss *him*, and lest he should miss *you* too much. So you must come back soon, or you will be superseded.

Alcott has heard that I laughed, and so set the people laughing, at his arbor, though I never laughed louder than when I was on the ridgepole. But now I have not laughed for a long time, it is so serious. He is very grave to look at. But, not knowing all this, I strove innocently enough, the other day, to engage his attention to my mathematics. "Did you ever study geometry, the relation of straight lines to curves, the transition from the finite to the infinite? Fine things about it in Newton and Leibnitz." But he would hear none of it,—men of taste preferred the natural curve. Ah, he is a crooked stick himself. He is getting on now so many *knots* an hour. There is one knot at present occupying the point of highest elevation,—the present highest point; and as many knots as are not handsome, I presume, are thrown down and cast into the pines. Pray show him this if you meet him anywhere in London, for I cannot make him hear much plainer words here. He forgets that I am neither old nor young, nor anything in particular, and behaves as if I had still some of the animal heat in me. As for the building, I feel a little oppressed when I come near it. It has no great disposition to be beautiful; it is certainly a wonderful structure, on the whole, and the fame of the

architect will endure as long as it shall stand. I should not show you this side alone, if I did not suspect that Lidian had done complete justice to the other.

Mr. Hosmer has been working at a tannery in Stow for a fortnight, though he has just now come home sick. It seems that he was a tanner in his youth, and so he has made up his mind a little at last. This comes of reading the New Testament. Was n't one of the Apostles a tanner? Mrs. Hosmer remains here, and John looks stout enough to fill his own shoes and his father's too.

Mr. Blood and his company have at length seen the stars through the great telescope, and he told me that he thought it was worth the while. Mr. [Benjamin] Peirce made him wait till the crowd had dispersed (it was a Saturday evening), and then was quite polite,—conversed with him, and showed him the micrometer, etc.; and he said Mr. Blood's glass was large enough for all ordinary astronomical work. [Rev.] Mr. [Barzillai] Frost and Dr. [Josiah] Bartlett seemed disappointed that there was no greater difference between the Cambridge glass and the Concord one. They used only a power of 400. Mr. Blood tells me that he is too old to study the calculus or higher mathematics. At Cambridge they think that they have discovered traces of another satellite to Neptune. They have been obliged to exclude the public altogether, at last. The very dust which they raised, "which is filled with minute crystals," etc., as professors declare, having to be wiped off the glasses, would erelong wear them away. It is true enough, Cambridge college is really beginning to wake up and redeem its character and overtake the age. I see by the catalogue that they are about establishing a scientific school in connection with the university, at which any one above eighteen, on paying one hundred dollars annually (Mr. [Abbott] Lawrence's fifty thousand dollars will probably diminish this sum), may be instructed in the highest branches of science,—in astronomy, "theoretical and practical, with the use of the instruments" (so the great Yankee astronomer may be born without delay), in mechanics and engineering to the last degree. Agassiz will erelong commence his lectures in the zoölogical department. A chemistry class has already been formed under the direction of Professor [Eben N.] Horsford. A new and adequate building for the purpose is already being erected. They have been foolish enough to put at the end of all this earnest the old joke of a diploma. Let every sheep keep but his own skin, I say.

I have had a tragic correspondence, for the most part all on one side,

with Miss [Ford]. She did really wish to—I hesitate to write—marry me. That is the way they spell it. Of course I did not write a deliberate answer. How could I deliberate upon it? I sent back as distinct a *no* as I have learned to pronounce after considerable practice, and I trust that this *no* has succeeded. Indeed, I wished that it might burst, like hollow shot, after it had struck and buried itself and made itself felt there. *There was no other way.* I really had anticipated no such foe as this in my career.

I suppose you will like to hear of my book, though I have nothing worth writing about it. Indeed, for the last month or two I have forgotten it, but shall certainly remember it again. Wiley & Putnam, Munroe, the Harpers, and Crosby & Nichols have all declined printing it with the least risk to themselves; but Wiley & Putnam will print it in their series, and any of them, anywhere, at *my* risk. If I liked the book well enough, I should not delay; but for the present I am indifferent. I believe this is, after all, the course you advised,—to let it lie.

I do not know what to say of myself. I sit before my green desk, in the chamber at the head of the stairs, and attend to my thinking, sometimes more, sometimes less distinctly. I am not unwilling to think great thoughts if there are any in the wind, but what they are I am not sure. They suffice to keep me awake while the day lasts, at any rate. Perhaps they will redeem some portion of the night erelong.

I can imagine you astonishing, bewildering, confounding, and sometimes delighting John Bull with your Yankee notions, and that he begins to take a pride in the relationship at last; introduced to all the stars of England in succession, after the lecture, until you pine to thrust your head once more into a genuine and unquestionable nebula, if there be any left. I trust a common man will be the most uncommon to you before you return to these parts. I have thought there was some advantage even in death, by which we "mingle with the herd of common men."

Hugh [the gardener] still has his eye on the Walden *agellum*, and orchards are waving there in the windy future for him. That's the where-I'll-go-next, thinks he; but no important steps are yet taken. He reminds me occasionally of this open secret of his, with which the very season seems to labor, and affirms seriously that as to his wants—wood, stone, or timber—I know better than he. That is a clincher which I shall have to avoid to some extent; but I fear that it is a wrought nail and will not break. Unfortunately, the day after cattle show—the day after small beer—he was among the missing, but not long this time. The

Ethiopian cannot change his skin nor the leopard his spots, nor indeed Hugh—his Hugh.

As I walked over Conantum, the other afternoon, I saw a fair column of smoke rising from the woods directly over my house that was (as I judged), and already began to conjecture if my deed of sale would not be made invalid by this. But it turned out to be John Richardson's young wood, on the southeast of your field. It was burnt nearly all over, and up to the rails and the road. It was set on fire, no doubt, by the same Lucifer that lighted Brooks's lot before. So you see that your small lot is comparatively safe for this season, the back fire having been already set for you.

They have been choosing between John Keyes and Sam Staples, if the world wants to know it, as representative of this town, and Staples is chosen. The candidates for governor—think of my writing this to you! —were Governor [George N.] Briggs and General [Caleb] Cushing, and Briggs is elected, though the Democrats have gained. Ain't I a brave boy to know so much of politics for the nonce? But I should n't have known it if Coombs had n't told me. They have had a peace meeting here,—I should n't think of telling you if I did n't know anything would do for the English market,—and some men, Deacon [Reuben] Brown at the head, have signed a long pledge, swearing that they will "treat all mankind as brothers henceforth." I think I shall wait and see how they treat me first. I think that nature meant kindly when she made our brothers few. However, my voice is still for peace. So good-by, and a truce to all joking, my dear friend, from

H. D. T.

When Sanborn printed this letter he left blank the name of the woman who proposed to Thoreau. But the catalogue of the William Harris Arnold sale of 1924, in an excerpt, includes the name "Miss Ford." This was unquestionably Sophia Foord (she frequently spelled her name "Ford"), who was about forty-five when Thoreau wrote his deliberate no. She had tutored the Alcott children in Concord, as well as the young Emersons, during parts of 1845 and 1846. In late 1846 and early 1847 she lived under the Emersons' roof. She left it for good April 1. Further details of this abortive romance are given in Walter Harding, "Thoreau's Feminine Foe," PMLA, LXIX (March 1954), 110–16.

As Raymond Adams has pointed out in "Emerson's House at Walden" (The Thoreau Society Bulletin, § 24 [July, 1948]), Bronson Alcott devoted the summer of 1847 to building a rustic summerhouse for Emerson; Thoreau was his assistant. The house, built of gnarled and knotted wood, was too fantastic ever to prove useful.

Thoreau sold his Walden cabin to Hugh Whelan, Emerson's gardener, soon after he left the pond. On Hugh's misadventures with the hut see Thoreau's sprightly account in the letter to Emerson of January 12, 1848. Some years later the hut was purchased by a Concord farmer and moved to the opposite end of the town, where it was used as a granary. Its timbers ultimately helped to make a barn.

The Lucifer was the railroad train that was constantly setting fire to Concord woods. Sam Staples was the village jailer who, in the summer of 1846, had arrested Thoreau for nonpayment of taxes. Text, Emerson-Thoreau, pp. 737–40.

To ABEL ADAMS

Concord Nov 15th—47

Dear Sir,

Mrs Emerson requests me to forward this circular to you. Mr E. had anticipated it, and, as she thinks, said that you would take care of it. She is sure that he will take new shares.

She desires to be kindly remembered to your family, and would have written herself, if not prevented by a slight indisposition.

We have not yet heard from Mr. E.

Yrs respectfully
H. D. Thoreau

To Mr. Abel Adams Boston,

The letter is written on the back of a notice from the Fitchburg Rail-Road Company, dated November 10, 1847, offering present owners of

stock in the company the opportunity to buy new shares. MS., Massachusetts Historical Society; *previously unpublished.*

From EMERSON

Manchester, 2 Dec. 1847.

Dear Henry,
    Very welcome in the parcel was your letter, very precious your thoughts & tidings. It is one of the best things connected with my coming hither that you could & would keep the homestead, that fireplace shines all the brighter,—and has a certain permanent glimmer therefor. Thanks, evermore thanks for the kindness which I well discern to the *youths* of the house, to my darling little horseman of pewter, leather wooden, rocking & what other breeds, destined, I hope, to ride Pegasus yet, and I hope not destined to be thrown, to Edith who long ago drew from you verses which I carefully preserve, & to Ellen who by speech & now by letter I find old enough to be companionable, & to choose & reward her own friends in her own fashions. She sends me a poem today, which I have read three times!—I believe, I must keep back all my communication on English topics until I get to London, which is England. Everything centralizes, in this magnificent machine which England is. Manufacturer for the world she is become or becoming one complete tool or engine in herself.—Yesterday the *time* all over the kingdom was reduced to Greenwich time. At Liverpool, where I was, the clocks were put forward 12 minutes. This had become quite necessary on account of the railroads which bind the whole country into swiftest connexion, and require so much accurate interlocking, intersection, & simultaneous arrival, that the difference of time produced confusion. Every man in England carries a little book in his pocket called "Bradshaws Guide," which contains time tables of arrival & departure at every station on all railroads of the kingdom. It is published anew on the first day of every month & costs sixpence. The proceeding effects of Electric telegraph will give a new importance to such arrangements.

194

—But lest I should not say what is needful, I will postpone England once for all,—and say that I am not of opinion that your book should be delayed a month. I should print it at once, nor do I think that you would incur any risk in doing so that you cannot well afford. It is very certain to have readers & debtors here as well as there. The Dial is absurdly well known here. We at home, I think, are always a little ashamed of it,—I am,—and yet here it is spoken of with the utmost gravity, & I do not laugh. Carlyle writes me that he is reading Dooms-day Book.—You tell me in your letter one odious circumstance, which we will dismiss from remembrance henceforward. Charles Lane en-treated me, in London, to ask you to forward his Dials to him, which must be done, if you can find them. Three bound vols are among his books in my library. The 4th Vol is in unbound numbers at J Munroe & Co.'s Shop, received there in a parcel to my address a day or two before I sailed & which I forgot to carry to Concord It must be claimed without delay It is certainly there—was opened by me, & left. And they can enclose all 4 vols to Chapman for me.— Well, I am glad the Pleasaunce at Walden suffered no more but it is a great loss as it is which years will not repair.— I see that I have baulked you by the promise of a letter which ends in as good as none But I write with counted minutes & a miscellany of things before me.

Yours affectionately,
R. W. E.

MS., Berg.

From EMERSON

Will Mr Thoreau please to bear in mind that when there is good mortar in readiness, Mr. Dean must be summoned to fit the airtight stove to the chimney in the Schoolroom; unless Mr. T. can do it with convenience himself

MS., Berg; *printed in* Emerson-Thoreau, *p. 742. Sanborn thinks that this letter accompanied the longer one of December 2. Rusk (Emerson Letters, III, 445) suggests that a much earlier date would seem more likely. Since there is no specific evidence for it, we tentatively accept Sanborn's date.*

To EMERSON

Concord Dec 15 1847

Dear Friend,

You are not so far off but the affairs of *this* world still attach to you. Perhaps it will be so when we are dead. Then look out.— Joshua R. Holman of Harvard, who says he lived a month with Lane at Fruitlands wishes to *hire* said Lane's farm for one or more years, and will pay $125 rent, taking out of the same what is necessary for repairs—as, for a new bank-wall to the barn cellar, which he says is indispensable. Palmer is gone, Mrs Palmer is going. This is all that is known, or that is worth knowing.

Yes or no—
What to do?

Hugh's plot begins to thicken. He starts thus. 80 dollars on one side— Walden field & house on the other. How to bring these together so as to make a garden & a palace.

$80 .... [field]   □   house

1st let   10 go over to unite the two last
        ――
          70   [□]

          6 for Wetherbee's rocks to found your palace on.
        ――
          64

          64 So far indeed we have already got.

$\dfrac{4}{60}$ to bring the rocks to the field.

save $\underline{20}$ by all means to manure the field, and you have

left   40 to complete the palace—build cellar— & dig well. Build the cellar yourself— & let well alone— & now how does it stand?

$40 to complete the palace somewhat like this

—for when one asks— ["]What do you want? Twice as much room more," the reply— Parlor kitchen & bedroom—these make the palace.— Well, Hugh, what will you do? Here are forty dollars to buy a new house 12 feet by 25 and add it to the old. — Well, Mr Thoreau, as I tell you, I know no more than a child about it. It shall be just as you say. — Then build it yourself—get it roofed & get in. Commence at one end & leave it half done, and let time finish what money's begun.

So you see we have forty dollars for a nest egg—sitting on which, Hugh & I, alternately & simultaneously, there may in course of time be hatched a house, that will long stand, and perchance even lay fresh eggs one day for its owner, that is, if when he returns he gives the young chick 20 dollars or more in addition by way of "swichin"—to give it a start in the world.

Observe this—I got your check changed into thirty dollars the other day, & immediately paid away sixteen for Hugh. To-day Mr Cheney says that they in Boston refuse to answer it—not having funds enough to warrant it. There must be some mistake &c — We shall pay back the thirty dollars & await your orders.

The Mass. Quart. Review came out on the 1st of Dec., but it does not seem to be making a sensation—at least not hereabouts. I know of none in Concord who takes, or has seen, it yet.

We wish to get by all possible means some notion of your success or failure in England—more than your two letters have furnished— Can't you send a fair sample both of Young & of Old England's criticism, if there is any printed? Alcott & Channing are equally greedy with myself.

Henry Thoreau

C T [Jackson] takes the Quarterly (new one) and will lend it to us. Are you not going to send your wife some news of your good or ill success by the newspapers?

The tribulations of Hugh Whelan over the remodeling of Thoreau's Walden cabin continue in this letter. The Massachusetts Quarterly Review *was founded late in 1847 by Theodore Parker and James Elliot Cabot as a successor to the* Dial. *C. T. Jackson was Emerson's brother-in-law.* MS., C. Waller Barrett; *the postscript is in a different handwriting, probably Mrs. Emerson's.*

To JAMES MUNROE & CO.

Concord Dec. 27th 1847

Gentlemen,

In a letter from R. W. Emerson, which I received this morning, he requests me to send him Charles Lane's Dials. Three bound vols accompany this letter to you—"The fourth," to quote his own words, "is in unbound numbers at J Munroe & Co's shop, received there in a parcel to my address a day or two before I sailed, and which I forgot to carry to Concord—It is certainly there, was opened by me, & left."

—And he wishes me to ask you to "enclose all four vols. to Chapman" for him (Emerson).

If all is right, will you please say so to the express-man—or at any rate give me an opportunity to look for the fourth vol, if it is missing.

I may as well inform you that I do not intend to print *my book* anywhere immediately.

Yrs Respectfully
Henry Thoreau

Thoreau had decided on further revision of A Week on the Concord and Merrimack Rivers *after its unsuccessful round of the publishers.* MS., Boston Public Library; *previously unpublished.*

To EMERSON

Concord Dec 29th 1847.

My Dear Friend,

I thank you for your letter. I was very glad to get it—And I am glad again to write to you. However slow the steamer, no time intervenes between the writing and the reading of thoughts, but they come freshly to the most distant port.

I am here still, & very glad to be here—and shall not trouble you with my complaints because I do not fill my place better. I have had many good hours in the chamber at the head of the stairs—a solid time, it seems to me. Next week I am going to give an account to the Lyceum of my expedition to Maine. Theodore Parker lectures tonight—We have had Whipple on Genius—too weighty a subject for him—with his _____ _____ antithetical definitions,—new-vamped—What it *is*, & what it is *not*—but altogether what it is *not*. Cuffing it this way, & cuffing it that, as if it were an India rubber ball. Really, it is a subject which should—expand & accumulate itself before the speaker's eyes, as he goes on,—like the snow balls which boys roll in the street— & when he stops, it should be so large that he cannot start it—but must leave it there— _____. [H. N.] Hudson too has been here with a dark shadow in the core of him, and his desperate wit so much indebted to the surface of him—wringing out his words and snapping them off like a dish-cloth—very remarkable but not memorable. Singular that these two best lecturers should have so much "wave" in their timber—Their solid parts too be made and kept solid by shrinkage and contraction of the whole—with consequent checks & fissures—Ellen and I have a good understanding—I appreciate her genuineness—Edith tells me after her fashion—"By & by, I shall grow up to be a woman, and then I shall remember how you exercised me."—Eddie has been to Boston to Christmas—but can remember nothing but the coaches—all Kendall's coaches. There is no variety of that vehicle that he is not familiar with.—He *did* try once to tell us something else, but, after thinking and stuttering a long time—said—"I dont know what the word is,"— the *one* word, forsooth that would have disposed of all that Boston phenomenon. If you did not know him better than I—I could tell you more. He is a good companion for me—& I am glad that we are

all natives of Concord—It is *Young Concord*—Look out—World.—Mr Alcott seems to have sat down for the winter. He has got Plato and other books to read. He is as large featured—and hospitable to traveling thoughts & thinkers as ever—but with the same creaking & sneaking Connecticut philosophy as ever, mingled with what is better. If he would only stand straight and toe the line!—though he were to put off several degrees of largeness—and put on a considerable degree of little- ness.—After all, I think we must call him particularly *your* man.—I have pleasant walks and talks with Channing.—James Clark—the Sweden- borgian that was—is at the Poor House—insane with too large views, so that he cannot support himself—I see him working with Fred and the rest. Better than be there not insane. It is strange that they will make an ado when a man's body is buried—and not when he thus really & tragically dies—or seems to die. Away with your funeral processions,— into the ballroom with them. I hear the bell toll hourly over there.

Lidian & I have a standing quarrel as to what is a suitable state of preparedness for a traveling Professor's visits—or for whomsoever else —but further than this we are not at war. We have made up a dinner— we have made up a bed—we have made up a party—& our own minds & mouths three several times for your Professor, and he came not—Three several turkeys have died the death—which I myself carved, just as if he had been there, and the company too, convened and demeaned themselves accordingly— Everything was done up in good style, I as- sure you with only the part of the Professor omitted. To have seen the preparation though Lidian says it was nothing extraordinary—I should certainly have said he was a coming—but he did not. He must have found out some shorter way to Turkey—some overland rout[e]—I think. By the way, he was complimented at the conclusion of his course in Boston by the Mayor moving the appointment of a committee to draw up resolutions expressive of &c &c which was done.

I have made a few verses lately—Here are some—though perhaps not the best—at any rate they are the shortest on that universal theme —yours as well as mine, & several other people's

> The good how can we trust?
> Only the wise are just.
> The good we use,
> The wise we cannot choose.
> These there are none above;

The good they know & love,
But are not known again
By those of lesser ken.
They do not charm us with their eyes,
But they transfix with their advice,
No partial sympathy they feel,
With private woe or private weal,
But with the Universe joy & sigh,
Whose knowledge is their sympathy.

Good night

Henry Thoreau

I am sorry to send such a medley as this to you. I have forwarded Lane's Dial to Munroe with the proper instructions and he tells the express man that all is right.

Thoreau delivered his lecture on the Maine Woods before the Concord Lyceum early in January. E. P. Whipple was a popular lecturer and essayist of the day. Sanborn identifies the traveling professor as Agassiz. The "few verses" were later incorporated by Thoreau in the essay on friendship in the Wednesday chapter of the Week. MS., Berg. The blanks indicate words crossed out by Thoreau and now undecipherable.

1848

A man named Marshall struck gold in Eldorado County, California while building a millrace for John Sutter. Mexico ceded a good part of the Southwest to the United States. John Jacob Astor died in New York at eighty-five. The Pacific Mail Steamship Company was organized to carry gold seekers to California. The cornerstone of the Washington Monument was laid. A congress of labor organizations met in Philadelphia, and the first women's rights convention was held in Seneca Falls, New York, with Lucretia Mott as speaker. In New York City William Tweed joined in organizing a volunteer fire company; on its engine he painted the tiger that he later adopted as the emblem of Tammany Hall. Slavery was prohibited in Oregon. For the fiscal year the United States Treasury had a deficit of $9,641,447.

For Thoreau the main literary event of the year was the publication in the *Union Magazine*, with Horace Greeley as agent, of five substantial excerpts from his Maine record, under the general title "Ktaadn and the Maine Woods." They were "The Wilds of the Penobscot," "Life in the Wilderness," "Boating on the Lakes," "The Ascent of Ktaadn," and "The Return Journey." Thoreau left the Emersons and went home to live. He walked and he wrote. Lecturing and pencil-making, with surveying beginning to be added, made some kind of living for him. His interest in nature study increased. His *Journal* for this year has not survived, but it is a safe enough guess that much of it went into the Maine Woods series. He wrote elevated essays to a new disciple, H. G. O. Blake, and corresponded with Emerson in England and Greeley in America.

Concord, January 12, 1848.

It is hard to believe that England is so near as from your letters it appears; and that this identical piece of paper has lately come all the way from there hither, begrimed with the English dust which made you hesitate to use it; from England, which is only historical fairyland to me, to America, which I have put my spade into, and about which there is no doubt.

I thought that you needed to be informed of Hugh's progress. He has moved his house, as I told you, and dug his cellar, and purchased stone of Sol Wetherbee for the last, though he has not hauled it; all which has cost sixteen dollars, which I have paid. He has also, as next in order, run away from Concord without a penny in his pocket, "crying" by the way,—having had another long difference with strong beer, and a first one, I suppose, with his wife, who seems to have complained that he sought other society; the one difference leading to the other, perhaps, but I don't know which was the leader. He writes back to his wife from Sterling, near Worcester, where he is chopping wood, his distantly kind reproaches to her, which I read straight through to her (not to his bottle, which he has with him, and no doubt addresses orally). He says that he will go on to the South in the spring, and will never return to Concord. Perhaps he will not. Life is not tragic enough for him, and he must try to cook up a more highly seasoned dish for himself. Towns which keep a bar-room and a gun-house and a reading-room should also keep a steep precipice whereoff impatient soldiers may jump. His sun went down, *to me,* bright and steady enough in the west, but it never came up in the east. Night intervened. He departed, as when a man dies suddenly; and perhaps wisely, if he was to go, without settling his affairs. They knew that that was a thin soil and not well calculated for pears. Nature is rare and sensitive on the score of nurseries. You may cut down orchards and grow forests at your pleasure. Sand watered with strong

beer, though stirred with industry, will not produce grapes. He dug his cellar for the new part too near the old house, Irish like, though I warned him, and it has caved and let one end of the house down. Such is the state of his domestic affairs. I laugh with the Parcæ only. He had got the upland and the orchard and a part of the meadow ploughed by [Cyrus] Warren, at an expense of eight dollars, still unpaid, which of course is no affair of yours.

I think that if an honest and small-familied man, who has no affinity for moisture in him, but who has an affinity for sand, can be found, it would be safe to rent him the shanty as it is, and the land; or you can very easily and simply let nature keep them still, without great loss. It may be so managed, perhaps, as to be a home for somebody, who shall in return serve you as fencing stuff, and to fix and locate your lot, as we plant a tree in the sand or on the edge of a stream; without expense to you in the mean while, and without disturbing its possible future value.

I read a part of the story of my excursion to Ktadn to quite a large audience of men and boys, the other night, whom it interested. It contains many facts and some poetry. I have also written what will do for a lecture on Friendship.

I think that the article on you in Blackwood's is a good deal to get from the reviewers,—the first purely literary notice, as I remember. The writer is far enough off, in every sense, to speak with a certain authority. It is a better judgment of posterity than the public had. It is singular how sure he is to be mystified by any uncommon sense. But it was generous to put Plato into the list of mystics. His confessions on this subject suggest several thoughts, which I have not room to express here. The old word *seer*,—I wonder what the reviewer thinks that means; whether that *he* was a man who could *see more than himself*.

I was struck by Ellen's asking me, yesterday, while I was talking with Mrs. Brown, if I did not use *"colored* words." She said that she could tell the color of a great many words, and amused the children at school by so doing. Eddy climbed up the sofa, the other day, *of his own accord,* and kissed the picture of his father,—"right on his shirt, I did."

I had a good talk with Alcott this afternoon. He is certainly the youngest man of his age we have seen,—just on the threshold of life. When I looked at his gray hairs, his conversation sounded pathetic; but I looked again, and they reminded me of the gray dawn. He is getting better acquainted with Channing, though he says that, if they

were to live in the same house, they would soon sit with their backs to each other.

You must excuse me if I do not write with sufficient directness to yourself, who are a far-off traveler. It is a little like shooting on the wing, I confess.

Farewell.
Henry Thoreau.

Although the Concord Lyceum records are not definite at this point, Thoreau probably delivered this Ktaadn lecture (later a part of The Maine Woods) *before the Lyceum. There is no record of his having used the "Friendship" essay for a lecture, but he did incorporate it in the text of the* Week. *The notice in* Blackwood's *Magazine was an anonymous one entitled simply "Emerson" in the December 1847 issue (LXII, 643–57). Text, Emerson-Thoreau, pp. 744–45.*

From EMERSON

2 Fenny Street; Higher Broughton; Manchester; 28 January, 1848

Dear Henry,

One roll of letters has gone today to Concord & to New York, and perhaps I shall still have time to get this into the leathern bag, before it is carted to the wharf. I have to thank you for your letter which was a true refreshment. Let who or what pass, there stands the dear Henry,—if indeed any body had a right to call him so,—erect, serene, & undeceivable. So let it ever be! I should quite subside into idolatry of some of my friends, if I were not every now & then apprised that the world is wiser than any one of its boys, & penetrates us with its sense, to the disparagement of the subtleties of private gentlemen. Last night, as I believe I have already told Lidian, I heard the best man in England make perhaps his best speech: Cobden, who is the *cor cordis*, the object of honor & belief to risen & rising England a man of great discretion, who never overstates, nor states prematurely, nor has

a particle of unnecessary genius or hope to mislead him, no wasted strength, but calm, sure of his fact, simple & nervous in stating it, as a boy in laying down the rules of the game of football which have been violated—above all educated by his dogma of Free Trade, led on by it to new lights & correlative liberalities, as our abolitionists have been by their principle to so many Reforms. Then this man has made no mistake he has dedicated himself to his work of convincing this kingdom of the impolicy of corn laws, lectured in every town where they would hear him, & at last carried his point against immense odds, & yet has never accepted any compromise or stipulation from the Government. He might have been in the ministry. He will never go there, except with absolute empire for his principle, which cannot yet be awarded. He had neglected & abandoned his prosperous calico printing to his partners. And the triumphant League have subscribed between 60 & 80000 pounds, as the Cobden Fund; whereby he is made independent.—It was quite beautiful, even sublime, last night, to notice the moral radiations which this Free Trade dogma seemed to throw out, all-unlooked-for, to the great audience, who instantly & delightedly adopted them. Such contrasts of sentiments to the vulgar hatred & fear of France & jealousy of America, that pervaded the Newspapers. Cobden himself looked thoughtful & surprised, as if he saw a new Future. Old Col. Perronet Thompson, the Father of Free Trade, whose catechism on the Corn Laws set all these Brights & Cobdens first on cracking this nut, was present, & spoke in a very vigorous rasp-like tone. [Milner] Gibson, a member of the Brit. government, a great Suffolk Squire, & a convert to these opinions, made a very satisfactory speech and our old Abolition Friend, George Thompson, brought up the rear, though he, whom I now heard for the first time, is merely a piece of rhetoric & not a man of facts & figures & English solidity, like the rest. The audience play no inactive part, but the most acute & sympathizing, and the agreeable result was the demonstration of the arithmetical as well as the moral optimism of peace and generosity.

Forgive, forgive this most impertient [sic] scribble.

Your friend,
R. W. E.

I really did not mean to put you off with a Report when I began. But—

MS., Berg.

To EMERSON

Concord Feb 23d, 1848

Dear Waldo,

For I think I have heard that that is your name,—My letter which was put last into the leathern bag arrived first. Whatever I may *call* you, I know you better than I know your name, and what becomes of the fittest name—if in any sense you are here with him who *calls,* and not there simply to be called.

I believe I never thanked you for your lectures—one and all—which I heard formerly read here in Concord—I *know* I never have—There was some excellent reason each time why I did not—but it will never be too late. I have had that advantage at least, over you in my education.

Lidian is too unwell to write to you and so I must tell you what I can about the children, and herself. I am afraid she has not told you how unwell she is, today perhaps we may say—has been. She has been confined to her chamber four or five weeks, and three or four weeks, at least to her bed—with the jaundice, accompanied with *constant* nausea, which makes life intolerable to her. This added to her general ill health has made her *very* sick. She is as yellow as saffron. The Doctor, who comes once a day does not let her read (nor can she now) nor *hear* much reading. She has written her letters to you till recently sitting up in bed—but he said that he would not come again if she did so. She has Abby and Almira to take care of her, & Mrs. Brown to read to her, and I also occasionally have something to read or to say. The Doctor says she must not expect to "take any comfort of her life" for a week or two yet. She wishes me to say that she has written 2 long and full letters to you about the household economies &c which she hopes have not been delayed.

The children are quite well and full of spirits—and are going through a regular course of picture seeing with commentary by me—every evening—for Eddy's behoof. All the annuals and "diadems" are in requisition, and Eddy is forward to exclaim when the hour arrives—"Now for the dem dems!" I overheard this dialogue when Frank came down to breakfast, the other morning.—Eddy.—Why Frank, I am *astonished* that you should leave your boots in the dining-room.—Frank. "I guess you

mean *surprised*, dont you? Eddy—"No—Boots!—"If Waldo were here," said he the other night at bed-time, "we'd be four going upstairs." Would he like to tell Papa anything? "No—not anything" but finally "Yes,"—he would—that one of the white horses in his new barouche is broken. Ellen and Edith will perhaps speak for themselves as I hear something about letters to be written by them.

Mr. Alcott seems to be reading well this winter Plato—Montaigne—Ben Jonson—Beaumont & Fletcher—Sir Thomas Browne &c &c—"I believe I have read them all now—or nearly all"—Those English authors He is rallying for another foray with his pen, in his latter years, not discouraged by the past—into that crowd of unexpressed ideas of his—that undisciplined Parthian army—which as soon as a Roman soldier would face retreats on all hands—occasionally firing behind—easily routed—not easily subdued—hovering on the skirts of society. Another summer shall not be devoted to the raising of vegetables (Arbors?) which rot in the cellar for want of consumers—but perchance to the arrangement of the material—the brain-crop which the winter has furnished. I have good talks with him.

His respect for Carlyle has been steadily increasing for some time. He has read him with new sympathy and appreciation.

I see Channing often. He also goes often to Alcott's, and confesses that he has made a discovery in him—and gives vent to his admiration or his confusion in characteristic exaggeration—but between this extreme & that you may get a fair report—& draw an inference if you can. Sometimes he *will* ride a broom stick still—though there is nothing to keep him or it up—but a certain centrifugal force of whim which is soon spent—and there lies your stick—not worth picking up to sweep an oven with now. His accustomed path is strewn with them. But then again & perhaps for the most part he sits on the Cliffs amid the lichens, or flits past on noiseless pinion like the Barred Owl in the daytime—as wise & unobserved.

He brought me a poem the other day—for me—on "Walden Hermitage," not remarkable.

Lectures begin to multiply on my desk. I have one on Friendship which is new—and the materials of some others. I read one last week to the Lyceum on The Rights & Duties of the Individual in relation to Government—much to Mr. Alcott's satisfaction.—Joel Britton has failed and gone into chancery—but the woods continue to fall before the axes of other men—Neighbor [Eseek] Coombs was lately found dead in the

woods near Goose Pond—with his half-empty jug—after he had been missing a week.—Hugh [Whelan] by the last accounts was still in Worcester County.—Mr. Hosmer who is himself again, and living in Concord—has just hauled the rest of your wood—amounting to about 10½ cords.—The newspapers say that they have printed a pirated edition of your Essays in England. Is it as bad as they say—an undisguised unmitigated piracy?

I thought that the printed scrap would entertain Carlyle—notwithstanding its history. If this generation will see out of its hindhead, why then you may turn your back on its forehead. Will you forward it to him from me?

This stands written in your Day Book. "Sept. 3d Recd of Boston Savings Bank—on account of Charles Lane his deposit with interest 131.33 16th. Recd of Joseph Palmer on account of Charles Lane Three hundred twenty three 36/100 dollars being the balance of a note on demand for four hundred dollars with interest. $323.36."

If you have any directions to give about the trees you must not forget that spring will soon be upon us.

Farewell from your friend
Henry Thoreau

Sanborn identifies Frank as the son of Mrs. Emerson's sister, Mrs. Lucy Brown. Channing's "Walden Hermitage" was later included in his 1873 Thoreau, the Poet-Naturalist (pp. 196–99). Thoreau delivered his lecture, later printed as "Civil Disobedience," before the Concord Lyceum on January 26, 1848, or so Alcott indicates in his Journals (p. 201). The daybook records were given to straighten out the finances of the Fruitlands experiment. Text, Emerson-Thoreau, pp. 746–48.

To JAMES ELLIOT CABOT

Concord, March 8, 1848.

Dear Sir,—

Mr. Emerson's address is as yet, "R. W. Emerson, care of Alexander Ireland, Esq., Examiner Office, Manchester, England." We had a letter from him on Monday, dated at Manchester, February 10, and he was then preparing to go to Edinburgh the next day, where he was to lecture. He thought that he should get through his northern journeying by the 25th of February, and go to London to spend March and April, and if he did not go to Paris in May, then come home. He has been eminently successful, though the papers this side of the water have been so silent about his adventures.

My book, fortunately, did not find a publisher ready to undertake it, and you can imagine the effect of delay on an author's estimate of his own work. However, I like it well enough to mend it, and shall look at it again directly when I have dispatched some other things.

I have been writing lectures for our own Lyceum this winter, mainly for my own pleasure and advantage. I esteem it a rare happiness to be able to *write* anything, but there (if I ever get there) my concern for it is apt to end. Time & Co. are, after all, the only quite honest and trustworthy publishers that we know. I can sympathize, perhaps, with the barberry bush, whose business it is solely to *ripen* its fruit (though that may not be to sweeten it) and to protect it with thorns, so that it holds on all winter, even, unless some hungry crows come to pluck it. But I see that I must get a few dollars together presently to manure my roots. Is your journal able to pay anything, provided it likes an article well enough? I do not promise one. At any rate, I mean always to spend only words enough to purchase silence with; and I have found that this, which is so valuable, though many writers do not prize it, does not cost much, after all.

I have not obtained any more of the mice which I told you were so numerous in my cellar, as my house was removed immediately after I saw you, and I have been living in the village since.

However, if I should happen to meet with anything rare, I will forward it to you. I thank you for your kind offers, and will avail myself of them so far as to ask if you can anywhere borrow for me for a short

time the copy of the "Revue des Deux Mondes," containing a notice of
Mr. Emerson. I should like well to read it, and to read it to Mrs. Emerson and others. If this book is not easy to be obtained, do not by any
means trouble yourself about it.

*The letter Thoreau refers to ("We had a letter") is clearly the one to
Lidian Emerson from Gateshead upon Tyne, not from Manchester.*
Text, Familiar Letters of Thoreau, *pp. 186–88.*

To EMERSON

Dear Fri[end,]
      Lid[ian] says I must write a sentence about the children [Ed]die
says he cannot sing "not till mother is agoing to be well." We shall hear
his voice very soon in that case I trust. Ellen is already thinking what
will be done when you come home, but then she thinks it will be some
loss that I shall go away. Edith says that I shall come and see them, and
always at teatime so that I can play with her. Ellen thinks she likes
father best because he jumps her sometimes
      This is the latest news from yours &c

                                                            Henry

P. S. I have received three newspapers from you duly which I have not
acknowledged. There is an anti-sabbath convention held in Boston to-
day to which Alcott has gone.

*The bracketed letters, easily restored, were erased by sealing wax. The
manuscript is postmarked March 24, 1848. MS., Frank Walters.*

From EMERSON

London, 25 March, 1848

Dear Henry,

Your letter was very welcome and its introduction heartily accepted. In this city & nation of pomps, where pomps too are solid, I fall back on my friends with wonderful refreshment. It is pity, however, that you should not see this England, with its indiscribable material superiorities of every kind; the just confidence which immense successes of all pasts have generated in this Englishman that he can do everything, and which his manners, though he is bashful & reserved, betray; the abridgment of all expression, which dense population & the roar of nations enforces; the solidity of science & merit which in any high place you are sure to find (the Church & some effects of primogeniture excepted) but I cannot tell my story now. I admire the English I think never more than when I meet Americans—as, for example, at Mr Bancroft's American Soiree, which he holds every Sunday night.—Great is the self-respect of Mr Bull. He is very shortsighted & without his eyeglasses cannot see as far as your eyes, to know how you like him, so that he quite neglects that point. The Americans see very well, too well, and the traveling portion are very light troops. But I must not vent my ill-humour on my poor compatriots. They are welcome to their revenge & I am quite sure have no weapon to shave me if they too are at this hour writing letters to their gossips. I have not gone to Oxford yet, though I still correspond with my friend there, Mr Clough. I meet many young men here, who come to me simply as one of their School of thought, but not often in this class any giants. A Mr [J. D.] Morell who has written a History of Philosophy, and [J. J. G.] Wilkinson who is a Socialist now & gone to France, I have seen with respect. I went last Sunday for the first time to see [Charles] Lane at Ham & dined with him. He was full of friendliness & hospitality has a School of 16 children, one lady as matron, then Oldham,—that is all the household. They looked just comfortable. Mr Galpin, tell the Shakers, has *married*. I spent the most of that day in visiting Hampton Court & Richmond & went also into Pope's Grotto at Twickenham, & saw Horace Walpole's Villa of Strawberry Hill.

Ever your friend,
Waldo E.

Although Emerson did not return from England until late July, this is his last extant letter of the trip to Thoreau. Arthur Hugh Clough had long been a friend and correspondent of Emerson's. MS., Berg.

From H. G. O. BLAKE

It [Thoreau's *Dial* article on Aulus Persius Flaccus] has revived in me a haunting impression of you, which I carried away from some spoken words of yours. . . . When I was last in Concord, you spoke of retiring farther from our civilization. I asked you if you would feel no longings for the society of your friends. Your reply was in substance, "No, I am nothing." That reply was memorable to me. It indicated a depth of resources, a completeness of renunciation, a poise and repose in the universe, which to me is almost inconceivable; which in you seemed domesticated, and to which I look up with veneration. I would know of that soul which can say "I am nothing." I would be roused by its words to a truer and purer life. Upon me seems to be dawning with new significance the idea that God is here; that we have but to bow before Him in profound submission at every moment, and He will fill our souls with his presence. In this opening of the soul to God, all duties seem to centre; what else have we to do? . . . If I understand rightly the significance of your life, this is it: You would sunder yourself from society, from the spell of institutions, customs, conventionalities, that you may lead a fresh, simple life with God. Instead of breathing a new life into the old forms, you would have a new life without and within. There is something sublime to me in this attitude,—far as I may be from it myself. . . . Speak to me in this hour as you are prompted. . . . I honor you because you abstain from action, and open your soul that you may *be* somewhat. Amid a world of noisy, shallow actors it is noble to stand aside and say, "I will simply *be*." Could I plant myself at once upon the truth, reducing my wants to their minimum, . . . I should at once be brought nearer to nature, nearer to my fellow-men,—and life would be infinitely richer. But, alas! I shiver on the brink. . . .

Here begins Thoreau's major correspondence devoted to his ideas, that with Harrison Gray Otis Blake of Worcester, Massachusetts. Blake, a Harvard graduate and onetime Unitarian minister, had long been acquainted with the Transcendentalists. Now by chance he reread Thoreau's article on Persius in the Dial *of July 1840 and found in it "pure depth and solidity of thought." The correspondence continued throughout Thoreau's life. Unfortunately this is the only letter from Blake to Thoreau that has been preserved, and it only in part. Since the letter of March 27, 1848 is obviously a reply to this, it can be dated as approximately the middle of March 1848.* Text, Familiar Letters of Thoreau, *pp. 190–91.*

To H. G. O. BLAKE

Concord, March 27, 1848.

I am glad to hear that any words of mine, though spoken so long ago that I can hardly claim identity with their author, have reached you. It gives me pleasure, because I have therefore reason to suppose that I have uttered what concerns men, and that it is not in vain that man speaks to man. This is the value of literature. Yet those days are so distant, in every sense, that I have had to look at that page again, to learn what was the tenor of my thoughts then. I should value that article, however, if only because it was the occasion of your letter.

I do believe that the outward and the inward life correspond; that if any should succeed to live a higher life, others would not know of it; that difference and distance are one. To set about living a true life is to go a journey to a distant country, gradually to find ourselves surrounded by new scenes and men; and as long as the old are around me, I know that I am not in any true sense living a new or a better life. The outward is only the outside of that which is within. Men are not concealed under habits, but are revealed by them; they are their true clothes. I care not how curious a reason they may give for their abiding by them. Circumstances are not rigid and unyielding, but our habits are rigid. We are apt to speak vaguely sometimes, as if a divine life were to be grafted on to

or built over this present as a suitable foundation. This might do if we could so build over our old life as to exclude from it all the warmth of our affection, and addle it, as the thrush builds over the cuckoo's egg, and lays her own atop, and hatches that only; but the fact is, we—so there is the partition—hatch them both, and the cuckoo's always by a day first, and that young bird crowds the young thrushes out of the nest. No. Destroy the cuckoo's egg, or build a new nest.

Change is change. No new life occupies the old bodies;—they decay. *It* is born, and grows, and flourishes. Men very pathetically inform the old, accept and wear it. Why put it up with the almshouse when you may go to heaven? It is embalming,—no more. Let alone your ointments and your linen swathes, and go into an infant's body. You see in the catacombs of Egypt the result of that experiment,—that is the end of it.

I do believe in simplicity. It is astonishing as well as sad, how many trivial affairs even the wisest man thinks he must attend to in a day; how singular an affair he thinks he must omit. When the mathematician would solve a difficult problem, he first frees the equation of all incumbrances, and reduces it to its simplest terms. So simplify the problem of life, distinguish the necessary and the real. Probe the earth to see where your main roots run. I would stand upon facts. Why not see,—use our eyes? Do men know nothing? I know many men who, in common things, are not to be deceived; who trust no moonshine; who count their money correctly, and know how to invest it; who are said to be prudent and knowing, who yet will stand at a desk the greater part of their lives, as cashiers in banks, and glimmer and rust and finally go out there. If they *know* anything, what under the sun do they do that for? Do they know what *bread* is? or what it is for? Do they know what life is? If they *knew* something, the places which know them now would know them no more forever.

This, our respectable daily life, in which the man of common sense, the Englishman of the world, stands so squarely, and on which our institutions are founded, is in fact the veriest illusion, and will vanish like the baseless fabric of a vision; but that faint glimmer of reality which sometimes illuminates the darkness of daylight for all men, reveals something more solid and enduring than adamant, which is in fact the corner-stone of the world.

Men cannot conceive of a state of things so fair that it cannot be realized. Can any man honestly consult his experience and say that it is so? Have we any facts to appeal to when we say that our dreams are

premature? Did you ever hear of a man who had striven all his life faithfully and singly toward an object and in no measure obtained it? If a man constantly aspires, is he not elevated? Did ever a man try heroism, magnanimity, truth, sincerity, and find that there was no advantage in them? that it was a vain endeavor? Of course we do not expect that our paradise will be a garden. We know not what we ask. To look at literature;—how many fine thoughts has every man had! how few fine thoughts are expressed! Yet we never have a fantasy so subtile and ethereal, but that *talent merely*, with more resolution and faithful persistency, after a thousand failures, might fix and engrave it in distinct and enduring words, and we should see that our dreams are the solidest facts that we know. But I speak not of dreams.

What can be expressed in words can be expressed in life.

My actual life is a fact in view of which I have no occasion to congratulate myself, but for my faith and aspiration I have respect. It is from these that I speak. Every man's position is in fact too simple to be described. I have sworn no oath. I have no designs on society—or nature —or God. I am simply what I am, or I begin to be that. I *live* in the *present*. I only remember the past—and anticipate the future. I love to live, I love reform better than its modes. There is no history of how bad became better. I believe something, and there is nothing else but that. I know that I am—I know that [ano]ther is who knows more than I who takes interest in me, whose creature and yet [whose] kindred, in one sense, am I. I know that the enterprise is worthy—I know that things work well. I have heard no bad news.

As for positions—as for combinations and details—what are they? In clear weather when we look into the heavens, what do we see, but the sky and the sun?

If you would convince a man that he does wrong do right. But do not care to convince him.—Men will believe what they see. Let them see.

Pursue, keep up with, circle round and round your life as a dog does his master's chaise. Do what you love. Know your own bone; gnaw at it, bury it, unearth it, and gnaw it [still. Do not be too] moral. You may cheat yourself out of much life so. Aim above morality. Be not *simply* good—be good for something.—All fables indeed have their morals, but the innocent enjoy the story.

Let nothing come between you and the light. Respect men as brothers only. When you travel to the celestial city, carry no letter of introduction. When you knock ask to see God—none of the servants. In what

concerns you much do not think that you have companions—know that you are alone in the world.

Thus I write at random. I need to see you, and I trust I shall, to correct my mistakes. Perhaps you have some oracles for me

[Henry Thoreau.]

Text, Familiar Letters of Thoreau, pp. 192–95, for all before the last six paragraphs; beginning with "My actual life," they are an undated fragment in Berg—perhaps the final portion of the letter itself or else the final portion of a draft Thoreau composed first. The bracketed portions have been cut or torn out; we replace them with Sanborn's printed text.

From HORACE GREELEY

New York, April 3, 1848

My Friend Thoreau:

I have but this moment received yours of 31st ult. and was greatly relieved by the breaking of your long silence. Yet it saddens and surprises me to know that your article was not paid for by Graham; and, since my honor is involved in the matter, I will see that you *are* paid, and that at no distant day. I shall not forget the matter, and hope you will not feel annoyed at my interference in the business. I choose to speak about it, and don't believe Graham will choose to differ with me. Don't fear for my time; I expect to visit Philadelphia on my own business next week, and will have time to look into the matter.

As to "Katahdin and the Maine Woods," I will take it and send you the money if I cannot dispose of it more to your advantage within the week ensuing. I hope I can.

Yours,
Horace Greeley.

For further details of the "Graham matter" see Greeley's letter of February 5, 1847. "Ktaadn and the Maine Woods," now the first portion of

The Maine Woods, was eventually placed by Greeley in John Sartain's Union Magazine, where it was serialized for five issues, July–November 1848. MS., Morgan.

From HORACE GREELEY

New York, April 17, 1848.

My Friend Thoreau,

I have been hurried about a thousand things, including a Charter Election, and have not yet settled your business with Graham. I went to Philadelphia last Wednesday, and called twice at Graham's office without finding him; and though I *did* see him in the evening, it was at a crowded dinner party where I had no chance to speak with him on business. But I have taken that matter in hand, and I will see that you are paid,—within a week, I hope, but at any rate soon.

I enclose you $25 for your article on Maine Scenery, as promised. I know it is worth more though I have not yet found time to read it; but I have tried once to sell it without success. It is rather long for my columns and too fine for the million; but I consider it a cheap bargain, and shall print it myself if I do not dispose of it to better advantage. You will not of course consider yourself under any sort of obligation to me, for my offer was in the way of business and I have got more than the worth of my money. Send me a line acknowledging the receipt of the money, and say if all is right between us. I am a little ashamed of Graham's tardiness, but I shall correct it, and I would have done so long ago if I had known he had neglected you. I shall make it come round soon.

If you will write me two or three articles in the course of the summer, I think I can dispose of them for your benefit. But write not more than half as long as your article just sent me, for that is too long for the Magazines. If that were in two it would be far more valuable.

What about your book? Is any thing going on about it now? Why did not Emerson try it in England? I think the Howitts could get it

favorably before the British public. If you can suggest any way wherein I can put it forward, do not hesitate, but command me.

Yours,
Horace Greeley.

With the manuscript there is a sheet stating:
$25 enclosed

$5. *Appleton Boston*
5. *Bridgeport, Conn.*
5   *Globe, Providence*
5   *Brattleboro, Vt.*
5   *FICU. Burlington Vt.*

But, although this letter is supposed to have enclosed the sum mentioned, we are not sure that this particular sheet belongs with the letter.
MS., Yale University Library.

To H. G. O. BLAKE

Concord, May 2, 1848.

"We must have our bread." But what is our bread? Is it baker's bread? Methinks it should be very *home-made* bread. What is our meat? Is it butcher's meat? What is that which we *must* have? Is that bread which we are now earning sweet? Is it not bread which has been suffered to sour, and then been sweetened with an alkali, which has undergone the vinous, acetous, and sometimes the putrid fermentation, and then been whitened with vitriol? Is this the bread which we must have? Man must earn his bread by the sweat of his brow, truly, but also by the sweat of his brain within his brow. The body can feed the body only. I have tasted but little bread in my life. It has been mere grub and provender for the most part. Of bread that nourished the brain and the heart, scarcely any. There is absolutely none even on the tables of the rich.

There is not one kind of food for all men. You must and you will feed those faculties which you exercise. The laborer whose body is weary does not require the same food with the scholar whose brain is weary. Men should not labor foolishly like brutes, but the brain and the body should always, or as much as possible, work and rest together, and then the work will be of such a kind that when the body is hungry the brain will be hungry also, and the same food will suffice for both; otherwise the food which repairs the waste energy of the over-wrought body will oppress the sedentary brain, and the degenerate scholar will come to esteem all food vulgar, and all getting a living drudgery.

How shall we earn our bread is a grave question; yet it is a sweet and inviting question. Let us not shirk it, as is usually done. It is the most important and practical question which is put to man. Let us not answer it hastily. Let us not be content to get our bread in some gross, careless, and hasty manner. Some men go a-hunting, some a-fishing, some a-gaming, some to war; but none have so pleasant a time as they who in earnest seek to earn their bread. It is true actually as it is true really; it is true materially as it is true spiritually, that they who seek honestly and sincerely, with all their hearts and lives and strength, to earn their bread, do earn it, and it is sure to be very sweet to them. A very little bread,—a very few crumbs are enough, if it be of the right quality, for it is infinitely nutritious. Let each man, then, earn at least a crumb of bread for his body before he dies, and know the taste of it,— that it is identical with the bread of life, and that they both go down at one swallow.

Our bread need not ever be sour or hard to digest. What Nature is to the mind she is also to the body. As she feeds my imagination, she will feed my body; for what she says she means, and is ready to do. She is not simply beautiful to the poet's eye. Not only the rainbow and sunset are beautiful, but to be fed and clothed, sheltered and warmed aright, are equally beautiful and inspiring. There is not necessarily any gross and ugly fact which may not be eradicated from the life of man. We should endeavor practically in our lives to correct all the defects which our imagination detects. The heavens are as deep as our aspirations are high. So high as a tree aspires to grow, so high it will find an atmosphere suited to it. Every man should stand for a force which is perfectly irresistible. How can any man be weak who dares *to be* at all? Even the tenderest plants force their way up through the hardest earth, and the crevices of rocks; but a man no material power can resist. What

a wedge, what a beetle, what a catapult, is an *earnest* man! What can resist him?

It is a momentous fact that a man may be *good,* or he may be *bad;* his life may be *true,* or it may be *false;* it may be either a shame or a glory to him. The good man builds himself up; the bad man destroys himself.

But whatever we do we must do confidently (if we are timid, let us, then, act timidly), not expecting more light, but having light enough. If we confidently expect more, then let us wait for it. But what is this which we have? Have we not already waited? Is this the beginning of time? Is there a man who does not see clearly beyond, though only a hair's breadth beyond where he at any time stands?

If one hesitates in his path, let him not proceed. Let him respect his doubts, for doubts, too, may have some divinity in them. That we have but little faith is not sad, but that we have but little faithfulness. By faithfulness faith is earned. When, in the progress of a life, a man swerves, though only by an angle infinitely small, from his proper and allotted path (and this is never done quite unconsciously even at first; in fact, that was his broad and scarlet sin,—ah, he knew of it more than he can tell), then the drama of his life turns to tragedy, and makes haste to its fifth act. When once we thus fall behind ourselves, there is no accounting for the obstacles which rise up in our path, and no one is so wise as to advise, and no one so powerful as to aid us while we abide on that ground. Such are cursed with *duties,* and the *neglect of their duties.* For such the decalogue was made, and other far more voluminous and terrible codes.

These departures,—who have not made them?—for they are as faint as the parallax of a fixed star, and at the commencement we say they are nothing,—that is, they originate in a kind of sleep and forgetfulness of the soul when it is naught. A man cannot be too circumspect in order to keep in the straight road, and be sure that he sees all that he may at any time see, that so he may distinguish his true path.

You ask if there is no doctrine of sorrow in my philosophy. Of acute sorrow I suppose that I know comparatively little. My saddest and most genuine sorrows are apt to be but transient regrets. The place of sorrow is supplied, perchance, by a certain hard and proportionably barren indifference. I am of kin to the sod, and partake largely of its dull patience,—in winter expecting the sun of spring. In my cheapest moments I am apt to think that it is not my business to be "seeking the

spirit," but as much its business to be seeking me. I know very well what Goethe meant when he said that he never had a chagrin but he made a poem out of it. I have altogether too much patience of this kind. I am too easily contented with a slight and almost animal happiness. My happiness is a good deal like that of the woodchucks.

Methinks I am never quite committed, never wholly the creature of my moods, being always to some extent their critic. My only integral experience is in my vision. I see, perchance, with more integrity than I feel.

But I need not tell you what manner of man I am,—my virtues or my vices. You can guess if it is worth the while; and I do not discriminate them well.

I do not write this time at my hut in the woods. I am at present living with Mrs. Emerson, whose house is an old home of mine, for company during Mr. Emerson's absence.

You will perceive that I am as often talking to myself, perhaps, as speaking to you.

Text, Familiar Letters of Thoreau, *pp. 197–203.*

From HORACE GREELEY

Dear Friend Thoreau,—

I trust you have not thought me neglectful or dilatory with regard to your business. I have done my very best, throughout, and it is only to-day that I have been able to lay my hand on the money due you from Graham. I have been to see him in Philadelphia, but did not catch him in his business office; then I have been here to meet him, and been referred to his brother, etc. I finally found the two numbers of the work in which your article was published (not easy, I assure you, for he has them not, nor his brother, and I hunted them up, and bought one of them at a very out-of-the-way place), and with these I made out a regular bill for the contribution; drew a draft on G. R. Graham

for the amount, gave it to his brother here for collection, and to-day received the money. Now you see how to get pay yourself, another time; I have pioneered the way, and you can follow it easily yourself. There has been no intentional injustice on Graham's part; but he is overwhelmed with business, has too many irons in the fire, and we did not go at him the right way. Had you drawn a draft on him, at first, and given it to the Concord Bank to send in for collection, you would have received your money long since. Enough of this. I have made Graham pay you $75, but I only send you $50, for, having got so much for Carlyle, I am ashamed to take your "Maine Woods" for $25.

I have expectations of procuring it a place in a new magazine of high character that will pay. I don't expect to get as much for it as for Carlyle, but I hope to get $50. If you are satisfied to take the $25 for your "Maine Woods," say so, and I will send on the money; but I don't want to seem a Jew, buying your articles at half price to speculate upon. If you choose to let it go that way, it shall be so; but I would sooner do my best for you, and send you the money.

Thoreau, if you will only write one or two articles, when in the spirit, about half the length of this, I can sell it readily and advantageously. The length of your papers is the only impediment to their appreciation by the magazines. Give me one or two shorter, and I will try to coin them speedily.

Sanborn assigns the date May 17, 1848 to this letter. Text, Sanborn's Henry D. Thoreau, *pp. 224–26, 228.*

To HORACE GREELEY

Concord May 19th 1848.

My Friend Greeley,
    I received from you fifty dollars today.—
    For the last five years I have supported myself solely by the labors of my hands— I have not received one cent from any other source, and

this has cost me so little time, say a month in the spring and another in the autumn, doing the coarsest work of all kinds, that I have probably enjoyed more leisure for literary pursuits than any contemporary. For more than two years past I have lived alone in the woods, in a good plastered and shingled house entirely of my own building, earning only what I wanted, and sticking to my proper work. The fact is man need not live by the sweat of his brow—unless he sweats easier than I do—he needs so little. For two years and two months all my expenses have amounted to but 27 cents a week, and I have fared gloriously in all respects. If a man must have money, and he needs but the smallest amount, the true and independent way to earn it is by day-labor with his hands at a dollar a day.—I have tried many ways and can speak from experience.—Scholars are apt to think themselves privileged to complain as if their lot was a peculiarly hard one. How much have we heard about the attainment of knowledge under difficulties of poets starving in garrets—depending on the patronage of the wealthy—and finally dying mad. It is time that men sang another song. There is no reason why the scholar who professes to be a little wiser than the mass of men, should not do his work in the ditch occasionally, and by means of his superior wisdom make much less suffice for him. A wise man will not be unfortunate. How then would you know but he was a fool?

This money therefore comes as a free and even unexpected gift to me—

My Friend Greeley, I know not how to thank you for your kindness—to thank you is not the way—I can only assure you that I see and appreciate it—To think that while I have been sitting comparatively idle here, you have been so active in my behalf!

You have done well for me. I only wish it had been a better cause—Yet the value of good deeds is not affected by the unworthiness of their object. Yes—that was the right way, but who would ever have thought of it? I think it might not have occurred to somewhat of a business man. I am not one in the common sense at all—that is, I am not acquainted with the forms—I might have way-laid him perhaps. I perceive that your way has this advantage too, that he who draws the draft determines the amount which it is drawn for. You prized it well, that was the exact amount.

If more convenient the Maine article might be printed in the form of letters; you have only to leave off at the end of a day, and put the date before the next one. I shall certainly be satisfied to receive $25.00

for it—that was all I expected if you *took* it—but I do not by any means consider you bound to pay me that—the article not being what you asked for, and being sent after so long a delay. You shall therefore, if you take it, send me 25 dollars now, or when you have disposed of it, which-ever is most convenient—that is, after deducting the necessary expenses which I perceive you must have incurred. This is all I ask for it.

The carrier it is commonly who makes the money—I am concerned to see that you as carrier make nothing at all—but are in danger of losing a good deal of your time as well as some of your money.

So I got off—rather so I am compelled to go off muttering my inef-fectual thanks. But believe me, my Friend, the gratification which your letter affords me is not wholly selfish.

Trusting that my good genius will continue to protect me on this accession of wealth, I remain

Yours
Henry Thoreau

P. S.   My book is swelling again under my hands, but as soon as I have leisure I shall see to those shorter articles. So, look out.

MS., Boston Public Library.

To EMERSON

Concord May 21st 1848

Dear Friend

Mrs. Emerson is in Boston whither she went with Eddy yester-day Saturday, and I do not know that my news will be worth sending alone. Perhaps she will come home in season to send with me from Concord. The Steam mill was burnt last night—it was a fine sight light-ing up the rivers and meadows. The owners who bought it the other day for seven thousand dollars, though it was indeed insured for six,

I hear since will be gainers rathers that losers—but some individuals who hired of them have lost—my Father probably more than any—from four to five hundred dollars, not being insured. Some think that it was set on fire. I have no doubt that the wise fates did set it on fire, I quite agree with them that that disgrace to Concord enterprise & skill needed to be burnt away. It was a real purification as far as it went, and evidence of it was come to every man's door. I picked up cinders *in your yard* this morning 6 inches long—though there was no wind.

Your trees are doing very well; but one died in the winter—the Watson pear, a native, which apparently grew more than any other last year, and hence it died. I am a constant foe to the caterpillars.

Mr. Alcott recommenced work on the Arbor yesterday, or rather commenced repairs— But enough of this

Mr. [Cyrus] Warren tells me that he is on the point of buying the hill field for you perhaps for a hundred dollars, and he remembers that you would allow him and [Cyrus ?] Stow the privilege of a *way* to their fields— I should beware how I suffered him to transact this business with such an implied privilege for his compensation. It would certainly greatly reduce the value of the field to you.

Your island wood was severely burnt—but Reuben Brown say[s] that it may stand till winter without harm before it is cut. He suffered his own to stand last year. There are applications for the Walden field and house which await your attention when you come home.

The proposition for a new journal is likely to fall among inflammable materials here—& excite another short and ineffectual blaze. As for me, I cannot yet join the *journalists* any more than the Fourierites—for I can not adopt their principles—one reason is because I do not know what they are. Men talk as if you couldn't get good things printed, but I *think* as if you couldn't get them written. That at least is the whole difficulty with me.

I am more interested in the private journal than the public one, and it would be better news to me to hear that there were two or three valuable papers being written in England & America—that might be printed sometime—than that there were 30,000 dollars to defray expenses—& forty thousand men standing *ready to write* merely, but no certainty of anything valuable being written. The blacksmiths met together looking grim and voted to have a thunderbolt; if they could only to get someone to launch it, but all the while there was not one man among them who could *make* anything better than a horse-shoe nail.

Who has any desire to split himself any further up, by straddling the Atlantic? We are extremities enough already. There is danger of one's straddling so far that he can never recover an upright position. There are certain men in Old & New England who aspire to the renown of the Colossus of Rhodes, and to have ships sail under them.

Those who build castles in the air generally have one foot in the moon.

What after all is the value of a journal, the best that we know—but a short essay once in 2 or 3 years which you can read—separated by impassable swamps of ink & paper— It is the combination that makes the swamp, but not the firm oasis—

A journal 2 or 3 times as good as the best English one even would not be worth the while— It would not interest you nor me.

To be sure there is no telling what an individual may do, but it is easy to tell what half a dozen men may *not* do unless they are to a certain extent united as one.

How was it with the Mass. Quart. Rev., several men undertook to make a small book for mankind to read—& advertised then what they were about some months before hand—and after considerable delay they brought it out—& I read it, or what I could of it, and certainly if one man had written it all a wise publisher would not have advised to print it. It should have been suppressed for nobody was starving for *that*. It probably is not so good a book as the Boston Almanack—or that little book about the same size which Mr Spaulding has just put out called his Practical Thoughts—for Mr Spaulding's contains more of autobiography at least. In this case there is nothing to come to the rescue of. Is it the publisher?—or the reputation of the editors? The journal itself has no character. Shall we make a rush to save a piece of paper which is falling to the ground? It is as good as anybody seriously designed that it should be or meant to make it.—But I am ashamed to write such things as these.

I am glad to hear that you are writing so much. Lecturing is of little consequence. Dont forget to inquire after Persian and Hindoo books in London or Paris. Ellen & Edith are as well as flies. I have had earnest letters from H. G. O. Blake. Greeley has sent me $100 dollars and wants more manuscript.

But this and all this letter are nothing to the purpose.

H. Thoreau

P. S. 22nd Mrs E. has come home tonight and opened your letter. I am glad to find that you are expecting a line from me, since I have a better excuse for sending this hard scrawl. I trust however that the most prosaic Concord news acquires a certain value by the time it reaches London, as Concord cranberries have done. But dont think that these berries have soured by the way, as did the first received— They are naturally harsh and sour. Yet I think that I could listen kindly and without selfishness to men's projected enterprises if they were not too easy.—if they were struggles not into death but even into life. I read in a Texas paper sent to you that there was a farm for sale in that country "suitable for a man of small force." You had better make a minute of this for the benefit of some of your literary acquaintances.

This is the last letter to Emerson in England. He returned to America in July. On May 20, 1848 a steam mill in Concord belonging to Abel Moore, Sherman Barrett, and others was completely destroyed by fire. Mrs. Caleb Wheeler, an authority on Concord history, believes that the Thoreau family rented part of this mill to manufacture the wooden part of the pencils. She states that a newspaper of the day lists it as a "sawmill, grist mill and lead pencil manufactury." MS., Harvard.

From HORACE GREELEY

[. . . Don't scold at my publishing a part of your last private letter (May 19, 1848) in this morning's paper. It will do great good. . . . I am so importuned by young loafers who want to be hired in some intellectual capacity so as to develope their minds—that is, get a broad-cloth living, without doing any vulgar labor—that I could not refrain from using against them the magnificent weapon you so unconsciously furnished me. . . .]

<I send you the $25 for your "Maine Woods," as you positively say that will be enough; but I shall feel like a Jew when I sell the article for more, and pocket the money.>

Write me something shorter when the spirit moves (never write a line otherwise, for the hack writer is a slavish beast, *I* know), and I will sell it for you soon. I want one shorter article from your pen that will be quoted, as these long articles cannot be, and let the public know something of your way of thinking and seeing. It will do good. What do you think of following out your thought in an essay on "The Literary Life?" You need not make a personal allusion but I know you can write an article worth reading on that theme when you are in the vein.

[Horace Greeley]

Sanborn assigns the date May 25, 1848 to the letter. Text, *Sanborn's* Henry D. Thoreau, *p. 228; printed with additions (in brackets) from the catalogue of the Kennard sale (Charles F. Libbie & Co., April 26–27, 1904) and an addition (in broken brackets) from the catalogue of the Gable sale (American Art Association, March 10–11, 1924).*

———————

To GEORGE THATCHER

Concord Aug. 24th 1848.

Dear Cousin,

If it is not too late I will thank you for your letter and your sympathy. I send you with this the third part, as they have chosen to call it, of that everlasting mountain story. I presume that the other two have reached you. They had bargained, as I thought to send me many copies for distribution, but I have received none. It should have been printed all together in some large newspaper—and then it would have gone down at one dose by its very gravity. I was sorry to hear that you came so near Concord without coming here. It always does us good to see you. Mr. Emerson came home on the Europa 3 or 4 weeks ago, in good health and spirits. I think that he has seen English men, such as are worth seeing, more thoroughly than any traveller. He has made them better acquainted with one another and with Americans. He had access

to circles which are inaccessible to most travellers, but which are none the better for that. He has seen the elephant—or perhaps I should say the British lion now, and was made a lion of himself. He found Carlyle the most interesting man—as I expected he would—Stonehenge the most interesting piece of antiquity—and the London Times newspaper the best book which England is printing nowadays.

Travelling is so cheap at present that I am tempted to make you a visit—but then, as usual, I have so much idle business that cannot be postponed—if any will believe it! The probable failure of the melon crop this season is *melon*choly—but fortunately *our* potatoes do not rot yet. I feel somewhat encouraged at the political prospects of the country, not because the new party have chosen such a leader, but because they are perhaps worthy of a better one. The N.E. delegation seems to have managed affairs in a bungling manner. If they had gone prepared they might have had their own man. But who is he? It is time to be done selecting available men; for what are they not available who do thus?

Father desires to be remembered to you & to Mrs. Thatcher—and to the last named does also

yours sincerely
Henry Thoreau

"That everlasting mountain story" was Thoreau's essay on Ktaadn, appearing serially that summer and fall in the Union Magazine. *The year brought forth many new political groups; Thoreau was probably referring to the Free Soil Party, which met in convention in Buffalo August 9, 1848 and nominated Van Buren.* MS., Abernethy (*typescript*).

From HAWTHORNE

Salem, October 21st, 1848.

My dear Sir,

    The Managers of the Salem Lyceum, some time ago, voted that you should be requested to deliver a Lecture before that Institution,

during the approaching season. I know not whether Mr Chever, the late corresponding Secretary, communicated the vote to you; at all events, no answer has been received, and, as Mr Chever's succesor in office, I am instructed to repeat the invitation. Permit me to add my own earnest wishes that you will accept it—and also, laying aside my official dignity, to express my wife's desire and my own that you will be our guest, if you do come.

In case of your compliance, the Managers would be glad to know at what time it will best suit you to deliver the Lecture.

Very truly Yours,
Nathl Hawthorne,
Cor. Secy Salem Lyceum.

P. S.   I live at No 14, Mall Street—where I shall be very happy to see you. The stated fee for Lectures is $20.

Here is the first extant letter from Hawthorne to Thoreau. Thoreau accepted this invitation from his old Concord friend and delivered a lecture on "Student life in New England, Its Economy," a portion of what was to be the first chapter of Walden, *before the Salem Lyceum on November 22, 1848. Probably his first lecture outside his native town, it was successful enough for him to be invited to deliver another in Salem before the winter was over. MS., Berg.*

From HORACE GREELEY

[October 28, 1848]

I break a silence of some duration to inform you that I hope on Monday to receive payment for your glorious account of "Ktaadn and the Maine Woods," which I bought of you at a Jew's bargain, and sold to the "Union Magazine." I am to get $75 for it, and, as I don't choose to *exploiter* you at such a rate, I shall insist on inclosing you $25 more

in this letter, which will still leave me $25 to pay various charges and labors I have incurred in selling your articles and getting paid for them,—the latter by far the more difficult portion of the business.

[You must write to the magazines in order to let the public know who and what you are. Ten years hence will do for publishing books.]

[Horace Greeley]

Text, *Sanborn's* Henry D. Thoreau, *p. 227; printed with additions (in brackets) from the catalogue of the Hathaway-Richardson sale (Charles F. Libbie & Co.; May 9–10, 1911).*

From HORACE GREELEY

New York, Nov. 19, 1848.

Friend Thoreau,

Yours of the 17th received. Say we are even on money counts, and let the matter drop. I have tried to serve you, and have been fully paid for my own disbursements and trouble in the business. So we will move on.

I think you will do well to send me some passages from one or both of your new works, to dispose of to the magazines. This will be the best kind of advertisement whether for a publisher or for readers. You may write with an angel's pen, yet your writings have no mercantile, money value till you are known and talked of as an author. Mr. Emerson would have been twice as much known and read if he had written for the magazines a little, just to let common people know of his existence. I believe a chapter from one of your books printed in Graham or The Union will add many to the readers of the volume when issued. Here is the reason why British books sell so much better among us than American—because they are thoroughly advertised through the British Reviews, Magazines and journals which circulate or are copied among us. —However, do as you please. If you choose to send me one of your MSS.

232

I will get it publisher, but I cannot promise you any considerable recompense; and, indeed, if Monroe will do it, that will be better. Your writings are in advance of the general mind here—Boston is nearer their standard.

I never saw the verses you speak of. Won't you send them again? I have been buried up in politics for the last six weeks.

Kind regards to Emerson. It is doubtful about my seeing you this season.

Yours,
Horace Greeley.

Thoreau's "new works" were his Week *and* Walden. *Munroe did finally take the first and publish it at the author's expense in 1849. Its complete failure postponed the publication of* Walden *until 1854. Then Thoreau, taking Greeley's advice, permitted him to publish excerpts in the* Tribune *to arouse interest in the book.* MS., Abernethy (*typescript*).

From HAWTHORNE

Boston, Nov 20th, 1848

My dear Thoreau,

I did not sooner write you, because there were pre-engagements for the two or three first lectures, so that I could not arrange matters to have you come during the present month. But, as it happens, the expected lectures have failed us; and we now depend on you to come this very next Wednesday. I shall announce you in the paper of tomorrow, so you *must* come. I regret that I could not give you longer notice.

We shall expect you on Wednesday, at No 14 Mall. Street.

Yours truly,
Nath Hawthorne.

If it is utterly impossible for you come, pray write me a line so that I may get it Wednesday morning. But, by all means, come.

This Secretaryship is an intolerable bore. I have travelled thirty miles, this wet day for no other business.

MS., Morgan.

———————————

To GEORGE THATCHER

I hear that the Gloucester paper has me in print again, and the Republican—whatever they may say is not to the purpose only as it serves as an advertisement of me. There are very few whose opinion I value.

The date December 26, 1848 is assigned in the catalogue. Text, catalogue of the Joline Sale (*Anderson Auction Co., April 28–29, 1915*).

1849

Gold fever became an American epidemic. On January 30 the *New-York Tribune* listed 131 vessels sailing for California and carrying more than 8,000 passengers to the gold fields. The overland trail was even more popular. On the basis of records kept at Fort Laramie it has been estimated that 30,000 people passed westward over the trail during this year. Beards were popular again, and not only in the West. The United States imported $148,000,000 worth of goods and metals and exported $2,000,000 less—a cause of some headshaking among old-line economists. Food cost roughly one quarter what it costs now. Hoop skirts were coming in. They could be bought or made at home; they were constructed of such materials as steel wires and webbing or reeds and muslin.

In May *A Week on the Concord and Merrimack Rivers* was published by the Boston firm of James Munroe. Book buyers ignored it. Thoreau finally had to make a thousand dollars' worth of pencils for enough profit to pay off the hundred dollars he owed Munroe. But the book was and is, as Alcott said, "purely American, fragrant with the lives of New England woods and streams." It is at least a minor classic. *Walden* itself was ready for publication this year; the lack of success, however, of the *Week* must have delayed it considerably. Even though *Walden* failed to appear, Thoreau was able to publish another and much shorter work that has had its own considerable influence. "Resistance to Civil Government," later called "Civil Disobedience," was included in a set of so-called *Aesthetic Papers* edited by Elizabeth Peabody. Again Thoreau's *Journal* for the year, if it has survived, has not been printed. His letters deal with publishing, lecturing, and nature study.

Boston Feb. 8, 1849

Henry D. Thoreau Esq.
Concord
Mass.

Dear Sir:
    We find on looking over publishing matters that we cannot well undertake anything more at present. If however you feel inclined we will publish "Walden or Life in the Woods" on our own acc, say one Thousand copies, allowing for 10 p^r.c^t. copyright on the Retail Price on all that are sold. The style of printing & binding to be like Emerson's Essays.

Respy
Ticknor & Co.

MS., Harvard (*typescript*).

To GEORGE THATCHER

Concord Feb. 16 1849

Dear George,
    I am going as far as Portland to lecture before their Lyceum on the 3d Wednesday in March.—By the way they pay me $25.00. Now I am not sure but I may have leisure then to go on to Bangor and so up river. I have a great desire to go up to Chesuncook before the ice breaks

up—but I should not care if I had to return down the banks and so saw the logs running; and I write you chiefly to ask how late it will probably do to go up the river—or when on the whole would be the best time for me to start? Will the 3d week in March answer?

I should be very glad if you would go with me, but I hesitate to ask you now, it is so uncertain whether I go at all myself. The fact is I am once more making a bargain with the Publishers Ticknor & Co., who talk of printing a book for me, and if we come to terms I *may* then be confined here correcting proofs—or at most I should have but a few days to spare.

If the Bangor Lyceum should want me about those times, that of course would be very convenient, and a seasonable aid to me.

Shall I trouble you then to give me some of the statistics of a winter excursion to Chesuncook?

Of Helen I have no better news to send. We fear that she may be very gradually failing, but it may not be so. She is not very uncomfortable and still seems to enjoy the day. I do not wish to foresee what change may take place in her condition or in my own.

The rest of us are as well off as we deserve to be.—

Yrs truly
Henry D. Thoreau

Helen Thoreau died May 2, 1849. MS., University of Texas Library; previously unpublished.

From TICKNOR & CO.

Boston, Feby. 16 1849

Henry D. Thoreau Esq
Dear Sir,

In reply to your fav. of 10th inst. we beg to say that we will publish for your acc "A Week on the Concord River."

The following general Estimate based upon vol. ⅓ larger than Emerson's Essays first series (as suggested by you) we present for your consideration—

Say—1000 Cops. 448 pages like Emerson's Essays 1st series printed on good paper @ $4.00 pr ream will cost in sheets $381.24. The binding in our style fine cloth.

12¢ pr Copy—or for the Edn   120.00
                                     $501.24

In the above Estimate we have included for alterations and extractions say $15.00—It may be more or less—This will depend on yourself. The book can be condensed & of course cost less. Our Estimate is in accordance with sample copy. As you would not perhaps, care to bind more than ½ the Edn at once,—you would need to send $450.—to print 1000 cops. & bind ½ of the same.

Your very truly,
W. D. Ticknor & Co.

Concord Mass.

Nothing came of this proposal to publish the Week; *it went instead to Munroe. MS., Harvard (typescript); previously unpublished.*

From HAWTHORNE

Salem, Feb. 19th 1849

My dear Thoreau,

The managers request that you will lecture before the Salem Lyceum on Wednesday evening *after* next—that is to say, on the 28th inst. May we depend on you? Please to answer immediately, if convenient.

Mr. Alcott delighted my wife and me, the other evening, by announcing that you had a book in prep. I rejoice at it, and nothing doubt of such success as will be worth having. Should your manuscripts all be in the

printer's hands, I suppose you can reclaim one of them, for a single evening's use, to be returned the next morning; or perhaps that Indian lecture, which you mentioned to me, is in a state of forwardness. Either that, or a continuation of the Walden experiment (or, indeed, anything else,) will be acceptable.

We shall expect you at 14 Mall Street.

Very truly yours,
Nathl Hawthorne.

Again Thoreau gladly accepted an invitation to the Salem Lyceum and delivered a second lecture on his Walden experiment there on February 28, 1849. There is no other record of his having an Indian lecture; possibly Hawthorne was referring to the lecture on the Maine Woods delivered in Concord the preceding winter. MS., Morgan.

From BRONSON ALCOTT

12 West Street, Boston, Feb. 20, 1849.

Dear Sir,—

I send you herewith the names of a select company of gentlemen, esteemed as deserving of better acquaintance, and disposed for closer fellowship of Thought and Endeavor, who are hereby invited to assemble at No. 12 West Street, on Tuesday, the 20th of March next, to discuss the advantages of organizing a Club or College for the study and diffusion of the Ideas and Tendencies proper to the nineteenth century; and to concert measures, if deemed desirable, for promoting the ends of good fellowship. The company will meet at 10 a.m. Your presence is respectfully claimed by

Yours truly,
A. Bronson Alcott.

*The New England liberals to whom, according to Sanborn, Alcott
sent his circular of invitations were Emerson, William Lloyd Garrison,
Theodore Parker, William Henry Channing, Wendell Phillips, Thomas
T. Stone, F. Henry Hedge, Samuel G. Howe, J. Freeman Clarke, Ed-
mund Quincy, John W. Browne, J. Elliot Cabot, T. Starr King, Lowell,
Samuel G. Ward, John L. Weiss, Edwin P. Whipple, T. Wentworth
Higginson, Parker Pillsbury, Thoreau, Henry I. Bowditch, Henry C.
Wright, John S. Dwight, Francis Jackson, W. Ellery Channing, William
B. Greene, Caleb Stetson, George P. Bradford, Adin Ballou, Jones Very,
William F. Channing, Elizur Wright, Stephen S. Foster, Charles C.
Shackford, Emanuel Scherb, E. P. Clarke, Samuel D. Robbins, Joshua
Melroy, J. T. Fisher, Oliver Johnson, O. B. Frothingham, C. K. Whipple,
Samuel Johnson, James N. Buffum, William H. Knapp, Samuel May,
Jr., Otis Clapp, J. M. Spear, Charles Spear, W. R. Alger, Edward Bangs,
R. F. Walcott, and A. D. Mayo. Out of Alcott's efforts the Town and
Country Club was established in July. It had its ups and downs, includ-
ing an attempt—repelled by Emerson—to admit female intellectuals.
It became the ancestor of a much more famous group, the Saturday
Club, out of which grew the idea for the* Atlantic Monthly. *It does not
appear that Thoreau ever wanted to be active in either club; in fact,
we know that he declined to take part in the Saturday Club. For a full
but rambling discussion of the background to this letter see Sanborn's
memoir of Alcott in his and William T. Harris's* A. Bronson Alcott: His
Life and Philosophy, *II, 459–94; text, p. 461.*

To GEORGE THATCHER

Concord, March 16, 1849

Dear Cousin:

    I shall lecture in Portland next Wednesday. It happens, as I
feared it would, that I am now receiving the proof sheets of my book
from the printers, so that without great inconvenience I can not make
you a visit at present. I trust that I shall be able to ere long. I thank you
heartily for your exertions in my behalf with the Bangor Lyceum—but

unless I should hear that they want *two* lectures to be read in *one* week or nearer together, I shall have to decline coming, this time.

Helen remains about the same.

Yours in haste,
Henry D. Thoreau

Thoreau repeated his Salem lecture in Portland during this month. Maria Thoreau, in a letter to "P" quoted in Canby's Thoreau *(p. 248), states: "George wants him to keep on to Bangor they want to have him there, and if their funds hold out they intend to send for him, they give 25 dollars." But apparently the Bangor lecture was never delivered. MS., Miss Charlotte Thatcher; previously unpublished.*

To GEORGE THATCHER

[March 22, 1849]

The first thing I saw on being introduced to the Portland Lyceum last evening was your letter. . . . Mr. Emerson follows me here. I am just in the midst of printing my book, which is likely to turn out much larger than I expected. I shall advertise another, "Walden, or Life in the Woods," in the first which by the way I call "A Week on the Concord and Merrimack Rivers."

Text, catalogue of the Haber sale (*Anderson Galleries; December 7–8, 1909*).

To ELIZABETH PEABODY

Concord April 5th 1849

Miss Peabody,

I have so much writing to do at present, with the printers in the rear of me, that I have almost no time left, but for bodily exercise; however, I will send you the article in question before the end of next week. If this will not be soon enough will you please inform me by the next mail.

Yrs respectly
Henry D. Thoreau

P.S.   I offer the paper to your *first volume* only.

Thoreau's "Resistance to Civil Government" (later better known as "Civil Disobedience") appeared in the first and only volume of Elizabeth Peabody's Aesthetic Papers *in May 1849. MS., Historical Society of Pennsylvania; previously unpublished.*

To H. G. O. BLAKE

Concord Ap. 17th 1849

Dear Sir,

It is my intention to leave Concord for Worcester, via Groton, at 12 o'clock on Friday of this week. Mr Emerson tells me that it will take about two hours to go by this way. At any rate I shall try to [secure] 3 or 4 hours in which to see you & Worcester before the lecture.

Yrs in haste
Henry D. Thoreau

H. G. O. Blake took a decided interest in Thoreau's lecture career and saw to it that he was offered the opportunity to speak in Worcester at least once almost every winter. This first Worcester lecture was delivered in City Hall April 20, 1849. It was followed by a second on April 27. MS., Berg; copy in Blake's hand; previously unpublished. There is some question whether the month is "Ap." or "Sp.", but the only record of Thoreau's lecturing in Worcester in 1849 is of April. The bracketed word read as "secure" is partly torn from Blake's copy.

To LOUIS AGASSIZ

Concord *Mass* June 30th -49

Dear Sir,

Being disappointed in not finding you in Boston a week or two since, I requested Dr. [Augustus A.] Gould to make some inquiries of you for me; but now, as I shall not be able to see that gentleman for some time, I have decided to apply to you directly.

Suffice it to say, that one of the directors of the Bangor (Me.) Lyceum has asked me to ascertain simply—and I think this a good Yankee way of doing the business—whether you will read *two* or *three* lectures before that institution early in the next lecture season, and if so, what remuneration you will expect. Of course they would be glad to hear more lectures, but they are afraid that they may not have money enough to pay for them.

You may recognize in your correspondent the individual who forwarded to you through Mr Cabot many firkins of fishes and turtles a few years since and who also had the pleasure of an introduction to you at Marlboro' Chapel.

Will you please to answer this note as soon as convenient?

Yrs. respectfully,
Henry D. Thoreau

It was probably at the request of Thoreau's cousin George Thatcher that Thoreau tried to obtain Agassiz as a speaker for the Bangor Lyceum. MS., Harvard; previously unpublished.

From LOUIS AGASSIZ

Dear Sir,

I remember with much pleasure the time you used to send me specimens from your vicinity and also our short interview in the Marlborough Chapel. I am under too many obligations of your kindness to forget it, and I am very sorry that I missed your visit in Boston, but for 18 months I have now been settled in Cambridge.

It would give me great pleasure to engage for the lectures you ask from me, on behalf of the Bangor Lyceum; but I find it has been last winter such an heavy tax upon my health, that I wish *for the present* to make no engagements, as I have some hopes of making my living this year by other efforts and beyond the necessity of my wants, both domestic and scientific, I am determined not to exert myself, as all the time I can thus secure to myself must be exclusively devoted to science. You see this does not look much like business making; but my only business is my intercourse with nature and could I do without draughtsmen, lithographers &c &c I would live still more retired. This will satisfy you, that whenever you come this way, I shall be delighted to see you, since I have also heard something of your mode of living.

With great regard
Sincerely yours
L R Agassiz

Henry D. Thoreau

Agassiz has moved to Cambridge to take up his new professorship at Harvard. His letter to Thoreau, undated, is postmarked Cambridge, July 5 (no year). It clearly answers Thoreau's of June 30. MS., Morgan.

To ELLEN EMERSON

Concord July 31st 1849

Dear Ellen,
        I think that we are pretty well acquainted, though we never had any very long talks. We have had a good many short talks, at any rate. Dont you remember how we used to despatch our breakfast two winters ago, as soon as Eddy could get on his feeding tire, which was not always remembered, before the rest of the household had come down? Dont you remember our wise criticisms on the pictures in the portfolio and the Turkish book with Eddy and Edith looking on,—how almost any pictures answered our purpose, and we went through the Penny Magazine, first from beginning to end, and then from end to beginning, and Eddy stared just as much the second time as the first, and Edith thought that we turned over too soon, and that there were some things which she had not seen—? I can guess pretty well what interests you, and what you think about. Indeed I am interested in pretty much the same things myself. I suppose you think that persons who are as old as your father and myself are always thinking about very grave things, but I know that we are meditating the same old themes that we did when we were ten years old, only we go more gravely about it. You love to write or to read a fairy story and that is what you will always like to do, in some form or other. By and by you will discover that you want what are called the necessaries of life only that you may realize some such dream.
        Eddy has got him a fish-pole and line with a pin-hook at the end, which he flourishes over the dry ground and the carpet at the risk of tearing out our eyes; but when I told him that he must have a cork and a sinker, his mother took off the pin and tied on a cork instead; but he doubts whether that will catch fish as well. He tells me that he is five years old. Indeed I was present at the celebration of his birthday lately, and supplied the company with onion and squash pipes, and rhubarb whistles, which is the most I can do on such occasions. Little Sammy Hoar blowed them most successfully, and made the loudest noise, though it almost strained his eyes out to do it. Edith is full of spirits. When she comes home from school, she goes hop skip and jump down into the field to pick berries, currants, gooseberries, raspberries, and thimbleberries; if there is one of these that has thoughts of changing its

245

hue by to-morrow morning, I guess that Edith knows something about it and will consign it to her basket for Grandmama.

Children may now be seen going a-berrying in all directions. The white-lillies are in blossom, and the john'swort and goldenrod are beginning to come out. Old people say that we have not had so warm a summer for thirty years. Several persons have died in consequence of the heat,—Mr [Obadiah] Kendal, perhaps, for one. The Irishmen on the railroad were obliged to leave off their work for several days, and the farmers left their fields and sought the shade. William Brown of the poor house is dead,—the one who used to ask for a cent—"Give me a cent?" I wonder who will have his cents now!

I found a nice penknife on the bank of the river this afternoon, which was probably lost by some villager who went there to bathe lately. Yesterday I found a nice arrowhead, which was lost some time before by an Indian who was hunting there. The knife was a very little rusted; the arrowhead was not rusted at all.

You must see the sun rise out of the ocean before you come home. I think that Long Island will not be in the way, if you climb to the top of the hill—at least, no more than Bolster Island, and Pillow Hill and even the Lowlands of Never-get-up are elsewhere.

Do not think that you must write to me because I have written to you. It does not follow at all. You would not naturally make so long a speech to me here in a month as a letter would be. Yet if sometime it should be perfectly easy, and pleasant to you, I shall be very glad to have a sentence

Your old acquaintance
Henry Thoreau

In June 1849 Emerson's eldest child, then ten, went to Staten Island to visit her cousins for the summer. MS., Raymond Emerson.

To H. G. O. BLAKE

Concord, August 10, 1849

Mr. Blake,—

I write now chiefly to say, before it is too late, that I shall be glad to see you in Concord, and will give you a chamber, etc., in my father's house, and as much of my poor company as you can bear.

I am in too great haste this time to speak to your, or out of my, condition. I might say,—you might say,—comparatively speaking, be not anxious to avoid poverty. In this way the wealth of the universe may be securely invested. What a pity if we do not live this short time according to the laws of the long time,—the eternal laws! Let us see that we stand erect here, and do not lie along by our *whole length* in the dirt. Let our meanness be our footstool, not our cushion. In the midst of this labyrinth let us live a *thread* of life. We must act with so rapid and resistless a purpose in *one* direction, that our vices will necessarily trail behind. The nucleus of a comet is almost a star. Was there ever a genuine dilemma? The laws of earth are for the feet, or inferior man; the laws of heaven are for the head, or superior man; the latter are the former sublimed and expanded, even as radii from the earth's centre go on diverging into space. Happy the man who observes the heavenly and the terrestrial law in just proportion; whose every faculty, from the soles of his feet to the crown of his head, obeys the law of its level; who neither stoops nor goes on tiptoe, but lives a balanced life, acceptable to nature and to God.

These things I say; other things I do.

I am sorry to hear that you did not receive my book earlier. I addressed it and left it in Munroe's shop to be sent to you immediately, on the twenty-sixth of May, before a copy had been sold.

Will you remember me to Mr. Brown, when you see him next: he is well remembered by

Henry Thoreau.

I still owe you a worthy answer.

This is our first reference to the actual publication of the Week, *which fell so far short of adequate recognition. Mr. Brown was Theophilus Brown, an earnest-eyed, bearded Worcester tailor and frequent com-*

panion of Blake on his visits to Thoreau. Text, Familiar Letters of Thoreau, *pp. 208–9.*

From J. A. FROUDE

S. D. Darbishire Esq. Manchester Sept 3 1849

Dear Mr Thoreau

    I have long intended to write you, to thank you for that noble expression of yourself you were good enough to send to me. I know not why I have not done so; except from a foolish sense that I should not write till I had thought of something to say which it would be worth your while to read.

    What can I say to you except express the honour & the love I feel for you. An honour and a love which Emerson taught me long ago to feel, but which I feel now "not on account of his word, but because I myself have read & know you."

    When I think of what you are—of what you have *done* as well as of what you have written, I have a right to tell you that there is no man living upon this earth at present, whose friendship or whose notice I value more than yours; What are these words? Yet I wished to say something—and I must use words though they serve but seldom in these days for much but lies.

    In your book and in one other also from your side of the Atlantic "Margaret" I see hope for the coming world. all else which I have found true in any of our thinkers, (or even of yours) is their flat denial of what is false in the modern popular jargon—but for their positive affirming side they do but fling us back upon our human nature, stoically to hold on by that with our own strength—A few *men* here & there may do this as the later Romans did—but *mankind* cannot and I have gone near to despair—I am growing not to despair, and I thank you for a helping hand.

    Well I must see you sometime or other. It is not such a great matter with these steam bridges. I wish to shake hands with you, and look a brave honest man in the face. In the mean time I will but congratulate

you on the age in which your work is cast, the world has never seen one more pregnant.

God bless you
Your friend (if you will let him call you so)
J A Froude

This letter from the English historian, who was also an intimate friend and biographer of Thomas Carlyle, is one of the few evidences Thoreau ever received that he might someday have a wide influence abroad. The "noble expression of yourself" was a copy of the Week *inscribed to Froude, now in* Berg. Margaret: A Tale of the Real and Ideal *was a novel by the minor Transcendentalist Sylvester Judd.* MS., Hosmer collection; *copy in an unknown hand.*

To JARED SPARKS

Concord Mass. Sep 17—'49

Sir,

Will you allow me to trouble you with my affairs?

I wish to get permission to take books from the College library to Concord where I reside. I am encouraged to ask this, not merely because I am an alumnus of Harvard, residing within a moderate distance of her halls, but *because I have chosen letters for my profession,* and so am one of the clergy embraced by the spirit at least of her rule. Moreover, though books are to some extent my stock and tools, I have not the usual means with which to purchase them. I therefore regard myself as one whom especially the library was created to serve. If I should change my pursuit or move further off, I should no longer be entitled to this privilege.—I would fain consider myself an *alumnus* in more than a merely historical sense, and I ask only that the University may help to finish the education, whose foundation she has helped to lay. I was not then ripe for her higher courses, and now that I am riper I trust that I am not too far away to be instructed by her. Indeed I see not how her

children can more properly or effectually keep up a living connexion with their Alma Mater than by continuing to draw from her intellectual nutriment in some such way as this.

If you will interest yourself to obtain the above privilege for me, I shall be truly obliged to you.

Yrs respectly
Henry D. Thoreau

Perry Miller, in Consciousness in Concord, *where this letter was first printed (p. 37), points out that it puts the lie to Emerson's anecdote (in his funeral address for Thoreau) of Thoreau's interview with Sparks, the president of Harvard, to obtain use of the library. Miller also notes that while Sparks simply wrote "one year" in the margin of this letter, Thoreau continued to use the privilege for the rest of his life. How Thoreau managed to borrow volumes from the Harvard Library in 1841 and on September 11, 1849, before this letter was written (as is indicated in Kenneth Cameron's* Emerson the Essayist, *pp. 194, 195), is not known.* MS., Harvard College Library.

To H. G. O. BLAKE

Concord Nov. 20th 1849

Mr Blake,

I have not forgotten that I am your debtor. When I read over your letters, as I have just done, I feel that I am unworthy to have received or to answer them, though they are addressed, as I would have them to the ideal of me. It behoves me, if I would reply, to speak out of the rarest part of myself.

At present I am subsisting on certain wild flowers which Nature wafts to me, which unaccountably sustain me, and make my apparently poor life rich. Within a year my walks have extended themselves, and almost every afternoon, (I read, or write, or make pencils, in the forenoon, and by the last means get a living for my body.) I visit some new

hill or pond or wood many miles distant. I am astonished at the wonderful retirement through which I move, rarely meeting a man in these excursions, never seeing one similarly engaged, unless it be my companion, when I have one. I cannot help feeling that of all the human inhabitants of nature hereabouts, only we two have leisure to admire and enjoy our inheritance.

"Free in this world, as the birds in the air, disengaged from every kind of chains, those who have practiced the *yoga* gather in Brahma the certain fruit of their works."

Depend upon it that rude and careless as I am, I would fain practise the *yoga* faithfully.

"The yogin, absorbed in contemplation, contributes in his degree to creation: he breathes a divine perfume, he hears wonderful things. Divine forms traverse him without tearing him, and united to the nature which is proper to him, he goes, he acts, as animating original matter."

To some extent, and at rare intervals, even I am a yogin.

I know little about the affairs of Turkey, but I am sure that I know something about barberries and ches[t]nuts of which I have collected a store this fall. When I go to see my neighbor he will formally communicate to me the latest news from Turkey, which he read in yesterday's Mail—how Turkey by this time looks determined, & Lord Palmerston —Why, I would rather talk of the bran, which, unfortunately, was sifted out of my bread this morning and thrown away. It is a fact which lies nearer to me. The newspaper gossip with which our hosts abuse our ears is as far from a true hospitality as the viands which they set before us. We did not need them to feed our bodies; and the news can be bought for a penny. We want the inevitable news, be it sad or cheering —wherefore and by what means they are extant, this *new* day. If they are well let them whistle and dance; If they are dyspeptic, it is their duty to complain, that so they may in any case be *entertaining*. If words are invented to conceal thought, I think that newspapers are a great improvement on a bad invention. Do not suffer your life to be taken by newspapers.

I thank you for your hearty appreciation of my book. I am glad to have had such a long talk with you, and that you had patience to listen to me to the end. I think that I have the advantage of you, for I chose my own mood, and in one sense your mood too, that is a quiet and attentive reading mood. Such advantage has the writer over the talker.

I am sorry that you did not come to Concord in your vacation. Is it not time for another vacation? I am here yet, and Concord is here.

You will have found out by this time who it is that writes this, and will be glad to have you write, to him, without his subscribing himself,

Henry D. Thoreau

P. S.   It is so long since I have seen you, that as you will perceive, I have to speak as it were *in vacuum*, as if I were sounding hollowly for an echo, & it did not make much odds what kind of a sound I made. But the gods do not hear my rude or discordant sound, as we learn from the echo; and I know that the nature toward which I launch these sounds is so rich that it will modulate anew and wonderfully improve my rudest strain.

MS., Hosmer collection.

From SAMUEL ? CABOT

[December 18, 1849]

It [the American goshawk] was first described by Wilson; lately Audubon has identified it with the European goshawk, thereby committing a very flagrant blunder. It is usually a very rare species with us. The European bird is used in hawking; and doubtless ours would be equally *game*. If Mr. Farmer skins him now, he will have to take second cut; for his skin is already off and stuffed,—his remains dissected, measured, and deposited in alcohol.

Jacob Farmer, one of Thoreau's Concord friends, shot or captured an American goshawk, and Thoreau presented the specimen to the Boston Society of Natural History. Sanborn implies that the author was James Elliot Cabot; he was probably James's brother Samuel, then Curator of Birds. Text, Familiar Letters of Thoreau, *p. 227.*

1850

Life expectancy in Massachusetts was thirty-eight years for the male babies born this year and forty for the female. Nine of the slaveholding states met in convention at Nashville and came out in favor of disunion. A treaty of amity and commerce was signed with Borneo. On the death of President Zachary Taylor, he was succeeded in office by one of the least remembered of American presidents. The decennial census gave the population as 23,191,876—an increase of more than one third over 1840. Only 262 slaves were counted in the North. Flogging was abolished in the Navy and on vessels of commerce, partly through the efforts of Herman Melville, in spite of the fact that several admirals appeared before Congress with the assertion that naval discipline would end the moment the lash was voted away. On March 7 Webster aligned himself with Henry Clay in favor of what is now called the Compromise of 1850; this omnibus bill of concessions to the South kept the Union together for a while longer.

The *Journal* for this year is full, even though eighty-four pages, apparently Thoreau's account of his trip to Canada, are missing. There is little philosophy left, but much naturalizing, with a good deal of lively observation of human nature. Among the best pieces are a sketch of a drunken Dutchman and Thoreau's dry recital of how he had accidentally set fire years earlier to some Concord woods and of the consequences. By now he had become as much of a settled man as he was ever to be. His walking and writing continued, but the writing was seldom superlative. His work as a surveyor took more of his time, and he was not, one would judge, discontent that it did so. Though one or two flibbertigib-

253

bets were to shout "burnt woods" at him for some years, Thoreau was in general accepted by his townsmen. If they did not praise him, they no longer paused to condemn him as a college graduate too indifferent to his opportunities. The Thoreaus moved to the "Yellow House" on Concord's Main Street. Lecturing and looking for the dead body of Margaret Fuller are two of the various doings the letters for this year are concerned with.

Saco, Maine, Wednesday 6 Feb

Dear Henry

I was at *South Danvers* on Monday Evening, & promised Mr C.
Northend, Secretary of the Lyceum, to invite you for Monday 18th
Feb. to read a lecture to his institution. I told him there were two lectures to describe Cape Cod, which interested him & his friends, & they
hoped that the two might somehow be rolled into one to give them some
sort of complete story of the journey. I hope it will not quite discredit
my negotiation if I confess that they heard with joy that Concord people
laughed till they cried, when it was read to them. I understand Mr N.,
that there is a possibility but no probability that his absent colleague of
the Lyceum has filled up that evening by an appointment But Mr N.
will be glad to hear from you that you will come, & if any cause exist
why not, he will immediately reply to you. They will pay your expenses,
& $10.00. You will go from the Salem depot in an omnibus to Mr N.'s
house. Do go if you can. Address *Charles Northend, Esq. South Danvers.*

Yours ever
R. W. Emerson.

MS., Berg; *previously unpublished. For dating, see* Emerson Letters
*(IV, 178), where the context of other letters makes 1850 the logical
year.*

From EMERSON

Concord, 11 March 1850

Mr Henry D. Thoreau,
My dear Sir,
I leave town tomorrow & must beg you, if any question arises between Mr [Charles] Bartlett & me, in regard to boundary lines, to act as my attorney, & I will be bound by any agreement you shall make. Will you also, if you have opportunity, warn Mr Bartlett, on my part, against burning his woodlot, without having there present a sufficient number of hands to prevent the fire from spreading into my wood,—which, I think, will be greatly endangered, unless much care is used.
Show him too, if you can, where his cutting & his post-holes trench on our line, by *plan* and, so doing, oblige as ever,

Yours faithfully,
R. W. Emerson.

MS., Morgan.

———————

To H. G. O. BLAKE

Concord, April 3, 1850.

Mr. Blake,—
I thank you for your letter, and I will endeavor to record some of the thoughts which it suggests, whether pertinent or not. You speak of poverty and dependence. Who are poor and dependent? Who are rich and independent? When was it that men agreed to respect the appearance and not the reality? Why should the appearance *appear*? Are we well acquainted, then, with the reality? There is none who does not lie hourly in the respect he pays to false appearance. How sweet it would be to treat men and things, for an hour, for just what they are! We

wonder that the sinner does not confess his sin. When we are weary with travel, we lay down our load and rest by the wayside. So, when we are weary with the burden of life, why do we not lay down this load of falsehoods which we have volunteered to sustain, and be refreshed as never mortal was? Let the beautiful laws prevail. Let us not weary ourselves by resisting them. When we would rest our bodies we cease to support them; we recline on the lap of earth. So, when we would rest our spirits, we must recline on the Great Spirit. Let things alone; let them weigh what they will; let them soar or fall. To succeed in letting only one thing alone in a winter morning, if it be only one poor frozen-thawed apple that hangs on a tree, what a glorious achievement! Methinks it lightens through the dusky universe. What an infinite wealth we have discovered! God reigns, *i. e.*, when we take a liberal view,—when a liberal view is presented us.

Let God alone if need be. Methinks, if I loved him more, I should keep him,—I should keep myself rather,—at a more respectful distance. It is not when I am going to meet him, but when I am just turning away and leaving him alone, that I discover that God is. I say, God. I am not sure that that is the name. You will know whom I mean.

If for a moment we make way with our petty selves, wish no ill to anything, apprehend no ill, cease to be but as the crystal which reflects a ray,—what shall we not reflect! What a universe will appear crystallized and radiant around us!

I should say, let the Muse lead the Muse,— let the understanding lead the understanding, though in any case it is the farthest forward which leads them both. If the Muse accompany, she is no muse, but an amusement. The Muse should lead like a star which is very far off; but that does not imply that we are to follow foolishly, falling into sloughs and over precipices, for it is not foolishness, but understanding, which is to follow, which the Muse is appointed to lead, as a fit guide of a fit follower.

Will you live? or will you be embalmed? Will you live, though it be astride of a sunbeam; or will you repose safely in the catacombs for a thousand years? In the former case, the worst accident that can happen is that you may break your neck. Will you break your heart, your soul, to save your neck? Necks and pipe-stems are fated to be broken. Men make a great ado about the folly of demanding too much of life (or of eternity?), and of endeavoring to live according to that demand. It is much ado about nothing. No harm ever came from that quarter. I am

not afraid that I shall exaggerate the value and significance of life, but that I shall not be up to the occasion which it is. I shall be sorry to remember that I was there, but noticed nothing remarkable,—not so much as a prince in disguise; lived in the golden age a hired man; visited Olympus even, but fell asleep after dinner, and did not hear the conversation of the gods. I lived in Judæa eighteen hundred years ago, but I never knew that there was such a one as Christ among my contemporaries! If there is anything more glorious than a congress of men a-framing or amending of a constitution going on, which I suspect there is, I desire to see the morning papers. I am greedy of the faintest rumor, though it were got by listening at the key-hole. I will dissipate myself in that direction.

I am glad to know that you find what I have said on Friendship worthy of attention. I wish I could have the benefit of your criticism; it would be a rare help to me. Will you not communicate it?

"What I have said on Friendship" was in all probability the essay on friendship imbedded in the Wednesday chapter of A Week. *Text, Familiar Letters of Thoreau, pp. 213–16.*

From C. H. DUNBAR

Haverhill May 1st 1850

Cousin H.—

You probably think ere this I have forgotten to answer your letter but it is not so. I have waited untill now that I might send some definite word about that Job I spoke of. You will recollect I told you one of the owners lived in Cincinate. He has come on and wishes to have the farm immediately surveyed and laid into house lots. There is some twenty acres of it. So you see it is *quite a Job* and there will be probably some small Jobs. Mr. Emmerson will wait untill you come which must by as soon as Thursday. I hope it will be so you can come

as I have some Jobs to do on the lots as soon as laid out & I think we both can make a good living at it Let me see you if possible if not drop a line that we may not be in suspense. All well as usual. Give my best respects to all and say to them we should be happy to see them at Haverhill

Yours
C H Dunbar

Charles Dunbar was Thoreau's cousin in nearby Haverhill. That Thoreau accepted the offer is indicated by the many Haverhill entries in his Journal *for May 1850. MS., Harvard; previously unpublished.*

To H. G. O. BLAKE

Concord May 28 1850

Mr Blake,

I "never found any contentment in the life which the newspapers record"—any thing of more value than the cent which they cost. Contentment in being covered with dust an inch deep! We who walk the streets and hold time together, are but the refuse of ourselves, and that life is for the shells of us—of our body & our mind—for our scurf—a thoroughly *scurvy* life. It is coffee made of coffee-grounds the twentieth time, which was only coffee the first time—while the living water leaps and sparkles by our doors. I know some who in their charity give their coffee grounds to the poor! We demanding news, and putting up with *such* news! Is it a new convenience or a new accident or rather a new perception of the truth that we want?

You say that ["]the serene hours in which Friendship, Books, Nature, Thought, seem above primary considerations, visit you but faintly"— Is not the attitude of expectation somewhat divine?—a sort of home-made divineness? Does it not compel a kind of sphere music to attend

259

on it? And do not its satisfactions merge at length by insensible degrees in the enjoyment of the thing expected?

What if I should forget to write about my not writing. It is not worth the while to make that a theme. It is as if I had written every day— It is as if I had never written before— I wonder that you think so much about it, for not writing is the most like writing in my case of anything I know.

Why will you not relate to me your dream? That would be to realize it somewhat. You tell me that you dream, but not what you dream.— I can *guess* what comes to pass. So do the frogs dream. Would that I knew what. I have never found out whether they are awake or asleep —whether it is day or night with them.

I am preaching, mind you, to bare walls, that is to myself; and if you have chanced to come in and occupy a pew—do not think that my remarks are directed at you particularly, and so slam the seat in disgust. This discourse was written long before these exciting times.

Some absorbing employment on your higher ground—your upland farm, whither no cartpath leads—but where you mount alone with your hoe—Where the life-ever-lasting grows—you raise a crop which needs not to be brought down into the valley to a market, which you barter for heavenly products.

Do you separate distinctly enough the support of your body from that of your essence? By how distinct a course commonly are these two ends attained! Not that they should not be attained by one & the same means—that indeed is the rarest success—but there is no half and half about it.

I shall be glad to read my lecture to a small audience in Worcester, such as you describe, and will only require that my expenses be paid. If only the parlor be large enough for an echo, and the audience will embarrass themselves with hearing as much as the lecturer would otherwise embarrass himself with reading. But I warn you that this is no better calculated for a promiscuous audience than the last two which I read to you. It requires in every sense a concordant audience

I will come on Saturday next and spend Sunday with you, if you wish it. Say so if you do.

Drink deep or taste not of the Pierian spring. Be not deterred by melancholy on the path which leads to immortal health & joy. When they tasted of the water of the river over which they were to go, they

thought that tasted a little bitterish to the palate, but it proved sweeter
when it was down.

HDT

MS., C. Waller Barrett.

————————

To HORACE GREELEY

Wedns. Morn.

Dear Sir—
  If Wm E Channing calls—will you say that I am gone to Fire-
Island by cars at 9 this morn. via Thompson. with Wm. H. Channing
Yrs

Henry D. Thoreau

*It is clear that when the shocking news of Margaret Fuller Ossoli's
death reached Concord Emerson asked Thoreau to hurry to Fire Island, where the ship bringing Margaret and her husband and child to
America had been wrecked. Emerson said in a letter of July 23 to
Greeley that he had charged Thoreau to gather all the news of the
wreck that could be got at the beach and to recover any of Margaret's
manuscripts or other property that could be salvaged. Her ship, however, had been wrecked on the 19th; so that by the time the report
reached Concord and Thoreau arrived on his sad errand it was the 24th
and there was little to salvage. MS., Berg; the manuscript, undated, is
attached to the letter from Emerson to Greeley; but Thoreau set out for
Fire Island on the 24th, a Wednesday.*

To EMERSON

Fire Island Beach Monday morn. July 25 '50

Dear Friend,

I am writing this at the house of Smith Oakes, within one mile of the wreck. He is the one who rendered the most assistance. W*m* H Channing came down with me, but I have not seen Arthur Fuller—nor Greeley, nor Spring. Spring & Sumner were here yesterday, but left soon. Mr Oakes & wife tell me (all the survivors came or were brought dir[ec]tly to their house) that the ship struck at 10 minutes after 4 A M. and all hands, being mostly in their night clothes made haste to the forecastle—the water coming in [at o]nce. There they remained the, passengers *in* the forecastle, the crew *above* it doing what they could. Every wave lifted the forecastle roof & washed over those within. The first man got ashore at 9. many from 9 to noon—. At floodtide about 3½ o'clock when the ship broke up entirely—they came out of the forecastle & Margaret sat with her back to the foremast with her hands over her knees—her husband & child already drowned—a great wave came & washed her off. The Steward? had just before taken her child & started for shore; both were drowned.

The broken desk in a bag—containing no very valuable papers—a large black leather trunk—with an upper and under apartment—the upper holding books & papers—A carpet bag probably Ossolis and one of his? shoes—are all the Ossolis' effects known to have been found.

Four bodies remain to be found—the two Ossoli's—Horace Sumner—& a sailor.

I have visited the child's grave—Nobody will probably be taken away today.

The wreck is to be sold at auction—excepting the hull—today The mortar would not go off. Mrs Hartz the Captain's wife, told Mrs Oakes that she & Margaret divided their money—& tied up the halves in handkerchiefs around their persons that Margaret took 60 or 70 dol[lars.] Mrs Hartz who can tell all about Margaret up to 11 'oclock on Friday is said to be going to Portland Me. today—She & Mrs Fuller must & probably will come together. The cook, the last to leave, & the Steward? will know the rest. I shall try to see them. In the meanwhile I shall do what I can to recover property & obtain particulars here abouts. W*m*

H. Channing—did I write it? has come with me. Arthur Fuller has this moment reached this house. He reached the beach last night—we got here yesterday noon. A good part of the wreck still holds together where she struck, & something may come ashore with her fragments. The last body was found on Tuesday 3 miles west. Mrs Oakes dried the papers which were in the trunk—and she says they appeared to be of various kinds. "Would they cover that table"?, a small round one— "They would spread out"—Some were tied up. There were 20 or 30 books in the same half of the trunk. Another, smaller trunk empty, came ashore, but there is no mark on it—She speaks of [Celesta] Pardena as if she might have been a sort of nurse to the child"—I expect to go to Patchogue whence the pilferers must have chiefly come—& advertise &c &c.

MS., Harvard.

To CHARLES SUMNER

Springfield Depot noon July 29th 1850.

Dear Sir,

I left Fire Island Beach on Saturday between nine & ten o'clock A. M. The same morning I saw on the beach, four or five miles west of the wreck, a portion of a human skeleton, which was found the day before, probably from the Elisabeth, but I have not knowledge enough of anatomy to decide *confidently,* as many might, whether it was that of a male or a female. I therefore hired Selah Strong, Keeper of the Light, to bury it simply for the present, and mark the spot, leaving it to future events, or a trustworthy examination, to decide the question.

Yrs in haste
Henry D. Thoreau

P. S.   No *more* bodies had then been found.

In searching Thoreau came across a body that he thought might be that of Horace Sumner, brother of Charles Sumner the famed abolitionist, later senator from Massachusetts. MS., Harvard; previously unpublished.

From CHARLES SUMNER

Boston July 31st 50

My dear Sir,

I desire to thank you for your kindness in writing me with regard to the remains of a human body found on the beach last Saturday.

From what you write & from what I hear from others, it seems impossible to identify them.

If the body of my brother could be found, it would be a great satisfaction to us to bury him with those of his family who have gone before him.

Believe me, dear Sir, faithfully & gratefully Yours,
Charles Sumner

MS., Abernethy (*typescript*); *previously unpublished.*

To H. G. O. BLAKE

Concord, August 9, 1850.

Mr. Blake,—

I received your letter just as I was rushing to Fire Island beach to recover what remained of Margaret Fuller, and read it on the way. That

event and its train, as much as anything, have prevented my answering it before. It is wisest to speak when you are spoken to. I will now endeavor to reply, at the risk of having nothing to say.

I find that actual events, notwithstanding the singular prominence which we all allow them, are far less real than the creations of my imagination. They are truly visionary and insignificant,—all that we commonly call life and death,—and affect me less than my dreams. This petty stream which from time to time swells and carries away the mills and bridges of our habitual life, and that mightier stream or ocean on which we securely float,—what makes the difference between them? I have in my pocket a button which I ripped off the coat of the Marquis of Ossoli, on the seashore, the other day. Held up, it intercepts the light,—an actual button,—and yet all the life it is connected with is less substantial to me, and interests me less, than my faintest dream. Our thoughts are the epochs in our lives: all else is but as a journal of the winds that blew while we were here.

I say to myself, Do a little more of that work which you have confessed to be good. You are neither satisfied nor dissatisfied with yourself, without reason. Have you not a thinking faculty of inestimable value? If there is an experiment which you would like to try, try it. Do not entertain doubts if they are not agreeable to you. Remember that you need not eat unless you are hungry. Do not read the newspapers. Improve every opportunity to be melancholy. As for health, consider yourself well. Do not engage to find things as you think they are. Do what nobody else can do for you. Omit to do anything else. It is not easy to make our lives respectable by any course of activity. We must repeatedly withdraw into our shells of thought, like the tortoise, somewhat helplessly; yet there is more than philosophy in that.

Do not waste any reverence on my attitude. I merely manage to sit up where I have dropped. I am sure that my acquaintances mistake me. They ask my advice on high matters, but they do not know even how poorly on 't I am for hats and shoes. I have hardly a shift. Just as shabby as I am in my outward apparel, ay, and more lamentably shabby, am I in my inward substance. If I should turn myself inside out, my rags and meanness would indeed appear. I am something to him that made me, undoubtedly, but not much to any other that he has made.

Would it not be worth while to discover nature in Milton? be native to the universe? I, too, love Concord best, but I am glad when I discover,

in oceans and wildernesses far away, the material of a million Concords: indeed, I am lost, unless I discover them. I see less difference between a city and a swamp than formerly. It is a swamp, however, too dismal and dreary even for me, and I should be glad if there were fewer owls, and frogs, and mosquitoes in it. I prefer ever a more cultivated place, free from miasma and crocodiles. I am so sophisticated, and I will take my choice.

As for missing friends,—what if we do miss one another? have we not agreed on a rendezvous? While each wanders his own way through the wood, without anxiety, ay, with serene joy, though it be on his hands and knees, over rocks and fallen trees, he cannot but be in the right way. There is no wrong way to him. How can he be said to miss his friend, whom the fruits still nourish and the elements sustain? A man who missed his friend at a turn, went on buoyantly, dividing the friendly air, and humming a tune to himself, ever and anon kneeling with delight to study each little lichen in his path, and scarcely made three miles a day for friendship. As for conforming outwardly, and living your own life inwardly, I do not think much of that. Let not your right hand know what your left hand does in that line of business. It will prove a failure. Just as successfully can you walk against a sharp steel edge which divides you cleanly right and left. Do you wish to try your ability to resist distension? It is a greater strain than any soul can long endure. When you get God to pulling one way, and the devil the other, each having his feet well braced,—to say nothing of the conscience sawing transversely,—almost any timber will give way.

I do not dare invite you earnestly to come to Concord, because I know too well that the berries are not thick in my fields, and we should have to take it out in viewing the landscape. But come, on every account, and we will see—one another.

Text, Familiar Letters of Thoreau, *pp. 223–26.*

[1850]

From JOSIAH PIERCE, JR.

Portland, Oct. 18, 1850.

Dear Sir,

In behalf of its Managing Committee, I have the honor of inviting you to lecture before the "Portland Lyceum" on some Wednesday evening during the next winter. Your former animated and interesting discourse is fresh in the memory of its members, and they are very anxious to have their minds again invigorated, enlivened and instructed by you. If you consent to our request, will you be pleased to designate the time of the winter when you would prefer to come here?

The Managers have been used to offer gentlemen who come here to lecture from a distance equivalent to your own, only the sum of twenty-five dollars, not under the name of pecuniary compensation for the lectures but for traveling expenses—

An early and favorable reply will much oblige us.

With great respect, Your obedient Servant,
Josiah. Pierce, Jr.

Henry D. Thoreau, Esq.

Thoreau had read a portion of Walden *as a lecture in Portland in March of 1849. MS., Berg; previously unpublished.*

———————

From FRANKLIN FORBES

Clinton Nov 14, 1850

Henry D. Thoreau Esq
Dear Sir

As one of the Committee on Lectures of the Bigelow Mechanic Institute of this town, I wish to ascertain if you will deliver your lecture

on "Cap[e] Cod" before the Institute on either Wednesday Evening of the month of January—

An early answer will much oblige

Yrs respectfully,
Franklin Forbes.

P. S.   If you prefer any other lecture of yours to the above mentioned, please name a day on which you can deliver it.

MS., Berg; *previously unpublished.*

To FRANKLIN FORBES

Concord Nov. 15 1850

Dear Sir,

I shall be happy to lecture before your Institution this winter, but it will be most convenient for me to do so on the 11*th* of December. If, however, I am confined to the month of January I will choose the first day of it. Will you please inform me as soon as convenient whether I can come any earlier.

Yrs respectfully
Henry D. Thoreau.

Thoreau delivered a lecture on Cape Cod at the Bigelow Mechanic Institute in Clinton on January 1, 1851. MS., Estelle Doheny Collection, St. John's Seminary, Camarillo, California (typescript); previously unpublished.

From JOSIAH PIERCE, JR.

Portland, Nov. 20th 1850.

Dear Sir,

You may perhaps believe that I am writing to you from Ireland and not from Portland, making a blunder even in the date of the letter, when you read that this is for the purpose of apologizing for and correcting another error—I intended and ought to have designated the evening of January 15th and not of January 8th or 10th, as that on which we hoped to hear a lecture from you.

With the wish that this newly appointed time, the fifteenth of January next, may be equally acceptable to you,

I am With great respect, Yours truly

J. *Pierce,* Jr

MS., Berg; *previously unpublished.*

From T. W. HIGGINSON

Newburyport, Dec. 3, 1850.

My Dear Sir

I hear with pleasure that you are to lecture in Newburyport this week. Myself & wife are now living in town again, & we shall be very glad to see you at our house, if you like it better than a poor hotel. And you shall go as early as you please on Saturday—which is the great point, I find, with guests, however unflattering to the hosts.

If I do not hear to the contrary I shall expect you, & will meet you at the cars.

Very sincerely yours
T. W. Higginson.

Thoreau delivered a lecture in Newburyport on December 6. Higginson, a Unitarian clergyman, was active in the Transcendentalist movement and wrote much about it in his various memoirs. MS., Berg; previously unpublished.

From SAMUEL CABOT

In his *Familiar Letters of Thoreau* (pp. 226–27) Sanborn notes: "On the 27th of December, 1850, Mr. Cabot wrote to say that the Boston Society of Natural History, of which he was secretary, had elected Thoreau a corresponding member, 'with all the *honores, privilegia, etc., ad gradum tuum pertinentia,* without the formality of paying any entrance fee, or annual subscription. Your duties in return are to advance the interests of the Society by communications or otherwise, as shall seem good.' . . . The immediate occasion of this election was the present, by Thoreau, to the Society, of a fine specimen of the American goshawk, caught or shot by Jacob Farmer." For Mr. Cabot's letter acknowledging receipt of the goshawk see December 18, 1849. For a further contribution to the society by Thoreau see his letter to Dr. Samuel Kneeland of October 13, 1860.

1851

This was the peak year for the immigration of the Irish, whom Thoreau always regarded with interest. Population reports state that more than 221,000 were admitted to the United States during the year. The Hungarian patriot Louis Kossuth reached America and began his triumphal tour. He was received with great enthusiasm but soon found that Congressional support and American money were not forthcoming for the cause of Hungarian independence. Henry Clay resigned from Congress. John Audubon and James Fenimore Cooper died. The first electric railroad was established between Washington and nearby Bladensburg, Maryland. The Committee of Vigilance organized itself in San Francisco. Its record of sentences ran: four men hanged, one whipped, fourteen deported, one ordered to leave California, fifteen handed over to the authorities, and forty-one discharged. A Negro named Shadrach was arrested in Boston as a fugitive slave, rescued from jail at night by a mob of colored men, and sent off in safety to Canada.

Thoreau became thirty-four during this year. He had to have some dentistry done and acquired false teeth—to him a strong sign of man's mortality. No Yankee ascetic, though plainly no sensualist either, he thought and wrote about love and marriage. He disliked feminists, however, and complained about having to squire one of them, Elizabeth Oakes Smith, to a lecture. While respectable Boston obeyed the Fugitive Slave Law, his sympathies swung over to the abolitionists, although he was still ready to point out that there were many more forms of slavery than Negro slavery. There were strongly marked trends in his writing for 1851. The year saw no publications but a good deal of composition. The *Journal* is full—full and rich. There are several different kinds of writings in it, and they are all good. Oddly enough, only one letter has been found.

Concord Feb 10th 1851

Dear Sir,
    I return by the bearer De Laet's "Novus Orbis" &c. Will you please send me Alfred Hawkins' "Picture of Quebec" and "Silliman's Tour of Quebec"?
    If these are not in—then Wytfliet's *"Descriptionis Ptolemaicae Argumentum* &c and Lescarbot *"Les Muses de la Nouvelle France."*

Yrs respectly
Henry D. Thoreau

The year before this Thoreau had gone with Ellery Channing on a trip to Montreal and Quebec. Dr. Harris was naturalist as well as Harvard librarian; he and Thoreau became friends primarily through Thoreau's growing interest in nature study. J. S. Wade, "The Friendship of Two Old-Time Naturalists," The Scientific Monthly, *XXIII (August, 1926), 152–60, chronicles the relationship between Harris and Thoreau. MS., Harvard; previously unpublished.*

From WILLIAM W. GREENOUGH ET AL.

Boston, March 7th, 1851.

Dear Sir:
    It is proposed that a meeting of the Class of 1837 be held at the Revere House, on Wednesday, at 5 P. M., on the 19th of March next.

[1851]

There are reasons for a deviation from the usual custom of the Class in assembling during the week of the annual Commencement.

In Boston and its vicinity are now collected a larger number of the Class than at any time since we left the University. A general desire has been expressed to take advantage of this circumstance, and to endeavor to re-awaken the interest natural to those who have been pleasantly associated together at an early period of life. Nearly fourteen years have elapsed since we left Cambridge, and but few have been in situations to bring them much into contact with any considerable number of their Class.

There is a manifest advantage in holding a meeting at this season of the year. Upon Commencement week, other engagements are liable to interfere, and the usual heat and fatigue of the days preclude any long duration of the meeting either in the afternoon or evening.

On the present occasion a dinner is proposed of which the expense will not exceed one dollar to each person.

It is desirable that a definite answer to this letter should be returned to the Committee previous to the 17th inst. If circumstances should compel the absence of any member, it is expected that he will contribute to the interest of the occasion by writing some account of himself since he left College.

Very truly,

Your friends and Classmates,
William W. Greenough,
William J. Dale,
David Greene Haskins,
J. H. Adams, Jr.

Class Committee.

Annexed is a list of the members of the Class supposed to be in this vicinity.

Allen,	Dall,	Holmes, 2d.
Bacon,	Davis, 1st.	Hubbard,
Belcher,	Davis, 2d.	Kimball,
Bigelow,	Dana,	Lane,
Clap,	Greenough,	March,
Clarke,	Haskins,	Peabody,
Dale,	Hawes,	Perry,

273

Phelps,	Tuckerman,	Wight,
Richardson,	Vose,	Williams, 1st.
Russell,	Weiss,	Williams, 3d.
Thoreau,	Whitney,	

A form letter. There is no indication that Thoreau either replied or attended the dinner. MS., Harvard.

1852

Massachusetts enacted a prohibition law. Isaac Singer patented a new and improved sewing machine. Daniel Webster died at Marshfield; Henry Clay died in Washington. Commodore Matthew C. Perry sailed for Japan to negotiate a treaty with the Japanese. In a four-hour speech in the Senate Charles Sumner bitterly attacked the Fugitive Slave Law. Total tonnage of the American merchant marine, including canal boats and barges, was 4,138,440. The Post Office, after a decade of either profits or else relatively small losses, went spectacularly into the red. The year before, it had shown a surplus of $131,000; now it showed a deficit of almost $2,000,000, and this trend was to continue for a good many years.

This was a year when Horace Greeley bulked large. He was a vigorous and helpful literary agent for Thoreau. Greeley advised him about the proper length for his manuscripts, negotiated with magazine editors to place Thoreau's work, offered him good terms for a long review article on Emerson, which Thoreau rejected, and lent him money. (Probably the best tribute to Greeley is that Thoreau was able to make himself ask Greeley for a loan.) Most of the time Thoreau spent in following the pleasant routine he had set up for himself in Concord: writing, and some surveying, in the morning as a rule, walking in the country in the afternoon, and more writing at night, or a midnight walk if the moon were up. By now he could drive his pen ahead with the efficiency of a well-trained professional author. There is little waste motion to be noted in the manuscripts that survive; there are few corrections; and the handwriting has all the oversimplification of speed and fluency. The *Journal* for the year is copious. The writing in it is most frequently sensitive and accurate description of the Concord woods.

275

To MARSTON WATSON

I have not yet seen Mr. [Ellery] Channing, though I believe he is in town,—having decided to come to Plymouth myself,—but I will let him know that he is expected. Mr. [Daniel] Foster wishes me to say that he accepts your invitation, and that he would like to come Sunday after next; also that he would like to know before next Sunday whether you will expect him. I will take the Saturday afternoon train. I shall be glad to get a winter view of Plymouth Harbor, and to see where your garden lies under snow.

After leaving Harvard Marston Watson took up the kind of pastoral life that probably met with Thoreau's approval. He bought a pretty farm near Plymouth and devoted himself to raising ornamental trees and flowering plants. In Plymouth he organized a number of series of what were conveniently called "Marston's meetings" in Leyden Hall. They were held on Sundays; some of the speakers were clerical and some not. Thoreau delivered a lecture to Watson's group on February 22; the probable date of this letter is February 17. Text, Sanborn's memoir of Alcott in A. Bronson Alcott: His Life and Philosophy, I, 483 n.

From HORACE GREELEY

New York, *February* 24, 1852.

My Friend Thoreau,—
Thank you for your remembrance, though the motto you suggest is impracticable. The People's Course is full for the season; and even

276

if it were not, your name would probably not pass; because it is not merely necessary that each lecturer should continue *well* the course, but that he shall be *known* as the very man beforehand. Whatever draws less than fifteen hundred hearers damages the finances of the movement, so low is the admission, and so large the expense. But, Thoreau, you are a better speaker than many, but a far better writer still. Do you wish to swap any of your "wood-notes wild" for dollars? If yea, and you will sell me some articles, shorter, if you please, than the former, I will try to coin them for you. Is it a bargain? Yours,

Horace Greeley.

Text, *Sanborn's* Henry D. Thoreau, *p. 231.*

From HORACE GREELEY

New York, Mar. 18, 1852.

My Dear Sir:

I ought to have responded before this to yours of the 5th inst. but have been absent—hurried, &c &c. I have had no time to bestow upon it till to-day.

I shall get you some money for the articles you send me, though not immediately.

As to your longer account of a canadian tour, I don't know. It looks unmanageable. Can't you cut it into three or four, and omit all that relates to time? The cities are described to death; but I know you are at home with Nature, and that she rarely and slowly changes. Break this up if you can, and I will try to have it swallowed and digested.

Yours,
Horace Greeley.

Henry D. Thoreau, Esq. Concord, Mass.

Thoreau apparently took Greeley's advice, for when the account of the Canadian tour was printed in Putnam's *it appeared in three separate parts.* MS., Morgan.

From HORACE GREELEY

Sanborn, in his *Henry D. Thoreau* (pp. 232–33), states that Greeley, a week after his letter of March 18, wrote Thoreau that the publisher Sartain had accepted his articles "for a low price," and adds: "If you break up your 'Excursion to Canada' into three or four articles, I have no doubt I could get it published on similar terms." He also enclosed the following letter from Sartain:

Philadelphia, *March* 24, 1852.

Dear Sir,—

I have read the articles of Mr. Thoreau forwarded by you, and will be glad to publish them if our terms are satisfactory. We generally pay for prose composition per printed page, and would allow him three dollars per page. We do not pay more than four dollars for any that we now engage. I did not suppose our maximum rate would have paid you (Mr. Greeley) for your lecture, and therefore requested to know your own terms. Of course, when an article is unusually desirable, we may deviate from rule; I now only mention ordinary arrangement. I was very sorry not to have your article, but shall enjoy the reading of it in Graham. Mr. T. might send us some further contributions, and shall at least receive prompt and courteous decision respecting them.

Yours truly,
John Sartain.

To T. W. HIGGINSON

Concord April 2nd 52

Dear Sir,

I do not see that I can refuse to read another lecture, but what makes me hesitate is the fear that I have not another available which

will *entertain* a large audience, though I have thoughts to offer which I think will be quite as worthy of their attention. However I will try, for the prospect of earning a few dollars is alluring. As far as I can foresee, my subject would be Reality rather transcendentally treated. It lies still in "Walden or Life in the Woods." Since you are kind enough to undertake the arrangements, I will leave it to you to name an evening of next week—decide on the most suitable room—and advertise (?)— if this is not taking you too literally at your word

If you still think it worth the while to attend to this, will you let me know as soon as may be what evening will be most convenient

Yrs with thanks
Henry D. Thoreau

MS. (facsimile), *T. W. Higginson's* Part of a Man's life, *opp. p. 16.*

From HORACE GREELEY

Friend Thoreau,—

I wish you to write me an article on Ralph Waldo Emerson, his Works and Ways, extending to one hundred pages, or so, of letter sheet like this, to take the form of a review of his writings, but to give some idea of the Poet, the Genius, the Man,—with some idea of the New England scenery and home influence, which have combined to make him what he is. Let it be calm, searching, and impartial; nothing like adulation, but a just summing up of what he is and what he has done. I mean to get this into the "Westminster Review," but if not acceptable there, I will publish it elsewhere. I will pay you fifty dollars for the article when delivered; in advance, if you desire it. Say the word, and I will send the money at once. It is perfectly convenient to do so. Your "Carlyle" article is my model, but you can give us Emerson better than you did Carlyle. I presume he would allow you to write extracts for this purpose from his lectures not yet published. I would delay the

publication of the article to suit his publishing arrangements, should that be requested.

Yours,
Horace Greeley.

Text, *Sanborn's* Henry D. Thoreau, *pp. 233–34. Sanborn dates the letter April 3, 1852.*

To T. W. HIGGINSON

Concord, 2 pm Ap. 3d./52

I certainly do not feel prepared to offer myself as a lecturer to the Boston public, and hardly know whether more to dread a small audience or a large one. Nevertheles I will repress this squeamishness, and propose no alterations in your arrangements. I shall be glad to accept of your invitation to tea.

Henry D. Thoreau.

Thoreau delivered the lecture at the Mechanics Apprentices Library in Boston. The audience was small. Bronson Alcott, there with him, urged the clerks and apprentices reading their newspapers at the other end of the lecture room to listen to Thoreau; but they would not. MS. (facsimile), T. W. Higginson & H. W. Boynton, A Reader's History of American Literature, *p. 196.*

From HORACE GREELEY

New York, April 20, 1852.

Dear Sir:
I have yours of the 17th. I am rather sorry you will not do the
Works and Ways; but glad that you are able to employ your time to
better purpose.
But your Quebeck notes don't reach me yet, and I fear the 'good time'
is passing. They ought to have appeared in the June Nos. of the Month-
lies, but now cannot before July. If you choose to send them to me all
in a bunch, I will try to get them printed in that way. I don't care about
them if you choose to reserve or to print them elsewhere; but I can
better make a use for them at this season than at any other.

Yours,
Horace Greeley.

H. D. Thoreau, Concord, Mass.

*In a letter we have been unable to find, Thoreau declined to exploit his
friendship with Emerson by writing the article that Greeley had suggested. When the "Quebeck notes" did arrive Greeley offered them to
the American Whig Review and other magazines, but they were not
then accepted. MS., Lawrence A. Averill, Wiscasset, Maine.*

From HORACE GREELEY

New York, May 26, 1852

Friend Thoreau:
I duly received your package and letter, and immediately
handed over the former to C. Bissell Editor of the Whig Review, asking
him to examine it fully and tell me what he could give for it, which
he promised to do. Two or three days afterward, I left for the West

without having heard from him. This morning, without having seen your letter, having reached home at 1 o'clock, I went to Bissell at 9, and asked him about the matter. He said he had not read all the MSS. but had part of it, and inquired if I would be willing to have him print part and pay for it. I told him I could not consent without consulting you, but would thank him to make me a proposition in writing, which I would send you. He said he would do so very soon, whereupon I left him.

I hope you will acquit me of negligence in the matter, though I ought to have acknowledged the receipt of your package. I did not, simply because I was greatly hurried, trying to get away, and because I momently expected some word from Bissell.

Yours,
Horace Greeley.

H. D. Thoreau, Esq.

The package presumably contained the "Quebeck notes" (Greeley's letter of April 20). Thoreau apparently sent a covering letter. MS., Berg; previously unpublished.

From HORACE GREELEY

New York June 25, 1852

Dear Thoreau:
  I have had only bad luck with your manuscript. Two magazines have refused it on the ground of its length, saying that articles 'To be continued' are always unpopular, however good. I will try again.

Yours,
Horace Greeley

H. D. Thoreau, Esq.

MS., Hosmer collection.

From HORACE GREELEY

New York, *July* 8, 1852.

Dear Thoreau,—

Yours received. I was absent yesterday. I *can* lend you the seventy-five dollars, and am very glad to do it. Don't talk about security. I am sorry about your MSS., which I do not quite despair of using to your advantage.

Yours,
Horace Greeley.

Text, *Sanborn's* Henry D. Thoreau, *p. 235.*

To SOPHIA THOREAU

Concord July 13th '52

Dear Sophia,

I am a miserable letter writer, but perchance if I should say this at length and with sufficient emphasis & regret, it could make a letter. I am sorry that nothing transpires here of much moment; or, I should rather say that I am so slackened and rusty, like the telegraph wire this season, that no wind that blows can extract music from me. I am not on the trail of any elephants or mastodons, but have succeeded in trapping only a few ridiculous mice, which can not feed my imagination. I have become sadly scientific. I would rather come upon the vast valley-like "spore" only of some celestial beast which this world's woods can no longer sustain, than spring my net over a bushel of moles. You must do better in those woods where you are. You must have some adventures to relate and repeat for years to come—which will eclipse even Mother's voyage to Goldsborough & Sissiboo. They say that Mr Pierce the presidential candidate was in town last 5th of July visiting Hawthorne whose college chum he was, and that Hawthorne is writing a life of him for electioneering purposes. Concord is just as idiotic as

283

ever in relation to the spirits and their knockings. Most people here believe in a spiritual world which no respectable junk bottle which had not met with a slip—would condescend to contain even a portion of for a moment—whose atmosphere would extinguish a candle let down into it, like a well that wants airing—in spirits which the very bull frogs in our meadows would blackball. Their evil genius is seeing how low it can degrade them. The hooting of owls—the croaking of frogs—is celestial wisdom in comparison. If I could be brought to believe in the things which they believe—I should make haste to get rid of my certificate of stock in this & the next world's enterprises, and buy a share in the first Immediate Annihilation Company that offered—I would exchange my immortality for a glass of small beer this hot weather. Where *are* the heathen? Was there ever any superstition before? And yet I suppose there may be a vessel this very moment setting sail from the coast of North America to that of Africa with a missionary on board! Consider the dawn & the sun rise—the rain bow & the evening,—the words of Christ & the aspirations of all the saints! Hear music? See—smell—taste—feel—hear—anything—& then hear these idiots inspired by the cracking of a restless board—humbly asking "Please spirit, if you cannot answer by knocks, answer by tips of the table."!!!!!!

Yrs
H. D. Thoreau

MS., Huntington.

To H. G. O. BLAKE

Concord July 21st '52.

Mr Blake,

 I am too stupidly well these days to write to you. My life is almost altogether outward, all shell and no tender kernel; so that I fear the report of it would be only a nut for you to crack, with no meat in it for you to eat. Moreover, you have not cornered me up, and I enjoy

such large liberty in writing to you that I feel as vague as the air. However, I rejoice to hear that you have attended so patiently to anything which I have said heretofore, and have detected any truths in it. It encourages me to say more—not in this letter I fear—but in some book which I may write one day. I am glad to know that I am as much to any mortal as a persistent and *consistent* scarecrow is to a farmer—such a bundle of straw in a man's clothing as I am—with a few bits of tin to sparkle in the sun dangling about me. As if I were hard at work there in the field. However, if this kind of life saves any man's corn,— why he is the gainer. I am not afraid that you will flatter me as long as you know what I am, as well as what I think, or aim to be, & distinguish between these two, for then it will commonly happen that if you praise the last, you will condemn the first.

I remember that walk to Asnebumskit very well;—a fit place to go on a Sunday, one of the true temples of the earth. A temple you know was anciently "an open place without a roof," whose walls served merely to shut out the world, and direct the mind toward heaven; but a modern *meeting house* shuts out the heavens, while it crowds the world into still closer quarters. Best of all is it when as on a *Mt.* top you have for all walls your own elevations and deeps of surrounding ether. The partridge berries watered with *Mt* dews, which are gathered there, are more memorable to me than the words which I last heard from the pulpit at least, and for my part I would rather walk toward Rutland than Jerusalem. Rutland—modern town—land of ruts—trivial and worn—not too sacred—with no holy sepulchre, but prophane green fields and dusty roads,—and opportunity to live as holy a life as you can;—where the sacredness if there is any is all in yourself and not in the place.

I fear that your Worcester people do not often enough go to the hilltops, though, as I am told, the springs lie nearer to the surface on your hills than in your valleys. They have the reputation of being Free Soilers—Do they insist on a free atmosphere too, that is, on freedom for the head or brain as well as the feet? If I were consciously to join any party it would be that which is the most free to entertain thought.

All the world complain now a days of a press of trivial duties & engagements which prevents their employing themselves on some higher ground they know of,—but undoubtedly if they were made of the right stuff to work on that higher ground, provided they were released from all those engagements—they would now at once fulfill the superior engagement, and neglect all the rest, as naturally as they breathe. They

would never be caught saying that they had no time for this when the dullest man knows that this is all that he has time for. No man who acts from a sense of duty ever puts the lesser duty above the greater. No man has the desire and the ability to work on high things but he has also the ability to build himself a high staging.

As for passing *through* any great and glorious experience, and rising *above* it,—as an eagle might fly athwart the evening sky to rise into still brighter & fairer regions of the heavens, I cannot say that I ever sailed so creditably, but my bark ever seemed thwarted by some side wind and went off over the edge and now only occasionally tacks back toward the center of that sea again. I have outgrown nothing good, but, I do not fear to say, fallen behind by whole continents of virtue which should have been passed as islands in my course; but I trust—what else can I trust?—that with a stiff wind some Friday, when I have thrown some of my cargo over board, I may make up for all that distance lost.

Perchance the time will come when we shall not be content to go back & forth upon a raft to some huge Homeric or Shakspearean India-man that lies upon the reef, but build a bark out of that wreck, and others that are buried in the sands of this desolate island, and such new timber as may be required, in which to sail away to whole new worlds of light & life where our friends are.

Write again. There is one respect in which you did not finish your letter, you did not write it with ink, and it is not so good therefore against or for you in the eye of the law, nor in the eye of

H. D. T.

Rutland, Massachusetts is near the base of Mount Wachusett, the destination of many of Thoreau's walks with Blake. MS., C. Waller Barrett.

From WILLIAM H. SWEETSER

Charlestown, Mass. July 21 1852.

Sir,
    I am a boy 15 years of age collecting autographs and should be very much obliged if you would send me yours.

                                        Yours respectfully,
                                            Wm. H. Sweetser.

To Henry Thoreau Esq.

MS., Berg; *previously unpublished.*

———————

To WILLIAM H. SWEETSER

Concord July 26 '52

Wm H. Sweetser
    This is the way I write when I have a poor pen and still poorer ink.

                                            Yrs,
                                        Henry D. Thoreau

MS., New York.

To H. G. O. BLAKE

Mr. Blake,

Here come the sentences which I promised you. You may keep them if you will regard & use them as the disconnected fragments of what I may find to be a completer essay, on looking over my journal at last, and may claim again.

I send you the thoughts on chastity & sensuality with diffidence and shame, not knowing how far I speak to the condition of men generally, or how far I betray my peculiar defects. Pray enlighten me on this point if you can.

Henry D. Thoreau

Sanborn prints the brief essays headed "Love" and "Chastity and Sensuality" as part of this letter, but Thoreau's signature preceding them seems to make them an enclosure. For the essays, see Familiar Letters of Thoreau, *pp. 238–51. MS., Iowa State Department of History and Archives. Except for "1852" penciled at a later date in the margin, the manuscript is undated; but Emerson and Sanborn, both of whom consulted directly with Blake, ascribe the letter to September 1852.*

To GEORGE WILLIAM CURTIS

Concord Nov 16th 1852

Dear Sir,

I send you herewith 100 pages of "Cape Cod." It is not yet half the whole. The remainder of the narrative is more personal, as I reach the scene of my adventures. I am a little in doubt about the extracts from the old ministers. If you prefer to, you may omit from the middle of the 86th page to the end of this parcel; (the rest being respected); or perhaps a smaller type will use it up fast enough.

As for the conditions of sale; if you accept the paper, it is to be mine to reprint, if I think it worth the while, after it has appeared in your journal.

I shall expect to be paid *as fast as* the paper is printed, and if it is likely to be on hand long, to receive reasonable warning of it.

I have collected this under several heads for your convenience. The next subject is "The Beach," which I will copy out & forward as soon as you desire it.

Yrs
Henry D. Thoreau.

If we judge by this letter, Thoreau's account of his experiences on Cape Cod was now well on its way to publication. But the unhappy circumstances that attended so many of his contacts with magazines recur; the Cape Cod articles did not actually appear until 1855—and then Thoreau stopped them because of a controversy with Curtis. Why they took so long to reach print we do not know. MS., Harvard; previously unpublished.

From HORACE GREELEY

New York, Nov. 23, 1852.

My Dear Thoreau,

I have made no bargain— none whatever—with [George Palmer] Putnam, concerning your MS. I have indicated no price to him. I handed over the MS. because I wish it published, and presumed that was in accordance both with your interest and your wishes.

And I now say to you that if he will pay you $3 per printed page, I think that will be very well. I have promised to write something for him myself, and shall be well satisfied with that price. Your 'Canada' is not so fresh and acceptable as if it had just been written on the strength of a last summer's trip, and I hope you will have it printed in Putnam's

Monthly. But I have said nothing to his folks as to price, and will not till I hear from you again.

Very probably, there was some misapprehension on the part of Geo. Curtis. I presume the price now offered you is that paid to writers generally for the Monthly.

As to Sartain, I know his magazine has broken down, but I guess he will pay you. I have not seen but one of your articles printed by him, and I think the other may be reclaimed. Please address him at once. I have been very busy the past season, and had to let every thing wait that could till after Nov. 2d.

Yours,
Horace Greeley.

H. D. Thoreau Esq

Greeley erred in thinking that only one of Thoreau's articles had been printed in Sartain's Union Magazine. *"The Iron Horse" appeared in XI (July 1852), 66–68, and "A Poet Buying a Farm" in XI (August 1852), 127. Both have been overlooked by the bibliographers of Thoreau. They are excerpts from* Walden. *MS., Huntington.*

To MARSTON WATSON

Concord, December 31, 1852.

Mr. Watson,—

I would be glad to visit Plymouth again, but at present I have nothing to read which is not severely heathenish, or at least secular,— which the dictionary defines as "relating to affairs of the present world, not holy,"—though not necessarily unholy; nor have I any leisure to prepare it. My writing at present is profane, yet in a good sense, and, as it were, sacredly, I may say; for, finding the air of the temple too close, I sat outside. Don't think I say this to get off; no, no! It will not do to read such things to hungry ears. "If they ask for bread, will you give

them a stone?" When I have something of the right kind, depend upon it I will let you know.

After having lectured for Watson once before, Thoreau—in spite of Watson's invitation—did not lecture in Plymouth again until October 8, 1854. Text, Familiar Letters of Thoreau, *p. 230.*

1853

Hawthorne's friend Frank Pierce became president. The railroad systems expanded in the West through the help of munificent land grants received from the government. Nine small railroads in the East between Albany and Buffalo merged as the New York Central system. The coinage of $3 gold pieces was authorized. A law was enacted in Illinois to the effect that any Negro who came into the state and stayed for ten days was to be fined $50 or sold into slavery until the fine was worked out. Basques, or bodices with short skirts or tails below the waist line, were popular items of ladies' wear and continued to be for several years.

Three parts of the story of Thoreau's excursion to Canada were printed in *Putnam's Monthly Magazine*. The rest was withdrawn by Thoreau because the editor of *Putnam's* reserved the right to censor the manuscript. Thoreau made a third trip into Maine, which was also to bear literary fruit. Greeley continued to be as good a friend as any writer in search of markets could want. Munroe, the Boston publisher of the *Week*, sent back 700 copies of the work, bound or in sheets, to its depressed but ironical author. The few letters for this year are often concerned with business matters. In the extensive *Journal* there is less reflection and more observation than earlier. Thoreau's eye for nature has sharpened, but his eye for Transcendentalism has definitely clouded. It is perhaps symptomatic that this is the year in which he was suggested for membership in the Association for the Advancement of Science.

From HORACE GREELEY

New York, *January* 2, 1853.

Friend Thoreau,—

I have yours of the 29th, and credit you $20. Pay me when and in such sums as may be convenient. I am sorry you and C [urtis] cannot agree so as to have your whole MS. printed. It will be worth nothing elsewhere after having partly appeared in Putnam's. I think it is a mistake to conceal the authorship of the several articles, making them all (so to speak) *editorial;* but *if* that is done, don't you see that the elimination of very flagrant heresies (like your defiant Pantheism) becomes a necessity? If you had withdrawn your MS., on account of the abominable misprints in the first number, your ground would have been far more tenable.

However, do what you will.

Yours,
Horace Greeley.

George William Curtis, the editor of Putnam's *and an old friend of Thoreau, insisted on omitting certain "heretical" passages from his "Excursion to Canada" without consulting the author. As a result the manuscript was withdrawn after only three of the five installments had appeared.* Text, *Sanborn's* Henry D. Thoreau, *p. 237.*

To HORACE GREELEY

Concord Feb. 9th '53

Friend Greeley,

I send you inclosed Putnam's cheque for 59 dollars, which together with the 20" sent last December—make, nearly enough, principal & interest of the $75 which you lent me last July—However I regard that loan as a kindness for which I am still indebted to you both principal and interest. I am sorry that my manuscript should be so mangled, insignificant as it is, but I do not know how I could have helped it fairly, since I was born to be a pantheist—if that be the name of me, and I do the deeds of one.

I suppose that Sartain is quite out of hearing by this time, & it is well that I sent him no more.

Let me know how much I am still indebted to you pecuniarily for trouble taken in disposing of my papers—which I am sorry to think were hardly worth our time.

Yrs with new thanks
Henry D. Thoreau

MS., Morgan; *previously unpublished.*

To ELIJAH WOOD

Concord Feb. 26th '53 [?]

Mr Wood,

I mentioned to you that Mr. Flannery had given me an order on you for ¾ of his wages. I have agreed with him that that arrangement shall not begin to take effect until the first of March 1854.

yrs
Henry D. Thoreau

One of Thoreau's best friends among the Irish was Michael Flannery, "industrious Irishman from Kerry." According to Sanborn (The Life of Henry David Thoreau, p. 435), Flannery gave at least one note of hand to the Thoreaus "for money lent him in some pinch." This note Sophia Thoreau kept for many years and then turned over to Sanborn with instructions to collect the money if possible but in any event to surrender the note to Flannery. A number of the Concord farmers employed such Irishmen as Flannery for odd jobs. Thoreau notes, for instance, in his Journal for September 28, 1857, "that E. Wood has sent a couple of Irishmen. . .to cut off the natural hedges. . .on this hill farm." It is probable that the order on Flannery's wages is addressed to old Elijah Wood, but it may have been to his son. The year of this letter is either 1853 or 1854; it is impossible to tell from the manuscript. We incline to 1853, in which Thoreau was "borrowing money for a poor Irishman who wishes to get his family to this country" (Journal, October 12, 1853). If it had been 1854, it is questionable whether Thoreau would have written "March 1854" instead of merely "March." MS., Huntington; previously unpublished.

To H. G. O. BLAKE

Concord Feb. 27 '53

Mr Blake,

I have not answered your letter before because I have been almost constantly in the fields surveying of late. It is long since I have spent so many days so profitably in a pecuniary sense; so unprofitably, it seems to me, in a more important sense. I have earned just a dollar a day for 76 days past; for though I charge at a higher rate for the days which are seen to be spent, yet so many more are spent than appears. This is instead of lecturing, which has not offered to pay for that book which I printed. I have not only cheap hours, but cheap weeks and months, i.e. weeks which are bought at the rate I have named. Not that they are quite lost to me, or make me very melancholy, alas! for I too often take a cheap satisfaction in so spending them,—weeks of pasturing

and browsing, like beeves and deer, which give me animal health, it may be, but create a tough skin over the soul and intellectual part. Yet if men should offer my body a maintenance for the work of my head alone, I feel that it would be a dangerous temptation.

As to whether what you speak of as the "world's way" (Which for the most part is my way) or that which is shown me, is the better, the former is imposture, the latter is truth. I have the coldest confidence in the last. There is only such hesitation as the appetites feel in following the aspirations The clod hesitates because it is inert, wants *animation*. The one is the way of death, the other of life everlasting. My hours are not "cheap in such a way that *I* doubt whether the world's way would not have been better," but cheap in such a way, that I doubt whether the world's way, which I have adopted for the time, could be worse. The whole enterprise of this nation which is not an upward, but a westward one, toward Oregon California, Japan &c, is totally devoid of interest to me, whether performed on foot or by a Pacific railroad. It is not illustrated by a thought it is not warmed by a sentiment, there is nothing in it which one should lay down his life for, nor even his gloves, hardly which one should take up a newspaper for. It is perfectly heathenish—a flibustiering *toward* heaven by the great western route. No, they may go their way to their manifest destiny which I trust is not mine. May my 76 dollars whenever I get them help to carry me in the other direction. I see them on their winding way, but no music 'is' wafted from their host, only the rattling of change in their pockets. I would rather be a captive knight, and let them all pass by, than be free only to go whither they are bound. What end do they propose to themselves beyond Japan? What aims more lofty have they than the prairie dogs?

As it respects these things I have not changed an opinion one iota from the first. As the stars looked to me when I was a shepherd in Assyria, they look to me now a New Englander. The higher the *mt.* on which you stand, the less change in the prospect from year to year, from age to age. Above a certain height, there is no change. I am a Switzer on the edge of the glacier, with his advantages & disadvantages, goitre, or what not. (You may suspect it to be some kind of swelling at any rate). I have had but one *spiritual* birth (excuse the word,) and now whether it rains or snows, whether I laugh or cry, fall farther below or approach nearer to my standard, whether Pierce or Scott is elected,

296

—not a new scintillation of light flashes on me, but ever and anon, though with longer intervals, the same surprising & everlastingly new light dawns to me, with only such variations as in the coming of the natural day, with which indeed, it is often coincident.

As to how to preserve potatoes from rotting, your opinion may change from year to year, but as to how to preserve your soul from rotting, I have nothing to learn but something to practise.

Thus I declaim against them, but I in my folly am the world I condemn.

I very rarely indeed, if ever, "feel any itching to be what is called useful to my fellowmen." Sometimes, it may be when my thoughts for want of employment, fall into a beaten path or humdrum, I have dreamed idly of stopping a man's horse that was running away, but perchance I wished that he might run in order that I might stop him,—or, of putting out a fire, but then of course it must have got well a-going. Now, to tell the truth, I do not dream much of acting upon horses before they run, or of preventing fires which are not yet kindled. What a foul subject is this, of doing good, instead of minding ones life, which should be his business—doing good as a dead carcass, which is only fit for manure, instead of as a living man,—Instead of taking care to flourish & smell & taste sweet and refresh all mankind to the extent of our capacity & quality. People will sometimes try to persuade you that you have done something from that motive, as if you did not already know enough about it. If I ever *did* a man any good, in their sense, of course it was something exceptional, and insignificant compared with the good or evil which I am constantly doing by being what I am. As if you were to preach to ice to shape itself into burning glasses, which are sometimes useful, and so the peculiar properties of ice be lost—Ice that merely performs the office of a burning glass does not do its duty.

The problem of life becomes one cannot say by how many degrees more complicated as our material wealth is increased, whether that needle they tell of was a gate-way or not,—since the problem is not merely nor mainly to get life for our bodies, but by this or a similar discipline to get life for our souls; by cultivating the lowland farm on right principles, that is with this view, to turn it into an upland farm. You have so many more talents to account for. If I accomplish as much more in spiritual work as I am richer in worldly goods, then I am just as worthy, or worth just as much as I was before, and no more. I see that,

in my own case, money *might* be of great service to me, but probably it would not be, for the difficulty ever is that I do not improve my opportunities, and therefore I am not prepared to have my opportunities increased. Now I warn you, if it be as you say, you have got to put on the pack of an Upland Farmer in good earnest the coming spring, the lowland farm being cared for, aye you must be selecting your seeds forth with and doing what winter work you can; and while others are raising potatoes and Baldwin apples for you, you must be raising apples of the Hesperides for them. (Only hear how he preaches!) No man can suspect that he is the proprietor of an Upland farm, upland in the sense that it will produce nobler crops and better repay cultivation in the long run, but he will be perfectly sure that he ought to cultivate it.

Though we are desirous to earn our bread, we need not be anxious to *satisfy* men for it—though we shall take care to pay them, but Good [sic] who alone gave it to us. Men may in effect put us in the debtors jail, for that matter, simply for paying our whole debt to God which includes our debt to them, and though we have his receit for it, for his paper is dishonored. The carrier will tell you that he has no stock in his bank.

How prompt we are to satisfy the hunger & thirst of our bodies; how slow to satisfy the hunger & thirst of our *souls*. Indeed we [who] would be practical folks cannot use this word without blushing because of our infidelity, having starved this substance almost to a shadow. We feel it to be as absurd as if a man were to break forth into a eulogy on *his dog* who has n't any. An ordinary man will work every day for a year at shovelling dirt to support his body, or a family of bodies, but he is an extraordinary man who will work a whole day in a year for the support of his soul. Even the priests, the men of God, so called, for the most part confess that they work for the support of the body. But he alone is the truly enterprising & practical man who succeeds in *maintaining* his soul here. Haven't we our everlasting life to get? And isn't that the only excuse at last for eating drinking sleeping or even carrying an umbrella when it rains? A man might as well devote himself to raising pork, as to fattening the bodies or temporal part merely of the whole human family. If we made the true distinction we should almost all of us be seen to be in the almshouse for souls.

I am much indebted to you because you look so steadily at the better side, or rather the true center of me (for our true center may & perhaps oftenest does lie entirely aside from us, and we are in fact ec-

centric,) and as I have elsewhere said "Give me an opportunity to live." You speak as if the image or idea which I see were reflected from me to you, and I see it again reflected from you to me, because we stand at the right angle to one another; and so it goes, zig-zag, to what successive reflecting surfaces, before it is all dissipated, or absorbed by the more unreflecting, or differently reflecting,—who knows? Or perhaps what you see directly you refer to me. What a little shelf is required, by which we may impinge upon another, and build there our eyrie in the clouds, and all the heavens we see above us we refer to the crags around and beneath us. Some piece of mica, as it were, in the face or eyes of one, as on the Delectable *Mts.*, slanted at the right angle, reflects the heavens to us. But in the slow geological depressions & upheavals, these mutual angles are disturbed, these suns set & new ones rise to us. That ideal which I worshipped was a greater stranger to the mica than to me. It was not the hero I admired but the reflection from his epaulet or helmet. It is nothing (for us) permanently inherent in another, but his attitude or relation to what we prize that we admire. The meanest man may glitter with micacious particles to his fellow's eye. There are the spangles that adorn a man. The highest union—the only *un*-ion (don't laugh) or central oneness, is the coincidence of visual rays. Our club room was an apartment in a constellation where our visual rays met (and there was no debate about the restaurant) The way between us is over the mount.

Your words make me think of a man of my acquaintance whom I occasionally meet, whom you too appear to have met, one Myself, as he is called. Yet why not call him *Your*-self? If you have met with him & know him it is all I have done, and surely where there is a mutual acquaintance the my & thy make a distinction without a difference.

I do not wonder that you do not like my Canada story. It concerns me but little, and probably is not worth the time it took to tell it. Yet I had absolutely no design whatever in my mind, but simply to report what I saw. I have inserted all of myself that was implicated or made the excursion. It has come to an end at any rate, they will print no more, but return me my mss. when it is but little more than half done— as well as another I had sent them, because the editor Curtis requires the liberty to omit the heresies without consulting me—a privilege California is not rich enough to bid for.

I thank you again & again for attending to me; that is to say I am

glad that you hear me and that you also are glad. Hold fast to your most indefinite waking dream. The very green dust on the walls is an organized vegetable; the atmosphere has its fauna & flora floating in it; & shall we think that dreams are but dust & ashes, are always disintegrated & crumbling thoughts and not dust like thoughts trooping to its standard with music systems beginning to be organized. These expectations these are roots these are nuts which even the poorest man has in his bin, and roasts or cracks them occasionally in winter evenings, which even the poor debtor retains with his bed and his pig, i.e. his idleness & sensuality. Men go to the opera because they hear there a faint expression in sound of this news which is never quite distinctly proclaimed. Suppose a man were to sell the hue the least amount of coloring matter in the superficies of his thought,—for a farm—were to exchange an absolute & infinite value for a relative & finite one—to gain the whole world & lose his own soul!

Do not wait as long as I have before you write. If you will look at another star I will try to supply my side of the triangle

Tell Mr Brown that I remember him & trust that he remembers me.

Yrs
H.D.T.

PS. Excuse this rather flippant preaching—which does not cost me enough—and do not think that I mean you *always*—though your letter *requested* the subjects.

Thoreau's Week *was selling so poorly that the publisher insisted on Thoreau's taking the unsold remainder off his hands and settling the printing debt. Theo Brown, a fellow townsman of Blake, was one of Thoreau's friends and occasional companions.* MS., Berg.

To G. W. CURTIS

Concord Mar. 11 '53

Mr. Curtis:

Together with the ms of my Cape Cod adventures Mr [George Palmer] Putnam sends me only the first 70 or 80 (out of 200) pages of the "Canada," all which having been printed is of course of no use to me. He states that "the remainder of the mss. *seems* to have been lost at the printers'." You will not be surprised if I wish to know if it *actually is* lost, and if reasonable pains have been taken to recover it. Supposing that Mr. P. may not have had an opportunity to consult you respecting its whereabouts—or have thought it of importance enough to inquire after particularly—I write again to you to whom I entrusted it to assure you that it is of more value to me than may appear.

With your leave I will improve this opportunity to acknowledge the receipt of another cheque from Mr. Putnam.

I trust that if we ever have any intercourse hereafter it may be something more cheering than this curt business kind.

Yrs,
Henry D. Thoreau

For earlier details of the controversy over the publication of "Excursion to Canada," see the letter from Greeley of January 2, 1853. MS., John Cooley (typescript).

From HORACE GREELEY

New York, *March* 16, 1853.

Dear Sir,—

I have yours of the 9th, inclosing Putnam's check for $59, making $79 in all you have paid me. I am paid in full, and this letter is your receipt in full. I don't want any pay for my "services," whatever they

301

may have been. Consider me your friend who *wished* to serve you, however unsuccessfully. Don't break with C[urtis] or Putnam.

Text, *Sanborn's* Henry D. Thoreau, *pp. 237–38.*

To H. G. O. BLAKE

Concord, April 10, 1853.

Mr. Blake,—
    Another singular kind of spiritual foot-ball,—really nameless, handleless, homeless, like myself,—a mere arena for thoughts and feelings; definite enough outwardly, indefinite more than enough inwardly. But I do not know why we should be styled "misters" or "masters": we come so near to being anything or nothing, and seeing that we are mastered, and not wholly sorry to be mastered, by the least phenomenon. It seems to me that we are the mere creatures of thought,—one of the lowest forms of intellectual life, we men,—as the sunfish is of animal life. As yet our thoughts have acquired no definiteness nor solidity; they are purely molluscous, not vertebrate; and the height of our existence is to float upward in an ocean where the sun shines,—appearing only like a vast soup or chowder to the eyes of the immortal navigators. It is wonderful that I can be here, and you there, and that we can correspond, and do many other things, when, in fact, there is so little of us, either or both, anywhere. In a few minutes, I expect, this slight film or dash of vapor that I am will be what is called asleep,—resting! forsooth from what? Hard work? and thought? The hard work of the dandelion down, which floats over the meadow all day; the hard work of a pismire that labors to raise a hillock all day, and even by moonlight. Suddenly I can come forward into the utmost apparent distinctness, and speak with a sort of emphasis to you; and the next moment I am so faint an entity, and make so slight an impression, that nobody can find the traces of me. I try to hunt myself up, and find the

little of me that is discoverable is falling asleep, and then I assist and tuck it up. It is getting late. How can *I* starve or feed? Can *I* be said to sleep? There is not enough of me even for that. If you hear a noise,— 't aint I,—'t aint I,—as the dog says with a tin-kettle tied to his tail. I read of something happening to another the other day: how happens it that nothing ever happens to me? A dandelion down that never alights,— settles,—blown off by a boy to see if his mother wanted him,—some divine boy in the upper pastures.

Well, if there really is another such a meteor sojourning in these spaces, I would like to ask you if you know whose estate this is that we are on? For my part I enjoy it well enough, what with the wild apples and the scenery; but I should n't wonder if the owner set his dog on me next. I could remember something not much to the purpose, probably; but if I stick to what I do know, then—

It is worth the while to live respectably unto ourselves. We can possibly *get along* with a neighbor, even with a bedfellow, whom we respect but very little; but as soon as it comes to this, that we do not respect ourselves, then we do not get along at all, no matter how much money we are paid for halting. There are old heads in the world who cannot help me by their example or advice to live worthily and satisfactorily to myself; but I believe that it is in my power to elevate myself this very hour above the common level of my life. It is better to have your head in the clouds, and know where you are, if indeed you cannot get it above them, than to breathe the clearer atmosphere below them, and think that you are in paradise.

Once you were in Milton doubting what to do. To live a better life —this surely can be done. Dot and carry one. Wait not for a clear sight, for that you are to get. What you see clearly you may omit to do. Milton and Worcester? It is all Blake, Blake. Never mind the rats in the wall; the cat will take care of them. All that men have said or are is a very faint rumor, and it is not worth the while to remember or refer to that. If you are to meet God, will you refer to anybody out of that court? How shall men know how I succeed, unless they are in at the life? I did not see the "Times" reporter there.

Is it not delightful to provide one's self with the necessaries of life, —to collect dry wood for the fire when the weather grows cool, or fruits when we grow hungry?—not till then. And then we have all the time left for thought!

303

THE CORRESPONDENCE OF THOREAU

Of what use were it, pray, to get a little wood to burn, to warm your body this cold weather, if there were not a divine fire kindled at the same time to warm your spirit?

> "Unless above himself he can
> Erect himself, how poor a thing is man!"

I cuddle up by my stove, and there I get up another fire which warms fire itself. Life is so short that it is not wise to take roundabout ways, nor can we spend much time in waiting. Is it absolutely necessary, then, that we should do as we are doing? Are we chiefly under obligations to the devil, like Tom Walker? Though it is late to leave off this wrong way, it will seem early the moment we begin in the right way; instead of mid-afternoon, it will be early morning with us. We have not got half way to dawn yet.

As for the lectures, I feel that I have something to say, especially on Traveling, Vagueness, and Poverty; but I cannot come now. I will wait till I am fuller, and have fewer engagements. Your suggestions will help me much to write them when I am ready. I am going to Haverhill to-morrow, surveying, for a week or more. You met me on my last errand thither.

I trust that you realize what an exaggerater I am,—that I lay myself out to exaggerate whenever I have an opportunity,—pile Pelion upon Ossa, to reach heaven so. Expect no trivial truth from me, unless I am on the witness-stand. I will come as near to lying as you can drive a coach-and-four. If it isn't thus and so with me, it is with something. I am not particular whether I get the shells or meat, in view of the latter's worth.

I see that I have not at all answered your letter, but there is time enough for that.

Thoreau's account of his surveying trip to Haverhill may be found in the Journal *(V, 109–14), where it concentrates on botanical observation. The reference to Tom Walker derives from Washington Irving's* Tales of a Traveller. Text, Familiar Letters of Thoreau, *pp. 261–65.*

From JAMES MUNROE & CO.

We send by express this day a box & bundle containing 250 copies of Concord River, & also 450. in sheets. All of which we trust you will find correct.

Munroe now insisted on returning the unsold copies of Thoreau's first book, which were taking up needed storage space in his cellar. It was thus that Thoreau acquired "a library of nearly nine hundred volumes, over seven hundred of which I wrote myself." For Thoreau's further comments on the return of the unsold remainder, see his Journal *for October 25, 1853, the day he received the books from Munroe. (V, 459–60). MS., Huntington, in a letter from Thoreau to Ticknor & Fields, February 24, 1862; previously unpublished.*

To FRANCIS H. UNDERWOOD

Concord Nov. 22d '53

Dear Sir,
    If you will inform me in season at what rate per page, (describing the page) you will pay for accepted articles,—returning the rejected within a reasonable time—and your terms are satisfactory, I will forward something for your Magazine before Dec 5th, and you shall be at liberty to put my name in the list of contributors.

Yours
Henry D. Thoreau.

In the summer and fall of 1853 Underwood wrote to numerous literary men of New England in an attempt to round up literary material for a projected antislavery magazine to be issued by the Boston publisher John P. Jewett. Jewett had already made his name and had begun to make his fabulous profits the year before out of one item, Mrs. Stowe's Uncle Tom's Cabin. *The new magazine was supposed to begin publication in December of 1853. MS., Berg..*

Concord Nov. 22ᵈ 53

Dear Sir,

If you will inform
me in season at what rate
per page, (describing the page)
you will pay for accepted articles,
— returning rejected within a
reasonable time — and your
terms are satisfactory, I will
forward something for your
Magazine before Dec 5ᵗʰ,
and you shall be at liberty
to put my name in the
list of Contributors.

Yours
Henry D. Thoreau

To FRANCIS H. UNDERWOOD

Concord, *Dec.* 2d, 1853.

Dear Sir,—

I send you herewith a complete article of fifty-seven pages. *Putnam's Magazine* pays me four dollars a page, but I will not expect to receive more for this than you pay to anyone else. Of course you will not make any alterations or omissions without consulting me.

Yours,

Henry D. Thoreau

Apparently Underwood's reply to Thoreau's letter of November 22 was acceptable. The article was probably "Chesuncook," an account of the trip to the Maine Woods of September 1853. Because the launching of the magazine was postponed the article was not published in the At-lantic until 1858. Then James Russell Lowell deleted the line about the pine tree: "It is as immortal as I am, and perchance will go to as high a heaven, there to tower above me still," without consulting Thoreau and brought down the wrath of the author on his head. Text, Bliss Perry's Park Street Papers, p. 217.

From FRANCIS H. UNDERWOOD

Boston Dec. 5, 1853

Dear Sir,

I am extremely sorry to inform you that Mr. Jewett has decided not to commence the Magazine as he proposed. His decision was made too late to think of commencing this year with another publisher. His ill health and already numerous cares are the reasons he gives. The en-

terprise is therefore postponed—but not indefinitely it is to be hoped. Should the fates be favorable I will give you the earliest information.

Very sincerely yours,
F. H. Underwood

Mr. H. D. Thoreau

The decision of the Boston publisher John P. Jewett not to issue his antislavery magazine provided Thoreau with still another unhappy experience in the periodical field. However, Underwood continued to work toward the establishment of a "free" magazine, and he deserves the main credit for starting the Atlantic Monthly, *which ultimately appeared (with Lowell as editor at Underwood's suggestion) in November of 1857. MS., Berg; previously unpublished.*

To SPENCER F. BAIRD

Concord Dec. 19th 1853

Spencer F. Baird,
Dear Sir,
    I wish hereby to convey my thanks to the one who so kindly proposed me as a member of the Association for the Advancement of Science, and also to express my interest in the Association itself. Nevertheless, for the same reason that I should not be able to attend the meetings, unless held in my immediate vicinity, I am compelled to decline the membership.

Yrs, with hearty thanks,
Henry D. Thoreau

(To be returned to S. F. Baird, Washington, with the blanks filled.)
Name Henry D(avid) Thoreau

Occupation (Professional, or otherwise). Literary and Scientific, combined with Land-surveying

Post-office address Henry D. Thoreau Concord Mass.

Branches of science in which especial interest is felt The Manners & Customs of the Indians of the Algonquin Group previous to contact with the civilized man.

Remarks I may add that I am an observer of nature generally, and the character of my observations, so far as they are scientific, may be inferred from the fact that I am especially attracted by such books of science as White's Selborne and Humboldt's "Aspects of Nature."

With thanks for your "Directions," received long since I remain

Yrs &c

Henry D. Thoreau.

Early in March of 1853, according to Thoreau's Journal entry for March 5, he received a circular letter from the Association for the Advancement of Science asking him "to fill the blank against certain questions, among which the most important one was what branch of science I was specially interested in. . . . I felt that it would be to make myself the laughing-stock of the scientific community to describe or attempt to describe to them that branch of science which specially interests me, inasmuch as they do not believe in a science which deals with the higher law. So I was obliged to speak to their condition and describe to them that poor part of me which alone they can understand." MS., John Cooley; the italicized portions are a printed form.

To H. G. O. BLAKE

Concord, December 19, 1853.

Mr. Blake,—

My debt has accumulated so that I should have answered your last-letter at once, if I had not been the subject of what is called a press of engagements, having a lecture to write for last Wednesday, and sur-

veying more than usual besides. It has been a kind of running fight with me,—the enemy not always behind me, I trust.

True, a man cannot lift himself by his own waistbands, because he cannot get out of himself; but he can expand himself (which is better, there being no up nor down in nature), and so split his waistbands, being already within himself.

You speak of doing and being, and the vanity, real or apparent, of much doing. The suckers—I think it is they—make nests in our river in the spring of more than a cart-load of small stones, amid which to deposit their ova. The other day I opened a muskrat's house. It was made of weeds, five feet broad at base, and three feet high, and far and low within it was a little cavity, only a foot in diameter, where the rat dwelt. It may seem trivial, this piling up of weeds, but so the race of muskrats is preserved. We must heap up a great pile of doing, for a small diameter of being. Is it not imperative on us that we *do* something, if we only work in a treadmill? And, indeed, some sort of revolving is necessary to produce a centre and nucleus of being. What exercise is to the body, employment is to the mind and morals. Consider what an amount of drudgery must be performed,—how much humdrum and prosaic labor goes to any work of the least value. There are so many layers of mere white lime in every shell to that thin inner one so beautifully tinted. Let not the shell-fish think to build his house of that alone; and pray, what are its tints to him? Is it not his smooth, close-fitting shirt merely, whose tints *are not* to him, being in the dark, but only when he is gone or dead, and his shell is heaved up to light, a wreck upon the beach, do they appear. With him, too, it is a Song of the Shirt, "Work,—work,—work!" And the work is not merely a police in the gross sense, but in the higher sense a discipline. If it is surely the means to the highest end we know, can any work be humble or disgusting? Will it not rather be elevating as a ladder, the means by which we are translated?

How admirably the artist is made to accomplish his self-culture by devotion to his art! The wood-sawyer, through his effort to do his work well, becomes not merely a better wood-sawyer, but measurably a better *man*. Few are the men that can work on their navels,—only some Brahmins that I have heard of. To the painter is given some paint and canvas instead; to the Irishman a hog, typical of himself. In a thousand apparently humble ways men busy themselves to make some

right take the place of some wrong,—if it is only to make a better paste-blacking,—and they are themselves *so much* the better morally for it.

You say that you do not succeed much. Does it concern you enough that you do not? Do you work hard enough at it? Do you get the benefit of discipline out of it? If so, persevere. Is it a more serious thing than to walk a thousand miles in a thousand successive hours? Do you get any corns by it? Do you ever think of hanging yourself on account of failure?

If you are going into that line,—going to besiege the city of God,—you must not only be strong in engines, but prepared with provisions to starve out the garrison. An Irishman came to see me to-day, who is endeavoring to get his family out to this New World. He rises at half past four, milks twenty-eight cows (which has swollen the joints of his fingers), and eats his breakfast, without any milk in his tea or coffee, before six; and so on, day after day, for six and a half dollars a month; and thus he keeps his virtue in him, if he does not add to it; and he regards me as a gentleman able to assist him; but if I ever get to be a gentleman, it will be by working after my fashion harder than he does. If my joints are not swollen, it must be because I deal with the teats of celestial cows before breakfast (and the milker in this case is always allowed some of the milk for his breakfast), to say nothing of the flocks and herds of Admetus afterward.

It is the art of mankind to polish the world, and everyone who works is scrubbing in some part.

If the work is high and far,

> You must not only aim aright,
> But draw the bow with all your might.

You must qualify yourself to use a bow which no humbler archer can bend.

"Work,—work,—work!"

Who shall know it for a bow? It is not of yew-tree. It is straighter than a ray of light; flexibility is not known for one of its qualities.

December 22.

So far I had got when I was called off to survey. Pray read the life of Haydon the painter, if you have not. It is a small revelation for these

latter days; a great satisfaction to know that he has lived, though he is now dead. Have you met with the letter of a Turkish cadi at the end of Layard's "Ancient Babylon"? that also is refreshing, and a capital comment on the whole book which precedes it,—the Oriental genius speaking through him.

Those Brahmins "put it through." They come off, or rather stand still, conquerors, with some withered arms or legs at least to show; and they are said to have cultivated the faculty of abstraction to a degree unknown to Europeans. If we cannot sing of faith and triumph, we will sing our despair. We will be that kind of bird. There are day owls, and there are night owls, and each is beautiful and even musical while about its business.

Might you not find some positive work to do with your back to Church and State, letting your back do all the rejection of them? Can you not *go* upon your pilgrimage, Peter, along the winding mountain path whither you face? A step more will make those funereal church bells over your shoulder sound far and sweet as a natural sound.

"Work,—work,—work!"

Why not make a *very large* mud-pie and bake it in the sun! Only put no Church nor State into it, nor upset any other pepper-box that way. Dig out a woodchuck,—for that has nothing to do with rotting institutions. Go ahead.

Whether a man spends his day in an ecstasy or despondency, he must do some work to show for it, even as there are flesh and bones to show for him. We are superior to the joy we experience.

Your last two letters, methinks, have more nerve and will in them than usual, as if you had erected yourself more. Why are not they good work, if you only had a hundred correspondents to tax you?

Make your failure tragical by the earnestness and steadfastness of your endeavor, and then it will not differ from success. Prove it to be the inevitable fate of mortals,—of one mortal,—if you can.

You said that you were writing on Immortality. I wish you would communicate to me what you know about that. You are sure to live while that is your theme.

Thus I write on some text which a sentence of your letters may have furnished.

313

I think of coming to see you as soon as I get a new coat, if I have money enough left. I will write to you again about it.

On December 14, 1853 Thoreau delivered before the Concord Lyceum a lecture on his journey to Moosehead Lake. Text, Familiar Letters of Thoreau, *pp. 266–71.*

1854

A treaty between Japan and the United States was signed after Commodore Perry had presented American gifts to the Japanese commissioners, the gifts including a fully equipped miniature railroad, a telegraph line, and a steamboat, all intended to represent the arts of Western civilization. Abram Gessner patented kerosene, thus carrying the arts a step farther. The first international convention of the Young Men's Christian Association assembled in Buffalo. A convention of Whigs and Free Soilers met in Detroit and adopted the name "Republican." The Kansas-Nebraska Bill, introduced by Senator Stephen Douglas, was passed; it repealed the Missouri Compromise of 1820 and allowed the two new territories to decide for themselves whether they wanted slavery or not. Settlers from the North, including New England, and from the South streamed into Kansas. Proslavery men formed secret societies called "Blue Lodges," which were effective in carrying the congressional election in November for a proslavery candidate. An agreement with Russia was signed respecting rights of neutrals at sea. In Boston the runaway slave Anthony Burns was arrested; his arrest caused riots and an attack on the courthouse, but he was returned to slavery in a cutter provided by the government.

On August 9 the firm of Ticknor and Fields, at a cost to themselves of 43 cents a copy, published *Walden*. It sold for $1.00; though the American public did not know it then, few better bargains were offered in 1854. The book was not widely reviewed. However, the few reviews were appreciative. In the *Journal* for June—to take a month at random —Thoreau wrote about oak galls; the birth of a shadow; a flight of

ephemerae; the river clams; the injustice of fame; a nighthawk; painted
tortoises laying eggs; oak leaves; tracks of turtles; a snapping turtle;
"artificial wants"; the great fringed orchis; the Anthony Burns affair;
the upper Sudbury River; the evergreen forest bird; river plants; the
cricket's homely chirp; harvest flies; dew; the waterlily; flowers and
morality; the Anthony Burns affair again; beauty and baseness; wild
roses; mountain laurel; an ocean of fog; the Fugitive Slave Law and
the Constitution; the season of small fruits; the Burns affair; a snapping
turtle's nest; the "tweezer-bird"; a free-man party wanted; a thunder-
shower; a school of young pouts; grassy hollows; miscellaneous notes;
and large black birches. This year Thoreau found a new disciple—or,
rather, the disciple found him—and a new friend from England. The
disciple was the Quaker Daniel Ricketson of New Bedford. The Englishman was the cultivated and well traveled Thomas Cholmondeley.

Concord 1 Jany 1854

Dear Henry,

    I meant to have seen you, but for delays that grew out of the snowbanks, to ask your aid in these following particulars. On the 8 February, Professor Horsford is to lecture at the Lyceum; on the 15th Feb.y, Theodore Parker. They are both to come to my house for the night. Now I wish to entreat your courtesy & counsel to receive these lonely pilgrims, when they arrive, to guide them to our house, & help the alarmed wife to entertain them, & see that they do not lose the way to the Lyceum, nor the hour. For, it seems pretty certain that I shall not be at home until perhaps the next week following these two. If you shall be in town, & can help these gentlemen so far, you will serve the whole municipality as well as

Yours faithfully,
R. W. Emerson

Emerson had been elected a curator of the Concord Lyceum on No-
vember 16, 1853. Theodore Parker delivered a lecture, "The Function
of Beauty." Professor Eben N. Horsford's lecture was postponed be-
cause of inclement weather. MS., Morgan.

From L. MARETT

Middlesex. S[ummon]S *To* Henry D. Thoreau of Concord in said County of Middlesex.

Greeting.
     You are hereby required, in the name of the Commonwealth of Massachusetts, to make your appearance before Justices of the Court of Common Pleas now *holden at* Cambridge *within and for the County of* Middlesex *on* Thursday the Twentieth day of January instant at 9 Oclock A.M. *and from day to day until the Action herein named is heard by the court, to give evidence of what you know relating to an Action or Plea of* Tort *then and there to be heard and tried betwixt* Leonard Spaulding Lots [?] *Plaintiff and* William C. Benjamin *Defendant*
     Hereof fail not, as you will answer your default under the pains and penalty in the law in that behalf made and provided. Dated at Cambridge *the* Eighteenth *day of* January *in the year of our Lord one thousand eight hundred and* fifty four   .
L. Marett Justice of the Peace

Thoreau's work as a surveyor was herein used as court testimony. Leonard Spaulding was a contemporary resident of Concord. MS., Huntington; previously unpublished; the italicized portions were part of a printed form.

———————

To H. G. O. BLAKE

Concord Jan 21st '54

Mr Blake,
     My coat is at last done, and my mother & sister allow that I am *so far* in a condition to go abroad. I feel as if I had gone abroad the

moment I put it on. It is, as usual a production strange to me, the wearer, invented by some Count D'Orsay, and the maker of it was not acquainted with any of my real depressions or elevations. He only measured a peg to hang it on, and might have made the loop big enough to go over my head. It requires a not quite innocent indifference not to say insolence to wear it. Ah, the process by which we get over-coats is not what it should be. Though the church declare it righteous & its priest pardons me, my own Good Genius tells me that it is hasty & coarse & false. I expect a time when, or rather an integrity by which a man will get his coat as honestly, and as perfectly fitting as a tree its bark. Now our garments are typical of our conformity to the ways of the world, i.e. of the Devil, & to some extent react on us and poison us like that shirt which Hercules put on.

I think to come & see you next week on Monday if nothing hinders. I have just returned from Court at Cambridge, whither I was called as a witness, having surveyed a water-privilege about which there is a dispute since you were here.

Ah! what foreign countries there are, greater in extent than the U. S. or Russia, and with no more souls to a square mile—stretching away on every side from every human being with whom you have no sympathy. Their humanity affects me as simply monstrous. Rocks—earth—brute beasts comparatively are not so strange to me. When I sit in the par-lors or kitchens of some with whom my business brings me— I was going to say in contact—(business, like misery, makes strange bedfellows) I feel a sort of awe and as forlorn as if I were cast away on a desolate shore—I think of Riley's Narrative & his sufferings. You who soared like a merlin with your mate through the realms of ether—in the presence of the unlike drop at once to earth a mere amorphous squab—divested of your air inflated pinions. (By the way, excuse this writing, for I am using the stub of the last feather I chance to possess.) You travel on, however, through this dark & desert world. You see in the distance an intelligent & sympathizing lineament,—stars come forth in the dark & oases appear in the desert.

But (to return to the subject of coats), we are well nigh smothered under yet more fatal coats, which do not fit us, our whole lives long. Consider the cloak that our employment or station is—how rarely men treat each other for what in their true & naked characters they are. How we use & tolerate pretension; how the judge is clothed with dignity which does not belong to him, and the trembling witness with humility

319

that does not belong to him, and the criminal perchance with shame or impudence which no more belong to him. It does not matter so much then what is the fashion of the cloak with which we cloak these cloaks. Change the coat—put the judge in the criminal box & the criminal on the bench, and you might think that you had changed the men.

No doubt the thinnest of all cloaks is conscious deception or lies it is sleazy & frays out, it is not close woven like cloth—but its meshes are a coarse net-work. A man can afford to lie only at the intersection of the threads, but truth puts in the filling & makes a consistent stuff.

I mean merely to suggest how much the station affects the demeanor & self-respectability of the parties, & that the difference between the judge's coat of cloth & the criminal's is insignificant compared with—or only partially significant of—the difference between the coats which their respective stations permits them to wear. What airs the judge may put on over his coat which the criminal may not! The judge's opinion (*sententia*) of the criminal *sentences* him & is read by the clerk of the court, & published to the world, & executed by the sheriff—but the criminal's opinion of the judge has the weight of a sentence & is published & executed only in the supreme court of the universe—a court not of common pleas. How much juster is the one than the other? Men are continually *sentencing* each other, but whether we be judges or criminals, the sentence is ineffectual unless we condemn ourselves.

I am glad to hear that I do not always limit your vision when you look this way—that you sometimes see the light through me, that I am here & there windows & not all dead wall. Might not the community sometimes petition a man to remove himself as a nuisance—a darkener of the day—a too large mote?

H. D. T.

This letter shows a greater debt, perhaps, to Sartor Resartus *than anything else Thoreau wrote. The volume referred to is James Riley's* Authentic Narrative of the Loss of the American Brig Commerce. *MS., Percy Brown.*

From THOMAS B. SMITH

New York Feby 23/54

Mr Henry Thoreau

Dear Sir
        Enclosed I send Ten Dollars for which send me 5 pounds best Plumbago for Electrotype purposes. The pound you sent before I found very good. Please send me a small quantity of the $1.50 per pound Black Lead that I may try it.

Yours Truly
Thomas B Smith per R.H.S.

This is the earliest of many extant letters written to Thoreau ordering materials manufactured by the family. Apparently Thoreau was gradually taking over some responsibility for the business from his aging father. MS., Berg; previously unpublished.

To GEORGE THATCHER

Concord Feb 25 '54.

Dear Cousin,—
        I should have answered you earlier if a wood merchant whom I engaged had kept his appointment. Measuring on Mr. Hubbard's plans of '36 and '52, which I enlarged, [word] the whole area wanted for a cemetery 16 acres & 114 rods. This includes a path one rod wide on the north side of the wood next to the meadow, and is all of the Brown Farm north of the New Road, except the meadow of about 7 acres and a small triangle of about a dozen rods next to the Agricultural Land. The above result is probably accurate within half an acre; nearer I cannot come with certainty without a resurvey.

9 acres & 9 rods are woodland, whose value I have got Anthony Wright, an old Farmer & now measurer of wood at the Depot, to assist me in determining. This is the result

			cord standing large & small	
Oak chiefly 4A 53rd 156 Cords at $2.75			cord standing large & small	429
White & Pitch Pine 3A 30rd		143½ Cords 2		287
Pitch Pine	146rd	16½ Cords 2		41 25
Young P Pine	100rd	5 cord 2		10
				$767 25

Merchantable green oak wood, piled on the cars, brings
here   4.75   pr cord.
Pitch pine   4.25.
White   2 50

An acquaintance in Boston applied to me last October for a small farm in Concord, and the small amount of land & the want of a good house may prevent his thinking of the Dutch House place. & besides circumstances have transpired which I fear will prevent his coming here; however I will inform him at once that it is on the market. I do not know about the state of his funds, only that he was in no hurry, though in earnest, & limited me to $2000.

All well

Yours
Henry D. Thoreau

According to Miss Sarah Bartlett of the Concord Free Public Library (letter of August 17, 1951) the land Thoreau surveyed was probably for Sleepy Hollow cemetery; and it was probably Cyrus Hubbard whose plan Thoreau used. The Brown farm belonged to Deacon Reuben Brown. MS., Edward Wannemacher (typescript); previously unpublished.

Concord March 1st 1854

Dear Sir,
I return herewith—three volumes viz. **Price on the Picturesque**
1st vol. McCulloh's Researches, and Josselyn's Voyages.

Yrs
Henry D. Thoreau

The letter is addressed to "Librarian of Harvard University Politeness
of Mr. Gerrish." Gerrish is identified by Kenneth Cameron as Charles
Pickering Gerrish, of the Class of 1854. MS. facsimile, Kenneth Walter
Cameron, The Transcendentalists and Minerva, *II, 481.*

From HORACE GREELEY

March 6 1854

Dear Sir,—
I presume your first letter containing the $2 was robbed by our
general mail robber of New Haven, who has just been sent to the State's
Prison. Your second letter has probably failed to receive attention owing
to a press of business. But I will make all right. You ought to have the
Semi-weekly, and I shall order it sent to you one year on trial; if you
choose to write me a letter or so some time, very well; if not, we will
be even without that.
Thoreau, I want you to do something on *my* urgency. I want you to
collect and arrange your "Miscellanies" and send them to me. Put in
"Ktaadn," "Carlyle," "A Winter Walk," "Canada," etc., and I will try
to find a publisher who will bring them out at his own risk, and (I hope)
to your ultimate profit. If you have anything new to put with them, very

323

well; but let me have about a 12mo volume whenever you can get it ready, and see if there is not something to your credit in the bank of Fortune.

Yours,
Horace Greeley.

Text, *Sanborn's* Henry D. Thoreau, *pp. 238–39.*

To ?

In his *Journal* for March 8, 1854 (VI, 158) Thoreau records: "I wrote a letter for an Irishman night before last [March 6], sending for his wife in Ireland to come to this country. One sentence which he dictated was, 'Don't mind the rocking of the vessel, but take care of the children that they be not lost overboard.' "

From HORACE GREELEY

New York, Mar. 23, '54.

Dear Thoreau,

I am glad your "Walden" is coming out. *I* shall announce it at once, whether Ticknor does or not.

I am in no hurry now about your Miscellanies; take your time, select a good title, and prepare your articles deliberately and finally. Then if Ticknor will give you something worth having, let him have this too; if proffering it to him is to glut your market, let it come to me. But take your time. I was only thinking you were hybernating when you ought to be doing something. I referred (without naming you) to your 'Walden' experience in my lecture on "Self-Culture," with which I have

bored ever so many audiences. This episode excited much interest and I have repeatedly been asked who it is that I refer to.

Yours,
Horace Greeley.

H. D. Thoreau, Concord, Ms.

P.S. You must know Miss Elizabeth Hoar, whereas I hardly do. Now I have agreed to edit Margaret's works, and I want of Elizabeth a letter or memorandum of personal recollections of Margaret and her ideas. Can't you ask her to write it for me?

Yours,
H. G.

MS., Princeton University Library.

From HORACE GREELEY

[April 2, 1854]

Dear Thoreau,—
Thank you for your kindness in the matter of Margaret. Pray take no further trouble; but if anything should come in your way, calculated to help me, do not forget.

Yours,
Horace Greeley.

Text, *Sanborn's* Henry D. Thoreau, *p. 240.*

To DR. THADDEUS W. HARRIS

Concord April 18th '54

Dear Sir,
 I return by Mr. Gerrish three vols. viz Agassiz sur les Glaciers Shepard's Clear Sunshine and New England in 1652

Yrs
Henry D. Thoreau

MS., Harvard.

From CHARLES SCRIBNER

145 Nassau Street, New York, May 1854

As it is my intention to publish the coming season a work, entitled *An Encyclopaedia of American Literature*, embracing Personal and Critical Notices of Authors, with passages from their Writings, from the earliest period to the present day, with Portraits, Autographs, and other illustrations, I have adopted the method of addressing to you a Circular letter, as the best means of rendering the book as complete in regard to points on which you may be interested, as possible, and as faithful as may be to the memories and claims of the families and personages whose literary interests will be represented in it. The plan of the work is to furnish to the public, at one view, notices of the Lives and Writings of all American authors of importance. As it is quite probable you may have in your possession material or information which you would like the opportunity of seeing noticed in such a publication, you will serve the objects of the work by a reply to this circular, in such answers to the following suggestions as may appear desirable or convenient to you.

1. Dates of birth, parentage, education, residence, with such biographical information and anecdote; as you may think proper to be employed in such a publication.
2. Names and dates of Books published, references to Articles in Reviews, Magazines, &c., of which you may be the author.
3. Family notices and sources of information touching American authors no longer living, of whom you may be the representative.

Dates, facts, and precise information, in reference to points which have not been noticed in collections of this kind, or which may have been misstated, are desirable. Your own judgment will be the best guide as to the material of this nature which should be employed in a work which it is intended shall be of general interest and of a National character. It will represent the whole country, its only aim being to exhibit to the readers a full, fair, and entertaining account of the literary products thus far of America.

It is trusted that the plan of the work will engage your sympathy and concurrence, and that you will find in it a sufficient motive for a reply to this Circular. The materials which you may communicate will be employed, so far as is consistent with the limits and necessary unity of the work, for the preparation of which I have engaged Evert A. and George L. Duyckinck, who have been prominently before the public for several years in a similar connection, as Editors of the "Literary World."

Yours, respectfully,
Charles Scribner

The volume was published by Scribner in 1855 under the title of Cyclopaedia of American Literature, *and a notice of Thoreau's writings was included* (*II, 653–56*). MS., Huntington; *previously unpublished. Except for the date the letter is printed.*

From TICKNOR & CO.

Boston June 10 1854

Dear Sir

Our Mr. Fields who left by the steamer of the 7th for England took the proof sheets of Walden—In order to secure a copt in England the book must be published there as soon as here and at least 12 copies published and offered for sale. If Mr. F. succeeds in making a sale of the early sheets, it will doubtless be printed in London so as to cause very little delay here but if it be necessary to print and send out the copies it will delay us 3 or 4 weeks. Probably not more than three weeks. You will probably prefer to delay the publication that you may be sure of your cop't in England.

Truly yours
W. D. Ticknor & Co.

H. D. Thoreau

On that trip James Fields never reached England; he became so seasick that he had to leave ship at Halifax and return home. Nevertheless, as Tryon and Charvat point out in The Cost Books of Ticknor & Fields, *he continued his efforts on behalf of* Walden. *He recommended the book to the London publisher Richard Bentley, as Emerson had done, and he added: "The book is sure to make a noise in the literary world." Fields also wrote his firm's agent, Trübner, asking him to dispose of the English rights to some publisher, Bentley preferably. In the Trübner letter Fields said of* Walden: *"It belongs to the same class of works with Mr. Emerson's writings & will be likely to attract attention. . . . Walden is no common book" (The Cost Books, p. 290). In spite of these and other efforts,* Walden *was not published in England until 1884. MS., Harvard (typescript).*

From DR. THADDEUS W. HARRIS

Cambridge, Mass. June 27, 1854.

Mr. Henry D. Thoreau,
Dear Sir.

 Your letter of the 25th, the books, and the *Cicada* came to hand this evening,—and I am much obliged to you for all of them;—for the books,—because I am very busy with putting the Library in order for examination, & want every book to be in its place;—for the letter, because it gives me interesting facts concerning Cicadas; and for the specimen because it is *new* to me, as a species or as a variety.

 The *Cicada* seems to be a *female,* and of course when living could not make the noise peculiar to the other sex. It differs from my specimens of *Cicada septemdecim* (& indeed still more from all the other species in my collection). It is not so large as the *C.17;* it has more orange about its thorax; the wing-veins are not so vividly stained with orange, and the dusky zigzag W on the anterior or upper wings, which is very distinct in the *C.17,* is hardly visible in this specimen. It has much the same form as the female *C.17;* but I must see the *male* in order to determine positively whether it be merely a variety or a different species. I should be very glad to get more specimens and of both sexes. Will you try for them?

Your much obliged
Thaddeus William Harris.

Harris, the Harvard librarian and a leading entomologist, was the author of the classic Report on Insects Injurious to Vegetation (*Boston, 1841*). *Thoreau reports the discovery of this cicada in his* Journal *for June 13, 1854.* MS., Morgan; *previously unpublished.*

To H. G. O. BLAKE

Concord, August 8, 1854.

Mr. Blake,—

Methinks I have spent a rather unprofitable summer thus far. I have been too much with the world, as the poet might say. The completest performance of the highest duties it imposes would yield me but little satisfaction. Better the neglect of all such, because your life passed on a level where it was impossible to recognize them. Latterly, I have heard the very flies buzz too distinctly, and have accused myself because I did not still this superficial din. We must not be too easily distracted by the crying of children or of dynasties. The Irishman erects his sty, and gets drunk, and jabbers more and more under my eaves, and I am responsible for all that filth and folly. I find it, as ever, very unprofitable to have much to do with men. It is sowing the wind, but not reaping even the whirlwind; only reaping an unprofitable calm and stagnation. Our conversation is a smooth, and civil, and never-ending speculation merely. I take up the thread of it again in the morning, with very much such courage as the invalid takes his prescribed Seidlitz powders. Shall I help you to some of the mackerel? It would be more respectable if men, as has been said before, instead of being such pigmy desperates, were Giant Despairs. Emerson says that his life is so unprofitable and shabby for the most part, that he is driven to all sorts of resources [recources?], and, among the rest, to men. I tell him that we differ only in our resources. Mine is to get away from men. They very rarely affect me as grand or beautiful; but I know that there is a sunrise and a sunset every day. In the summer, this world is a mere wateringplace,—a Saratoga,—drinking so many tumblers of Congress water; and in the winter, is it any better, with its oratorios? I have seen more men than usual, lately; and, well as I was acquainted with one, I am surprised to find what vulgar fellows they are. They do a little business commonly each day, in order to pay their board, and then they congregate in sitting-rooms and feebly fabulate and paddle in the social slush; and when I think that they have sufficiently relaxed, and am prepared to see them steal away to their shrines, they go unashamed to their beds, and take on a new layer of sloth. They may be single, or have families in their *faineancy*. I do not meet men who can have nothing to do with me because they have so much to do with themselves. However, I trust

that a very few cherish purposes which they never declare. Only think, for a moment, of a man about his affairs! How we should respect him! How glorious he would appear! Not working for any corporation, its agent, or president, but fulfilling the end of his being! A man about *his business* would be the cynosure of all eyes.

The other evening I was determined that I would silence this shallow din; that I would walk in various directions and see if there was not to be found any depth of silence around. As Bonaparte sent out his horsemen in the Red Sea on all sides to find shallow water, so I sent forth my mounted thoughts to find deep water. I left the village and paddled up the river to Fair Haven Pond. As the sun went down, I saw a solitary boatman disporting on the smooth lake. The falling dews seemed to strain and purify the air, and I was soothed with an infinite stillness. I got the world, as it were, by the nape of the neck, and held it under in the tide of its own events, till it was drowned, and then I let it go down stream like a dead dog. Vast hollow chambers of silence stretched away on every side, and my being expanded in proportion, and filled them. Then first could I appreciate sound, and find it musical.

But now for your news. Tell us of the year. Have you fought the good fight? What is the state of your crops? Will your harvest answer well to the seed-time, and are you cheered by the prospect of stretching corn-fields? Is there any blight on your fields, any murrain in your herds? Have you tried the size and quality of your potatoes? It does one good to see their balls dangling in the lowlands. Have you got your meadow hay before the fall rains shall have set in? Is there enough in your barns to keep your cattle over? Are you killing weeds nowadays? or have you earned leisure to go a-fishing? Did you plant any Giant Regrets last spring, such as I saw advertised? It is not a new species, but the result of cultivation and a fertile soil. They are excellent for sauce. How is it with your marrow squashes for winter use? Is there likely to be a sufficiency of fall feed in your neighborhood? What is the state of the springs? I read that in your country there is more water on the hills than in the valleys. Do you find it easy to get all the help you require? Work early and late, and let your men and teams rest at noon. Be careful not to drink too much sweetened water, while at your hoeing, this hot weather. You can bear the heat much better for it.

Text, Familiar Letters of Thoreau, *pp. 275–79.*

From DANIEL RICKETSON

Brooklawn, near New Bedford Mass. Aug. 12th, 1854

Dear Sir,

I have just finished reading "Walden" and hasten to thank you for the great degree of satisfaction it has afforded me. Having always been a lover of Nature, in man, as well as in the material universe, I hail with pleasure every original production in literature which bears the stamp of a genuine and earnest love for the true philosophy of human life.—Such I assure you I esteem your book to be. To many, and to most, it will appear to be the wild musings of an eccentric and strange mind, though all must recognize your affectionate regard for the gentle denizens of the woods and pond as well as the great love you have shewn for what are familiarly called the beauties of Nature. But to me the book appears to evince a mind most thoroughly self possessed, highly cultivated with a strong vein of common sense. The whole book is a prose poem (pardon the solecism) and at the same time as simple as a running brook.

I have always loved ponds of pure translucent water, and some of my happiest and most memorable days have been passed on and around the beautiful Middleboro' Ponds, particularly the largest, Assawampset —here King Philip frequently came, and a beautiful round hill near by, is still known as "King Philip's look-out." I have often felt an inclination when tired of the noise and strife of society, to retire to the shores of this noble old pond, or rather lake, for it is some 5 or 6 miles in length and 2 broad. But I have a wife and four children, & besides have got a *little* too far along, being in my forty-second year, to undertake a new mode of life. I strive however, and have striven during the whole of my life, to live as free from the restraint of mere forms & ceremonies as I possibly can. I love a quiet, peaceful rural retirement; but it was not my fate to realize this until a little past thirty years of age— since then I have been a sort of rustic, genteel perhaps, rustic. Not so very genteel you might reply, if you saw the place where I am writing. It is a rough board shanty 12 × 14 three miles from New Bedford in a quiet & secluded spot—here for the present I eat, & sleep, read, write, receive visitors &c. My house is now *undergoing* repairs &c and my family are in town. A short time since a whip-poor-will serenaded me,

and later at night I hear the cuckoos near my windows. It has long been my delight to observe the feathered tribes, and earlier in life I was quite an ornithologist. The coming of the first Blue bird in early Spring is to me still a delightful circumstance. But more particularly soothing to me is the insect hum so multitudinous at this season.—Now as I write the crickets & other little companions are sweetly & soothingly singing around my dwelling, & occasionally in my room. I am quite at home with partridges, Quails, rabbits skunks & woodchucks. But Winter is my best time, then I am a great tramper through the woods. O how I love the woods. I have walked thousands of miles in the woods hereabouts. I recognize many of my own experiences in your "Walden." Still I am not altogether given up to these matters—they are my pastimes. I have a farm to attend to, fruit trees & a garden & a little business occasionally in town to look after, but much leisure nevertheless. In fact I am the only man of leisure I know of, every body here as well as elsewhere is upon the stir. I love quiet, this you know friend Thoreau dont necessarily imply that the body should be still all the time. I am often quietest, arn't you, when walking among the still haunts of Nature or hoeing perhaps beans as I have oftentimes done as well as corn & potatoes &c &c.

Poetry has been to me a great consolation amid the jarring elements of this life. The English poets some of them at least, and one Latin, our good old Virgil, have been like household gods to me.—Cowper's Task, my greatest favorite now lies before me in which I had been reading & alternately looking at the western sky just after sunset before I commenced this letter. Cowper was a true lover of the country. How often have I felt the force of these lines upon the country in my own experience

> "I never framed a wish or formed a plan,
> That flattered me with hopes of earthly bliss
> But there I laid the scene."

All through my boyhood, *the country* haunted my thoughts. Though blessed with a good home, books & teachers, the latter however with one exception were not blessings, I would have exchanged all for the life of a rustic. I envied as I then thought the freedom of the farmer boy. But I have long thought that the life of the farmer, that is most farmers, possessed but little of the poetry of labour. How we accumulate cares around us. The very repairs

I am now making upon my house will to some considerable extent increase my cares. A rough board shanty, rye & indian bread, water from the spring, or as in your case, from the pond, and other things in keeping, do not burden the body & mind. It is fine houses, fine furniture, sumptuous fare, fine clothes, and many in number, horses & carriages, servants &c &c &c, there are the harpies, that so disturb our real happiness.

My next move in life I hope will be into a much more simple mode of living. I should like to live in a small house, with my family, uncarpeted white washed walls, simple old fashioned furniture & plain wholesome old fashioned fare. Though I have always been inclined to be a vegetarian in diet & once lived in capital health two years on the Graham system.

Well this will do for myself. Now for you friend Thoreau. Why return to the world again? a life such as you spent at Walden was too true & beautiful to be abandoned for any slight reason.

The ponds I allude to are much more secluded than Walden, and really delightful places—Should you ever incline again to try your "philosophy of living" I would introduce you into haunts, that your very soul would leap to behold. Well I thought I would just write you a few lines to thank you for the pleasure I have received from the reading of your "Walden," but I have found myself running on till now. I feel that you are a kindred spirit and so fear not. I was pleased to find a kind word or two in your book for the poor down trodden slave. Wilberforce, Clarkson and John Woolman & Anthony Benezet were household words in my father's house.—I early became acquainted with the subject of slavery for my parents were Quakers, & Quakers were then all Abolitionists. My love of Nature, absolute, undefiled Nature makes me an abolitionist. How could I listen to the woodland songs—or gaze upon the outstretched landscape, or look at the great clouds & the starry heavens and be aught but a friend of the poor and oppressed coloured race of our land But why do I write—it is in vain to portray these things—they can only be felt and lived, and to you of all others I would refrain from being prolix.

I have outlived, or nearly so, all ambition for notoriety. I wish only to be a simple, good man & so live that when I come to surrender up my spirit to the Great Father, I may depart in peace.

I wrote the above last evening. It is now Sunday afternoon, and alone in my Shanty I sit down at my desk to add a little more. A great white

cloud which I have been watching for the past half hour is now majestically moving off to the north east before the fine S. W. breeze which sets in here nearly every summer afternoon from the ocean. We have here the best climate in New England—sheltered on the north & east by dense pine woods from the cold winds which so cut up the healths of eastern folks, or rather are suffered to—but I think if the habits of our people were right the north easters would do but little harm. I never heard that the Indians were troubled by them—but they were nature's philosophers and lived in the woods. I *love* to go by my instincts, inspiration rather. O how much we lose by civilization! In the eyes of the world you & I are demi savages— But I rather think we could stand our hand at the dinner table or in the drawing room with most of folks. I would risk you anywhere, and as for myself I have about done with the follies of "society." I never was trump'd yet.

I have lived out all the experiences of idle youth—some gentle, & some savage experiences but my heart was not made of the stuff for a sportsman or angler—early in life I ranged the woods, fields & shores with my gun, or rod, but I found that all I sought could be obtained much better without the death dealing implements. So now my rustic staff is all the companion I usually take, unless my old dog joins me— taking no track as he often does, and bounding upon me in some distant thicket. My favorite books are—Cowper's task, Thomson's Seasons Milton, Shakespeare, &c &c— Goldsmith Gray's Elegy— Beattie's Minstrel (parts) Howitt, Gil. White, (Selbourne) Bewick (wood-engraver) moderns—Wordsworth Ch. Lamb—De Quiney, Macauly, Kit. North, &c &c

These and others are more my companions than men. I like talented women & swear lustily by May Wolstoncroft, &c &c—Roland, Joan d'arc & somewhat by dear Margaret Fuller.

The smaller fry, let go by—

Again permit me to thank you for the pleasure & strength I have found in reading "Walden."

Dear Mr Walden good bye for the present.

Yours most respectfully
Daniel Ricketson

Henry D. Thoreau Esq

This new disciple became remarkably faithful, writing many more let-
ters than he received and extending more invitations than were recipro-
cated. Thoreau learned to view him with affection not unmixed with
exasperation. MS., Huntington.

From T. W. HIGGINSON

Newburyport, Aug 13, 1854.

Dear Sir:
    Let me thank you heartily for your paper on the present condi-
tion of Massachusetts, read at Framingham and printed in the *Liberator.* As a literary statement of the truth, which every day is making more
manifest, it surpasses everything else (so I think), which the terrible
week in Boston has called out. I need hardly add my thanks for
"Walden," which I have been awaiting for so many years. Through Mr.
Field's kindness, I have read a great deal of it in sheets:—I have just
secured two copies, one for myself, and one for a young girl here, who
seems to me to have the most remarkable literary talent since Margaret
Fuller,—and to whom your first book has been among the scriptures,
ever since I gave her that. [No doubt your new book will have a larger
circulation than the other, but not, I think, a more select or appreciate
one.]

The paper that so impressed Higginson was "Slavery in Massachu-
setts." The young girl he mentions was Harriet Prescott, who later con-
tributed numerous articles to the Atlantic Monthly. *Text, Sanborn's*
Recollections of Seventy Years, *p. 399; the manuscript was sold by*
Charles F. Libbie & Co. at the Garfield sale of January 27–28, 1914; the
sale catalogue quotes the bracketed sentence.

To SARAH E. WEBB

Concord *Mass.* Sep. 15 '54

Sarah E. Webb,
    Your note, which was directed to Concord *N.H.*, has just reached me. The address to which you refer has not been printed in a pamphlet form. It appeared in the Liberator, from which it was copied into the Tribune, &, with omissions, into the Anti-Slavery Standard. I am sorry that I have not a copy to send you. I have published "A Week on the Concord & Merrimack Rivers," as well as "Walden, or Life in the Woods," and some miscellaneous papers. The "Week" probably is not for sale at any bookstore. The greater part of the edition was returned to me.

Respectfully
Henry D. Thoreau.

Undoubtedly "Slavery in Massachusetts," which Thoreau had delivered before the Anti-slavery Convention at Framingham the preceding July 4, was the address Miss Webb had in mind. MS., Berg; previously unpublished.

From MARSTON WATSON

Plymouth Mass Sept 17

My dear Sir—
    Mr James Spooner and others here, your friends, have clubbed together and raised a small sum in hope of persuading you to come down and read them a paper or two some Sunday. They can offer you $10 at least. Mr Alcott is now here, and I thought it might be agreeable to you to come down next Saturday and read a paper on Sunday morn-

ing and perhaps on Sunday evening also, if agreeable to yourself. I can
assure you of a very warm reception but from a small party only.

Very truly yours
B. M. Watson

I will meet you at the Depot on Saturday evening, if you so advise
me. Last train leaves at 5—

This is not a "Leyden Hall Meeting" but a private party—social gathering—almost sewing circle. Tho' perhaps we may meet you at Leyden
Hall.

*Watson, a friend of Thoreau's at Harvard, had in Plymouth an estate,
"Hillside," that was a favorite spot for most of the Transcendentalists.
Leyden Hall is a public hall in Plymouth. MS., Mrs. Robert Bowler,
previously unpublished.*

To MARSTON WATSON

Concord Mass Sep 19th '54

Dear Sir

I am glad to hear from you & the Plymouth men again. The
world still holds together between Concord and Plymouth, it seems. I
should like to be with you while Mr Alcott is there, but I cannot come
next Sunday. I will come Sunday after next, that is Oct 1st, if that will
do,—and look out for you at the depot.

I do not like to promise now more than one discourse. Is there a good
precedent for 2?

Yrs Concordially
Henry D. Thoreau.

MS., Huntington.

To H. G. O. BLAKE

Concord, September 21, 1854.

Blake,—

I have just read your letter, but do not mean now to answer it, solely for want of time to say what I wish. I directed a copy of "Walden" to you at Ticknor's, on the day of its publication, and it should have reached you before. I am encouraged to know that it interests you as it now stands,—a printed book,—for you apply a very severe test to it,— you make the highest demand on me. As for the excursion you speak of, I should like it right well,—indeed I thought of proposing the same thing to you and [Theo] Brown, some months ago. Perhaps it would have been better if I had done so then; for in that case I should have been able to enter into it with that infinite margin to my views,—spotless of all engagements,—which I think so necessary. As it is, I have agreed to go a-lecturing to Plymouth, Sunday after next (October 1) and to Philadelphia in November, and thereafter to the West, *if they shall want me;* and, as I have prepared nothing in that shape, I feel as if my hours were spoken for. However, I think that, after having been to Plymouth, I may take a day or two—if that date will suit you and Brown. *At any rate* I will write you then.

Text, Familiar Letters of Thoreau, *p. 281.*

From MARSTON WATSON

Plymouth Mass. Sept 24.

My dear Sir:

There is to be a meeting here on Oct 1st that we think will interfere with yours, and so if the Lord is willing and you have no objections we will expect you on the next Sunday 8th October.

I think Mr A. will stay till that time.

I have been lately adding to my garden, and now have all that joins me—so I am ready to have it surveyed by you; a pleasure I have long promised myself. So, if you are at leisure and inclined to the field I hope I may be so fortunate as to engage your services

Very truly yrs
B. M. Watson

The survey might be before the Monday or after as you please, and I will meet you at the Depot any time you say.

Thoreau did make the survey of "Hillside," and the original survey is in the possession of Mrs. Bowler. He also delivered his lecture on "Moonlight" on the evening of October 8, 1854, as is reported by Bronson Alcott in his manuscript Journal *in the Concord Free Public Library. MS., Mrs. Robert Bowler; previously unpublished.*

From MARSTON WATSON

Plymouth Oct [*sic*] 30

My dear Sir—

I am glad to learn from Mr. Spooner that you are really coming down, with the tripod too, which is so good news that I hardly dared to expect it.

It seems a little uncertain whether you intend to read in the morning as well as evening, and so I write to enquire, that there may be no mistake in the announcement. Please let me know by return mail which will be in time.

Very truly yours
B. M. Watson

Although the letter is dated October 30, it is obviously a sequel to Watson's letter of September 24, written before Thoreau's lecture engagement of October 8. MS., Mrs. Robert Bowler; previously unpublished.

To DANIEL RICKETSON

Concord Mass, Oct 1st '54

Dear Sir,

I had duly received your very kind and frank letter, but delayed to answer it thus long because I have little skill as a correspondent, and wished to send you something more than my thanks. I was gratified by your prompt and hearty acceptance of my book. Yours is the only word of greeting I am likely to receive from a dweller in the woods like myself, from where the whippoorwill and cuckoo are heard, and there are better than moral clouds drifting over, and real breezes blow.

Your account excites in me a desire to see the Middleboro Ponds, of which I had already heard somewhat; as also of some very beautiful ponds on the Cape, in Harwich I think, near which I once passed. I have sometimes also thought of visiting that remnant of *our* Indians still living near you.— But then, you know there is nothing like ones native fields and lakes. The best news you send me is, not that Nature with you is so fair and genial, but that there is one there who likes her so well. That proves all that was asserted.

Homer, of course, you include in your list of lovers of Nature—and, by the way, let me mention here,—for this is "my thunder" lately—*Wm* Gilpin's long series of books on the Picturesque, with their illustrations. If it chances that you have not met with these, I cannot just now frame a better wish than that you may one day derive as much pleasure from the inspection of them as I have.

Much as you have told me of yourself, you have still I think a little the advantage of me in this correspondence, for I have told you still more in my book. You have therefore the broadest mark to fire at.

341

A young English author, Thomas Cholmondeley, is just now waiting for me to take a walk with him—therefore excuse this very barren note from

Yrs, hastily at last,
Henry D. Thoreau

Ricketson jotted in his journal: "Received a letter from Henry D. Thoreau to-day in reply to mine to him. Letter hastily written and hardly satisfactory, evidently well meant though overcautious" (Ricketson, *p. 280). For a discussion of Thoreau's interest in Gilpin see W. D. Templeman, "Thoreau, Moralist of the Picturesque," PMLA, XLVII (September 1932), 864–89. The young English author Thoreau mentions at the end of his letter was to become his good friend. Cholmondeley had arrived in America in August 1854. He went to Concord originally for the purpose of seeing Emerson, but soon developed more interest in Thoreau and corresponded with him until the end of his life. The most notable event in their friendship was probably Cholmondeley's gift to Thoreau, after Cholmondeley returned to England, of a rich library of Hindu writings in translation. They arrived in Concord at the end of November 1855, a treasure for Thoreau, forty-four volumes in all, as he noted in his* Journal *at the time. MS., Huntington.*

To H. G. O. BLAKE

Concord Oct. 5 '54

Mr. Blake,

After I wrote to you Mr. Watson postponed my going to Plymouth one week i.e. till next Sunday, and now he wishes me to carry my instruments & survey his grounds, to which he has been adding. Since I want a little money, though I contemplate but a short excursion, I do not feel at liberty to decline this work. I do not know exactly how long it will detain me—but there is plenty of time yet—& I will write to you again—perhaps from Plymouth—

There is a Mr. Thomas Cholmondeley (pronounced Chumly) a young English author, staying at our house at present—who asks me to teach him *botany*—i.e. anything which I know—and also to make an excursion to some mountain with him. He is a well-behaved person, and *possibly* I may propose his taking that run to Wachusett with us—if it will be agreeable to you. Nay If I do not hear any objection from you I will consider myself *at liberty* to invite him.

In haste,
H. D. Thoreau

MS., Berg, *in Blake's hand.*

From DANIEL RICKETSON

Brooklawn, near New Bedford, Oct. 12th, 1854.

Dear Mr. Walden,—

Your long delayed, but very acceptable acknowledgment of the 1st inst. came duly to hand. It requires no answer, and I trust you will not esteem this as such. I simply wish to say, that it will afford me pleasure to show you the Middleborough ponds, as well as the other Indian water spoken of by you, which I conclude to be what is called "Wakeebe Pond," at Mashpee near Sandwich.

Since I first wrote you my rough board shanty, which I then inhabited and from which I now write, has been partially forsaken, thro' the house of which I spoke to you as being built, having been completed and my family moved into it; so the shanty is somewhat shorn of its beams to the public or vulgar eye at least, but none the less prized by me. Here I spend a considerable part of my time in study and meditation, and here I also entertain my best and most welcome friends. Now, friend Walden, if it should be agreeable to you to leave home at this pleasant season, I shall be happy to receive you as my guest. Making my farm, which lies about three miles north of New Bedford, headquarters, we can sally

forth into the adjoining country—to the fine ponds in question and visit other objects of interest hitherward. I am just now quite busily engaged in the improvement of the grounds near my house, but expect to conclude them by the end of next week, when, should it meet your pleasure, I shall be very happy to see you here.

I am quite a *tramper* as well as yourself, but have horse-flesh and carriages at hand if preferable, which certainly for long distances, with all my antediluvian taste, I deem it to be.

Perhaps your young English friend and author, Mr. Cholmondeley, would like to accompany you, should you conclude to come. If so, please extend the invitation to him should you deem it proper.

I do not wish to push matters at all, but am of the opinion, if you are not too *learned*, we shall affiliate nicely in our rustic feelings—at any rate it will do no harm to try.

Your short and hastily written note embarrasses me, and I hardly know whether it best or no to send what I have now written, and so conclude, whether this shall reach you or not,

Your friend and fellow-worshipper at Nature's great shrine,

Daniel Ricketson.

Apparently Ricketson did not mail this letter for a while: he said in his journal, December 14, 1854: "Wrote an invitation to H. D. Thoreau of Concord, author of Walden, and sent a letter which I had had on hand some time" (Ricketson, p. 280). Text, Ricketson, pp. 32–34.

To H. G. O. BLAKE

Concord Sat. pm. Oct 14 '54

Blake,

I have just returned from Plymouth, where I have been detained surveying much longer than I expected.

What do you say to visiting Wachusett next Thursday? I will start

at 7¼ a.m. *unless there is a prospect of a stormy day,* go by cars to West-minster, & thence on foot 5 or 6 miles to the *mt* tops, where I may engage to meet you at (or before) 12. *m.*

If the weather is unfavorable, I will try again—on Friday,—& again on Monday.

If a storm comes on after starting, I will seek you at the tavern in Princeton Center, as soon as circumstances will permit.

I shall expect an answer to clinch the bargain.

Yrs
Henry D. Thoreau.

Blake apparently accepted Thoreau's invitation, for the Journal *entry on the following Thursday, October 19, reads: "7:15 a.m.—To West-minster by cars; thence on foot to Wachusett Mountain, four miles to Foster's and two miles thence to mountain-top by road." MS., Miss Charlotte Thatcher.*

From A. FAIRBANKS

Providence Oct 14, 1854

Mr Henry D Thoreau
Dear Sir

Our Course of Independent, or reform Lectures (ten in number) we propose to commence Next Month. Will you give me liberty to put your name in the program, and say when it will suit your convenience to come   every Lecturer will choose his own Subject, but we expect *all,* whether Antislavery or what else, will be of a *reformatory Character* We have engaged Theodore Parker, who will give the Introductory Nov. 1st (Garrison, W. Phillips Thos W. Higginson Lucy Stone (Mrs Rose of New York Antoinett L Brown and hope to have Cassius N Clay, & Henry Ward Beecher, (we had a course of these lectures last year and the receipts from tickets at a low price paid expenses and fifteen to twenty dollars to the Lecturers. We think we shall do as well this year

345

as last, and perhaps better. The Anthony Burns affair and the Nebraska bill, and other outrages of Slavery has done much to awaken the feeling of a class of Minds heretofore quiet, on all questions of reform In getting up these popular Lectures we thought at first, it would not do as well to have them too radical, or it would be best to have a part of the Speakers of the conservative class, but experience has shown us in Providence surely, that the Masses who attend such Lectures are better suited with reform lectures than with the old school conservatives. I will thank you for an early reply

Yours Respectfully for true freedom
A. Fairbanks

This is, in some respects, the kind of letter that made Thoreau's hackles rise. He never liked to be told what to say, even if it were to be "of a reformatory Character." Although he accepted the invitation and lectured in Providence on December 6, his irritation overflowed into his Journal *entry for the next day: "I would rather write books than lectures. That is fine, this coarse." We are not sure of the identity of Fairbanks.* Brown's Providence Directory *for 1853–54 lists two Fairbankses whose first names begin with "A": Addison M., a machinist, and Asa, a paper and paper stock dealer. MS., Huntington; previously unpublished.*

To DR. THADDEUS W. HARRIS

Concord Oct 23d '54

Sir,

I return herewith the "Bhagvat Geeta." Will you please send me the "Vishnoo Purana" a single volume—translated by Wilson.

Yrs respecty
Henry D. Thoreau

MS., Berg; *previously unpublished.*

From C. B. BERNARD

Akron Oct 26, 1854

Henry D. Thoreau Esq Concord Mass
Dear Sir

Seeing your name announced as a Lecturer, I write you a line to see if your services could be secured to give a Lecture before the Library Association of this place.

We can give #50—

Thinking you might have other calls this way, we thought we would add our solicitation with the rest—

Yours Respectfully
C B Bernard Cor Sec

Thoreau, probably because he was unable to arrange a large enough schedule to make the trip worth while, made no lecture tours so far west. MS., Berg; previously unpublished.

To CHARLES SUMNER

"These faithful reports with their admirable maps and plates, are some atonement for the mistakes of our Government," Thoreau wrote in a letter that was sold by the Anderson Galleries at the Manning sale of February 1–3, 1926. The catalogue of that sale described the documents merely as "some Government reports." Earlier, Francis H. Allen's *Bibliography of Henry David Thoreau* (p. 161) lists the letter as a "1 page, 4to" manuscript sold by Charles F. Libbie & Co. at the Stickney sale of December 18–19, 1907.

From CHARLES SUMNER

Boston 31st Oct. '54

My dear Sir,

I am glad to send books where they are so well appreciated as in your chamber.

Permit me to say that the courtesy of your letter admonishes me of my short-coming in not sooner acknowledging the gift of your book. Believe me I had not forgotten it, but I proposed to write you, when I had fully read & enjoyed it. At present I have been able to peruse only the early chapters, & have detected parts enough, however, to satisfy me that you have made a contribution to the permanent literature of our mother tongue, & to make me happy in your success.

Believe me, dear Sir,

Sincerely Yours,
Charles Sumner

Henry D. Thoreau Esq.

MS., University of Texas Library; *previously unpublished.*

———

From A. FAIRBANKS

Providence Nov. 6, 1854

Mr Henry D Thore[a]u
Dear Sir

I am in receipt of yours of the 4th inst, You stating explicitly that the 6th December would suit you better than any other time. I altered other arrangements on purpose to accommodate you, and notified you as *soon* as I was able to *accomplish* them. Had you named the last Wednsday in Nov. or the second Wednsday in December, I could have replied to you at once *or* any time in Janury or Feb it would have

been the same I shall regret the disappointment very much but must submit to it if you have such overtures as you cannot avoid. I hope however you will be able to come at the time appointed

Truly
A. Fairbanks

Thoreau lectured in Providence on December 6. MS., Huntington; previously unpublished.

To REVEREND ADRIEN ROUQUETTE

Rev*d* Adrien Rouquette

Concord Mass. Nov. 13th 1854

Dear Sir

I have just received your letter and the 3 works which accompanied it—and I make haste to send you a copy of "A Week on the Concord & Merrimack Rivers"—in the same mail with this. I thank you heartily for the interest which you express in my Walden—and also for the gift of your works. I have not had time to peruse [?] the books attentively but I am

In his Journal *for November 11, 1854 Thoreau records that he had received a letter in French and three "ouvrages" from the Abbé Rouquette in Louisiana. In the catalogue of his library Thoreau lists Rouquette's* La Thébaïde en Amérique *and* Wild Flowers. *The third volume was probably* Les Savanes, Poésies Américaines. *MS., Harvard; previously unpublished; this is apparently Thoreau's rough draft of the letter, the latter part of which is missing.*

To BRONSON ALCOTT

Concord Nov. 15, 1854

Mr. Alcott,

I wish to introduce to you Thomas Cholmondeley, an English man, of whom and his work in New Zealand I have already told you. He proposes to spend a part of the winter in Boston, pursuing his literary studies, at the same time that he is observing our institutions.

He is an English country gentleman of simple habits and truly liberal mind, who may one day take a part in the government of his country.

I think that you will find you[r] account in comparing notes with him.

MS., Concord Free Public Library; *the signature has been cut from the manuscript.*

––––––––––––

To DR. THADDEUS W. HARRIS

Concord Nov. 15 1854

Dr Harris
Dear Sir,

Will you allow me to introduce to you the bearer—Thomas Cholmondeley, who has been spending some months with us in Concord He is an English country gentleman, and the author of a political work on New Zealand called "Ultima Thule" He wishes to look round the Library.

If you can give him a few moments of your time, you will confer a favor on both him & me.

I have taken much pains, but in vain, to find another of those locusts for you—I have some of the grubs from the nuphar buds in spirits.

Yrs. truly
Henry D. Thoreau

Five days before sending this introduction to the Harvard librarian Thoreau had written in the Journal: *"Got some donacia grubs for Harris, but find no chrysalids." And then he observed about the Nuphar or yellow pond lily: "The sight of the masses of yellow . . . leaves and flower-buds of the yellow lily, already five or six inches long, at the bottom of the river, reminds me that nature is prepared for an infinity of springs yet." Harris once remarked rather condescendingly that if Emerson had not spoiled Thoreau he would have been a good naturalist, but Thoreau's observation comprehended much more than most trained naturalists'. MS., Harvard; previously unpublished. In the manuscript 1854 looks at first glance to be 1853, but the external evidence is decisive.*

———

To WILLIAM E. SHELDON

Concord Nov. 17, 1854.

W*m* E. Sheldon Esq.
Dear Sir

Thinking it possible that you might be expecting me [to] lecture before your Society on the 5th of December as I offered—I write to ask if it is so.

I am still at liberty for that evening—and will read you a lecture either on the Wild or on Moosehunting as you may prefer.

Yrs respectfully

We find no record of a lecture on December 5, 1854, and the Journal *entry for the day implies that Thoreau remained in Concord. We have been unable to discover where Mr. Sheldon lived or for what society he labored. MS., Harvard; previously unpublished; apparently Thoreau's rough copy; it lacks a signature.*

To C. B. BERNARD

Concord Mass Nov 20th 1854

C. B. Bernard Esq.
Dear Sir,
   I expect to lecture in Hamilton C[anada] W[est], once or twice during the first week of January. In that case, how *soon* after (or before) that week will you hear me in Akron? My subject will

As we have noted, these plans for lecturing in Canada and the Middle West were apparently later abandoned. Bernard was the corresponding secretary of the Library Association in Akron, Ohio. MS., Harvard; previously unpublished; this is Thoreau's rough draft of the letter, the bottom portion of which has been torn away.

From ANDREW WHITNEY

Nantucket Nov 27, 1854

Dear Sir
   Your favor of 25th is at hand this evening.
  We cannot have you between the 4 & 15th of Dec. without bringing two lecturers in one week—which we wish to avoid if possible.

If you cannot come the 28th of Dec. will the 2d week in January either the 9th 10th 11th or 12th of the month suit you?—if not, perhaps you can select a day in the 4th week in Jany., avoiding Monday and Saturday.

Write us as soon as possible and make the day as early as you can.—

Yours truly,
Andrew Whitney.

The lecture, a month later, turned out unusually well. Thoreau's topic was "Getting a Living." MS., Huntington; previously unpublished.

To CHARLES SUMNER

Concord Mass Dec 5 1854

Mr Sumner,
Dear Sir,

Allow me to thank you once more for the Report of Sittgreaves, the Patent Office 2d part, and on Emigrants Ships.

At this rate there will be one department in my library, and not the smallest one, which I may call the Sumnerian—

Yours sincerely
Henry D. Thoreau.

The government documents that Sumner sent were Lorenzo Sitgreaves' Report of an Expedition down the Zuni and Colorado Rivers, the second part of the Patent Office Report, which dealt with agriculture, and probably the Message on Health of Emigrants, which dealt with the "health and comfort of emigrants by sea to the United States." MS., Harvard; previously unpublished.

Concord, December 19, 1854.

Mr. Blake,—

I suppose you have heard of my truly providential meeting with Mr T[heo] Brown; providential because it saved me from the suspicion that my words had fallen altogether on stony ground, when it turned out that there was some Worcester soil there. You will allow me to consider that I correspond with him through you.

I confess that I am a very bad correspondent, so far as promptness of reply is concerned; but then I am sure to answer sooner or later. The longer I have forgotten you, the more I remember you. For the most part I have not been idle since I saw you. How does the world go with you? or rather, how do you get along without it? I have not yet learned to live, that I can see, and I fear that I shall not very soon. I find, however, that in the long run things correspond to my original idea,—that they correspond to nothing else so much; and thus a man may really be a true prophet without any great exertion. The day is never so dark, nor the night even, but that the laws at least of light still prevail, and so may make it light in our minds if they are open to the truth. There is considerable danger that a man will be crazy between dinner and supper; but it will not directly answer any good purpose that I know of, and it is just as easy to be sane. We have got to know what both life and death are, before we can begin to live after our own fashion. Let us be learning our a-b-c's as soon as possible. I never yet knew the sun to be knocked down and rolled through a mud-puddle; he comes out honor-bright from behind every storm. Let us then take sides with the sun, seeing we have so much leisure. Let us not put all we prize into a foot-ball to be kicked, when a bladder will do as well.

When an Indian is burned, his body may be broiled, it may be no more than a beefsteak. What of that? They may broil his *heart*, but they do not therefore broil his *courage*,—his principles. Be of good courage! That is the main thing.

If a man were to place himself in an attitude to bear manfully the greatest evil that can be inflicted on him, he would find suddenly that there was no such evil to bear; his brave back would go a-begging. When Atlas got his back made up, that was all that was required. (In

this case *a priv.*, not *pleon.*, and τλῆμι [a subtraction, not an addition, and therefore not a burden].) The world rests on principles. The wise gods will never make underpinning of a man. But as long as he crouches, and skulks, and shirks his work, every creature that has weight will be treading on his toes, and crushing him; he will himself tread with one foot on the other foot.

The monster is never just there where we think he is. What is truly monstrous is our cowardice and sloth.

Have no idle disciplines like the Catholic Church and others; have only positive and fruitful ones. Do what you know you ought to do. Why should we ever go abroad, even across the way, to ask a neighbor's advice? There is a nearer neighbor within us incessantly telling us how we should behave. But we wait for the neighbor without to tell us of some false, easier way.

They have a census-table in which they put down the number of the insane. Do you believe that they put them all down there? Why, in every one of these houses there is at least one man fighting or squabbling a good part of his time with a dozen pet demons of his own breeding and cherishing, which are relentlessly gnawing at his vitals; and if perchance he resolve at length that he will courageously combat them, he says, "Ay! ay! I will attend to you after dinner!" And, when that time comes, he concludes that he is good for another stage, and reads a column or two about the *Eastern War!* Pray, to be in earnest, where is Sevastopol? Who is Menchikoff? and Nicholas behind there? who the Allies? Did not we fight a little (little enough to be sure, but just enough to make it interesting) at Alma, at Balaclava, at Inkermann? We love to fight far from home. Ah! the Minié musket is the king of weapons. Well, let us get one then.

I just put another stick into my stove,—a pretty large mass of white oak. How many men will do enough this cold winter to pay for the fuel that will be required to warm them? I suppose I have burned up a pretty good-sized tree to-night,—and for what? I settled with Mr. Tarbell for it the other day; but that wasn't the final settlement. I got off cheaply from him. At last, one will say, "Let us see, how much wood did you burn, sir?" And I shall shudder to think that the next question will be, "What did you do while you were warm?" Do we think the ashes will pay for it? that God is an ash-man? It is a fact that we have got to render an account for the deeds done in the body.

Who knows but we shall be better the next year than we have been

355

the past? At any rate, I wish you a really *new* year,—commencing from the instant you read this,—and happy or unhappy, according to your deserts.

Text, Familiar Letters of Thoreau, *pp. 291–94.*

———————

To DANIEL RICKETSON

Concord Mass. Dec 19 1854.

Dear Sir,

I wish to thank you again for your sympathy. I had counted on seeing you when I came to New Bedford, though I did not know exactly how near to it you permanently dwelt; therefore I gladly accept your invitation to stop at your house.

I am going to lecture at Nantucket the 28th and as I suppose I must improve the earliest opportunity to get there from New Bedford, I will endeavor to come on Monday that I may see yourself and New Bedford before my lecture.

I should like right well to see your ponds, but that is hardly to be thought of at present. I fear that it is impossible *for me* to combine such things with the business of lecturing. You cannot serve God and Mammon. However perhaps I shall have time to see something of your country. I am aware that you have not so much snow as we. There has been excellent sleighing here ever since the 5th ult.

Mr Cholmondeley has left us; so that I shall come alone.

Will you be so kind as to warn Mr Mitchell that I accepted at once his invitation to lecture on the 26th of this month, for I do not know that he has got my letter.

Excuse this short note from yours truly

Henry D. Thoreau.

Thoreau delivered "Getting a Living" in New Bedford December 26. Two days later he delivered the same lecture at Nantucket. As usual, he confused ult. *with* inst. MS., Huntington.

From DANIEL RICKETSON

H. D. Thoreau.
Dear Sir,—
　　　Yours of the 19th came to hand this evening. I shall therefore look for you on Monday next.

　　My farm is three miles north of New Bedford. Say to the conductor to leave you at the Tarkiln Hill station, where I or some of my folks will be in readiness for you on the arrival of the evening train. Should you intend coming earlier in the day, please inform me in time.

　　I will get word to the Committee of the N. B. Lyceum, as you desire.

　　If I do not hear from you again, I shall prepare for your arrival as before.

　　In the meantime, I remain,

Yours very truly,
Dan'l Ricketson.

Brooklawn, near New Bedford, Wednesday Eve'g, Dec. 20, '54.

The first meeting of the two friends occurred December 25, 1854 at Ricketson's home. An amusing account with a pencil sketch of Thoreau is given in Ricketson, *pp. 11–12. Text, Ricketson, p. 35.*

To H. G. O. BLAKE

Concord Dec. 22nd '54

Mr Blake,

[I w]ill lecture for your [Lyceum on the 4]th of January next; and I hope that I shall have time for that good day out of doors. Mr Cholmondeley is in Boston, yet *perhaps* I may write him to accompany me.

I have engaged to lecture at New Bedford on the 26 inst, stopping with Daniel Ricketson 3 miles out of town; and at Nantucket on the 28th; so that I shall be gone all next week. They say there is some danger of being weather-bound at Nantucket, but I see that others run the same risk.

You had better acknowledge the receit of this at any rate, though you should write nothing else, otherwise I shall not know whether you get it; but perhaps you will not wait till you have seen me to answer my letter. I will tell you what I think of lecturing when I see you.

Did you see the notice of Walden in the last Anti-Slavery Standard? You will not be surprised if I tell you that it reminded me of you.

Yrs,

[Henry D. Thoreau.]

MS., Miss Charlotte Thatcher; *portions in brackets have been clipped from the manuscript but are rewritten in another hand, probably Blake's.*

1855

Congress appropriated $30,000 for the Secretary of War to import camels and dromedaries from the Orient and test them in Texas for military purposes. Iowa, Michigan, Indiana, Delaware, Nebraska, New York, and New Hampshire passed prohibition laws, most of which were repealed the moment the tide of reform receded. Henry Bessemer received his first patent for his process of producing steel. The war in Kansas went on throughout the year, nor was it resolved by the adoption in December of a state constitution that prohibited slavery. The Arctic expedition of Dr. Elisha Kane returned after severe hardships. California wrote a law imposing a "passenger tax" of $50 on every Chinese entering the state. Our country's imports totaled $257,809,000, our exports $192,751,000. There were 1,307 banks reporting their assets and liabilities; their total resources were $816,729,000.

Thoreau gradually so expanded his journalizings that a printed volume of more than 500 pages is needed to contain his observations for the year as preserved in the standard edition of his works. He is the "reporter of woods and fields"—never exclusively so and never dully so, but nonetheless a hard-working reporter rather than a poet. *Putnam's Monthly* published four selections from *Cape Cod*, "The Shipwreck," "Stage-Coach Views," "The Plains of Nanset" (a Putnam misprint for "Nauset"), and "The Beach." There were to have been more parts, but Thoreau and the editor disagreed about the price and the tone of the articles. (During his life Thoreau made four trips to Cape Cod, two with his friend Ellery Channing and two by himself. The first trip, in 1849 with Channing, was the main basis for the series of articles.) A

little over a year after the publication of *Walden* the publisher Ticknor sent Thoreau his profits. The check was for $51.60; 344 copies had been sold during the year, and Thoreau received fifteen cents on each. A high light of the year was Thomas Cholmondeley's gift of a library of Hindu classics in translation, which fed Thoreau's interest in the East. This was the year of his only serious illness since his student days at Harvard. He became sick in spring, rested through the summer, and by fall was almost—but not quite—his old self again. His illness bore the marks of tuberculosis; whatever it was, Thoreau would never feel so well after this year as before.

Shanty, Brooklawn, Thursday p.m., Jan. 4, 1855.

Dear Walden,—

We should be glad to hear of your safe arrival home from your "perils by land and by flood," and as we are not likely to know of this unless you receive a strong hint, I just drop a line for that end.

Your visit, short as it was, gave us all at Brooklawn much satisfaction.

I should be glad to have you come again next summer and *cruise* around with me.

I regret I was unusually unwell when you were here, as you undoubtedly perceived by my complaints.

I am just starting for a walk, and as I expect to pass our village post-office, thought it a good time to write you.

I trust you and your comrade [Ellery] Channing will have many good times this winter.

I may possibly drop in on you for a few hours at the end of this month, when I expect to be in Boston.

Excuse haste.

Yours very truly,
Daniel Ricketson.

P.S.   Mrs. R. and children sent kind regards.

Text, Ricketson, *p. 36.*

361

To DANIEL RICKETSON

Concord Mass Jan 6th 1855

Mr Ricketson,

I am pleased to hear from the shanty whose inside and occupant I have seen. I had a very pleasant time at Brooklawn, as you know,— and thereafter at Nantucket. I was obliged to pay the usual tribute to the sea, but it was more than made up to me by the hospitality of the Nantucketers. Tell Arthur [Ricketson] that I can now compare notes with him, for though I went neither before nor behind the mast, since we hadn't any—I went with my head hanging over the side all the way.

In spite of all my experience I persisted in reading to the Nantucket people the lecture which I read at New Bedford, and I found them to be the very audience for me. I got home Friday night after being lost in the fog off Hyannis.

I have not yet found a new jacknife but I had a glorious skating with Channing the other day on the skates found long ago.

Mr Cholmondeley sailed for England direct in the America on the 3d—after spending a night with me. He thinks even to go to the east & enlist!

Last night I returned from lecturing at Worcester.

I shall be glad to see you when you come to Boston, as will also my mother & sister who know something about you as an abolitionist. Come directly to our house.

Please remember me to Mrs Ricketson, & also to the [young folks

Yrs

Henry D Thoreau]

MS., Huntington; *printed in* Ricketson, *pp. 36–37. The bracketed final portion is not in the manuscript; a note, apparently in Sanborn's hand, says, "The close given for autograph to Mary Wall."*

From DANIEL RICKETSON

Shanty, Brooklawn, 9 Jan., '55.

Dear Walden,—

I have just received your very welcome reply. I am also happy to learn of your safe arrival home, and was much amused by your account of your voyage to Nantucket—also that you found an appreciative audience there.

You address me as Mr. Ricketson. What did I do while you were here to warrant so much deference—I pass for a rather aristocratic man among *big* folk, but didn't suppose you knew it! You should have addressed "Dear Brooklawn." Johnson in his Tour to the Hebrides says they have a custom, in those isles, of giving their names to their chieftans or owners—as Col. Rasay, Much, etc., of which they are the Lairds. You are the true and only Laird of Walden, and as such I address you. You certainly can show a better title to Walden Manor than any other. It is just as we lawyers say, and you hold the *fee.* You didn't think of finding such knowing folks this way, altho you had travelled a good deal in Concord.

By the way, I have heard several sensible people speak well of your lecture before the New Bedford Lyceum, but conclude it was not generally understood.

My son Arthur and I have begun a series of pilgrimages to old farm-houses—we don't notice any short of a hundred years old.

I am much obliged to you and your mother for your kind invitation. My intention is to attend the Anti-slavery meetings in Boston, Wednesday and Thursday, 24th and 25th this month, and shall endeavor to get up to Concord for part of a day.

I wish you would come to Boston at that time. You will find me at the Tremont House, where I shall hope to see you.

Mrs. Ricketson and the "young folks" wish to be kindly remembered to you.

I have had a present of a jack-knife *found* upon a stick of timber in an old house, "built in" and supposed to have been left there by the carpenter. The house is over one hundred years old, and the knife is very *curious.*

So I conclude this rambling epistle,

Yours exceedingly,
"Mr. Ricketson."

Present my compliments to Mr. Channing.

Text, Ricketson, *pp. 37–38.*

From THOMAS CHOLMONDELEY

Hodnet Salop Tuesday 1855

My dear Thoreau
You will be glad to hear that I am safe at my Mothers home in Salop after a most disagreeable passage to England in the steamer America.

I have accepted the offer of a Captaincy in the Salop Militia, & it is probable that we shall be sent before very long to relieve other troops who are proceeding to the seat of the war: but if the strife continues to consume men at its present rate of 1000 a week we shall be involved in it before the year is out by volunteering into the Line.

Meanwhile I shall use my best diligence to learn all I can of my men & prepare myself for the active service to which I impatiently look forward. Nothing can be more awful than the position of our poor army. At the present rate of mortality they will be finished up by the time they are most wanted; & it will be reserved for the French to take Sevastopol.

We are learning a tremendous lesson: I hope we shall profit by it & so far from receding I trust we shall continue hostilities with greater energy & greater wisdom than before.

I would rather see the country decimated than an unglorious or even an accomodating peace.

My passion is to see the fellow crushed or to die in the attempt.

Lord John [Russell] has resigned & the ministry is, we all think, breaking up. It was high time considering the mismanagement of New-Castle.

We are in the midst of a great snow (great at least for us). Colds are rife in the Parish so that "coughing drowns the Parsons saw."

I find the red brick houses are the most striking feature on revisiting this country. Though a great deal smaller than your elegant villas our cottages on the whole please my eyes & look more homey, a very suggestion of good cheer.

There is such a quietness & excessive sleepiness about Shropshire—the only excitement being an occasional alehouse brawl—that it is hardly possible to imagine we are at war!

The fact is the common people never see a newspaper—& such is their confidence in "the Queen's army" that they believe prolonged resistance on the part of any power would be impossible & absurd. My cousin in the Crimea still survives contrary to my expectations. We have heard a good anecdote from him. Early on Christmas morning the remains of the regiment to wh. he belongs gathered painfully together, & as day dawned they all sung the fine English Carol "Christmas Awake." It is rather touching.

I find all here quite well & hearty & hope your people will be the same when this arrives at Concord—a place I shall often revisit in spirit. Pray remember me to your father mother & sister—to Mr. Emerson, Channing & Do not forget your promise to come over sometime to England, which you will find a very snug & hospitable country—though perhaps decaying, & not on such a huge scale as America.

My romance—the Dream of my life—without which it is not worth living for me—is a *glorious commonwealth*. I am persuaded that things must in their way to this, be greatly worse before they can become better. Turn it how you will, our English nation *no longer stands upon the Living Laws of the Eternal God*—we have turned ourselves to an empire & cotton bags & the leprosy of prodigious manufacture. Let that all go & let us grow great men again instead of dressing up dolls for the market. I feel we are strong enough to live a better life than this one which now festers in all our joints.

So much for the confession of a thorough English conservative as you know me to be!

You have my direction so pray write. Your letter will be forwarded to wherever I may be.

> Dear Thoreau
> Ever affectionately yours
> Thos Cholmondeley

Henry Thoreau Esq Concord Massachusetts U.S. North America

We are not sure when Cholmondeley wrote this letter. The manuscript is dated only "Tuesday 1855." When Sanborn printed the letter in Cholmondeley (1893) *he added "January 20"; when he referred to the letter in* Familiar Letters of Thoreau (1894) *and* Familiar Letters (1906) *he gave the date January 27. Neither fell on a Tuesday. February 20 did, but Thoreau had answered the letter on February 7. The normal interval for transatlantic mail and the ease of mistaking a hand-written "3" for a "7" suggest Tuesday, January 23. We assume that Sanborn did not invent the two dates he assigned. MS., Hosmer.*

From DANIEL RICKETSON

Brooklawn, N. Bedford, 26 Jan., 1855.

Dear Sir,—

I fully intended to have gone to Boston yesterday; but not being very well, deferred it until to-day, and now we are visited by a severe snowstorm, so that I fear the railway track may be obstructed. I shall not, therefore, be able to reach Concord this time. My only fear is that you may have gone to Boston in expectation of meeting me there; but as I have not heard from you to this effect I have no very strong reason to think so, and hope that you have not.

I should like very much to see Concord and its environs with the Laird of Walden, and hope at no very distant time to do so, should it

meet his pleasure. I hope also to see your lordship again here, and to visit with you some of our rural retreats.

Yours,
D. Ricketson

H. D. Thoreau, Esq. Concord, Mass.

Text, Ricketson, *pp. 39–40.*

From F. B. SANBORN

Hampton Falls, N.H., *Jan'y* 30th, '55.

My dear Sir,—

I have had it in mind to write you a letter ever since the day when you visited me, without my knowing it, at Cambridge. I saw you afterward at the Library, but refrained from introducing myself to you, in the hope that I should see you later in the day. But as I did not, will you allow me to seek you out, when next I come to Concord?

The author of the criticism in the "Harvard Magazine" is Mr. [Edwin] Morton of Plymouth, a friend and pupil of your friend, Marston Watson, of that old town. Accordingly I gave him the book which you left with me, judging that it belonged to him. He received it with delight, as a gift of value in itself, and the more valuable for the sake of the giver.

We who at Cambridge look toward Concord as a sort of Mecca for our pilgrimages, are glad to see that your last book finds such favor with the public. It has made its way where your name has rarely been heard before, and the inquiry, "Who is Mr. Thoreau?" proves that the book has in part done its work. For my own part, I thank you for the new light it shows me the aspects of Nature in, and for the marvelous beauty of your descriptions. At the same time, if any one should ask me what I think of your philosophy, I should be apt to answer that it is not worth a straw. Whenever again you visit Cambridge, be assured,

367

sir, that it would give me much pleasure to see you at my room. There, or in Concord, I hope soon to see you; if I may intrude so much on your time.

Believe me always, yours very truly,

F. B. Sanborn.

In Henry D. Thoreau (*pp. 195–96*) *Sanborn gives the following note on this letter:*

My own acquaintance with Thoreau . . . sprang from the accident of my editing for a few weeks the "Harvard Magazine," a college monthly, in 1854–55, in which appeared a long review of "Walden" and the "Week." In acknowledgment of this review, which was laudatory and made many quotations from his two volumes, Thoreau, whom I had never seen, called at my room in Holworthy Hall, Cambridge, in January, 1855, and left there in my absence, a copy of the "Week" with a message implying it was for the writer of the magazine article. It so happened that I was in the College Library when Thoreau was calling on me, and when he came, directly after, to the Library, some one present pointed him out to me as the author of "Walden." I was then a senior in college, and soon to go on my winter vacation; in course of which I wrote to Thoreau from my native town.

Ultimately Sanborn became the chief, if not the most meticulous, historian of the Concord group. Throughout his life he was a vigorous humanitarian in addition to being a historian of literature; he was the first secretary of the Massachusetts State Board of Charities and helped to found several national professional organizations, among them the American Social Science Association. Text, Sanborn's Henry D. Thoreau, *pp. 196–97.*

To DANIEL RICKETSON

Concord, February 1st, 1855.

Dear Sir,—

I supposed, as I did not see you on the 24th or 25th, that some track or other was obstructed, but the solid earth still holds together between New Bedford and Concord, and I trust that as this time you stayed away, you may live to come another day.

I did not go to Boston, for with regard to that place, I sympathize with one of my neighbors, an old man, who has not been there since the last war, when he was compelled to go—No, I have a real genius for staying at home.

I have been looking of late at Bewick's tailpieces in the "Birds"—all they have of him at Harvard. Why will he be a little vulgar at times?

Yesterday I made an excursion up our river—skated some thirty miles in a few hours if you will believe it. So with reading and writing and skating the night comes round again.

Yours,
Henry D. Thoreau.

The elderly neighbor, according to Sanborn (Henry D. Thoreau, *p. 274*), *was George Minott. The noted English illustrator Thomas Bewick prepared a* History of British Birds. *Text, Ricketson, p. 40.*

———

To F. B. SANBORN

Concord Feb 2nd '55

Mr F. B. Sanborn.
Dear Sir,

I fear that you did not get the note which I left with the Librarian for you, and so will thank you again for your politeness. I was sorry that

I was obliged to go into Boston almost immediately. However, I shall be glad to see you whenever you come to Concord, and I will suggest nothing to discourage your coming, so far as I am concerned, trusting that you know what it is to take a partridge on the wing.

You tell me that the author of the criticism is Mr. Morton. I had heard as much, & indeed guessed more. I have latterly found Concord nearer to Cambridge than I believed I should, when I was leaving my Alma Mater, and hence you will not be surprised if even I feel some interest in the success of the Harvard Magazine.

Believe me

Yrs truly
Henry D. Thoreau

Edwin Morton, who prepared the criticism of Walden *and the* Week *for his college monthly, was a member of the Harvard class of 1855. MS.,* C. Waller Barrett.

To THOMAS CHOLMONDELEY

Concord Mass. Feb 7 1855

Dear Cholmondeley,

I *am* glad to hear that you have arrived safely at Hodnet, and that there is a solid piece of ground of that name which can support a man better than a floating plank in that to me as yet purely historical England.

But have I not seen you with my own eyes, a piece of England herself? And has not your letter come out to me thence? I have now reason to believe that Salop is as real a place as Concord, with, at least, as good an underpinning of granite floating in liquid fire. I congratulate you on having arrived safely at that floating isle, after your disagreeable passage in the steamer America. So are we not all making a passage, agreeable or disagreeable in the steamer Earth, trusting to arrive at last at some less undulating Salop and Brother's house?

I cannot say that I am surprised to hear that you have joined the

militia, after what I have heard from your lips, but I am glad to doubt if there will be occasion for your volunteering into the line. Perhaps I am thinking of the saying that it is always darkest just before day. I believe that it is only necessary that England be fully awakened to a sense of her position, in order that she may right herself—especially as the weather will soon cease to be her foe.

I wish I could believe that the cause in which you are embarked is the cause of the people of England. However, I have no sympathy with the idleness that would contrast this fighting with the teachings of the pulpit, for perchance more true virtue is being practised at Sebastopol than in many years of peace. It is a pity that we seem to require a war from time to time to assure us that there is any manhood still left in man.

I was much pleased by [J. J. G.] Wilkinson's vigorous & telling assault on Allopathy, though he substitutes another and perhaps no stronger *thigh* for that. Something as good on the whole conduct of the war would be of service. Cannot Carlyle supply it? We will not require him to provide the remedy. Every man to his trade.

As you know, I am not in any sense a politician. You who live in that snug and compact isle may dream of a glorious Commonwealth, but I have some doubts whether I and the new king of the Sandwich Islands shall pull together. When I think of the gold-diggers and the Mormons, the slaves and slave-holders, and the *flibustiers,* I naturally dream of a glorious *private life.* No—I am not patriotic; I shall not meddle with the gem of the Antilles; Gen. Quitman cannot count on my aid [in capturing Cuba], alas for him! nor can Gen. Pierce.

I still take my daily walk or skate over Concord fields or meadows, and on the whole have more to do with nature than with man. We have not had much snow this winter, but have had some remarkably cold weather, the mercury Feb 6 not rising above 6° below zero during the day, and the next morning falling to 25°. Some ice is still 20 inches thick about us. A rise in the river has made uncommonly good skating which I have improved to the extent of some 30 miles at a time, 15 out & 15 in.

Emerson is off westward, enlightening the Hamiltonians & others, mingling his thunder with that of Niagara. Since his themes are England & slavery some begin to claim him as a practical man.

Channing still sits warming his 5 wits—his sixth you know is always limber—over that stove, with the dog down cellar.

Lowell has just been appointed Professor of Belles Lettres in Harvard University, in place of Longfellow, resigned, and will go very soon to spend another year in Europe before taking his seat.

I am from time to time congratulating myself on my *general* want of success as a lecturer—*apparent* want of success, but is it not a real triumph? I do my work clean as I go along, and they will not be likely to want me anywhere again. So there is no danger of my repeating myself and getting to a barrel of sermons which you must upset & begin again with.

My father & mother & sister all desire to be remembered to you, & trust that you will never come within range of Russian bullets.

Of course I would rather think of you as settled down there in Shropshire, in the camp of the English people, making acquaintance with your men—striking at the root of the evil—perhaps assaulting that rampart of cotton bags that you tell of. But it makes no odds where a man goes or stays if he is only about his business.

Let me hear from you, wherever you are, and believe me yours ever in the good fight,—whether before Sebastopol or under the wreken—

Henry D. Thoreau.

MS., Richard Cholmondeley.

_____

To ELIZABETH OAKES SMITH

Concord, Feb. 19, '55

My Dear Madam,

I presume you will like an early, though it should be an unfavorable, answer to your note. After due consultation and inquiry, I am sorry to be obliged to say that we cannot make it worth your while to come to Concord at this season. The curators of the Lyceum, before which you lectured three years ago, tell me that they have already exceeded their means,—our N. E. towns are not so enterprising as some Western ones, in this respect—and Mr. [Daniel?] Foster's society,

which used to be our next resource, furnishing a meeting-house and an audience, no longer exists. He is settled in Princeton, in this state.

Mrs. Emerson sends love, and wishes me to say that she would be glad to have you spend a day or two with her after Mr. E's return, which will probably be before the middle of March,—*and she will not forget that you have a lecture on Margaret Fuller* in your bag.

I remember well meeting you at Mr. Emerson's, in company with Mr. Alcott, and that we did not fatally disagree. You were fortunate to be here at the same time with Mr. A. who diffuses sunshine wherever he goes. I hear that he says the times are so hard that the people cannot have him to converse. Are not those *hard* times indeed?

As for the good time that is coming, let us not forget that there is a good time *going* too, and see that we dwell on that eternal ridge between the two which neither comes nor goes.

Yrs truly
Henry D. Thoreau

Mrs. Smith was a professional feminist and one of the earliest lecturers of her sex in America. MS., Daniel J. Bernstein.

To DR. THADDEUS W. HARRIS

Concord Mass Feb 27 1855

Dear Sir,

> I return to the Library, by Mr Frost, the following books, viz
> Wood's N. E. Prospect,
> Sagard's "Histoire du Canada,"
> & Bewick's "British Birds."

Yrs respectfully
Henry D. Thoreau

MS., C. Waller Barrett; *previously unpublished.*

To CHARLES SUMNER

Concord Mar. 12 1855

Dear Sir

Allow me to thank you for the Comp'd'm of the U. S. census, which has come safely to hand. It looks as full of facts as a chestnut of meat. I expect to nibble at it for many years.

I read with pleasure your pertinent Address before the Merc. Lit. Association, sent me long ago.

Yrs truly
Henry D. Thoreau

Charles Sumner.

MS., Harvard; *previously unpublished.*

To GEORGE WILLIAM CURTIS

Mr. Editor

. . . I see that I was not careful enough to preserve the past tense. I suppose that your objection will be avoided by writing the passage this,—"Not one of those moderate Calvanist, said to be common in the writers day, who, by giving up or explaining away the peculiar doctrines of the party, became, like a porcupine disarmed of its quills, but a consistent Calvanist. . ." By "Scripture" I mean the bible. I suspected that the line was derived from Elliot's Indian bible. It will be better if it is printed "the Scripture" . . .

Apparently Thoreau herein made some attempt to compromise the controversy with Curtis over his "heretical" views in Cape Cod, *appearing serially in* Putnam's. *The passage in question may be found in* Cape

Cod (*IV, 49*). Text, Catalogue of the Graham Sale (*New York, Parke-Bernet, April 30, 1958*), *p. 118. The letter is dated Concord, April 13, 1855, in the catalogue.*

To TICKNOR & FIELDS ?

Concord Ap. 30th 1855

Gentlemen,

Is it not time to republish "A Week on the Concord & Merrimack Rivers"? You said you would notify me when it was; but I am afraid that it will soon be too late for this season.

I have, with what were sent to you, about 250 bound, and 450 in sheets.

Yrs truly
Henry D. Thoreau

The recipient has been identified in the Berg collection as James Monroe & Co., who originally published the Week *in 1849. But since Thoreau purchased all the remaining copies from them in 1853, and since, according to F. H. Allen in his* Bibliography of Henry David Thoreau (*p. 4*), *Thoreau sent Fields twelve copies of the book on October 18, 1854, it is almost certain that the letter was to Ticknor & Fields. The book was not republished until 1862. Dr. Raymond Adams, in his* Thoreau Newsletter *for March 1942, questions the disposal of the 250 bound copies. Did Ticknor & Fields unbind them and then, rebinding them, issue them along with the 450 copies bound from the sheets as the 1862 edition? Dr. Adams concludes that, since the 1862 edition is extremely rare, in all probability they were destroyed to get them out of the way.* MS., Berg.

To H. G. O. BLAKE

Concord June 27th 1855

Mr Blake,

I have been sick and good for nothing but to lie on my back and wait for something to turn up, for two or three months. This has *compelled* me to postpone several things, among them writing to you to whom I am so deeply in debt, and inviting you and [Theo] Brown to Concord—not having brains adequate to such an exertion. I should feel a little less ashamed if I could give any name to my disorder, but I cannot, and our doctor cannot help me to it, and I will not take the name of any disease in vain. However, there is one consolation in being sick, and that is the possibility that you may recover to a better state than you were ever in before. I expected in the winter to be deep in the woods of Maine in my canoe long before this, but I am so far from that that I can only take a languid walk in Concord streets.

I do not know how the mistake arose about the Cape Cod excursion. The nearest I have come to that with anybody is that about a month ago Channing proposed to me to go to Truro, on Cape Cod, with him & board there awhile, but I declined. For a week past however I have been a little inclined to go there & sit on the sea-shore a week or more, but I do not venture to propose myself as the companion of him or of any peripatetic man. Not that I should not rejoice to have you and Brown or C. sitting there also. I am not sure that C. really wishes to go now—and as I go simply for the medicine of it, while I need it, I should not think it worth the while to notify him when I am about to take my bitters.

Since I began this, or within 5 minutes, I have begun to think that I will start for Truro next Saturday morning—the 30th. I do not know at what hour the packet leaves Boston, nor exactly what kind of accommodation I shall find at Truro.

I should be singularly favored if you and Brown were there at the same time, and though you speak of the 20th of July, I will be so bold as to suggest your coming to Concord Friday night (when, by the way, Garrison & Phillips hold forth here) & going to the Cape with me. Though we take short walks together there we can have *long* talks, and you & Brown will have time enough for your own excursions besides

I received a letter from Cholmondeley last winter, which I should

like to show you, as well as his book. He said that he had "accepted the offer of a captaincy in the Salop Malitia," and was hoping to take an active part in the war before long.

I thank you again and again for the encouragement your letters are to me. But I must stop this writing, or I shall have to pay for it

Yours Truly

H. D. Thoreau

MS. of the first four paragraphs (*up to and including the words "Brown will"*), Miss Charlotte Thatcher; *the rest is a copy in the hand of B. B. Thatcher.*

To H. G. O. BLAKE

North Truro, July 8, 1855.

There being no packet, I did not leave Boston till last Thursday, though I came down on Wednesday, and Channing with me. There is no public house here; but we are boarding with Mr. James Small, the keeper, in a little house attached to the Highland Lighthouse. It is true the table is not so clean as could be desired, but I have found it much superior in that respect to the Provincetown hotel. They are what is called "good livers." Our host has another larger and very good house, within a quarter of a mile, unoccupied, where he says he can accommodate several more. He is a very good man to deal with,—has often been the representative of the town, and is perhaps the most intelligent man in it. I shall probably stay here as much as ten days longer: board $3.50 per week. So you and [Theo] Brown had better come down forthwith. You will find either the schooner Melrose or another, or both, leaving Commerce Street, or else T Wharf, at 9 A. M. (it commonly means 10), Tuesdays, Thursdays, and Saturdays,—if not other days. We left about 10 A. M., and reached Provincetown at 5 P. M.,—a very good run. A stage runs up the Cape every morning but Sunday, starting at

4½ A. M., and reaches the postoffice in North Truro, seven miles from Provincetown, and one from the lighthouse, about 6 o'clock. If you arrive at P. before night, you can walk over, and leave your baggage to be sent. You can also come by cars from Boston to Yarmouth, and thence by stage forty miles more,—through every day, but it costs much more, and is not so pleasant. Come by all means, for it is the best place to see the ocean in these States. I *hope* I shall be worth meeting.

Text, Familiar Letters of Thoreau, *pp. 303–4.*

To H. G. O. BLAKE

July 14.

You say that you hope I will excuse your frequent writing. I trust you will excuse my infrequent and curt writing until I am able to resume my old habits, which for three months I have been compelled to abandon. Methinks I am beginning to be better. I think to leave the Cape next Wednesday, and so shall not see you here; but I shall be glad to meet you in Concord, though I may not be able to go *before the mast,* in a boating excursion. This is an admirable place for coolness and sea-bathing and retirement. You must come prepared for cool weather and fogs.

P.S.—There is no mail up till Monday morning.

Thoreau is evidently still in North Truro. Text, Familiar Letters of Thoreau, *pp. 304–5.*

378

To MESSRS. DIX AND EDWARDS

Concord Aug 3d 1855

Messrs Dix & Edwards

Your check for thirty-five dollars in payment for my article in the August number of Putnam's Monthly has come duly to hand—for which accept the acknowledgments of

Yrs respectfully
Henry D. Thoreau

PS. Will you please forward the following note to the Editor

"The Beach," now a part of Cape Cod, *appeared in the August 1855 number of* Putnam's Monthly Magazine. *MS. facsimile,* Clara Louise Dentler, A Privately-owned Collection of Letters, Autographs, and Manuscripts with Many Association Items (*Florence, Italy, n. d., Plate VII*). *"The following note" has not been included in the facsimile, and we have been unable to trace it.*

To GEORGE WILLIAM CURTIS

Mr. Editor

Will you allow me to trouble you once more about my Cape Cod paper. I would like to substitute the accompanying sheets for about ten pages of my MS, in the Chapter called "The Beach Again," . . .

Thoreau finally withdrew the manuscript of Cape Cod *before the chapter "The Beach Again" could be published.* Text, Catalogue of the Graham Sale (*New York, Parke-Bernet, April 30, 1958*), p. 118. *The letter is dated Concord, August 8, 1855 in the catalogue.*

From HORACE GREELEY

New York, Aug. 17, 1855.

Friend Thoreau,
    There is a very small class in England who ought to know what
you have written, and for whose sake I want a few copies of "Walden"
sent to certain periodicals over the water—for instance, to

> Westminster Review,
> 8 King Wm. St. Strand London.
> The Reasoner, 147 Fleet St. London
> Gerald Massey, office of The News
>   Edinburgh.
> —Willy, Esq. of
>   Dickens's Household Words,
>   Fleet. St. London.

    I feel sure your publishers would not throw away copies sent to these
periodicals; especially if your "Week on the Concord and Merrimac"
could accompany them. Chapman, Ed Westminster Rev. expressed
surprise to me that your book had not been sent him, and I could find
very few who had read or seen it. If a new edition should be called for,
try to have it better known in Europe; but have a few copies sent to those
worthy of it at all events.

                                            Yours,
                                            Horace Greeley
H. D. Thoreau, Concord, Mass.

Thoreau took Greeley's advice, and a review of Walden *by no less a
person than George Eliot appeared in the* Westminster Review, LXV
(*January 1856*), 302–3. MS., Daniel Gregory Mason, *lent through the
courtesy of Van Wyck Brooks.*

To HORACE GREELEY

Concord Sep 7th 55

Friend Greeley,

I have just returned from Boston where I showed your note to [William D.] Ticknor. He says he will put the books into the next package which he sends to England. I did not send a single copy of Walden across the water, though Fields did two or three, to private persons alone I think.

Thank you for the suggestion.

I am glad to hear that you are on this side again—though I should not care if you had been detained somewhat longer, if so we could have had a few more letters from Clichy.

Yrs
Henry D. Thoreau

Greeley, while on his European summer tour, sent back a series of travel letters, published in the New-York Tribune *under the title "Europe Revisited." One of the liveliest, "Two Days at Clichy," was written from jail. Greeley was thrown into the famous French debtors' prison because he was a stockholder in the Crystal Palace Exposition in New York, to which a French sculptor named Lechesne had shipped a statue that was broken on the way. Under French law Greeley was liable for part of the damages Lechesne wanted. However, an imposing number of officials from the United States embassy came to Greeley's aid, and he was quickly released. MS., Morgan; previously unpublished.*

From DANIEL RICKETSON

Brooklawn, Sunday p.m., Sept. 23d, 1855.

Dear Thoreau,—

Here am I at home again seated in my Shanty. My mind is constantly reverting to the pleasant little visit I made you, and so I thought I would sit down and write you.

I regret exceedingly that I was so interrupted in my enjoyment while at Concord by my "aches and pains." My head troubled me until I had got within about 20 miles of home, when the pain passed off and my spirits began to revive. I hope that your walks, &c, with me will not harm you and that you will soon regain your usual health and strength, which I trust the cooler weather will favor; would advise you not to doctor, but just use your own good sense. I should have insisted more on your coming on with me had I not felt so ill and in such actual pain the day I left—but I want you to come before the weather gets uncomfortably cool. I feel much your debtor, for through you and your Walden I have found my hopes and strength in those matters which I had before found none to sympathize with. You have more than any other to me discovered the true secret of living comfortably in this world, and I hope more and more to be able to put it into practice, in the mean time you will be able to extend your pity and charity. You are the only "millionaire" among my acquaintance. I have heard of people being "independently rich," but you are the only one I have ever had the honor of knowing.

How charmingly you, Channing, and I dovetailed together! Few men smoke such pipes as we did—the real Calumet—the tobacco that we smoked was free labor produce. I have n't lost sight of Solon Hosmer, the wisest looking man in Concord, and a real *"feelosopher"!* I want you to see him and tell him not to take down the old house, where the *feelosofers met.* I think I should like to have the large chamber, for an occasional sojourn to Concord. It might be easily tinkered up so as to be a comfortable roost for a *feelosofer*—a few old chairs, a table, bed, &c, would be all-sufficient, then you and C. could come over in your punt and rusticate. What think of it? In the mean time come down to Brooklawn, and look about with me. As you are a little under the weather, we will make our peregrinations with horse and wagon.

382

With much regard to Channing and my kind remembrances to your parents and sister, I remain,

Yours very truly,
D'l Ricketson.

P.S.   Please come by Saturday next, as the weather is getting cool. I would like to have Channing to come with you. Please invite him from me. You can wear your old clothes here.

Text, Ricketson, *pp. 40–42*.

To H. G. O. BLAKE

Concord, September 26, 1855.

Mr. Blake,—

The other day I thought that my health must be better,—that I gave at last a sign of vitality,—because I experienced a slight chagrin. But I do not see how strength is to be got into my legs again. These months of feebleness have yielded few, if any, thoughts, though they have not passed without serenity, such as our sluggish Musketaquid suggests. I hope that the harvest is to come. I trust that you have at least warped up the stream a little daily, holding fast by your anchors at night, since I saw you, and have kept my place for me while I have been absent.

Mr. Ricketson of New Bedford has just made me a visit of a day and a half, and I have had a quite good time with him. He and Channing have got on particularly well together. He is a man of very simple tastes, notwithstanding his wealth; a lover of nature; but, above all, singularly frank and plain-spoken. I think that you might enjoy meeting him.

Sincerity is a great but rare virtue, and we pardon to it much complaining, and the betrayal of many weaknesses. R. says of himself, that

he sometimes thinks that he has all the infirmities of genius without the genius; is wretched without a hair-pillow, etc.; expresses a great and awful uncertainty with regard to "God," "Death," his "immortality"; says, "If I only knew," etc. He loves Cowper's "Task" better than anything else; and thereafter, perhaps, Thomson, Gray, and even Howitt. He has evidently suffered for want of sympathizing companions. He says that he sympathizes with much in my books, but much in them is naught to him,—"namby-pamby,"—"stuff,"—"mystical." Why will not I, having common sense, write in plain English always; *teach* men in detail how to live a simpler life, etc.; not go off into ——? But I say that I have no scheme about it,—no designs on men at all; and, if I had, my mode would be to tempt them with the fruit, and not with the manure. To what end do I lead a simple life at all, pray? That I may teach others to simplify their lives?—and so all our lives be *simplified* merely, like an algebraic formula? Or not, rather, that I may make use of the ground I have cleared, to live more worthily and profitably? I would fain lay the most stress forever on that which is the most important,—imports the most to me,—though it were only (what it is likely to be) a vibration in the air. As a preacher, I should be prompted to tell men, not so much how to get their wheat-bread cheaper, as of the bread of life compared with which *that* is bran. Let a man only taste these loaves, and he becomes a skillful economist at once. He'll not waste much time in earning those. Don't spend your time in drilling soldiers, who may turn out hirelings after all, but give to undrilled peasantry a *country* to fight for. The schools begin with what they call the elements, and where do they end?

I was glad to hear the other day that [T. W.] Higginson and _____ were gone to Ktaadn; it must be so much better to go to than a Woman's Rights or Abolition Convention; better still, to the delectable primitive mounts within you, which you have dreamed of from your youth up, and seen, perhaps, in the horizon, but never climbed.

But how do *you* do? Is the air sweet to you? Do you find anything at which you can work, accomplishing something solid from day to day? Have you put sloth and doubt behind, considerably?—had one redeeming dream this summer? I dreamed, last night, that I could vault over any height it pleased me. That was *something;* and I contemplated myself with a slight satisfaction in the morning for it.

Methinks I will write to you. Methinks you will be glad to hear. We will stand on solid foundations to one another,—I a column planted on

this shore, you on that. We meet the same sun in his rising. We were built slowly, and have come to our bearing. We will not mutually fall over that we may meet, but will grandly and eternally guard the straits. Methinks I see an inscription on you, which the architect made, the stucco being worn off to it. The name of that ambitious worldly king is crumbling away. I see it toward sunset in favorable lights. Each must read for the other, as might a sailer-by. Be sure you are star-y-pointing still. How is it on your side? I will not require an answer until you think I have paid my debts to you.

I have just got a letter from Ricketson, urging me to come to New Bedford, which possibly I may do. He says I can wear my old clothes there.

Let me be remembered in your quiet house.

Text, Familiar Letters of Thoreau, *pp. 305–8; the catalogue of the Hathaway-Richardson sale (Charles F. Libbie & Co. May 9–10, 1911) fills in the blank near the end of the letter with the name "Brown"— probably Theo Brown.*

To DANIEL RICKETSON

Concord Sep 27 '55

Friend Ricketson,

I am sorry that you were obliged to leave Concord without seeing more of it—its river and woods, and various pleasant walks, and its worthies. I assure you that I am none the worse for my walk with you, but on all accounts the better. Methinks I am regaining my health, but I would like to know first what it was that ailed me.

I have not yet conveyed your message to Hosmer, but will not fail to do so. That idea of occupying the old house is a good one—quite feasible,—and you could bring your hair-pillow with you. It is an *inn* in Concord which I had not thought of—a philosophers inn. That large

chamber might make a man's ideas expand proportionately. It would be well to have an interest in 'some old chamber in' a desserted house in every part of the country which attracted us. There would be no such place to receive one's guests as that. If old furniture is fashionable, why not go the whole—house at once? I shall endeavor to make Hosmer believe that the old house is the chief attraction of his farm, & that it is his duty to preserve it by all honest appliances. You might take a lease of it *in perpetuo*, and done with it.

I am so wedded to my way of spending a day—require such broad margins of leisure, and such a complete ward-robe of old clothes, that I am ill fitted for going abroad. Pleasant is it sometimes to sit, at home, on a single egg all day, in your own nest, though it may prove at last to be an egg of chalk. The old coat that I wear is Concord—it is my morning robe & study gown, my working dress and suit of ceremony, and my night-gown after all. Cleave to the simplest ever—Home—home—home. *Cars* sound like *cares* to me.

I am accustomed to think very long of going anywhere—am slow to move. I hope to hear a response of the oracle first.

However I think that I will try the effect of your talisman on the iron horse next Saturday, and dismount at Tarkiln Hill. Perhaps your sea air will be good for me.

I conveyed your invitation to Channing but he apparently will not come.

Excuse my not writing earlier—but I had not decided.

Yrs
Henry D. Thoreau.

MS., Huntington; *beginning with the third paragraph additional punctuation is in an ink now blacker than Thoreau's.*

[1855]

From TICKNOR & CO.

Boston Sept. 29, 1855

H. D. Thoreau
        In acc with W. D. Ticknor & Co.
Walden—
On hand last settlement   600 cops.
    Sold since last acc   344
    Remaining on hand   256
    Sales 344 Cops @ 15 cents is $51.60

Dear Sir,
        We regret for your sake as well as ours that a larger number of
Walden has not been sold.
        We enclose our check for Fifty-one $^{60}/_{100}$ Dollars for sales to date.
                                                                Ever Respy
                                                        W. D. Ticknor & Co.
Henry D. Thoreau Concord Mass.

*W. D. Ticknor & Co. had already become Ticknor & Fields, but for
some reason the old style is used here. MS., Harvard (typescript);
previously unpublished.*

———————

From THOMAS CHOLMONDELEY

Octr 3

My dear Thoreau
        I have been busily collecting a nest of Indian Books for you,
which, accompanied by this note, Mr [John] Chapman will send you—
& you will find them at Boston carriage-paid (mind that, & don't let
them cheat you) at Crosby & Nichols.

387

I hope dear Thoreau you will accept this trifle from one who has received so much from you & one who is so anxious to become your friend & to induce you to visit England. I am just about to start for the Crimea, being now a complete soldier—but I fear the game is nearly played out—& all my friends tell me I am just too late for the fair. When I return to England (if ever I do return) I mean to buy a little cottage somewhere on the south coast where I can dwell *in Emersonian leisure* & where I have a plot to persuade you over.

Give my love to your Father & Mother & sister & my respects to Mr Emerson & Channing, & the painter who gave me Websters Head—

I think I never found so much kindness anywhere in all my travels as in your country of New England—& indeed—barring its youth—it is very like *our old country* in my humble judgment

Adieu dear Thoreau & immense affluence to you

Ever yours
Thos Cholmondeley.

P.S.   Excuse my bad writing. *Of course it is the Pen.* Chapman will send a list of your books—by which you can see whether they are all right because I hate to have anything lost or wasted, however small.

The year must be 1855. Cholmondeley's gift left Liverpool November 10, 1855 (Thoreau's Journal, VIII, 36). For the place of writing there is no known evidence. MS., Berg.

To DANIEL RICKETSON

Concord Oct 12 1855

Mr Ricketson,

I fear that you had a lonely and disagreeable ride back to New Bedford, through the Carver woods & so on,—perhaps in the rain too, and I am in part answerable for it. I feel very much in debt to you & your

family for the pleasant days I spent at Brooklawn. Tell Arthur & Walter [Walton; perhaps a slip of Thoreau's pen] that the shells which they gave me are spread out, and make quite a show to inland eyes. Methinks I still hear the strains of the piano the violin & the flageolet blend together. Excuse *me* for the noise which I believe drove you to take refuge in the shanty. That shanty is indeed a favorable place to expand in, which I fear I did not enough improve.

On my way through Boston I inquired for Gilpin's works at Little Brown & Co's, Monroes, Ticknor's & Burnham's. They have not got them. They told me at Little Brown & Co's that his works (not complete) in 12 vols 8vo, were imported & sold in this country 5 or 6 years ago for about 15 dollars. Their terms for importing are 10 per cent on the cost. I copied from "The London Catalogue of Books, 1816–51" at their shop, the following list of Gilpin's books—

	L	S	d	
"Gilpin (W*m*) Dialogues on Various Subjects 8vo	0	9	0	Cadell
Essays on Picturesque Subjects 8vo	"	15	"	"
Exposition of the New Testament 2 vols 8vo	0	16	0	Longman.
Forest Scenery, by Sir T. D. Lauder 2 vols 8vo	0	18	0	Smith & E
Lectures on the Catechism, 12mo	0	3	6	Longman
Lives of the Reformers 2 v. 12mo	"	8	"	Rivington
Sermons Illustrative & Practical 8vo	0	12	0	Hatchard.
to Country Congregations, 4 v. 8*vo*	1	16	0	Longman
Tour in Cambridge Norfolk &c 8*vo*	0	18	0	Cadell
" of the River Wye, 12*mo*	"	4	"	, with plate 8vo
	0	17	0	Cadell
Gilpin (W S (?)) Hints on Landscape Gardening				"
Roy. 8*vo*	1	0	0	Cadell.

Beside these I remember to have read 1 volume on Prints
His Southern Tour (1775)
Lakes of Cumberland 2 vols—
Highlands of Scotland "   "   NB. There *must* be plates
& West of England.   in every volume.

I still see an image of those Middleborough Ponds in my mind's eye— broad shallow lakes with an iron mine at their bottom—comparatively unvexed by sails—only by Tom Smith & his squaw Sepit's "sharper." I find my map of the state to be the best I have seen of that district. It is

a question whether the islands of Long Pond or Great Quitticus offer the most attractions to a Lord of the Isles. That plant which I found on the Shore of Long Pond chances to be a rare & beautiful flower—the *Sabbatia chloroides*—referred to Plymouth.

In a Description of Middleborough in the Hist. Coll. vol 3d 1810—signed Nehemiah Bennet Middleborough 1793—it is said "There is on the easterly shore of Assawampsitt Pond, on the shore of Betty's Neck, two rocks which have curious marks thereon (supposed to be done by the Indians) which appear like the steppings of a person with naked feet which settled into the rocks, likewise the prints of a hand on several places, with a number of other marks; also there is a rock on a high hill a little to the eastward of the old stone fishing wear, where there is the print of a person's hand in said rock."

It would be well to look at those rocks again more carefully—also at the rock on the hill.

I should think that you would like to explore Shipatuct Pond in Rochester [it] is so large & near. It is an interesting fact that the alewives used to ascend to it—if they do not still—both from Mattapoisett & through Great Quitticus.

There will be no trouble about the chamber in the old house, though, as I told you, Hosmer counts his coppers and *may* expect some compensation for it. He says "Give my respects to Mr R. & tell him that I cannot be at a large expense to preserve an antiquity or curiosity. Nature must do its work." "But" say I, ["]R asks you only not to assist Nature."

I find that Channing is gone to his wife at Dorchester—perhaps for the winter—& both *may* return to Concord in the Spring.

yrs

Henry D. Thoreau

MS., Huntington; *beginning with the word "piano" in the first paragraph additional punctuation is in an ink now blacker than Thoreau's.*

From DANIEL RICKETSON

Brooklawn, 13 Oct., '55.

Dear Thoreau,—

Your long lost letter came to hand last Monday, and I concluded that you had safely arrived in Concord and had forwarded it yourself.

One week ago this morning we parted in Plymouth. I looked out of my window and got the last glimpse of you going off with your umbrella and carpet-bag or valise.

Your visit here was very agreeable to us all, and particularly to me. In fact your visit was highly successful except in duration—being much too short.

But the principal object in my now writing is, to assure you that I expect to spend a *few* days in Concord next week, and I shall leave here by the middle or towards the end of the week. I shall bring my hair pillow and some old clothes. I shall not consider it obligatory on you to devote much time to me, particularly as you are an *invalid,* but such time as you can spare I shall be glad to avail myself of, but I hope that Channing, you, and I will be able to *feelosophize* a little occasionally.

I shall go directly to the Tavern, and shall insist upon putting you to no trouble or attention.

I conclude in haste, breakfast waiting.

Yours truly,
Dan'l Ricketson.

Tell Channing I hope to smoke my pipe with him soon.

Text, Ricketson, *pp. 47–48.*

From DANIEL RICKETSON

Brooklawn, Saturday noon, 13 Oct., 1855.

Dear Thoreau,—

I wrote a few lines to you this morning before breakfast, which I took to the post-office, but since, I have received yours of yesterday, which rather changes my mind as to going to Concord. I thank you for your kindness in procuring for me information concerning Gilpin's work, which I shall endeavor to procure.

My ride home, as you anticipate, was somewhat dull and dreary through Carver woods, but I escaped the rain which did not come on until after my arrival home, about tea-time. I think that you hurried away from Brooklawn. We had just got our affairs in good train. I hope, however, that you will soon be able to come again and spend several weeks, when we will visit the pond in Rochester which you mentioned, and review our rides and rambles. The Middleborough ponds and their surroundings never tire me. I could go every day for a long time to them. I give my preference to the isles in Long Pond—we must get the Indian name of this favorite lake of ours.

The principal reason for my changing my mind in regard to going to Concord is that you say Channing has gone, and perhaps for the winter. Although I intended to board and lodge at the Tavern, I expected to philosophize with you and C. by his wood-fire. But this is only a good reason for you to come to Brooklawn again. We have some weeks of good rambling weather yet before winter sets in. You will be very welcome to us all, and don't feel the least hesitation about coming if you have the desire so to do.

I am in the Shanty—Uncle James is here with me. He came up as soon as he heard you had gone. I have endeavored to convince him that you are perfectly harmless, but I think he still retains a portion of his fears. I think you would affiliate well if you should ever come together.

Yours truly,
D. Ricketson.

H. D. Thoreau, Esq., Concord, Mass.

Text, Ricketson, *pp. 48–49.*

Concord Oct 16th 1855

Friend Ricketson,

I have got both of your letters at once. You must not think Concord so barren a place when Channing is away. There are the river & fields left yet, and I, though ordinarily a man of business, should have some afternoons and evenings to spend with you, I trust; that is: if you could stand so much of me. If you can spend your time profitably here, or without ennui, having an occasional ramble or tete-a-tete with one of the natives, it will give me pleasure to have you in the neighborhood. You see I am preparing you for our awful unsocial ways,—keeping in our dens a good part of the day, sucking our claws perhaps.—But then we make a religion of it, and that you cannot but respect.

If you know the taste of your own heart and like it—come to Concord, and I'll warrant you enough here to season the dish with,—aye, even though C and E[merson] and I were all away. We might paddle quietly up the river—then there are one or two more ponds to be seen, &c.

I should very much enjoy further rambling with you in your vicinity, but must postpone it for the present. To tell the truth, I am planning to get seriously to work after these long months of inefficiency and idleness. I do not know whether you are haunted by any such demon which puts you on the alert to pluck the fruit of each day as it passes, and store it safely in your bin. True, it is well to live abandonedly from time to time, but to our working hours that must be as the spile to the bung. So for a long season I must enjoy only a low slanting gleam in my mind's eye from the Middleborough Pond far away.

Methinks I am getting a little more strength into those knees of mine; and, for my part, I believe that God *does* delight in the strength of a man's legs.

Yours
Henry D. Thoreau

MS., Abernethy (*typescript*).

From DANIEL RICKETSON

Brooklawn, Oct. 18th, 1855.

Dear Thoreau,—

I received yours of the 16th inst. yesterday. I am very sorry that you did not conclude at once to come to Brooklawn and finish the visit which you so unceremoniously curtailed. But I cannot release you on so light grounds. I thought that you were a man of leisure. At any rate by your philosophy which I consider the best, you are so. You appear to be hugging your chains or endeavoring so to do. I approve of your courage, but cannot see the desperate need of your penance.

But I must appeal to you as a brother man, a philanthropist too. I am in need of help. I want a physician, and I send for you as the one I have the most confidence in.

You can bring your writing with you, but I can furnish you with stationery in abundance, and you can have as much time for "sucking your claws" as you wish.

Don't fail to come by Saturday noon the 20th.

Yours truly,
D. Ricketson.

I am in need of a physician—so Dr. Thoreau, come to my relief. I need dosing with country rides and rambles, lake scenery, cold viands and jack-knife dinners.

I find the following in Sterne's Koran, which is the best thing I have seen for a long time:—

"Spare diet and clear skies are Apollo and the Muses."

Text, Ricketson, *p. 51.*

From JOHN CHAPMAN

London 8 King William St Strand, Octr 26, 1855.

Dear Sir,
        Enclosed is the list of book[s] referred to in Mr Thos Cholmonde-
ley's note. The parcel I have forwarded to Messrs Crosby Nichols &
Co of Boston, and have requested them to deliver it to you free of all
expense. As Mr Cholmondeley has gone to the East I should be glad
of a note from you acknowledging the receipt of the parcel. I am, dear
Sir

                                Very truly yours
                                John Chapman

List of Books (made up in one parcel) for *Henry D. Thoreau* Esq.,
enclosed by John Chapman, to Messrs. Crosby Nichols & Co Boston
U S A.

Wilsons Rig Veda Sanhita Vols 1 & 2	8vo	*RWE*
Translation of Mandukya Upanishads	2v	*RWE*
Nala & Damyanta by Milman	8vo	*RWE*
Vishnu Purana by Wilson	4to	*RWE*
Haughtons Institutes of Menu	4to	*RWE*
Colebrookes Two Treatises	4to bds	*RWE*
Sankhya Karika	4to	*RWE*
Aphorisms of the Mimasma	8vo	*RWE*
— " " Nayaya (4 books)	8vo	*RWE*
Lecture on the Vedanta	8vo	*RWE*
Bhagavat Gheeta & translation 2 Volumes	8vo	*RWE*
Wilsons "Theatre of the Hindoos 2 Volumes	8vo	*RWE*
Williams' Translation of "Sakoontala," or The Lost Ring 4to gilt		
		E. Hoar
Colebrookes' Miscellaneous Essays 2 Vols	8vo	*RWE*
Hardys Eastern Monachism 8vo		
" Manual of Buddhism 8vo		
Mills' History of British India 9 volumes 8vo		*Town Library*

The Chevalier Bunsens Christianity & Mankind
- I. "Hippolytus & his Age" 2 Vols
- II. "Outlines of the Philosophy of Universal Religion applied to Language & Religion" 2 Vols *Ripley*
- III. Analecta Ante Nicana 3 Vols
  Together 7 Volumes 8vo cloth.

The Chevalier Bunsens Egypts Place in Universal History
2 Volumes 8vo *Sanborn*
The Bhagavita Purana Bournouf 3 Vols. *RWE*
Lotus de la Bonnes Lois Bournouf 4to *RWE*
Halsteads Code of Gentoo Laws 4to. *E R Hoar*

The books of Cholmondeley's shipment are described in detail in Walter Harding, Thoreau's Library *(Charlottesville, 1957). MS. of letter, Berg; MS. of list, Abernethy (typescript); the italicized portions are Thoreau's annotations indicating to whom he wished the volumes given after his death.*

From JOHN CHAPMAN

Strand London: 8 King William Street, Novr— 2nd, 1855.

H. D. Thoreau Esqr,
Dear Sir
    The parcel of books advised by me on the 26th of October, as having been sent by the "Asia" Steamer, from Liverpool, has been shut out of that vessell on account of her cargo being complete several days previous to her sailing. Under these circumstances I have therefore ordered the parcel to be shipped by the "Canada" of the 10th proximo,

and trust that you will not experience any inconvenience from this unavoidable delay—

I am, dear Sir,

Yours very truly
John Chapman
A D Ferguson

I have written to Messrs Crosby Nichols & Co, Boston, respecting your package—

MS., Berg.

To THOMAS CHOLMONDELEY

Concord Nov. 8th 1855.

Dear Cholmondeley,

I must endeavor to thank you for your magnificent, your princely gift to me. My father, with his hand in his pocket, and an air of mystery and importance about him suggests that I have another letter from Mr. Cholmondeley, and hands me a ship letter. I open eagerly upon a list of books (made up in one parcel) for Henry D. &c &c"; and my eye glances down a column half as long as my arm, where I already detect some eminences which I had seen or heard of, standing out like the peaks of the Himalayas. No! it is not Cholmondeley's writing.—But what good angel has divined my thoughts? Has any company of the faithful in England passed a resolution to overwhelm me with their munificent regards "Wilsons Rig Veda Sanhitu" [*sic*] Vols 1 & 2 8*vo*. "Translation of Mandukya Upanishads." I begin to step from pinnacle to pinnacle. Ah! but here it is "London, King William Street. truly yours John Chapman." Enclosed is the list. "Mr Thomas Cholmondeley" and now I see through it, and here is a hand I know and father was right after all. While he is

397

gone to the market I will read a little further in this list "Nala & Da-myanta" "Bhagavita Purana," "Institutes of Menu."—

How they look far away and grand!

That will do for the present: a little at a time of these rich dishes. I will look again by and by. "Per Asia" too they have come, as I read on the envelope! Was there any design in that? The very nucleus of her cargo; Asia carried them in her womb long ago. Was not the ship conscious of the freight she bore Insure her for nothing ye Jews; she and all her passengers and freight are destined to float serene through whatever seas. Immobility itself is tossed on Atlantic billows to present the gift to me. Was not there an omen for you? No Africa; no Europe—no Baltic, but it would have sunk. And now we will see if America can sustain it. Build new shelves—display, unfold your columns. What was that dim peak that loomed for an instant far behind, representative of a still loftier and more distant range. "Vishnu Purana," an azure mountain in itself.—gone again, but surely seen for once. And what was that which dimmed the brightness of the day, like an apex of Cotopaxi's cone, seen against the disk of the sun by the voyager of the South American coast "Bhagavat Geeta"! whose great unseen base I can faintly imagine spreading beneath. "History of British India nine vols"!! Chevalier Bunsen nine vols 8vo cloth"!! Have at them! who cares for numbers in a just cause England expects every man to do his duty. Be sure you are right and then go ahead. I begin to think myself learned for merely possessing such works: If here is not the wealth of the Indies, of what stuff then is it made? They may keep their rupees this and the like of this is what the great company traded and fought for, to convey the light of the East into the West:—this their true glory and success.

And now you have gone to the East or Eastward, having assisted its light to shine westward behind you; have gone towards the source of light! to which I pray that you may get nearer and nearer.

Dec. 1st—

After a fortnights delay, owing to the cargo of the Asia being complete when the parcel reached Liverpool, my Indian library was sent by the Canada and at length reached my door complete and in good order, last evening. After overhauling my treasures on the carpet, wading knee deep in Indian philosophy and poetry—with eager eyes around ready to admire the splendid binding and illumination at least, drawing them forth necessarily from amidst a heap of papers, every scrap of which bore some evidence of having come from that fabulous

region the "Strand," not far this side Colchis toward which you are gone. I placed them in the case which I had prepared, and went late to bed dreaming of what had happened. Indeed it was exactly like the realization of some dreams which I have had; but when I woke in the morning I was not convinced that it was reality until I peeped out and saw their bright backs. They are indeed there and I thank you for them. I am glad to receive them from you, though notwithstanding what you say, if I should stop to calculate I should find myself very much your debtor. I shall not soon forget your generous entertainment of some thoughts which I cherish and delight in an opportunity to express. If you thought that you met with any kindness in New England I fear that it was partly because you had lately come from New Zealand. At any rate excuse our hard and cold New England manners, lay it partly to the climate: granite and ice, you know, are our chief exports. B. (of the mountain) was here when your note and the list of books arrived, and enjoyed the perusal with me. E. whose constant enquiry for the last fortnight has been, "Have your books come?["] is about starting for the west on a lecturing tour. The papers say he is to lecture *in nine cities on the Mississippi.*

I hope that the trumpet and the drum will sound to you as they do in dreams, and that each night you may feel the satisfaction of having fought worthily in a worthy cause.

I shall depend on hearing from you in the camp. My father and mother and sister send their hearty good wishes. If I am ever rich enough I shall think seriously of going to England and finding you out in your cottage on the south shore. That you may return home safely and in good time to carry out that project, your country's glory being secured, is the earnest wish of one by whom you will ever be well remembered.

Henry Thoreau.

MS., Berg, *copy in an unknown hand; previously unpublished.*

From CROSBY & NICHOLS?

H D Thoreau Esq.
De Sir,
      The parcel of books referred to in your letter of the 9th has not yet reached us.
      We suppose that our case whi contained it was left behind at Liverpool and shall expect it by next Steamer

This fragment was probably from Crosby & Nichols about Cholmondeley's shipment of books. It seems unlikely that Thoreau could have received Cholmondeley's letter of October 3 before October 9. And since he did not receive the books until November 30 (see his letter of November 8–December 1), he probably wrote the Boston firm on November 9. Therefore their letter was probably written shortly after that latter date. MS., Harvard; previously unpublished.

To H. G. O. BLAKE

Concord, December 9, 1855.

Mr. Blake,—
      Thank you! thank you for going a-wooding with me,—and enjoying it,—for being warmed by my wood fire. I have indeed enjoyed it much alone. I see how I might enjoy it yet more with company,—how we might help each other to live. And to be admitted to Nature's hearth costs nothing. None is excluded, but excludes himself. You have only to push aside the curtain.
      I am glad to hear that you were there too. There are many more such voyages, and longer ones, to be made on that river, for it is the water of life. The Ganges is nothing to it. Observe its reflections,—no idea but is familiar to it. That river, though to dull eyes it seems terrestrial wholly, flows through Elysium. What powers bathe in it invisible to

villagers! Talk of its shallowness,—that hay-carts can be driven through it at midsummer; its depth passeth my understanding. If, forgetting the allurements of the world, I could drink deeply enough of it; if, cast adrift from the shore, I could with complete integrity float on it, I should never be seen on the Mill-dam again. If there is any depth in me, there is a corresponding depth in it. It is the cold blood of the gods. I paddle and bathe in their artery.

I do not want a stick of wood for so trivial a use as to burn even, but they get it over night, and carve and gild it that it may please my eye. What persevering lovers they are! What infinite pains to attract and delight us! They will supply us with fagots wrapped in the daintiest packages, and freight paid; sweet-scented woods, and bursting into flower, and resounding as if Orpheus had just left them,—these shall be our fuel, and we still prefer to chaffer with the wood-merchant!

The jug we found still stands draining bottom up on the bank, on the sunny side of the house. That river,—who shall say exactly whence it came, and whither it goes? Does aught that flows come from a higher source? Many things drift downward on its surface which would enrich a man. If you could only be on the alert all day, and every day! And the nights are as long as the days.

Do you not think you could contrive thus to get woody fibre enough to bake your wheaten bread with? Would you not perchance have tasted the sweet crust of another kind of bread in the mean while, which ever hangs ready baked on the bread-fruit trees of the world?

Talk of burning your smoke after the wood has been consumed! There is a far more important and warming heat, commonly lost, which precedes the burning of the wood. It is the smoke of industry, which is incense. I had been so thoroughly warmed in body and spirit, that when at length my fuel was housed, I came near selling it to the ashman, as if I had extracted all its heat.

You should have been here to help me get in my boat. The last time I used it, November 27th, paddling up the Assabet, I saw a great round pine log sunk deep in the water, and with labor got it aboard. When I was floating this home so gently, it occurred to me why I had found it. It was to make wheels with to roll my boat into winter quarters upon. So I sawed off two thick rollers from one end, pierced them for wheels, and then of a joist which I had found drifting on the river in the summer I made an axletree, and on this I rolled my boat out.

Miss Mary Emerson [R. W.'s aunt] is here,—the youngest person

in Concord, though about eighty,—and the most apprehensive of a genuine thought; earnest to know of your inner life; most stimulating society; and exceedingly witty withal. She says they called her old when she was young, and she has never grown any older. I wish you could see her.

My books did not arrive till November 30th, the cargo of the Asia having been complete when they reached Liverpool. I have arranged them in a case which I made in the mean while, partly of river boards. I have not dipped far into the new ones yet. One is splendidly bound and illuminated. They are in English, French, Latin, Greek, and Sanscrit. I have not made out the significance of this godsend yet.

Farewell, and bright dreams to you!

Text, *Familiar Letters of Thoreau, pp. 316–19.*

To DANIEL RICKETSON

Concord Dec 25 '55

Friend Ricketson,

Though you have not shown your face here, I trust that you did not interpret my last note to my disadvantage. I remember that, among other things, I wished to break it to you that, owing to engagements, I should not be able to show you so much attention as I could wish, or as you had shown to me.—How we did scour over the country! I hope your horse will live as long as one which I hear just died in the south of France at the age of 40.—Yet I had no doubt you would get quite enough of me. Do not give up so easily—the old house is still empty —& Hosmer is easy to treat with.

Channing was here about ten days ago. I told him of my visit to you, and that he too must go and see you & your country. This may have suggested his writing to you.

That island lodge, especially for some weeks in a summer, and new

402

explorations in your vicinity are certainly very alluring; but *such are my engagements to myself* that I dare not promise to wend your way —but will for the present only heartily thank you for your kind & generous offer. When my vacation comes, then look out.

My legs have grown considerably stronger, and that is all that ails me.

But I wish now above all to inform you—though I suppose you will not be particularly interested—that Cholmondeley has gone to the Crimea "a complete soldier," with a design when he returns, if he ever returns, to buy a cottage in the south of England and tempt me over,— but that, before going, he busied himself in buying, & has caused to be forwarded to me by Chapman, a royal gift, in the shape of 21 distinct works (one in 9 vols—44 vols in all) almost exclusively relating to ancient Hindoo literature, and scarcely one of them to be bought in America. I am familiar with many of them & know how to prize them.

I send you information of this as I might of the birth of a child.

Please remember me to all your family—

Yrs truly
Henry D. Thoreau.

MS., Huntington.

From EMERSON

American House, Boston, December 26, 1855.

Dear Henry,—

It is so easy, at distance, or when going to a distance, to ask a great favor which one would haggle at near by. I have been ridiculously hindered, and my book is not out, and I must go westward. There is one chapter yet to go to the printer; perhaps two, if I decide to send the second. I must ask you to correct the proofs of this or these chapters. I hope you can and will, if you are not going away. The printer will send you the copy with the proof; and yet, 't is likely you will see good

cause to correct copy as well as proof. The chapter is Stonehenge, and I may not send it to the printer for a week yet, for I am very tender about the personalities in it, and of course you need not think of it till it comes. As we have been so unlucky as to overstay the market-day,— that is, New Year's—it is not important, a week or a fortnight, now.

If anything puts it out of your power to help me at this pinch, you must dig up Channing out of his earths, and hold him steady to this beneficence. Send the proofs, if they come, to Phillips, Sampson & Co., Winter Street.

We may well go away, if, one of these days, we shall really come home.

Yours,
R. W. Emerson

Mr. Thoreau.

The book was Emerson's English Traits (*1856*). Text, Emerson-Thoreau, *p. 751.*

1856

In Kansas the war or, as the acting governor of the territory termed it, the "state of open insurrection and rebellion" went on. Charles Sumner of Massachusetts made his "Crime against Kansas" speech on the floor of the Senate, adding a personal arraignment of his fellow senators Douglas of Illinois and Butler of South Carolina. Two days afterward he was beaten into insensibility by Butler's nephew, Representative Preston Brooks. James Buchanan of Pennsylvania was elected president with a popular vote of 1,838,169. He defeated that free-wheeling military man and explorer, John Fremont, and a former president, Millard Fillmore. The first street railroad in New England was opened between Boston and Cambridge. Congress made grants of public land to Iowa, Alabama, Florida, Louisiana, Michigan, and Mississippi that they might subsidize railroads within their boundaries. A treaty of friendship and commerce with Persia was signed.

Superficially Thoreau was active enough during this year. By spring he felt well again and did much surveying and much walking. His new throat beard is pictured in the daguerreotype of him that a man named Maxham made when Thoreau journeyed to Worcester. In fall he visited Bronson Alcott in Walpole, N. H., and then did his customary stint of lecturing. He gave five lectures, three of them at a onetime utopian settlement near Perth Amboy, the others at Philadelphia and Amherst, New Hampshire. Toward the end of the year he was introduced to Walt Whitman. Each man was reserved during the meeting, but Thoreau's enthusiasm for Walt grew remarkably. "We ought to rejoice greatly in him," he said in a letter to H. G. O. Blake. Blake and Daniel Ricketson of New Bedford continued to be the two disciples Thoreau corresponded with most.

405

377–379 Broadway New York Jany 4 '56

Mr. Thoreau
Dear Sir
    Inclosed please find $10, for which please to send me 5 lbs of blacklead for electrotyping purposes:—such as Mr. Filmore has sent for occasionally.

Respectfully yours
John F. Trow

MS., Abernethy (*typescript*); *previously unpublished.*

Concord Jan. 18th 1856.

Dear Sir,
    I am glad to hear that my "Walden" has interested you—that perchance it holds some truth still as far off as Michigan. I thank you for your note.
    The "Week" had so poor a publisher that it is quite uncertain whether you will find it in any shop. I am not sure but authors must turn booksellers themselves. The price is $1.25 If you care enough for it to send me that sum by mail, (stamps will do for change) I will forward you the copy by the same conveyance.

406

As for the "more" that is to come, I cannot speak definitely at present, but I trust that the mine—be it silver or lead—is not yet exhausted. At any rate, I shall be encouraged by the fact that you are interested in its yield.

Yrs respectfully
Henry D. Thoreau

Calvin H. Greene

The fullest account of the relationship between these two correspondents is to be found in Samuel Arthur Jones, Some Unpublished Letters of Henry D. and Sophia E. Thoreau, *pp. 25–49. MS., Princeton University Library.*

To CALVIN GREENE

Concord Feb 10th '56

Dear Sir,

I forwarded to you by mail on the 31st of January a copy of my "Week," post paid, which I trust that you have received. I thank you heartily for the expression of your interest in "Walden" and hope that you will not be disappointed by the "Week." You ask how the former has been received. It has found an audience of excellent character, and quite numerous, some 2000 copies having been dispersed. I should consider it a greater success to interest one wise and earnest soul, than a million unwise & frivolous.

You may rely on it that you have the best of me in my books, and that I am not worth seeing personally—the stuttering, blundering, clod-hopper that I am. Even poetry, you know, is in one sense an infinite brag & exaggeration. Not that I do not stand on all that I have written—but what am I to the truth I feebly utter!

I like the name of your county. May it grow men as sturdy as its trees. Methinks I hear your flute echo amid the oaks. Is not yours too a good place to study theology? I hope that you will ere long recover

your turtle-dove, and that it will bring you glad tidings out of that
heaven in which it disappeared.

Yrs Sincerely
Henry D. Thoreau

Calvin H. Greene Esq

Greene's county is Oakland. The reference to the turtledove is from
Walden; *in the most famous set of symbols in the book Thoreau wrote
that he had long ago lost a hound, a bay horse, and a turtledove and
was still on their trail. MS., Princeton University Library.*

From DANIEL RICKETSON

The Shanty, Brooklawn, 26th Feb., 1856.

Dear Thoreau,—

I often think of you and nearly as often feel the prompting to
write you, and being alone in the Shanty this afternoon I have concluded to obey the prompting. I say alone, but I can fancy you seated
opposite on the settee looking very *Orphic* or something more mystical.
This winter must have been a grand one for your ruminations and I conclude that you will thaw out in the spring with the snakes and frogs,
more of a philosopher than ever, which perhaps is needless. It has
required all my little share of *feelosofy* to keep up my fortitude during
the past Hyperborean interregnum. We have usually flattered ourselves
that our winters were much milder than of most places in New England
or even in the same latitude farther inland, on account of our vicinity
to the sea and the Gulf stream in particular. But O! the cold, cold days
and weeks we have had in common with the rest of our country North,
South, East and West!

But we are beginning to relax a little, and like barn-yard fowls begin
to plume ourselves again and pick about, but we hardly begin to lay
and cackle yet—that will all come in due season, and such a crowing
some of us old cocks will make that if you are awake you will perhaps
hear at Concord.

408

The snow has nearly gone, but our river is still firmly bound, and great sport have gentle and simple, young and old, thereon—skating, ice-boats, boys holding sails in their hands are shooting like "mercurial trout" in every direction up and down, even horses and sleighs and loaded wagons have passed where large ships float.

But I glory in none of this, on the contrary sigh for the more genial past, and hope for no more such desperate seasons. Ah! but March is close here, and she wears at least the gentle name of Spring as Bryant says—and soon may we expect to hear the bluebird and song sparrow again. Then let "Hope rule triumphant in the breast," and buckling our girth a little tighter journey on.

Dear Thoreau, I am under the greatest obligations to you. Before your Walden I felt quite alone in my best attainments and experiences, but now I find myself sustained and strengthened in my hopes of life. Can we not meet occasionally ere the evil days, should there be any in store for us, come? The accumulated years "notched upon my stick" warn me not to be too prodigal of time. By April then I hope you will be ready to wend this way, and take Spring a little in advance of Concord; then with the bluebirds and sparrows, the robins and thrushes, will I welcome you and associate you.

I should have told you before that Channing is here in New Bedford. I had but just written his name, when old Ranger announced him, and he is now quietly smoking his pipe by the shanty fire. He arrived on Christmas day, and his first salutation on meeting me at the front door of my house was, "That's your shanty," pointing towards it. He is engaged with the editor of the N. B. Mercury, and boards in town, but whereabouts I have not yet discovered. He usually spends Saturday and a part of Sunday with me, and seems to enjoy himself pretty well.

Mr. Emerson is expected to lecture before our Lyceum to-morrow evening, but from a note I received from him in answer to an invitation to Brooklawn I should think it quite uncertain whether he be here.

I too have written and delivered a lecture this winter before the Lyceum of our village, Acushnet, on Popular Education, into which I contrived to get a good deal of radicalism, and had a successful time.

Should your Lyceum be in want of a lecture you might let me know, although I should hardly dare to promise to come,—that is, gratuitously except incidental expenditures. I have commenced a new lecture of a little higher literary tone upon "The Poet Cowper and his Friends," and am meditating a grand affair wherein I expect to introduce some of

the philosophy I have found in solitude, or rather to publish some of the communications and revelations received from a certain *old neighbor and visitor,* who occasionally favors by his presence, the world's outcasts, holding them up by the chin, and occasionally whispering weighty matters into their ears, which at these times are particularly free from wax.

Channing is not here now, that is in the Shanty, but it being after tea, is chatting by the fireside with my wife and daughters, and I am writing by the humming of my fire and the music of my Eolian harp. These are fine things to have in your windows, and lest you are not acquainted with them I will describe the way to make them.

Make two wedges of soft wood—make a slight incision in the top of thick part of the wedges and another in the thin part, which should be shaved down quite thin—then take a string of saddler's silk, or several strands of fine silk twisted to the size of the other, waxed or not, as you may see fit, make a knot in each end, the length of the string to be governed by the width of the window-sash where it is to be placed. Put one end of the string into the incision upon the top of the wedge and then down the side through the other split in the thin end and the other end likewise on the other wedge, then place the two wedges drawing the string tight between the upper and lower sashes of your window and if the wind be favorable, it will give you a pleasing serenade.

Write soon and believe me,

Yours very truly,

D. R.

Thursday a.m., 29th.

Another pleasant day—the song sparrows singing from the old rail fences, and whortleberry bushes—the last day of winter. How rich we are!

My dear old Northman, sitting by the sea,
Whose azure tint is seen, reflected in thy e'e,
Leave your sharks and your dolphins, and eke the sporting whale,
And for a little while on milder scenes regale:
My heart is beating strongly to see your face once more,
So leave the land of *Thor,* and *row* along our shore!

D. R.

Pax vobiscum

[1856]

Thoreau was already fully familiar with the Aeolian harp and had built himself one, which is now in the collection of the Concord Antiquarian Society. Text, Ricketson, *pp. 53–57.*

From HORACE GREELEY

[March ? 4, 1856]

Our home is two hours (36 miles) from New York . . . in a quiet Quaker neighborhood. . . . You would be out of doors nearly all pleasant days, under a pleasant shade, with a pleasant little landscape in view from the open hill just back of our house.

Charles F. Libbie & Co. sold the manuscript of an autograph letter from Greeley to Thoreau at the Garfield sale of January 27–28, 1914. The firm described it as "4 pp., 8vo. Washington. Nov. 4, 1856, to 'My Friend Thoreau.' Asking Thoreau to come and live with him and teach his two young children." We feel, however, that the letter is wrongly dated. By November the offer to Thoreau had already been made and the details had been discussed. Unless the letter is a restatement of the original invitation, it should be dated at least several months earlier than it now is. At least once before, Greeley's bad handwriting had caused someone to date his letter March 18, 1852, as November 18. This is an easy error to make, furthermore, because of Greeley's use of "Mar." and "Nov." If the letter of invitation could be placed in March, a perfectly logical sequence would develop. It would begin with the letter from Greeley to Thoreau of March 4, when the invitation was extended. Next would come Thoreau's answer of March 10. (We do not have this letter, but Greeley acknowledged it.) Greeley's letter of March 12 would follow, and the rest of their correspondence would continue from there. One other possibility that should be mentioned, though, is that the letter supposedly dated March 2 (and listed in our check list) contained the original invitation.

411

Against our general line of argument, however, is the fact that the catalogue of the Gable sale (American Art Association, March 10–11, 1924) notes what is obviously the same letter, although it is described as 12mo instead of 8vo, and dates it November 9. Two auction catalogues, then, read the month as "Nov." One, though, reads the day as "4," the other as "9," further illustrating the difficulty of Greeley's hand. Here we feel that the 4th is a more logical date than the 9th, because Greeley, writing to Thoreau from Washington, acknowledged what was probably the answer to him as of March 10 (in his letter to Thoreau of March 12). Text, catalogue of the Garfield sale.

To DANIEL RICKETSON

Concord Mar. 5 '56

Friend Ricketson,

I have been out of town, else I should have acknowledged your letters before. Though not in the best mood for writing I will say what I can now. You plainly have a rare, though a cheap, resource in your shanty. Perhaps the time will come when every country-seat will have one—when every country-seat will *be* one. I would advice you to see that shanty business out, though you go shanty mad. Work your vein till it is exhausted, or conducts you to a broader one; so that C[hanning] shall stand before your shanty, & say "That is your house."

This has indeed been a grand winter for me & for all of us. I am not considering how much I have enjoyed it. What matters it how happy or unhappy we have been, if we have minded our business and advanced our affairs I have made it a part of my business to wade in the snow & take the measure of the ice. The ice on one of our ponds was just two feet thick on the first of March—and I have to-day been surveying a wood-lot where I sank about two feet at every step.

It is high time that you, fanned by the warm breezes of the Gulf Stream, had begun to "lay"—for even the Concord hens have—though one wonders where they find the raw material of egg-shells here. Be-

ware how you put off your laying to any later spring, else your cackling will not have the inspiring *early* spring sound.

I was surprised to hear the other day that Channing was in New Bedford. When he was here last (in Dec., I think) he said, like himself, in answer to my inquiry where he lived, that he did not know the name of the place; so it has remained in a degree of obscurity to me. As you have made it certain to me that he is in New Bedford, perhaps I can return the favor by putting you on the track to his boarding house there. Mrs Arnold told Mrs Emerson where it was—and the latter thinks, though she may be mistaken, that it was at a Mrs Lindsey's

I am rejoiced to hear that you are getting on so bravely with him & his verses. He and I, as you know, have been old cronies.

> "Fed the same flock, by fountain, shade, & rill.
> Together both, ere the high lawns appeared
> Under the opening eye-lids of the morn,
> We drove afield, and both together heard &c &c &c"

"But O the heavy change" now he is gone!

The C you have seen & described is the real Simon Pure. You have seen him. Many a good ramble may you have together. You will see in him still more *of the same kind*—to attract & to puzzle you. How to serve him most effectually has long been a problem with his friends. Perhaps it is left for you to solve it. I suspect that the most that you or any one can do for him is to appreciate his genius—to buy & read, & cause others to buy & read his poems. That is the hand which he has put forth to the world—Take hold of that. Review them if you can. Perhaps take the risk of publishing something more which he may write.

Your knowledge of Cowper will help you to know C. He will accept sympathy & aid, but he will not bear questioning—unless the aspects of the sky are particularly auspicious. He will even be "reserved & enigmatic," & you must deal with him at arm's length.

I have no secrets to tell you concerning him, and do not wish to call obvious excellences & defects by far-fetched names. I think I have already spoken to you more, and more to the purpose, on this theme, than I am likely to write now—nor need I suggest how witty & poetic he is—and what an inexhaustible fund of good-fellowship you will find in him.

As for visiting you in April,—though I am inclined enough to take some more rambles in your neighborhood, especially by the sea-side—

I dare not engage myself, nor allow you to expect me. The truth is, I have my enterprises now as ever, at which I tug with ridiculous feebleness, but admirable perseverance—and cannot say when I shall be sufficiently fancy-free for such an excursion.

You have done well to write a lecture on Cowper. In the expectation of getting you to read it here, I applied to the curators of our Lyceum but alas our Lyceum has been a failure this winter for want of funds. It ceased some weeks since, with a debt—they tell me, to be carried over to the next years' account. Only one more lecture is to be read by a Signor somebody—an Italian—paid for by private subscription—as a deed of charity to the lecturer. They are not rich enough to offer you your expenses even, though probably a month or two ago they would have been glad of the chance.

However the old house has not failed yet. That offers you lodging for an indefinite time after you get into it—and in the mean while I offer you bed & board in my father's house—always excepting hair pillows & new-fangled bedding.

Remember me to your family.

Yrs
H. D. T.

If there was ever a Transcendentalist more individual than Thoreau, it was Ellery Channing. Here in this letter is the clearest picture of him to be found anywhere in a small space. MS., Huntington.

From DANIEL RICKETSON

The Shanty, 7th March, 1856.

To My dear Gabriel,
    Who like the one of old that appeared to Daniel, Zachariah, &c. hath in these latter days appeared unto the least of all Daniels,—Greetings,—

I have just received and read your genuine epistle of the 5th Inst. You satisfy me fully in regard to C and I trust we shall draw with an even yoke in future. I had thought of attempting something by way of reviving his poems. A new public has grown up since their appearance, and their assasinator Poe, lies in the Potter's Field at Baltimore, without a stone to mark his grave, as somebody in the Home Journal of this week, says: and thus hath Nemesis overtaken him.

Mrs Ricketson as well as myself have felt a good deal of sympathy for Mrs. C. but of course the matter cannot be spoken of to C.

I think, however, that he is now working for his family. His courage and endurance under the circumstances are wonderful. Unless he has a very strong physical as well as mental constitution, I fear he will suffer, & perhaps break down. I conclude you received my newspaper notice of Mr. Emerson's explosion before the N. B. Lyceum, although you make no mention of it. You may be surprised at my sudden regard for his genius, but not more so than myself. It came by revelation. I had never, I believe, read a page of his writings when I heard his lecture. How I came to go to hear him I hardly know, and must conclude that my good Gabriel led me there.

Dont despair of me yet, I am getting along bravely in my shanty & hope to* crow in due time. Somehow too, I am getting wonderfully interested in ancient lore, and am delighted to find that there were odd fellows like you & I & C. some hundreds of years before our *data*.

How wonderfully daylight shines upon us at times.

I no longer wonder that you had Homer, Valmiki, Vyasa &c in your Walden Shanty. They have already peeped into my windows & I shall not be surprised to have them seated within as my guests ere long. You need not be astonished if you hear of my swearing in Sanscrit or at least in Pan scrit!

I have just got a taste of these old fellows, and what a glorious feast awaits me. What a lucky mortal are you to be the possessor of these priceless treasures, sent you from England. I am about starting upon a pilgrimage into the country of those ancient Hindus, and already in fancy at least see the "gigantic peaks of the Himalayas" and sit beneath "the tremendous heights of the Dhawalagiri range"—so far as the railway of books can convey me there. Give me your hand Gabriel, and lead the way.†

* a true shanty clear (chanticleer!)
† My lamp has soiled my paper.—

415

Now for the present time. We are beginning to have spring here—and I have already heard the warbling of the blue-bird near the Shanty —but did not get a sight of one. The bluebird once appeared here as early as the middle of February, but disappeared as the weather proved colder & did not return until about the middle of March. I am sorry you talk so discouragingly about coming this way this spring. Dont be afraid of me dear Gabriel—I will do you no harm. I have my fears also. I conclude that I am too social for you, although this is a *sin* I have never been accused of. Think of it again, about coming here; but dont come unless you get a clear '*response from your oracle*' I quote Gabriel himself. I am quite humbled at your halting—the cords of love do not draw you and I have none stronger to bring into requisition, but I shall not release you without a struggle.—May I not then expect you in May —things *may* be done in that month which none other in the calendar admit of. It is the month of May bees—so some fine morning may you alight here a *thoro' maybee* fresh from Musketaquid. Then you and Channing & I can sit in the little hermitage like the Gymnosophists of old, and you may do the stamping on the ground to any Alexander that may offer himself as intruder.

I copy from my Journal of this day the following for your *edification!*
"Orphics" by a Modern Hindu.

The ancient Hindus of course wrote no "orphics."—the gentleman is a Modern.

In proportion as we see the merits of others we add to our own.

Mind is ever in the Spring—one eternal May morning—the same in its original freshness whether in the Sanscrit, the Greek and other languages or the English as a Medium of expression.

Mind has an eternal youth.

"Haunted forever by the eternal mind" is a fine thought of Words-worth, himself a philosopher and priest of Nature. Man must ever find this to be true—the thoughtful man.

A Diurnal Rhyme

Time Evening

In my humble shanty rude,
Where I pass the graceful hours,
Sweetened by sweet solitude—
The true springtime with its flowers,

Many solemn truths I learn,
That are found not in the books,
Ne'er denied to those who yearn,
For them in their chosen nooks:—
For primeval wisdom here
Finds me ready at her call,
And upon my listening ear,
Oft her kindly whisperings fall,—
Telling me in accents clear,—
Known but to the ear within,
That the source of all I hear,
Did with Man at first begin.
And in silence as I sit,
Calmly waiting for the Power,
Knowledge to my soul doth flit,
That no learning e'er could shower:—
Sempiternal wisdom deep,
From the endless source divine,
Not as creeds and dogmas creep,
But as doth the day-god shine—
With broad beams of amber light,
Reaching into every cell,
Driving out the ancient night,
That my soul in peace may dwell.—
Thus I'm taught to look & learn,
Rather calmly to receive,
And from stupid schoolmen turn,
To that which will ne'er deceive.

❋ ❋ ❋ ❋ ❋ ❋ ❋

I copy the above as the shortest way of informing you how I am
getting along & so abruptly close.

My dear Gabriel Jungfung [Jung*fang*?: cheerful one]

Yours warmly
D. <i>the least</i></div>

How is she of the 'lotus eyes'? since her perilous journey—

417

"A foolish letter," Daniel Ricketson wrote wryly on the top of the first page when he reread his epistle a dozen years later. Emerson had lectured before the New Bedford Lyceum on February 28, 1856. Ms., Hosmer; printed in Ricketson, pp. 61–63 and 64–65, where another letter, undated and beginning "Your letter as usual was full of wisdom," is inserted ahead of "A Diurnal Rhyme." For the inserted letter, see below.

From DANIEL RICKETSON

(Parachute)

Solar lamp, 10 p.m.

Dear T.

Your letter as usual was full of wisdom and has done me much good. Your visit here last fall did much to carry me well through the winter. I consider a visit from you a perfect benison, & hope that you will get a good response for May. I must try to get a look at the old house during the spring.—I thank you for your kind invitation but I am already too much in debt to you. Should I visit Concord it must be in a way not to incommode your household. I think I will set up a bed at once in the old house, to be kept as a kind of retreat for a few days at a time occasionally. I should have stated before that Channing and I have passed a word in relation to going to Concord together. So look out!

I wish to know if you think my sketch of the Concord sage was right —if you received the paper.

With kind remembrances to your family—Good night.

I go to bed.

his

D.   R.

a la Bewick   mark

MS., Hosmer; *the manuscript contains a fingerprint, doubtless Ricketson's, in the midst of "D. R. his mark." Here Ricketson was imitating a volume of Thomas Bewick from his library on which Thoreau commented in his* Journal *for October 1, 1855.*

From HORACE GREELEY

Washington, March 12, '56.

My Friend Thoreau,

I thank you for yours of the 10th. I hope we shall agree to know each other better, and that we shall be able to talk over some matters on which we agree, with others on which we may differ.

I will say now that money shall not divide us—that is, I am very sure that I shall be willing to pay such sum as you will consider satisfactory. I will not attempt to fix on a price just now, as I wish to write to Mrs. Greeley in Europe and induce her (if I can) to return somewhat earlier in view of the prospect of securing your services.

I concur entirely in your suggestion that both parties be left at liberty to terminate the engagement when either shall see fit. But I trust no such termination will be deemed advisable, for a year or two at least; and I hope at least a part of your books and other surroundings will follow you to our cottage in the woods after you shall have had time to pronounce us endurable.

I will write by Saturday's steamer to Mrs. Greeley, and trust you will make no arrangements incompatible with that we contemplate until further communication between us. I expect to have you join us, if you will, in early summer.

Your obliged friend,
Horace Greeley.

Henry D. Thoreau, Concord, Mass.

In spite of good will on both sides, the idea of having Thoreau tutor the Greeley children at their "farm" in Chappaqua was never put into

effect. MS., Daniel Gregory Mason, *lent through the courtesy of Van Wyck Brooks; previously unpublished.*

To H.G.O. BLAKE

Concord Mar. 13 1856.

Mr Blake—

It is high time I sent you a word. I have not heard from Harrisburg since offering to go there, and have not been invited to lecture anywhere else the past winter. So you see I am fast growing rich. This is quite right, for such is my relation to the lecture-goers. I should be surprised and alarmed if there were any great call for me. I confess that I am considerably alarmed even when I hear that an individual wishes to meet me, for my experience teaches me that we shall thus only be made certain of a mutual strangeness, which otherwise we might never have been aware of.

I have not yet recovered strength enough for such a walk as you propose, though pretty well again for circumscribed rambles & chamber work. Even now I am probably the greatest walker in Concord— to its disgrace be it said. I remember our walks & talks & sailing in the past, with great satisfaction, and trust that we shall have more of them ere long—have more woodings-up—for even in the spring we must still seek "fuel to maintain our fires."

As you suggest, we would fain value one another for what we are absolutely, rather than relatively. How will this do for a symbol of sympathy?

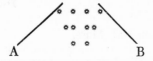

As for compliments,—even the stars praise me, and I praise them,— they & I sometimes belong to a mutual admiration society. Is it not so with you? I know you of old. Are you not tough & earnest to be talked

at, praised or blamed? Must *you* go out of the room because you are the subject of conversation? Where will you go to—pray? Shall we look into the "Letter Writer" to see what compliments are admissible. I am not afraid of praise for I have practised it on myself. As for my deserts, I never took an account of that stock, and in this connection care not whether I am deserving or not. When I hear praise coming do I not elevate & arch myself to hear it like the sky, and as impersonally? Think I appropriate any of it to my weak legs? No—praise away *till all is blue.*

I see by the newspapers that the season for making sugar is at hand. Now is the time, whether you be rock or white maple,—or hickory. I trust that you have prepared a store of sap tubs and sumach spouts, and invested largely in kettles. Early the first frosty morning tap your maples—the sap will not run in summer, you know—It matters not how little juice you get, if you get all you can, and boil it down. I made just one crystal of sugar once, one twentieth of an inch cube out of a pumpkin, & it sufficed. Though the yield be no greater than that,—this is not less the reason for it, & it will be not the less sweet,—nay, it will be infinitely the sweeter.

Shall then the maple yield sugar, & not man? Shall the farmer be thus active, & surely have so much sugar to show for it before this very March is gone,—while I read the newspaper? While he works in his sugar camp, let me work in mine—for sweetness is in me, & to sugar it shall come;—it shall not all go to leaves & wood. Am I not a *sugar maple* man then?

Boil down the sweet sap which the spring causes to flow within you —Stop not at syrup; go on to sugar,—though you present the world with but a single crystal—a crystal not made from trees in your yard, but from the new life that stirs in your pores. Cheerfully skim your kettle, & watch it set & crystalize—making a holiday of it, if you will. Heaven will be propitious to you as to him.

Say to the farmer,—There is your crop,—Here is mine. Mine is sugar to sweeten sugar with. If you will listen to me, I will sweeten your whole load,—your whole life.

Then will the callers ask—Where is Blake?—He is in his sugar-camp on the *Mt.* side.—Let the world await him.

Then will the little boys bless you, & the great boys too,—for such sugar is the origin of many condiments—Blakeians, in the shops of Worcester, of new form, with their mottos wrapped up in them.

Shall men taste only the sweetness of the maple & the cane, the coming year?

A walk over the crust to Asnybumskit, standing there in its inviting simplicity,—is tempting to think of,—making a fire on the snow under some rock! The very poverty of outward nature implies an inward wealth in the walker. What a Golconda is he conversant with, thawing his fingers over such a blaze! —But—but—

Have you read the new poem—"The Angel in the House"?—perhaps you will find it good for you.

H. D. T.

Thoreau's plan for a Western lecture tour was canceled through lack of engagements. Ticknor & Fields had just published Coventry Patmore's Angel in the House, *which Thoreau recommends to Blake. MS., C. Waller Barrett.*

From HORACE GREELEY

New York, Wednesday, April 30, '56

Friend Thoreau,

Immediately on the receipt of your letter, I wrote to Mrs. Greeley its substance. She was then in Dresden, but I wrote to Paris, and she did not receive my letter till the 9th inst. I have now her response, and she is heartily gratified with the prospect that you will come to us and teach our children. She says she thinks it may at least sometimes be best to have instruction communicated by familiar oral conversations while walking in the fields and woods, and that it might not be well to be confined always to the same portion of each day. However, she hopes, as I do, that interest in and love for the children would soon supersede all formal stipulations, and that what is best for them will also be found consistent with what is most agreeable for you.

Mrs. Greeley will not be home till the middle of June, so that I sup-

pose the 1st of July will be about as soon as we should be snugly at home in our country cottage, ready for instruction and profit. Please write me your ideas with regard to the whole matter, including the amount of compensation that you consider fair and just. I prefer that you should come to us feeling at perfect liberty to leave at any time when you think best to do so; but I hope you will be reconciled to stay with us for one year at least. Of course, this would not preclude your going away to lecture or visit when you should see fit. Please write me soon and fully, and oblige

Yours,
Horace Greeley

Henry D. Thoreau Concord Mass.

MS., Abernethy (*typescript*).

———————————

To H.G.O. BLAKE

Concord May 21st '56

Mr. Blake,

I have not for a long time been *putting such thoughts together* as I should like to read to the company you speak of. I have enough of that sort to say, or even read, but not time now to arrange it. Something I have prepared might prove for their entertainment or refreshment perchance, but I would not like to have a hat carried round for it. I have just been reading some papers to see if they would do for your company; but though I thought pretty well of them as long as I read them to myself, when I got an auditor to try them on, I felt that they would not answer. How could I let you drum up a company to hear them?— In fine, what I have is either too scattered or loosely arranged, or too light, or else is too scientific and matter of fact (I run a good deal into that of late) for so hungry a company.

I am still a learner, not a teacher, feeding somewhat omnivorously,

423

browsing both stalk & leaves—but I shall perhaps be enabled to speak with the more precision & authority by & by—if philosophy & sentiment are not buried under a multitude of details.

I do not refuse, but accept your invitation—only changing the time —I consider myself invited to Worcester once for all—& many thanks to the inviter.

As for the Harvard excursion, will you let me suggest another? Do you & Brown come to Concord on Saturday, if the weather promises well, and spend the Sunday here on the river or hills or both. So we shall save some of our money, (which is of next importance to our souls) and lose—I do not know what. You say you *talked* of coming here before, now *do* it. I do not propose this because I think that I am worth your spending time with—but because I hope that we may prove flint & steel to one another. It is at most only an hour's ride further, & you can at any rate do what you please when you get here.

Then we will see if we have any apology to offer for our existence. So come to Concord!—come to Concord!—come to Concord! or — — — — — your suit shall be defaulted.

As for the dispute about solitude & society any comparison is im- pertinent. It is an idling down on the plain at the base of a mountain instead of climbing steadily to its top. Of course you will be glad of all the society you can get to go up with. Will you go to glory with me? is the burden of the song. I love society so much that I swallowed it all at a gulp—i.e. all that came in my way. It is not that we love to be alone, but that we love to soar, and when we do soar, the company grows thinner & thinner till there is none at all. It is either the Tribune on the plain, a sermon on the mount, or a very private *extacy* still higher up. We are not the less to aim at the summits, though the multitude does not ascend them. Use all the society that will abet you. But perhaps I do not enter into the spirit of your talk.

H.D.T.

There is no record of Thoreau's delivering a lecture in Worcester at this time. MS., Massachusetts Historical Society.

To JOHN LANGDON SIBLEY, Harvard Librarian

Concord May 27 56

Dear Sir
    I return herewith the following books to the Library—viz—"Columella of Husbandry" 1. v. "Pennsylvania, Ohio, & Delaware" 1. v. Jesuit Relations for 1639 & 1642 & 3 2. vols.

Yrs
Henry D. Thoreau

There is a discussion of Thoreau's use of Columella in Francis L. Utley, "Thoreau and Columella: A Study in Reading Habits," The New England Quarterly, XI (March 1938), 171–80, and a reply to this article in Odell Shepard, "Thoreau and Columella: A Comment," The New England Quarterly, XI (September 1938), 605–6. MS., Harvard; previously unpublished.

To CALVIN GREENE

Concord May 31st '56

Dear Sir,
    I forwarded by mail a copy of my "Week" post paid to James Newberry, Merchant, Rochester, Oakland Co Mich., according to your order, about ten days ago, or on the receit of your note.
    I will obtain and forward a copy of "Walden" & also of the "Week," to California, to your order, post paid, for $2.60 The postage will be between 60 & 70 cts.
    I thank you heartily for your kind intentions respecting me. The West has many attractions for me, particularly the lake country & the Indians. Yet I do not foresee what my engagements may be in the fall. I have once or twice come near going West a-lecturing, and perhaps

425

some winter may bring me into your neighborhood, in which case I should probably see you. Yet lecturing has commonly proved so foreign & irksome to me, that I think I could only use it to acquire the means with which to make an independent tour another time.

As for my pen, I can say that it is not altogether idle, though I have finished nothing new in the book form. I am drawing a rather long bow, though it may be a feeble one, but I pray that the archer may receive new strength before the arrow is shot.

With many thanks

Yrs truly
Henry D. Thoreau

Calvin H. Greene

MS., Princeton University Library.

To CALVIN GREENE

Concord Saturday June 21st '56

Dear Sir

On the 12 ult I forwarded the two books to California, observing your directions in every particular, and I trust that Uncle Sam will discharge his duty faithfully. While in Worcester this week I obtained the accompanying daguerreotype—which my friends think is pretty good—though better looking than I.

Books & postage — — — — — —	$2.64
Daguerreotype	.50
Postage — — — —	.16
	3.30

5 00
3.30   You will accordingly
find 1.70   enclosed with my shadow

Yrs
Henry D. Thoreau

The picture was the Maxham daguerreotype showing Thoreau with Galway whiskers underneath his chin. F. H. Allen notes Thoreau's habitual misuse of "ult." for "inst." (A Bibliography of Henry David Thoreau, p. xiii.) MS., Princeton University Library.

From MARY MOODY EMERSON

Saturday Noon, July 12, 1856.

Will my young friend visit me tomorrow early as he can? This evening my Sister [Sarah Alden] Ripley sends word she will come, and go to see Mrs. William Emerson, who is in town. I wish for your writings, hoping they will give me a clearer clue to your faith,—its nature, its destination and object. While excited by your original wit and thoughts, I lose sight, perhaps, of the motive and end and infinite responsibility of talent, in any of its endless consequences. To enter the interior of a peculiar organization of mind is desirable to all who think and read in intermitted solitude. They believe, when the novelty of genius opens on their unpractised eye, that the spirit itself must own and feel its natural relations to their God of revelation, where alone every talent can be perfected and bring its additions to the owner; that faith in the discipline towards moral excellence can alone insure an immortal fame,—or even success and happiness here. God bless you, and thus make you useful to your Country and kind, prays

M E

Slight, waspish, and brilliant, Mary Moody Emerson left few persons indifferent to her. She had been a great stimulant to her nephew Ralph Waldo when he was a youth, and although she was later much disappointed by his deserting Unitarianism for Transcendentalism she maintained an affection for him throughout her long life. Now at eighty-two she was visiting him and also seeing Henry Thoreau frequently. Per-

427

haps she saw in him an individualism as striking as her own. Text, F. B.
Sanborn, "A Concord Note-Book," The Critic, XLVIII (April 1906),
344.

From MARY MOODY EMERSON

Dear Henry:

I expect to set out to-morrow morning for Goshen,—a place
where wit and gaiety never come "that comes to all." But hope lives,
and travels on with the speed of suns and stars; and when there are
none but clouds in the sky,

> "Its very nakedness has power
> To aid the hour,"

says old Sir Walter. However, the "old Bobbin Woman was steady to
her Bible," where each page unfolded words of comfort and assurance. Yet the memory of intelligence and extensive mentality will never
fail to give a vivid pleasure to reflection,—if shaded by the faith of
future uncertainties,—'t is well to admit the decrees of unerring recti-
tude. If you write to M.E. it will brighten the solitude so desired. Had
I been detained by nothing but weather! but I must pack up by daylight.

Mary Emerson

*This note from Emerson's indomitable aunt was written on the inside
page of a letter dated July 17, 1856 from her to Thoreau's mother,
father, and family.* Text, F. B. Sanborn, "A Concord Note-Book," The
Critic, XLVIII (April 1906), 345.

[1856]

To F. B. SANBORN

Friday eve

If you chance to be going to Cambridge. . . will. . . you take a small volume to the library. . . It is so rare a book I do not like to trust the expressmen with it. . . .

We are not sure when Thoreau wrote this penciled note, which the auction catalogue describes as 1 p. 12mo. It was almost certainly after August 1856. He and Sanborn were friends by the summer of 1856, and Thoreau might have asked this favor any time after that. Sanborn says that, starting during this summer, he "began to dine daily at [Thoreau's] mother's table, and thus saw him almost every day for three years" (Familiar Letters of Thoreau, p. 301). It may be argued that if Thoreau saw Sanborn, he would not have had to write him; and so this letter could be dated after the three-year period was over. Such a case, however, for dating the letter after 1859 is rather tenuous. Nor does the rarity of the book mentioned in the letter help us much. Kenneth Walter Cameron, in the second volume of his Emerson the Essayist, *prints a chronological list (pp. 192–98) through 1860 of the books Thoreau borrowed from the Harvard library, but there are too many of them to determine what the book was and consequently when it was borrowed and when it was returned.* Text, catalogue of the Hess sale (*Anderson Auction Co., January 24, 1908*).

To BRONSON ALCOTT

Concord Sep 1st 56

Mr Alcott,
I remember that in the spring you invited me to visit you. I feel inclined to spend a day or two with you and on your hills at this season,

returning perhaps by way of Brattleboro. What if I should take the cars for Walpole next Friday morning? Are you at home? And will it be convenient and agreeable to you to see me then?—I will await an answer.

I am but poor company, and it will not be worth the while for you to put yourself out on my account; yet from time to time I have some thoughts which would be the better for an airing. I also wish to get some hints from September on the Connecticut to help me understand that season on the Concord;—to snuff the musty fragrance of the decaying year in the primitive woods. There is considerable cellar room in my nature for such stores, a whole row of bins waiting to be filled before I can celebrate my Thanksgiving. Mould is the richest of soils, yet *I* am not mould. It will always be found that one flourishing institution exists & battens on another mouldering one. The Present itself is parasitic to this extent.

Your fellow traveller
Henry D. Thoreau

According to his Journal (*IX, 61 ff.*), *Thoreau started September 5 for Brattleboro, where he visited Charles Frost and Mary Brown. On September 10 he went on to Walpole, New Hampshire, to visit the Alcotts; on the 12th he returned to Concord.* MS., F. W. Pratt.

To DANIEL RICKETSON

Concord Sep 2d '56

Friend Ricketson,

My father & mother regret that your indisposition is likely to prevent your coming to Concord at present. It is as well that you do not, if you depend on seeing me, for I expect to go to New Hampshire the latter part of the week. I shall be glad to see you afterward, if you are prepared for & can endure my unsocial habits.

430

I would suggest that you have one or two of the teeth—which you can best spare, extracted at once—for the sake of your general no less than particular health. This is the advice of one who has had quite his share of toothache in this world.—I am a trifle stouter than when I saw you last, yet far—far short of my best estate. I thank you for two newspapers which you have sent me—am glad to see that you have studied out the history of the ponds, got the Indian names straightened—which means made more crooked—&c &c I remember them with great satisfaction. They are all the more interesting to me for the lean & sandy soil that surrounds them. Heaven is not one [of] your fertile Ohio bottoms, you may depend on it. Ah, the Middleboro Ponds!—Great Platte Lakes! Remember me to the perch in them. I trust that I may have some better craft than that oarless pumpkin-seed the next time I navigate them.

From the size of your family I infer that Mrs. Ricketson & your daughters have returned from Franconia. Please remember me to them, & also to Arthur & Walton, & tell the latter that if in the course of his fishing he should chance to come across the shell of a terrapin & will save it for me, I shall be exceedingly obliged to him.

Channing dropped in on us the other day, but soon dropped out again.

Yrs
Henry D. Thoreau.

MS., Huntington.

———

From B. B. WILEY

Providence R.I. Sep 4, 1856

Henry D. Thoreau Esq Concord
Dear Sir
    Having read your "Week on the Concord" which you sent D W Vaughan a short time since, I enclose $1.27 for which will you please send me a copy of the same.

I have your "Walden" which I have read several times. If you can send me any writings of yours besides the above works I will esteem it a favor and will immediately remit you the amount due

I consider that the moderate price I pay for excellent writings does not remove my obligation to their author and I most gladly take this occasion to tender you my warmest thanks for the pleasure and improvement you have afforded me

Yours very truly
B. B. Wiley

Benjamin Wiley, when he first wrote Thoreau, was a Providence business man active as broker and banker. D. W. Vaughan, who lent Wiley his own copy of the Week, *was also a Providence banker. MS., Berg; previously unpublished.*

To DANIEL RICKETSON

Concord Sep 23 '56

Friend Ricketson,

I have returned from New Hampshire, and find myself *in statu quo*. My journey proved one of business purely. As you suspected, I saw Alcott, and I spoke to him of you, and your good will toward him; so now you may consider yourself introduced. He would be glad to hear from you about a conversation in New Bedford. He was about setting out on a conversing tour to Fitchburg, Worcester, & 3 or 4 weeks hence Waterbury Ct, New York, Newport (?) & Providence (?). You may be sure that you will not have occasion to repent of any exertions which you may make to secure an audience for him. I send you one of his programmes, lest he should not have done so himself.

I am sorry to hear so poor an account of C[hanning]. Perhaps he will turn up & show his better side again.

You propose to me teaching the following winter. I find that I can-

not entertain the idea. It would require such a revolution of all my habits, I think, as would sap the very foundation of me. I am engaged to Concord & my very private pursuits by 10,000 ties, & it would be suicide to cut them. If I were weaker, & not somewhat stronger physically, I should be more tempted. I am so busy that I cannot even think of visiting you. The days are not long enough or I am not strong enough to do the work of the day before bed-time.

Excuse my paper. It chances to be the best I have.

Yrs
Henry D. Thoreau

Alcott accepted Ricketson's invitation, according to Familiar Letters *(p. 304), and visited New Bedford in the spring of 1857. MS., Hosmer.*

From DANIEL RICKETSON

Brooklawn, 24 Sept. 1856.

Dear Friend,—

Yours of the 23rd is received, and I notice what you say in regard to Mr. Alcott's class; but I fear that I shall hardly prove able to undertake the business of obtaining one for him. It is entirely out of my line and very much *averse* to my taste, to solicit from any one. People are so ready to ride a "high horse," as soon as you present anything to them that is left for their consideration or decision, that I shrink at once from any such collision. Still should anything turn up whereby I may effect the object through a third party, I shall be very glad so to do. In the mean time I am ready to listen to any suggestions Mr. Alcott may make to me in the premises.

I am sorry that I shall not have the pleasure of a visit from you this fall, but as you need companionship so much less than I do I suppose the pleasure would not be reciprocal were we to meet. I am becoming quite a historical sketcher, and have already commenced publishing

a history of New Bedford, or rather of the old township of Dartmouth, which included New Bedford, also the townships of Westport, Fair-haven, and the present Dartmouth.

Have you ever observed how many of the Indian names of rivers, lakes, &c, end in et? Assawampsett, Acushnet, Pascamanset, &c., &c. I am informed by a person who appeared to have some knowledge of Indian words that *et* signifies water—the Taunton river was called Nemasket for several miles from its outlet from the Middleborough Ponds—then Tetiquet or Tetiquid. Now I come to my object—did not your own Musketaquid have the final syllable *quet?* If the fact can be established that *et* meant water, I should have no hesitation in making the alteration.

Please remember me most truly to your family, and to Mr. Emerson and his, when you next meet him.

Trusting that when the right time comes around we shall meet once more, I remain,

Yours faithfully,
D. Ricketson.

Text, Ricketson, *pp. 68–69.*

From SARAH ALDEN RIPLEY

My dear friend,

a story you once told me about the spontaneous generation of your butterfly was brought to mind by an article in Blackwood's maga-zine on "Sea side studies." I thought you would like to look at it, if you have not seen it. *The* Magazine belongs to Mr. Ames.

With much regard
S. A. Ripley

Mr Henry Thoreau

Sarah Alden Ripley, Emerson's widowed aunt, was noted for her knowledge of foreign languages. Then living in Concord, she knew and liked Thoreau. On the day of his death, she wrote: "This morning is sad for those of us who sympathize with the friends of Henry Thoreau, the philosopher and the woodman."

A series of articles entitled "Sea-Side Studies" and "New Sea-Side Studies" appeared in Volumes LXXX and LXXXI of Blackwood's Edinburgh Magazine. This letter apparently refers to the second installment of the series, which appeared in the September 1856 issue. On this evidence we date the letter conjecturally as of September 1856; of course it may have been written at any time from this date to Thoreau's death. MS., Berg; previously unpublished.

To THOMAS CHOLMONDELEY

Concord Mass. Oct 20th 1856.

Dear Cholmondeley

    I wish to thank you again for those books. They are the nucleus of my library. I wrote to you on the receipt of them last winter, (directing as now) but not having heard from you, do not know in what part of the world this may find you. Several here are enquiring if you have returned to England, as you had just started for the Crimea at the last account. The books have long been shelved in cases of my own construction made partly of the driftwood of our river. They are the admiration of all beholders. Alcott and Emerson, besides myself, have been cracking some of the nuts.

    Certainly I shall never pay you for them. Of those new to me the Rig Veda is the most savory that I have yet tasted. As primitive poetry, I think as any extant. Indeed all the Vedantic literature is priceless. There they stand occupying two shelves, headed by Froissart, stretching round Egypt and India "Ultima Thule," as a fit conclusion. What a world of variety. I shall browse there for some winters to come. While war has given place to peace on your side, perhaps a more serious war still is breaking out here. I seem to hear its distant mutterings,

435

though it may be long before the bolt will fall in our midst. There has not been anything which you could call union between the North and South in this country for many years, and there cannot be so long as slavery is in the way. I only wish that Northern—that any men—were better material, or that I for one had more skill to deal with them; that the north had more spirit and would settle the question at once, and here instead of struggling feebly and protractedly away off on the plains of Kansas. They are on the eve of a Presidential election, as perhaps you know. and all good people are praying that of the three candidates Fremont may be the man; but in my opinion the issue is quite doubtful. As far as I have observed, the worst man stands the best chance in this country. But as for politics, what I most admire now-a-days, is not the regular governments but the irregular primitive ones, like the Vigilance committee in California and even the free state men in Kansas. They are the most divine.—I have just taken a run up country, as I did with you once, only a little farther, this time; to the Connecticut river in New Hampshire, where I saw Alcott, King of men. He is among those who ask after you, and takes a special interest in the oriental books. He cannot say enough about them. "And then that he should send you a library! Think of it!"

I am sorry that I can give but a poor account of myself. I got "run down" they say, more than a year ago, and have not yet got fairly up again. It has not touched my spirits however, for they are as indifferently tough, as sluggishly resilient, as a dried fungus. I would it were the kind called punk; that they might catch and retain some heavenly spark. I dwell as much aloof from society as ever: find it just as impossible to agree in opinion with the most intelligent of my neighbors; they not having improved one jot, nor I either. I am still immersed in nature, have much of the time a living sense of the breadth of the field on whose verge I dwell. The *great west* and *north west* stretching on infinitely far and grand and wild, qualifying all our thoughts. That is the only America I know. I prize this western reserve chiefly for its intellectual value. That is the road to new life and freedom,—if ever we are dissatisfied with this and not to exile as in Siberia and knowing this, one need not travel it. That great northwest where several of our shrubs, fruitless here, retain and mature their fruits properly.

I am pleased to think of you *in* that England, where we all seem to have originated, or at least sojourned which Emerson values so much, but which I know so little about. That island seems as full of good things

436

as a nut is of meat: and I trust that it still is a sound nut without mould or worm. I hope that by this time you are settled in your mind and satisfactorily employed there.

My father mother and sister send their best wishes, and would be glad to see you in this country again. We are all quite anxious to hear that you are safe and sound: I in particular hope that you are in all respects unscathed by the battle of life, ready for still worthier encounters.

Yours,
H. D. T.

MS., Berg, *copy in an unknown hand; previously unpublished.*

From B. B. WILEY

Providence Oct 31, 1856

H D Thoreau Concord
Dear Sir

In Worcester I saw Theo Brown who was very glad to hear from you. In the evening we went together to see Harry Blake. Both these gentlemen were well. Mr Blake is an enthusiast in matters which the world passes by as of little account. Since I returned here I have taken two morning walks with Chas Newcomb. He suggested that he would like to walk to the White Mountains with me some time and it may yet be done. He walks daily some miles and seems to be in pretty good health. He says he would like to visit Concord, but named no time for that purpose.

I am anxious to know a little more of Confucius. Can you briefly, so that it will not take too much of *your* time, write me his views in regard to Creation, Immortality, man's preexistence if he speaks of it, and generally anything relating to man's Origin, Purpose, & Destiny.

I would also like much to know the names of the leading Hindu philosophers and their ideas on the preceding topics

Is Swedenborg a valuable man to you, and if so, why?

Do not think me too presuming because I ask you these questions. I am an inquirer (as indeed I always hope to be) and have to avail myself of the wisdom of those who have commenced life before me. Though I cannot hope that my existence will be of any direct benefit to you, yet I cannot fail to exert influence somewhere, and that it may be of an elevating character, I wish to make my own the experience of collective humanity.

I shall leave here next Thursday Nov 6 for Chicago. My address there will be *care of Strong & Wiley*. I shall undoubtedly spend the winter there and how much longer I shall stay I cannot tell.

I suggested brevity in your remarks about the views of those philosophers. This was entirely for your convenience. I shall read appreciatingly and most attentively whatever you find time to write.

Yours truly
B. B. Wiley

Newcomb was Emerson's Providence friend and correspondent. Thoreau found him an interesting walking companion (Journal, *VII, 79*). *MS,. Berg; previously unpublished.*

To SOPHIA THOREAU

Direct

Eagleswood—Perth Amboy N. J. Sat. Eve Nov. 1st '56

Dear Sophia,

I have hardly had time & repose enough to write to you before. I spent the afternoon of Friday (it seems some months ago) in Worcester, but failed to see Blake, he having "gone to the horse race"! in

Boston;—to atone for which I have just received a letter from him, asking me to stop at Worcester & lecture on my return—I called on [Theo] Brown & [T. W.] Higginson, & in the evening came by way of Norwich to N. Y. in the steamer Commonwealth, and though it was so windy in land, had a perfectly smooth passage, and about as good a sleep as usually at home. Reached N Y about 7 Am, too late for the John Potter (there was'nt any Jonas) so I spent the forenoon there, called on Greeley, (who was not in) met [F. A. T.] Bellew in Broadway and walked into his workshop, read at the Astor Library &c &c—I arrived here about 30 miles from N. Y. about 5 pm Saturday, in company with Miss E. Peabody, who was returning in the same covered wagon from the Landing to Eagleswood, which last place she has just left for the winter. This is a queer place— There is one large long stone building, which cost some $40000, in which I do not know exactly who or how many work—(one or two familiar faces, & more familiar names have turned up)—a few shops & offices, an old farm house and Mr [Marcus] Spring's perfectly private residence within 20 rods of the main building. "The City of Perth Amboy" is about as big as Concord, and Eagleswood is 1¼ miles S W of it, on the bay side. The central fact here is evidently Mr [Theodore] Weld's school—recently established—around which various other things revolve. Saturday evening I went to the school room, hall, or what not, to see the children & their teachers & patrons dance. Mr Weld, a kind looking man with a long white beard, danced with them, & Mr [E. J.] Cutler his assistant, lately from Cambridge, who is acquainted [with] Sanborn, Mr Spring—and others. This Sat. eve-dance is a regular thing, & it is thought something strange if you dont attend. They take it for granted that you want *society!*

Sunday forenoon, I attended a sort of Quaker meeting at the same place—(The Quaker aspect & spirit prevails here— Mrs Spring says "—does thee not?") where it was expected that the spirit would move me (I having been previously spoken to about it) & it, or something else, did, an inch or so. I said just enough to set them a little by the ears & make it lively. I had excused myself by saying that I could not adapt myself to a particular audience, for all the speaking & lecturing here has reference to the children, who are far the greater part of the audience, & they are not so bright as N. E. children Imagine them sitting close to the wall all around a hall—with old Quaker looking men & women here & there. There sat Mrs. Weld (Grimke) & her sister, two

elderly grayheaded ladies, the former in extreme Bloomer costume, which was what you may call remarkable; Mr [Arnold] Buffum with broad face & a great white beard, looking like a pier head made of the cork tree with the bark on, as if he could buffet a considerable wave;— James G. Birney, formerly candidate for the Presidency, with another particularly white head & beard—Edward Palmer, the anti-money man (for whom communities were made) with [word] ample beard somewhat grayish. Some of them I suspect are very worthy people. Of course you are wondering to what extent all these make one family— to what extent 20. Mrs [Caroline] Kirkland, and this [a] name only to me, I saw— She has just bought a lot here. They all know more about your neighbors & acquaintances than you suspected.

On Sunday evening, I read the moose-story to the children to their satisfaction. Ever since I have been constantly engaged in surveying Eagleswood—through woods ravines marshes & along the shore, dodging the tide—through cat-briar mud & beggar ticks—having no time to look up or think where I am—(it takes 10 or 15 minutes before each meal to pick the beggar ticks out of my clothes—burrs & the rest are left—rents mended at the first convenient opportunity) I shall be engaged perhaps as much longer. Mr Spring wants me to help him about setting out an orchard & vineyard—Mr Birney asks me to survey a small piece for him, & Mr Alcott who has just come down here for the 3d Sunday—says that Greeley (I left my name for him) invites him & me to go to his home with him next Saturday morning & spend the Sunday.

It seems a twelve-month since I was not here—but I hope to get settled deep into my den again ere long. The hardest thing to find here is solitude & Concord. I am at Mr Spring's house— Both he & she & their family are quite agreeable.

I want you to write to me immediately— (just left off to talk French with the servant man—) & let Father & Mother put in a word—to them & to aunts—

Love from
Henry.

MS., Huntington.

To H. G. O. BLAKE

Eagleswood, N. J., November 19, 1856.

Mr. Blake,—

I have been here much longer than I expected, but have deferred answering you, because I could not foresee when I shall return. I do not know yet within three or four days. This uncertainty makes it impossible for me to appoint a day to meet you, until it shall be too late to hear from you again. I think, therefore, that I must go straight home. I feel some objection to reading that "What shall it profit" lecture *again* in Worcester; but if you are quite sure that it will be worth the while (it is a grave consideration), I will even make an independent journey from Concord for that purpose. I have read three of my old lectures (that included) to the Eagleswood people, and, unexpectedly, with rare success—*i. e.*, I was aware that what I was saying was silently taken in by their ears.

You must excuse me if I write mainly a business letter now, for I am sold for the time,—am merely Thoreau the surveyor here,—and solitude is scarcely obtainable in these parts.

Alcott has been here three times, and, Saturday before last, I went with him and Greeley, by invitation of the last, to G.'s farm, thirty-six miles north of New York. The next day A. and I heard Beecher preach; and what was more, we visited Whitman the next morning (A. had already seen him), and were much interested and provoked. He is apparently the greatest democrat the world has seen. Kings and aristocracy go by the board at once, as they have long deserved to. A remarkably strong though coarse nature, of a sweet disposition, and much prized by his friends. Though peculiar and rough in his exterior, his skin (all over (?)) red, he is essentially a gentleman. I am still somewhat in a quandary about him,—feel that he is essentially strange to me, at any rate; but I am surprised by the sight of him. He is very broad, but, as I have said, not fine. He said that I misapprehended him. I am not quite sure that I do. He told us that he loved to ride up and down Broadway all day on an omnibus, sitting beside the driver, listening to the roar of the carts, and sometimes gesticulating and declaiming Homer at the top of his voice. He has long been an editor and writer for the newspapers,—was editor of the "New Orleans Crescent" once; but

now has no employment but to read and write in the forenoon, and walk in the afternoon, like all the rest of the scribbling gentry.

I shall probably be in Concord next week; so you can direct to me there.

A penciled draft of the last part of this letter—the draft begins with "A remarkably strong," in Abernethy—includes an interesting addition to Thoreau's comments on Whitman as printed in Familiar Letters of Thoreau. *Whitman spoke to Thoreau about his having published Emerson's letter of endorsement of* Leaves of Grass, *an action that created a stir at the time and is still debated. Thoreau says: "In his apologizing account of the matter he made the printing of Es letter seem a simple thing—& to some extent throws the burden of it—if there is any, on the writer," that is, on Emerson—the sentence omitted from the published version.* Text, Familiar Letters of Thoreau, *pp. 339–41; the manuscript of the finished letter was sold by the Anderson Auction Co. at the Haber sale on December 7–8, 1909; the sale catalogue quotes some of the omitted sentence.*

To H. G. O. BLAKE

Concord Dec 6 '56

Mr Blake,

What is wanting above is merely an engraving of Eagleswood, which I have used. I trust that you got a note from me at Eagleswood about a fortnight ago. I passed thru' Worcester on the morning of the 25th of November, and spent several hours (from 3.30 to 6.20) in the travellers' room at the Depot, as in a dream, it now seems. As the first Harlem train unexpectedly connected with the first from Fitchburg, I did not spend the forenoon with you, as I had anticipated, on account of baggage &c— If it had been a seasonable hour I should have seen you, i.e. if you had not been gone to a horse-race. But think of making a call

at half past three in the morning! (Would it not have implied a 3 o clock in the morning courage in both you & me?) As it were ignoring the fact that mankind are really not at home—are not out, but so deeply in that they cannot be seen—nearly half their hours at this season of the year. I walked up & down the Main Street at half past 5 in the dark, and paused long in front of [Theo] Brown's store trying to distinguish its features; considering whether I might safely leave his "Putnam" in the door handle, but concluded not to risk it. Meanwhile a watchman (?) seemed to be watching me, & I moved off. Took another turn around there, a little later, and had the very earliest offer of the Transcript from an urchin behind, whom I actually could not see, it was so dark. So I withdrew, wondering if you & B. would know that I had been there. You little dream who is occupying Worcester when you are all asleep. Several things occurred there that night, which I will venture to say were not put into the Transcript. A cat caught a mouse at the depot, & gave it to her kitten to play with. So that world famous tragedy goes on by night as well as by day, & nature is *emphatically* wrong.* Also I saw a young Irishman kneel before his mother, as if in prayer, while she wiped a cinder out of his eye with her tongue; and I found that it was never too late (or early?) to learn something.—These things transpired while you and B. were, to all practical purposes, no where, & good for nothing—not even for society,—not for horse-races,—nor the taking back of a Putnam's Magazine. It is true I might have recalled you to life, but it would have been a cruel act, considering the kind of life you would have come back to.

However, I would fain write to you now by broad daylight, and report to you some of my life, such as it is, and recall you to your life, which is not always lived by you, even by day light.

Blake! Blake! Are you awake? Are you aware what an ever-glorious morning this is? What long expected never to be repeated opportunity is now offered to get life & knowledge?

For my part I am trying to wake up,—to wring slumber out of my pores;—For, generally, I take events as unconcernedly as a fence post,—absorb wet & cold like it, and am pleasantly tickled with lichens slowly spreading over me. Could I not be content then to be a cedar post, which lasts 25 years? Would I not rather be that than the farmer that set it? or he that preaches to that farmer?—& go to the heaven of posts at last? I think I should like that as well as any would like it. But

* Left on the stove too long. [Thoreau's note.]

443

I should not care if I sprouted into a living tree, put forth leaves & flowers, & have fruit.

I am grateful for what I am & have. My thanksgiving is perpetual. It is surprising how contented one can be with nothing definite—only a sense of* existance. Well anything for variety. I am ready to try this for the next 1000 years, & exhaust it. How sweet to think of! My extremities well charred, and my intellectual part too, so that there is no danger of worm or rot for a long while. My breath is sweet to me. O how I laugh when I think of my vague indefinite riches. No run on my bank can drain it—for my wealth is not possession but enjoyment.

What are all these years made for? and now another winter comes, so much like the last? Cant we satisfy the beggars once for all? Have you got in your wood for this winter? What else have you got in? Of what use a great fire on the hearth & a confounded little fire in the heart? Are you prepared to make a decisive campaign—to pay for your costly tuition—to pay for the suns of past summers—for happiness & unhappiness lavished upon you?

Does not Time go by swifter than the swiftest equine trotter or racker?

Stir up Brown—Remind him of his duties, which outrun the date & span of Worcester's years past & to come. Tell him to be sure that he is on the Main Street, however narrow it may be—& to have a lit sign, visible by night as well as by day.

Are they not patient waiters—They who wait for us? But even they shall not be losers.

———————————

Dec. 7

That Walt Whitman, of whom I wrote to you, is the most interesting fact to me at present. I have just read his 2nd edition (which he gave me) and it has done me more good than any reading for a long time. Perhaps I remember best the poem of Walt Whitman an American & the Sun Down Poem. There are 2 or 3 pieces in the book which are disagreeable to say the least, simply sensual. He does not celebrate love at all. It is as if the beasts spoke. I think that men have not been ashamed of themselves without reason. No doubt, there have always been dens where such deeds were unblushingly recited, and it is no merit to com-

* Eagleswood again all cut off! [Thoreau's note, referring to the letterhead.]

444

pete with their inhabitants. But even on this side, he has spoken more truth than any American or modern that I know. I have found his poem exhilirating encouraging. As for its sensuality,—& it may turn out to be less sensual than it appeared—I do not so much wish that those parts were not written, as that men & women were so pure that they could read them without harm, that is, without understanding them. One woman told me that no woman could read it as if a man could read what a woman could not. Of course Walt Whitman can communicate to us no experience, and if we are shocked, whose experience is it that we are reminded of?

On the whole it sounds to me very brave & American after whatever deductions. I do not believe that all the sermons so called that have been preached in this land put together are equal to it for preaching—

We ought to rejoice greatly in him. He occasionally suggests something a little more than human. You cant confound him with the other inhabitants of Brooklyn or New York. How they must shudder when they read him! He is awefully good.

To be sure I sometimes feel a little imposed on. By his heartiness & broad generalities he puts me into a liberal frame of mind prepared to see wonders—as it were sets me upon a hill or in the midst of a plain— stirs me well up, and then—throws in a thousand of brick. Though rude & sometimes ineffectual, it is a great primitive poem,—an alarum or trumpet-note ringing through the American camp. Wonderfully like the Orientals, too, considering that when I asked him if he had read them, he answered, "No: tell me about them."

I did not get far in conversation with him,—two more being present,— and among the few things which I chanced to say, I remember that one was, in answer to him as representing America, that I did not think much of America or of politics, and so on, which may have been somewhat of a damper to him.

Since I have seen him, I find that I am not disturbed by any brag or egoism in his book. He may turn out the least of a braggart of all, having a better right to be confident.

He is a great fellow.

One measure of the stature of the two leading Transcendentalists, Emerson and Thoreau, is that both praised Walt Whitman. It would have

been unusually easy for them to be repelled by so different a personality and so physical a poem as Leaves of Grass. *MS., Berg.*

To B. B. WILEY

Concord Dec 12 '56

Dear Sir,

I but recently returned from New Jersey after an absence of a little over a month, and found your letter awaiting me. I am glad to hear that you have walked with [Charles] Newcomb, though I fear that you will not have many more opportunities to do so. I have no doubt that in his company you would ere long find yourself, if not on those White Mountains you speak of, yet on some equally high, though not laid down in the geographies.

It is refreshing to hear of your earnest purposes with respect to your culture, & I can send you no better wish, than that they may not be thwarted by the cares and temptations of life. Depend on it, *now* is the accepted time, & probably you will never find yourself better disposed or freer to attend to your culture than at this moment. When *They* who inspire us with the idea are ready, shall not we be ready also?

I do not now remember anything which Confucius has said directly respecting man's "origin, purpose, and destiny." He was more practical than that. He is full of wisdom applied to human relations—to the private life—the Family—Government &c. It is remarkable that according to his own account the sum & substance of his teaching is, as you know, to Do as you would be done by.

He also said—(I translate from the French) ["]Conduct yourself suitably toward the persons of your family, then you will be able to instruct and to direct a nation of men."

"To nourish ones self with a little rice, to drink water, to have only his bended arm to support his head, is a state which has also its satisfaction. To be rich and honored by iniquitous means, is for me as the floating cloud which passes."

446

"As soon as a child is born he must respect its faculties; the knowledge which will come to it by & by does not resemble at all its present state. If it arrives at the age of 40 or 50 years, without having learned anything, it is no more worthy of any respect."

This last, I think, will speak to your condition.

But at this rate I might fill many letters.

Our acquaintance with the Ancient Hindoos is not at all personal. The few names that can be relied on are very shadowy. It is however tangible works that we know. The best I think of are the Bhagvat-Geeta (an episode in an ancient heroic poem called the Mahabarata)— the Vedas—the Vishnu Purana—The Institutes of Menu—&c

I cannot say that Swedenborg has been directly & practically valuable to me, for I have not been a reader of him, except to a slight extent —but I have the highest regard for him and trust that I shall read all his works in some world or other. He had a wonderful knowledge of our interior & spiritual life—though his illuminations are occasionally blurred by trivialities. He comes nearer to answering, or attempting to answer, literally, your questions concerning man's origin, purpose & destiny than any of the worthies I have referred to. But I think that this is not *altogether* a recommendation; since such an answer to these questions cannot be discovered, any more than perpetual motion, for which no reward is now offered. The noblest man it is, methinks, that knows, & by his life suggests, the most about these things. Crack away at these nuts however as long as you can—the very exercise will ennoble you—& you may get something better than the answer you expect—

Yrs
Henry D. Thoreau

MS., Berg.

From THOMAS CHOLMONDELEY

Rome, December 16, 1856.

My dear Thoreau,—

I wish that I was an accomplished young American lady, for then I could write the most elegant and "recherché" letters without any trouble or thought. But now, being an Englishman, even my pleasures are fraught with toil and pain. Why, I have written several letters to you, but always, on reading them over to myself, I was obliged to burn them, because I felt they were bad letters, and insufficient for a passage of the ocean. To begin, then, a new and a good letter, I must acquaint you that I received your former communication, which gave me *the sincerest pleasure,* since it informed me that the books which I sent came to hand, and were approved of. I had indeed studied your character closely, and knew what you would like. Besides, I had, even from our first acquaintance, a previous memory of you, like the vision of a landscape a man has seen, he cannot tell where.

As for me, my life still continues (through the friendship of an unseen hand) a fountain of never-ending delight, a romance renewed every morning, and never smaller to-day than it was yesterday, but always enhancing itself with every breath I draw. I delight myself, I love to live, and if I have been "run down" I am not aware of it.

I often say to God, "What, O Lord, will you do with me in particular? Is it politics, or philosophical leisure, or war, or hunting, or what?" He always seems to answer, "Enjoy yourself, and leave the rest to itself." Hence everything always happens at the right time and place, and rough and smooth ride together. There is an old Yorkshire gentleman—a great-grandfather of ninety—who promises to see his hundred yet, before he flits. This man was asked lately (he has had his troubles, too) "what of all things he should like best." The merry old squire laughed, and declared that "he should like of all things to begin and live his life over again, in any condition almost,—he was not particular." Now, I am like the squire in my appreciation of life. It is so great a matter to exist pleasurably. The sensation of Being!

Thus much about myself. As for my Phenomena, I have seen and thought and done quite up to my highest mark; but I will not weary you with descriptions of the Crimea, Constantinople, or even Rome, whence I am now writing.

448

But one thing I will attempt to tell you. I saw the great explosion when the Windmill Magazine blew up. I was out at sea, a good ten miles from the spot. The day was fine; suddenly the heaven was rent open by a pillar of fire, which seemed ready to tear the very firmament down. It was like the "idea" of the hottest oven. As it hung (for it lasted while you might count) on the horizon, the earth shook and the sea trembled, and we felt the ship quivering under us. It was felt far and wide like an earthquake. We held our breath and felt our beating hearts. Presently we recovered, and the first feeling in every heart was, "Better go home after that!" The *roaring noise* was, I am told, tremendous. Strange that I cannot at all recollect it! I only saw the apparition and felt the shock. . . .

The English temper keeps very war-like. They want another turn with Russia. But since Europe is now pretty well closed up, it seems to be the general impression that Asia will be the field of the next Russian war: and who knows how long it may last when once it begins? They descending from their Riphean hills, hordes of poor and hardy Tartars,—Gog and Magog and their company; we ascending, with the immense resources of India behind us, towards the central regions, the scarce-explored backbone of Asia. The ruins of long-forgotten cities half buried in sand, the shattered temples of preadamite giants, the Promethean cliffs themselves, will ring with the clang of many a battle, with the wail of great defeats and the delirious transports of victory. There is a very old English prophecy now in circulation, "that the hardest day would come when we should have to fight against men having snow on their helmets." So that superstition swells the anti-Russian tide.

I have seen something of Turks, Greeks, Frenchmen, and Italians, and they impress me thus: the Turk, brave, honest, religious; the Greek, unclean, lying, a slave, and the son of a slave; the Frenchman, light-hearted, clever, and great *in small things;* the Italian, great, deep, ingenious. I would put him first. He is greater than the Frenchman.

Having been in the Redan, the Malakoff, etc., I am truly astonished at the endurance of the Russians. The filth and misery of those horrid dens were beyond expression. Even the cleanest part of our own camp swarmed with vermin. I caught an aristocrat—a member of Parliament —one day stopped for a flea-hunt in his tent. Though too late for any regular engagement, I managed to experience the sensation of being under fire. It is only pleasurable for about a quarter of an hour; in short,

it soon fatigues, like a second-rate concert. The missiles make strange and laughable sounds sometimes,—whistling and crowing and boiling. Watching them moving through the air from the north side of the harbor, they seemed to come so slow!

The Crimea is a beautiful country,—the air clear, hilly, clothed with brushwood; the pine on the hill, and the vine in the valley. It is a fine country for horseback, and many a good ride I had through it. I see that I am falling into description, whether I will or no. The Bosphorus and the Sea of Marmora—indeed, all the neighborhood of Stamboul —are charming, in spite of rags, dirt, and disease. Nature has done her utmost here, and the view from the Seraskier's Tower is the finest in the world. The Turkish ladies (for I saw plenty of beauties in the bazaars) are, in figure, like our own; that is, "very fat." The Turk and the Briton seem to agree that a good breed cannot be got out of lean kine. In the face, however, they excel ours; the lines are more regular. In expression, *babies;* in gait, waddling; the teeth often rotten from too much sweetmeat.

There was an English lady at Stamboul who had traveled with a bashaw's favorite wife. They were put in one cabin on board a ship. She told us how the favorite behaved; how she was laughing and crying and praying in a breath; how she was continually falling fast asleep and snoring loudly, waking up again in a few minutes; she was the merest infant, and as fat as a little pig; lastly, how the bashaw was always popping into the cabin, to see what she was about, at all hours, and cared nothing for the English lady, though she was sometimes quite *en déshabillé.*

I met Abdel Kadir in the East. He is a very handsome man, with mild, engaging manners, a face deadly pale, very fine eyes, beard, and hands. Very like one of your Southerners, some of whom are not to be surpassed. He is now residing at Damascus. I noted the Circassians to be a fine race, very tall and well made, with high features; grave and fierce, and yet sweet withal. They wear high caps, and carry an armful of daggers and pistols. The feet and hands long and small. They have, too, a fine, light, high-going step, full of spring and elasticity, like the gait of a high-mettled horse. "*Incessu patuit.*" But every nation has a motion of its own. Among the boatmen on the Bosphorus I saw many faces and figures very like the same class at Hong-Kong and on the Canton River in China. Both have a Tartar look. Mongolians, I imagine.

450

I think I should like, as I grow older and more stay-at-home, to pay attention to the subject of "breeding." Astonishing facts come out upon inquiry. Now, *sheep, horses, dogs, and men* should be more closely watched. I see already some things. I see that Nature is always flowing. *She will not let you fix her,* and she refuses to be caught out by an process of exhaustion. There is always somewhat unknown, and that somewhat is everything. You may think that you have exhausted the chances of vice and disease by putting the best always together. Now, if you merely put the best together, you will have either no breed or a very bad one. There is something in the "black sheep" which the better one loses. There is something divine, which is pity to lose, even in the most barbarous stock. Lord Byron said that the finest man and the best boxer he ever met told him that he was the offspring of positive deformity, and that he had brothers still finer than himself. On the other hand, I know a young gentleman who is an absolute baboon, but the son of a good-looking father and a mother of a race famous for beauty. But the family crest is a baboon, and it came out after the lapse of centuries.

A student of family pictures will observe, in a good gallery, how the same face comes and goes. It will sometimes sleep for three hundred years. A certain expression of countenance is in a certain family; some change takes place,—perhaps they lose an estate or gain a peerage; it goes, and turns up again in another branch which never had it before. Is not Walker the best representative of old Rolf Granger? I think that both *gang* the same gait.

This is enchanted ground,—St. Peter's, the Pantheon, the Coliseum, etc. But let me tell you what attracts me most in Rome and its neighborhood. It is the lake and woods of the ancient Alba Longa, the mother city of Rome, which you see clearly and well in the distance (about 14 miles off). The lake, which is very large, many miles round, is in the crater of an old volcano, and therefore high up. It is surrounded by woods, chiefly of holm oaks; but here are also the stone pine, the common deciduous oak, and other fine trees. These woods are pierced by numerous beautiful walks.

This little map [a sketch of the neighborhood of the Alban Lake] will give you some inkling of these beautiful hills, of the lake of Alba and its sister Nemi. You will see that the colonists moved northwest to found Rome; you will imagine, when you stand on the bank of the lake, where is the long ridge or street whence the old city (all long ago

gone) took its name, that you are at a height sufficient to see all the country round; yet you have got the Monte Calvo, with the old temple (now a convent) of Jupiter Latiaris at your back and many hundred feet above you (perhaps a thousand). What a position for a city! What an eagle's nest! Here is every variety of scenery, with the sea quite plainly seen to the west. Hence you wind up through a modern town, called Rocca di Papa, and across a section of *Hannibal's camp* (you remember when he came so near Rome), which is another mountain basin, towards the temple aforesaid, where the thirty Latin cities used to sacrifice. The holy road to the top of the mountain still remains. It is very narrow, and flagged with great uneven stones. Algidus (not so high) lies behind. To the east, across the Campagna, are the Sabine hills, with Tibur in their bosom, and the old temple of Bona Dea on a great hill near it. The Etrurian hills are to the north, behind Rome, and Soracte, a little isolated shelf of rock, stands midway between them and the Sabine. Snow on Soracte marks a very hard winter. You remember the ode, "*Vides ut alta, etc.*, . . . *Soracte*" [Horace's Ode IX, Book I].

And now to come to yourself. I have your two letters by me, and read them over with deep interest. You are not living altogether as I could wish. You ought to have society. A college, a conventual life is for you. You should be the member of some society not yet formed. You want it greatly, and without this you will be liable to moulder away as you get older. *Forgive my English plainness of speech.* Your love for, and intimate acquaintance with, Nature is ancillary to some affection which you have not yet discovered.

The great Kant never dined alone. Once, when there was a danger of the empty dinner table, he sent his valet out, bidding him catch the first man he could find and bring him in! So necessary was the tonic, the effervescing cup of conversation, to his deeper labors. Laughter, chatter, politics, and even the prose of ordinary talk is better than nothing. Are there no clubs in Boston? The lonely man is a diseased man, I greatly fear. See how carefully Mr. Emerson avoids it; and yet, who dwells, in all essentials, more religiously free than he? Now, I would have you one of a well-knit society or guild, from which rays of thought and activity might emanate, and penetrate every corner of your country. By such a course you would not lose Nature. But supposing that reasons, of which I can know nothing, determine you to remain in "quasi" retirement; still, let not this retirement be too lonely.

Take up every man as you take up a leaf, and look attentively at him. This would be easy for you, who have such powers of observation, and of attracting the juices of all you meet to yourself. Even I, who have no such power, somehow find acquaintances, and nobody knows what I get from those about me. They give me all they have, and never suspect it. What treasures I gleaned at Concord! And I remember at Boston, at my lodgings, the worthy people only held out a week, after which I was the friend of the family, and chattered away like a magpie, and was included in their religious services. I positively loved them before I went away. I wish I lived near you, and that you could somehow originate some such society as I have in my head.

What you are engaged in I suspect to be Meditations on the Higher Laws as they show themselves in Common Things. This, if well weaved, may become a great work; but I fear that this kind of study may become too desultory. Try a history. How if you could write the sweet, beautiful history of Massachusetts? Positively, there is an immense field open. Or take Concord,—still better, perhaps. As for myself, so enamored am I of history that it is my intention, if I live long enough, to write a history of Salop; and I will endeavor to strike out something entirely new, and to put county history where it ought to be. Take the spirit of Walton and a spice of White! It would be a great labor and a grand achievement,—one for which you are singularly qualified.

By being "run down" I suppose you mean a little "hipped,"—a disorder which no one escapes. I have had it so badly as to have meditated suicide more than once. But it goes away with the merest trifle, and leaves you stronger than ever. Ordinary men of the world defeat the enemy with a sop, such as getting drunk or having a woman; but this is a bad plan, and only successful for a time. He is better defeated by sobriety or a change of scene, such as your trip to the Connecticut River. *"He is beginning to preach now,"* you will say. Well, then, let us have a turn at politics and literature. I was certain from the first that Buchanan would be President, because I felt sure that the Middle States are not with the North. Nor is the North itself in earnest. You are fond of humanity, but you like commerce, and a great heap, and a big name better. Of course you do. Besides, your principle and bond of union appears to be most negative,—you do not like slavery. Is there any positive root of strength in the North? Where and what? Your civilization is all in embryo, and what will come out no one can predict. At present, is there not a great thinness and poverty? *Magnas inter opes*

inops! You have indeed in New England the genius of liberty, and for construction and management; you have a wonderful *aplomb,* and are never off your feet. But when I think of your meagreness of invention, and your absurd whims and degraded fancies of spirit-rapping, etc., and the unseemly low ebb of your ordinary literature, I tremble.

You have one Phoenix,—the greatest man since Shakespeare, I believe, —but where is the rest of the choir? Why, the men that promise best— such as Channing, some of whose poems are admirable—do not go down; and they never will as long as newspaper novels are in request. It is the same as in England,—all is fragmentary, poor, and draggletail. There is no continence. A perfectly beautiful conception, generously born and bred, such as Schiller's Cranes of Ibycus or The Diver, is simply impossible in such a state of things. And observe, I would affirm the very same thing of England as it is at this hour. There is no poetry, and very little or no literature. We are drenched with mawkish lollipops, and clothed in tawdry rags. I am sorry to see even in Mr. Emerson's Traits of England that one or two chapters are far inferior to the rest of the book. He knows it, no doubt. He has sinned against his conception herein in order to accommodate the public with a few sugarplums. Those chapters will hurt the book, which would otherwise be, like his Essays, of perfect proportion and of historical beauty. I have seen some fragments by a certain W. Whitman, who appears to be a strong man. But why write fragments? It is not modest. Completeness of conception is the very first element of that sweet wonder which I know not how to call by its right name. There is a man we both of us respect and admire,— Carlyle; but has he not damaged his own hand beyond cure? He drives a cart, and strikes against every stone he sees. He has no "perception" of the highest kind. A good preacher, but after all a creaking, bumping, tortuous, involved, and visionary author.

I wonder what Emerson will give us for his next book. The only new books in England I have seen are Froude's History, of which I cannot speak too highly, and a report on India by Lord Dalhousie, very able and businesslike. There are also the Russian accounts of the battle of Inkerman (which were printed in the Times), curious and able. Grey's Polynesian legend is getting old, but we have Sandwich on Kars and Russell's admirable account of the Crimean campaign, of which I need say nothing. His excellent letters from Moscow will also form a good book. I had forgot Maurice's and Kingsley's last, and Mansfield's Paraguay. (Read that.) Truly the list grows. Our poems, such as Arnold's,

Sydney Dobell's, and Owen Meredith's, are the very dregs and sweepings of imitation. Alexander Smith's last I have not seen, but it is no great haul, I hear,—small potatoes! But they talk of a Catholic priest of the name of Stoddart,—that he has written well.

Burton's African and Arabian travels, Arthur Stanley's Palestine, Cotton's Public Works of India, are all good and sound. We ought to have a book from Livingstone before long. He is now on his way home, after having succeeded in traversing Africa,—a feat never accomplished before. (He is at home, and going out again.) Newman on Universities ought to be good. The other day a man asked me, "Have you ever read the Chronicles of the Emperor Baber?" I had never even heard of them before. He said they outdid Caesar's. Was he imposing upon my ignorance?

The books above mentioned I will endeavor to get when I visit England in the spring; some indeed I have already, and will send them to you. I want you to send me a copy of Emerson's Poems, which I cannot obtain, do what I will. Also please obtain for me a catalogue (you'll hear of it at the Boston Athenaeum) of your local histories in the United States. There are hundreds of them, I believe; a list has been made which I want to examine. I suppose you are well versed in the French works written by early travelers and missioners on America. Would you tell me one or two of the best authors of Canadian or Louisianian research? I am at present working at an essay on America, which gives me great pleasure and no little pain. I have a conception of America surveyed as "one thought"; but the members are not yet forthcoming. I have not yet written above a page or two. I have also been engaged upon Shakespeare's Antony and Cleopatra, and indeed in other ways. For my daily reading I am taking Tasso's Jerusalem, Chateaubriand's Génie, and sometimes a little Tacitus; and I also read the Bible every day.

Farewell, dear Thoreau. Give my best love to your father, mother, and sister, and to old Channing; and convey my respect to Mr. Emerson and Mr. Alcott; and when next you go to Boston, call at my old lodgings, and give my regards to them there. If you write to Morton, don't forget me there. He is a clever lad, is n't he? Also my respect to Mr. Theodore Parker, whose sermons are rather to be heard than read.

Ever yours, and not in haste,

Thos. Cholmondeley.

Posted in London February 22, 1857.

Cholmondeley kept this letter by him until he arrived in London. There he added some more to it on February 22, 1857, and mailed the whole thing to Thoreau on the same day. Text, Cholmondeley, pp. 746–51. The Life of Henry David Thoreau (*p. 306*) *transcribes the sentence in the sixteenth paragraph as "A college, a conventual life is not for you." Since we have not been able to locate the manuscript, we have been unable to determine which is the correct reading.*

From B. B. WILEY

Chicago Dec 21, 1856

Mr Thoreau

So much time had elapsed since I wrote you that I feared I should get no reply; I was therefore surprised & delighted as well as encouraged when your letter of 12th reached me. I do not want to encroach on your time but I shall take the liberty of writing to you occasionally, in hopes of drawing out a response, even though it be a criticism, for this would be valuable to me, as I do not want to slumber in false security. Like those knights who loudly sang hymns while they were passing the enchanted isle, I will remember that I am going to tell you some of my outward, though more of my inward life. This of itself will be a strong incentive to virtue.

The arrival of your letter at this time makes me think of Napoleon's practice of leaving letters unopened for weeks till in many cases there was no necessity for a reply. Though I wanted your views, I kept on in my path and already more than dimly apprehended that no man can penetrate the secrets of creation & futurity—Still I like to dwell on those themes, particularly the latter, as I have never found a present worthy to have permanent dominion over me. I like to send my thoughts forward to meet my destiny more than half way and prepare myself to meet with alacrity any decree of Eternal Fate. I am obliged for the excellent quotations from Confucius and the idea given of his teachings. I trust that if on this planet I attain the age of 40 years, I shall by the wisdom that may be mine merit the respect of those whose standard is in-

finitely high and whose motto is excelsior. "To be rich & honored by iniquitous means is for me as the floating cloud which passes" speaks to me with power. The last No of the Westminster magazine contains an article on Buddhism which I presume you may have seen. It does not mention him (Confucius) though as you told me he was above all sects

On my way back to Providence after my unforgotten Concord visit, I pondered deeply on what you had told me "to follow the faintest aspiration &c." I perhaps almost resolved to give up my Western plans of trade. Soon after, I walked with Newcomb and I of course fully agree with you in your high estimate of him and when you speak of my few opportunities for repeating these walks, I hope you only refer to my distance—not to his health. He asked me if I knew any active outdoor sphere he was qualified to fill and from what he said I doubt not he would come here did such a place present itself. He could much better than I afford to let books alone, as he has studied much more and has a more original and powerful mind, at least for metaphysical thoughts. It would give me deep satisfaction to have him here if I am to remain here. Just before your letter reached me I had been thinking of a future White Mountain trip with him and was not putting it far off. It is a good plan for traders to go to higher spheres occasionally.

I will give you some of my reasons for coming here though I withhold such as these from "business men" or "worldlings" technically so called. (I have told these to no other person) I think I can truly say that I am content with my outward circumstances but I hope at some future day to sustain a refined intercourse with some good & gentle being whom I can call *wife*, or better still *companion* and I know that all persons would not be satisfied to live on what would content me. At that time I should want to carry out my ideas of life as well as I *can* now but I should want to give my companion the facilities to carry out her views. Again, unless I deceive myself, I wish to be liberal beyond the sphere of my own family. The perfect transparency of soul that I would have between us leads me to say that I also had some thought of reputation. While in business formerly I travelled courses that I shall never tread again, and this, united with the success that generally accompanies able industry but which at the same time whets the edge of envy & malice & also my habit of refusing to justify my acts raised against me in some quarters the voice of calumny, though it is true that it is most often applied to those concerns where I feel that censure may be due. Not

457

from any inconvenience of this kind however did I leave Providence, for such would have been the very thing to make me remain there, as I am ready and like to face difficulties & dangers. My former partner is my personal friend, but as partners I feel that we were entirely unsuited to each other and I dissolved the connection against his will and that of his present associate Had it not been for my personal relations to him I should have recommenced there, as my friends wished me to do, but such a course would have brought me into direct competition with him and would inevitably have taken away much of his profit and that I *will not* do particularly as here is a field large enough for all and where I am specially invited to take a prominent part in a large house. Do not imagine from what I said that my former cause was a type of all that is disgraceful in man. I was intensely busy and acted thoughtlessly & unintelligently and my acts were such as are all the time adroitly done by *decent* men rather with eclat than with damage to their *reputation.* That other men do the same however is no excuse for me and having during the quiet of my past summer drunk somewhat of eternal truth I see & feel my errors and so help me God shall not again fall into them. My very retirement from trade was in the eyes of my detracting neighbors not the least of my short-comings though *I* know it to be one of the most fortunate things I ever did. As I place character however infinitely before reputation, I am not necessarily pledged to trade again. The fact that I am almost invariably popular and flattered & courted in Providence circles shows me that I need a higher monitor than the voice of the multitude who must necessarily know so little of the motives that actuate me. So little do detracting remarks puzzle my temper that were it in my way I should gladly assist any of the *quintette club* that try to injure me though of course with the littleness of soul which they display I cannot have particular love for them. I trust that if I have future antagonists they may be greater than these little men who have never had the manliness to face me. I expect to find in Montaigne somewhere the story of Alexander the Great who when urged to punish a slanderer, refused, saying he would live so purely that all men would see the fellow spoke falsely

I thus give you the leading motives that influenced me to come here. Since I arrived I heard that one of my leading prospective partners is dissatisfied with the determination I have shown to attend to higher things than trade. I am perfectly aware that I have lost caste with mere traders. The gentleman referred to is now here and our grand council

will soon begin. Walden will not change color during its continuance nor the Concord stop flowing. I am here at the wish of others as well as the result of my own reasoning but I will not become a common business drudge for all the wealth of Chicago. Instead of a trader I am going to be a man. I believe a divine life can be nourished even in this Western Shrine of Mammon. Should our Council not end in a partnership, I have no settled plans for the future. I should in all probability soon favor myself with a visit to Concord. Were I more gifted I would now leave trade forever and be your Plato. I freely admit to you that this kind of life is not what pleases me. Do not interpret my remarks into the grumblings of disappointment, for I am what the world calls singularly favored by fortune. I await the result of our Council calmly though my wishes would lead me to the haunts of Nature. If you think my ideas erroneous write a severe criticism for me. I would like to have you tell me just what you think

I have a good deal of leisure now. I have read Montaigne's Essays to some extent & with unfailing interest. The ancient anecdotes make the valuable part of the book to me though they are so well incorporated with his generally sensible & pithy remarks that no common man can approach him. I have read some of Emerson, a man to whom I am much indebted. I saw his notice of Mr [Samuel] Hoar. You mentioned to me Miss [Elizabeth] Hoar when I was there. In one respect of *infinite* moment I think Emerson has put in for me the key-stone of an arch which has cost me much labor & travail to build. He will be here next month to lecture and I shall call on him, as he asked me to do. Most men here are intensely devoted to trade but I have found one with whom I have unreserved & delightful intercourse—Rev Rush R Shippen the Unitarian minister. Mr Emerson will remember him. He is no ways priestly but has that open guileless countenance that wins the fullest confidence. He is of course intelligent & well-informed. He generously places his library at my disposal. I gladly accepted an invitation to take tea with him tomorrow as there is entire absence of ceremony. I am glad to find such a man with whom I can talk of the Infinite & Eternal. In addition to his library I have access to a public one of about 2000 volumes & I think I can largely extend my facilities. *Very* few books I *read* but I like to look at the tables of contents the engravings & portraits of others. The N.Y. Tribune often has things of more than transient interest. Some of their political articles are most powerful. Their notice of "Walden" introduced it to me.

I take walks of considerable length almost daily and think I am in that respect the most enthusiastic of the plus 100,000 people here. I generally go along the Lake shore. I have to go 3 miles to reach woods any way. The Lake is the great feature of the place. Everything being level I have nothing on the land to meet my New England bred eyes and have learned (from Newcomb) to watch the clouds and I find it not the least valuable of his suggestions. One cloudy morning I saw in the East over the Lake as the moon rose what resembled a vast bird with outstretched wings holding her course towards the East. I recorded in my Journal that I might consider it emblematic of my own desire of progress towards the source of [word torn out] inward illumination. One morning I saw in the East a perpendicular pillar of cloud that would have answered well enough to guide any Israelites that were going in that dirction—another morning I saw on the hitherto level surface of the frozen lake ice-hills of considerable size. I was glad to see hills anywhere.

The Lake water is carried over the city for drinking &c. It is almost always discolored by storms. That which comes moderately clear I fancy I can render white by beating with my hands and if allowed to stand, a sediment of lime is deposited. It makes some trouble with strangers' digestive organs and I am not entirely accustomed to it. If you have at your tongue's end a description of your own way to make a filter, I should probably put it in practice & should appreciate your kindness. I have been wondering how you know the different species of plants as described by science. Is the description so accurate that you know them at sight?

Are millers that come round our summer lamps Chrysalides and into what are they next transformed?

I have written much more than I expected to do. I hope I may ere long have a reply from you. Please remember me to Mr Emerson if you meet him. I am

Yours sincerely
B B Wiley

Ms., Berg; *previously unpublished.*

To H. G. O. BLAKE

Concord, December 31, 1856.

Mr. Blake,—

I think it will not be worth the while for me to come to Worcester to lecture at all this year. It will be better to wait till I am—perhaps unfortunately—more in that line. My writing has not taken the shape of lectures, and therefore I should be obliged to read one of three or four old lectures, the best of which I have read to some of your auditors before. I carried that one which I call "Walking, or the Wild," to Amherst, N.H., the evening of that cold Thursday, and I am to read another at Fitchburg, February 3. I am simply their hired man. This will probably be the extent of my lecturing hereabouts.

I must depend on meeting Mr. [David A.] Wasson some other time.

Perhaps it always costs me more than it comes to to lecture before a promiscuous audience. It is an irreparable injury done to my modesty even,—I become so indurated.

O solitude! obscurity! meanness! I never triumph so as when I have the least success in my neighbor's eyes. The lecturer gets fifty dollars a night; but what becomes of his winter? What consolation will it be hereafter to have fifty thousand dollars for living in the world? I should like not to exchange *any* of my life for money.

These, you may think, are reasons for not lecturing, when you have no great opportunity. It is even so, perhaps. I could lecture on dry oak leaves; I could, but who could hear me? If I were to try it on any large audience, I fear it would be no gain to them, and a positive loss to me. I should have behaved rudely toward my rustling friends.

I am surveying instead of lecturing, at present. Let me have a skimming from your "pan of unwrinkled cream."

H. D. T.

Thoreau did finally agree to lecture in Worcester that season, but not without further warnings that he had used up his best lectures. MS., Abernethy (*typescript*).

461

From WILLIAM D. TUTTLE

made a very small plan of it (about 2 rods to an inch I should judge) & cast it up making 14A 22 rods The plan was so small (& so unskillfully drawn) that I told Mr W that very little reliance could be placed upon it in computing areas. Since then I have computed the area several times by the aid of traverse tables finding the Lat & Dep both in chains & decimals of a chain & in rods & dec of a rod & obtaining answers varying from 13a–106½r to 13a–11.9r. By calling the bearing of the 3d course N 57E & taking out the Lat & dep in rods & decimals of a rod I made the area to be 13a–109.57r. I find but little (.01 of a rod) diff between the Eastings & Westings & but .19 of a rod between the Northings & Southings. & in ballancing the survey I subtracted the Diff between the North & Southings from the Southing of the 7th course.

Will you have the kindness to inform me by what method you computed the Lat in question: if by plotting to what scale your plan was drawn, or if by the traverse table whether you took out the distances in chains or rods & to how many decimal places you found the Lat & Dep of each course

What is your general method of computing areas? & What is the present variation of the needle in Concord?

Yours very respectfully,
Wm D. Tuttle.

Mr H. D. Thoreau Surveyor Concord Mass.

The Huntington Library chronology suggests that this letter, only the final page of which remains, should be dated between 1854 and 1856. MS., Huntington; previously unpublished.

To ?

Dear Sir,

    I would advise not to take a revolver or other weapon of defense. It will affect the innocence of your enterprise. If you chance to

meet with a wolf or a dangerous snake, you will be luckier than I have been, or expect to be. When I went to the White Mts. I carried a gun to kill game with, but finally left it at Concord, N.H. As for a knapsack, I should say wear something water-tight & comfortable, with two or three pockets to keep things separate. Wear old shoes; carry no thin clothes. Do not forget needle and thread and pins, a compass, and the best pocket map of the country attainable.

Yours in haste,
Henry D. Thoreau.

Text, Goodspeed's Catalogue No. 189, *Item 247, p. 28, where it is dated only "1856."*

1857

A Negro named Dred Scott maintained that he had become free by staying with his owner in the free state of Illinois and the free territory of Minnesota. His case finally went up to the Supreme Court. Chief Justice Roger Taney presided and read the opinion. Taney ruled that Negroes were property, had no rights of citizenship, and could not sue in the federal courts. It followed that the Missouri Compromise and similar legislation were unconstitutional. There were other signs of crisis as well. The boom that had followed the discovery of gold in California collapsed. Over five thousand banks and railroads failed within the year, and in October there was a general suspension of specie payments by banks. A mass meeting of the unemployed in Philadelphia was attended by some 10,000 men. The tariff was reduced by Congressional action to the lowest point since 1815. The warfare in Kansas went on.

Out of Kansas came John Brown of Osawatomie. Thoreau met him twice when he came to Concord asking for support. Frank Sanborn, a young Harvard graduate acquaintance of Thoreau's, brought him to Thoreau's house the first evening, and Thoreau met him again at Emerson's the next night. Thoreau was deeply impressed by Brown's fanatical integrity; the later essays will bear witness to the impression. This year Thoreau visited both the Maine woods and Cape Cod. A new pair of corduroy trousers cost him $1.60. The letters for this year are scattered and miscellaneous. Thoreau's correspondents include Blake and his wandering English friend Thomas Cholmondeley.

To H. G. O. BLAKE

Concord Feb. 6th 57

Mr. Blake,

I will come to you on Friday Feb. 13th with that lecture. You may call it "The Wild"—or "Walking" or both—whichever you choose. I told [Theo] Brown that it had not been much altered since I read it in Worcester, but now I think of it, much of it must have been new to you, because, having since divided it into two, I am able to read what before I omitted. Nevertheless, I should like to have it understood by those whom it concerns, that I am invited to read in public (if it be so) what I have already read, in part, to a private audience.

Henry D. Thoreau.

MS., Berg, *copy in Blake's hand.*

From TICKNOR & FIELDS

H. D. Thoreau Esq
    In acc with Ticknor & Fields Co.

1856	By copy't on 240 Walden	36.00
	12 Concord River	9.00
		$45.00

[?] Jan 31
1857

| Feb. 16 | Cash Check | $45.00 |

Boston Feby 16/57

465

Dear Sir

Enclosed we beg to hand our check for forty Five Dollars in accordance with above statement.

Please acknowledge its receipt
And oblige
Your obdt servant
Ticknor & Fields
Clark

MS., Harvard *(typescript); previously unpublished.*

From ?

Buffalo Feb 17th 1857

Henry D. Thoreau Esq Concord Mass
My Dear Sir,

I came home from Cleveland and found yours of the 7th inst. I had an idea the map of Superior [indecipherable word]

MS., Harvard; *previously unpublished.*

From THOMAS CHOLMONDELEY

Feb. 22, 1857   *Town.*

Dear Thoreau

You see I've *saved* this letter which is the best I ever wrote you (for I burnt the rest) & posted it in Town. For Rome being so uncertain a Post I thought 'better wait till I get to Town'; & send it properly.

466

I am just going now on an expedition to search for a little cottage somewhere in Kent or Sussex where I may henceforth dwell & endeavour to gather a little moss. I hope to get a few acres of land with it on lease—for as to *buying,* it is almost out of the question They ask about £500 an acre now for anything like decent land in England. In fact land is worth too much. It is a shame. I suppose I could buy a *good farm* in New England for £2000 couldnt I? I shouldn't wonder if I was to settle in New England after all—for the ties which hold me here are very slender.

However if I *do* succeed in getting my cottage in Kent remember there will be a room for you there, & as much as ever you can eat & drink. I am staying in town with my brother Reginald who is a painter, & has very agreeable rooms. He is very good to me & trots me out to see people whom otherwise I should scarcely be able to meet.

I heard [Frederick] Maurice preach today in Lincolns Inn. It was on Faith, Hope & Charity. He explained that this charity is not human—but Divine—& to be enjoyed in communion with God. It was a good & strictly orthodox sermon, & not extempore in any sense. I called at John Chapmans the other day, but he was out, being they said engaged in one of the Hospitals. He has turned Doctor it seems. The fact is I fear that Chapman has done himself mischief by publishing books containing new views & philosophy which the English from the Lord to the Cabman hate & sneer at. The very beggars in the streets are all conservatives except on the subject of their sores. To speculate in thought in this country is *ruin*—& sure to lead if pursued long enough —to the Queens Bench or Bedlam. I am persuaded that the Turks & the chinese are *nothing* to us. Perhaps we are more like the Japanese than any other people—I mean as regards what Swedenborg would call "our interiors." The prophets prophesy as they did among the ancient Hebrews & the smooth prophets bear away the bells.

I met [James] Spedding the other day & had much talk with him—but nothing *real*—but he is a good man & in expression like your Alcott. He is now bringing out his Bacon the work of his whole life. Farewell

Ever yrs

Thos Chol.ley

I mean within hail of Town—for I dont want to settle finally in Wales or Yorkshire

This is Cholmondeley's addendum to his letter of December 16, 1856.
MS., Berg.

From JOHN BURT

Bellvale[?] Feb. 23rd '57

Dear Sir,
　　If I was in a Lyceum Lecture Committee I would use my greatest efforts to engage you to deliver a Lecture as I perceive your name in among a list published a short time since. But as I do not occupy any such influential position in this Community I suppose I will have to forgo for the present a long cherished wish to see and hear you. To compensate for this deprivation I would most respectfully solicit your Autograph.
　　I have read your Hermit Life and also a very appropriate Fourth of July Oration on Slavery in Massachusetts. To say that I greatly admired both would be but an inadequate expression.
　　A compliance with the above request will be gratefully remembered by

Yours Truly
John Burt
Bellvale Orange Co N. Y.

We discover no Bellvale post office in Orange County, but the word appears to be clearly that. MS., Harvard; previously unpublished.

To JOHN BURT

Concord Feb. 26th 1857

"Herein is the tragedy; that men doing outrage to their proper natures, even those called wise & good, lend themselves to perform the office of inferior and brutal ones. Hence come war and slavery in; and what else may not come in by this opening?"
A Week on the Concord & Merrimack Rivers—p 137.

Henry D. Thoreau

The quotation is from the Monday chapter of A Week. *The letter is addressed to John Burt, Esq., Bellvale, Orange Co., New York. MS., Chapin Library, Williams College; previously unpublished.*

_____

From TICKNOR & CO.

Boston, 27 Feb. 1857

H. Thoreau Esq. Concord Mass.

Dear Sir
    Please send us as soon as convenient twelve copies of the "Week &c" on sale and oblige

Truly yours
Ticknor & Co.
per J.R. Osgood

MS., Harvard (*typescript*); *previously unpublished.*

469

To DANIEL RICKETSON

Concord, March 28, 1857.

Friend Ricketson,—

If it chances to be perfectly agreeable and convenient to you, I will make you a visit next week, say Wednesday or Thursday, and we will have some more rides to Assawampset and the seashore. Have you got a boat on the former yet? Who knows but we may camp out on the island?

I propose this now, because it will be more novel to me at this season, and I should like to see your early birds, &c.

Your historical papers have all come safely to hand, and I thank you for them. I see that they will be indispensable, *memoires pour servier*. By the way, have you read Church's History of Philip's War, and looked up the localities? It should make part of a chapter.

I had a long letter from Cholmondeley lately, which I should like to show you.

I will expect an answer to this straightaway—but be sure you let your own convenience and inclinations rule it.

Yours truly,
Henry D. Thoreau.

P.S.—Please remember me to your family.

The phrase in French makes no apparent sense; lacking the manuscript, we cannot tell whether the error was Thoreau's or his editor's. Apparently he was trying to say that the papers sent would help him. Text, Ricketson, pp. 70–71.

From DANIEL RICKETSON

New Bedford, Sunday a.m., 29 March, '57

Dear Thoreau,—

I have just received your note of the 28th at my brother's, and hasten a reply for the Post Office before I leave for Brooklawn.

Nothing would give me more pleasure than a visit from you at any time. It will be perfectly agreeable to myself and family at this present time, and I shall duly expect you on Wednesday or Thursday. Should this reach you in time for an answer, I will be at Tarkiln Hill station to meet you; if not, make your appearance as early as you wish. You can leave your baggage at the depot, and I will send for it if you do not find me or our carriage in waiting.

As Channing did not make his usual appearance, yesterday p.m., I conclude that he is with you today, and if he leaves before Wednesday or Thursday, you may like to have his company hereward. We are getting on very nicely together.

The early birds are daily coming. Song sparrows, bluebirds, robins, meadow larks, blackbirds ("Gen. Abercrombies") are already here, frogs croaking, but not piping yet, and the spring quite genial.

My historical sketches have kept me quite busy, but agreeably so during the past winter. They are quite to my surprise, very popular. I should have hardly supposed that my homely habits and homelier style of composition would have suited many.

Should Channing be in Concord and in the humor, he can report my home affairs more fully, if you wish.

Remember me to your parents and sister and other friends, particularly the Emersons.

I write at my brother's, and in the midst of conversation, in which I am participating. You will perceive this is not a Shanty letter, but I am none the less cordially yours,

D. Ricketson.

The Shanty was Ricketson's retreat from, among other things, a disputatious wife. Text, Ricketson, *pp. 71–72.*

To MARY BROWN

Mrs. Elizabeth B. Davenport, in "Thoreau in Vermont in 1856" in the *Vermont Botanical Club Bulletin* No. 3 (April 1908), 36–38, quotes from a letter from Mrs. Mary Brown Dunton: "Among my most cherished possessions are three letters from [Thoreau]. The first dated March, 1857, was written on sending me a spray of 'Lygodium palmatum,' a little known fern to me at that time. He gave directions for opening and mounting it and added 'The Climbing Fern' would have been a pretty name for some delicate Indian maiden,' also 'Please give my regards and thanks to your mother and to the rest of your family if they chance to be with you.' "

Thoreau visited the Addison Browns, Mary's parents, in Brattleboro during the fall of 1856 on his way to see Bronson Alcott in Walpole, New Hampshire. He gives a full account of the trip, with much botanical detail, in his Journal *(IX, 61–80).*

To DANIEL RICKETSON

Concord Ap. 1 1857

Dear Ricketson,
     I got your note of welcome night before last. Channing is not here, at least I have not seen nor heard of him, but depend on meeting him in New Bedford. I expect if the weather is favorable, to take the 4:30 train from Boston tomorrow, Thursday, *pm*—for I hear of no noon train, and shall be glad to find your wagon at Tarkiln Hill, for I see it will be rather late for going across lots.
     Alcott was here last week, and will probably visit New Bedford within a week or 2.
     I have seen all the spring signs you mention and a few more, even here. Nay I heard one frog peep nearly a week ago, methinks the very first one in all this region. I wish that there were a few more signs of

spring in myself—however, I take it that there *are* as many within us as we think we hear *without* us. I am decent for steady pace but not yet for a race. I have a little cold at present, & you speak of rheumatism about the head & shoulders. Your frost is not quite out. I suppose that the earth itself has a little cold & rheumatism about these times, but all these things together produce a very fair general result. In a concert, you know, we must sing our parts feebly sometimes that we may not injure the general effect. I shouldn't wonder if my two-year old in-validity had been a positively charming feature to some amateurs favor-ably located. Why not a blasted man, as well as a blasted tree, on your lawn?

If you should happen not to see me by the train named, do not go again, but wait at home for me, or a note from

Yrs

Henry D Thoreau

MS., Thoreau Museum, Middlesex School.

From B. B. WILEY

Chicago Apl 7, 1857

Mr Thoreau

In January I was in Providence a short time and had a walk with Newcomb at Narragansett Bay. Since you heard from me I have learned more of him and I find your statements fall short of the truth. He has thrown light on doubts with which I was wrestling. Reading is useful but it may be long before one finds what he is in search of and when a man or saint appears who can help us solve the problem we cannot be too grateful. This acquaintance is one of the results of my pregnant Concord visit. Then Emerson told me that if we needed each other we should be brought together. I have had some illustrations of this and perhaps accept the remark as irrefragably true

473

I want in this material atmosphere some breath from the hills of Concord. Will you favor me with a copy of the "Wild & Walking" Do not disappoint me. I want it for my own reading mainly, though I may sometimes read it to friends. I of course do not want it for publication. I trust I shall have a copy in your own hand

I have read much of Plato; some of it with almost a wild delight. Many of the biographies I have read with equal or perhaps greater interest. I like to have the principles illustrated by an actual life. He (Carlyle) is a wondrous clear & reverent thinker. As for an obscure faulty style in him, I have yet to discover it.

Leaves of Grass I read and I appreciate Walt's pure freedom & humanity

Plutarch's Morals I have more recently commenced. This I shall take in gradually as I did the Iliad. I could have wished that in the latter those good enough fellows had been less ready to annihilate each other with big stones "such as two men could not now lift." The morning of the 1st we had a hard storm on the Lake and I walked along the "much-resounding sea" for a long distance seeing it dash grandly against the pier. I wish you had been there with me.

Heroes & Hero Worship I intend to read soon. Montaigne I have read with much interest. I have given you those names to inquire whether you think of any other valuable books not too abstruse for me. Books of a half biographical character have great charm for me. I have read none of the German authors. I think Wilhelm Meister may be full of meaning to me. I hope Goethe is that great universal man that Carlyle accounts him. His auto-biography I suppose is valuable. Dont think I am reading at random. I have a place for all true thoughts on my own subjects. Now and then I return and read again and again my leading books so that they become my intimate friends and help me to test my own life.

If it be not unfair to ask an author what he means I would inquire what I am to understand when in your list of employments given in Walden you say "I long ago lost a hound a bay-horse and a turtle-dove." If I transgress let the question pass unnoticed.

For myself I make fictitious employments. I am not satisfied with much that I do. Exultingly should I hail that wherein I could give exercise to my best powers for an end of unquestionable value

With one and only one here do I have really valuable hours. Rev R R Shippen. He is a true man—working, living, hoping, strong. I have

not been to his church yet, wicked rebel that I am, but I may soon attend, though again I may not. In private however he tells me of his sermons and necessarily speaks to me as he could not in an assembly. He tells me that lately from "we are members one of another" he told them of their duties as members of a Christian church and threatened if he were not more zealously seconded to "shake off the dust from his feet and depart out of their city." I am sorry that this is not a mere rhetorical flourish. He will probably leave in the Fall as he must at any rate have rest.

Among other works you recommended some of Coleridge. I took up his books, but was so repelled by the Trinitarian dogmas that I read almost none. I am very sensitive to that theological dust. As a child I was kept in it too much

Please give my love to Emerson. I trust he carried home pleasanter experiences than the measles

Your friend
B B Wiley

Thoreau had read his lecture on walking several times during the pre-ceding winter; it was not to be printed until just after his death. For the answer to Wiley's question about hound, bay horse, and turtledove see the letter to him dated April 26, 1857. MS., Berg; previously un-published.

To CAROLINE C. ANDREWS

Concord, Ap. 16[?], '57

Miss Caroline C. Andrews,

I send to you by the same mail with this a copy of my "Week." I was away from home when your note arrived, and have but just re-turned; otherwise you would have received the book earlier.

Henry D. Thoreau

The dating of the letter is difficult to decipher, but Thoreau's Journal *records a visit to New Bedford April 2–15. MS., William Cummings (typescript); previously unpublished.*

To H. G. O. BLAKE

Concord Ap. 17th 1857

Mr Blake,

 I returned from New Bedford night before last. I met Alcott there & learned from him that probably you had gone to Concord. I am very sorry that I missed you. I had expected you earlier, & at last thought that I should get back before you came, but I ought to have notified you of my absence. However, it would have been too late, after I had made up my mind to go. I hope you lost nothing by going a little round.

 I took out the Celtis seeds at your request, at the time we spoke of them, and left them in the chamber on some shelf or other. If you have found them, very well; if you have not found them, very well; but tell [Edward Everett] Hale of it, if you see him.

 My mother says that you & [Theo] Brown & [Seth] Rogers & [David A.] Wasson (titles left behind) talk of "coming down on" me some day. Do not fail to come one & all, and within a week or two, if possible, else I *may* be gone again. Give me a short notice, and then come & spend a day on Concord River—or say that you will come if it is fair, unless you are confident of bringing fair weather with you. Come & be Concord, as I have been Worcestered.

 Perhaps you came nearer to me for not finding me at home, for trains of thought the more connect when trains of cars do not. If I had actually met you, you would have gone again, but now I have not yet dismissed you.

 I hear what you say about personal relations with joy. It is as if you were to say, I value the best & finest part of you, & not the worst. I can even endure your very near & real approach, & prefer it to a shake of the hand. This intercourse is not subject to time or dis[tance.

476

I have a very long new and faithful le]tter from Cholmondeley which I wish to show you. He speaks of sending me more books!!

If I were with you now I could tell you much of Ricketson, and my visit to New Bedford, but I do not know how it will be by & by. I should like to have you meet R—who is the frankest man I know. Alcott & he get along very well together.

Channing has returned to Concord with me, probably for a short visit only.

Consider this a business letter, which you know *counts* nothing in the game we play.

Remember me particularly to Brown.

MS., Abernethy (*typescript*); *Familiar Letters of Thoreau, pp. 357–59; bracketed portion, torn from the original, is supplied from the printed text; most of the identifications are Sanborn's.*

To B. B. WILEY

Concord April 26th 1857

Dear Sir

I have been spending a fortnight in New Bedford, and on my return find your last letter awaiting me.

I was sure that you would find Newcomb inexhaustible, if you found your way into him at all. I might say, however, by way of criticism, that he does not take firm enough hold on this world, where surely we are bound to triumph.

I am sorry to say that I do not see how I can furnish you with a copy of my essay on the wild. It has not been prepared for publication, only for lectures, and would cover at least a hundred written pages. Even if it were ready to be dispersed, I could not easily find time to copy it. So I return the order.

I see that you are turning a broad furrow among the books, but I

trust that some very private journal all the while holds its own through their midst. Books can only reveal us to ourselves, and as often as they do us this service we lay them aside. I should say read Goethe's Autobiography, by all means, also Gibbon's Haydon the Painter's—& our Franklin's of course; perhaps also Alfieris, Benvenuto Cellini's, & DeQuincey's Confessions of an Opium Eater—since you like Autobiography.

I think you must read Coleridge again & further—skipping all his theology—i. e. if you value precise definitions & a discriminating use of language. By the way, read DeQuincey's reminiscences of Coleridge & Wordsworth.

How shall we account for our pursuits if they are original? We get the language with which to describe our various lives out of a common mint. If others have their losses, which they are busy repairing, so have I *mine,* & their hound & horse may *perhaps* be the symbols of some of them. But also I have lost, or am in danger of losing, a far finer & more etherial treasure, which commonly no loss of which they are conscious will symbolize—this I answer hastily & with some hesitation, according as I now understand my own words.

I take this occasion to acknowledge, & thank you for, your long letter of Dec. 21st. So poor a correspondent am I. If I wait for the fit time to reply, it commonly does not come at all, as you see. I require the presence of the other party to suggest what I shall say.

Methinks a certain polygamy with its troubles is the fate of almost all men. They are married to two wives—their genius (a celestial muse) and also to some fair daughter of the earth. Unless these two were fast friends before marriage, and so are afterward, there will be but little peace in the house.

In answer to your questions, I must say that I never made, nor had occasion to use a filter of any kind; but, no doubt, they can be bought in Chicago.

You cannot surely identify a plant from a scientific description until after long practice.

The "millers" you speak of are the perfect or final state of the insect. The chrysalis is the silken bag they spun when caterpillars, & occupied in the nymph state.

Yrs truly

Henry D. Thoreau

The famous "hound, bay horse and turtle dove" symbolism, one of the most intriguing problems of Thoreau scholarship, will probably never be solved to everyone's satisfaction. Sanborn records (in his footnote to this letter in Familiar Letters of Thoreau, *p. 353) a conversation between Thoreau and Uncle Ed Watson of Plymouth in 1855 or 1856: "'You say in one of your books,' said Uncle Ed, 'that you once lost a horse and a hound and a dove,—now I should like to know what you meant by that?' 'Why, everybody has met with losses, have n't they?' 'H'm,—pretty way to answer a fellow!' said Mr. Watson; but it seems this was the usual answer."* MS. Berg.

To DANIEL RICKETSON

Concord May 13 57

Friend Ricketson

A recent neighbor of ours, W*m*. W. Wheildon, having heard that you talked somewhat of moving to Concord (for such things will leak out) has just been asking me to inform you that he will rent his house, which is a *furnished one*, with a garden, or sell the same, if you like them. It is a large house, the third below (East of) us on the same side of the street—was built some 20 years ago partly of old material, & since altered. The garden is a very good one, of about 2 1/2 acres, with many fruit trees &c &c. Channing can tell you about it. When I ask his price, he merely answers 'I think it worth $ 8000. But I would rather have Mr R. see it before I speak of the price." It could probably be bought for a thousand or two less. Indeed I have heard $ 6000 named. If you think seriously of coming to Concord to live, it will be worth your while to see it. His address is "W*m* W. Wheildon, Editor of the Bunker Hill Aurora, Charlestown Mass."—for he lives there at present. You would see his name over his office if you went there. Since you are so much attracted to New Bedford that it is doubtful if you can live any where else—would it not be safer—if you do anything about it —to hire first, with liberty to buy afterward at a price before agreed on?

My mother & sister join with me in saying that if you think it worth your while to look at the premises, we shall be glad of the opportunity to receive you with any of your family under our roof.

Since I left N B I have made several voyages equal to the circumnavigation of the Middleboro Ponds, and have done much work beside with my hands— In short, I am suddenly become much stouter than for the past 2 years.

Let me improve this opportunity to acknowledge the receit of "Tom Bowling"—& the May-flower—for which convey my thanks to the donor. His soul is gone aloft—his body only is epigaea repens (creeping over the earth). It has been sung & encored several times—& is duly made over to my sister & her piano.

> In haste
> Yours truly
> Henry D. Thoreau

"Tom Bowling" was Thoreau's favorite song. MS., Huntington.

From THOMAS CHOLMONDELEY

May 26, 1857 London.

My dear Thoreau

I have received your four books & what is more I have read them. Olmstead was the only entire stranger. His book I think might have been shortened—& if he had indeed written only one word instead of ten—I should have liked it better. It *is* a horrid vice this *wordiness*—Emerson is beautiful & glorious—Of all his poems the *"Rhodora"* is my favorite. I repeat it to myself over & over again. I am also delighted with "Guy" "Uriel" & "Beauty" Of your own book I will say nothing but I will ask you a question, which perhaps may be a very ignorant one. I have observed a few lines about [sentence unfinished].

Now there is *something here* unlike anything else in these pages.

Are they absolutely your own, or whose? And afterward you shall hear what I think of them. Walt Whitmans poems have only been heard of in England to be laughed at & voted offensive—Here are "Leaves" indeed which I can no more understand than the book of Enoch or the inedited Poems of Daniel! I cannot believe that such a man lives unless I actually touch him. He is further ahead of me in yonder west than Buddha is behind me in the Orient. I find reality & beauty mixed with not a little violence & coarseness both of which are to me *effeminate*. I am amused at his views of sexual energy—which however are absurdly false. I believe that rudeness & excitement in the act of generation are injurious to the issue. The man appears to me not to know how to behave himself. I find the gentleman altogether left out of the book! Altogether these leaves completely puzzle me. Is there actually such a man as Whitman? Has anyone seen or handled him? His is a tongue "not understanded" of the English people. It is the first book I have ever seen which I should call 'a *new* book' & thus I would sum up the impression it makes upon me.

While I am writing, Prince Albert & Duke Constantine are reviewing the guards in a corner of St James Park. I hear the music. About two hours ago I took a turn round the Park before breakfast & saw the troops formed. The varieties of colour gleamed fully out from their uniforms. They looked like an Army of soldier butterflies just dropped from the lovely green trees under which they marched. Never saw the trees look so green before as they do this spring. Some of the oaks incredibly so. I stood before some the other day in Richmond & was obliged to pinch myself & ask "is this oak tree really growing on the earth they call so bad & wicked an earth; & itself so *undeniably* & astonishingly fresh & fair"? It did not look like magic. It *was* magic.

I have had a thousand strange experiences lately—most of them delicious & some almost awful. I seem to do so much in my life when I am doing nothing at all. I seem to be hiving up strength all the while as a sleeping man does; who sleeps & dreams & strengthens himself unconsciously; only sometimes half-awakes with a sense of cool refreshment. Sometimes it is wonderful to me that I say so little & somehow cannot speak even to my friends! Why all the time I was at Concord I never could tell you much of all I have seen & done! I never could somehow tell you anything! How ungrateful to my guardian genius to think any of it trivial or superfluous! But it always seemed already

481

told & long ago said. What is past & what is to come seems as it were all shut up in some very simple but very dear notes of music which I never can repeat.

Tonight I intend to hear Mr. [Neal] Dow the American lecture in Exeter Hall. I *believe* it is tonight. But I go forearmed against him—being convinced in my mind that a good man is all the better for a bottle of Port under his belt every day of his life.

I heard Spurgeon the Preacher the other day. He said some very good things: among others "If I can make the bells ring in *one* heart I shall be content." Two young men not behaving themselves, he called them as sternly to order as if they were *serving* under him. Talking of Jerusalem he said that "every good man had a mansion of his own there & a crown that would fit no other head save his." That I felt was true. It is the voice of Spurgeon that draws more than his matter. His organ is very fine—but I fear he is hurting it by preaching to too large & frequent congregations. I found this out—because he is falling into *two voices* the usual clerical infirmity.

The bells—church bells are ringing somewhere for the queens birthday they tell me. I have not a court-guide at hand to see if this is so. London is cram-full. Not a bed! Not a corner! After all the finest sight is to see such numbers of beautiful girls riding about & riding well. There are certainly no women in the world like ours. The men are far, far inferior to them.

I am still searching after an abode & really my adventures have been most amusing. One Sussex farmer had a very good little cottage close to Battle—but he kept "a few horses & a score or two of Pigs" under the very windows. I remarked that his stables were very filthy. The man stared hard at me—as an English farmer only can stare: ie, as a man stares who is trying to catch a thought which is always running away from him. At last he said striking his stick on the ground—"But that *is why* I keep the Pigs. I want their dung for my hop-grounds" We could not arrange it after that. I received a very kind note today from Concord informing me that there was a farm to be sold on the hill just over your river & nearly opposite your house. But it is out of the question buying land by Deputy! I have however *almost* decided to settle finally in America. There are many reasons for it. I think of running over in the trial-trip of the Great Eastern which will be at

the close of the year. She is either to be the greatest success—or else to sink altogether without more ado! She is to be something decided. I was all over her the other day. The immense creature musical with the incessant tinkling of hammers is as yet unconscious of life. By measurement she is larger than the Ark. From the promenade of her decks you see the town & trade of London; the river—(the sacred river) —; Greenwich with its park & palace; the vast town of Southwark & the continuation of it at Deptford; the Sydenham palace & the Surrey hills. Altogether a noble Poem. Only think, I am losing all my teeth. All my magnificent teeth are going. I now begin to know I *have* had good teeth. This comes of too many cups of warm trash. If I had held to cold drinks—they would have lasted me out; but the effeminacy of tea coffee chocolate & sugar has been my bane. Miserable wretches were they who invented these comforters of exhaustion! They could not afford wine & beer. Hence God to punish them for their feeble hearts takes away the grinders from their representatives one of whom I have been induced to become. But, Thoreau, if ever I live again I vow never so much as to touch anything warm. It is as dangerous as to take a Pill which I am convinced is a most immoral custom. Give me ale for breakfast & claret or Port or ale again for dinner. I should then have a better conscience & not fear to lose my teeth any more than my tongue.

Farewell Thoreau. Success & the bounty of the gods attend you

Yrs ever

Thos Chol.ley

In response to Cholmondeley's letter of December 16, 1856, mailed February 22, 1857, Thoreau—according to Sanborn (Cholmondeley, *p. 752)—sent the Englishman the first volume (that is, the first edition probably, since it came out only in a single volume) of Emerson's* Poems, Walden, *the first edition of Whitman's* Leaves of Grass, *and a book by F. L. Olmsted on the Southern States* (A Journey in the Seaboard Slave States, *evidently*). MS., Berg; *previously unpublished.*

To H. G. O. BLAKE

Concord, June 6, 1857, 3 p. m.

Mr. Blake,—

I have just got your note, but I am sorry to say that this very morning I sent a note to Channing, stating that I would go with him to Cape Cod next week on an excursion which we have been talking of for some time. If there were time to communicate with you, I should ask you to come to Concord on Monday, before I go; but as it is, I must wait till I come back, which I think will be about ten days hence. I do not like this delay, but there seems to be a fate in it. Perhaps Mr. Wasson will be well enough to come by that time. I will notify you of my return, and shall depend on seeing you all.

Text, Familiar Letters of Thoreau, *p. 359.*

To H. G. O. BLAKE

Concord Tuesday Morning June 23d 1857

Mr Blake,

I returned from Cape Cod last evening, and now take the first opportunity to invite you men of Worcester to this quiet *Mediterranean* shore. Can you come this week on Friday or next Monday? I mention the earliest days on which I suppose you can be ready. If more convenient name some other time *within ten days.* I shall be rejoiced to see you, and to act the part of skipper in the contemplated voyage. I have just got another letter from Cholmondeley, which may interest you somewhat.

H. D. T.

MS., Gunn Memorial Library.

484

To CALVIN GREENE

Concord July 8th '57

Dear Sir,

You are right in supposing that I have not been Westward. I am very little of a traveller. I am gratified to hear of the interest you take in my books; it is additional encouragement to write more of them. Though my pen is not idle, I have not published anything for a couple of years at least. I like a private life, & cannot bear to have the public in my mind.

You will excuse me for not responding more heartily to your notes, since I realize what an interval there always is between the actual & imagined author, & feel that it would not be just for *me* to appropriate the sympathy and good will of my unseen readers.

Nevertheless, I should like to meet you, & if I ever come into your neighborhood shall endeavor to do so. Cant you tell the world of *your* life also? Then I shall know you, at least as well as you me.

Yrs truly
Henry D. Thoreau

MS., Princeton University Library.

To GEORGE THATCHER

Concord July 11th 1857

Dear Cousin,

Finding myself somewhat stronger than for 2 or 3 years past, I am bent on making a leisurely & economical excursion into your woods —say in a canoe, with two companions, through Moosehead to the Allegash Lakes, and possibly down that river to the French settlements,

& so homeward by whatever course we may prefer. I wish to go at an earlier season than formerly or within 10 days, notwithstanding the flies &c and we should want a month at our disposal.

I have just written to Mr [Eben J.] Loomis, one of the Cambridge-port men who went through Bangor last year, & called on you, inviting him to be one of the party, and for a third have thought of your son Charles, who has had some fresh, as well as salt, water experience. The object of this note is to ask if he would like to go, and you would like to have him go, on such an excursion. If so, I will come to Bangor, spend a day or 2 with you on my way, buy a canoe &c & be ready by the time my other man comes along. If Charles cannot go, we may find another man here, or possibly take an Indian. A friend of mine would like to accompany me, but I think that he has neither woodcraft nor strength enough.

Please let me hear from you as soon as possible.

Father has arrived safe & sound, and, he says, the better for his journey, though he has no longer his Bangor appetite. He intends writing to you.

Yours truly,
Henry D. Thoreau.

Thoreau's Bangor cousin, George Thatcher, must have said no to the suggested excursion, for it was finally made with a Concord neighbor, Edward Hoar, and an Indian guide, Joe Polis, as Thoreau's only companions. The excursion lasted from July 20 to August 8 and furnished the basis for the final chapter of The Maine Woods. *MS., Berg.*

From EDWIN BROWN C——

Henry David Thoreau E[sq.] Concord M[ass.]

Dear [Sir:]
      W[ould you] have the kindness to s[ign your] Autograph (Paper
& add[ress] for which I enclose) [and] oblige

Very Respectfully,
      Yours
      Edwin Brown C[?]

Boston 14th July 1857

Half of the manuscript has been torn away, making it difficult if not im-
possible to identify the sender. The Boston Directory *for 1857 lists no*
appropriate candidate; there are some Edwins under last names begin-
ning with C, but no Edwin Browns or even Edwin B's. MS., Berg; pre-
viously unpublished.

To MARSTON WATSON

Concord, August 17, 1857.

Mr. Watson,
      I am much indebted to you for your glowing communication of
July 20th. I had that very day left Concord for the wilds of Maine;
but when I returned, August 8th, two out of the six worms remained
nearly, if not quite, as bright as at first, I was assured. In their best estate they had excited the admiration of many of the inhabitants of
Concord. It was a singular coincidence that I should find these worms
awaiting me, for my mind was full of a phosphorescence which I had
seen in the woods. I have waited to learn something more about them
before acknowledging the receipt of them. I have frequently met with
glow-worms in my night walks, but am not sure they were the same

kind with these. Dr. [Thaddeus] Harris once described to me a larger kind than I had found, "nearly as big as your little finger"; but he does not name them in his report.

The only authorities on Glow-worms which I chance to have (and I am pretty well provided), are Kirby and Spence (the fullest), Knapp ("Journal of a Naturalist"), "The Library of Entertaining Knowledge" (*Rennie*), a French work, etc., etc.; but there is no minute, scientific description in any of these. This is apparently a female of the genus *Lampyris;* but Kirby and Spence say that there are nearly two hundred species of this genus alone. The one commonly referred to by English writers is the *Lampyris noctiluca;* but judging from Kirby and Spence's description, and from the description and plate in the French work, this is not that one, for, besides other differences, both say that the light proceeds from the abdomen. Perhaps the worms exhibited by Durkee (whose statement to the Boston Society of Natural History, second July meeting, in the "Traveller" of August 12, 1857, I send you) were the same with these. I do not see how they could be the L. *noctiluca,* as he states.

I expect to go to Cambridge before long, and if I get any more light on this subject I will inform you. The two worms are still alive.

I shall be glad to receive the *Drosera* at any time, if you chance to come across it. I am looking over Loudon's "Arboretum," which we have added to our Library, and it occurs to me that it was written expressly for you, and that you cannot avoid placing it on your own shelves.

I should have been glad to see the whale, and might perhaps have done so, if I had not at that time been seeing "the elephant" (or moose) in the Maine woods. I have been associating for about a month with one Joseph Polis, the chief man of the Penobscot tribe of Indians, and have learned a great deal from him, which I should like to tell you sometime.

Text, Familiar Letters of Thoreau, *pp. 360–62.*

To DANIEL RICKETSON

Concord Aug 18th 1857

Dear Sir,

Your Wilson Flagg seems a serious person, and it is encouraging to hear of a contemporary who recognizes nature so squarely, and selects such a theme as "Barns." (I would rather "*Mt* Auburn" were omitted.) But he is not alert enough. He wants stirring up with a pole. He should practice turning a series of somersets rapidly, or jump up & see how many times he can strike his feet together before coming down. Let him make the earth turn round now the other way—and whet his wits on it, whichever way it goes, as on a grindstone;—in short, see how many ideas he can entertain at once.

His style, as I remember, is singularly vague (I refer to the book) and before I got to the end of the sentences I was off the track. If you indulge in long periods you must be sure to have a snapper at the end. As for style of writing—if one has any thing to say, it drops from him simply & directly, as a stone falls to the ground for there are no two ways about it, but down it comes, and he may stick in the points and stops wherever he can get a chance. New ideas come into this world somewhat like falling meteors, with a flash and an explosion, and perhaps somebody's castle roof perforated. To try to polish the stone in its descent, to give it a peculiar turn and make it whistle a tune perchance, would be of no use, if it were possible. Your polished stuff turns out not to be meteoric, but of this earth.—However there is plenty of time, and Nature is an admirable schoolmistress.

Speaking of correspondence, you ask me if I "cannot turn over a new leaf in this line." I certainly could if I were to receive it; but just then I looked up and saw that your page was dated "May 10th" though mailed in August, and it occurred to me that I had seen you since that date this year. Looking again, it appeared that your note was written in '56!! However, it was a *new* leaf to me, and I *turned it over* with as much interest as if it had been written the day before. Perhaps you kept it so long in order that the MS & subject matter might be more in keeping with the old fashioned paper on which it was written.

I travelled the length of Cape Cod on foot, soon after you were here,

and within a few days have returned from the wilds of Maine, where I have made a journey of 325 miles with a canoe & an Indian & a single white companion, Edward Hoar of this town, lately from California,—traversing the headwaters of the Kennebeck—Penobscot—& St Johns.

Can't you extract any advantage out of that depression of spirits you refer to? It suggests to me cider mills, wine-presses, &c &c. All kinds of pressure or power should be used & made to turn some kind of machinery.

Channing was just leaving Concord for Plymouth when I arrived, but said he should be here again in 2 or 3 days.

Please remember me to your family & say that I have at length learned to sing Tom Bowling according to the notes—

Yrs truly
Henry D. Thoreau

Daniel Ricketson Esq.

Wilson Flagg's Studies in the Field & Forest *came out in this year.* MS., Morgan.

To H. G. O. BLAKE

Concord, August 18, 1857.

Mr. Blake,—

Fifteenthly. It seems to me that you need some absorbing pursuit. It does not matter much what it is, so it be honest. Such employment will be favorable to your development in more characteristic and important directions. You know there must be impulse enough for steerage way, though it be not toward your port, to prevent your drifting helplessly on to rocks or shoals. Some sails are set for this purpose only. There

is the large fleet of scholars and men of science, for instance, always to be seen standing off and on every coast, and saved thus from running on to reefs, who will at last run into their proper haven, we trust.

It is a pity you were not here with [Theo] Brown and [B. B.] Wiley. I think that in this case, *for a rarity*, the more the merrier.

You perceived that I did not entertain the idea of our going together to Maine on such an excursion as I had planned. The more I thought of it, the more imprudent it appeared to me. I did think to have written to you before going, though not to propose your going also; but I went at last very suddenly, and could only have written a business letter, if I had tried, when there was no business to be accomplished. I have now returned, and think I have had a quite profitable journey, chiefly from associating with an intelligent Indian. My companion, Edward Hoar, also found his account in it, though he suffered considerably from being obliged to carry unusual loads over wet and rough "carries," —in one instance five miles through a swamp, where the water was frequently up to our knees, and the fallen timber higher than our heads. He went over the ground three times, not being able to carry all his load at once. This prevented his ascending Ktaadn. Our best nights were those when it rained the hardest, on account of the mosquitoes. I speak of these things, which were not unexpected, merely to account for my not inviting you.

Having returned, I flatter myself that the world appears in some respects a little larger, and not, as usual, smaller and shallower, for having extended my range. I have made a short excursion into the new world which the Indian dwells in, or is. He begins where we leave off. It is worth the while to detect new faculties in man,—he is so much the more divine; and anything that fairly excites our admiration expands us. The Indian, who can find his way so wonderfully in the woods, possesses so much intelligence which the white man does not,—and it increases my own capacity, as well as faith, to observe it. I rejoice to find that intelligence flows in other channels than I knew. It redeems for me portions of what seemed brutish before.

It is a great satisfaction to find that your oldest convictions are permanent. With regard to essentials, I have never had occasion to change my mind. The aspect of the world varies from year to year, as the landscape is differently clothed, but I find that the *truth* is still *true*, and I never regret any emphasis which it may have inspired. Ktaadn is there

still, but much more surely my old conviction is there, resting with more than mountain breadth and weight on the world, the source still of fertilizing streams, and affording glorious views from its summit, if I can get up to it again. As the mountains still stand on the plain, and far more unchangeable and permanent,—stand still grouped around, farther or nearer to my maturer eye, the ideas which I have entertained, —the everlasting teats from which we draw our nourishment.

Text, *Familiar Letters of Thoreau, pp. 368–70.*

From DANIEL RICKETSON

The Shanty, Sept. 7th, 1857.

Dear Thoreau,—

I wrote you some two weeks ago that I intended visiting Concord, but have not yet found the way there. The object of my now writing is to invite you to make me a visit. Walton's small sail boat is now in Assawampset Pond. We took it up in our farm wagon to the south shore of Long Pond (Apponoquet), visited the islands in course and passed through the river that connects the said ponds. This is the finest season as to weather to visit the ponds, and I feel much stronger than when you were here last Spring. The boys and myself have made several excursions to our favorite region this summer, but we have left the best of it, so far as the voyage is concerned, for you to accompany us.

We hear nothing of Channing, but conclude that he is with you— trust he has not left us entirely, and hope to see him again before long.

Now should my invitation prove acceptable to you, I should be glad to see you just as soon after the receipt of this as you like to come, immediately if you please.

If you cannot come and should like to see me in Concord, please inform me, but we all hope to see you here.

Mrs. R. and the rest join in regards and invitation.

Yours truly,
D. R.

Remember me to Channing.

Text, Ricketson, *p. 76.*

To DANIEL RICKETSON

Concord Sep 9 1857

Friend Ricketson

I thank you for your kind invitation to visit you—but I have taken so many vacations this year—at New Bedford—Cape Cod—& Maine—that any more relaxation, call it rather dissipation, will cover me with shame & disgrace. I have not earned what I have already enjoyed. As some heads cannot carry much wine, so it would seem that I cannot bear so much society as you can. I have an immense appetite for solitude, like an infant for sleep, and if I don't get enough of it this year I shall cry all the next.

I believe that Channing is here still—he was two or three days ago—but whether for good & all, I do not know nor ask.

My mother's house is full at present; but if it were not, I should have no right to invite you hither, while entertaining such designs as I have hinted at. However, if you care to storm the town, I will engage to take some afternoon walks with you—retiring into profoundest solitude the most sacred part of the day.

Yrs sincerely
H. D. T.

MS., Huntington; *printed in* Ricketson, *p. 77, with the postscript:* "(*Written before my late visit, as the date shows*)."

From DANIEL RICKETSON

The Shanty, 10th Sept 1857.

Dear Philosopher,

I received your note of yesterday this A.M. I am glad you write me so frankly. I know well how dear one's own time & solitude may be, and I would not on any consideration violate the sanctity of your prerogative.

I fear too that I may have heretofore trespassed upon your time too much If I have please pardon me as I did it unwittingly I felt the need of congenial society—& sought yours I forgot that I could not render you an equivalent. It is good for one to be checked—to be thrown more and more upon his own resources. I have lived years of solitude (seeing only my own family, & Uncle James occasionally,) and was never happier. My heart however was then more buoyant and the woods and fields—the birds & flowers, but more than these, my moral meditations afforded me a constant source of the truest enjoyment. I admire your strength & fortitude to battle the world. I am a weak and broken reed. Have charity for me, if not sympathy. Can any one heart know another's? If not let us suspend our too hasty judgment against those from whom we differ.

I hope to see you in due time at Brooklawn where you are always a welcome & instructive guest.

With my kind regards to your family, I remain

Yours faithfully
D. Ricketson

MS., Abernethy (*typescript*); *previously unpublished.*

To GEORGE THATCHER

Concord Nov 12 1857

Dear Cousin,

Father has received your letter of Nov. 10, but is at present unable to reply. He is quite sick with the jaundice, having been under the doctor's care for a week; this, added to his long standing cold, has reduced him very much. He has no appetite, but little strength and gets very little sleep. We have written to aunts Maria & Jane to come up & see him.

I am glad if your western experience has made you the more a New Englander—though your part of N.E. is rather cold—Cold as it is, however, I should like to see those woods and lakes, & rivers in mid-winter, sometime.

I find that the most profitable way to travel is, to write down your questions before you start, & be sure that you get them all answered, for when the opportunity offers you cannot always tell what you want to know, or, if you can will often neglect to learn it

Edward Hoar is in Concord still. I hear that the moose horns which you gave him make the principal or best part of an elaborate hat-tree

Sophia sends much love to Cousin Rebecca & expects an answer to her letter.

Yrs
Henry D. Thoreau

MS., Abernethy *(typescript); previously unpublished.*

To H. G. O. BLAKE

Concord, November 16, 1857.

Mr. Blake,—

You have got the start again. It was I that owed you a letter or two, if I mistake not.

They make a great ado nowadays about hard times; but I think that the community generally, ministers and all, take a wrong view of the matter, though some of the ministers preaching according to a formula may pretend to take a right one. This general failure, both private and public, is rather occasion for rejoicing, as reminding us whom we have at the helm,—that justice is always done. If our merchants did not most of them fail, and the banks too, my faith in the old laws of the world would be staggered. The statement that ninety-six in a hundred doing such business surely break down is perhaps the sweetest fact that statistics have revealed,—exhilarating as the fragrance of sallows in spring. Does it not say somewhere, "The Lord reigneth, let the earth rejoice"? If thousands are thrown out of employment, it suggests that they were not well employed. Why don't they take the hint? It is not enough to be industrious; so are the ants. What are you industrious about?

The merchants and company have long laughed at transcendentalism, higher laws, etc., crying, "None of your moonshine," as if they were anchored to something not only definite, but sure and permanent. If there was any institution which was presumed to rest on a solid and secure basis, and more than any other represented this boasted common sense, prudence, and practical talent, it was the bank; and now those very banks are found to be mere reeds shaken by the wind. Scarcely one in the land has kept its promise. It would seem as if you only need live forty years in any age of this world, to see its most promising government become the government of Kansas, and banks nowhere. Not merely the Brook Farm and Fourierite communities, but now the community generally has failed. But there is the moonshine still, serene, beneficent, and unchanged. Hard times, I say, have this value, among others, that they show us what such promises are worth,—where the *sure* banks are. I heard some merchant praised the other day because he had paid some of his debts, though it took nearly all he had (why, I've done as much as that myself many times, and a little more), and then gone to board. What if he has? I hope he 's got a good boarding-place, and can pay for it. It 's not everybody that can. However, in my opinion, it is cheaper to keep house,—*i. e.*, if you don't keep too big a one.

Men will tell you sometimes that "money's hard." That shows it was not made to eat, I say. Only think of a man in this new world, in his log cabin, in the midst of a corn and potato patch, with a sheepfold on one

side, talking about money being hard! So are flints hard; there is no alloy in them. What has that to do with his raising his food, cutting his wood (or breaking it), keeping in-doors when it rains, and, if need be, spinning and weaving his clothes? Some of those who sank with the steamer the other day found out that money was *heavy* too. Think of a man's priding himself on this kind of wealth, as if it greatly enriched him. As if one struggling in mid-ocean with a bag of gold on his back should gasp out, "I am worth a hundred thousand dollars." I see them struggling just as ineffectually on dry land, nay, even more hopelessly, for, in the former case, rather than sink, they will finally let the bag go; but in the latter they are pretty sure to hold and go down with it. I see them swimming about in their great-coats, collecting their rents, really *getting their dues*, drinking bitter draughts which only increase their thirst, becoming more and more water-logged, till finally they sink plumb down to the bottom. But enough of this.

Have you ever read Ruskin's books? If not, I would recommend you to try the second and third volumes (not parts) of his "Modern Painters." I am now reading the fourth, and have read most of his other books lately. They are singularly good and encouraging, though not without crudeness and bigotry. The themes in the volumes referred to are Infinity, Beauty, Imagination, Love of Nature, etc.,—all treated in a very living manner. I am rather surprised by them. It is remarkable that these things should be said with reference to painting chiefly, rather than literature. The "Seven Lamps of Architecture," too, is made of good stuff; but, as I remember, there is too much about art in it for me and the Hottentots. We want to know about matters and things in general. Our house is as yet a hut.

You must have been enriched by your solitary walk over the mountains. I suppose that I feel the same awe when on their summits that many do on entering a church. To see what kind of earth that is on which you have a house and garden somewhere, perchance! It is equal to the lapse of many years. You must ascend a mountain to learn your relation to matter, and so to your own body, for *it* is at home there, though *you* are not. It might have been composed there, and will have no farther to go to return to dust there, than in your garden; but your spirit inevitably comes away, and brings your body with it, if it lives. Just as awful really, and as glorious, is your garden. See how I can play with my fingers! They are the funniest companions I have ever found. Where did they come from? What strange control I have over them!

Who am I? What are they?—those little peaks—call them Madison, Jefferson, Lafayette. What is *the matter?* *My* fingers ten, I say. Why, erelong, they may form the top-most crystal of Mount Washington. I go up there to see my body's cousins. There are some fingers, toes, bowels, etc., that I take an interest in, and therefore I am interested in all their relations.

Let me suggest a theme for you: to state to yourself precisely and completely what that walk over the mountains amounted to for you,—returning to this essay again and again, until you are satisfied that all that was important in your experience is in it. Give this good reason to yourself for having gone over the mountains, for mankind is ever going over a mountain. Don't suppose that you can tell it precisely the first dozen times you try, but at 'em again, especially when, after a sufficient pause, you suspect that you are touching the heart or summit of the matter, reiterate your blows there, and account for the mountain to yourself. Not that the story need be long, but it will take a long while to make it short. It did not take very long to get over the mountain, you thought; but have you got over it indeed? If you have been to the top of Mount Washington, let me ask, what did you find there? That is the way they prove witnesses, you know. Going up there and being blown on is nothing. We never do much climbing while we are there, but we eat our luncheon, etc., very much as at home. It is after we get home that we really go over the mountain, if ever. What did the mountain say? What did the mountain do?

I keep a mountain anchored off eastward a little way, which I ascend in my dreams both awake and asleep. Its broad base spreads over a village or two, which do not know it; neither does it know them, nor do I when I ascend it. I can see its general outline as plainly now in my mind as that of Wachusett. I do not invent in the least, but state exactly what I see. I find that I go up it when I am light-footed and earnest. It ever smokes like an altar with its sacrifice. I am not aware that a single villager frequents it or knows of it. I keep this mountain to ride instead of a horse.

Do you not mistake about seeing Moosehead Lake from Mount Washington? That must be about one hundred and twenty miles distant, or nearly twice as far as the Atlantic, which last some doubt if they can see thence. Was it not Umbagog?

Dr. [Reinhold] Solger has been lecturing in the vestry in this town on Geography, to Sanborn's scholars, for several months past, at five

P. M. Emerson and Alcott have been to hear him. I was surprised when the former asked me, the other day, if I was not going to hear Dr. Solger. What, to be sitting in a meeting-house cellar at that time of day, when you might possibly be out-doors! I never thought of such a thing. What was the sun made for? If he does not prize daylight, I do. Let him lecture to owls and dormice. He must be a wonderful lecturer indeed who can keep me indoors at such an hour, when the night is coming in which no man can walk.

Are you in want of amusement nowadays? Then play a little at the game of getting a living. There never was anything equal to it. Do it temperately, though, and don't sweat. Don't let this secret out, for I have a design against the Opera. OPERA!! Pass along the exclamations, devil.

Now is the time to become conversant with your wood-pile (this comes under Work for the Month), and be sure you put some warmth into it by your mode of getting it. Do not consent to be passively warmed. An intense degree of that is the hotness that is threatened. But a positive warmth within can withstand the fiery furnace, as the vital heat of a living man can withstand the heat that cooks meat.

The starting point for this one of Thoreau's many sermons to Blake is the panic of 1857, the worst the country had experienced in a generation. A sidelight on the comments about mountains is the fact that he had had a "mountain dream" only a few days before (Journal, X, 141–44). Text, Familiar Letters of Thoreau, pp. 371–78.

From DANIEL RICKETSON

The Shanty, Friday Evening, Dec. 11, 1857.

Dear Thoreau,—

I expect to go to Boston next week, Thursday 17th, with my daughters Anna and Emma to attend the Anti-Slavery Bazaar. They will probably return home the next day, and I proceed to Malden for

a day or two. After which I may proceed to Concord, if I have your permission, and if you will be at home, for without you Concord would be quite poor and deserted, like to the place some poet, perhaps Walter Scott, describes,—

> "Where thro' the desert walks the lapwing flies
> And tires their echoes with unceasing cries."

Channing says I can take his room in the garret of his house, but I think I should take to the tavern. Were you at Walden I should probably storm your castle and make good an entrance, and perhaps as an act of generous heroism allow you quarters while I remained. But in sober truth I should like to see you and sit or lie down in your room and hear you growl once more, thou brave old Norseman—thou Thor, thunder-god-man. I long to see your long beard, which for a short man is rather a stretch of imagination or understanding. C[hanning] says it is terrible to behold, but improves you mightily.

How grandly your philosophy sits now in these *trying* times. I lent my Walden to a broken merchant lately as the best panacea I could offer him for his troubles.

You should now come out and call together the lost sheep of Israel, thou cool-headed pastor, no Corydon forsooth, but genuine Judean—fulminate from the banks of Concord upon the banks of Discord and once more set ajog a pure curren(t)cy whose peaceful tide may wash us clean once more again. *Io Paean!*

Is "Father Alcott" in your city? I should count much on seeing him too—a man who is All-cot should not be without a home at least in his chosen land.

Don't be provoked at my nonsense, for anything better would be like "carrying coals to Newcastle." I would sit at the feet of Gamaliel, so farewell for the present.

With kind remembrances to your family, I remain,

Faithfully your friend,

D. Ricketson

P.S.   If I can't come please inform me.

Text, Ricketson, *pp. 77–79.*

1858

The Sons of Vulcan were organized into a union, which later became the Amalgamated Association of Iron and Steel Workers and still later led, though not by the most direct descent, to the AFL and CIO. A free zone was decreed between our country and Mexico. In Ottawa, Illinois Abraham Lincoln debated with Stephen Douglas in the campaign for United States Senator. Lincoln said there that this country could not endure half slave and half free. Two months later William Seward, speaking in Rochester, agreed and maintained that this country was engaged in an "irrepressible conflict" and must become either slave or free. The first Atlantic cable was laid successfully. Queen Victoria and President Buchanan exchanged congratulations over it. The Overland Mail Company began carrying mail by stage coach from Memphis and St. Louis to San Francisco. The Crystal Palace in New York burned down.

Thoreau's essay "Chesuncook" was published in the *Atlantic Monthly*. The intention was to make it the beginning of a series. However, Editor James Russell Lowell blue-penciled a sentence in which Thoreau suggested that a pine tree might go to heaven. Thoreau of course resented the censoring, sent a blistering letter to Lowell, and published no more in the *Atlantic* until it had a new editor. Thoreau traveled a good deal during the year. He visited Worcester, New York City, and Cape Ann among other places; he climbed Monadnock with Ellery Channing and Mt. Washington with the young man who helped to start the fire that had burned so many Concord trees—all of which might or might not have gone to heaven. Thoreau also wrote extensively and did a good deal of surveying; 1858 summed up as an unusually active year for him. The *Journal* is filled with facts—Latin labels and botanical observations. "How differently the poet and the naturalist look at objects!" Thoreau notes in September, and he is right.

To GEORGE THATCHER

Concord Jan 1st 1858

Dear Cousin,

Father seems to have got over the jaundice some weeks since, but to be scarcely the better for all that. The cough he has had so long is at least as bad as ever, and though much stronger than when I wrote before he is not sensibly recovering his former amount of health. On the contrary we cannot help regarding him more & more as a sick man. I do not think it a transient ail—which he can entirely recover from— nor yet an acute disease, but the form in which the infirmities of age have come upon him. He sleeps much in his chair, & commonly goes out once a day in *pleasant* weather.

The Harpers have been unexpected enough to pay him—but others are owing a good deal yet. He has taken one man's note for $400.00, pay- able I think in April, & it remains to be seen what it is worth.

Mother & Sophia are as well as usual. Aunt returned to Boston some weeks ago.

Mr Hoar is still in Concord, attending to Botany, Ecology, &c with a view to make his future residence in foreign parts more truly profitable to him. I have not yet had an opportunity to convey your respects to him—but I shall do so.

I have been more than usually busy surveying the last six weeks run- ning & measuring lines in the woods, reading old deeds & hunting up bounds which have been lost these 20 years. I have written out a long account of my last Maine journey—part of which I shall read to our Lyceum—but I do not know how soon I shall print it.

We are having a remarkably open winter, no sleighing as yet, & but little ice.

I am glad to hear that Charles [Thatcher] has a good situation, but I thought that the 3rd mate lived with and as the sailors. If he makes a study of navigation &c, and is bent on being master soon, well & good.

502

It is an honorable & brave life, though a hard one, and turns out as good men as most professions. Where there is a good character to be developed, there are few callings better calculated to develop it.

I wish you a happy new year—

Henry D. Thoreau

MS., Berg; *previously unpublished.*

To JONES VERY

Concord Jan 16th 1858

My Dear Sir,

I received your note inviting me to Salem after my lecture Wednesday evening. My first impulse was to go to you; but I reflected that Mr [Parker] Pillsbury had just invited me to Lynn, thro' Mr Buffum, promising to be there to meet me, indeed, we had already planned some excursions to Nahant, &c—and he would be absent on Friday;—so I felt under obligations to him & the Lynn people to stay with them. They were very kind to me, and I had a very good time with them— Jonathan Buffum & Son, Pillsbury & Mr. [Benjamin?] Mudge—My reason for not running over to Salem for an hour, or a fraction of the day, was simply that I did not wish to impair my right to come by & by when I may have leisure to take in the whole pleasure & benefit of such a visit —for I hate to *feel* in a hurry.

I shall improve or take an opportunity to spend a day—or part of a day with you ere long, and I trust that you will be attracted to Concord again, and will find me a better walker than I chanced to be when you were here before.

I have often thought of taking a walk with you in your vicinity. I have a little to tell you, but a great deal more to hear from you. I had a grand time deep in the woods of Maine in July, &c &c. I suppose that I

saw the *genista tinctoria* in the N. W. part of Lynn—on my way to the boulders & the mill-stone ledge.

Please remember me to Mr. [George P.?] Bradford.

Yrs truly
Henry D. Thoreau

MS., Essex Institute; *previously unpublished.*

To JAMES RUSSELL LOWELL

Concord Jan. 23d 1858

Dear Sir,

I have been so busy surveying of late, that I have scarcely had time to "think" of your proposition, or ascertain what I have for you. The more fatal objection to printing my last Maine-wood experience, is that my Indian guide, whose words & deeds I report very faithfully,— and they are the most interesting part of the story,—knows how to read, and takes a newspaper, so that I could not face him again.

The most available paper which I have is an account of an excursion into the Maine woods in '53; the subjects of which are the Moose, the Pine Tree & the Indian. Mr. Emerson could tell you about it, for I remember reading it to his family, after having read it as a lecture to my townsmen. It consists of about one hundred manuscript pages, or a lecture & a half, as I measure. The date could perhaps be omitted, if in the way. On account of other engagements, I could not get it ready for you under a month from this date.

If you *think that you would like* to have this, and will state the rate of compensation, I will inform you at once whether I will prepare it for you.

Yrs truly
Henry D. Thoreau

J. R. Lowell Esq

Thoreau was evidently one of the prospective contributors to the new
Atlantic Monthly *whom Lowell, its initial editor, was definitely inter-*
ested in. The magazine had begun publication the year before. Thoreau
and its editor had been acquainted since Harvard days; then Lowell was
a year behind Thoreau. But there must have been little if anything in
common. Lowell, a vigorous dandy, moved in Harvard's shiniest circles,
while Thoreau was leading his own uncluttered life. After college their
careers continued to diverge markedly. Lowell became a very popular
poet, a married man, an abolitionist, and a professor. Thoreau hoed his
furrow. The surprising thing, one would judge, is that Lowell when he
came to the Atlantic *got in touch with Thoreau at all. (It may have*
been at the suggestion of Francis H. Underwood, who had approached
Thoreau in 1853 about contributing to a projected antislavery magazine
and who was now helping Lowell in the Atlantic *office.) Very probably*
Lowell approached Thoreau indirectly through Emerson. On Septem-
ber 14, 1857 Lowell wrote Emerson about some of his contributions
to the Atlantic *and also inquired "How about Mr. Thoreau?" On No-*
vember 19 Lowell was more specific: "Will not Thoreau give us some-
thing from Moosehead?" (H. E. Scudder's James Russell Lowell, *I, 415*
and 417), and that may have been the query that resulted in this letter.
MS., *Harvard; previously unpublished.*

From ?

Dear Sir:

Please send me a copy

This fragment is all that remains of what was probably a request for a
copy of one of Thoreau's books. The manuscript is postmarked "Athol,
January 25, 1858." MS., *Lownes; previously unpublished.*

From T. W. HIGGINSON

Worcester Jan 27, 1858

Dear Sir
    Would it not be practical to start from Moosehead Lake, with an Indian guide, reach the head water of the Allegash & so down to Madawaska—or farther West, under the Sugar Loaf Mts. to Quebec? What were the termini of your expedition in that direction & what time & cost?

Cordially
T. W. Higginson

MS., Harvard; *previously unpublished.*

To T. W. HIGGINSON

Concord Jan 28 1858

Dear Sir,
    It would be perfectly practicable to go the Madawaska the way you propose—As for the route to Quebec, I do not find the "Sugar-loaf Mts" on my maps. The most direct and regular way, as you know, is substantially Montresor's & Arnold's, and the younger John Smith's—by the Chaudiere; but this is less wild. If your object is rather to see the St. Lawrence River below Quebec, you will probably strike it at the Riviere du Loup. (V. Hodges' account of his excursion thither via the Allegash. I believe it is in the 2nd Report on the Geology of the Public Lands of Maine & Mass, in '37.) I think that our Indian last summer, when we talked of going to the St. Lawrence named another route, near the Madawaska—perhaps the St Francis, which would save the long portage which Hodge made.
    I do not know whether you think of ascending the St Lawrence in a

506

canoe—but if you should you might be delayed not only by the current, but by the waves, which frequently run too high for a canoe in such a mighty stream. It would be a grand excursion to go to Quebec by the Chaudiere—descend the St Lawrence to the Riviere du Loup—& so return by the Madawaska & St Johns to Frederickton, or further—almost all the way *down stream*—a very important consideration.

I went to Moosehead in company with a party of four who were going a hunting down the Allegash—& St Johns, and thence by some other stream over into the Restigouche & down that to the Bay of Chaleur—to be gone 6 weeks!

Our northern terminus was an island in Heron Lake on the Allegash (V. Colton's R. R. & Township map of Maine.) The Indian proposed that we should return to Bangor by the St Johns & Great Schoodic Lake —which we had thought of ourselves—and he showed us on the map where we should be each night. It was then noon, and the next day night, continuing down the Allegash, we should have been at the Madawaska settlements, having made only one or 2 portages, and thereafter, on the St Johns there would be but one or 2 more falls with short carries, and if there was not too much wind, we could go down that stream 100 miles a day. It is settled all the way below the Madawaska. He knew the route well. He even said that this was easier, and would take but little more time, though much further, than the route we decided on— i.e. by Webster Stream—the East Branch & Main Penobscot to Oldtown —but he may have wanted a longer job. We preferred the latter—not only because it was shorter, but because—as he said, it was wilder.

We went about 325 miles with the canoe (including 60 miles of Stage between Bangor & Oldtown) were out 12 nights, & spent about 40 dollars apiece, which was more than was necessary We paid the Indian, who was a very good one, $1.50 per day & 50 cts per week for his canoe. This is enough in ordinary seasons. I had formerly paid $2 00 for an Indian & for white batteau-men

If you go to the Madawaska in a leisurely manner, supposing no delay on account of rain or the violence of the wind, you may reach *Mt* Kineo by noon, & have the afternoon to explore it. The next day you may get to the head of the Lake before noon, make the portage of 2½ miles over a wooden R R & drop down the Penobscot half a dozen miles. The 3d morning you will perhaps walk half a mile about Pine Stream Falls, while the Indian runs down, cross the head of Chesuncook, & reach the junction of the Caucomgomock & Umbazookskus by noon, and

ascend the latter to Umbazookskus Lake that night. If it is lowwater, you may have to walk & carry a little on the Umbazookskus before entering the lake. The 4th morning you will make the carry of 2 miles to Mud Pond (Allegash water) & a very wet carry it is, & reach Chamberlain Lake by noon, & Heron Lake perhaps that night, after a couple of very short carries at the outlet of Chamberlain.

At the end of 2 days more, you will probably be at Madawaska.

Of course the Indian can paddle twice as far in a day as he commonly does.

Perhaps you would like a few more details—We *used* (3 of us) exactly 26 lbs of hard bread, 14 lbs of pork, 3 lbs of coffee 12 lbs of sugar (& could have used more) beside a little tea, Ind. meal, & rice & plenty of berries & moosemeat. This was faring very luxuriously. I had not formerly carried coffee—sugar, or rice. But for solid food, I decide that *it is not worth the while to carry anything but hard bread & pork*, whatever your tastes & habits may be. These wear best—& you have no time nor dishes in which to cook any thing else. Of course you will take a little Ind. meal to fry fish in—& half a dozen lemons also, if you have sugar—will be very refreshing—for the water is warm.

To save time, the sugar, coffee, tea salt &c &c should be in separate water tight bags labelled and tied with a leather string; and all the provisions & blankets should be put into 2 large India rubber bags, if you can find them water tight—Ours were not.

A 4-quart tin pail makes a good kettle for all purposes, & tin plates are portable & convenient. Dont forget an India rubber knapsack—with a large flap—plenty of *dish cloths*—old newspapers, strings, & 25 feet of strong cord.

Of India rubber clothing the most you can wear, if any, is a very light coat, and that you cannot work in.

I could be more particular, but perhaps have been too much so already.

Yrs truly

Henry D. Thoreau

MS., Berg.

To JAMES RUSSELL LOWELL

Concord, Feb. 22d 1858

My dear Sir,

I think that I can send you a part of the story to which I referred within a fortnight. I am to read some of my latest Maine wood experiences to my townsmen this week; and in this case I shall not hesitate to call names.

MS., Harvard; *previously unpublished; the signature has been clipped from the MS.*

To JAMES RUSSELL LOWELL

Concord Mar. 5 1858

Dear Sir,

I send you this morning, by the Concord & Cambridge expresses, some 80 pages of my Maine Story. There are about 50 pages more of it. I think that it is best divided thus. If, however, this is too long for you, there is a tolerable stopping place after the word "mouse" p. 74, which is about the middle of the whole.

If there is no objection you can print the whole date 1853.

I reserve the right to publish it in another form after it has appeared in your magazine.

Will you please send me the proofs on account of Indian names &c- and also, if you print this, inform me how soon you would like the rest?

Yrs truly
Henry D. Thoreau

MS., Harvard; *previously unpublished.*

From R. WARNER

Boston April 10 1858

Mr Henry D Thoreau
Sir
        I wish you would go & measure the piece of land that I bought
of Mr Brown immediately if you will call at my mill & tell Mr Smith
to let Thomas [name] go with you & shew the lines I shall be up next
week Wednesday or Saturday if you got the land measured before you
will send the measure to me by mail

yours Truly
R. Warner

The Boston City Directory *for 1858 lists a Richard Warner of Warner
& Son, marginal slaters, who may have been the writer of this note.
MS., Berg; previously unpublished.*

To MARY BROWN

        I think that they [Mayflowers] amount to more than grow in
Concord. The blood-root also, which we have not at all, had not suffered in the least. Part of it is transferred to my sister's garden. Preserving one splendid vase full, I distributed the rest of the Mayflowers
among my neighbors, Mrs. Emerson, Mrs. Ripley, Mr. Hoar and others.
. . . They have sweetened the air of a good part of the town ere this.
. . . I should be glad to show you my Herbarium, which is very large;
and in it you would recognize many specimens which you contributed.
. . . Please remember me to Father and Mother, whom I shall not fail
to visit whenever I come to Brattleboro, also to the Chesterfield mountain, if you can communicate with it; I suppose it has not budged an
inch.

510

Mrs. Mary Brown Dunton comments on this letter that it was written to
thank her for a box of mayflowers—i.e. trailing arbutus—which Thoreau
received April 23. She and Thoreau had become acquainted during
his visit to Brattleboro during the autumn of 1856. (Journal, IX, 61–
80.) Text, Vermont Botanical Club Bulletin *No. 3 (April 1908),* 37–38.

To MARSTON WATSON

Concord, April 25, 1858

Dear Sir,

Your unexpected gift of pear-trees reached me yesterday in good
condition, and I spent the afternoon in giving them a good setting out;
but I fear that this cold weather may hurt them. However, I am inclined
to think they are insured since you have looked on them. It makes ones
mouth water to read their names only. From what I hear of the extent
of your bounty, if a reasonable part of the trees succeed this trans-
planting will make a new era for Concord to date from.

Mine must be a lucky star, for day before yesterday I received a box
of May-flowers from Brattleboro, and yesterday morning your pear-
trees, and at evening a humming-bird's nest from Worcester. This looks
like fairy housekeeping.

I discovered two new plants in Concord last winter, the Labrador
Tea (Ledum latifolium), and Yew (Taxis baccata).

By the way, in January I communicated with Dr. Durkee, whose
report on glow-worms I sent you, and it appeared, as I expected, that he
(and by his account, Agassiz, Gould, Jackson, and others to whom he
showed them) did not consider them a distinct species, but a variety of
the common, or Lampyris noctiluca, some of which you got in Lincoln.
Durkee, at least, has never see the last. I told him that I had no doubt
about their being a distinct species. His, however, were luminous
throughout every part of the body, as those which you sent me were not,
while I had them.

Is nature as full of vigor to your eyes as ever, or do you detect some
falling off at last? Is the mystery of the hog's bristle cleared up, and

with it that of our life? It is the question, to the exclusion of every other interest.

I am sorry to hear of the burning of your woods, but, thank heaven, your great ponds and your sea cannot be burnt. I love to think of your warm sandy wood-roads, and your breezy island out in the sea. What a prospect you can get every morning from the hill-top east of your house! I think that even the heathen that I am, could say, or sing, or dance morning prayers there of some kind.

Please remember me to Mrs. Watson, and to the rest of your family who are helping the sunshine yonder.

Watson's villa in Plymouth, "Hillside," was a favorite spot for Thoreau and his friends to visit. Sanborn (Recollections of Seventy Years, II, 320) *reports that Thoreau and Alcott visited there "and in walks through the surrounding wood encountered the remains of a dead hog—his white firm jawbone, and his bristles quite untouched by decay. 'You see,' said Thoreau to his vegetarian friend, 'here is something that succeeded, beside spirituality, and thought,—here is the tough child of nature.'"*

Mrs. Watson, born Mary Russell, had lived in the Thoreau household before her marriage and was supposed by Marston Watson to be the Maiden of Thoreau's youthful poem "To the Maiden in the East." MS., Mrs. Robert Bowler.

From B. B. WILEY

Chicago Apl 26, 1858

H D Thoreau Esq
Dear Sir

May I ask you to send me or have sent to me Mr Emerson's lecture on "Country Life." I am told he is ready to lend his papers to earnest inquirers. I will pay all postages and return the Ms. as soon as

read, though, if Mr Emerson do not object, I might wish to copy it. Neither you nor he must think me impertinent. I am where I would almost give my life for light and hence the request.

Not having your "Wild & Walking" to read, I have been walking in the wild of my own Nature and I am filled with anxious inquiries as to whether I had better remain in this business into which I passively slided. At that time I had many misgivings that it was not a wise step and I have been on the anxious seat ever since. I want labor that I can contemplate with approval and continue to prosecute with delight in sickness, adversity, and old age, should I chance to meet with such. I object to this business that it does not use my faculties, and on the other hand I ask myself if all my trouble is not in me. You dont want to hear my reasons pro and con. You too have been at a parting of the ways and will understand me.

It is true that while here I have been much helped yet it is in spite of my trade connections which came near spoiling me.

If I now leave, I shall probably have very little money, but I think some "fire in my belly" which will in the long run do something for me, if I live in the freedom of obedience.

If I leave, it will be with the expectation of earnestly choosing some sort of "Country Life," or, if I remain in a city, something that will make me grow. I believe that am I once fairly on deck I should not want to go below again.

I am ready to tread cheerfully any path of Renunciation if Heavenly Wisdom demand it—with equal alacrity would I, in that high behest, go to the Devil by the most approved modern, respectable, orthodox methods. It is difficult to reconcile the Temporal and the Eternal. I must at some time so decide it that I can use all the "fire in my belly" to some purpose

I spent, in December, some weeks on a farm in the interior of the State. I walked some distance over the prairie to look at a farm a man wanted me to buy and when the next night I reached my host's house, I took up "Walden" and came across your translation of Cato's advice to those about buying farms. It was very welcome and I let this farm alone.

I would write you a long letter, but I suppose it would only make you smile benignly—and perhaps me, too, when, a year hence, I remembered it.

513

Remember me respectfully and lovingly to Mr Emerson
Your grateful friend
B. B. Wiley

MS., Berg; *previously unpublished.*

To JAMES RUSSELL LOWELL

Concord May 18 1858

Dear Sir,

The proofs, for which I *did* ask in the note which accompanied the ms, would have been an all sufficient "Bulletin."

I was led to suppose by Mr Emerson's account,—and he advised me to send immediately—that you were not always even *one* month ahead. At any rate it was important to me that the paper be disposed of soon.

I send by express this morning the remainder of the story—of which allow me to ask a sight of the proofs.

Yrs. truly
Henry D. Thoreau

MS., Harvard; *previously unpublished.*

To H. G. O. BLAKE

Concord Tuesday 4 *pm* June 1st 1858

Mr Blake—

It looks as if it might rain tomorrow; therefore this is to inform you—if you have not left Worcester on account of rain, that if the

weather prevents my starting tomorrow, I intend to start on Thursday morning—i.e. if it is not decidedly rainy—or something more than a shower, and I trust that I shall meet you at Troy as agreed on.

H. D. T.

MS., Hosmer; *previously unpublished.*

To JAMES RUSSELL LOWELL

Concord June 22d 1858.

Dear Sir,

When I received the proof of that portion of my story printed in the July number of your magazine, I was surprised to find that the sentence—"It is as immortal as I am, and perchance will go to as high a heaven, there to tower above me still."—(which comes directly after the words "heals my cuts," page 230, tenth line from the top,) have been crossed out, and it occurred to me that, after all, it was of some consequence that I should see the proofs; supposing, of course, that my "Stet" &c in the margin would be respected, as I perceive that it was in other cases of comparatively little importance to me. However, I have just noticed that that sentence was, in a very mean and cowardly manner, omitted. I hardly need to say that this is a liberty which I will not permit to be taken with my MS. The editor has, in this case, no more right to omit a sentiment than to insert one, or put words into my mouth. I do not ask anybody to adopt my opinions, but I do expect that when they ask for them to print, they will print them, or obtain my consent to their alteration or omission. I should not read many books if I thought that they had been thus *expurgated.* I feel this treatment to be an insult, though not intended as such, for it is to presume that I can be hired to suppress my opinions.

I do not mean to charge you with this omission, for I cannot believe that you knew anything about it, but there must be a responsible editor somewhere, and you, to whom I entrusted my MS. are the only

515

party that I know in this matter. I therefore write to ask if you sanction this omission, and if there are any other sentiments to be omitted in the remainder of my article. If you do not sanction it—or whether you do or not—will you do me the justice to print that sentence, as an omitted one, indicating its place, in the August number?

I am not willing to be associated in any way, unnecessarily, with parties who will confess themselves so bigoted & timid as this implies. I could excuse a man who was afraid of an uplifted fist, but if one habitually manifests fear at the utterance of a sincere thought, I must think that his life is a kind of nightmare continued into broad daylight. It is hard to conceive of one so completely derivative. Is this the avowed character of the Atlantic Monthly? I should like an early reply.

Yrs truly,
Henry D. Thoreau

The lines of force that converged in this letter could be detected in the earlier notes. Thoreau's insistence that he be allowed to read his printer's proofs is clear there. So is his cold and formal attitude toward Lowell—an attitude that Lowell doubtless matched. Canby has said that the letter should be framed in every editor's office as a reminder. If Thoreau ever received a reply, we have no record of it. MS., Harvard.

To H. G. O. BLAKE

Concord, June 29, 1858, 8 A.M.

Mr. Blake,—

Edward Hoar and I propose to start for the White Mountains in a covered wagon, with one horse, on the morning of Thursday the 1st of July, intending to explore the mountain tops botanically, and camp on them at least several times. Will you take a seat in the wagon with us? Mr. Hoar prefers to hire the horse and wagon himself. Let us hear by express, as soon as you can, whether you will join us here by the earliest train Thursday morning, or Wednesday night. Bring your map

of the mountains, and as much *provision* for the road as you can,—hard bread, sugar, tea, meat, etc.,—for we intend to live like gipsies; also, a blanket and some thick clothes for the mountain top.

Text, Familiar Letters of Thoreau, *p. 385.*

___

To DANIEL RICKETSON

Concord, June 30, 1858.

Friend Ricketson,—

I am on the point of starting for the White Mountains in a wagon with my neighbor Edward Hoar, and I write to you now rather to apologize for not writing, than to answer worthily your three notes. I thank you heartily for them. You will not care for a little delay in acknowledging them, since your date shows that you can afford to wait. Indeed, my head has been so full of company, &c., that I could not reply to you fitly before, nor can I now.

As for preaching to men these days in the Walden strain,—is it of any consequence to preach to an audience of men who *can* fail? or who can be *revived?* There are few beside. Is it any success to interest these parties? If a man has *speculated* and *failed,* he will probably do these things again, in spite of you or me.

I confess that it is rare that I rise to sentiment in my relations to men, —ordinarily to a mere patient, or may be wholesome good-will. I can imagine something more, but the truth compels me to regard the ideal and the actual as two things.

Channing has come, and as suddenly gone, and left a short poem, "Near Home," published (?) or printed by Munroe, which I have hardly had time to glance at. As you may guess, I learn nothing of you from him.

You already foresee my answer to your invitation to make you a summer visit—I am bound for the Mountains. But I trust that you have

517

vanquished, ere this, those dusky demons that seem to lurk around the Head of the River. You know that this warfare is nothing but a kind of nightmare—and it is our thoughts alone which give those *un-worthies* any body or existence.

I made an excursion with Blake, of Worcester, to Monadnoc, a few weeks since. We took our blankets and food, spent two nights on the mountain, and did not go into a house.

Alcott has been very busy for a long time repairing an old shell of a house, and I have seen very little of him. I have looked more at the houses which birds build. Watson made us all very generous presents from his nursery in the spring especially did he remember Alcott.

Excuse me for not writing any more at present, and remember me to your family.

Yours,

H. D. Thoreau.

Text, Ricketson, *pp. 79–80.*

To H. G. O. BLAKE

Concord, July 1, 1858

July 1st. Last Monday evening Mr. Edward Hoar said that he thought of going to the White Mountains. I remarked casually that I should like to go well enough if I could afford it. Whereupon he declared that if I would go with him, he would hire a horse and wagon, so that the ride would cost me nothing, and we would explore the mountain tops *botanically*, camping on them many nights. The next morning I suggested you and Brown's accompanying us in another wagon, and we could all camp and cook, gipsy-like, along the way,—or, perhaps, if the horse could draw us, you would like to bear half the expense of the horse and wagon, and take a seat with us. He liked either proposition, but said, that if you would take a seat with us, he would

prefer to hire the horse and wagon himself. You could contribute something else if you pleased. Supposing that Brown would be confined, I wrote to you accordingly, by *express* on Tuesday morning, *via* Boston, stating that we should start to-day, suggesting provision, thick clothes, etc., and asking for an answer; but I have not received one. I have just heard that you *may* be at Sterling, and now write to say that we shall still be glad if you will join us at Senter Harbor, where we expect to be next Monday morning. In any case, will you please direct a letter to us there *at once?*

Text, Familiar Letters of Thoreau, *pp. 385–86. Sanborn prints this letter and that of June 29 as one, with a white space between.*

To G. W. CURTIS

Concord Aug. 18th '58

Dear Sir,

Channing's poem "Near Home" was printed (if not published) by James Munroe and Co. Boston. C. brought it to me some seven weeks ago with the remark—"Knowing your objection to manuscript, I got it printed"—and I do not know that he presented it to anyone else. I have not been to the city of late, but Emerson told me that he found a small pile of them at Munroe's, and bought two or three; though Munroe said that he was forbidden to advertise it. Of course this is equivalent to dedicating it "to whom it may concern." Others also have bought it, for fifty cents; but C. still persists, in his way, in saying that it is not published. Ought not a poem to publish itself?

I am glad if you are not weary of the Maine Woods, partly because I have another and a larger slice to come.

As for the presidency,—I cannot speak for my neighbors, but, for my own part, I am politically so benighted (or belighted?) that I do not know what Seward's qualifications are. I know, however, that no one

in whom I could feel much interest would stand any chance of being elected. But the nail which is hard to drive is hard to draw.

Yours truly
Henry D. Thoreau

MS., Abernethy (*typescript*).

To JAMES RUSSELL LOWELL

I shall be glad to receive payment for my story as soon as convenient—will you be so good as to direct it this way.

So Thoreau wrote stiffly to Lowell in a letter that has been erroneously dated 1856. As of September 1858 the Atlantic *owed Thoreau $198 by his calculation for the Maine woods material it had printed, but it took at least one more note, that of October 4, 1858, to get him his money. Text, catalogue of the Moulton sale (Merwin-Clayton, November 9, 1905), where the letter is described as 1 p. 8vo, dated from Concord, September 1, 1856.*

To JAMES RUSSELL LOWELL

Concord Oct 4 1858

James R. Lowell Esq.
Dear Sir,

I wrote to you more than a month ago respecting what was due me from the Atlantic monthly, but I have not heard from you. Perhaps

520

you have not received my note. As I count, your magazine is indebted to me for thirty-three pages at six dollars a page—$198.00

I should be glad to know if you receive this, and also when I may expect to be paid.

Yrs
Henry D. Thoreau

This is the last communication to Lowell that we have. Presumably Thoreau was at length paid. He had nothing else to do with the Atlantic *until Lowell was succeeded in the summer of 1861 by James T. Fields. MS., Harvard; previously unpublished.*

To DANIEL RICKETSON

Concord Oct 31 1858

Friend Ricketson,

I have not seen anything of your English Australian yet. Edward Hoar, my companion in Maine and at the White *Mts.*, his sister Elizabeth, and a Miss Prichard, another neighbor of ours, went to Europe in the Niagara on the 6th. I told them to look out for you under the Yardley Oaks, but it seems that they will not find you there.

I had a pleasant time in Tuckerman's Ravine at the White *Mts* in July, entertaining four beside my self under my little tent through some soaking rains; & more recently I have taken an interesting walk with Channing about Cape Ann. We were obliged to "dipper it" a good way, on account of the scarcity of fresh water, for we got most of our meals by the shore.

C[hanning] is understood to be here for the winter,—but I rarely see him.

I should be pleased to see your face here in the course of the Indian summer, which may still be expected—if any authority can tell us when the phenomenon *does* occur. We would like to hear the story of your

travels—for if you have not been fairly intoxicated with Europe, you have been half-seas-over, & so probably can tell more about it—

[Yours truly
Henry D. Thoreau]

We do not know who Ricketson's English Australian was. When Ricketson's son and daughter printed this letter they misread the date as 1856 and, incidentally, read "English author" for "English Australian" (Ricketson, p. 69). MS., Huntington; part of the page has been cut out for the autograph, and the signature and complimentary close have been added in pencil in another hand.

From DANIEL RICKETSON

The Shanty, 9 p.m., Nov. 3d, 1858.

Dear Thoreau,—

Your truly welcome note of the 31st ult. reached me only this evening. I am sorry our English Australian has not been in Concord. He is quite an original, and appeared to be as familiar with the Concord worthies, as though he had been a fellow townsman of theirs. He is a young man, but has seen a good deal of the world, inside and outside—has lived some years in and about London, and fellowshipped with all sorts of folks, authors, gypsies, vagrants, &c., his accounts of which are entertaining—talks easy and well, has no vain pretensions, although I found incidentally that he is highly connected—I believe, with the family of the celebrated Lord Lyttleton, of monody memory—wears common cheap clothes, and carries his own baggage, a small leathern bag, is short and rather stout, full beard and of sandy complexion, smokes a pipe a good deal, likes malt liquor and an occasional glass of whiskey or gin, but is by no means intemperate, only English and cosmopolitan in his habits. He has a little book in project to be called "Pots of Beer," the chapters headed Pot First, Pot Second, &c., so on—

522

Conversations and reflections over these inspiring vessels. (P.S. Of wrath?)

I told Channing about him (who, by the way—C.—I found at his old post at the Mercury office, last week), and he said that you would not like his pipe. This puts me to thinking, as Jack Downing would say, and I want to take this opportunity to apologize for having so often offended you by my untimely *puffs*. I assure you, in future, that I will strive to refrain in your presence, for I am ready to "acknowledge the corn," and plead guilty, craving pardon for my manifold sins against your purer tastes.

I feel deeply disappointed and somewhat chagrined at my failure in going to Europe, and hope to master sufficient courage to embark again next spring, when I shall probably go from New York, whence like the *decensus averni* there is no return. You would like to know more about my voyage. I was really "half seas over," as you intimate, in more senses than one, for my sea-sickness operated on my brain like a potent stimulus, accompanied with the most painful vertigo. I felt somewhat as I conclude a dancing dervish might, after having spun round for some time, that is if they ever do so, or is it only the Shakers that perform these gyrations? But the newspaper I send you will give you an account of my experiences on board ship. The paragraph about the moose is quite Thoreau.$^{ish}_{ian}$—take your choice—and the phrase, *tribute to the sea,* is, I think, borrowed from your account of your winter voyage to Nantucket, some years ago.

I have published my history of New Bedford in a neat duodecimo of 400 pages, and am *prospecting* for a volume of poems—also writing some sketches called "Smoke from my Pipe"—in the second chapter of which I introduce a certain philosopher, a friend of mine, who built his own house, earned his own livelihood, and lived alone some years, a genial man, a scholar, &c. Can you guess him out? I think I may also introduce, all of course, in a respectful and quiet way, some other of the Concordian band—but more of this anon, as we authors say, when we run out our line.

I am quite tempted by your kind invitation to visit Concord during the "Indian summer," should such a boon come this month. I may go to Boston soon, and may also possibly get as far as Concord for a few days —but whether I do or not, I want you to come down and visit me. I value your acquaintance highly, and I want to see Mr. Emerson and Father

Alcott once more. Life is too short, and noble men and women too scarce, for me to lose any opportunity of enjoying the society of such, when I can do so without obtrusion.

With my warm regards to your family and my other Concord friends, and hoping to hear from you again very soon, I remain, yours faithfully,

Daniel Ricketson.

Please return the newspaper.

I am amused by your account of your party in the rain under your little tent. I trust your friends were quite contented with your hospitality.

Text, Ricketson, *pp. 81–83.*

To DANIEL RICKETSON

Concord Nov. 6 1858

Friend Ricketson,

I was much pleased with your lively and life-like account of your voyage. You were more than repaid for your trouble, after all. The coast of Nova-Scotia which you sailed along from Windsor westward is particularly interesting to the historian of this country, having been settled earlier than Plymouth. Your "Isle of Haut" is properly "Isle Haute" or the High Island of Champlain's map. There is another off the coast of Maine. By the way, the American elk, of *American authors,* (Cervus Canadensis) is a distinct animal from the moose (cervus alces), though the latter is also called elk by many.

You drew a very vivid portrait of the Australian—short & stout, with a pipe in his mouth, and his book inspired by beer, Pot 1st, Pot 2 &c. I suspect that he must be pot-bellied withal. Methinks I see the smoke going up from him as from a cottage on the moor. If he does not quench

his genius with his beer, it may burst into a clear flame at last. However, perhaps he intentionally adopts the low style.

What do you mean by that ado about smoking and my "purer tastes"? I should like his pipe as well as his beer, at least. Neither of them is so bad as to be "highly connected," which you say he is, unfortunately. Did you ever see an English traveller who was not? Even they who swing for their crimes may boast at last that they are *highly connected.*—No! I expect nothing but pleasure in "smoke from *your* pipe."

You & the Australian must have put your heads together when you concocted those titles—with pipes in your mouths over a pot of beer. I suppose that your chapters are Whiff the Ist—Whiff the 2nd &c But of course it is a more modest expression for "Fire from my Genius."

You must have been very busy since you came back, or before you sailed, to have brought out your History, of whose publication I had not heard. I suppose that I have read it in The Mercury. Yet I am curious to see how it looks in a volume, with your name on the title page.

I am more curious still about the poems. Pray put some sketches into the book—your shanty for frontispiece; Arthur & Walton's boat, (if you can) running for Cuttyhunk in a tremendous gale, not forgetting "Be honest boys" &c nearby; the Middleboro' Ponds with a certain island looming in the distance; the Quaker meetinghouse, and the Brady House, if you like; the villagers catching smelts with dip nets in the twilight, at the head of the River &c &c. Let it be a local and villageous book as much as possible. Let some one make a characteristic selection of mottoes from your shanty walls, and sprinkle them in an irregular manner, at all angles, over the fly leaves and margins, as a man stamps his name in a hurry; and also canes, pipes, and jacknives, of all your patterns, about the frontispiece. I can think of plenty of devices for tail-pieces. Indeed I should like to see a hair-pillow, accurately drawn, for one; a cat with a bell on, for another; the old horse with his age printed in the hollow of his back; half a cocoa-nut shell by a spring; a sheet of blotted paper; a settle occupied by a settler at full length, &c &c &c. Call all the arts to your aid. Dont wait for the Indian Summer, but bring it with you

Yrs, truly
H. D. T.

P. S. Let me ask a favor. I am trying to write something about the autumnal tints, and I wish to know how much our trees differ from

English & European ones in this respect. Will you observe, or learn for me what English or European trees, if any, still retain their leaves in Mr. [James] Arnold's garden (the gardener will supply the true names) & also if the foliages of any (& what) European or foreign trees there have been brilliant the past month. If you will do this, you will greatly oblige me. I return the newspaper with this.

No doubt the kind of good "local" book Thoreau advises Ricketson to write was the kind he himself hoped to prepare about Concord some day. The information on leaves that Thoreau requested in his postscript was put to excellent use in the essay "Autumnal Tints" in the Atlantic Monthly *for October 1862, after his death. MS., Huntington.*

From DANIEL RICKETSON

The Shanty, Nov. 10th, 1858.

Friend Thoreau,—

Your very pleasant and encouraging letter reached me on Monday (the 8th). Pleasant from the cheerful spirit in which it was written, and encouraging from the appreciation you express for the little portraits of my late travelling experiences I sent you.

This forenoon I made a visit to Arnold's grounds, walking to and from through the woods and fields most of the way on the route by the upper road by which the wind-mill stands. In company with the gardener, rejoicing in the appropriate and symphonious name of Wellwood Young, whose broad Gaelic accent rendered an attentive ear necessary to catch the names, I made the following list. The Scotch larch, for instance, he said came from Norroway (Norway), the yellow fringes of which were still hanging on the branches.

The following is the list I made in accordance with your request. I give the names without any order, just as we happened to meet the trees. Horse-chestnut, quite full of yellow and green foliage. English

walnut, do. Beech, Linden, Hawthorn (nearly perfect in green foliage, only a little decayed at the top, but in a sheltered place), Silver Linden, Copper Beech, Elm, Weeping Ash, Weeping Willow, Scotch Larch, Euanimus Europeus (Gardener's name), I suppose correct. These are all European or English, I believe.

I give a few others not European, viz: Osage orange (or Maclura), Cornus Florida (handsome) Tulip, three-thorned Acacia, Mexican Cypress.

There were numerous shrubs in full leaf, among them the Guelder Rose. Vines, Bignonia radicans and Bignonia cuminata.

I send a few leaves. The largest green leaf is the American Linden— the smaller, the European copper leaved Beech. One English Elm (green), and two smaller and narrower leaves, the *Euanimus Europeus.*

I am sorry the list is no fuller, but I think it includes all in these grounds. The location is quite sheltered. I could not ascertain from the gardener what trees exhibited particular brilliancy of foliage last month. I conclude, however, that these I have named were quite fresh up to the last of October.

It is barely possible I may reach Concord on Saturday next and remain over Sunday, but hardly probable as they say.

Channing I understand has been to Concord since I wrote you last, and is now here again. Is he not quite as much a "creature of moods" as old Sudbury Inn? But I am in poor mood for writing, and besides it is nearly dark (5 p.m.).

May I not hear from you again soon, and may I not expect a visit also ere long?

As this is only a business letter I trust you will excuse its dulness. Hoping I have supplied you (Channing has just come in) with what you wanted, I conclude.

Yours faithfully,
D. R.

P. S. If I should not go to Concord I will endeavor to get one of my books to you soon.

Text, Ricketson, *pp. 86–88.*

To DANIEL RICKETSON

Concord Nov. 22d 1858

Friend Ricketson
    I thank you for your "History." Though I have not yet read it again, I have looked far enough to see that I like the homeliness of it; that is the good old-fashioned way of writing as if you actually lived where you wrote. A man's interest in a single blue-bird, is more than a complete, but dry, list of the fauna & flora of a town. It is also a considerable advantage to be able to say at any time, if R. is not here, here in his book. Alcott, being here and inquiring after you (whom he has been expecting) I lent the book to him almost immediately. He talks of going west the latter part of this week.
    Channing is here again, as I am told, but I have not seen him.
    I thank you also for the account of the trees. It was to my purpose, and I hope that you got something out of it too. I suppose that the cold weather prevented your coming here. Suppose you try a winter walk or skate—Please remember me to your family.

Yrs H. D. T.

Ricketson's History of New Bedford, *published by its author, came out this year.* MS., Huntington.

From THOMAS CHOLMONDELEY

Donegana Friday 26th

My dear Thoreau
    I am at *Montreal* & I think I shall pass south not far from you. I shall be on Tuesday evening at the Revere at Boston. I am going to

spend the winter in the West Indies. What do you say to come there too?

Yrs ever
Thos Cholmondeley

Henry Thoreau Esq Concord Massachusetts

Donegana's was a Montreal hotel. Cholmondeley visited Thoreau in Concord a few days later. MS., Berg.

From THOMAS G. CARY, GEORGE LIVERMORE, AND HENRY G. DENNY

Boston, December 1st, 1858.

Sir:—

At the annual meeting of the Association of the Alumni of Harvard College, held in July last, a committee, appointed at a previous meeting "to take into consideration the state of the college library, and to devise means for its increase, maintenance, and administration," made their report in print, a copy of which has been sent to you. A committee has lately been appointed to carry the recommendations of this report into effect, in behalf of whom we now ask of you a contribution to aid in supplying the deficiencies that have been made known.

If you should not yet have examined the report, we earnestly ask that it may receive your particular attention, together with the statements appended thereto from the president, the librarians, and other officers of the college, showing such pressing want of means to keep up with the advance of the age, that professors and tutors are obliged to expend a portion of their moderate salaries in the purchase of new and expensive books, which should be found in the library, for their use and for that of the students.

The college has ever maintained the highest rank among the institutions of learning in the United States, and the influence which it has exerted on the intellectual and moral culture not only of this community, but, to a great extent, of the whole country, is very generally

acknowledged. In aiding it to maintain this pre-eminence and to continue the exercise of this salutary influence, the library is of the highest importance; yet the provision for its increase is utterly inadequate to supply, from year to year, even a moderate portion of the new works actually needed to meet the reasonable expectation of its friends and of the community.

This state of things seems to call earnestly upon all who have been at any time connected with the college, to make some return for the advantages which they have received from the munificence of its former benefactors, by providing in their turn for the wants that have arisen in the lapse of years and the progress of literature and science; it calls on the community, in the midst of which the college is situated, to sustain one of its noblest ornaments in a manner creditable to itself and to the country, and it calls on the friends of education generally to assist in maintaining at Cambridge the highest standard of scholarship.

Again referring to the printed statements for a more particular account of the wants of the library, we respectfully urge you to aid us in obtaining such a fund for investment as may be necessary for its proper support, feeling sure that only a general misapprehension of its resources has prevented the friends of the college and the community at large from placing it long ago beyond the need of such an appeal. To keep scholarship at Cambridge even with the advance of knowledge in this age, requires, for the annual purchase of new works, the income of a fund of not less than one hundred thousand dollars, and such a fund we hope to obtain.

While the exigencies of the case seem to demand a liberal subscription from those whose means will warrant it, we beg every one to respond to our call in some amount, however small, remembering that a few dollars from each one of the many who have not the ability to give largely, will in the aggregate be an important aid to the library.

We request you, therefore, on the receipt of this communication, or as soon after as may be convenient, to return the annexed paper, with your name and the amount of your donation, (either enclosing the money, or stating the time when we may expect to receive it,) to Henry G. Denny, Secretary and Treasurer of the Committee, 42, Court Street, or to Amos A. Lawrence, Esq., Treasurer of Harvard College, 30, Court Street, Boston. You will also confer a great favor by obtaining, as far as you have the power, further subscriptions, or by promoting bequests from those who are liberally disposed, in aid of the fund.

Should you not have received a copy of the report, please send your post-office address to the secretary of the committee, and one will be forwarded immediately.

We are, Sir, respectfully,

Your obedient servants,
Thomas G. Cary,
George Livermore,
Henry G. Denny.

A circular letter sent to all the Harvard College alumni. MS. facsimile, Kenneth Walter Cameron, The Transcendentalists and Minerva, *p. 486.*

To DANIEL RICKETSON

Concord Dec 6 1858

Friend Ricketson,

Thomas Cholmondeley, my English acquaintance, is here, on his way to the West Indies. He wants to see New Bedford, a whaling town. I told him that I would like to introduce him to you there, thinking more of his seeing you than New Bedford. So we propose to come your way tomorrow. Excuse this short notice, for the time is short. If, on any account, it is inconvenient to see us, you will treat us accordingly.

Yours truly
Henry D. Thoreau

The proposed visit was made, and there is a good account of it in Ricketson's journal (Ricketson, *pp. 309–10*). *Cholmondeley soon left New England, went to Jamaica, and finally returned to his own country before the summer of 1859. MS.*, Abernethy (*typescript*).

From TICKNOR & FIELDS

Boston Decr 7/58

Henry D. Thoreau Esq Concord Mass.
Dear Sir
    Referring to our file of letters from 1857 we find a note from you of which the enclosed is a copy.
    As our letter to which it is a reply was missent we doubt not but our answer to yours of a few months since has been subjected to the same, or a similar irregularity.

Respectfully yours &c.
Ticknor & Fields
pr Clark

There is no copy of Thoreau's letter in the letterbooks. MS., Harvard (typescript); previously unpublished.

———————

From TICKNOR & CO.

Boston Dec. 15 1858

Mr. H. D. Thoreau Concord Mass.
Dear Sir,
    In our last account we credited you capl [cash?] on the balance of copies of Walden, including quite a number of copies then on hand unsold—as the Edition was so nearly out we paid for all at that time. We have never been out of the book but there is very little demand for it so the 16 cops. rqd were in the edition printed. We enclose ck

$11 [16? 18?] .25 for 15 cops Concord River sold leaving in our hands 17 cops.

Truly yours
W. D. Ticknor & Co.

MS., Harvard (*typescript*); *previously unpublished.*

To JOHN LANGDON SIBLEY

Concord Dec 19 1858.

Dear Sir,
   I return to the Library Marquette's "Recit des Voyages" &c the unbound reprint, one volume.

Yrs respectfully
Henry D. Thoreau

This note is addressed merely to the "Librarian of Harvard College." MS., Yale University Library; *previously unpublished.*

1859

Gold was discovered in Colorado, gold and silver (the Comstock Lode) in Nevada. A treaty of friendship, commerce, and navigation was signed with Paraguay. At Vicksburg a commercial convention recommended that all laws prohibiting the African slave trade be repealed. John Wise started from St. Louis in a balloon and reached Henderson, New York, 802 miles away, in twenty hours. Emile Gravelet ("M. Blondin") crossed the Niagara River below the Falls on a tightrope. The first Pullman made its initial trip from Bloomington to Chicago. J. B. Clark introduced a resolution in the House of Representatives to the effect that a proposal to circulate H. R. Helper's book *The Impending Crisis* was incipient treason. The first oil well was drilled near Titusville, Pennsylvania. With the assistance of Colonel Robert E. Lee and a company of marines the local militia captured John Brown and his followers at the Harpers Ferry arsenal. On December 2 Brown was hanged at Charlestown, [West] Virginia.

Thoreau's father died in February. He had been a quiet man, interested in Concord town rather than Concord country. Added responsibilities came to Thoreau, for now he had to take over the running of the profitable graphite business. He also received his most extensive surveying contract. Because the Concord, Sudbury, and Assabet Rivers were backing up and flooding the adjoining hay meadows, the owners of these lands hired him to measure the water depths and write the history of the bridges and their abutments. Thoreau believed that he could rightly call himself a civil engineer, and he signed himself so. His health was not of the best. He found time to write a good deal in the *Journal*. Here are the subjects for the last month of the year: a ride with an insane man; a glaze on the trees; John Brown as a preacher;

Brown's translation; a lichen day; Walden in a mist; tansy; Brown's greatness; Brown and public opinion; present, past, and future; a warm, soft sky; Dr. Ripley's firewood; an Irish woodchopper; faery visitors; watching the clouds; snowballs made by the wind; from the first Georgic; a classification of snowstorms; the "philosophy" of wood; Gerard's Herbal; seeds as food for birds; the squirrels' winter food; the divinity of youth; a lodging snow; the snow wrinkled with age; a reminiscence of summer; fisherman's luck; a large blueberry bush; fishes in a newly dug pond; a flock of snow buntings; liatris in winter; a blueberry grove; a golden-crested wren; the artillery of the frozen pond; the life of the pickerel fisher; headgear of men and women; women and boot-heels; a brute with a gun; muskrat houses and muskrat food; scientific nomenclature; open places in the river; the breath of the river; remarkable clouds; a shrike; the musquash in winter; winter fog; our system of education; and thoughts and the man. Probably the most important item, mentioned four times in the printed headings in the *Journal*, was John Brown.

Concord, January 1, 1859.

Mr. Blake,—

It may interest you to hear that Cholmondeley has been this way again, *via* Montreal and Lake Huron, going to the West Indies, or rather to Weiss-nicht-wo, whither he urges me to accompany him. He is rather more demonstrative than before, and, on the whole, what would be called "a good fellow,"—is a man of principle, and quite reliable, but very peculiar. I have been to New Bedford with him, to show him a whaling town and Ricketson. I was glad to hear that you had called on R. How did you like him? I suspect that you did not see one another fairly.

I have lately got back to that glorious society called Solitude, where we meet our friends continually, and can imagine the outside world also to be peopled. Yet some of my acquaintance would fain hustle me into the almshouse for *the sake of society*, as if I were pining for that diet, when I seem to myself a most befriended man, and find constant employment. However, they do not believe a word I say. They have got a club, the handle of which is in the Parker House at Boston, and with this they beat me from time to time, expecting to make me tender or minced meat, so fit for a club to dine off.

> "Hercules with his club
> The Dragon did drub;
> But More of More Hall,
> With nothing at all,
> He slew the Dragon of Wantley."

Ah! that More of More Hall knew what fair play was. Channing, who wrote to me about it once, brandishing the club vigorously (being set on by another, probably), says *now*, seriously, that he is sorry to find by my letters that I am "absorbed in politics," and adds, begging my

pardon for his plainness, "Beware of an extraneous life!" and so he does his duty, and washes his hands of me. I tell him that it is as if he should say to the sloth, that fellow that creeps so slowly along a tree, and cries *ai* from time to time, "Beware of dancing!"

The doctors are all agreed that I am suffering from want of society. Was never a case like it. First, I did not know that I was suffering at all. Secondly, as an Irishman might say, I had thought it was indigestion of the society I got. [It is indispensable that I should take a dose of Lowell & Agassiz & Woodman.]

As for the Parker House, I went there once, when the Club was away, but I found it hard to see through the cigar smoke, and men were deposited about in chairs over the marble floor, as thick as legs of bacon in a smoke-house. It was all smoke, and no salt, Attic or other. The only room in Boston which I visit with alacrity is the Gentlemen's Room at the Fitchburg Depot, where I wait for the cars, sometimes for two hours, in order to get out of town. It is a paradise to the Parker House, for no smoking is allowed, and there is far more retirement. A large and respectable club of us hire it (Town and Country Club), and I am pretty sure to find some one there whose face is set the same way as my own.

My last essay, on which I am still engaged, is called Autumnal Tints. I do not know how readable (*i. e.*, by me to others) it will be.

I met Mr. [Henry] James the other night at Emerson's, at an Alcottian conversation, at which, however, Alcott did not talk much, being disturbed by James's opposition. The latter is a hearty man enough, with whom you can differ very satisfactorily, on account of both his doctrines and his good temper. He utters *quasi* philanthropic dogmas in a metaphysic dress; but they are for all practical purposes very crude. He charges society with all the crime committed, and praises the criminal for committing it. But I think that all the remedies he suggests out of his head—for he goes no farther, hearty as he is—would leave us about where we are now. For, of course, it is not by a gift of turkeys on Thanksgiving Day that he proposes to convert the criminal, but by a true sympathy with each one,—with him, among the rest, who lyingly tells the world from the gallows that he has never been treated kindly by a single mortal since he was born. But it is not so easy a thing to sympathize with another, though you may have the best disposition to do it. There is Dobson over the hill. Have not you and I and all the world been trying, ever since he was born, to sympathize with him? (as doubt-

537

less he with us), and yet we have got no farther than to send him to the House of Correction once at least; and he, on the other hand, as I hear, has sent us to another place several times. This is the real state of things, as I understand it, at least so far as James's remedies go. We are now, alas! exercising what charity we actually have, and new laws would not give us any more. But, perchance, we might make some improvements in the House of Correction. You and I are Dobson; what will James do for us?

Have you found at last in your wanderings a place where the solitude is sweet?

What mountain are you camping on nowadays? Though I had a good time at the mountains, I confess that the journey did not bear any fruit that I know of. I did not expect it would. The mode of it was not simple and adventurous enough. You must first have made an infinite demand, and not unreasonably, but after a corresponding outlay, have an all-absorbing purpose, and at the same time that your feet bear you hither and thither, travel much more in imagination.

To let the mountains slide, —live at home like a traveler. It should not be in vain that these things are shown us from day to day. Is not each withered leaf that I see in my walks something which I have traveled to find?—traveled, who can tell how far? What a fool he must be who thinks that his El Dorado is anywhere but where he lives!

We are always, methinks, in some kind of ravine, though our bodies may walk the smooth streets of Worcester. Our souls (I use this word for want of a better) are ever perched on its rocky sides, overlooking that lowland. (What a more than Tuckerman's Ravine is the body itself, in which the "soul" is encamped, when you come to look into it! However, eagles always have chosen such places for their eyries.)

Thus is it ever with your fair cities of the plain. Their streets may be paved with silver and gold, and six carriages roll abreast in them, but the real *homes* of the citizens are in the Tuckerman's Ravines which ray out from that centre into the mountains round about, one for each man, woman, and child. The masters of life have so ordered it. That is their *beau-ideal* of a country seat. There is no danger of being *tuckered* out before you get to it.

So we live in Worcester and in Concord, each man taking his exercise regularly in his ravine, like a lion in his cage, and sometimes spraining his ankle there. We have very few clear days, and a great many small plagues which keep us busy. Sometimes, I suppose, you hear a neigh-

bor halloo (Brown, may be) and think it is a bear. Nevertheless, on the whole, we think it very grand and exhilarating, this ravine life. It is a capital advantage withal, living so high, the excellent drainage of that city of God. Routine is but a shallow and insignificant sort of ravine, such as the ruts are, the conduits of puddles. But these ravines are the source of mighty streams, precipitous, icy, savage, as they are, haunted by bears and loup-cerviers; there are born not only Sacos and Amazons, but prophets who will redeem the world. The at last smooth and fertilizing water at which nations drink and navies supply themselves begins with melted glaciers, and burst thunder-spouts. Let us pray that, if we are not flowing through some Mississippi valley which we fertilize, —and it is not likely we are,—we may know ourselves shut in between grim and mighty mountain walls amid the clouds, falling a thousand feet in a mile, through dwarfed fir and spruce, over the rocky insteps of slides, being exercised in our minds, and so developed.

The Saturday Club met the last Saturday of each month at the Parker House. Among the members were Emerson, Longfellow, Lowell, Holmes, and other men of letters, as well as such semiliterary figures as Louis Agassiz and young Horatio Woodman. Text, Familiar Letters of Thoreau, *pp. 399–405. The manuscript was sold by Charles F. Libbie & Co. at the Hathaway-Richardson sale of May 9–10, 1911; the sale catalogue quotes the sentence bracketed.*

From HENRY WALKER FROST?

Boston Jan 7th 1859

Mr. H. D. Thoreau.
Dear Sir,
    Will you do me the favor of meeting me at the Probate Court in East Cambridge on Tuesday next (11th inst) at ten o'clock A.M. in order to prove my father's will to which [page torn] sness. My mother [page torn]

"Three years ago," Thoreau remarked to Ricketson in a letter dated February 12, "I was called with my Father to be a witness to the signing of our neighbor Mr Frost's will. . . . I was lately required to go to Cambridge to testify to the genuineness of the will." Barzillai Frost died December 8, 1858. The note given above is probably from his elder son. Young Frost, a member of the Harvard class of 1858, was living in Boston, reading law and attending the lectures of the Harvard Law School. MS., Morgan; previously unpublished. The remainder of the manuscript is torn away.

To H. G. O. BLAKE

Concord, January 19, 1859.

Mr. Blake,—

If I could have given a favorable report as to the skating, I should have answered you earlier. About a week before you wrote there was good skating; there is now none. As for the lecture, I shall be glad to come. I cannot now say when, but I will let you know, I think within a week or ten days at most, and will then leave you a week clear to make the arrangements in. I will bring something else than "What shall it profit a Man?" My father is very sick, and has been for a long time, so that there is the more need of me at home. This occurs to me, even when contemplating so short an excursion as to Worcester.

I want very much to see or hear your account of your adventures in the Ravine [Tuckerman's], and I trust I shall do so when I come to Worcester. Cholmondeley has been here again, returning from Virginia (for he went no farther south) to Canada; and will go thence to Europe, he thinks, in the spring, and never ramble any more. (January 29). I am expecting daily that my father will die, therefore I cannot leave home at present. I will write you again within ten days.

Thoreau's father died February 3. Text, Familiar Letters of Thoreau, pp. 405–6.

From THOMAS G. CARY AND HENRY G. DENNY

Boston, January 21st, 1859.

Sir,

In behalf of the library committee of the Association of the Alumni of Harvard College, we send you herewith copies of the circular which you have kindly undertaken to distribute among your class; together with copies of the report on the state of the library, which was presented to the association at their last annual meeting, to be forwarded to those who have not yet received it.

The committee would suggest that a personal interview with each one who is applied to for a subscription is highly important, and should be had when practicable; it being likely to command more attention than a written communication, and to afford a better opportunity for a full explanation of the subject. They hope also, that, in every case where a personal application cannot be made, a letter will be forwarded with the circular, advancing such special arguments as may occur to the writer as likely to be effective, from his knowledge of the disposition, habits, or taste of the person addressed.

It seems to the committee desirable that no graduate should be passed over in the distribution of the circulars, on account of any supposed inability or indisposition to contribute, as instances have come to their knowledge where interest in this movement has been expressed, and aid has been readily given, when there had seemed good reason to doubt the utility of any application for it.

Information concerning the library and of the progress of the subscription can be had at the office of the secretary of the committee, 42, Court Street, where additional copies of the circular and of the pamphlet containing the report, together with the addresses of the graduates so far as known, can be obtained if needed.

You are requested to make a return of the subscriptions procured by you, to the chairman of the committee or to the secretary, as often as once in three or four weeks, and to give immediate notice of any unusually large sum which may be subscribed, in order that accounts may

541

from time to time be published for the information and encouragement of those engaged in this work.

We are, Sir, respectfully yours,

> Thomas G. Cary, *Chairman.*
> Henry G. Denny, *Secretary.*

We hereby agree to contribute the sums set against our respective names towards a fund to be permanently invested, the income of which shall be applied to the purchase of books for the public library of Harvard College.

A form letter sent out, according to Kenneth Cameron, to all members of the alumni. The italicized last paragraph was returned by Thoreau in his letter of reply, p. 545. MS. facsimile, Kenneth Cameron, The Transcendentalists and Minerva, *p. 487.*

To H. G. O. BLAKE

Concord Feb. 7th 1859

Mr. Blake,

I will come and read you an extract from "Autumnal Tints," on Tuesday the 15th, of this month, if that is agreeable to you,—leaving here probably at noon. Perhaps you had better acknowledge the receipt of this.

H. D. T.

Apparently the lecture was postponed until February 22, for Sallie Holley, in A Life for Liberty *(p. 167), tells of hearing a lecture on "Autumnal Tints" in Worcester on that date. MS., Berg, copy in Blake's hand; previously unpublished.*

From DANIEL RICKETSON

The Shanty, 9 Feb. 1859.

My dear Friend,—

I received last evening a Boston newspaper with your super-scription, containing the record of the decease of your father. It had previously been published in the New Bedford Mercury, perhaps by Channing.

You must all feel his loss very much, particularly your mother. I have rarely, if ever, met a man who inspired me with more respect. He appeared to me to be a real embodiment of honest virtue, as well as a true gentleman of the old school. I also recognized in him a fund of good fellowship, or what would perhaps better and more respectfully express it, kindly friendship. I remember with pleasure, a ramble I took with him about Concord some two or three years ago, at a time when you were away from home, on which occasion I was much impressed with his good sense, his fine social nature, and genuine hospitality. He reminded me much of my own father, in fact, I never saw a man more like him even in his personal appearance and manners—both bore upon their countenances the impress of care and sorrow, a revelation of the experience of life, written in the most legible characters, and one which always awakens my deepest sympathy and reverence.

I doubt not but that he was a good man, and however we may be unable to peer beyond this sphere of experience, may we not trust that some good angel, perhaps that of his mother (was her name Jeanie Burns?), has already welcomed him to the spirit land? At any rate, if there be any award for virtue and well doing I think it is for such as he. Veiled as the future is in mystery profound, I think we may fully rely upon Divine Wisdom who has seen it proper not only to conceal from us knowledge beyond this life, but has also wrapped us in so much *obscurity* even here. But let us go on trustfully in Him—the sun yet shines, the birds sing, the flowers bloom, and Nature is still as exhaustless as ever in her charms and riches for those who love her.

I trust that your mother and sister will find that consolation which they so much need. They as well as you have my warmest sympathy, and it is a pleasurable sorrow for me to bear my poor tribute to the memory and worth of him from whom you have so lately parted.

It seems to me that Nature—and by this I always mean the out-o'-door life in woods and fields, by streams and lakes, etc.—affords the best balm for our wounded spirits. One of the best things written by Francis Jeffrey, and which I have tacked upon my Shanty wall, is, "If it were not for my love of beautiful nature and poetry, my heart would have died within me long ago."

Would not a little run from home soon, if you can be spared, be well for you? Can you not catch the early spring a little in advance? We are probably a week or two before you in her maiden steps. Soon shall we see the catkins upon the willows, and hear the bluebird and song-sparrow again—how full of hope and cheer! Even this morning (a soft, drizzling one) I have heard the sweet, mellow, long-drawn pipe of the meadow lark. I have also seen robins occasionally during the winter, and a flock of quails several times, besides numerous partridges and rabbits.

I see nothing of Channing of late.

With my best regards to your mother and sister, believe me

Very truly your friend,
D. Ricketson

Please write me.

P.S.   Your letter indicates health of mind and good pluck. In fact, Dr. Pluck is a capital physician. Glory in whortle and blackberries; eat them like an Indian, abundantly and from the bushes and vines. When you can, smell of sweet fern, bayberry, sassafras, yellow birch, and rejoice in the songs of crickets and harvest flies.

Io Paean

Text, Ricketson, *pp. 89–92.*

To H. G. DENNY

Henry G. Denny, Esq.
Dear Sir,
    Inclosed please find five dollars, for the object above described.
I would gladly give more, but this exceeds my income from all sources
together for the last four months.

Y'rs respectfully,
Henry D. Thoreau.

Text, catalogue of the Denny sale (*Charles F. Libbie & Co., January
30 ff., 1906*).

From HENRY G. DENNY

42, Court St., Boston February 11th, 1859

Henry D. Thoreau, Esq.,
Dear Sir,
    I am happy to acknowledge the receipt of five dollars from you,
as a contribution to the fund for the public library of Harvard College.

Respectfully yours,
Henry G. Denny, Sec'y Library Committee

MS., Goodspeed's Book Shop, Boston (*typescript*); *previously unpublished.*

To DANIEL RICKETSON

Concord Feb 12 1859

Friend Ricketson,

      I thank you for your kind letter. I sent you the notice of my Father's death as much because you knew him, as because you know me. I can hardly realize that he is dead. He had been sick about two years, and at last declined rather rapidly though steadily. Till within a week or ten days before he died, he was hoping to see another spring; but he then discovered that this was a vain expectation, and thinking that he was dying he took his leave of us several times within a week before his departure. Once or twice he expressed a slight impatience at the delay. He was quite conscious to the last, and his death was so easy, that though we had all been sitting around the bed for an hour or more, expecting that event, as we had sat before, he was gone at last almost before we were aware of it.

      I am glad to read what you say about his social nature. I think I may say that he was wholly unpretending; and there was this peculiarity in his aim, that, though he had pecuniary difficulties to contend with the greater part of his life, he always studied merely how to make a *good* article, pencil or other, (for he practised various arts) and was never satisfied with what he had produced,—nor was he ever in the least disposed to put off a *poor* one for the sake of pecuniary gain;—as if he labored for a higher end.

      Though he was not very old, and was not a native of Concord, I think that he was, on the whole, more identified with Concord street than any man now alive, having come here when he was about twelve years old, and set up for himself as a merchant here at the age of 21, fifty years ago.

      As I sat in a circle the other evening with my mother and sister, my mother's two sisters & my Father's two sisters, it occurred to me that my Father, though 71 belonged to the youngest four of the eight who recently composed our family.

      How swiftly, at last, but unnoticed, a generation passes away! Three years ago I was called with my Father to be a witness to the signing of our neighbor Mr Frost's will. Mr Samuel Hoar, who was there writing it, also signed it. I was lately required to go to Cambridge to testify to

546

the genuineness of the will, being the only one of the four who could be there; and now I am the only one alive.

My Mother & Sister thank you heartily for your sympathy. The latter in particular agrees with you in thinking, that it is communion with still living & healthy nature alone which can restore to sane and cheerful views.

I thank you for your invitation to New Bedford—but I feel somewhat confined here for the present. I did not know but we should see you the day after [William R.?] Alger was here. It is not too late for a winter walk in Concord.

It does me good to hear of spring birds, and singing ones too, for spring seems far away from Concord yet.

I am going to Worcester to read a parlor lecture on the 22nd, and shall see Blake & Brown. What if you were to meet me there! or go with me from here! You would see *them* to good advantage.

Cholmondeley has been here again, after going as far south as Virginia, and left for Canada about three weeks ago. He is a good soul, and I am afraid that I did not sufficiently recognize him.

Please remember me to Mrs Ricketson, and to the rest of your family.

Yrs
Henry D. Thoreau

MS., Huntington.

From DANIEL RICKETSON

The Shanty, Sunday a. m., 6 March, 1859.

Respected Friend,—

This fine spring morning with its cheering influences brings you to my mind; for I always associate you with the most genial aspects of our beloved Nature, with the woods, the fields, lakes and rivers, with the birds and flowers. As I write, the meadow lark is piping sweetly in

the meadows near by, and lo! at this instant, the very first I have heard this season, a bluebird has warbled on a tree near the Shanty. What salutation could be more welcome or more in unison with my subject? Yesterday, my son Walton saw and heard the red-winged Blackbird, and this morning robins are flying about. The song-sparrow (F. melodia) now singing, has also been in tune since the 23d of February. Truly may we say, "Spring is come!"

At my present writing, the thermometer at my north window indicates 44 degrees and is rising; yesterday p.m. 50 degrees, wind W. S. W. It seems to me quite time to stop the abuse of our climate. In my boyhood and even until after my marriage (1834), I do not remember it ever occurred to me but that our climate was a very good one. And had I never heard it complained of by others, should hardly have ever suspected it otherwise. A climate that has sustained such men as R. W. E., A. B. A., H. D. T., and other kindred natures, can't be a very bad one, and may be the very best.

March is to me *the month of hope.* I always look forward to its coming with pleasure, and welcome its arrival. Others may speak of it in terms of reproach, but to me it has much to recommend itself. The backbone of winter, according to the homely adage, is now broken. Every day brings us nearer to the vernal influences, to the return of the birds and the appearance of wild flowers. Mingled with storms are many warm sunny days. I am no longer in haste for finer weather, so near at hand. Each day has something to interest me, and even in a severe snow or rainstorm, accompanied with cold weather, I know that the glorious sun, when once he shines again, will dispel all gloom and soften the temperature. Although it is my custom to walk in the woods, fields, and by-places at all seasons of the year and in all weathers, the spring (and in this I include March as fairly belonging) is my most favorite time. Nature, ever attractive to me, is at this season particularly inviting, the kind solace and hope of my days. Although I am but an indifferent versifier, yet I fancy but few poets have experienced richer or happier emotions than myself from her benign spirit.

I am most happy to record, at this time, that I have, I trust, recovered my good spirits, such as blessed me in my earlier years of manhood. I shall endeavor by a life of purity and retirement to keep them as the choicest of blessings. My desires, I believe, are moderate, and not beyond my reach. So far as the false luxuries of life are concerned, I

548

have but little taste for them, and I would willingly dispense with almost every unnecessary article in the economy of living, for the sake of being the master of my own time, and the leisure to pursue the simple occupations and enjoyments of rural life. I do not covet wealth, I certainly do not wish it. With the intelligent and worthy poor, I feel far greater sympathy and affinity, than with a large portion of the rich and falsely great. I would give more for one day with the poet-peasant, Robert Burns, or Shakespeare, than for unnumbered years of entertainment at the tables of proud and rich men.

> "Behind the plough Burns sang his wood-notes wild,
> And richest Shakespeare was a poor man's child."

So sung Ebenezer Elliot, the Corn-law rhymer, himself a true poet and friend of the "virtuous and struggling poor."

I copy the foregoing, suggested by the season, from my Daily Journal, on the entrance of March. You may, therefore, read it as a soliloquy, by which it may savor less of egotism and bombast, to which objections it might otherwise be open.

During my walk, yesterday p.m., in a sunny spot, I found the "pussy willows" (S. eriocephala) and enclose one of the "catkins" or "woolly aments" in testimony thereof. I also enclose a pansy from the south side of the Shanty. How should I rejoice to have you as the companion of my walks!

I suppose you have some time since returned from your literary *exploit* into Worcester, and trust that you had a good time with your disciples, Blake, and Brown. They must be *thoreauly* brown by this time. "Arcades ambo" under your pupilage—though, I think, the classic term applies better to you and R. W. E. or W. E. C[hanning]. May I not also claim as a birthright to rank in your fraternity, as a disciple, at least? Please not reject me. Failing in you I shall be bankrupt, indeed. Shall echo respond, to my complaint, "Is there none for me in the wide world,—no kindred spirit?" "None"?

Don't be alarmed, "Amicus Mihi," you shall be as free as air for aught me.

During the past winter I have been reviewing somewhat my law studies, and what will not a little surprise you, have received and accepted a commission as justice of the peace. I have collected the relic of my law library, and ranged them in formidable array upon a shelf

in the Shanty. I find myself much better able to grasp and cope with these legal worthies than when a young man.

I don't suppose I shall do much in the way of my profession, but may assist occasionally the injured in the recovery of their rights. I have not done this hastily, as you may suppose. I intend to be free from all trammels, and believing, as I do, that law, or rather government, was made for the weal of all concerned, and particularly for the protection of the weak against the strong, and that, according to Blackstone, "What is not reason is not law," I shall act accordingly if I act at all.

I may make use of the elective franchise, but of this am as yet undetermined. It seems to me as though a crisis was approaching in the affairs of our government, when the use of every means that "God and nature affords" will be required to oppose tyranny. I trust that I shall have your sympathy in this matter.

I shall seek no opportunity for the exercise of my opposition, but "*bide my time.*"

A visit from you would be very welcome. With kind regards to your household and my Concord friends, one and all, I remain,

Yours truly,
D. R.

Yours of 12th Feb. came duly to hand.

Text, Ricketson, *pp. 94–98.*

From MARY BROWN

tleboro sometime before long—Father and Mother send kind regards. Hoping the May flowers will be fresh when they reach you:

yours truly
Mary H. Brown

[1859]

*Mary Brown sent mayflowers to Thoreau at least twice, in April 1858
and in May 1859. We prefer the latter date for her letter because the
fragment quoted above fits very well with Thoreau's answer of May 19.
Our dating is arbitrary, however; Mary Brown's note might equally
well have accompanied the large box of flowers he received on April
23, 1858 and noted in his* Journal *for that day.* MS., Huntington; previously unpublished. This is the lower part of a sheet of small stationery
that Thoreau tore off to use for a paragraph in* Cape Cod.

To MARY BROWN

Concord May 19th 1859

Miss Mary H. Brown,

Excuse me for not acknowledging before the receipt of your
beautiful gift of may-flowers. The delay may prove that I did not fear
I should forget it, though very busily engaged in surveying. The flowers
were somewhat detained on the road, but they were not the less
fragrant, and were very superior to any that we can show.

It chanced that on the very day they arrived, while surveying in the
next town, I found more of these flowers than I have ever seen hereabouts, and I have accordingly named a certain path "May-flower Path"
on my plan. But a botanist's experience is full of coincidences. If you
think much about some flower which you never saw, you will be
pretty sure to find it some day actually growing near by you. In the
long run, we find what we expect. We shall be fortunate then if we
expect great things.

Please remember me to your Father & Mother.

Yours truly
Henry D. Thoreau

For an account of Mary Brown's youthful acquaintance with Thoreau see Mrs. Elizabeth B. Davenport, "Thoreau in Vermont in 1856," Vermont Botanical Club Bulletin No. 3 (April 1908), 36–38. MS., Abernethy (typescript).

To DAVID(?) HEARD

Concord July 8 1859

Mr Heard
Dear Sir,

You did not give me any data concerning the Town or Causeway Bridge—that is the old wooden one—whether it was longer than the present one—&c By the vote of the Committee I am requested "To learn, if possible, the time of erection of each bridge, and if any abutments have been extended since the building of any bridge, & when." I think you told me that the stone one was built about 10 years ago.

I have done with your map, and, if you so direct, will leave it with Dr. Reynolds.

Yrs truly
Henry D. Thoreau

Thoreau was hired to survey the river, its depth, its bridges and dams because river haying land suffered from flooding with water backed up by various obstructions. His water survey papers are now in the Concord Public Library. In his Journal for June 24, 1859 he notes that he has been surveying the bridges and river from Heard's Bridge to the Billerica dam on the 22d, 23d, and 24th. Thoreau adds: "Colonel David Heard, who accompanied me . . . has worked at clearing out the river (I think about 1820)." David Heard, 1793–1881 according to Concord records, had a son, David, born in 1820, and in the same Journal passage Thoreau mentions a Deacon Richard Heard. The evidence leans to the senior David Heard as the recipient of Thoreau's letter. MS., Abernethy (typescript).

From LUCAS, BROTHERS

Balt. July 26, 1859

Mr Henry D. Thoreau
D Sir
    We enclose Ten dollars, Rockland Bank, in settlement of your bill of 21st inst
    Please acknowledge & oblige

Yours Respy
Lucas, Bros

The bill, in all probability, was for black lead, graphite, or plumbago. MS., Harvard; previously unpublished.

To WILLIAM A. WILSON

Concord, Mass. July 30th 1859

Mr. Wm. A. Wilson
Dear Sir,
    I send you by the same mail with this a copy of A Week on the Concord & Merrimack Rivers. The price is $1.25. The change can be sent in postage stamps. I have no copies of "Walden" to spare; and I learn that it is out of print

Yours respectfully
Henry D. Thoreau

P. S.   These are the only books I have published.

MS., Robert Miller (*typescript*); *previously unpublished.*

From THO. H. MUMFORD

Philad. Augs. 12th/ 59

Dear Sir

Please send us ten pounds of Plumbago for Electrotyping purposes, such as we got last from you—as it is some risk to send the money
by mail, we would prefer paying the Express agent on delivery of the
box—I suppose this arrangement will be satisfactory to you but if not
please let us know at once as we have but a very little on hand.

Respectfully Yours &c

Tho. H. Mumford

*This note and similar ones suggest how much time Thoreau was having
to spend on the family business since his father's death. MS., Berg;
previously unpublished.*

From WELCH, BIGELOW & CO.

Cambridge Aug 18

Mr Thoreau
Dear Sir

Inclosed please find $15 00 for which send us 10 lbs Blacklead by
return of express—directed as usual

Yours truly

Welch, Bigelow, & Co

Aug 18.

*The date on this order does not include the year, but the manuscript is
with other correspondence for 1859 among Thoreau's "Notes on Fruits."
MS., Berg; previously unpublished.*

From HOBART & ROBBINS

Boston Augt. 22d 1859

Mr Henry D. Thoreaux Concord, Mass.
    Please send by return Express 6 lbs best Black Lead & Enclosed please find Nine Dollars to pay for the same—
    Send a receipt.

Yrs Resp'y &c
Hobart & Robbins

One 5.00 bill	The Freemans Bank, No. 9				
One 3.00 "	"	"	"	"	864
One 1.00 "	"	"	"	"	1146

$9.00

MS., Berg; *previously unpublished.*

To GEORGE THATCHER

Concord Aug 25th '59

Dear Cousin,
    Mother unites with me in assuring Charles Benjamin & Caleb, that we shall be happy to see them, & trust that they will not be in a hurry to go hence to Peterboro, but will first exhaust at their leisure whatever entertainment the dull town may afford. Accommodations will be provided for them at any rate, and such visitors as come later must take their chance. The prospect is that Concord will not be herself that week. I fear it will be more like Discord. Thank fortune, the camp will be nearly 2 miles west of us; yet the *scamps* will be "all over the lot." The very anticipation of this muster has greatly increased the amount of travel past our house, for a month; & now, at last, whole houses have

begun to roll that way. I fear that we shall have no melons to speak of for either friends or foes, unless perchance the present rain may revive them, for we are in the midst of a severe drought. Sophia is on a short visit to Miss Swift in Roxbury. Please let aunts know that their letter to her reached us yesterday, & that we shall expect them muster [indecipherable word]. We hope that Aunt Jane will be able to travel without inconvenience. I believe that the soldiers will come over the road on Tuesday; & I hear that cars will be run between Boston & Concord at very short intervals on the days of the muster.

I should think that you might have a very pleasant journey to New Brunswick, & for my own part, I would rather go to where men will be mustered less thickly than they will be hereabouts next month.

Edward Hoar, with wife & sister, leave Liverpool for home the 27 inst.

I know the fatigue of much concentrating, especially of drawing accurate plans. It is the hardest work I can do. While following it, I need to go to Moosehead every afternoon, & camp out every night.

Yrs truly
Henry D. Thoreau

This letter was probably to George Thatcher of Bangor; he had accompanied Thoreau on visits to the Maine woods and would have known Edward Hoar of Concord, who accompanied Thoreau in 1857. A state muster was held in Concord September 7–9. MS., Historical Society of Pennsylvania; previously unpublished.

To E. G. DUDLEY

Concord Sep 5 1859

E. G. Dudley Esq.
Dear Sir
    I will read a lecture to your company on the 9th of October, for the compensation named. I should prefer, however, to bring one which I call "Life Misspent," instead of "Autumnal Tints."

Yrs truly
Henry D. Thoreau

MS., Lownes; *previously unpublished.*

To H. G. O. BLAKE

Concord, September 26, 1859.

Mr. Blake,—
    I am not sure that I am in a fit mood to write to you, for I feel and think rather too much like a business man, having some very irksome affairs to attend to these months and years on account of my family. This is the way I am serving King Admetus, confound him! If it were not for my relations, I would let the wolves prey on his flocks to their bellies' content. Such fellows you have to deal with! herdsmen of some other king, or of the same, who tell no tale, but in the sense of counting their flocks, and then lie drunk under a hedge. How is your grist ground? Not by some murmuring stream, while you lie dreaming on the bank; but, it seems, you must take hold with your hands, and shove the wheel round. You can't depend on streams, poor feeble things! You can't depend on worlds, left to themselves; but you've got to oil them and goad them along. In short, you've got to carry on two farms at once,—the farm on the earth and the farm in your mind. Those

Crimean and Italian battles were mere boys' play,—they are the scrapes into which truants get. But what a battle a man must fight everywhere to maintain his standing army of thoughts, and march with them in orderly array through the always hostile country! How many enemies there are to sane thinking! Every soldier has succumbed to them before he enlists for those other battles. Men may sit in chambers, seemingly safe and sound, and yet despair, and turn out at last only hollowness and dust within, like a Dead Sea apple. A standing army of numerous, brave, and well-disciplined thoughts, and you at the head of them, marching straight to your goal,—how to bring this about is the problem, and Scott's Tactics will not help you to it. Think of a poor fellow begirt only with a sword-belt, and no such staff of athletic thoughts! his brains rattling as he walks and *talks!* These are your prætorian guard. It is easy enough to maintain a family, or a state, but it is hard to maintain these children of your brain (or say, rather, these guests that trust to enjoy your hospitality), they make such great demands; and yet, he who does only the former, and loses the power to *think* originally, or as only he ever can, fails miserably. Keep up the fires of thought, and all will go well.

Zouaves?—pish! How you can overrun a country, climb any rampart, and carry any fortress, with an army of *alert* thoughts!—thoughts that send their bullets home to heaven's door,—with which you can *take* the whole world, without paying for it, or robbing anybody. See, the conquering hero comes! You *fail* in your thoughts, or you *prevail* in your thoughts only. Provided you *think* well, the heavens falling, or the earth gaping, will be music for you to march by. No foe can ever see you, or you him; you cannot so much as *think* of him. Swords have no edges, bullets no penetration, for such a contest. In your mind must be a liquor which will dissolve the world whenever it is dropt in it. There is no universal solvent but this, and all things together cannot saturate it. It will hold the universe in solution, and yet be as translucent as ever. The vast machine may indeed roll over our toes, and we not know it, but it would rebound and be staved to pieces like an empty barrel, if it should strike fair and square on the smallest and least angular of a man's thoughts.

You seem not to have taken Cape Cod the right way. I think that you should have persevered in walking on the beach and on the bank, even to the land's end, however soft, and so, by long knocking at Ocean's gate, have gained admittance at last,—better, if separately, and

in a storm, not knowing where you would sleep by night, or eat by day. Then you should have given a day to the sand behind Provincetown, and ascended the hills there, and been blown on considerably. I hope that you like to remember the journey better than you did to make it.

I have been confined at home all this year, but I am not aware that I have grown any rustier than was to be expected. One while I explored the bottom of the river pretty extensively. I have engaged to read a lecture to [Theodore] Parker's society on the 9th of October next.

I am off—a barberrying.

Text, Familiar Letters of Thoreau, *pp. 409–13; manuscript listed in* Stephen H. Wakeman Collection *sale catalogue as Item 1014, with these additional sentences: "Emerson has been seriously lame for 2 or three months past—Sprained his foot and does not yet get better. It has been a bad business for him."*

From EDWARD BANGS

Boston Oct 5 59

Mr. Henry Thoreau Concord
Dear Sir
        Your aunts wish you to come by the next train to the Superior Court 1st Session to testify that the family tradition is that they & you are descended from the Orrocks which is necessary to be proved in this case vs. Miss Palleis [Pallies.]

Very truly yours
Edward Bangs.

The case of Maria Thoreau and others vs. *Eliza Pallies was in court because Miss Pallies, a remarkably aggressive woman, had entered Aunt Maria's yard, thrown down the fence enclosing it, and then put*

up a spite fence within a foot and a half of the door and windows of Maria's house. Miss Pallies' only legal basis had been a right of way through the yard. She lost the case and was ordered to pay the court costs plus damages of one dollar (Allen, Cases . . . in the Supreme Judicial Court of Massachusetts, 1861, I, 425). Edward Bangs was Maria's lawyer. MS., Abernethy (typescript); previously unpublished.

From DANIEL RICKETSON

The Shanty, Oct. 14, 1859.

Friend Thoreau,—
    Shall I break our long silence, silence so much more instructive than any words I may utter? Yet should my rashness procure a response from you, I, at least, may be the wiser. Solemn though the undertaking be, I would fain venture.
    Well, *imprimis,* you have been talking, as I learn from various sources, in Boston. I hope you were understood, in some small measure, at least, though I fear not; but this is not your business—to find understanding for your audience. I respect your benevolence in thus doing, for I esteem it one of the most gracious and philanthropic deeds, for a wise, thoughtful man, a philosopher, to attempt, at least, to awaken his fellow men from their drunken somnolence, perhaps to elevate them.

> "But unimproved, Heaven's noblest brows are vain,
>   No sun with plenty crowns the uncultured vale;
> Where green lakes languish on the silent plain,
>   Death rides the billows of the western gale."

What are we to think of a world that has had a Socrates, a Plato, a Christ for its teachers, and yet remaining in such outer darkness?
    It appears to me it is only, age after age, the working over of the old original compound—man. We appear to gain nothing. A few noble, wise ones, mark the lustrums of the past—a few also will mark what we call the present. The things men rate so highly in modern times do not appear to me to be of very great value after all. What is it for a ship

to cross the ocean by steam if its passengers have no godlike errand to perform? We have enough to wonder at in Nature already, why seek new wonders?

I have passed some peaceful hours of late, sawing wood by moonlight, in the field near the lane to our cow-pastures—the work does not interfere with, but rather favors meditation, and I have found some solace in the companionship of the woods near by, and the concert of their wind harps.

During my evening walks I hear the flight of passenger birds overhead, probably those of noctural habits, as I suppose others rest at this season (Night).

A small flock, only ten wild geese, passed over a few days ago. The *Sylviacola coronata* [Myrtle Warbler] have arrived from the north, and will remain until driven away by the severe cold. I have often seen them in the company of snow buntings about the house and during snowstorms, but they suffer and often die at such times if the storm be severe. Quails are gradually increasing, though still scarce. Last winter I saw a covey of some twelve or more near here, and occasionally have heard their whistle during the early part of the past summer.

I made the acquaintance of your friends, Blake and Brown, very favorably at the Middleborough ponds, last June, on their way to Cape Cod. I had, however, seen Mr. Blake once before.

I should be happy to have a visit from you. Can you not come soon?

I have passed through some deep experiences since I last saw you. We are getting nearer. Is there not such a fact as human companionship? I need not add how much I owe you, and that I remain, faithfully your friend,

D. R.

Bluebirds are still here, and meadow-larks are tuneful.

Text, Ricketson, *pp. 99–101.*

From THEOPHILUS BROWN

Worcester Oct 19

Friend Thoreau,

The book came duly to hand, and as it was not for me, I *intend* to send you the money for it in this note—

Blake must speak for himself and not for me when speaking of that mountain walk of ours. I enjoyed it well enough, and ought to be ashamed of myself that I did, perhaps, since it yielded me so little.

Our Cape Cod walk salts down better with me, & yet there wasn't much salt in that,—enough to save it perhaps, but not enough of the sea & sand & sky. The good things I got in it were rather incidental— did not belong to the sea. But I did get some glimpses of the sea. I remember a smoke we had on a little barren knoll where we heard the plover, in North Dennis, in the twilight after a long & hot days walk. We heard the pounding of the surf against a shore twenty miles off (so said the man at whose house we passed the night,—) and we were expecting to arrive there the next day.

I have been in the habit of thinking our journey culminated in that smoke, if it did'nt *end* there, for, though we arrived at the beach the next day according to programme & found the thirty miles stretch of it, with its accompaniments too large to complain of, yet—our anticipations were immense. But now in thinking of it the actual sea & sky loom up larger, while our smoke & dreams—hold their own pretty well—

Your friend
Theo Brown

Although the name of Theo Brown, a Worcester man and partner in a tailoring establishment, appears often in Thoreau's correspondence, this is the first extant letter from him. He was a very close friend of H. G. O. Blake, the connecting link between him and Thoreau. Brown and Blake were with Thoreau during the excursion into the White Mountains early in July 1858. Thoreau notes in his Journal *for July 8, 1858 that he "went up the stream to meet Blake and Brown, wet, ragged, and bloody with*

black flies"; Brown is probably on the defensive in writing, "I enjoyed it well enough." Brown omits the year, but it is obviously 1859. MS., Berg; previously unpublished.

To H. G. O. BLAKE

Concord, Oct. 31st ['59.]

Mr. Blake,

    I spoke to my townsmen last evening on "The character of Capt. Brown, now in the clutches of the slaveholder." I should like to speak to any company in Worcester who may wish to hear me, & will come, if only my expenses are paid. I think that we should express ourselves at once, while Brown is alive. The sooner the better. Perhaps [T. W.] Higginson may like to have a meeting.

    Wednesday evening would be a good time.

    The people here are deeply interested in the matter.

    Let me have an answer as soon as may be.

Henry D. Thoreau.

[The following was written in pencil.]

    P. S.   I may be engaged toward the end of the week.

Thoreau's address in Concord on John Brown was probably the most successful of his life. He repeated it in Boston on November 1 and again in Worcester on November 3. MS., Berg; copy in Blake's hand; the second and last bracketed insertions are his.

From CHARLES W. SLACK

American Telegraph Company Boston Oct 31 1859

To Henry D. Thoreau or Ralph Waldo Emerson. Concord.
  Thoreau must lecture for Fraternity Tuesday Evening—Douglas fails
—Letter mailed

Charles W. Slack

11 Bs 28

The success of Thoreau's lecture of October 9 is evident in this tele-graphed invitation for him to fill in as a last-minute substitute for Fred-erick Douglass. This second lecture in the Fraternity Course sponsored by Theodore Parker's congregation was given November 1. It was "A Plea for Captain John Brown." MS., Berg; previously unpublished.

From MONCURE CONWAY

Cin. Novr. 19, 1859.

My dear Mr. Thoreau,
      I trust that you also, with Emerson, will be moved by old and high memories to help us in starting out here a new incarnation of the old Dial. It certainly will prove worthy to be so called if we can obtain help from R. W. E. yourself and others. We will not be able at once to pay contributors, and the Editor expects to lose; but in due time we shall reap if we faint not. Will you not give the babe a birth-present? One of those fresh wood-zephyrs that fan our fevered hearts and bring health to *blasé* cheeks! You are the man, the only man, who can make green grass and flowers grow upon the pages of our *Dial*.
      What is my chief wish of you? It is to have you interested in us: willing to send us a love-gift of thought: noting, now and then on paper, the form and [?] of some pearls, which I know you are constantly

564

finding in that Oriental Sea of yours upstairs. So now Mr. Pearl-Diver,
I await your word of cheer! May I say that I shall be assisted by H. D.
Thoreau of Concord? Pray let me hear at once.

Your friend,
M. D. Conway.

*Conway was an active young liberal when he wrote Thoreau. A graduate
of Harvard Divinity School in 1854, he had gone to Cincinnati as minister
of the First Congregational Church when he was twenty-four. There he
aroused a good deal of controversy by advocating unorthodox causes.
"The papers teemed with controversial letters," he explained in his
Autobiography, "and a magazine became inevitable." Conway, who had
once lived in Concord, wrote to several other Transcendentalist acquaintances about contributions. The new* Dial *appeared in January
1860 and ended in December.* MS., University of Rochester Library
(typescript).

To MONCURE CONWAY

Concord Nov 23 '59

Mr. Conway

Let me thank you for your earthy and [word] of Capt. Brown.
As for your new Dial I do not think of any Thing which I have available
for your purpose & other engagements prevent my preparing it. While
I wish you success I know at [word]your assistance knowing myself so
well—

I can only say that if I [word] [word] on any & the [word] I will
remember your magazine

To follow out your simile I find in my sea some mother o' pearl—it
may be but very few pearls as yet—may I now good wishes & more
[word] and [word] [word?] ment—

But this will not be worth an advertisement.

565

Crossed out were (1) "perhaps" after "it may be" and (2) the first three letters of "offer" after "may I now." Apparently Thoreau never found any material for Conway's Dial, *for none was ever printed there.* MS., University of Rochester Library (*typescript*); *it is Thoreau's draft on the back of Conway's letter of November 19; previously unpublished.*

To CALVIN GREENE

Concord Nov. 24. '59

Dear Sir,

The lectures which you refer to were reported in the newspapers, *after a fashion,* the last one in some half dozen of them, and if I possessed one, or all, of those reports I would send them to you, bad as they are. The best, or at least longest one of the Brown Lecture was in the Boston "Atlas & Bee" of Nov 2nd. Maybe half the whole. There were others in the Traveller—the Journal &c of the same date.

I am glad to know that you are interested to see my things. & I wish that I had them in a printed form to send to you. I exerted myself considerably to get the last discourse printed & sold for the benefit of Brown's family—but the publishers are afraid of pamphlets & it is now too late.

I return the stamps which I have not used.

I shall be glad to see you if I ever come your way

Yours truly
Henry D. Thoreau

MS., Princeton University Library.

1860

It was a bitter, wrangling year. The Democratic national convention split; the majority nominated Douglas of Illinois for president and, in a vain gesture, a Georgian for vice-president. The Southern seceders nominated John Breckinridge of Kentucky for president and an Oregonian for vice-president. At the Republican convention William Seward led on the first ballot by 173½ votes to Lincoln's 102, but Lincoln soon overcame Seward's lead. In the fall election Lincoln received 1,866,452, Douglas 1,375,157, and Breckinridge 847,953. South Carolina passed an ordinance of secession and appointed three commissioners to go to Washington and treat with the government about the disposition of federal property within the state. President Buchanan received the commissioners as private gentlemen and shortly afterward announced in a letter to them that Fort Sumter would be defended to the last extremity. But he was not always so firm. The eighth decennial census gave the total population of the United States as 31,443,321—26,922,537 white, 3,953,760 Negro slaves, and 488,070 free Negroes. The center of population had moved to twenty miles south of Chillicothe. At mid-year the United States Army consisted of 1,080 officers and 14,926 enlisted men.

Business this year, as last, took an important part of Thoreau's time. His family now owned two houses, and Henry as executor of his father's estate could give bond for $10,000. Still, he managed to fill up many pages of the *Journal* and found time for sauntering and traveling in addition. He published "A Plea for Captain John Brown" in an anthology called *Echoes of Harper's Ferry* and "The Succession of the Forest Trees" in Greeley's *Tribune*. In summer he spent most of a week on Monadnock with Ellery Channing. The letters are almost invariably

567

short except for a few to Blake and Ricketson. The best thing, it may be, coming out of this year is the continued fluency and precision of the nature writing in the *Journal*. The worst is the illness, only a cold to begin with, that Thoreau contracted in December while counting tree rings.

Jany 9th 1860

Mr. H. D. Thoreau Concord Mass.
Dear Sir:
    Enclosed please find $10 Amt of your bill of 27th Ult. Please acknowledge recpt and oblige

Yours truly
R. Allison Supt.

Allison was superintendent of the Franklin Type and Stereotype Foundry in Cincinnati. MS., Berg; previously unpublished.

From EDWARD BANGS

[January 9, 1860]

Dear Sir:
    Your Aunts case vs. Miss Pallies will be tried tomorrow—will you please come down by the first train?

Very truly yours
Edward Bangs

See Bangs's letter to Thoreau of October 5, 1859. MS., Berg; previously unpublished.

569

From HOBART & ROBBINS

Boston Jany 9, 1860

Mr. Henry D. Thoreaux Concord, Mass.

Enclosed are Nine Dollars, for which, please send at once 6 lbs best (ground) plumbago, with bill

Yrs &c
Hobart & Robbins

MS., Berg; *previously unpublished.*

From DANIEL RICKETSON

The Shanty, 15 Jan., 1860.

Friend Thoreau,—

We've been having a good deal of wintry weather for our section of late, and skating by both sexes is a great fashion. On the 26th of last month, Arthur, Walton, and I skated about fifteen miles. We rode out to the south end of Long pond (Aponoquet), and leaving our horse at a farmer's barn, put on our skates, and went nearly in a straight line to the north end of said pond, up to the old herring weir of King Philip, where we were obliged to take off our skates, as the passage to Assawamset was not frozen. We stopped about an hour at the old tavern and had a good solid anti-slavery, and John Brown talk with some travellers. One, a square-set, red-bearded farmer, said among other rough things, that *he would like to eat Southerners' hearts! and drink their blood! for a fortnight, and would be willing to die if he could not live on this fare!* This was said in reply to a spruce young fellow who had been in New Orleans, and *knew all about slavery*—damned the abolitionists most lustily, and John Brown and his associates in particular. Oaths flew like shot from one side to the other, but the renegade

570

Northerner was no match for the honest farmer, who met him at every point with facts, statistics, oaths, and arguments, and finally swore his antagonist down flat. He "burst the bully" in good earnest. Occasionally I had interspersed a few words, and others present, but our farmer was the champion of the field, and a more complete annihilation of a dough-face I never witnessed.

My boys seemed to enjoy it well. After this scene we again assumed our skates from the Assawamset shore, near by, and skated down to the end of the East Quitticus pond, the extreme southern end of the ponds; thence crossing to West Quitticus, we skated around it, which with the return from the south end of the former pond to our crossing place, we estimated at something over 15 miles. Taking off our skates we took a path through the woods, and walking about a mile came out in some old fields near our starting point. We put on our skates at 10.30 o'clock a.m., and at 3 p.m. were eating dinner at the old farm-house of William A. Morton, near the south shore of Long Pond.

I, as well as my boys, enjoyed the excursion very much. We saw our favorite pond under entirely new aspects, and visited many nooks that we had never before seen—sometimes under the boughs of the old cedars, draped in long clusters of moss, like bearded veterans, and anon farther out on the bosom of the lake, with broad and refreshing views of wild nature, taking the imagination back to the times of the Indians and early settlers of these parts—shooting by little islands and rocky islets, among them the one called "Lewis Island," which you thought would do for a residence. I got a fresh hold of life that day, and hope to repeat the pleasure before winter closes his reign. I found myself not only not exhausted, as I had expected, but unusually fresh and cheerful on my arrival home about 5 p.m. The boys stood it equally well. So my friend we shall not allow you all the glory of the skating field, but must place our Aponoquet, Assawamset and Quitticas-et, in the skating account with your own beloved Musketaquid exploits.

Well, since I saw you, dear old John Brown has met, and O! how nobly, his death, at the hands of Southern tyrants. I honor him and his brave associates in my "heart of hearts"; but my voice is for peaceable measures henceforth, doubtful, alas! as their success appears.

I expect to be in Boston at the annual meeting of the Mass. A[nti] S[lavery] Society, near at hand, and hope to see you there, and if agreeable should like to have you return home with me, when, D.V., we may try our skates on the Middleborough ponds.

We all spoke of you and wished you were with us on our late excursion there.

With kind regards to your family and my other Concord friends, I remain,

Yours faithfully,
D. Ricketson.

H. D. Thoreau, Concord.

Text, Ricketson, *pp. 101–3.*

To SAMUEL RIPLEY BARTLETT

Concord Jan 19th 1860

Mr S. Ripley Bartlett,
Dear Sir,
 I send you with this a letter of introduction to Ticknor & Fields, as you request; though I am rather remote from them.

I think that your poem was well calculated for our lyceum, and the neighboring towns, but I would advise you, if it is not impertinent, not to have it printed, as you propose. You might keep it by you, read it as you have done, as you may have opportunity, and see how it wears with yourself. It may be in your own way if printed. The public are very cold and indifferent to such things, and the publishers still more so. I have found that the precept "Write with fury, and correct with flegm" required me to print only the hundredth part of what I had written. If you print at first in newspapers, you can afterward collect survives [survivors?]—what your readers demand. That, I should say, is the simplest and safest, as it is the commonest, way. You so get the criticism of the public, & if you fail, no harm is done.

You may think this harsh advice, but, believe me, it is sincere.

Yrs truly
Henry D. Thoreau

572

[1860]

*According to the records of the Concord Lyceum, now in the Concord
Public Library, young Samuel Ripley Bartlett delivered his poem "The
Concord Fight" on January 4, 1860. Sumner, Emerson, and Thoreau
lectured in the same lyceum course. Thoreau's letter to Ticknor & Fields
proved useless, as he thought it would; however, Bartlett got the Boston
firm of A. Williams & Co. to print his poem, a tediously sentimental and
patriotic affair in alternately rhyming pentameters. MS., Library of
Congress; previously unpublished.*

From CHAUNCEY SMITH

Boston Jan 23d 1860

Mr Henry D Thoreau
Dear Sir

Enclosed please find note of my brother L. L. Smith for $100
payable in three months with my endorsement and acknowledge the
receipt thereof to him

Yours truly
Chauncey Smith

*Smith was a patent lawyer who practiced in Boston. We can only con-
jecture that his brother was in business and bought plumbago from
Thoreau. MS., Huntington; previously unpublished.*

573

From JAMES REDPATH

Feby 6, 1860

Henry D Thoreau
Dear Sir—

If you do not desire to know my address, (which you had better not know if you have any prospect of being summoned to Washington) please hand the enclose *knot* to F. B. S[anborn] who, perhaps, may wish to see me to consult as to our future course. I have been regularly summoned, but have resolutely refused to obey the summons; & am in the country, now, to have quiet until I shall complete the forthcoming Volume. I directed your Lecture to be sent to you for correction; which —I am told—has been done.

Can *you* furnish me with an a/c of the B[attle] of B[lack] J[ack]? I was very conscious of the defects of the a/c I copied; but as I recollect very little about the B, I cd not undertake to describe it from my own resources. I shall however yet obtain the testimony of the eye witnesses; as I have all their names (the "Orderly Book" that you allude to) & will either see or write to every man who was present, as soon as I can get their addresses or leave Mass. for K. Territory. I shall probably visit the ground in the spring.

For the Private Life I have already a number of very interesting letters from Kansas men,—just such plain, matter of fact statements as you are greedy for, & which, better than any rhetorical estimates of John Brown's character or cause, exhibit to the intelligent reader the spirit & life of the old warrior.

The very numerous faults of language (there have been very few of facts) & the imperfect estimates of character which disfigure my book warn me—& I will heed the hint—to take more time in fixing another original volume. As for my forthcoming book, as it is an *edited* volume only, I have nothing to fear in that a/c.

I have not even yet attempted to arrange my voluminous newspaper materials, & do not see that I shall be able to commence it for some weeks to come This is my apology or reason rather for neglecting (in appearance) my promise with reference to Miss Thoreau's Scrap Book.

I find that the extracts that [word] made in my book for your lecture were incorrectly reported. Do you desire that they shall be altered? If

so, *please return the volume I sent you* properly marked; & I will return you as many vols as you desire with the latest corrections. The 33d thousand has been printed & contains many corrections *not* in the edition I sent you. The prospect is that it will reach over 50000 at least. I think it will do good among the masses; that is all I tried to do—for the educated have teachers enough; & over them I do not expect to have influence.

Remember me to Mrs Thoreau & thank her, in my own name & in behalf of my wife, also—for her kind invitation; which we shall, as soon as possible, accept.

Very truly yours
Jas Redpath

James Redpath had assisted John Brown in his preparations for the Harpers Ferry excursion and was now afraid of being summoned to Washington to testify before a Senate committee investigating the affair. Indeed, on February 16, 1860 an order for his arrest was issued by the Senate committee. In that same year Redpath published The Public Life of Capt. John Brown, *dedicated to Thoreau, Emerson, and Wendell Phillips, and* Echoes of Harper's Ferry, *a collection of tributes to Brown that included "A Plea for Captain John Brown" and Thoreau's remarks at the memorial service in Concord. The "Private Life" of Brown that Redpath mentions seems not to have been printed. Sophia Thoreau's scrapbook of antislavery clippings is in the hands of a private collector. Redpath, once the storm of civil war was over, became the most noted of American lecture managers. The Battle of Black Jack was Brown's most noted encounter at arms in Kansas; with nine men of his own he captured over twice that number of his proslavery enemy. According to Sanborn* (Recollections of Seventy Years, I, 103) *Brown told Thoreau about it in detail. MS., Abernethy (typescript); previously unpublished.*

From WELCH, BIGELOW & CO.

Cambridge Feb 7, 60

Mr Thoreau
Dear Sir
 Enclosed please find draft on Boston for thirty-seven 50/100 dollars the amt of your bill due By receipting the same and returning it you will oblige

Yours truly
Welch, Bigelow & Co.

MS., Berg; *previously unpublished.*

From HENRY WILLIAMS

Boston, February 9, 1860

My Dear Sir:
 At the last annual meeting of the Class of '37, a vote was passed, that the members of the Class be requested to furnish the Secretary with their photographs, to be placed in the Class Book. Several fellows, in accordance with the above vote, have already sent me their pictures, and I trust that you will feel disposed, at an early date, to follow their example. You can send to me through the Post Office, at 18 Concord Square.

Very truly yours,

A printed form letter sent out by the secretary of Thoreau's class. There is no indication that Thoreau replied. MS., Harvard.

From JANE ANDREWS

Mr. Thoreau,

Please send me by mail a copy of your "Week on the Concord and Merrimack Rivers."

Enclosed please find one dollar and a quarter ($1.25), which I believe you consider the pecuniary value of the book.

Address Jane Andrews, Newburyport, Mass. March 22, 1860.

MS., Harvard; *previously unpublished.*

From L. JOHNSON & CO.

L. Johnson & Co. Type Founders No. 606 Sansom St. Philadelphia

April 20, 1860

Mr. Henry D. Thoreau Concord, Mass.
Dear Sir—

Send us immediately by Express 10 lbs. Plumbago with bill to

Yours Respt
L. Johnson & Co.

MS., Morgan; *previously unpublished.*

From L. JOHNSON & CO.

L. Johnson & Co. Type Founders No. 606 Sansom St. Philadelphia

May 2nd 1860

Mr. Henry D. Thoreau Concord Mass.
Dear Sir—
 Enclosed find Fifteen dollars in notes amt of your bill of 21st ult. Please acknowledge receipt.

        Yours truly
        L. Johnson & Co

MS., Morgan; *previously unpublished.*

To H. G. O. BLAKE

        Concord May 20 1860

Mr Blake,
 I must endeavor to pay some of my debts to you.
 To begin where we left off then.
 The presumption is that *we* are always the same; our opportunities & Nature herself fluctuating. Look at mankind. No great difference between two, apparently; perhaps the same height and breadth and weight; and yet to the man who sits most E. this life is a weariness, routine, dust and ashes, and he drowns his imaginary cares (!) (a sort of friction among his vital organs), in a bowl. But to the man who sits most W., his *contemporary* (!) it is a field for all noble endeavors, an elysium, the dwelling place of heroes & knights. The former complains that he has a thousand affairs to attend to; but he does not realize, that his affairs, (though they may be a thousand,) and he are one.
 Men & boys are learning all kinds of trades but how to make *men* of themselves. They learn to make houses, but they are not so well

housed, they are not so contented in their houses, as the woodchucks in their holes. What is the use of a house if you haven't got a tolerable planet to put it on? If you can not tolerate the planet it is on? Grade the ground first. If a man believes and expects great things of himself, it makes no odds where you put him, or what you show him, (of course, you cannot put him anywhere nor show him anything), he will be surrounded by grandeur. He's in the condition of a healthy & hungry man, who says to himself—How sweet this crust is!

If he despairs of himself, then Tophet is his dwelling place, and he is in the condition of a sick man who is disgusted with the fruits of finest flavor.

Whether he sleeps or wakes, whether he runs or walks, whether he uses a microscope or a telescope, or his naked eye, a man never discovers anything, never overtakes anything or leaves anything behind, but himself. Whatever he says or does he merely reports himself. If he is in love, he *loves;* if he is in heaven he *enjoys,* if he is in hell he *suffers.* It is his condition that determines his locality.

The principal, the only thing a man makes is his condition, or fate. Though commonly he does not know it, nor put up a sign to this effect, "My own destiny made & mended here." [not *yours*] He is a master-workman in this business. He works 24 hours a day at it and gets it done. Whatever else he neglects or botches, no man was ever known to neglect this work. A great many pretend to make *shoes* chiefly, and would scout the idea that they make the hard times which they experience.

Each reaching and aspiration is an instinct with which all nature consists & cooperates, and therefore it is not in vain. But alas! each relaxing and desperation is an instinct too. To be active, well, happy, implies rare courage. To be ready to fight in a duel or a battle implies desperation, or that you hold your life cheap.

If you take this life to be simply what old religious folks pretend, (I mean the effete, gone to seed in a drought, mere human galls stung by the Devil once), then all your joy & serenity is reduced to grinning and bearing it. The fact is, you have got to take the world on your shoulders like Atlas and put along with it. You will do this for an idea's sake, and your success will be in proportion to your devotion to ideas. It may make your back ache occasionally, but you will have the satisfaction of hanging it or twirling it to suit yourself. Cowards suffer, heroes enjoy. After a long day's walk with it, pitch it into a hollow place, sit

down and eat your luncheon. Unexpectedly, by some immortal thoughts, you will be compensated. The bank whereon you sit will be a fragrant and flowery one, and your world in the hollow a sleek and light gazelle.

Where is the "Unexplored land" but in our own untried enterprises? To an adventurous spirit any place,—London New York, Worcester, or his own yard, is "unexplored land," to seek which Freemont & Kane travel so far. To a sluggish & defeated spirit even the Great Basin & the Polaris are trivial places. If they ever get there (& indeed they are there now) they will want to sleep & give it up, just as they always do. These are the regions of the Known & of the Unknown. What is the use of going right over the old track again? There is an adder in the path which your own feet have worn. You must make tracks into the Unknown. That is what you have your board & clothes for. Why do you ever mend your clothes, unless that, wearing them, you may mend your ways?

Let us sing

H.D.T.

MS., Scripps College Library. *The brackets are Thoreau's.*

From MRS. BRONSON ALCOTT

My dear friend Mr Thoreau
    Will you join us for one hour (11 ocl to 12.) at our home this day to celebrate the marriage of our dear Anna and John
                                                    Yrs affectionately
                                                    Abby Alcott

According to The Journals of Bronson Alcott *Anna Alcott and John Pratt were married May 23, 1860. MS., Berg; previously unpublished.*

From CHAUNCEY SMITH

Boston June 1st 1860

Mr Henry D Thoreau
Dear Sir
    I enclose to you my brothers note with my endorsement, at his request.
    Please acknowledge to him its reception

Yours truly
Chauncey Smith

Smith **had** *endorsed an earlier note for his brother, L. L. Smith, and sent it to Thoreau on January 23, 1860. MS., Huntington; previously unpublished.*

To SOPHIA THOREAU

Concord July 8 1860

Dear Sophia,
    Mother reminds me that I must write to you, if only a few lines, though I have sprained my thumb so that it is questionable whether I can write legibly, if at all. I can't bear on much. What is worse, I believe that I have sprained my brain too—i.e it sympathizes with my thumb. But there is no excuse, I suppose, for writing a letter in such a case, is, like sending a newspaper, only a hint to let you know that "all is well"—but my thumb.
    I hope that you begin to derive some benefit from that more mountainous air which you are breathing Have you had a distinct view of the Franconia Notch mts (blue peaks in the N horizon)? which I told you that you could get from the road in Campton, & probably from some

other points nearer. Such a view of the *mts* is more memorable than any other.

Have you been to Squam Lake, or overlooked it— I should think that you could easily make an excursion to some *mt* in that direction from which you could see the lake & the *mts* generally.

Is there no friend of N.P.Rogers who can tell you where the "lions" are. Of course I did not go to North Elba, but I sent some reminiscences of last fall

I hear that John Brown jr has just come to Boston for a few days. Mr Sanborn's case, it is said, will come on after some murder cases have been disposed of—here.

I have just been invited, formally, to be present at the annual picnic of Theodore Parker's society (that was) at Waverly next Wednesday, & to make some remarks. But that is wholly out of my line— I do not go to picnics even in Concord you know.

Mother & Aunt Sophia rode to Acton in time yesterday. I suppose that you have heard that Mr Hawthorne has come home. I went to meet him the other evening & found that he has not altered except that he was looking pretty brown after his voyage He is as simple & child-like as ever.

I believe that I have fairly scared the kittens away, at last, by my pretended fierceness—which was humane merely.

& now I will consider my thumb— & your *eyes*

Henry

According to Sanborn (Familiar Letters of Thoreau, p. 419), Sophia was in Campton, New Hampshire when her brother wrote this geo-graphical-political letter. Rogers (he died in 1846) had been a strong New Hampshire antislavery man; presumably the "lions" Thoreau mentions in connection with him are abolitionist ones. Thoreau had been invited to North Elba, an upstate New York village, to attend services for John Brown on his burial there on July 4, 1860. "Mr. San-born's case" was the indictment against not Sanborn but the federal deputies who had attempted to arrest him for not testifying before the Senate in its John Brown investigation (see also Thoreau to Sumner, July 16, 1860). MS., Morgan; the writing is frequently slurred because of Thoreau's injury.

From CHARLES C. MORSE

Atheneum & Mechanics Association Rochester N. Y.

Henry D. Thoreau
Dear Sir: I have been unable to obtain from our booksellers your "Week on the Concord & Merrimack Rivers" and therefore enclose you the supposed price. You will please send it to my address by mail.

I would also inquire if you are in the lecture field and whether you could be obtained to deliver two or more lectures upon some[?] scientific subjects before our association this coming winter?

Yours Respectfully
Chas C. Morse

The rough draft of Thoreau's answer to this undated letter is dated July 12. MS., Huntington; previously unpublished.

To CHARLES C. MORSE

Conc[or]d July 12 1860

Mr Charles C Morse
Dear Sir—
    I mail to your address today a copy of my "Week" as you request—
    I *am* in the lecture field—but my subjects are not *scientific*—rather [Transcendentalist & aesthetic. I devote myself to the absorption of nature generally.] Such as "Walking or *the Wild*" "Autumnal tints" &c— [Even if the utterances were scientific, the treatment would hardly bear that sense]
less in a popular vein if you think that your audience will incline or erect[?] their ears to such themes as these. I shall be happy to read to them.

Yr respect[ful]ly
Hen. D. Thoreau

We cannot be sure whether Morse's group was depressed or not by the prospect of Transcendentalist and aesthetic lectures, but there is no record of further negotiations, nor does the final copy of Thoreau's draft survive in the files of the Rochester Athenaeum (now the Rochester Institute of Technology). (But see also Thoreau to Benjamin Austin, Jr., July 16, 1860.) MS., Huntington, a penciled scrawl on the back of Morse's letter; printed with additions (given here in brackets) in the catalogue of the Bixby sale (Anderson Auction Co., February 28, 1917).

————

To BENJAMIN H. AUSTIN, JR.

Concord July 16 1860

Mr Benjamin H Austin Jr
Dear Sir

    I shall be very happy to read to your association three lectures on the evenings named, but the question is about their character. They will not be scientific in the common, nor, perhaps, in any sense. They will be such as you might infer from reading my books. As I have just told Mr. Morse, they will be *transcendental*, that is, to the mass of hearers, probably *moonshine*. Do you think that this will do? Or does your audience prefer lamplight, or total darkness these nights? I dare say, however, that they would interest those who are most interested in what is called nature.

    Mr Morse named no evenings & I have not had time to hear from, or make any arrangement with him.

Yrs respectfully
Henry D. Thoreau

Austin was one of the lecture managers for the Young Men's Association of Buffalo. Thoreau was apparently trying to arrange something of a lecture tour, with Rochester and Buffalo as two of his stops. His apparently talking about Mr. Morse of Rochester as if Austin knew of him

is puzzling. Is there a lost letter? (Thoreau, however, had written Morse only four days before.) Had Morse written Austin about Thoreau's coming to Rochester? Another possibility is that Thoreau was referring to a Charles H. Morse of Buffalo who became the corresponding secretary of the Young Men's Association in 1861, though not listed as an officer in 1860. According to Miss Margaret H. Evans of the Buffalo Public Library there is no mention of Thoreau in the reports of the Young Men's Association there, though other speakers are listed. Probably he never spoke in either Buffalo or Rochester. MS., Buffalo Public Library; previously unpublished.

To CHARLES SUMNER

Concord July 16 1860

Mr Sumner
Dear Sir,

Allow me to thank you for your two speeches on the Hyatt case, & for two Patent Office Reports on Agriculture

Especially, I wish to thank you for your speech on the Barbarism of Slavery, which, I hope and suspect, commences a new era in the history of our Congress; when questions of national importance have come to be considered occasionally from a broadly ethical, and not from a narrowly political point of view alone.

It is refreshing to hear some naked truth, moral or otherwise, uttered there—which can always take care of itself when uttered, and of course belongs to no party. (That was the whole value of Gerrit Smith's presence there, methinks, though he did go to bed early.) Whereas this has only been employed occasionally to perfume the wheel-grease of party or national politics.

The Patent Office Reports on Agriculture contain much that concerns me, & I am very glad to possess now a pretty complete series of them.

Yrs truly
Henry D. Thoreau

Charles Sumner made two speeches in the Senate on behalf of Thaddeus Hyatt of New York. The Senate had appointed a special committee to investigate John Brown's raid on Harpers Ferry. The committee summoned a large number of citizens suspected of having had some connection with Brown, among them F. B. Sanborn, James Redpath (see his letter of February 6, 1860), and Hyatt. Hyatt appeared, refused to testify as the committee desired, and was charged with contempt of the Senate and thrown into the District of Columbia jail. Sumner spoke against his imprisonment. Thoreau's dig at the wealthy agrarian abolitionist Gerrit Smith was based on the rumor that Smith had failed to vote against the Kansas-Nebraska Bill because it came up for passage after his customary bedtime, nine o'clock. MS., Harvard; previously unpublished.

To WELCH, BIGELOW & CO.

Concord July 27 1860

Messrs Welch, Bigelow, & *Co*
    Below you will find my bill for plumbago. I will thank you to send a Draft for the amount on a Boston bank, as heretofore. Trusting that you will not require me to wait so long, without explanation, as the last time, I remain

Yrs truly
Henry D. Thoreau

Concord July 27 1860

Messrs Welch Bigelow & Co
    Bought of Henry D. Thoreau
    Twenty-four lb of Plumbago $36.00
sent April 27
                Recd Payt

MS., Berg, *Thoreau's manuscript draft; previously unpublished.*

Concord July 27' 1860

Messrs Welch, Bigelow, & Co

    Below you will find my bill
for Plumbago. I will thank you to
send a Draft for the amount on a
Boston bank, as heretofore. Trusting
that you will not require me to
wait so long without explanation,
as the last time, I remain
       Yrs truly
       Henry D. Thoreau

Concord July 27' 1860

Messrs Welch Bigelow & Co
       Bought of Henry D. Thoreau

Twenty four lb of Plumbago $ 36,00
sent April 27" - - - -

    Recd Pay'd

587

To H. G. O. BLAKE

Concord, August 3, 1860.

Mr. Blake,—

I some time ago asked Channing if he would not spend a week with me on Monadnoc; but he did not answer decidedly. Lately he has talked of an excursion somewhere, but I said that *now* I must wait till my sister returned from Plymouth, N.H. She has returned,—and accordingly, on receiving your note this morning, I made known its contents to Channing, in order to see how far I was engaged with him. The result is that he decides to go to Monadnoc to-morrow morning; so I must defer making an excursion with you and Brown to another season. Perhaps you will call as you pass the mountain. I send this by the earliest mail.

P. S.—That was a very insufficient visit you made here the last time. My mother is better, though far from well; and if you should chance along here any time after your journey, I trust that we shall all do better.

Text, Familiar Letters of Thoreau, *pp. 421–22.*

From CHARLES P. RICKER

Lowell, Aug 31 1860

Mr. Thoreau:
Dear Sir:

By the instructions of our Committee I am requested to write, that we have two lectures on the Sabbath.

If you could give us two lectures instead of one for the terms you state we shall be happy to hear you. Otherwise we shall be obliged to

wait till we gain a stronger hold on the public mind, and chiefly increase or better our financial condition.

Please answer if possible by return of mail.

Yours Respectfully
Charles P. Ricker

MS., Berg; *previously unpublished.*

From CHARLES P. RICKER

Lowell, Sept. 6 / 60

Mr. H. D. Thoreau:

Yours of the 31st. is recieved. We shall expect you to address our people next Sabbath. Arriving at Lowell, you will find me at No 21 Central Street, or at residence No. 123 East Merrimack Street, or you can take a coach direct to Mr. Owen's, No 52 East Merrimack Street, who will be in readiness to entertain you, and with whom you will find a pleasant home during your stay among us.

Hoping to see you soon I remain

Yours Respectfully
Charles P. Ricker

Thoreau's Journal *shows that he went to Lowell as agreed, leaving Concord on the 8th and returning on the 10th.* MS., Berg; *previously unpublished.*

To THE PUBLISHERS OF "THE WORLD," September 17, 1860

This letter asked the publishers of a newly organized New York newspaper to include Thoreau's name in their list of lecturers, according to the catalogue of the E. C. Stedman sale (Anderson Galleries, January 24–25, 1911), which listed the manuscript. It was later listed in the catalogue of the John Heise sale (American Art Association, May 6, 1915), with one sentence quoted: "I should like to have my name included in your list."

———————

To HORACE GREELEY

Concord Sep 29 1860

Friend Greeley,
        Knowing your interest in whatever relates to Agriculture, I send you with this a short address delivered by me before "the Middlesex Agricultural Society," in this town, Sep. 20, on The Succession of Forest Trees. It is part of a chapter on the Dispersion of Seeds. If you would like to print it, please accept it. If you do not wish to print it entire, *return it to me* at once, for it *is due to the Societys* "Report" a month or 6 weeks hence

Yours truly
Henry D. Thoreau

Greeley accepted the address and printed it in the October 6, 1860 New-York Weekly Tribune. *It was also printed in the* Transactions of the Middlesex Agricultural Society for the Year 1860. *But Thoreau never completed "The Dispersion of Seeds."* MS., New York; *previously unpublished.*

From A. S. CHASE

Waterbury Conn Oct 5 1860

Dear Sir
    I have yours of the 22nd ult— We accept your offer to lecture here and have assigned you for Tuesday evening December 11th. We have Rev. H. H. Bellows for the 4th & Bayard Taylor for the 18th. Please name your subject in advance of the time if convenient as we would like to be able to state it.

Truly yours
A. S Chase Cor Sy

Mr Henry D. Thoreau

Thoreau lectured on "Autumnal Tints." He was suffering from a severe cold, and the strain of the journey probably brought on a succeeding attack of bronchitis. The report in the Waterbury American *spoke caustically of his performance: "it was dull, commonplace and unsatisfactory." MS., Berg; previously unpublished.*

To DR. SAMUEL KNEELAND

Concord Oct 13 1860

Dr. Samuel Kneeland
Dear Sir;
    The members of the Nat. Hist. Soc. may be interested to hear, that a female Canada Lynx (L. Canadensis, or Loup Cervier) was killed, on the 9th of September, in Carlisle, about three miles from the middle of Concord. I saw the carcase, & have the skin & skull, which I have set up. It is as large as any of its kind which I find described. I was at first troubled to identify it in the books, because it has naked soles, though I believed it to be the *Canadensis*. Audubon & Bachman give

591

THE CORRESPONDENCE OF THOREAU

"soles hairy" as one of the specific characters of this species, and "soles naked" as a specific character of L. Rufus. Emmons (in the Massachusetts' Reports) says further & more particularly, "The two most remarkable characters of the Lynx [i.e. The *Canadensis*] are the beautiful pencils of black hair which ornament the ears, and the perfect hairiness of the soles of the feet, which have no naked spots or tubercles like the other species of the feline race." And, speaking of the Bay Lynx, he says that it "is easily distinguished from the preceding by the shorter pencils of hair upon the ear, and by the nakedness of the balls of the toes. This last character, it appears to me, is sufficiently important in the *borealis* [i.e. *Canadensis*] to constitute it a genus by itself."

At length, I obtained a copy of Bairds' "Mammals"; but still I was not satisfied till I had read to near the end of his account, when he says that he has received a second specimen, "in summer pelage," and that "the pads of the feet in this specimen are distinctly visible, not being at all overgrown, as in winter specimens." This is my animal, both in this and in other respects. I am thus minute because it is not yet made quite distinct enough, that hairy soles are no more characteristic of this Lynx than naked soles are.

Judging from the above descriptions, the only peculiarity in my specimen is a distinct black line commencing at the eye and terminating in the black portion of the ruff.

I suspect that some of the Lynxes killed in this vicinity of late years, and called the Bay Lynx, were the Canada Lynx.

Yrs truly
Henry D. Thoreau

Dr. Kneeland was recording secretary of the Boston Society of Natural History. Thoreau had been elected a corresponding member in 1850 and for the rest of his life kept in contact with the Society's activities. The brackets are Thoreau's. MS., Boston Society of Natural History.

From DANIEL RICKETSON

The Shanty, Oct. 14, 1860.

Friend Thoreau,—

Am I to infer from your silence that you decline any farther correspondence and intercourse with me? Or is it that having nothing in particular to communicate you deem silence the wiser course? Yet, between friends, to observe a certain degree of consideration is well, and as I wrote you last, and that some nine or ten months ago, inviting you to visit me, I have often felt disappointed and hurt by your almost sepulchral silence towards me.

I am aware that I have no claims upon you, that I voluntarily introduced myself to your notice, and that from the first you have always behaved toward me with a composure which leads me not to judge too severely your present neutrality. I know also that I have but little to give you in return for the edification and pleasure I have derived from your society, and of which to be deprived not only myself but my family would deem a great and irreparable loss. I readily admit that this gives me no claim upon your friendship, but having passed so much of my life in the want of rural companionship I cannot easily surrender the opportunity of occasionally conversing and rambling among the scenes of our beloved neighborhood, here and at Concord, with you. I trust you will now pardon me for again obtruding myself upon you. I am not accustomed to be humble, nor do I intend to be at this time, for I am not conscious of having committed any offence of sufficient magnitude to forfeit your regard for me.

I would, however, state, that you have probably never seen me under the most favorable circumstances, that is, in my *calmest* hours. I am by nature very easily disturbed, mentally and physically, and this tendency, or infirmity, has been increased by smoking. I have, at last, abandoned the use of the weed. It is now about four months since I have made any use whatever of tobacco, and nearly a year since I began to battle seriously with this enemy of my soul's and body's peace. When I was last at Concord, owing to bad sleep, and the consequent nervous irritability aggravated by smoking, I was particularly out of order, and like an intoxicated or crazed man, hardly responsible for my conduct. Wherefore, if I betrayed any want of kind or gentlemanly feeling, which, I fear, may

593

have been the case, I trust you will pardon the same and attribute it to a source not normal with me.

In conclusion, I would add that it would give me much pleasure to continue our friendship and occasional intimacy. Still I would not press it, for in so doing I should be selfish, as I have so little to return you for your favors. But ah! me, what is this life worth, if those of congenial tastes and pursuits cannot exchange common courtesies with each other?

Channing is occasionally in New Bedford, but he never comes to see me, nor writes me. I endeavored to be to him a good friend, and his cold, strange ways hurt and grieve me. Would to God that he were able to be true to his higher nature, so beautiful and intelligent.

It is possible you may not have got the last letter I wrote you, which was in December last, if so, the cause of your silence will prove less painful to me.

I write under embarrassment, and must trust to your generosity for the want of felicity of expression in my attempt to convey to you my estimation of the value of your friendship, and my unwillingness to lose it.

I remain, truly and faithfully your friend,

D. Ricketson

Ricketson's reference to a letter of "December last" is probably a slip of memory: we have a letter of January 1860, but none for December. Text, Ricketson, pp. 104–6.

From WELCH, BIGELOW & CO.

Oct 30, 1860

Mr H D Thoreau
Dear Sir
    Please send us another installment of Black Lead as before. Only you should pay express chg. to Boston as heretofore with the exception of the last

Yours truly
Welch Bigelow & Co

MS., Berg; *previously unpublished.*

———————

To H. G. O. BLAKE

Concord Nov. 4 1860

Mr Blake,
    I am glad to hear any particulars of your excursion. As for myself, I looked out for you somewhat on that Monday, when, it appears, you passed Monadnock—turned my glass upon several parties that were ascending the mountain half a mile on one side of us. In short, I came as near to seeing you as you to seeing me. I have no doubt that we should have had a good time if you had come, for I had, all ready, two good spruce houses, in which you could stand up, complete in all respects, half a mile apart, and you & B[rown] could have lodged by yourselves in one, if not with us.
    We made an excellent beginning of our *mt* life. You may remember that the Saturday previous was a stormy day. Well, we went up in the rain—wet through, and found ourselves in a cloud there at mid *pm.* in no situation to look about for the best place for a camp. So I proceded at once, through the cloud, to that memorable stone "chunk yard," in

595

which we made our humble camp once, and there, after putting our packs under a rock, having a good hatchet, I proceded to build a substantial house, which C[hanning] declared the handsomest he ever saw. (He never camped out before, and was, no doubt, prejudiced in its favor.) This was done about dark, and by that time we were nearly as wet as if we had stood in a hogshead of water. We then built a fire before the door, directly on the site of our little camp of two years ago, and it took a long time to burn thro' its remains to the earth beneath. Standing before this, and turning round slowly, like meat that is roasting, we were as dry if not drier than ever after a few hours, & so, at last we "turned in."

This was a great deal better than going up there in fair weather, & having no adventure (not knowing how to appreciate either fair weather or foul) but dull common-place sleep in a useless house, & before a comparatively useless fire—such as we get every night. Of course, we thanked our stars, when we saw them, which was about midnight, that they had seemingly withdrawn for a season. We had the *mt* all to ourselves that *pm* & night. There was nobody going up that day to engrave his name on the summit, nor to gather blueberries. The Genius of the *mts.* saw us starting from Concord & it said,— There come two of our folks. Let us get ready for them— Get up a serious storm, that will send a packing these holiday guests (They may have their say another time) Let us receive them with true *mt.* hospitality—kill the fatted cloud—Let them know the value of a spruce roof, & of a fire of dead spruce stumps. Every bush dripped tears of joy at our advent. Fire did its best & received our thanks.—What could fire have done in fair weather?—Spruce roof got its share of our blessings. And then such a view of the wet rocks with the wet lichens on them, as we had the next morning, but did not get again!

We & the *mt* had a sound season, as the saying is. How glad we were to be wet in order that we might be dried!—how glad we were of the storm which made our house seem like a new home to us! This day's experience was indeed lucky for we did not have a thunder shower during all our stay. Perhaps our host reserved this attention in order to tempt us to come again.

Our next house was more substantial still. One side was rock, good for durability, the floor the same, & the roof which I made would have upheld a horse. I stood on it to do the shingling.

I noticed, when I was at the White *Mts* last, several nuisances which render travelling there-abouts unpleasant. The chief of these was the

mt houses. I might have supposed that the main attraction of that region even to citizens, lay in its wildness and unlikeness to the city, & yet they make it as much like the city as they can afford to. I heard that the Crawford House was lighted with gas, & had a large saloon, with its band of music, for dancing. But give me a spruce house made in the rain.

An old Concord farmer tells me that he ascended Monadnock once, & danced on the top. How did that happen? Why, he being up there, a party of young men & women came up bringing boards & a fiddler, and having laid down the boards they made a level floor, on which they danced to the music of the fiddle. I suppose the tune was "Excelsior." This reminds me of the fellow who climbed to the top of a very high spire, stood upright on the ball, & then hurrahed for—what? Why for Harrison & Tyler. That's the kind of sound which most ambitious people emit when they culminate. They are wont to be singularly frivolous in the thin atmosphere they can't contain themselves, though our comfort & their safety require it; it takes the pressure of many atmospheres to do this; & hence they helplessly evaporate there. It would seem, that, as they ascend, they breathe shorter and shorter, and at each *expiration,* some of their wits leave them, till, when they reach the pinnacle, they are so light headed as to be fit only to show how the wind sits. I suspect that Emersons criticism called Monadnock was inspired not by remembering the inhabitants of N. H. as they are in the valleys, so much as by meeting some of them on the *mt* top.

After several nights' experience C came to the conclusion that he was "lying out doors," and inquired what was the largest beast that might nibble his legs there. I fear that he did not improve all the night, as he might have done, to sleep. I had asked him to go and spend a week there. We spent 5 nights, being gone 6 days, for C suggested that 6 working days made a week, & I saw that he was ready to *de-camp.* However, he found his account in it, as well as I.

We were seen to go up in the rain, grim & silent like 2 Genii of the storm, by Fassett's men or boys, but we were never identified afterward, though we were the subject of some conversation which we overheard. Five hundred persons at least came onto the *mt.* while we were there, but not one found our camp. We saw one party of three ladies & two gentlemen spread their blankets and spend the night on the top, & heard them converse, but they did not know that they had neighbors, who were

comparatively old settlers. We spared them the chagrin which that knowledge would have caused them, & let them print their story in a newspaper accordingly.

From what I heard of Fassett's infirmities I concluded that his partner was Tap. He has moved about thirty rods further down the *mt.*, & is still hammering at a new castle there when you go by, while Tap is probably down cellar. Such is the Cerberus that guards *this* passage. There always is one you know. This is not so bad to go by as the Glen House. However, we left those Elysian fields by a short cut of our own which departed just beyond where he is stationed.

Yes, to meet men on an honest and simple footing, meet with rebuffs, suffer from sore feet, as you did, aye & from a sore heart, as perhaps you also did,—all that is excellent. What a pity that that young prince could not enjoy a little of the legitimate experience of travelling, be dealt with simply & truly though rudely. He might have been invited to some hospitable house in the country, had his bowl of bread & milk set before him, with a clean pin-a-fore, been told that there were the punt & the fishing rod, and he could amuse himself as he chose—might have swung a few birches, dug out a woodchuck, & had a regular good time, & finally been sent to bed with the boys,—and so never have been introduced to Mr. [Edward] Everett at all. I have no doubt that this would have been a far more memorable & valuable experience than he got.

The snow-clad summit of *Mt.* Washington must have been a very interesting sight from Wachusett. How wholesome winter is seen far or near, how good above all mere sentimental warm-blooded—short-lived, soft-hearted *moral* goodness, commonly so called. Give me the goodness which has forgotten its own deeds,—which God has seen to be good and let be. None of your *just made perfect*—pickled eels! All that will save them will be their picturesqueness, as with blasted trees Whatever is and is not ashamed to be is good. I value no moral goodness or greatness unless it is good or great even as that snowy peak is. Pray how could thirty feet of bowels improve it? Nature is goodness crystalized. You looked into the land of promise. Whatever beauty we behold, the more it is distant, serene, and cold, the purer & more durable it is. It is better to warm ourselves with ice than with fire.

Tell Brown that he sent me more than the price of the book—viz a word from himself, for which I am greatly his debtor.

H. D. T.

This was to be Thoreau's last visit to Monadnock. The young prince he mentions became Edward VII. MS., Lownes.

To DANIEL RICKETSON

Concord Nov. 4 1860

Friend Ricketson,

I thank you for the verses. They are quite too good to apply to me. However, I know what a poet's license is, and will not get in the way.

But what do you mean by that prose? Why will you waste so many regards on me, and not know what to think of my silence? Infer from it what you might from the silence of a dense pine wood. It is its natural condition, except when the winds blow, and the jays scream, & the chickadee winds up his clock. My silence is just as inhuman as that, and no more.

You know that I never promised to correspond with you, & so, when I do, I do more than I promised.

Such are my pursuits and habits that I rarely go abroad, and it is quite a habit with me to decline invitations to do so. Not that I could not enjoy such visits, if I were not otherwise occupied. I have enjoyed very much my visits to you and my rides in your neighborhood, and am sorry that I cannot enjoy such things oftener; but life is short, and there are other things also to be done. I admit that you are more social than I am, and far more attentive to "the common courtesies of life" but this is partly for the reason that you have fewer or less exacting private pursuits.

Not to have written a note for a year is with me a very venial offence. I think that I do not correspond with any one so often as once in six-months.

I have a faint recollection of your invitation referred to, but I suppose that I had no new nor particular reason for declining & so made no new statements. I have felt that you would be glad to see me almost whenever I got ready to come, but I only offer myself as a rare visitor, & a still rarer correspondent.

I am very busy, after my fashion, little as there is to show for it, and feel as if I could not spend many days nor dollars in travelling, for the shortest visit must have a fair margin to it, and the days thus affect the weeks, you know. Nevertheless, we cannot forego these luxuries altogether.

You must not regard me as a regular diet, but at most only as acorns, which too are not to be despised, which, at least, we love to think are edible in a bracing walk. We have got along pretty well together in several directions, though we are such strangers in others.

I hardly know what to say in answer to your letter.

Some are accustomed to write many letters, others very few. I am one of the last. At any rate, we are pretty sure, if we write at all, to send those thoughts which we cherish, to that one, who, we believe, will most religiously attend to them.

This life is not for complaint, but for satisfaction. I do not feel addressed by this letter of yours. It suggests only misunderstanding. Intercourse may be good, but of what use are complaints & apologies? Any complaint *I* have to make is too serious to be utterred, for the evil cannot be mended.

Turn over a new leaf

My out-door harvest this fall has been one Canada Lynx, a fierce looking fellow, which, it seems, we have hereabouts; eleven barrels of apples from trees of my own planting; and a large crop of white oak acorns which I did not raise.

Please remember me to your family. I have a very pleasant recollection of your fireside, and I trust that I shall revisit it—also of your shanty & the surrounding regions.

Yrs truly
Henry D. Thoreau

The gap of which Ricketson complained is apparently considerable: the last extant letter before this one is dated February 12, 1859. Thoreau's opening reference to some verses is obscure. They must have been original ones—Ricketson fancied himself as a poet—but we are not sure which. The admonition to "Turn over a new leaf," at the bottom of a sheet, is a typically Thoreauvian pun. MS., Huntington.

From MONCURE CONWAY

Cincinnati, Nov. 26.

My dear Mr. Thoreau,

We are thinking of issuing the *Dial* next year as a Quarterly instead of a Monthly; and I wish to ask if you will be so bountiful as to let me publish therein your Agricultural Address.

Your friend,
M. D. Conway.

Mr H D Thoreau.

The "Agricultural Address" was probably "The Succession of Forest Trees." But neither it nor any other work by Thoreau ever appeared in Conway's Dial. *The year is omitted, but the letter is included in* Berg *with other manuscripts for 1860, the year of Thoreau's address. MS.,* Berg; *previously unpublished.*

To H. G. O. BLAKE

Concord Dec 2d '60

Mr Blake,

I am going to Waterbury Ct. to lecture on the 11th inst. If you are to be at home, & it will be agreeable to you, I will spend the afternoon & night of the 10th with you & Brown.

H. D. Thoreau

MS., *Berg, copy in Blake's hand; previously unpublished.*

From HOBART & ROBBINS

Boston 3d Dec'r, 1860.

Mr. Henry D. Thoreau Concord, N. H.
Dr. Sir
    Enclosed are Nine Dollars, to pay our order of the 26th. Return the enclosed bill receipted.

Yr's Resp'y
Hobart & Robbins

$9.00

MS., Berg; *previously unpublished.*

To LOUIS A. SURETTE

Concord Dec 17 '60

Mr Surette
Dear Sir
    I am very sorry to say that the illness of my mother, who is confined to her bed, will prevent her showing to Mr Phillips the attention which she desired to. The prospect is also that I shall be kept at home Wednesday evening by an influenza— My mother wishes me to say, however, that Mrs Brooks will be happy to entertain Mr Phillips at her home.

Yrs truly
Henry D. Thoreau

Surette, the curator of the Concord Lyceum, had evidently tried to make arrangements for hospitality for Wendell Phillips, who lectured two

days after Thoreau wrote this note. Mrs. Nathan Brooks was a good friend of Thoreau's womenfolk. MS., Huntington; previously unpublished.

To E. H. RUSSELL

The book to which I referred was "Heywood's New England Gazeteer Concord, New Hampshire, 1839." There are later and probably better editions. I am glad to hear that my own book has afforded you any pleasure.

Yours truly,
Henry D. Thoreau.

Elias Harlow Russell was an elocutionist and teacher in Worcester and a good friend of H. G. O. Blake and Theo Brown. At one time, after Thoreau's death, Russell became his literary executor. Text, Goodspeed's Catalogue No. 271, Item 221, p. 28.

1861

Mayor Fernando Wood of New York proposed to his City Council that in the event of disunion New York should constitute itself a free city and trade with both the North and the South. Throughout the South federal arsenals and army posts were seized by local forces. The Confederate Provisional Congress met in Montgomery, adopted a constitution, and elected Jefferson Davis president of the Confederate States and Alexander Stephens vice-president. William Seward, now Lincoln's Secretary of State, suggested to the President that a foreign war be declared in order to take the people's minds off disunion and unite them again. On April 13 Fort Sumter fell. The Northern states and the Confederacy responded to the call for troops. Lee accepted command of the Confederate Army and was made a full general on June 14. In November General George McClellan was appointed commander of the United States Army. The battle lines were drawn swiftly throughout the nation. Both armies swelled in strength. The skirmishes and bloodless victories ended; the pitched battles began, with the Union forces losing most of them.

Thoreau started the year by concentrating on nature. His *Journal* entries are reasonably full for the first few months, but by spring they dwindle into jottings, and by fall they are finished. On the chance that better health might be found through travel, he and young Horace Mann, Jr. took a trip to Minnesota from May to July. Good health for Thoreau was not to be discovered there, however. Even the Indian council failed to stir him deeply, although he had for many years been filling notebooks with information about Indians. By late fall he was gravely ill.

Office of The Adams Express Company 164 Baltimore Street

Baltimore, Jany 31 1861

Mr Hy. D. Thoreau Concord
      Your *Pcl* and *Bill* for Collection, *$10 oo* on *H. A. Lucas Balto* has been presented and *Payment Refused*
Please advise us at once what disposition we shall make of the Goods, as they are held subject to your order, and at your RISK AGAINST FIRE, AND OTHER DANGERS.
Answer on THIS SHEET.

Respectfully yours,
For the Company
Jos. Stubbs

This is a form letter with all but the italicized words printed. MS., Berg; previously unpublished.

From FREDERIC TUDOR

Boston February 12th 1861

Mr. Henry D. Thoreau Concord Mass.
Dear Sir
      I have to acknowledge receipt of your favor of 11*th* instant enclosing a Check by the Concord Bank on the Suffolk Bank of this City

for *Forty three & 03/100 Dollars* to my order being in full for amount of Bill of 2 Bbls Black Lead forwarded you on the 10th inst per your order & I remain

Yr. Ob. St.
Frederic Tudor
Per Benj. F. Field

$43.03

MS., Berg; *previously unpublished.*

From DANIEL RICKETSON

Wednesday, 9 a.m., 27th Feb., 1861.

Dear Thoreau,—

> "The bluebird has come, now let us rejoice!
> This morning I heard his melodious voice."

But a more certain herald of spring, the pigeon woodpecker, a few of which remain with us during the winter, has commenced his refreshing call. While I sit writing with my Shanty door open I hear, too, the sweet notes of the meadow-lark, which also winters here, and regales us with his song nearly every fine morning. I have seen and heard the black-bird flying over, not his song, but crackle; the redwing, I doubt not he is quite garrulous in the warmer nooks of low and open woodlands and bushy pastures. There goes the woodpecker, rattling away on his "penny trumpet!"

It is one of those exquisitely still mornings when all nature, without and within, seems at peace. Sing away, dear bluebird! My soul swells with gratitude to the great Giver of all good and beautiful things. As I go to my Shanty door to dry my ink in the sun, I see swarms of little flies in the air near by. The crows are cawing from the more distant

pine-woods, where you and I and my other dear poetic friends have walked together. Now I hear the lonely whistle of the black-cap, followed by his strange counterpart in song, the "chickadee" chorus.

2 p.m. Wind S. W. Thermometer 52 deg. in shade. I suppose that you are also enjoying somewhat of this spring influence, if not as fully as we. The winter has passed away thus far quite comfortably with us, and though not severe, with a few occasional exceptions, yet we have had a good deal of good skating, which has been well improved by both sexes, old and young. My sons and I again made a circuit of the Middleborough ponds on the 17th December, at which we should have liked very much your company. Our river has also been frozen strong enough, and we have had several afternoons' skating there, visiting our friends below on the Fairhaven side. It was really a cheerful sight to see the large number—sometimes a thousand or more—enjoying the pastime and recreation. Many of our young women skate well, and among them our Emma. Walton makes his own skates, and really elegant affairs are they, and he is also very agile upon them. We have a large ship building a little below us, but far enough off not to interfere with the inland quiet of my rambles along shore, which I sometimes take in foggy weather, when I suppose I am [a] little more of a Hollander than usual.

As my object was principally to announce the bluebird, which may have reached you by the time this letter shall, I will soon close. March is close at hand again, and may be here by the time you read this. It is "a welcome month to me." I call it the month of hope, and can patiently wait for the spring flowers and the songs of birds so near by. Soon the willow will put forth its catkins, and your friends the piping or peeping frogs set up their vernal choir, so gentle and soothing to the wounded spirit, where there is also a poetic ear to listen to it.

4 p.m. I fear, after all, that this will prove rather a disjointed letter, for I have been interrupted several times in its progress. During the intervals I have been to town—helped load a hay-wagon with hay, and am just returned from a short drive with my wife and daughters. The only objects of particular attraction were the pussies or catkins on the willows along the lower part of the Nash road, and the aments of the alder, the latter not much advanced.

Now that spring is so near at hand may I not expect to see you here once more? Truly pleasant would it be to ramble about with you, or

607

sit and chat in the Shanty or with the family around our common hearthstone.

I send you this day's Mercury with a letter and editorial (I suppose) of Channing's.

Hoping to hear from you soon, or, what is better, to see you here, I remain,

Yours truly,
Dan'l Ricketson.

H. D. Thoreau.

Your welcome letter of Nov. 4th last was duly received. I regret that mine which prompted it should have proved mystical to you. We must "bear and forbear" with each other.

Text, Ricketson, *pp. 108–11.*

From L. JOHNSON & CO.

[Philadelphia] March 22d 1861

Mr. Henry D. Thoreau Concord, Mass.
Dear Sir—
Enclosed find $2. Note on Bank of Kenduskeag to replace the one returned. Of course we were not aware that there was any thing wrong with the one you returned.

Truly Yours
L. Johnson & Co

MS., Berg; *previously unpublished.*

To DANIEL RICKETSON

Concord Mar 22d 1861

Friend Ricketson,

The bluebirds were here the 26 of Feb. at least, which is one day earlier than your date; but I have not heard of larks nor pigeon woodpeckers.

To tell the truth, I am not on the alert for the signs of Spring, not having had any winter yet. I took a severe cold about the 3 of Dec. which at length resulted in a kind of bronchitis, so that I have been confined to the house ever since, excepting a very few experimental trips as far as the P. O. in some particularly mild noons. My health otherwise has not been affected in the least, nor my spirits. I have simply been imprisoned for so long; & it has not prevented my doing a good deal of reading & the like.

Channing has looked after me very faithfully—says he has made a study of my case, & knows me better than I know myself &c &c. Of course, if I knew how it began, I should know better how it would end. I trust that when warm weather comes I shall begin to pick up my crumbs. I thank you for your invitation to come to New Bedford, and will bear it in mind, but at present my health will not permit my leaving home.

The day I received your letter Blake & Brown arrived here, having walked from Worcester in two days, though Alcott who happened in soon after could not understand what pleasure they found in walking across the country at this season when the ways were so unsettled. I had a solid talk with them for a day & a half—though my pipes were not in good order—& they went their way again.

You may be interested to hear that Alcott is at present perhaps the most successful man in the town. He had his 2d annual exhibition of all the schools in the town at the Town Hall last Saturday—at which all the masters & misses did themselves great credit, as I hear, & of course reflected some on their teachers & parents. They were making their little speeches from 1 till 6 o'clock p*m*, to a large audience which patiently listened to the end. In the meanwhile the children made Mr A. an unexpected present, of a fine edition of Pilgrim's Progress & Herberts Poems—which, of course, overcame all parties. I inclose our order of exercises.

We had, last night, an old fashioned N. E. snow storm, far worse than any in the winter, & the drifts are now very high above the fences. The inhabitants are pretty much confined to their houses, as I was already. All houses are one color white with the snow plastered over them, & you cannot tell whether they have blinds or not. Our pump has another pump, its ghost, as thick as itself, sticking to one side of it. The town has sent out teams of 8 oxen each to break out the roads & the train due from Boston at 8½ am has not arrived yet (4 *pm*) All the passing has been a train from above at 12 m—which also was due at 8½ am. Where are the bluebirds now think you? I suppose that you have not so much snow at New Bedford, if any.

Yrs Henry D. Thoreau

Alcott was now superintendent of Concord schools. MS., Huntington.

From PARKER PILLSBURY

A friend of mine away in New York, wishes very much a copy of each of your "Memoirs"—"In the Woods" and On the Rivers." . . . Can you & will you cause a copy of each to meet me at the Anti-Slavery Office. . . .

Pillsbury, one of the outstanding antislavery orators, had long been a friend of the Thoreau family. The tenor of Thoreau's letter of April 10 makes it clear that Pillsbury had said something to Thoreau about potential readers distracted by the onset of the Civil War. Text, catalogue of the Abbott-Sprague sale (*Charles F. Libbie & Co., February 25–26, 1909*), *which also mentions that Pillsbury "Refers to 'Old Abe.'"*

To PARKER PILLSBURY

Concord Ap. 10th 1861

Friend Pillsbury,

I am sorry to say that I have not a copy of "Walden" which I can spare, and know of none, unless possibly, Ticknor & Fields have one. I send, nevertheless a copy of the "Week," the price of which is $1.25 which you can pay at your convenience.

As for my prospective reader, I hope that he *ignores* Fort Sumpter, & Old Abe, & all that, for that is just the most fatal and indeed the only fatal, weapon you can direct against evil ever; for as long as you *know of* it, you are *particeps criminis*. What business have you, if you are "an angel of light," to be pondering over the deeds of darkness, reading the New York Herald, & the like? I do not so much regret the present condition of things in this country (provided I regret it at all) as I do that I ever heard of it. I know one or 2 who have this year, for the first time, read a president's message; but they do not see that this implies a fall in themselves, rather than a rise in the president. Blessed were the days before you read a president's message. Blessed are the young for they do not read the president's message.

Blessed are they who never read a newspaper, for they shall see Nature, and through her, God.

But alas *I* have heard of Sumpter, & Pickens, & even of Buchanan, (though I did not read his message).

I also read the New York Tribune, but then I am reading Herodotus & Strabo, & Blodget's Climatology, and Six Years in the Deserts of North America, as hard as I can, to counterbalance it.

By the way, Alcott is at present our most popular & successful man, and has just published a volume on "vice," in the shape of the annual school report, which, I presume, he has sent to you.

Yours, for remembering all good things,

Henry D. Thoreau

Two days after Thoreau answered Pillsbury's request for Walden *the attack on Sumter began. In the last paragraph "vice" is probably a*

glancing reference to the scandal caused by Alcott's earlier publication of the reports on his work at the Temple School in Boston. MS., Boston Public Library.

From THOMAS CHOLMONDELEY

Shrewsbury April 23, 1861

My dear Thoreau—

It is now some time since I wrote to you or heard from you but do not suppose that I have forgotten you or shall ever cease to cherish in my mind those days at dear old Concord. The last I heard about you all was from Morton who was in England about a year ago; & I hope that he has got over his difficulties & is now in his own country again. I think he has seen rather more of English country life than most Yankee tourists; & appeared to find it *curious*, though I fear he was dulled by our ways, for he was too full of ceremony & compliments & bows, which is a mistake here; though very well in Spain. I am afraid he was rather on pins & needles; but he made a splendid speech at a volunteer supper, & indeed the *very best*, some said, ever heard in this part of the country.

We are here in a state of alarm & apprehension the world being so troubled in East & West & everywhere. Last year the harvest was bad & scanty. This year, our trade is beginning to feel the events in America. In reply to the northern tariff, of course we are going to smuggle as much as we can. The supply of cotton being such a necessity to us—we must work up India & South Africa a little better.

There is war even in old New Zealand but not in the same island where my people are! Besides we are certainly on the eve of a continental blaze. *So we are making merry & living while we can:* not being sure where we shall be this time year.

Give my affectionate regards to your father mother & sister & to Mr Emerson & his family, & to Channing Sanborn Ricketson Blake & Morton & Alcott & Parker. A thought arises in my mind whether I may not be enumerating some dead men! Perhaps Parker is! These rumors of wars make me wish that we had got done with this brutal stupidity of war

612

altogether; & I believe, Thoreau, that the human race will at last get rid of it, though perhaps not in a creditable way—but such *powers* will be brought to bear that it will become monstrous even to the French.

Dundonald declared to the last that he possessed secrets which from their tremendous character would make war impossible. So peace may be begotten from the machinations of evil.

Have you heard of any good books lately? I think *"Burnt Njal"* good & believe it to be genuine. "Hast thou not heard (says Steinrora to Thangbrand how Thor challenged Christ to single combat & how he did not dare to fight with Thor" When Gunnar brandishes his sword three swords are seen in air. The account of Ospah & Brodir & Brians battle is the only historical account of that engagement which the Irish talk so much of; for I place little trust in OHallorans authority though the outline is the same in *both*.

Darwin's origin of species may be fanciful but it is a move in the right direction.

Emersons Conduct of Life has done *me* good; but it will not go down in England for a generation or so.

But *these* are some of them already a year or two old. The book of the season is DeChaillu's Central Africa with accounts of the *Gorilla*, of which you are aware that you have had a skeleton at Boston for many years. There is also one in the British Museum; but they have now several stuffed specimens at the Geographical Societys rooms in Town.

I suppose you will have seen Sir Emerson Tennent's Ceylon, which is perhaps as *complete* a book as ever was published; & a better monument to a governors-residence in a great province was never made.

We have been lately astonished by a foreign *Hamlet*, a supposed impossibility; but Mr Fechter does real wonders. No doubt he will visit America & then you may see the best actor in the world. He has carried out Goethes idea of Hamlet as given in the Wilhelm Meister showing him forth as a fair hair'd & fat man. I suppose you are not yet fat yet!

Yrs ever truly
Thos Cholomondeley

Sanborn identifies Morton as Edwin Morton of Plymouth, Massachusetts, a friend of John Brown who went to England to avoid testifying against him. MS., Berg.

From MRS. HORACE MANN

Dear Mr. Thoreau,

Mrs. Josiah Quincy, a lady who reads & admires your books very much, is passing a few days with me. Will you come in and dine with us to-day—It will give her much pleasure to see you, & when you are tired of talking with ladies, Horace will be glad to have his promised visit & you shall release yourself when you please.

With much regard,
Mary Mann.

We dine at one.

The widow of the noted educator was now living in Concord with her children, among them her son Horace, who, though only in his teens, was already an interested naturalist; Thoreau's Journal for April mentions him four times. Mary Mann's guest was presumably the daughter-in-law of the same Josiah Quincy who had been president of Harvard and had helped Thoreau in his job seeking. She was also a friend of Emerson's, and her husband, Josiah Quincy, Jr., had been Emerson's classmate at Harvard. MS., Huntington; the heading is torn away, but the Huntington chronology supplies the date April 1861, which Sanborn believed probable.

To H. G. O. BLAKE

Concord May 3d 1861

Mr Blake,

    I am still as much an invalid as when you & Brown were here, if not more of one, and at this rate there is danger that the cold weather may come again, before I get over my bronchitis. The Doctor accordingly tells me that I must "clear out," to the West Indies, or elsewhere, he does not seem to care much where. But I decide against the West Indies, on account of their muggy heat in the summer, & the S. of Europe, on ac of the expense of time & money, and have at last concluded that it will be most expedient for me to try the air of Minnesota, say somewhere about St Paul. I am only waiting to be well enough to start—hope to get off within a week or 10 days.

    The inland air may help me at once, or it may not. At any rate I am so much of an invalid that I shall have to study my comfort in traveling to a remarkable degree—stopping to rest &c &c if need be. I think to get a through ticket to Chicago—with liberty to stop frequently on the way, making my first stop of consequence at Niagara Falls—several days or a week, at a private boarding house—then a night or day at Detroit —& as much at Chicago, as my health may require.

    At Chicago I can decide at what point (Fulton, Dunleith or another) to strike the Mississippi & take a boat to St. Paul.

    I trust to find a private boarding house in one or various agreeable places in that region, & spend my time there.

    I expect, and shall be prepared to be gone 3 months—& I would like to return by a different route—perhaps Mackinaw & Montreal.

    I have thought of finding a companion, of course, yet not seriously, because I had no right to offer myself as a companion to anybody— having such a peculiarly private & all absorbing but miserable business as *my* health, & not altogether *his*, to attend to—causing me to stop here & go there &c &c unaccountably.

    Nevertheless, I have just now decided to let you know of my intentions, thinking it barely possible that you might like to make a part or the whole of this journey, at the same time, & that perhaps your own health may be such as to be benefitted by it.

Pray let me know, if such a statement offers any temptations to you. I write in great haste for the mail & must omit all the moral.

H. D Thoreau

Thoreau did not find it easy to secure a companion. Blake evidently declined; and when Thoreau did go he took along the talented young naturalist Horace Mann, Jr. MS., New York Historical Society.

From EMERSON

Concord, Mass., 11 May, 1861.

My dear Thoreau,

I give you a little list of names of good men whom you may chance to see on your road. If you come into the neighborhood of any of them, I pray you to hand this note to them, by way of introduction, praying them, from me, not to let you pass by, without salutation, and any aid and comfort they can administer to an invalid traveler, one so dear and valued by me and all good Americans.

Yours faithfully,
R. W. Emerson

Henry D. Thoreau.

MS., Concord Antiquarian Society (*typescript*); *previously unpublished. The list of names does not accompany the manuscript.*

From ROBERT COLLYER

Mr. Thoreau
Dear Sir

You will find herein the thing you wanted to know. Mr. Whitfield is very well posted about the country and what he says is reliable. I hope you will have a pleasant time get heartily well and write a book about the great West that will be to us what your other books are. A friend, I want you to stop in Chicago as you come back if it can be possible, and be my guest a few days. I should be very much pleased to have you take a rest and feel at home with us, and if you do please write in time so that I shall be sure to be at home.

I am very truly

Robert Collyer

Chicago May 22d.

Collyer was a Unitarian minister in Chicago. MS., Concord Antiquarian Society (typescript); previously unpublished. Although the year is not given, it is obviously that of Thoreau's 1861 excursion to the West.

To SOPHIA THOREAU

I last evening called on Mr. Thatcher. He is much worse in consequence of having been recently thrown from a carriage,—so as to have had watchers within a few nights past. He was, however, able to give me a letter to a Dr. Anderson of Minneapolis, just over the river. You may as well direct to Mr. Thatcher's care still; for I cannot see where I may be a fortnight hence.

Samuel Thatcher, Jr., born in Warren, Maine, was probably the person Thoreau visited. He lived in St. Anthony, Minnesota when Thoreau

saw him and died there August 31. Dr. Anderson was Charles L. Anderson, the state botanist. Text, First and Last Journeys of Thoreau, *II, 44.*

Robert L. Straker in "Thoreau's Journey to Minnesota," *New England Quarterly,* XIV (September 1941), 553, quotes letters of June 9 and 14 from Mary Mann to Horace. The first states: "Mr. Thoreau wrote his sister that you were having a nice time in Natural History. I was amused to hear from Miss Thoreau that the last war news Mr. T. had heard was of the killing of seven hundred men at Leavall's Point, because that was a hoax and a fortnight old." (The passage referred to may have been part of this letter of May 27.) The second letter adds:

"Mrs. Thoreau called this morning to say she had heard from Mr. T. again. It was delightful to his mother to hear that Mr. T. has been swimming. He tells her that he does not pay any attention to his health, though he feels weak. . . . He tells his mother that you and he are having a fine time."

To F. B. SANBORN

Redwing Minnesota June 25th 1861

Mr. Sanborn,
Dear Sir,

I was very glad to find awaiting me, on my arrival here on Sunday afternoon, a letter from you. I have performed this journey in a very dead and alive manner, but nothing has come so near waking me up as the receipt of letters from Concord. I read yours, and one from my sister (and Horace Mann, his four) near the top of a remarkable isolated bluff here, called Barn Bluff or the Grange, or Redwing Bluff, some 450 feet high and half a mile long—a bit of the main bluff or bank standing alone. The top, as you know, rises to the general level of the surrounding country, the river having eaten out so much. Yet the valley just above & below this (we are at the head of Lake Pepin) must be 3 or 4 miles wide.

I am not even so well informed as to the progress of the war as you

suppose. I have seen but one eastern paper (that, by the way, *was* the Tribune) for 5 weeks. I have not taken much pains to get them; but, necessarily, I have not seen any paper at all for more than a week at a time. The people of Minnesota have *seemed* to me more cold—to feel less implicated in this war, than the people of Massachusetts. It is apparent that Massachusetts, for one state at least, is doing much more than her share, in carrying it on. However, I have dealt partly with those of southern birth, & have seen but little way beneath the surface. I was glad to be told yesterday that there was a good deal of weeping here at Redwing the other day, when the volunteers stationed at Fort Snelling followed the regulars to the seat of the war. They do not weep when their children go *up* the river to occupy the deserted forts, though they *may* have to fight the Indians there.

I do not even know what the attitude of England is at present.

The grand feature hereabouts is, of course, the Mississippi River. Too much can hardly be said of its grandeur, & of the beauty of this portion of it—(from Dunleith, and prob. from Rock Island to this place.) St. Paul is a dozen miles below the Falls of St. Anthony, or near the head of uninterrupted navigation on the main stream about 2000 miles from its mouth. There is not a "rip" below that, & the river is almost as wide in the upper as the lower part of its course. Steamers go up to the Sauk Rapids, above the Falls, near a hundred miles farther, & then you are fairly in the pine woods and lumbering country. Thus it flows from the pine to the palm.

The lumber, as you know, is sawed chiefly at the Falls of St. Anthony (what is not rafted in the log to ports far below) having given rise to the towns of St. Anthony, Minneapolis, &c &c In coming up the river from Dunleith you meet with great rafts of sawed lumber and of logs —20 rods or more in length, by 5 or 6 wide, floating down, all from the pine region above the Falls. An old Maine lumberer, who has followed the same business here, tells me that the sources of the Mississippi were comparatively free from rocks and rapids, making easy work for them, but he thought that the timber was more knotty here than in Maine.

It has chanced that about half the men whom I have spoken with in Minnesota, whether travelers or settlers, were from Massachusetts.

After spending some three weeks in and about St. Paul, St. Anthony, and Minneapolis, we made an excursion in a steamer some 300 or more miles up the Minnesota (St. Peter's) River, to Redwood, or the Lower Sioux Agency, in order to see the plains & the Sioux, who were to receive

619

their annual payment there. This is eminently *the* river of Minnesota, for she shares the Mississippi with Wisconsin, and it is of incalculable value to her. It flows through a very fertile country, destined to be famous for its wheat; but it is a remarkably winding stream, so that Redwood is only half as far from its mouth by land as by water. There was not a straight reach a mile in length as far as we went,—generally you could not see a quarter of a mile of water, & the boat was steadily turning this way or that. At the greater bends, as the Traverse des Sioux, some of the passengers were landed & walked across to be taken in on the other side. Two or three times you could have thrown a stone across the neck of the isthmus while it was from one to three miles around it. It was a very novel kind of navigation to me. The boat was perhaps the largest that had been up so high, & the water was rather low (it had been about 15 feet higher). In making a short turn, we repeatedly and designedly ran square into the steep and soft bank, taking in a cart-load of earth, this being more effectual than the rudder to fetch us about again; or the deeper water was so narrow & close to the shore, that we were obliged to run into & break down at least 50 trees which overhung the water, when we did not cut them off, repeatedly losing a part of our outworks, though the most exposed had been taken in. I could pluck almost any plant on the bank from the boat. We very frequently got aground and then drew ourselves along with a windlass & a cable fastened to a tree, or we swung round in the current, and completely blocked up & block-aded the river, one end of the boat resting on each shore. And yet we would haul ourselves round again with the windlass & cable in an hour or 2, though the boat was about 160 feet long & drew some 3 feet of water, or, often, water and sand. It was one consolation to know that in such a case we were all the while damming the river & so raising it. We once ran fairly on to a concealed rock, with a shock that aroused all the passengers, & rested there, & the mate went below with a lamp expecting to find a hole, but he did not. Snags & sawyers were so common that I forgot to mention them. The sound of the boat rumbling over one was the ordinary music. However, as long as the boiler did not burst, we knew that no serious accident was likely to happen. Yet this was a singularly navigable river, more so than the Mississippi above the Falls, & it is owing to its very crookedness. Ditch it straight, & it would not only be very swift, but soon run out. It was from 10 to 15 rods wide near the mouth & from 8 to 10 or 12 at Redwood. Though the current was swift, I did not see a "rip" on it, & only 3 or 4 rocks. For 3

months in the year I am told that it can be navigated by small steamers about twice as far as we went, or to its source in Big Stone Lake, & a former Indian agent told me that at high water it was thought that such a steamer might pass into the Red River.

In short this river proved so very *long* and navigable, that I was reminded of the last letter or two in the Voyages of the Baron la Hontan (written near the end of the 17 century, I think) in which he states that after reaching the Mississippi (by the Illinois or Wisconsin), the limit of previous exploration westward, he voyaged up it with his Indians, & at length turned up a great river coming in from the west which he called "La Riviere Longue" & he relates various improbable things about the country & its inhabitants, so that this letter has been regarded as pure fiction—or more properly speaking a lie. But I am somewhat inclined now to reconsider the matter.

The Governor of Minnesota, (Ramsay)—the superintendent of Ind. Affairs in this quarter,—& the newly appointed Ind. agent were on board; also a German band from St. Paul, a small cannon for salutes, & the money for the Indians (aye and the gamblers, it was said, who were to bring it back in another boat). There were about 100 passengers chiefly from St. Paul, and more or less recently from the N. Eastern states; also half a dozen young educated Englishmen. Chancing to speak with one who sat next to me, when the voyage was nearly half over, I found that he was a son of the Rev. Samuel [No; Joseph] May, & a classmate of yours, & had been looking for us at St. Anthony.

The last of the little settlements on the river, was New Ulm, about 100 miles this side of Redwood. It consists wholly of Germans. We left them 100 barrels of salt, which will be worth something more when the water is lowest, than at present.

Redwood is a mere locality, scarcely an Indian village—where there is a store & some houses have been built for them. We were now fairly on the great plains, and looking south, and after walking that way 3 miles, could see no tree in that horizon. The buffalo was said to be feeding within 25 or 30 miles—

A regular council was held with the Indians, who had come in on their ponies, and speeches were made on both sides thro' an interpreter, quite in the described mode; the Indians, as usual, having the advantage in point of truth and earnestness, and therefore of eloquence. The most prominent chief was named Little Crow. They were quite dissatisfied with the white man's treatment of them & probably have reason to be so.

This council was to be continued for 2 or 3 days—the payment to be made the 2d day—and another payment to other bands a little higher up on the Yellow Medicine (a tributary of the Minnesota) a few days thereafter.

In the afternoon the half naked Indians performed a dance, at the request of the Governor, for our amusement & their own benefit & then we took leave of them & of the officials who had come to treat with them.

Excuse these pencil marks but my ink stand is *unscrewable* & I can only direct my letter at the bar. I could tell you more & perhaps more interesting things, if I had time. I am considerably better than when I left home, but still far from well.

Our faces are already set toward home. Will you please let my sister know that we shall *probably* start for Milwaukee & Mackinaw in a day or 2 (or as soon as we hear from home) *via Prairie du Chien* & not La Crosse.

I am glad to hear that you have written to Cholmondeley, as it relieves me of some *responsibility*.

Yrs truly
Henry D. Thoreau

Sanborn, in his Life of Henry David Thoreau *(p. 401), apparently adds the following paragraph to the letter:*
"Fort Snelling is built of limestone (tawny or butterish) ten feet high, at an angle of the two rivers, St Peter's and the Mississippi. I overlook the broad valley of the St. Peter's River, bounded on the south, as I look, by a long range of low hills. The government buildings are handsome; there was a mill here before the settlement. Steamers go up to the Sauk Rapids, above the Falls of St. Anthony, near a hundred miles farther, and then you are fairly in the pine woods and the lumbering country. The St. Paul Mission to the Indians was not far south of the Fort." MS., Abernethy (typescript).

Concord, July 15, 1861.

Dear Sir:—

For such an excursion as you propose I would recommend you to carry as food for one for six days:

2 or 3 lbs. of boiled corned beef (I and my companions have preferred it to tongue).

2 lbs. of sugar.

¼ lb. of tea (or ½ lb. of coffee).

2 lbs. of hard bread, and a half a large loaf of home-made bread, (ready buttered if you like it), consuming the last first; or 4½ lbs. of hard bread alone.

Also a little *moist* and *rich* plum cake, of which you can take a pinch from time to time.

2 or 3 lemons will not come amiss to flavor poor water with.

If you multiply this amount by 8, the number of your party, subtract from 5 to 10 per cent.

Carry these different articles in separate cotton or linen bags labelled, and a small portion of the sugar in a box by itself for immediate use. (The same of salt, if you expect to get game or fish.)

As for clothing and other articles, I will state exactly what I should take in such a case (besides what I wore and what were already in my pockets), my clothes and shoes being old, but thick and stout.

1 shirt.

1 pair socks.

2 pocket-handkerchiefs.

1 thick waist-coat.

1 flannel   "

India rubber coat.

6 bosoms (or dickies).

Towel and soap.

Pins, needles, and thread.

A blanket.

A thick night cap (unless your day cap is soft and close fitting.)

A map of the route, and a compass.

(Such other articles as your peculiar taste and pursuits require.)

A hatchet, (for a party of half a dozen a light but long handled axe),

623

for you will wish to make a great fire, however warm, and to cut large logs.

Paper and stamps.

Jack knife.

Matches; some of these in a water-tight vial in your vest pocket.

A fish line and hooks, a piece of salt pork for bait, and a little salt always in your pocket, so as to be armed in case you should be lost in the woods.

Waste paper and twine.

An iron spoon and a pint tin dipper for each man, in which last it will be well to insert a wire handle, whose curve will coincide with that of the dipper's edge, and then you can use it as a kettle, if you like, and not put out the fire.

A four quart tin pail will serve very well for your common kettle.

An umbrella.

For shelter, either a tent or a strong sheet large enough to cover all. If a sheet, the tent will be built shed-fashion, open to the fair weather side; two saplings, either as they stand or else stuck in the ground, serving for main posts, a third being placed horizontally in the forks of these, 6 or 7 feet from the ground, and two or three others slanted backward from it. This makes the frame on which to stretch your sheet, which must come quite down to the ground on the sides and the back.

You will lie, of course, on the usual twigged bed, with your feet to the front.

When the National Baptist *printed this letter it explained:*

"In 1861, eight ministers residing in Worcester, Mass. and the immediate vicinity, who had long been united in very intimate and friendly ties, planned a foot excursion into the mountain region of New Hampshire, to occupy the period between two Sabbaths.

"One of the number wrote to that king of all woodcraft, the late Henry D. Thoreau, the author of 'Walden,' and other books redolent of the woods and the streams, asking him for information as to the preparation needed for the tramp. Mr. T. most kindly replied, in a letter which we publish, both because it is his, and also because of the valuable practical information it will afford to many who may be contemplating such a trip." Text, The National Baptist, *July 20, 1876.*

To DANIEL RICKETSON

Concord Aug. 15th '61

Friend Ricketson,

When your last letter was written I was away in the far North-West, in search of health. My cold turned to bronchitis which made me a close prisoner almost up to the moment of my starting on that journey, early in May. As I had an incessant cough, my doctor told me that I must "clear out"—to the West Indies or elsewhere, so I selected Minnesota. I returned a few weeks ago, after a good deal of steady travelling, considerably, yet not essentially better, my cough still continuing. If I do not mend very quickly I shall be obliged to go to another climate again very soon.

My ordinary pursuits, both indoor and out, have been for the most part omitted, or seriously interrupted—walking, boating, scribbling, &c. Indeed I have been sick so long that I have almost forgotten what it is to be well, yet I feel that it all respects only my envelope.

Channing & Emerson are as well as usual, but Alcott, I am sorry to say, has for some time been more or less confined by a lameness, perhaps of a neuralgic character, occasioned by carrying too great a weight on his back while gardening.

On returning home, I found various letters awaiting me, among others one from Cholmondeley & one from yourself.

Of course I am sufficiently surprised to hear of your conversion, yet I scarcely know what to say about it, unless that judging by your account, it appears to me a change which concerns yourself peculiarly, and will not make you more valuable to mankind. However, perhaps, I must see you before I can judge.

Remembering your numerous invitations, I write this short note now chiefly to say that, if you are to be at home, and it will be quite agreeable to you, I will pay you a visit next week, & take such rides or sauntering walks with you as an invalid may.

Yrs
Henry D. Thoreau

Ricketson's conversion was (according to Familiar Letters of Thoreau, *p. 456) "a return to religious Quakerism, of which [Ricketson] had written enthusiastically." News of it evidently formed part of the letter written while Thoreau was in the "far Northwest." MS., Huntington.*

From DANIEL RICKETSON

New Bedford, Sept. 1, 1861.

Dear Thoreau,—

Dr. Denniston, to whom I recommended you to go, has kindly consented on his way from New Bedford to Northampton, to go to Concord to see you. He has had much experience and success in the treatment of bronchitis, and I hope his visit to you will result in your placing yourself under his care, which I much desire.

Should the Doctor have the time, and you feel able, please show him a little of the Concord worthies and much oblige,

Yours truly,
D. Ricketson.

It is possible that this letter was never mailed, for Ricketson records in his journal (September 2) that he went to Concord with Denniston (Ricketson, p. 320). Dr. Edward E. Denniston was a "water-cure" physician and Thoreau would not submit to his treatment. Text, Ricketson, p. 319.

From DANIEL RICKETSON

The Shanty, Tuesday 6-h. 20-m. a.m., 17 Sept., '61.

Dear Friend,—

I am desirous to hear how you are getting along, although I have an impression that you are improving. I would not put you to the trouble to write me, could I fairly call upon any one else.

I look back with pleasure upon my late visit to Concord. The particularly bright spots are my walks with you to Farmer Hosmer's and to Walden Pond, as well as our visit to friend Alcott.

I should like to have you make us a good long visit before cold weather sets in, and should this meet your approval please inform me when you answer this.

I expect to be absent from home for a few days the last of this month, but after that time I shall be at home for some time.

Our Indian Summer weather is very charming, and probably the air softer than more inland if a season so delightful has any difference in this section of New England.

I suppose you have hardly needed a fresh doctor since the bountiful supply I brought you. I was much pleased at the unceremonious way in which you described him. I hope the dread of another holocaust of the same kind will keep you in good heart for some time, for, assuredly, as soon as you begin to complain, which is hardly possible, after so great a feast as you have had of late, a bigger victim will be forthcoming upon whom the eagle-eye of some friend of yours is already fixed.

You will pardon my seeming levity, and attribute it to the fresh morning air and increasing health and spirits. I have tasted no sugar-plums of any kind since I left you. I thank you for the friendly caution. I need more. Come then, and be my kind Mentor still further.

With kind regards to all your family and to Mr. Alcott, Channing, Hosmer, &c.

Yours truly,
D. Ricketson.

P. S.   Mrs Ricketson and our daughters join in regards and invitation to visit us soon. You will be welcome at any time. This is a good time to

ride out to the ponds, &c. We are having beautiful weather here, calm and mild.

Please ask Channing if he received a book I sent him in care of Dr. W. Channing, Boston.

Text, Ricketson, *pp. 115–16.*

To DANIEL RICKETSON

Concord Oct 14th '61

Friend Ricketson

I think that, on the whole, my health is better than when you were here; & my faith in the doctors has not increased.

I thank you all for your invitation to come to New Bedford, but I suspect that it must still be warmer here than there, that, indeed, New Bedford is warmer than Concord only in the winter, & so I abide by Concord.

September was pleasanter & much better for me than August, and October thus far has been quite tolerable. Instead of riding on horseback, I take a ride in a wagon about every other day. My neighbor, Mr [E. R.] Hoar, has two horses, & he being away for the most part this fall has generously offered me the use of one of them, and, as I notice, the dog throws himself in, and does scouting duty.

I am glad to hear that you no longer chew, but eschew, sugar plums. One of the worst effects of sickness even is that it may get one into the *habit* of taking a little something, his bitters or sweets, as if for his bodily good, from time to time, when he does not need it. However, there is no danger of this if you do not dose even when you are sick.

I met with a Mr Rodman, a young man of your town, here the other day—or week, looking at farms for sale, and rumor says that he is inclined to buy a particular one.

C[hanning] says that he received his book, but has not got any of yours.

It is easy to talk, but hard to write.

From the worst of all correspondents

Henry D. Thoreau

This is Thoreau's last letter to Ricketson, though Ricketson himself wrote several more. MS., Huntington.

To W. & C. H. SMITH

Concord Nov. 13 61

Messrs W & C H Smith

I received on the 8th inst your draft in payment for plumbago sent to you Oct 23d I forgot to deduct the interest, but when I remarked it supposed that you would correct the mistake before I could—for I had agreed to make the deduction.

But the case is now altered for if I have to pay for the draft (which in any other conditions are not to be sent without cost) I think that you should not expect me to make any further deduction for interest

Yours truly
Henry D. Thoreau

A letter may have accompanied the draft of November 8; we have no positive evidence. MS., Abernethy, in pencil (typescript); previously unpublished.

To GEORGE THATCHER

Concord Nov 15 1861

Dear Cousin,

We are glad to hear that you are in the neighborhood, and shall be much disappointed if we do not see you & Caleb.

Come up any day that is most convenient to you—or, if you stay so long, perhaps you will spend Thanksgiving (the 21st) with us.

Yrs, in haste,
Henry D. Thoreau.

This note was presumably to Thatcher; all the other Thoreau letters addressed "Dear Cousin" that we have are to him. Caleb was probably Caleb Billings, a Bangor stablekeeper who had married Nancy Thoreau. MS., Frank Jewett Mather; previously unpublished.

From L. JOHNSON & CO.

Philadelphia, Dec. 6th 1861

Mr. Henry D. Thoreau Concord Mass.

Dear Sir,—Enclosed find Fifteen Dollars ($15.00) in eastern funds in settlement of your bill of 28th. ulto. Please acknowledge receipt to

Yours Truly
L. Johnson & Co

MS., Huntington; previously unpublished.

1862

The war went on with enormous impact. The North continued to lose.

Thoreau lay on his day bed in the parlor. He dictated a few letters to his sister Sophia and revised his lectures on "Walking," "Autumnal Tints," "Wild Apples," and "Night and Moonlight" for a publication that he surely knew was to be posthumous. He coughed a great deal. Death by tuberculosis was in store for him; yet he awaited death with a peace of mind that impressed everyone who saw him. He died on the morning of May 6, 1862, at the age of forty-four.

From MYRON BENTON

According to Sanborn, Benton wrote that the news of Thoreau's illness had affected him as if it were that "of a personal friend whom I had known a long time," and he went on:

The secret of the influence by which your writings charm me is altogether as intangible, though real, as the attraction of Nature herself. I read and re-read your books with ever fresh delight. Nor is it pleasure alone; there is a singular spiritual healthiness with which they seem imbued,—the expression of a soul essentially sound, so free from any morbid tendency. [After mentioning that his own home was in a pleasant valley, once the hunting-ground of the Indians, Benton said:] I was in hope to read something more from your pen in Mr. Conway's "Dial," but only recognized that fine pair of Walden twinlets. Of your two books, I perhaps prefer the "Week,"—but after all, "Walden" is but little less a favorite. In the former, I like especially those little snatches of poetry interspersed throughout. I would like to ask what progress you have made in a work some way connected with natural history,—I think it was on Botany,—which Mr. Emerson told me something about in a short interview I had with him two years ago at Poughkeepsie. . . . If you should feel perfectly able at any time to drop me a few lines, I would like much to know what your state of health is, and if there is, as I cannot but hope, a prospect of your speedy recovery.

Benton was not personally acquainted with Thoreau. Ultimately he became a fairly good regional poet. According to Sanborn, he was then living in Dutchess County, New York. Sanborn dates the letter January 6, 1862. Text, Familiar Letters of Thoreau, *pp. 461–62.*

From DANIEL RICKETSON

Brooklawn, 7th Jan., 1862.

My dear Friend,—

I thought you would like to have a few lines from me, providing they required no answer.

I have quite recovered from my illness, and am able to walk and skate as usual. My son, Walton, and I do both nearly every day of late. The weather here—as I suppose has been the case with you at Concord—has been very cold, the thermometer as low one morn (Saturday last) as five degrees above zero.

We propose soon to take our annual tour on skates over the Middle-boro' ponds.

I received your sister's letter in reply to mine inquiring after your health. I was sorry to hear of your having pleurisy, but it may prove favorable after all to your case, as a counter-irritant often does to sick people. It appears to me you will in time recover—Nature can't spare you, and we all, your friends, can't spare you. So you must look out for us and hold on these many years yet.

I wish I could see you oftener. I don't believe in your silence and absence from congenial spirits. Companionship is one of the greatest blessings to me.

Remember me kindly to my valued friends Mr. and Mrs. Alcott.

Yours truly, in haste,

D. R.

P.S. Thank your sister for her letter.

At any time when you wish to visit us, just send a line. You are always welcome.

Text, Ricketson, *pp. 117–18.*

From THEOPHILUS BROWN

Worcester Jan. 10, 1862

Friend Thoreau—

The demand for your books here seems to be rather on the increase. Two copies of the Week are wanted & I am requested to write for them.

Walden also is wanted but I presume you can't help us to that.

You will have to get out another edition of that. I hope the next edition of both books will be small in size & right for the pocket, & for "field service"

Is it discouraging to you to have me speak thus of your books?—to see me sticking at what you have left? *Have you* left it?

Whether it be discouraging to you or the contrary, I have long desired to acknowledge my indebtedness to you for them & to tell you that through them the value of everything seems infinitely enhanced to me.

We took to the river and our skates, instead of the cars, on leaving you. & had a good time of it, *keeping above* the ice all the way.

The little snow-storm that we started in grew into quite a large one, or fast one, & made the day all the better. There was a sober cheer in the day, such as belongs to stormy days.

But to come back to business. I was requested to ask you to write your name in one of the books. & I would like to have you write it in the other—

I have forgotten the price of your books but I have the impression that it is $1.25 and accordingly will enclose $2.50. If I am not right you will tell me.

Your friend
Theo. Brown.

This is one of the few pieces of correspondence between the Worcester tailor and Thoreau. Evidently their common friend H. G. O. Blake normally acted as the channel of communication: Thoreau says as much in one of his letters to Blake. MS., Berg; previously unpublished.

From F. B. SANBORN

Sunday morning Jan'y 12th

My dear Friend;

If you have read the magazine which I loaned you the other day, (The Continental) will you have the goodness to give it to the bearer who will take it to Mrs [Sarah Bradford?] Ripley's for Miss [Amelia?] Goodwin.

Yours truly
F. B. Sanborn

H. D. Thoreau, Esq

No year is given in the manuscript of this letter, but the Continental Monthly, *a Boston publication devoted to literature and national affairs, issued its first number under date of January 1862. Furthermore, 1862 was the only year during the friendship of Sanborn and Thoreau in which January 12 fell on a Sunday. MS., Huntington; previously unpublished.*

To THE EDITORS OF "THE ATLANTIC MONTHLY"

Concord Feb. 11th 62

Messrs, Editors,

Only extreme illness has prevented my answering your note earlier. I have no objection to having the papers you refer to printed in your monthly—if my feeble health will permit me to prepare them for the printer. What will you give me for them? They are, or have been used as, lectures of the usual length,—taking about an hour to read & I dont see how they can be divided without injury—How many pages

can you print at once?— Of course, I should expect that no sentiment or sentence be altered or omitted without my consent, & to retain the copyright of the paper after you had used it in your monthly.— Is your monthly copyrighted?

> Yours respectfully,
> S. E. Thoreau
> for H. D. Thoreau.

Ticknor & Fields took over the Atlantic Monthly *in November 1859, having paid $10,000 for it to its original publishers, Phillips, Sampson & Co. James Russell Lowell remained as editor under the new owners until June 1861 and was then succeeded by one of them, James T. Fields. Fields, who had come to Boston as a shrewd New Hampshire youth, gradually distinguished himself in two ways: by his remarkable understanding of the public's taste and by his ability to cultivate good writers. Now he was evidently intent on bringing back to the* Atlantic *a writer whom Lowell had grossly offended.*

By this time the most that Thoreau could manage was rough drafts in pencil, which his devoted sister Sophia copied in ink. Ultimately unable to do even that, he dictated. MS., Huntington, in Sophia Thoreau's hand from Thoreau's penciled draft.

To TICKNOR & FIELDS

Concord Feb 20th 1862

Messrs Ticknor & Fields,

I send you herewith, the paper called Autumnal Tints. I see that it will have to be divided, & I would prefer that the first portion terminate with page 42, in order that it may make the more impression. The rest I think will take care of itself.

I may as well say now that on pages 55–6–7–8 I have described the Scarlet Oak leaf very minutely. In my lecturing I have always carried a

very large & handsome one displayed on a white ground, which did me great service with the audience. Now if you will read those pages, I think that you will see the advantage of having a simple outline engraving of this leaf & also of the White Oak leaf on the opposite page, that the readers may the better appreciate my words— I will supply the leaves to be copied when the time comes.

When you answer the questions in my last note, please let me know about how soon this article will be published.

> Yours respectfully,
> Henry D. Thoreau.
> by S. E. Thoreau.

MS., Huntington, *in Sophia Thoreau's hand.*

To TICKNOR & FIELDS

Concord Feb 24th 1862

Messrs Ticknor & Fields

Oct. 25*th* 1853 I received from Munroe & Co. the following note; "We send by express this day a box & bundle containing 250 copies of Concord River, & also 450. in sheets. All of which we trust you will find correct."

I found by count the number of bound volumes to be correct. The sheets have lain untouched just as received, in stout paper wrappers ever since.

I find that I now have 146 bound copies. Therefore the whole number in my possession is,

Bound copies	146
In sheets	450
	596

You spoke when here, of printing a new edition of the Walden. If you incline to do so, I shall be happy to make an arrangement with you to that effect.

Yours respectfully
H. D. Thoreau
by S. E. Thoreau

P S.   I will send you an article as soon as I can prepare it, which has no relation to the seasons of the year.

MS., Huntington, *in Sophia Thoreau's hand.*

To TICKNOR & FIELDS

Concord Feb 28th 1862.

Messrs Ticknor & Fields,
        I send you with this a paper called The Higher Law, it being much shorter & easier to prepare than that on Walking. It will not need to be divided on account of its length, as indeed the subject does not permit it. I should like to know that you receive it & also about what time it will be published.

Yours truly
H D. Thoreau
by S. E. Thoreau.

Ticknor & Fields—vice Fields himself, we presume—liked the essay but objected to its title. Thoreau substituted the more forceful "Life without Principle" (Thoreau to Ticknor & Fields, March 4, 1862). MS., Huntington, in Sophia Thoreau's hand.

To TICKNOR & FIELDS

Concord March 1st 1862

Messrs Ticknor & Fields,

This Scarlet Oak leaf is the smallest one in my collection, yet it must lose a bristle or two to gain admittance to your page.

I wish simply for a faithful outline engraving of the leaf bristles & all. In the middle of page 57 or of a neighboring page, is a note in pencil —The leaf should be opposite to this page & this note to be altered into a note for the bottom of the page like this—viz "The original of the leaf on the opposite page was picked from such a pile"

Yours truly
Henry D Thoreau,
by S. E. Thoreau.

MS., Huntington, *in Sophia Thoreau's hand.*

To TICKNOR & FIELDS

Concord March 4th 62.

Messrs Ticknor & Fields,

I hereby acknowledge the receipt of your check for one hundred dollars on account of manuscript sent to you.—As for another title for the Higher Law article, I can think of nothing better than, Life without Principle. The paper on Walking will be ready ere long.

I shall be happy to have you print 250. copies of Walden on the terms mentioned & will consider this answer as settling the business. I wish to make one alteration in the new edition viz, to leave out from the title the words "Or Life in the Woods."

Yours truly
H. D. Thoreau
by S. E. Thoreau

According to Warren S. Tryon and William Charvat, The Cost Books of Ticknor and Fields *(p. 290), a second printing of* Walden *amounting to 280 (rather than 250) copies was manufactured by the firm in March and April of 1862. MS., Huntington, in Sophia Thoreau's hand.*

To TICKNOR & FIELDS

Concord Mar. 11th 1862

Messrs Ticknor & Fields,

I send with this the paper on Walking & also the proofs of Autumnal Tints.

The former paper will bear dividing into two portions very well, the natural joint being, I think at the end of page 44. At any rate the two parcels being separately tied up, will indicate it—

I do not quite like to have the Autumnal Tints described as in two parts, for it appears as if the author had made a permanent distinction between them; Would it not be better to say at the end of the first portion "To be continued in the next number"?

As for the leaf, I had not thought how it should be engraved, but left it to you. Your note suggests that perhaps it is to be done at my expense. What is the custom? and what would be the cost of a steel engraving? I think that an ordinary wood engraving would be much better than nothing.

Yours truly
Henry D. Thoreau
by S. E. Thoreau.

MS., Huntington, *in Sophia Thoreau's hand.*

To MYRON BENTON

Concord, March 21, 1862.

Dear Sir,—

I thank you for your very kind letter, which, ever since I received it, I have intended to answer before I died, however briefly. I am encouraged to know, that, so far as you are concerned, I have not written my books in vain. I was particularly gratified, some years ago, when one of my friends and neighbors said, "I wish you would write another book,—write it for me." He is actually more familiar with what I have written than I am myself.

The verses you refer to in Conway's "Dial," were written by F. B. Sanborn of this town. I never wrote for that journal.

I am pleased when you say that in "The Week" you like especially "those little snatches of poetry interspersed through the book," for these, I suppose, are the least attractive to most readers. I have not been engaged in any particular work on Botany, or the like, though, if I were to live, I should have much to report on Natural History generally.

You ask particularly after my health. I *suppose* that I have not many months to live; but, of course, I know nothing about it. I may add that I am enjoying existence as much as ever, and regret nothing.

Yours truly,
Henry D. Thoreau,
by Sophia E. Thoreau.

Text, Familiar Letters of Thoreau, *pp. 463–64.*

From DANIEL RICKETSON

SPRING NOTES

New Bedford, 23d March, '62.

My dear Friend,—

As it is some time since I wrote you, I have thought that as a faithful chronicler of the season in this section, I would announce to you the present stage of our progress. I will not begin with the origin of creation as many worthy historians are wont, but would say that we have had a pretty steady cold winter through the months of January and February, but since the coming in of March the weather has been mild, though for the past week cloudy and some rain. Today the wind is southerly and the thermometer—3 p.m.—46°, north side of our house. A flock of wild geese flew over about an hour ago, which I viewed with my spy-glass—their course about due east. Few things give me a stronger sense of the sublime than the periodical flight of these noble birds. Blue-birds arrived here about a fortnight ago, but a farmer who lives about 1½ miles from here north, says he heard them on the 7th Feb'y. I hear the call of the golden winged woodpecker, and the sweet notes of the meadow lark in the morning, and yesterday morning for the first time this spring, we were saluted with the song of a robin in a tree near our house. The song sparrow has been calling the *maids to hang on their teakettles* for several weeks, and this morning I heard the *crackle* of the cow-bunting. I must not forget, too, that last evening I heard the ground notes *speed, speed* of the woodcock and his warbling while descending from his spiral flight. The catkins begin to expand upon the willows, and the grass in warm and rich spots to look green.

Truly spring is here, and each day adds to the interest of the season. I hope you will catch a share of its healthful influences; at least feast upon the stock you have in store, for as friend Alcott says, in his quaint way, you have all weathers within you. Am I right in my intimations that you are mending a little, and that you will be able once more to resume your favorite pursuits so valuable to us all as well as to yourself? May I not hope to see you the coming season at Brooklawn where you are always a welcome guest? I see that you are heralded in the Atlantic

for April, and find a genial appreciative notice of you under the head of "Forester," which I suppose comes from either Alcott or Emerson, and Channing's lines at the close, which I was also glad to see.

I am reading a very interesting book called "Footnotes from the page of Nature, or first forms of vegetation." By Rev. Hugh Macmillan, Cambridge and London, 1861. It treats of Mosses, Lichens, Fresh Water Algae and Fungi. The author appears to be rich in lore and writes in an easy manner with no pretension to science. Don't fail to read it if you can obtain it. It is lent to me by a friendly naturalist.

Hoping to hear of your improved state of health, and with the affectionate regards of my whole family, as well as my own,

I remain, dear friend,
Yours faithfully,
Dan'l Ricketson.

P.S.   I notice that Walden is to appear in a second edition, and hope that your publishers will consider your interests as well as their own. Would they not like to buy your unbound copies of "The Week"?

"*The Forester,*" *in the April* Atlantic Monthly, *was by Bronson Alcott.* Text, Ricketson, *pp. 119–21.*

From DANIEL RICKETSON

The Shanty, Brooklawn, 30 March, 1862.

Dear Thoreau,—

Alone, and idle here this pleasant Sunday p.m., I thought I might write you a few lines, not that I expect you to answer, but only to bring myself a little nearer to you. I have to chronicle this time, the arrival of the purple Finch, and a number of warblers and songsters of the sparrow tribe.

The spring is coming on nicely here, and to-day it is mild, calm, and sunny. I hope you are able to get out a little and breathe the pure air of your fields and woods. While sawing some pine wood the other day, the fragrance suggested to my mind that you might be benefited by living among, or at least frequenting pine woods. I have heard of people much improved in health who were afflicted in breathing, from this source, and I once seriously thought of taking my wife to the pine woods between here and Plymouth, or rather between Middleborough and Plymouth, where the pine grows luxuriantly in the dry yellow ground of that section.

I have thought you might, if still confined, transport yourself in imagination or spirit to your favorite haunts, which might be facilitated by taking a piece of paper and mapping out your usual rambles around Concord, making the village the centre of the chart and giving the name of each part, marking out the roads and footpaths as well as the more prominent natural features of the country.

I have had two unusually *dreamy* nights—last and the one before. Last night I was climbing mountains with some accidental companion, and among the dizzy heights when near the top I saw and pointed out to my fellow-traveller two enormous birds flying over our heads. These birds soon increased, and, from being as I at first supposed eagles of great size, became griffins! as large as horses, their huge bodies moved along by broadspread wings. The dream continued, but the remainder is as the conclusion of most dreams in strange contrast. I found myself passing through a very narrow and filthy village street, the disagreeable odor of which so quickened my speed as to either awake me or cut off my dream. At any rate, when I awoke my head was aching and I was generally exhausted. But enough of this.

Two young men in a buggy-wagon have just driven up the road singing in very sonorous strains the "John Brown" chorus. I wish its pathetic and heart-stirring appeals could reach the inward ears of Congress and the President. I hope you can see some light on our present benighted way, for I cannot except by the exercise of my faith in an overruling Providence.

I may write you again soon, and hope I do not tire you.

With kind regards to your family and my other Concord friends, I remain,

Yours affectionately,
Dan'l Ricketson.

P.S. I have just seen a cricket in the path near the house. Flies are very lively in my shanty windows. Two flocks wild geese just passed, 4 p.m., N.E. by N. Honk-honk! Honk-honk!

Text, Ricketson, *pp. 121–23.*

To TICKNOR & FIELDS

Concord Apr. 2nd "62

Messrs Ticknor & Fields,
    I send you herewith the paper on Wild Apples.
    You have made me no offer for The "Week." Do not suppose that I rate it too high, I shall be glad to dispose of it; & it will be an advantage to advertize it with Walden.

Yours truly,
Henry D. Thoreau
by S. E. Thoreau.

MS., Huntington, *in Sophia Thoreau's hand.*

From TICKNOR & FIELDS

Boston April 6, 1862

H D Thoreau Esq
Dear Sir,

Your paper on Wild Apples is rece'd. In a few days we will send proof of the article on 'Walking.' Touching the "Week on [page torn] we find by yours of [page torn] those already in cloth if we found them rusty. Since the volume was published prices have changed materially and discounts to Booksellers have largely increased. We now make ⅓ & 40% to the Trade as a matter of course. What with bad [page torn] we could not [page torn] our check for the amount.

Yours very truly
Ticknor & Fields

In spite of the perhaps pessimistic tone of this letter, Ticknor & Fields reissued Thoreau's first book within the year. They bound the sheets that James Munroe & Co. had printed for publication in 1849, and possibly they gave a new binding and title page to the copies Munroe had bound himself. However, they neglected to remove the back leaf that announced in each copy that Walden *would soon be published. MS., Huntington.*

From DANIEL RICKETSON

The Shanty, April 6th, 1862.

My dear Philomath,—

Another Sunday has come round, and as usual I am to be found in the Shanty, where I should also be glad to have you bodily present. We have had a little interruption to our fine weather during the past

week in the shape of a hail-storm yesterday p.m. and evening, but it is clear again to-day, though cooler.

I have to *Kronikle* the arrival of the white-bellied swallow and the commencement of the frog choir, which saluted my ear for the first time on the evening of the 3d inst. The fields are becoming a little greener, and the trailing moss is already waving along the sides of the rivulets. I have n't walked much, however, as I have been busy about farm work, the months of April and May being my busiest time, but as my real business is with Nature, I do not let any of these "side issues" lead me astray. How serenely and grandly amid the din of arms Nature preserves her integrity, nothing moved; with the return of spring come the birds and the flowers, the swollen streams go dancing on, and all the laws of the great solar system are perfectly preserved. How wise, how great, must be the Creator and Mover of it all! But I descend to the affairs of mortals, which particularly concern us at this time. I do not think that the people of the North appear to be awakened, enlightened, rather, to their duty in this great struggle. I fear that there is a great deal of treachery which time will alone discover and remove, for the Right must eventually prevail. Can we expect when we consult the page of history that this revolution will be more speedily terminated than others of a like nature? The civil war of England lasted, I think, some ten years, and the American Revolution some seven or eight years, besides the years of antecedent agitation. We have no Cromwell, unless Wendell Phillips shall by and by prove one; but at present he rather represents Hampden, whose mournful end was perhaps a better one than to be killed by a rotten-egg mob. The voice of Hogopolis (the mob portion of Cincinnati), if such grunts can be thus dignified, must prove a lasting disgrace. The government party, if we have a government, seems to continue with a saintly perseverance their faith in General McClellan. How much longer this state of delay will continue to be borne it is difficult to foresee, but I trust the force of circumstances (*sub Deo*) will soon require a move for the cause of liberty.

I read but little of the newspaper reports of the war, rather preferring to be governed by the general characteristics of the case, as they involuntarily affect my mind.

4 p.m. Since writing the foregoing, somewhat more than an hour ago, I have taken a stroll with my son Walton and our dog through the woods and fields west of our house, where you and I have walked several times; the afternoon is sunny and of mild temperature, but the wind

from the N.W. rather cool, rendering overcoat agreeable. Our principal object was to look at lichens and mosses, to which W. is paying some attention. We started up a woodcock at the south edge of the woods, and a large number of robins in a field adjoining, also pigeon-woodpeckers, and heard the warble of bluebirds.

I remain, with faith in the sustaining forces of Nature and Nature's God,

Yours truly and affectionately,
Daniel Ricketson.

Henry D. Thoreau, Concord, Mass.

Text, Ricketson, *pp. 123–25.*

From DANIEL RICKETSON

The Shanty, Brooklawn, 13th April, 1862.

My dear Friend,—

I received a letter from your dear Sister a few days ago, informing me of your continued illness and prostration of physical strength, which I was not altogether unprepared to learn, as our valued friend Mr. Alcott wrote me by your sister's request in February last, that you were confined at home and very feeble. I am glad, however, to learn from Sophia that you still find comfort and are happy, the reward I have no doubt of a virtuous life, and an abiding faith in the wisdom and goodness of our Heavenly Father. It is undoubtedly wisely ordained that our present lives should be mortal. Sooner or later we must all close our eyes for the last time upon the scenes of this world, and oh! how happy are they who feel the assurance that the spirit shall survive the earthly tabernacle of clay, and pass on to higher and happier spheres of experience.

"It must be so—Plato, thou reasonest well:—
Else, whence this pleasing hope, this fond desire,
This longing after immortality."

(Addison, *Cato*.)

"The soul's dark cottage, battered, and decayed,
Lets in new light through chinks that time has made:
Stronger by weakness, wiser men become,
As they draw near to their eternal home.
Leaving the old both worlds at once they view
Who stand upon the threshold of the new."

(Waller.)

It has been the lot of but few, dear Henry, to extract so much from life as you have done. Although you number fewer years than many who have lived wisely before you, yet I know of no one, either in the past or present times, who has drank so deeply from the sempiternal spring of truth and knowledge, or who in the poetry and beauty of every-day life has enjoyed more or contributed more to the happiness of others. Truly you have not lived in vain—your works, and above all, your brave and truthful life, will become a precious treasure to those whose happiness it has been to have known you, and who will continue to uphold though with feebler hands the fresh and instructive philosophy you have taught them.

But I cannot yet resign my hold upon you here. I will still hope, and if my poor prayer to God may be heard, would ask, that you may be spared to us a while longer, at least. This is a lovely spring day here—warm and mild—the thermometer in the shade at 62 above zero (3 p.m.). I write with my shanty door open and my west curtain down to keep out the sun, a red-winged blackbird is regaling me with a querulous, half-broken song from a neighboring tree just in front of the house, and the gentle southwest wind is soughing through my young pines. Here where you have so often sat with me, I am alone. My dear Uncle James whom you may remember to have seen here, the companion of my woodland walks for more than quarter of a century, died a year ago this month: my boys and girls have grown into men and women, and my dear wife is an invalid still, so, though a pater familias, I often feel quite alone. Years are accumulating upon me, the buoyancy of youth has erewhile departed, and with some bodily and many mental infirmities I sometimes feel that the cords of life are fast separating. I wish at least

to devote the remainder of my life, whether longer or shorter, to the cause of truth and humanity—a life of simplicity and humility. Pardon me for thus dwelling on myself.

Hoping to hear of your more favorable symptoms, but committing you (all unworthy as I am) unto the tender care of the great Shepherd, who "tempers the wind to the shorn lamb,"

I remain, my dear friend and counsellor,

Ever faithfully yours,
Dan'l Ricketson.

P.S.   It is *barely* possible I may come to see you on Sat'y next.

Text, Ricketson, *pp. 125–28.*

From DANIEL RICKETSON

The Shanty, Sunday, 7.30 a.m., 4th May, 1862.

My dear Friend,—

I have just returned from driving our cow to pasture and assisting in our usual in and outdoor work, the first making a fire in our sitting-room, a little artificial warmth being still necessary for my invalid wife, although I sit most of the time as I do now, with my Shanty door open, and without fire in my stove.

Well, my dear friend and fellow-pilgrim, spring has again come, and here appears in full glow. The farmers are busy and have been for some weeks, ploughing and planting,—the necessity of paying more attention to agriculture being strongly felt in these *hard* times,—old fields and neglected places are now being brought into requisition, and with a good season our former neglected farms will teem with abundance.

I, too, am busy in my way, but on rather a small scale, principally in my garden and among my fruit trees. Walton, however, is head man, and I am obliged generally to submit to his superior judgment.

About all the birds have returned—the large thrush (T. rufus) [Brown Thrasher] arrived here on the 25th last month. I am now daily expecting the catbird and ground robin, and soon the Bob-o-link and golden robin. With the arrival of the two last our vernal choir becomes nearly complete. I have known them both to arrive the same day. Of the great variety of little woodland and wayside warblers, I am familiar with but few, yet some of them are great favorites of mine, particularly the oven bird, warbling vireo, veery (T. Wilsonii), etc., etc. The wind flower and blue violet have been in bloom some time, and I suppose the columbine and wild geranium are also, although I have not been to visit them as yet. How beautiful and how wonderful indeed is the return of life—how suggestive and how instructive to mankind! Truly God is great and good and wise and glorious.

I hope this will find you *mending*, and as I hear nothing to the contrary, I trust that it may be so that you are. I did expect to be able to go to Concord soon; I still may, but at present I do not see my way clear, as we "Friends" say. I often think of you, however, and join hands with you in the spirit, if not in the flesh, which I hope always to do.

I see by the papers that Concord has found a new voice in the way of a literary journal y'clept "The Monitor," which has my good wishes for its success. I conclude that Mr. Sanborn is the pioneer in this enterprise, who appears to be a healthy nursing child of the old mother of heroes. I do not mean to be classic, and only intend to speak of old Mother Concord. I hope Channing will wake up and give us some of his lucubrations, and father Alcott strike his Orphic lyre once more, and Emerson discourse wisdom and verse from the woods around. There sings a whortleberry sparrow (F. juncorum) from our bush pasture beyond the garden. I hear daily your sparrow (F. Graminus) [vesper sparrow] with his "here! here! there! there! come quick or I'm gone!" By the way, is not Emerson wrong in his interpretation of the whistle of the Chickadee as "Phoebe"? The low, sweet whistle of the "black cap" is very distinct from the clearly expressed Phoebe of the wood pewee. But I must not be hypercritical with so true a poet and lover of Nature as E.

How grandly is the Lord overruling all for the cause of the slave—defeating the evil machinations of men by the operation of his great universal and regulating laws, by which the universe of mind and matter is governed! I do not look for a speedy termination of the war, although matters look more hopeful, but I cannot doubt but that slavery will

soon find its exodus. What a glorious country this will be for the next generation should this *curse* be removed!

Amid the song of purple finches, robins, meadow-larks, and sparrows —a kind of *T. solitarius* [hermit thrush] myself—and with a heart full of kind wishes and affection for you, I conclude this hasty epistle.

As ever, yours faithfully,

D. R.

P.S.   I believe I answered your sister's kind and thoughtful letter to me.

Sophia Thoreau had written Ricketson on April 7. Two days after he wrote the present letter Thoreau died. Text, Ricketson, *pp. 128–31.*

Undated Letters

From W. ELLERY CHANNING

Dear H.

    How would you like to go up to Holt's point to-day or will you

Yrs

W E C

There is no clue to the dating of this note. Channing was probably referring to a point of land on the Concord River just west of Ball's Hill that Thoreau called "The Holt." MS., Harvard; previously unpublished.

———

From W. CUSHING

    Will you please give us an answer—and your subject—if you consent to come—by Mr. Charles Bowers, who is to lecture here tomorrow evening.

Respectfully yours

W. Cushing

Chairman Ex. Comtee—

Mr. Henry D. Thoreau Concord

We have been unable to identify further or date this request for a lecture. MS., Scribner Book Store, New York (typescript); previously unpublished.

From MARY MOODY EMERSON

With her characteristic mixture of bitter and sweet, Emerson's aunt signed the two-page 4to letter she wrote Thoreau, "Your admirer often and your friend always." She signed the letter with her initials only. We do not know when it was written; the catalogue dates it only "May 3." The manuscript was sold by Charles F. Libbie & Co. at the Willard sale of February 15–16, 1910.

To HENRY WILLIAMS, JR.

Though bodily I have been a member of Harvard University, heart and soul I have been far away among the scenes of my boyhood. Those hours that should have been devoted to study, have been spent in scouring the woods and exploring the lakes and streams of my native village. Immured within the dark but classic walls of a Stoughton or a Hollis, my spirit yearned for the sympathy of my old and almost forgotten friend, Nature.

These sentences may or may not have come from a letter Thoreau wrote to the secretary of his Harvard class of 1837. The entry in the Memorials, *where the sentences are found, is ambiguous. Williams, the class secretary, quotes first from a letter Thoreau sent him on September 30, 1847 and then from the Class Book in which Thoreau must have written either during or shortly after his period in college. (He heads the autobiographical entry "David Henry" instead of the later "Henry David.")*

654

Williams then prefaces his third quotation from Thoreau, reproduced here, with merely "Again." Its third sentence is practically duplicated in the Class Book entry, but the two preceding ones do not appear there. All have the same ornate style. If they are from a letter Thoreau wrote, it must have been an early one. Text, *Henry Williams,* Memorial of the Class of 1837, *p.* 38.

Addendum

To REVEREND ANDREW BIGELOW

Concord Oct. 6*th* -38

Sir,

I learn from my brother and sister, who were recently employed as teachers in your vicinity, that you are at present in quest of some one to fill the vacancy in your high school, occasioned by Mr. Bellows' withdrawal. As my present school, which consists of a small number of well advanced pupils, is not sufficiently lucrative, I am advised to make application for the situation now vacant. I was graduated at Cambridge in –37, and have since had my share of experience in school-keeping.

I can refer you to the President and Faculty of Harvard College— to Rev. Dr. Ripley, or Rev. R. W. Emerson—of this town, or to the parents of my present pupils, among whom I would mention—Hon. Samuel Hoar—Hon. John Keyes—& Hon. Nathan Brooks. Written recommendations by these gentlemen will be procured if desired.

If you will trouble yourself to answer this letter immediately, you will much oblige your humble Servant,

Henry D. Thoreau

The letter is addressed to Rev. Andrew Bigelow, Taunton, Massachusetts. MS., Carl W. H. Cowdrey, Fitchburg, Massachusetts; previously unpublished.

Index

Before *to* and *from*, "letter" is to be understood.

657

Bigelow, Rev. Andrew
  to 656
Bigelow, Henry Jacob 5, 6, 142
Bigelow, Dr. Jacob 23
Birney, James G. 440
Bissell, C. 281, 282
Black, Mrs. Rebecca 104, 111
Blackwood's Magazine 204, 205
Blake, H. G. O.
  mentioned 30, 227, 437, 438, 518,
    547, 561, 562, 609, 634
  from 213
  to 214–17, 219–22, 242, 243, 247,
    250–52, 256–58, 259–61, 264–66,
    284–86, 288, 295–300, 302–4, 310–
    14, 318–20, 330–31, 339, 342–43,
    344–45, 354–56, 358, 376–77, 377–
    78, 378, 383–85, 400–2, 420–22,
    423–24, 441–42, 442–45, 461, 465,
    476–77, 484, 490–92, 495–99, 514–
    15, 516–17, 518–19, 536–39, 540,
    542, 557–59, 563, 578–80, 588,
    595–98, 601, 615–16
Blood, Perez 187, 190
Boston Miscellany 73, 123
Boston Review 20
Boston Society of Natural History 270,
  591, 592
Bowditch, Henry I. 240
Bowen, Francis 5, 6
Bradbury, Wymond 112, 113
Bradbury and Soden 113, 126, 134
Bradford, George Partridge 44, 91, 137,
  138, 155, 240, 504
Briggs, Governor George N. 192
Brisbane, Albert 81, 82, 111
Britton, Joel 137, 208
Brooks, Nathan 656
Brother Jonathan 139
Brown, John 464, 563, 566, 567, 570,
  574, 586
Brown, Lucy Jackson 33, 126, 137, 138,
  142
  to 44–45, 46–47, 50–51, 62–63, 75–
    76, 79–80
Brown, Mary
  from 550
  to 472, 510, 551
Brown, Deacon Reuben 126, 127, 192,
  226, 322
Brown, Theophilus 247, 300, 339, 354,

376, 377, 424, 437, 439, 443, 465,
  476, 491, 518, 519, 547, 561, 595,
  609, 615
  from 562, 634
Browne, John W. 240
Brownson, Orestes 21, 150
  to 19–20
Buffum, Arnold 440
Buffum, James N. 240
Buffum, Jonathan 503
Burnham's (booksellers) 389
Burt, John
  from 468
  to 469

Cabot, James Elliot 198, 240
  from 177–78, 181, 183
  to 179–80, 182–83, 210–11
Cabot, Samuel
  from 252, 270
"Cape Cod" 288, 289, 301, 374–75, 379
Cary, Thomas G.
  from 529–31, 541–42
Carlyle, Thomas 454, 474
Channing, Ellery
  'Letters' 118; moves to Red Lodge,
    Concord 96–97; Thoreau's com-
    ments on 208; mentioned 74, 102,
    108, 123, 126, 137, 138, 140, 145,
    147, 148–49, 153, 200, 204, 240,
    276, 359, 361, 371, 382, 383, 391,
    393, 402, 409, 410, 412, 413, 432,
    471, 472, 479, 484, 492, 500, 501,
    517, 519, 521, 523, 527, 528, 536–
    37, 567, 594, 596, 597, 609, 625,
    628, 651
  from 96, 97, 161–63, 653
Channing, W. H. 81, 82, 111, 116, 128,
  133, 143, 144, 147, 161, 240, 262
Channing, William F. 240
Chapin, E. H. 89
Chapman, John 387, 403, 467
  from 395–96, 396–97
Chase, A. S.
  from 591
Chesuncook 236, 237
"Chesuncook" 501, 515–16, 520
Cholmondeley, Thomas 316, 342, 343,
  344, 350, 358, 360, 362, 376–77,
  403, 404, 536, 540, 547

DATE DUE

AG 10 '64			
MR 31 '65			
MR 16 '66			
(14)			
MR 16 '66			
(14)			
MAY 12 1979			
	Withdrawn From		
	Ohio Northern		
	University Library		
GAYLORD			PRINTED IN U.S.A.

For my little chili peppers, Sophia and Matthew
—S.S.C.

For Julia and Joe, my Klondike bears,
and for our newest nuggets, Micah and Jillian
—D.D.

Library of Congress Cataloging-in-Publication Data
Crummel, Susan Stevens.
Ten-Gallon Bart beats the heat / by Susan Stevens Crummel ; illustrated by Dorothy Donohue. — 1st ed.
   p. cm.
Summary: Tired of the blistering heat in Dog City, Ten-Gallon Bart departs for the frozen north, where he gets lost in a blizzard.
ISBN 978-0-7614-5634-6
[1. Blizzards—Fiction. 2. Dogs—Fiction. 3. Animals—Fiction.] I. Donohue, Dorothy, ill. II. Title.
PZ7.C88845Tj 2010
[E]—dc22   2009006342

The illustrations are rendered with textured papers, layered and pasted down.
Book design by Virginia Pope
Editor: Margery Cuyler

Printed in China (E)
First edition
1 3 5 6 4 2

mc **Marshall Cavendish**
Children

It was hot in Dog City.

HoT. Hot. HOT.

Scorching hot.

Blistering hot.

Tongue-hanging-out hot.

It was so hot, the pigs were frying

like bacon.

But Ten-Gallon Bart didn't care.

He was happy.

He was hot.

He was home.

Paradise.

Everyone huddled around Bart.

"We're here," sobbed Buffalo Gal.

"We need you!" wailed Miss Pixie and Miss Dixie.

"You're our buddy!" blubbered Wyatt Burp and Wild Bill Hiccup.

"We missed you, Bart," bawled Miss Kitty.

Bart blinked one eye. He blinked the other. He began
to shake from head to tail. Then he slowly smiled at his friends.
"I m-m-m-issed you, too. T-T-Take me back t-t-to Dog City."

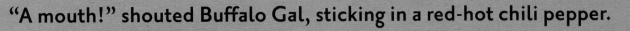
"A mouth!" shouted Buffalo Gal, sticking in a red-hot chili pepper.

Wyatt Burp and Wild Bill Hiccup wrapped the blanket around Bart.

But Bart didn't move. He was shiverin'cold. Teeth-chatterin' cold. Bone-chillin' cold.

Bart was frozen stiff.

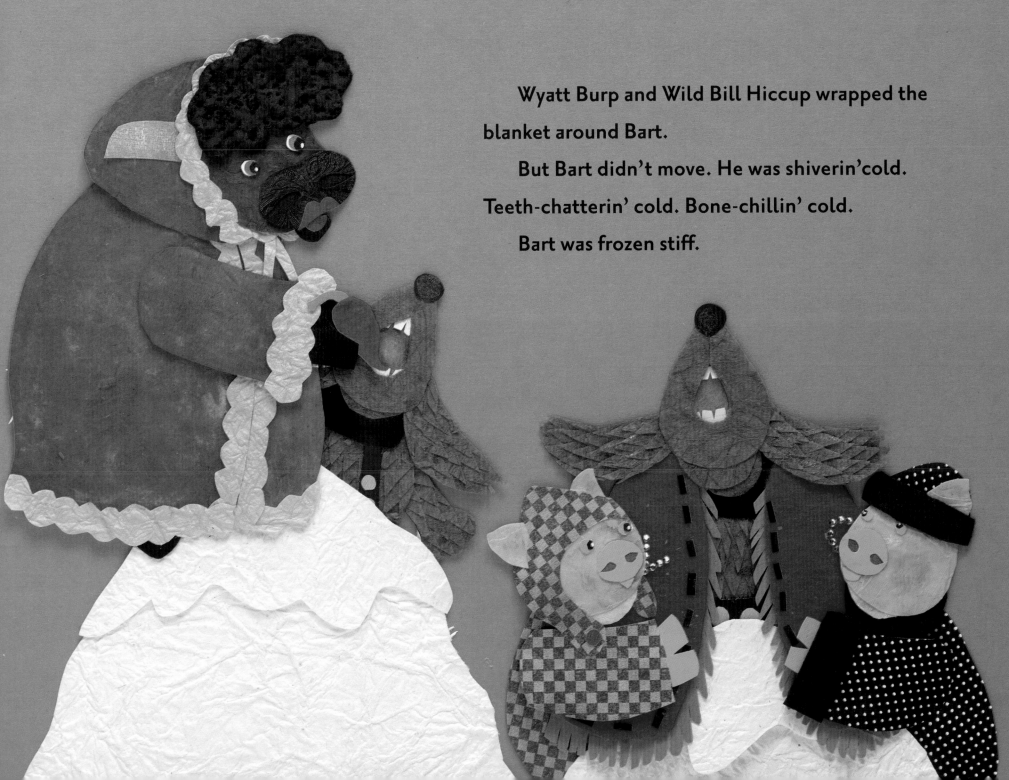

"We're coming! We're coming!" everyone hollered as they raced up the mountain.

They dug fast and furiously.

"Paws!" cried Pixie and Dixie.

"Here's our piggy bank," snorted Wyatt Burp and Wild Bill Hiccup.

"And Crazy Bull's blanket—that'll warm Bart on the outside."

"Look, two pigs in a blanket!" snickered Buffalo Gal. "I brought red-hot chili peppers—that'll warm Bart on the inside."

"I have a little nest egg," chirped Miss Pixie, "to pay for the tickets."

"And there's some cash in the kitty," added Miss Kitty.

"Hang on, Ten-Gallon Bart, we're on our way!"

"Read the headlines!" cried Wyatt Burp and Wild Bill Hiccup.

"That hat!" hollered Buffalo Gal. "It's Bart's hat! He's buried in the snow!"

"He'll freeze! We have to help him!" squawked Miss Pixie, running around like a chicken with her head cut off.

"Don't get your feathers ruffled," warned Miss Kitty. "Calm down. Think. We need warm stuff for Bart and money for tickets. Hurry! Let's meet back here in five minutes!"

owever, Mr. |
|ompany is d|
business, de|
calamity in|
sleds. Gold|
suspended |
mountains |

Meanwhile, back in Dog City . . .

By morning, all you could see of Bart was his ten-gallon hat.

All you could hear of Bart was a faint grumbling, "S-s-s-so much for g-g-g-gold-diggin'."

Digging and snowing.

Snowing and snowing.

Bart reached the top and started digging. The snow was falling.

And so it went all night long.

Snowing and snowing.

Digging and snowing.

THWUMP!

Ten-Gallon Bart belly flopped into a snowbank.

Bart grumbled, "So much for dogsleddin'." Then he spotted a sign and perked up.

"YIPPEE! It's diggin' time! I'm gonna git rich so's I can buy my own sled—an' fishin' hole, too."

"TAKE COVER!" yelled a miner. "Storm's a-comin'—looks like a big'n. Weather's gone haywire!"

"Couldn't be worse than a Dog City sandstorm," Bart howled. "I'm goin' up that mountain and dig me some GOLD!"

Bart went sliding. He slid up. He slid down.
He slid frontward. He slid backward. He slid sideways
and in circles. He did loop-de-loops and somersaults.

"H-E-E-E-L-L-L-P-P-P-P!" Bart shrieked.
"I can't stop!"

. . . a glacier.

SNAP!

The sled broke loose.

He slipped a harness onto Ten-Gallon Bart, tied him to the sled, and hopped on.

"Wait a cotton-pickin' minute," growled Bart. "When do I get to go dogsleddin'?"

"You ARE dogsledding," yelled Mr. Moose. "Now, MUSH!"

"Mush?" Bart asked.

"GO!" shouted Mr. Moose.

"Oh, you mean GIDDYUP!" hollered Bart.

"I said MUSH!" roared Mr. Moose, snapping his whip.

CRACK!

"YEOW!" Ten-Gallon Bart took off across the frozen tundra. The more Mr. Moose cracked the whip, the faster Bart ran.

"GEE! HAW!" screamed Mr. Moose. "RIGHT! LEFT!"

"YEE-E-E-HAW!" echoed Bart as he plunged forward, faster and faster, right onto . . .

Bart climbed down the tree and waved to Mr. Moose. "Howdy! I'm Ten-Gallon Bart from Dog City, an' I'm just itchin' to go sleddin'."

"Ever been dogsledding?" asked Mr. Moose.

"No . . . but I'm a dog—an' I've ridden a goat and a bull," bragged Bart. "Sleddin' should be a cinch."

Mr. Moose chuckled. "That's what YOU think! Let's go!"

"Holy mackerel!" Ten-Gallon Bart tossed the fish and ran for his life.

He bolted over the mountains, through the snow, and up a tree.

GRRRRRRRRRRRRRRRRRRRRRRRRRRRRRRR

"Stay away from our lake!" warned the three bears, ambling off.

Bart grumbled, "So much for fishin'." Then he spotted a small shack and perked up.

"YIPPEE! It's sleddin' time!"

MR. MOOSE'S
DOG
SLEDDING

GRRRRRRRRRRRRRRRRRRRRRRRR

"Who's been catching MY fish?" growled White Bear.

GRRRRRRRRRRRRRRRRRRRRR

"Who's been catching MY fish?" growled Brown Bear.

"Somethin' fishy's goin' on here!" snarled the three bears.

The Cats in
Krasinski Square

The Cats in Krasinski Square

By KAREN HESSE

Illustrated by WENDY WATSON

SCHOLASTIC PRESS · NEW YORK

Library of Congress Cataloging-in-Publication Data is available upon request

ISBN 0-439-43540-4

10 9 8 7 6 5 4 3 2 1   04 05 06 07 08

Printed in Singapore 46 · First edition, September 2004

The text type was set in Antykwa Poltawskiego, designed and cast by a Polish typographer,
Adam Jerzy Poltawski, in the late 1940s. The display type was set in Dalliance Roman.
The illustrations were created using pencil, ink, and watercolors
on Strathmore drawing paper.
Book design by Elizabeth B. Parisi

The cats
come
from the cracks in the Wall,
the dark corners,
the openings in the rubble.

They know

I can offer only

a gentle hand,

a tender voice.

They have no choice but to come.

They belonged once to someone.

They slept on sofa cushions

and ate from crystal dishes.

They purred,

furrowing the chests,

nuzzling the chins of their beloveds.

Now they have no one to kiss their
velvet heads. I whisper,
"I have no food to spare."
The cats don't care.
I can keep my fistful of bread,
my watery soup, my potato,
so much more
than my friend Michal gets
behind the Wall of the Ghetto.
The cats don't need me feeding them.
They get by nicely on mice.

I look like any child
playing with cats
in the daylight
in Warsaw,
my Jewish armband
burned with the rags I wore
when I escaped the Ghetto.

I wear my Polish look,

I walk my Polish walk.

Polish words float from my lips

and I am almost safe,

almost invisible,

moving through Krasinski Square

past the dizzy girls riding the merry-go-round.

My brave sister,

Mira,

all that is left of our family,

my brave sister

tells me the plan,

the newest plan

to smuggle food inside the Ghetto.

Her friends will come on the train,

carrying satchels

filled

not with clothes or books,

but bread, groats, and sugar.

I know the openings in the Wall.

The cats have taught me.

I show Mira on a map her friend Arik has drawn.

"Every crack will be filled with food," Mira says,

bringing our thin soup to simmer on the ring.

I ask to smuggle the bread

through the spot near Krasinski Square

where Michal lives on the other side of the Wall.

Mira knows the danger,

but she nods.

I fall back onto the mattress

and the big room dances with light.

But on the day,

when the train is already rolling toward Warsaw,

Arik, breathless, bursts into our room

and says the Gestapo

knows of the train and the satchels,

and they'll be waiting at the station with their dogs

to sniff out the smugglers.

The look that passes between Arik and Mira

frightens me more

than a knock on the door in the night.

I cannot remain inside.

Instead,

I wear my Polish look,

I walk my Polish walk.

Polish words float from my lips

as I move through Krasinski Square,

singing a nonsense song.

The cats come from the cracks in the Wall,

the dark corners,

the openings in the rubble.

And I know what we must do.

We gather the cats,

one by one,

Mira and Arik, Henryk and Marek,

Hanna and Anna, Tosia and Stasia,

we gather the cats into baskets

and head to the station,

where we spread out,

waiting for the train,

behind the Gestapo and their straining,

snarling dogs.

Suddenly steam and the scream of the whistle.

The train pulls in,

passengers stream off.

The dogs are set loose,

their sharp barks echo through the station.

They fly toward

the men and women,

the girls and boys

with the strong scent of bread, groats, and sugar about them.

But before the dogs can reach their prey,

we open our
baskets
and let the cats
loose.

The station explodes into chaos
as frenzied dogs turn
their wild hunger on the cats,
who flee in every direction,
slipping through cracks,
into dark corners,
between openings.

The smuggled food

vanishes from the station,

vanishes from our side of Warsaw,

through the Wall, over the Wall, under the Wall,

into the Ghetto.

Including my basket,

with a loaf of bread

for Michal,

taken by grateful hands.

And the music from the merry-go-round
floats in the air, rising, tinsel-bright,
above Krasinski Square.

AUTHOR'S NOTE

In 2001, I came across a short article about cats outfoxing the Gestapo at the train station in Warsaw during World War II. I couldn't get the story out of my mind, so I went in search of accounts of the Warsaw Ghetto and the Jewish Resistance in Poland. The two most valuable sources I found were the Ringelblum archives and Adina Blady Szwajger's book, *I Remember Nothing More*. Mira, the fictional older sister of the narrator in *The Cats in Krasinski Square*, was inspired by Adina Blady Szwajger. I owe the texture and substance of this book to Szwajger's account of her experience with the Jewish Resistance.

HISTORICAL NOTE

In late September 1939, at the beginning of World War II, Warsaw, the capital of Poland, fell into the hands of the attacking Germans. The Gestapo (German State Police) forced all Jewish men, women, and children from Warsaw and its surrounding towns to live on certain streets within the invaded city. If non-Jews lived in any of the buildings on these streets, they received orders to move out. A high brick wall was built to keep the Jewish people in, separated from the Aryans (non-Jewish "whites") who lived on the other side. By the time the Gestapo collected all the local Jewish people, the overcrowding inside the Warsaw Ghetto created conditions ripe for disease and hunger. Every day, hundreds of men, women, and children fell in the streets, too ill to take another step. And in those streets, they died.

In July 1942, the Germans began carrying out their plan to relocate the Warsaw Jews. The youngest and oldest disappeared from the Ghetto first, at the rate of 2,000, then 10,000, then 20,000 people per day. The weakest were killed before they ever left Warsaw. Eventually the Germans emptied the Ghetto of all Jews but those working in war plants.

Even though they were physically and emotionally exhausted, many Jews fought back. Thousands of brave young men and women planned ways to upset the Nazis' plans. These Jews formed an opposition group, causing trouble for the Germans whenever possible. At great risk, these daring Jews snuck people out of, and weapons, food, and medicine, into the Ghetto, saving thousands of Jewish lives.

In April 1943, the German army had every advantage when the last battle against the Warsaw Ghetto fighters began. And yet this handful of sick, starving, and injured civilians held off an army of trained German soldiers for over forty days. As the Germans bombed and set buildings on fire, the Jewish Resistance, leading their attacks from basements, attics, and hidden passages, knew the chance for a victory over the Germans was impossible. Yet even after the buildings within the Ghetto were flattened, small pockets of fighters rose up and did battle against the Nazis, waging a war until death.

Not every Jew died. Those who passed as Polish on the Aryan side of the Wall aided the escape of several hundred Jewish fighters. These daring warriors struggled out of the Ghetto toward freedom, neck-deep through the filth and stench of the sewers beneath Warsaw. The last survivors of the Jewish Ghetto came forward at war's end to tell the terrible truth of the deeds carried out by the Nazis.

In memory of my mother, Fran Levin
— K.H.

For my father, Aldren Auld Watson —
my teacher, mentor, colleague, and collaborator
— W.W.